Raven Wolf

An American Odyssey

by

Joel B. Reed

White Turtle Books
Canby, Minnesota

Published by:
White Turtle Books
Canby, Minnesota
www. whiteturtlebooks.com

ISBN 978-1-933482-09-5
Library of Congress Control Number 2006928320
Cover photos and design: Joel B. Reed
Cover ceramic figure: Gollum by Gem Mercer

DEDICATION

This work is dedicated to all those lovers, remembered and not, who have been messengers of grace in my life in my own quest for love and wholeness and completion. Some of these were lovers to me, and some were lovers to others. And while all of these loves were flawed in one way and another through our mutual humanity, it remains my conviction that each of them reflects to some degree the passion of the One who is the source of all being and the Author of love itself.

Above all, this book is about the quest for self-love and self-acceptance. I believe one must learn this first so one can come to accept others, however imperfectly, and through learning this, to become a lover of souls in the likeness and image of the One who created us. So at the bottom line, this book is about coming to embrace love in a world of madness. It is written in love to love and for love, and with Love surely kibitzing over my shoulder...

JBR

A Recalling

Our dearest Martin,

How good to see you again. How good to hear your voice, to see you smile. How sad to have so little time. And is it not incredible? After all these years to walk through a dark city surrounded by strangers, to make a chance turn, to find an old and beloved friend waiting there....

At first we were so afraid. The time away has changed you, marked you. There you were sitting in your dark suit and staring into the fountain. And so angry. So very angry we almost went away. How could we know you were so close to despair? Who were we, two aging hippies, to approach so austere and forbidding a Man?

Then you saw us. You smiled and the years went almost away. How the man in the taxi squeaked his brakes when you ran to meet us! How the policeman on the corner stared! Then, almost as soon as we found you, we had to leave again. When we did, the look in your eyes.....

You should see the Canyon. The fall came early this year and the aspens are almost completely changed. The nights are cool and in the mornings you can smell the piñon smoke from the night before. I cannot remember a more beautiful autumn, and this year, for some reason, it is very important for us to see it all. So in the warm afternoons the two of us take long walks up to the rim and look out over the plain. Down in the canyon are the little match box houses and tiny ant people. We can see our house clearly from there, not far from yours. And looking at it now, it is as if the years since you were here had never been.

Did you know Max was living in your place now? When some of the boys from town came to party and trashed it out he moved in so it would not be ruined. He cleaned it up—not as big a job as you had!—and finished the greenhouse you started, but very little else has changed. The gardens are still where you first planted them and the orchard did well this year. Up there on the rim life seems so simple, so beautiful. All

1

the troubles are smoothed by distance and all that is left is a peaceful procession of life by the river. How I wish you were home to see it.

Oh, Martin, forgive me. I promised myself in writing I would not do that. Yet the fact remains we love you, and we miss you, and not just me, but Jack Bear and Max. Many of the people you knew are still here, although some have moved away, and your name comes up far more often than you might think. Nor do any of us really understand why you went away, or when you went, why you never came back, even for a visit. I have come to understand it was not just us, not just the breaking off of our engagement which drove you away, and kept you away, and perhaps still drives you from place to place. I understand it is something within you that does this. Yet I often wonder if there was something we could have done to help you, to help you in the way you helped so many of us. Perhaps, but I think probably not. When I go to Mass, as I strangely have begun to do again in recent years, I light a candle for you in the terrible solitude of your journey....

The bread is done and the child is home from school, so I must be a mother for a while. Please come to see us, even just to visit for a few hours, if you can. You know there is always a place for you here, and always will be. This is your home. And if you cannot come, please write to let us know more of you and how it is with you. We love you so very much...

Stephania

Part I. The Canyon

How blessed are those whose strength is in Thee
and whose hearts are set on the pilgrim's way;
as they go through the Valley of the Weeper
they shall make it a place of springs....
Psalm of David, 84

Hear my prayer, O Lord,
and give ear to my cry;
hold not your peace
at my tears.
For I am but a
sojourner with
you, a wayfarer
as all my ancestors
were before me.
Psalm 39

1. Peregrino

Nothing Mexico. *The broad plain is still. The bright yellow sun has reached midday zenith and the wind is dead. Even in early spring heat waves radiate from the bleached yellow earth. Nothing moves, for this is the desert. The gila monster peers out from his dark lair beneath a rock. A scorpion hides in the shelter of a cactus. The coyote sleeps in its den and the jack rabbit has scraped out a shelter for itself below a clump of scrub. These creatures must hide through the day. For the sun is merciless. It gives no quarter. It dries the water holes, cracks the yellow earth. It claims its homage from the weak, the foolish, and only its partners in death are spared. A thousand feet above the desert floor the condor soars cool in its dark vestments. And beneath the surface the fiery red ants build their underground cities oblivious to the heat. These clean the sun's domain, obliterate all traces of its victims. Only the bones are left to bleach and crumble or be gnawed by desert rats....* (Martin Quinn's Journal)

April 1962. The jeep wagon made its way cautiously over ruts and small ravines scoring the rough road. As the wheels churned along, dust puffed up and hung in clouds in the still desert air. From time to time the belly of the machine touched scorched rock or plowed into the high center hump, giving rise to a metallic scream, and sometimes a small rock would rise like a fish from beneath the wheels and whang loudly off the undercarriage, startling the men inside.

"Jesus!" said Dickman, who was driving. "I'd forgot how rough this road can be." He reached up to wipe the sweat from his eyes with a bright calico bandanna. The back and arms of the light sport shirt covering his enormous bulk were soaked through and dust from the open windows stained his features. His handkerchief left streaks across his face. "Hell of a day for the air conditioner to go out! Sorry."

"Don't worry about it," said the other man. He grimaced as the Jeep

5

hit a particularly rough patch. "Doesn't the county ever grade this road?" He was young, perhaps twenty-five, and while his features gave little evidence of Nordic ancestry, his name was Lundberg. Yet where most of his ancestors were tall and fair he stood at medium height, with the broad heavy shoulders that spoke of immense physical power. His skin was a pleasant deep olive set below straight black hair, and only his clear grey eyes hinted at something beyond the area of the Mediterranean.

"About once in a blue moon," said Dickman, then added an explanation. "There's just one family lives up here. Bunch of Meskins. Hardly ever come to town."

"I see," said Lundberg. He smiled to himself, wondering how Dickman would react to knowing Lundberg's mother was a "Meskin". Not that it mattered so much growing up in St. Paul, Minnesota. American Indians were the scapegoat there. Yet now he was in the Southwest and a long way from town. He decided to say nothing to Dickman, at least not yet. "What kind of people are they?" he asked. "The people who live up here."

"Well, between you and me and the gatepost, old Ramos is a pretty good fellow," Dickman responded. "People say he's a little crazy and maybe he is at that. He's got some funny ideas and lives up here by hisself most of the time. Sometimes his family comes up to visit but they don't never stay too long. Can't blame them this far from town." Then Dickman grinned. "Old Ramos don't have no trouble with stealing. Local Meskins think he's a witch. Meskins down here is as superstitious as niggers back home. They paint their window frames blue to keep the devils out of the house."

"I wondered about that," Lundberg answered. "I thought it was just a local custom for decorating houses." He lapsed into silence for a while. Then curiosity overcame his reticence. If he were going to be here a while he might as well get to know people when he had a chance. "Where's home?"

"Mississippi. I moved out here when the niggers got so bad." Suddenly Dickman became aware of what he was saying. Some people from the North had strange ideas on the subject of race and Dickman didn't want to lose a sale. He glanced at Lundberg to see if the young man was offended, then went on. "Now don't get me wrong. I ain't got much use for niggers but Meskins is all right. They're a lot like white folks in some ways. Give a Mex a job and he'll do it. May take his time but he will do it. And they ain't like niggers about their women. A nigger will sell his mother for a quart of whiskey, but not a Meskin. You kind of got to watch it. Take up with a Meskin girl and her brother's like to pull a knife on you. They all carry them and they like to use them. I know a guy got cut up pretty bad once."

Lundberg said nothing. He didn't want to hear the story and hoped the other man would drop the subject, but Dickman overlooked Lundberg's lack of enthusiasm. "Yeah, he got cut up pretty bad but he lived. Twenty-three stitches and the Mex got off free."

"That's a shame," said Lundberg but Dickman was on a roll and his sarcasm slid by like an outside curve.

"You damn right. All he did was ask a girl to dance. He was down at Pete Gallegos'. That's a Meskin hangout and he should have had better sense than go in there in the first place. He seen her sitting by herself and asked her to dance. Of course, she pretended like he wasn't even there. They're like that. Flirt like hell and then act like you're dirt. Real prick tease."

"How much farther to the place?" asked Lundberg, trying to change the subject, but Dickman was not to be deflected.

"About thirty or forty minutes," the man said. "Where was I? Oh, yeah. This guy asks her to dance again and this time she tells him to go to hell so he starts dragging her across the dance floor. Joe didn't mean nothing by it. He was just making his point and he comes across kind of strong when he's had a few. Anyway, this pachuco jumps on Joe and pulls the girl away from him. When Joe takes a swing at him the Mex pulls a knife and starts carving. Joe said the Mex was going for his nuts but he jumped back and took it in the gut. He was lucky it didn't kill him. The Mex must of thought it did because he didn't finish Joe off. Just went back to his table and drank his beer until the police came."

"So the Mexican got off free," Lundberg murmured, shaking his head.

"Yeah, he got off free," Dickman nodded, glancing at Lundberg. "Didn't even spend one night in jail or anything. All the Meskins around here is cousins and they stick together. White jury would have hung his ass or at least sent him to the pen. Not here. They was even talking about having Joe up for assaulting the girl. Can you imagine that!"

"Sounds like your friend, Joe, got off pretty lucky." the younger man observed.

"What do you mean?" Dickman's face was a stone mask.

Lundberg did not feel like starting an argument, so he said, "Oh, nothing. I suppose the judge was named Garcia."

"Matter of fact it was Ramirez. How did you know he was Mex?" Dickman was truly puzzled.

"It figures," Lundberg said.

Dickman stared hard at the younger man for a long moment. Then his face cleared. "Oh, I get you. Since most people around here's Meskin they'd elect a Meskin judge."

Lundberg nodded. "Something like that." He stared out the window, but the scenery was still much the same.

"Yeah," Dickman continued. "Old Ramos is a good old boy. He don't mind scratching your back if you'll scratch his." He paused and looked at the younger man. "Look, what I'm telling you all this for is so you won't get yourself in a jam, see." A smart reply was on the tip of Lundberg's tongue, but the other man looked genuinely concerned, and so he nodded. "Watch yourself and you won't have no trouble. Most of them's good people. I do a lot of trading with them, but you got to watch them. Give a Mex half a chance and every one of them will cheat you if he can, but I kind of like them. They're a lot like white folk most ways, except you can't understand them when they get to jabbering Mex."

"You don't speak Spanish?" asked Lundberg, surprised.

"No," said Dickman, "but I hear tell what they speak ain't exactly Spanish neither. Most of them speak English and when you run into one that don't, it ain't hard to find one that does to tell you what they are saying. Mostly it's the old folks that don't."

"You've been here eight years without learning to speak Spanish?" Lundberg smiled. Dickman nodded. "Tell me something. How do you know they're not talking about you?"

"What? Well...I mean...." Dickman was completely flustered. Lundberg was amazed the question had apparently never occurred to the man. Then Dickman saw Lundberg was smiling. "Aw, come on. You're just pulling my leg, ain't you?"

"Yeah, I'm just kidding." Lundberg said. "I couldn't resist that one. I'm sure they don't."

"Yeah," said Dickman and smiled. "You had me going for a minute." Yet small lines of worry appeared above his eyes.

Dickman glanced at Lundberg again and started to say something, but the younger man was looking out the window and he refrained. For the next half hour the two rode in silence, Lundberg lost in the stark beauty of the passing countryside, and Dickman, trying to figure whether he'd offended the young man and if his first assessment were correct. For when Lundberg first came into his office the realtor mistook him for a well dressed *chicano*. Yet his "American" name and Lundberg's casual confidence confused Dickman, as did the way the young man spoke. Nor was the color of the eyes quite right. Then Dickman decided the young man must be Greek. He'd known many Greeks during the World War and came to like them despite their strange ways. The Greek men were good old boys to his mind for they loved to drink and carouse and to have a good time. And the women! Dickman felt the stirring of an erection as he remembered the time a Greek friend took him on a wild four-day tour of Athenean brothels.

Dickman glanced at Lundberg again, but the young man was still absorbed in the scenery. As he looked out the window Lundberg was intrigued. At the outset the road they traveled led across a broad desert plain, flat dry land broken only by deep ravines and sparse desert plants. Now, as they approached the mountains, the countryside as hilly and there were many more signs of life. The cactus and greasewood gradually turned into grass and scrub brush, and then to juniper and stunted cedar. The bare spots between the cactus plants became covered first with a few clumps of thin stemmed native grass, and then with more and more. Then, a bit higher up, Lundberg saw a faint trace of color hinting at early wild flowers. Even in early spring it seemed terribly hot for this hour of the morning, but Lundberg thought he noticed a slight difference. Turning to Dickman, he asked, "Is it my imagination or is it getting cooler?"

The realtor grinned. 'You wouldn't think so but we're already more than a thousand feet higher than town. You'd need a jacket if we was to go clear to the top." He pointed to the white crown covering the high peaks. "Funny, ain't it? It's like to hit a hundred in town today and there's still snow not thirty miles away. It's all due to elevation."

"How much higher are we going?" Lundberg asked.

"Not much. The place is at the foot of the mountains. Maybe another three, four hundred feet." They'd come to a particularly difficult stretch and the realtor was giving his whole attention to his driving.

"Sounds like the best of both worlds."

"I don't get you," Dickman replied, sparing Lundberg a brief glance from his attention to the deeply rutted road.

"What I mean is it's a lot cooler here than in town in the summer and a lot milder than higher up when the snows come."

"Yeah, I guess you're right. Makes it nice for you either way." Dickman devoted his attention to negotiating a deep ravine. Water was running as high as the floor boards, but the bottom of the ford was rock and the Jeep made it safely across.

"I wonder where that comes from?" Lundberg said to himself.

"What?" asked Dickman, distracted. "Oh, that's the Rio Enojado. It goes right by the place." Dickman's pronunciation was so atrocious it took the younger man a moment to translate.

"Angry River," he said softly.

"What?" asked Dickman.

"I was just wondering why it was called that."

"Oh, it's supposed to mean 'wild river'. Don't look like much up here and it ain't, but two years ago it washed out a bridge in town. Took out four, five houses, too, right in the middle of the night. Killed eight people."

Lundberg nodded and resumed his survey of the countryside. He could feel it growing cooler, almost as they drove, and the scrub brush was now scattered with low trees resembling pines. He asked Dickman what they were.

"Them's piñon pines." Again the man's pronunciation was confusing. To Lundberg it sounded as if he were talking about the steering assembly of a sports car. "I never seen them, either, until I come out here," Dickman added, nodding. "The Meskins come out here in the fall and pick up the nuts. Ain't that funny? A pine tree producing nuts!" Dickman laughed. "They is little bitty things, look like deer shit. They ain't bad eating, though. Taste sort of like a pecan, but a little different. The Meskins harvest them and sell them in town. Get a pretty good price I hear."

"That's good to know. If I'm around this fall I'll come out and gather some myself."

"Oh, I wouldn't do that!" Dickman protested.

"Why not?" Lundberg wanted to know.

"Well, the Meskins don't like white people to get the nuts. You're liable to get in trouble with some of them," Dickman advised, shaking his head.

"Is it really that bad around here?" Lundberg asked.

"What do you mean?"

"You make it sound like there's a war going on."

"No, it ain't like that. There's just some things you don't want to do, like messing with their women. They live in their place and we live in ours. There's only trouble when you try to mix them together."

"I see," said Lundberg, wondering just how much of what Dickman said could be believed. Very little, he suspected. Yet, there was probably a grain of truth in what the man told him, if only a grain. It made sense to find out local customs before blundering in blindly. He decided to move slowly and find out for himself. Caution would not hurt.

"Almost there!" Dickman called out. They were crossing the Rio Eno-jado again and turning to follow it up a deep canyon. On one side the canyon rose in a bold, sheer face of granite. The stream flowed around the base of the face and disappeared around a bend farther up. A flat stretch of land a hundred yards wide lay in the valley before the ground began a moderate slope toward the other side of the canyon. Even with the presence of the stream it was dry in the canyon and there were obvious signs of the desert everywhere. Cactus grew in the grass along the streambed and mounted the slope. Along the top of the ridges framing the canyon they could see evergreens, but these stopped about half way down the slope. Lundberg started to ask Dickman why this was, but something caught his eye. High on the rock face, about half way to the top, a pine had gained a tenuous foothold in the rock and near that he could see a small patch of brown moving along the face. He pointed it out to Dickman, asked what it might be.

"That's one of old Ramos' goats," the realtor replied. "Listen."

After a moment Lundberg could hear the faint tinkling of small bells over the noise of the stream. "He bells them so he knows where they are," Dickman explained. "Most of the Meskins keep goats around here. Eat them and drink the milk. Ain't bad barbecued, but sure as hell ain't good American beef!"

Dickman stopped the Jeep a little farther up the canyon. "The property begins about here," he said, pointing, "and runs about five hundred feet up the creek. Actually, it begins on top the cliff there." He grinned."But that part ain't much good but to look at and lean against."

The younger man was forced to smile. It was the first thing the other had said all afternoon that was really funny. "Do water rights go with the property?" he asked casually.

"Yeah, but they're a little tricky." Dickman looked at the younger man. "Where'd you hear about water rights?"

"History class," Lundberg replied. "Anywhere water is scarce it stands to reason that water rights will be important." He looked around. "Where's the house?" he inquired.

"Up yonder." Lundberg looked where Dickman was pointing. Up the sloping side of the canyon, and just below the tree line, he could see the corner of a tin roof. He climbed out of the Jeep and began walking rapidly up the hill. After a few dozen steps he had to stop to catch his breath. "It must be steeper than it looks," he said.

"No, you just ain't used to the altitude," Dickman answered. "It's close to seven thousand feet right here. Take you a few months to get used to it." The other man's grin and slow, even breathing did nothing to lessen Lundberg's growing dislike for him. After a moment Lundberg resumed his ascent at a more leisurely pace. Even so he was out of breath again when he reached the plateau where the house sat.

From where Lundberg stood the ground was about seventy-five feet higher than the valley floor and formed a high bench about a hundred feet in depth. The house sat well back from the edge of the bench and behind it Lundberg could see the point where the trees started on the high slope. As he looked around, his first impression was mixed. Set high on the bench, the house commanded a startling view of the canyon and the desert beyond.

At the same time, there was little else to commend the place. It was quite apparent it had not been occupied in years and it was equally obvious that the previous tenants had not bothered to keep it up. All the windows were broken out and the front door swung freely in its frame. At several points in the outer walls, plaster was falling away and the long tin roof line was beginning to sag. A pile of rubble, remnants of a stacked stone fence, outlined a garden where only traces of lawn could still be seen. As if abusing the house were not enough, the former inhabitants had further desecrated the site by leaving relics of their existence strewn about. Old tires, shards of glass, and pieces of furniture and household goods covered the site, together with enough random parts to complete four or five automobiles. Off to one side, congregated beyond the stone fence, lay the rusting bodies of the cars themselves, and beyond that was an enormous pile of bottles and tin cans. Someone apparently had also decided the garden was more convenient than the outhouse, for between two large rocks in a corner of the fence lay numerous piles of dried human feces.

As he looked over the scene, two disparate thoughts struck Lundberg at once. One was how animals mark their territories with urine and scats. The other was a treasure trove this would be to archaeologists of a later age.

Shaking his head, Lundberg turned to Dickman and said. "Nice people who lived here last."

"Yeah, it's kind of junky, ain't it?" the man agreed, nodding. "Probably a bunch of Meskins. Maybe squatters or wetbacks moving north."

Lundberg sighed. To the Rossiters there would always be Mexicans or Indians or Negroes to blame for all the ills of the world. Or *rednecks*, he thought wryly, laughing at himself. Cautiously he climbed over the stone rubble and examined the grass that remained. When he stooped to pick up a handful of the yellow dirt, he found it too hard to scrape up with his bare hand.

"Adobe dirt," Dickman explained when he said something. "Turns to mud when it rains then dries hard as rock when it dries. That's what the Meskins use to build their walls with. Mix up mud and throw in some straw to keep it all together, and then let it dry in the sun. Ain't bad, neither. Some of their houses around here been standing a couple of hundred years."

"And the plaster keeps the walls from washing away when it rains?" the younger man asked.

"Yeah, and it helps to hang the roof over like they done here." Dickman shrugged. "Don't rain much out here no way."

Lundberg took another brief look around the garden and made his way over to the house. Along the wall facing the canyon was a long gallery porch littered with large animal droppings. "It looks like the place was used for a barn," he remarked.

"No, it's probably the old man's goats," Dickman answered. "Maybe a cow or two now and then come in out of the weather, but it won't hurt none. Them floors is good stone."

Lundberg stepped into the house and was immediately aware of a drop in temperature. Despite the elevation the day was warm even in the valley, but inside the house it was quite cool even with open windows. He commented on this to Dickman.

"That's a nice thing about adobe," the realtor replied. "Them walls are at least a foot thick. Makes them cool in summer and warm in winter. I call it poor man's central air. Of course, it ain't as good as real air but it sure is cheap."

"Feels good to me." Lundberg said as he moved on to explore the rest of the house. It took a few moments for his eyes to adjust to the gloom of the interior and he groped his way into the next room. There he startled a small animal which scurried between his legs and through a window before he could identify it, almost causing him to fall over a broken table near the door. He decided to wait until his eyes adjusted to continue his tour.

The house turned out to have four large rooms and a small pantry off what was once a kitchen. Despite Dickman's claim, the stone floors were liberally covered with manure and two bales of very old hay were stacked against one wall. Lundberg wondered whether the animals had been housed here before or after the last tenants, or whether the people here had allocated two rooms to their animals and lived in the other two. He scraped the dry manure aside with his foot and examined the stone floor. It seemed to be sound and he made his way back to the front room where Dickman waited. "No plumbing?" he asked.

"No, but it wouldn't be too hard to put in. I know a contractor in town who will give you a good deal."

"Where's the water supply?"

"There's a spring back up the hill," Dickman said. "They tell me it runs all year long. Good water, too. Course, the best thing would be to dig you a well."

"And you just happen to know a contractor who would give me a good price," Lundberg grinned.

Dickman squinted in the gloom. "Yeah, as a matter of fact, I do. How'd you know?"

Lundberg was examining the roof through a hole in the ceiling. "It figures," he said. "A man in your business would need to get to know all the local building contractors."

"Yeah, I do. Pretty good bunch of old boys, but you got to watch some of them. They'll cheat you every time."

"Must be Mexicans," Lundberg observed dryly. Dickman glanced sharply at the younger man but Lundberg was already moving out of the house and up the slope toward the spring.

Lundberg found the state of things at the back of the house pretty much complimented the front, although there didn't seem to be quite so much junk thrown around. He wondered idly whether it was a local custom to take pride in how much junk one could accumulate and display in the front of one's house, a conspicuous consumption in poverty. He also was curious about what sort of people would let such a beautiful place go to ruin. For there was clear evidence that someone had once cared a great deal. Behind the house there was a large overgrown plot which had once apparently been a garden, and the remains of a wooden corral. Beyond the corral were three adobe outbuildings of different size, but the roofs had long been scavenged for their sheet metal and the walls were badly eroded near the top. Below the wall of one of the buildings some animal had burrowed out a dark den and the heavy, aromatic stench of skunk identified the occupant. Elsewhere, mounds of dirt were scattered at random, suggesting a colony of prairie dogs had homesteaded, and squatting by one of the mounds, Lundberg reached out a hand to feel the dirt. It was soft, slightly moist, and smelled rich with promise.

A bit farther up the slope Lundberg found the charred outline of a very small building. He stopped to examine this, puzzled at what it might have been. Then he realized what he was seeing explained the squatting stones by the fence in the front yard. He wondered whether the outhouse had been occupied at the time the fire started, and almost laughed aloud at the images which followed.

Unlike the other buildings, the one around the spring was built of natural stone, carefully fitted. The roof was intact and it was obvious someone had gone to a great deal of trouble to keep the spring house in good repair. This was surprising in contrast to the rest of the place.

While the source of water may be the least likely thing to be abused in a dry land, Lundberg would not have been surprised to find the previous tenants had literally shat in their own well. He opened the door and immediately jumped back as a harsh buzz reached his ears. Coiled at the foot of the wide stone cistern, where the ground was cool and damp, was a large rattlesnake.

For a moment Lundberg stood stock still, not knowing quite what to do. He heard Dickman coming up behind him and pointed to the snake. "Prairie rattler," said the realtor. He looked around and picked up a heavy stick. "Here, let me kill the bastard."

"Wait a minute," said Lundberg, stepping between Dickman and the snake. "There's no need to kill him. Just move him out of the way."

"What? You don't want one of them things around!" Dickman tried to step around Lundberg but the younger man countered his moves. "You're crazy!" said Dickman. "That thing will kill you!"

"Not if you leave it alone," the younger man replied. "Rattlesnakes serve a purpose and he's not in our way."

The snake took advantage of the confusion and slipped from the spring house into a nearby gopher hole. "Now look what you did," said Dickman. "We'll never get him now!"

"Good!" Lundberg turned and cautiously entered the spring house, leaving the realtor staring after him. "Looks good," he said. "Spring's still flowing."

Lundberg dipped up a handful of water and smelled it. There was no odor of minerals or other matter so he took a small sip. The water was cool and pleasant with a faint taste Lundberg could not identify at first. Then he realized what he was "tasting" was a lack of chlorine and other substances which find their way into city water. "Tastes good," he said. "Care for a drink?" He almost laughed aloud when he saw the expression on Dickman's face.

"No thanks," Dickman answered." I ain't thirsty just yet." His statement was almost true. Even though he was raised on a farm in northern Mississippi, he preferred the city tap water he was accustomed to drink. Somehow drinking from the same spring as the rattlesnake had seemed to him unclean. A more accurate statement would have indicated he was not *that* thirsty yet.

"Suit yourself." Lundberg carefully lowered himself and drank deeply. When he was done he sat on the edge of the cistern and lit a cigarette. "Let's talk business," he said. "How much are taxes here?"

"Oh, they ain't bad. Wouldn't cost you much."

"How much is not bad?"

"Hell, I can't remember. Got the figures back at my office. Seems like they was about twenty-five dollars a year."

"What's the local mill assessment?" Dickman gave him an approximate figure and Lundberg thought for a few moments. The realtor looked at him with new interest. He wondered how much the young man knew about the local real estate market.

"That would put the assessed value in the neighborhood of about six-fifty, or maybe seven hundred," Lundberg observed. "How much did you say they were asking?"

"Ten thousand for the twenty-five acres, the house and water. If you're interested I might talk them down a little."

"Seems a bit high, doesn't it? The house isn't worth much," Lundberg said. "The land isn't good for much, either. The main asset is the water."

For the first time Dickman felt himself on familiar ground. He sensed the young man was seriously interested and would probably buy if the price were right. The problem was no longer a matter of selling but of price, and the years had made him a skilled negotiator. "Forget the house for a minute. It's solid and won't take much fixing up. Look at what else you're getting. Twenty-five acres of land. That works out to two-fifty an acre and land around here's hard to get at that price. You got the stream and a lot of good bottom land if you was to want to keep a couple of horses. Besides, look at the view you got. Lots of folk pay a lot more for a view that ain't half this." He pointed toward the desert plain and then to the trees on the high face opposite the house.

Lundberg shrugged and said nothing. After a long silence the realtor went on. "Two-fifty ain't bad and you know you got good water with this spring. That counts for a lot around here."

"I know nothing of the sort," answered Lundberg. "I know it's good right now. What I don't know is how much volume flows or even if it's good all year around."

"I told you it was good all year. Don't you believe me?" Dickman's tone was wounded, as if his feelings were hurt,

"It's not a question of believing you or not. You said you *thought* it ran all year around. There's a big difference and I want to know for sure. I'm the one who has to live with the decision. So I'm not about to buy a pig in a poke."

"Hell, I wouldn't let you go wrong," Dickman protested. "You know there's water around here somewhere. You could always put in a well."

"For another two to three thousand? No thanks. Not at that price. It's too far to haul water even if the county graded the road."

"Oh, they'd grade it if there was somebody else living up here," Dickman assured him. "Besides, you could pump water up from the creek if you had to."

"Does it run all year, too?" Lundberg gave Dickman a sardonic grin. "Who owns the rest of the land around here?"

Dickman was stung by the question but decided to ignore it. He pointed toward the top of the ridge. "It's government land up there. Forest Service, but they never do much cutting down this low. Trees ain't big enough. They own the other side, too, from the top of the ridge back." Dickman pointed farther up the canyon. From where he sat Lundberg could see a house surrounded by tall trees and several acres of greenery. "Old man Ramos owns the rest of the canyon clear to the top."

Lundberg regretted his jibe. It was a cheap shot. After all, Dickman was only doing his job as best he knew how. He was simply looking out for his own interests and those of his client, the owner of the property. Lundberg's personal dislike of the man had little to do with working out a deal. As a matter of fact, it could well work against him. He considered an apology but decided against it. Dickman would take it as a sign of weakness at this point in the negotiations. Instead, he made himself respond with a friendly tone of voice. "Do you suppose he's home now?" he asked. "I'd like to meet him and he might know something about the water."

"Yeah, I bet he would," Dickman answered. "He's lived here long enough. I bet he's there. Hardly ever see him in town any more."

The two men walked back down the slope toward the Jeep. On the way by the house Lundberg wanted another look at the roof so they stopped. When he disappeared through a hole in the ceiling Dickman could follow his movements by the creaking of the boards across the *vigas*. Suddenly there was a muffled cry of, "Shit!"

"What's the matter?" shouted Dickman.

"A scorpion," came the muffled reply. "I almost put my hand down on it."

Dickman laughed. "Better watch out. Them things will eat you up. May not kill you but they can make you wish they did."

Lundberg eased himself down and dusted himself off. "From what I see the roof isn't too bad. Shouldn't take much to fix the sag and the iron is good."

"No," Dickman answered. "I didn't think so. There's a guy in town who'd fix it up real good and it wouldn't cost you much, neither."

The young man looked at him squarely. "Look Mr. Dickman, if I decide to buy this place, and I do mean 'if, it will be a straight cash deal. No financing, no strings, and no kickbacks from contractors."

Dickman flushed. "Are you calling me a cheat?"

"No, I am not," Lundberg answered. "You're a businessman and I'm telling you I know the business. My dad is a contractor and my older brother is in real estate. So I know how it works. They have a very cozy arrangement."

"Hell, if I'd known that... Why didn't you say so?" Dickman demanded.

"I didn't say so because I am not terribly proud of either of them," the younger man replied. "Now, could we go see Ramos?"

A few minutes later the Jeep stopped in front of the house they'd seen from the springhouse. Lundberg was startled by the contrast from the first place, so much so he simply sat and stared. Here there were no signs of the desert at all. Tall ponderosa pines shaded the house and the cool green lawn. Flower beds lined the walk and ran along the porch facing them, full of bright flowers. Off to the right of the house the slope dropped away to the creek in a deep green carpet of alfalfa and fruit trees in bright plumage dotted the slope. A brown milk cow grazed peacefully in the pasture beyond the creek, occasionally sounding the deep tone of her bell, and tame ducks paddled a pond where the creek was damned.

Below the pond several white bee hives sat like sentry boxes guarding the field and Lundberg thought he could hear the faint hum of tiny wings working the forage. Even the air had changed, full with the light smells of pine and flowers mixed with the deep rich smells of manure and fertile ground. From somewhere came a hint of roasting meat tinged with the spicy aroma of chile and the sharper smell of wood smoke.

Suddenly Lundberg felt at home. He felt the house reaching out to enfold him, inviting him to share its shelter. For a moment the world fell away, leaving him alone with the house in a tiny microcosm of infinity. There Lundberg felt a deep and abiding sense of rightness, of peace and harmony as if the years never touched this place, nor the anxious concerns of a frantic world.

"Nice, ain't it?" For a moment Lundberg was enraged, almost angry enough to attack the man for breaking the mood. A blazing retort formed itself in his mind. Then he realized Dickman was as deeply affected by the place as he. The retort died, unuttered. "Yeah," he said, almost in a whisper. *Perhaps there's hope for him yet*, he thought as he climbed out of the Jeep to ring the bronze watch bell hanging by the gate.

An elderly man appeared in the doorway of the house and waved them in. "Heidy, Ramos!" the realtor called out as they walked up the slope to the porch. "I brought somebody to see you. He's thinking about being your neighbor." The old man met them on the porch. "Ramos, this here's Marty Lundberg," said Dickman.

Lundberg wondered why the realtor was shouting. Perhaps the old man was deaf. He shook hands and said softly, "*Buenos dias, señor. Me gusto a conocer Usted. Se llamo Martin.*"

The old man smiled. "*Buenos dias, muchacho. Usted se habla espanol muy bien.*"

"Hey, I didn't know you spoke Mex...Spanish," said Dickman.

"I learned it in school," replied Lundberg. To the old man he continued in Spanish, "Thank you, sir, but you flatter me. I speak the language very poorly."

"You sell yourself short, young man. You speak the mother tongue very well, indeed. Too well to have learned it strictly in school," the old man replied.

Lundberg grinned and responded, again in Spanish. "A small lie for the *gringo*," he said. "I first learned it from my mother. She was a Delgado before she married."

"I thought so" said Ramos. "Blood will tell. Where was her family from?"

"Jalisco, originally," Lundberg answered. "They moved to Texas before she was born. She grew up in a small town no one ever heard of in the western part of the state. A place called Terlingua."

"Terlingua? I used to work there when the mines were still going." The old man thought a moment. "Delgado? The only Delgado I knew there was the *jeffe*. He was a very good friend of mine. I don't suppose she was related to him, was she? Ignacio Delgado."

"That was my grandfather!" Lundberg said, excited to make connection in such a remote part of the world.

Ramos laughed. "Your grandfather? Aiee! The sins of my youth! Some of the things he and I did! He must have saved my life three times, at least! Which one of his daughters was she, Rosa or Anita?"

"Rosa." Lundberg answered.

"Ah, Rosa," the old man sighed. "The last time I saw her she was still in pigtails. Boy, that's a long time ago! I used to frighten her and her sisters with stories of Pancho Villa. I guess she must have been five, maybe six, when I left." The old man was silent a minute, thinking. Dickman fidgeted nervously but Lundberg simply ignored him. When the old man spoke again, it was with a smile. "You know, you and I are almost relatives. Ignacio was my brother-in-law's wife's cousin." He pointed back and forth between them. "I don't know what that would make us."

"I don't know the Spanish equivalent, but in English that would be what are called 'shirt-tail' cousins." Ramos laughed at Lundberg's attempt to render this in Spanish.

"Hey, what are you two talking about?" Dickman demanded a little sharply. "Speak English."

"I beg your pardon," said Lundberg. "I forgot you don't speak Spanish. We were just exchanging greetings. He thinks my schoolboy's Spanish is funny."

"I don' spik so good the Englis'," said Ramos.

"I'll translate for you," Lundberg said, smiling to the old man. To Dickman he added. "He's more comfortable in Spanish."

Lundberg turned back to Ramos, speaking Spanish. "Tell me, sir, are you acquainted with this man. Is he a friend of yours?"

"I have known him for several years. He is always trying to persuade me to sell this place and move to town. But a friend, no."

"Am I right in mistrusting his word?"

Ramos gave the young man a smile of approval. "You are quite correct. They call him '*el zapo gordo*', the fat toad. I have not had dealings with him but some of my family have. They say he is not cursed with the vice of honesty. It is wise to watch him closely."

"I thought so. I have already caught him in two lies. Besides that, he smells like an old he-goat!" Ramos cackled at the play on words. While *cabrón* literally means "billy goat", to a *chicano* of the American Southwest it is a deadly insult. The only English vernacular equivalent is "motherfucker".

Dickman sensed something going on. "What did you say?" he demanded.

"It was just an old joke about the toad on the road," Lundberg answered easily. "I asked him why he didn't get the county to grade the road so he could have more visitors. He says he really doesn't want them."

"Oh," said Dickman. He was obviously still uneasy.

"Why don't you ask him about the water and let's get back to town. I need to get there before the Post Office closes."

Lundberg nodded and spoke to Ramos. "I must apologize for the manners of this pig," he said. "I would very much like to visit longer but I am riding with him. Could I perhaps come back tomorrow if you wouldn't mind?"

"Why don't you stay the night? My nephew will be coming out tomorrow morning to bring my mail and some supplies. You could catch a ride back into town with him. Unless you're in a hurry."

"You're very kind, but I would not think of imposing."

"Nonsense! We should get acquainted if you are to be my neighbor. Besides, we are shirt-tail cousins." Lundberg laughed at the play on words and Ramos went on. "You want the truth? I would like the company. It is lonely here since my family left."

"Then I accept on one condition. You must let me be useful." Ramos laughed. "Marvelous! My mule died and I need someone to pull the plows. Send the smelly he-goat on his way."

"What did he say?" Dickman wanted to know.

"He asked me to spend the night," Lundberg replied. "I'll catch a ride into town tomorrow with his nephew."

"What?" Dickman was flabbergasted. "Why, you can't be serious."

22

Lundberg decided to be obtuse. "Why not?"

"Look, you're from up north. They do things different. You don't know how things are around here."

"What do you mean?" Lundberg asked quietly.

"I mean they have their place and we have ours. You can't go mixing them. It just won't work."

Lundberg was tired of Dickman and his stupidity. "Look, Mr. Dickman, there is a possibility this man will be my neighbor. He has very kindly offered me the hospitality of his house. What do you expect me to do, throw it back in his face?"

"Well, no, that's not what I meant."

"That's what it would be where I come from. Manners are manners, no matter where you are." Lundberg's voice was very quiet.

"Like I said, they got their place and we got ours. Maybe it's done where you come from but folks think different down here. You can't...."

Lundberg cut him off. Anger put a chill edge to his voice. "I could give a shit what people think! I'll be damned before I let a bunch of stupid assholes tell me how to live."

Dickman flushed, but the prospect of a sale kept him civil. "Now look here, Marty, you don't want to go borrowing trouble. Like it or not you got to live with them. You can't go badmouthing people and expect them to like you for it."

"Jesus Christ, man! Didn't you hear what I just told you? I could care less if they like me. You may have to live with them but I don't. They don't sound like my kind of people and I could give a shit if they decided to drop that fucking little town off the map. I don't live there. I don't ever intend to."

"Hey, they ain't no call to get personal." Dickman was truly offended. "I'm telling you the truth."

"Personal? What else is it? You tell me I can't associate with the people I like and then you say it isn't personal? What the hell else is it?"

Ramos broke in in Spanish, "Easy, young man. He does not understand your anger. He may be stupid but it is not intentional."

"If it were I would not be so angry. Is this how things are around here? Is this what you have to put up with?" Lundberg answered, still seething.

"Not entirely. This one is worse than most but there are many like him. He is right, you know. We do live apart from them, but it is we who prefer it that way." Ramos was clearly trying to avoid trouble. Sensing Ramos was trying to calm the young man, Dickman chose to say nothing.

Lundberg respected his wish. "I can see why. Perhaps you would rather not have a *gringo* in your house. Perhaps you would like to reconsider your offer."

"Of course not! There is only one *gringo* here and he is not invited. One does not invite toads and dogs to the table." The old man grinned.

Lundberg laughed and the tension was gone. Dickman smiled and nodded and the old man continued, "If you think it would be better, then go back into town with him and come out tomorrow. There will be other times we can visit."

"*Mañana no se viene,*" Lundberg replied. Tomorrow never comes. "No, my nose tells me I'll gladly stay."

Dickman sensed the change in mood. "What are you all talking about?" he asked politely.

"If you bothered to learn the language, you'd know," Lundberg pointed out. Dickman flushed and the young man relented. "I beg your pardon. That was a low blow. Among other things I was offering Ramos an apology for our rude behavior."

"Our rude behavior?" Dickman protested. "You was the one with your tail over a rope."

"Mine then." Lundberg glanced at Ramos, then back to the realtor. "Look, this isn't getting us anywhere. I'm going to spend the night here and that's that. I'll let you know what I decide about the place. It will probably be within a week." He hesitated a moment, then added, "I regret flying off the handle like that. You're right. Things are a bit different down here."

"Well, if that's the way you want it," Dickman said.

"That's the way it's going to be."

Dickman shrugged. "All right, then Your choice. You know where to find me." He returned to the Jeep and Lundberg and Ramos watched until it was out of sight. "Eight years!" said the young man. "He's been here eight years and has never learned the language."

"Few of them do. They seem to believe English is the language God speaks." Ramos shrugged.

"I'm sure you're right. Money is their god."

"Yes," said Ramos. "And those of us in *la raza* who wish to make money become *gringos* and join the *gringo* church. It's very sad." Then he suddenly laughed. "Hey, what are we doing moping like two old nuns? There's good food to eat and wine. You like *cabrito*?"

"Never had any," Lundberg grinned. "Although my mother really used to like it. Is it better than *cabrón*?"

"Aiee, much better!" laughed Ramos." *Cabrón* tastes like boiled fat toad! Come on, then. Let's eat and then I'll show you around. It's not much but I am indecently proud of it."

2. La Casa Ramos

J *ackson, Mississippi. When Aubrey James Norvell shot James Meredith that should have been an end of it. After all, the nation was tired of marches. Civil rights was old news and by all rights the man who integrated Old Miss almost four years before should have become just another martyr to the cause of justice for Negroes in the South. For when he crossed the state line, James Meredith had only four companions marching with him, and a major news weekly had written him off as a black Quixote jousting a way of life which left many like him crushed in its wake.*

Then Aubrey Norvell raised his gun and fired, and the South began to change. Then Aubrey Norvell squeezed the trigger three times and the battle cry of "Black Power" went up from Greenville, Mississippi. Then Aubrey Norvell vented his rage and what started as a seemingly pointless gesture by a lone man suddenly became the fulfillment of the worst nightmare of any white supremacist. For James Meredith lived and James Meredith won. James Meredith rejoined the march, and when James Meredith led it into Jackson just three weeks after he began, over four thousand Negro voters had been added to the voter lists in Mississippi. The South would never be the same, ever again.

Even so, the change went far deeper than a change for the South. For Greenville, Mississippi, was a watershed for black-white relations in the whole nation. The cry of "Black Power" echoed across the land from Greenville to Bangor to Tacoma to Phoenix and Houston, touching buried hatreds within the black community and stirring the deepest fears of a white America whose American Dream had begun to fade.... (Martin Quinn's Journal)

Late April 1962. An hour after Dickman left, Lundberg and the old man were sitting on top of a small rise behind Ramos' house. Lundberg was in a torpor, full and content, watching the smoke from his cigarette curl lazily toward the sky. He could still taste the delicate flavor of the cabrito and the chile sauce the old man used to prepare it left a pleasant afterglow in his mouth. "Tell me," he said, "where did you learn to cook like that?"

"Here and there," the old man answered with a careless wave. "I used to cook for a ranch. Did you like it?"

"Too much, I think," Lundberg answered, patting his distended belly. "I wish I could have eaten more. As it is I had to loosen my belt."

"Good," Ramos nodded lazily. "A man should enjoy his food. How about the chile? Do they eat much of that where you come from?"

"Not really," the younger man answered. "They have a watered down version that's more like stew. My mother used to fix the real thing, but not too often. She and I were the only ones who could enjoy it. It tore my father and my brother apart."

Ramos nodded. "We have a saying about chile. It fires you up coming, going, and staying. Some of it is so hot even *chicanos* can't eat it without blowing smoke rings from both ends. Tomorrow you may wish you had never tasted it."

"Maybe so, but right now I'm content. *Mañana no se viene.* Tomorrow never comes. Don't I wish?"

Ramos laughed and nodded agreement. For a few minutes they sat saying nothing and gazing at the peaceful scene below. The sun was almost touching the top of the mountains and the subdued light gave the valley a golden cast. The adobe walls of the house were now a deep gold and the tin roof a fiery bronze. Lundberg liked this house. Set as it was against the mountain, it seemed to rise from the earth as if it were some natural part of creation which had grown there of its own accord. Only the tin roof and the sharp, straight lines of the walls gave any indication it was anything else, and these were softened by the deep shadow of the pines.

As Lundberg watched the shadow of the mountain crept gradually crept over the garden behind the house and then touched the walls, turning gold back into mud and plaster again. Looking farther down the valley he saw a glint from the roof of the other house and turned to Ramos. "What do you know about that place," he said, pointing.

"The old Vasques place?" the old man asked, following his gaze. "As much as anyone, I suppose. I haven't been up there for two, three years."

"Could it ever be made like this?" Lundberg waved an arm to indicate Ramos' homestead.

"Oh, yes, of course," Ramos nodded. "You would not know it now, but at one time that place put this one to shame. But that's been years and years ago." The old man thought a moment. "Yes, you could do it but only with a lot of work. The pigs who lived there before almost destroyed it."

"I was surprised they left the spring in such good shape. Does it run all year?"

"Yes, it is a good spring. I do not remember it ever running dry, but they didn't even take care of that. I had to completely rebuild the cistern and the walls to the spring house."

Lundberg started to ask the old man why he had taken such trouble for a spring not on his land, then decided it was a stupid question. Some things people simply do because they are the people they are and because it needs being done. Instead he said, "You must have been glad to see them go."

"I was. The only time I have had to lock things up was when those *ladrónes* were here. Even then I didn't until things began to disappear." He sighed. "It is sad. That was such a beautiful place once. The Vasques were good people, too, but they had many misfortunes. Some of the old women say it was because they were cursed. I don't know. They were such good friends of mine I cannot understand why they were picked for so much grief. First the father died. Then the sons were taken by the war. Then the mother lived up here alone after the daughters married and left. She went insane for a while. I think it was grief. Then people started saying she was a witch and they took her away to a mental hospital. She died there and for years no one would live there. Then those thieves moved in. They had bad luck, too, but they deserved it." He smiled at Lundberg. "Perhaps I shouldn't tell you these things. You may be superstitious and not want to live there."

"Who isn't superstitious?" Lundberg observed. "But, no, that doesn't bother me. Sometimes people have unexplainable misfortune, but from what I've seen most people who have bad luck make it themselves. Mostly, I think, because they don't think things through. Or don't even try to see things except the way they want them."

"Like a certain young man I met recently, perhaps?"

Lundberg blushed. "Yeah, it was kind of dumb letting Dickman get to me like that. I just hope I didn't make trouble for you."

"Me?" Ramos mimicked. "I'm just a dumb Mesikin. I don' know nahsing." He smiled. "Seriously, think nothing of it. 'Sufficient unto the day is the Dickman thereof.'"

"Something like that." Lundberg grinned. "Still, I'm going to paint my window frames blue."

"I doesn't hurt to be sure," said Ramos, looking at his own windows which were dark blue. "I tell myself I did it because my wife wanted it that way, but that would not be altogether true. Some people laugh and call it superstition, but if you watch you will usually find they carry a rabbit's foot or follow the zodiac or something." He glanced down the canyon. "Still, the old women say it is cursed and no one who lives there will ever find happiness."

"Who does?" asked Lundberg. "Are those frightened old women happy?"

"A good point." Ramos glanced toward the sun which was now behind the mountains. "Aiee! It's getting late and here I sit talking like an old fool. I must care for the animals."

"Let me help you." Lundberg rose and followed Ramos down the slope from the house toward the barns. With the sun gone the breeze turned back down the valley draining air down from the snow-covered peaks. By the time they reached the back door Lundberg was shivering.

Ten days later Martin Lundberg was back at the Ramos place sitting through the afternoon heat on the cool of the front porch. It was quiet and still with only the rush of the stream along the canyon floor breaking the silence. As they sat the two men sipped wine Ramos made himself and Lundberg reported the results of his trip to Santa Fe.

The trip had been a success. After he left the canyon with Luis, Ramos' nephew, Lundberg spent a great deal of time searching courthouse and state records, then making long distance calls. Between telephone calls he'd sold his sports car and bought a sound, but ancient Ford pickup. With his business done he loaded the truck with tools and supplies and camping gear, and then headed back to the canyon. There he found Ramos glad to see him, and full of his usual humor.

The truck Lundberg bought was the center of a great deal of lively talk. At some point in its career someone painted it a bright, electric purple. Someone later on decided the trim should be contrasting and painted the fenders and the wheels bright orange, then added a diesel truck horn as an afterthought. A long whip antenna attached to the rear bumper was apparently never meant to be functional, for there was no sign of a radio ever being mounted in the cab. The effect was rather striking and unique, and the two men decided something with such character deserved to be named.

They considered many names, then discarded them all. Finally Lundberg said, "Well, maybe I'll just call it *El Burro*. After all, it's like a donkey, built for work."

"Yes," said Ramos, "but this truck has soul. Surely it needs something more than that, something that describes it without question. Something like *El Burro Colorado*."

"Or *El Burro Morado*." Lundberg laughed and switched to English. "Well, I guess we could call it the Purple Ass." He took a sip of wine.

"*El Burro Morado*," mused Ramos. "Aiee!" he shouted. "That's it! *Un Burro Morado ... El Obispo*! Call it *El Burro Obispo*."

Lundberg almost choked on his wine. "All right," he laughed, "that's what it will be. The Bishop's Ass."

The men sat in silence for a long while. Then Ramos said, "So we are going to be neighbors. I'm glad."

"That's what it looks like," said Lundberg. "I've got to go back to Santa Fe next week and close the deal. The lawyer there said the title's in good shape. So there shouldn't be any trouble closing." He grinned. "Then the work begins."

"You have bought yourself a lot of work, my friend," said the old man. "And you were wise to hire a lawyer in Santa Fe. These local *putos* know when each other break wind. It is not good to let them know your business."

"I thought so. From what I've seen they have got things tied up pretty tight in town." Lundberg shrugged. "Dickman's not going to like it much, but there's not much he can do."

"You've not told him yet, have you?" The old man looked worried.

"No, but I don't see what he can do about it even if he knows. The people in California are anxious to sell and angry that he's not done so. It's been on the market two years."

"They are good people," said Ramos. "It is a shame they could not move here themselves, but then, I wouldn't have you for a neighbor." He smiled and raised his glass. "As the *gringos* say, 'Here's to good neighbors.'"

They drank the toast. Then Lundberg said, "You forget. I'm half *gringo*."

"There's no half way," replied Ramos. "If you were *gringo* you would be in Santa Fe stealing money from other *gringos*. It's the soul that counts and your mother gave you the soul of *la raza*. Your father only gave you a *gringo* face." He shrugged. "Even so, it's a useful gift. With it you can fool the *gringos* and still be a *chicano* where it counts. In your heart!"

Lundberg flushed and the old man hurried on. "Forgive me. I embarrass You. I get too personal. When one gets to my age one knows there is little time to be wasted on lies, even polite ones. It's the wine. '*In vino veritas.*'"

Lundberg glanced up, amazed to hear such clear classic Latin coming from the mouth of someone he'd thought essentially a rustic. "You are surprised?" laughed Ramos. "A priest told me that. What he didn't 't tell me was '*sapientam vino adumbrairi*'"

"I'm afraid you'll have to translate," Lundberg confessed.

"A beautiful paradox. In wine there is truth, but wisdom is clouded by wine. I've thought about it for years and have not decided which is better to have, wisdom or truth. At the moment, however, dear *Martus Aurelius,* we seem to be more in pursuit of Truth. Lady Wisdom must await the morrow, alas."

Ramos laughed at the bewildered expression on Lundberg 's face. "You're wondering where this old *pendejo* came up with such pleasant nonsense. It is really quite simple. I was once a Jesuit novitiate. Aiee, they drilled us in Latin!"

" 'I don' spik so good the Englis'.'" mimicked Lundberg.

"Precisely, " replied Ramos in perfect English. "It is never wise to let the world know how much one knows. Only a fool flaunts his knowledge. We can speak English, if you wish."

"No, I prefer Spanish. I need the practice."

"Good. That's as it should be. It 's a much better language for anything but making money, and the Spaniards were not bad at that." Ramos took a sip of his wine. "Tell me, why did you come here to live?"

"This was the first place I found that suited me. Actually, it was the first place I looked at seriously. Chance, I suppose. Nowhere else really felt right."

"Very little is due to chance," answered the old man. He waved a hand toward the desert outside the canyon. "What I mean is why did you come here to the ends of the earth to look?"

"Oh, a number of reasons. To put it in a nutshell, I want a better way to live. Have you ever lived in the city?" Ramos nodded and the young man went on. "Then you know what I mean. It's not something easy to explain." He lapsed into thought.

"Ah!" exclaimed Ramos. "There I go being a nosy old *brujo* again. I beg your pardon."

"No, I don't mind. Not at all. I've spent a lot of time trying to figure it out myself. What it boils down to is rather simple. There were so many things I didn't like about the way I was living, but there didn't seem much choice. Most of what I was doing seemed rather pointless and there didn't seem many alternatives there. So I started looking. Mostly for time and a place to think."

Lundberg looked at the old man. The grey eyes were compelling and Ramos was startled by the power and depth of pain he saw there. "Other people don't seem to be bothered, but I am. They don't seem able to see what I see. I see it so clearly it hurts. I don't like it and I don't know why I'm this way, but I don't seem to have much choice."

He shrugged. "I've got to honor the way I am, so here I am. I don't really know what I'm looking for or where to find it, but this seems like a place to start. Does that make any sense to you?"

"Yes, it does," the old man answered softly. "A great deal of sense. I came here for much the same reason, to think." Ramos looked around. "Now I've been thinking for forty years and I'm not much farther along than when I first began." He regarded the young man closely. "But that's not all of it, is it?"

Lundberg laughed. "Old Man Moses! You're too smart for your own good. They lost a good confessor when they let you go. No, that's not all of it." Once again they grey eyes caught Ramos' own. The old man felt like they were seeing the depths of his soul. The younger man smiled and went on. "I suspect the biggest reason I'm here is probably the same reason you're not a priest."

"Aiee! Who's being Old Man Moses now? I'm not a priest because I had too much fire in my loins."

"Yes, and that's what makes a man a man, isn't it?" the young man asked. "You're not talking about heat for a woman and neither am I."

"You should have been a lawyer," the old man asserted. "When you get your teeth into something you don't let go."

Lundberg's gaze softened and he started to apologize, but the old man waved it off. "No," he said, "it's my own fault for bringing it up. Please, do go on. I don't have much chance to talk of such things these days."

Lundberg grinned. "Well, as a matter of fact, I was a lawyer. Or almost. I finished law school and passed the bar but never really practiced law. Perhaps I should have, but I never did. I simply didn't have the heart for it. I don't know about being a priest but being a lawyer seemed an equally cloistered existence. When I told Dickman I didn't want anyone telling me how to live I meant it. That's what was happening back home. I saw myself locked into the professional thing and ending up dried up with nothing left but a thousand unfulfilled dreams to show for having never lived."

Lundberg sighed deeply. "Nothing else I looked at seemed much different. Lead a safe, bland life and at the end they seal you in a marble tomb and forget you. So what's the point?"

"Ah, but perhaps you are looking at a dried up old man with a thousand unfulfilled dreams," Ramos said. "Have you considered that?"

"Yes, but I see a difference," the young man replied. "A real difference. You made a conscious choice. At least that's what I think." Ramos nodded and Lundberg went on. "Besides, you have something to show for having lived. Few men have accomplished what you have here."

"Yes, but you only see a small part of what I hoped to do. You don't know of all I dreamed of doing and never accomplished."

"Yes, but damn it you tried!" Lundberg answered passionately. "You haven't given up yet. You could have lead a comfortable life as a priest. I could have as a lawyer. You chose not to. The way I see it looking in from the outside, you took responsibility for your own life. That's better than letting others make decisions for you and drifting along with the crowd like a sheep, isn't it?"

"I like to think so, my friend," the old man said somewhat sadly.

"Yet, you are wrong about one thing. One can do that as a lawyer or even a priest. The point is nothing comes easy. There is a price one pays for being his own man. You see, I did not quit the novitiate. They dismissed me, and from their point of view, for a good reason. There is a price one pays."

"Yes, but I don't see there's much choice," Lundberg said. "Even when your friends become strangers and your family abandons you I don't see what else one can do. What are we supposed to do, sell our souls for a little comfort? What's the point in that? I tried to live that way and I damned near died! I tried to make some sense of it, but it just didn't work. The harder I tried, the more pointless it became, until all I was doing was taking up space. So I just quit. In the end it was that or blow my brains out."

"So now you chase the rainbow," Ramos nodded approval. "Good. Too much sanity is not good for a man." He considered the other for a long moment. "So what do you do now? Where do you go from here?"

Lundberg laughed. "The Vasques place will give me more than enough to do for a year or two. While I'm working on that I'll have time to sort things out. After that, who knows? I might be a writer." He grinned. "Or a priest."

Ramos gave him a strange look. "Well," he said casually, "when you're ready, let me know. One of the novice masters is an old friend of mine from the seminary. Our lives have gone in different ways but we stay in touch."

"Hey!" Lundberg protested. "I was just kidding. I can't imagine myself...." He stopped, then laughed. Ramos was grinning. "All right, you caught me there. Still, I am serious about the writing."

Ramos thought a moment. "The Vasques place is a good plan. Something to occupy your hands and time to think. As for the other, I don't know."

"Why do you say that?" Lundberg asked, puzzled.

"It was just a thought. I do not know much about writing. I never tried that." Ramos waved his hand over his farm. "I do know this. I think you may find yourself so busy there is no time for much else."

Lundberg nodded. "I hope not. There's only one way I know to find out. Try it and see if it works. I'm not in any rush."

"Good. Too many people try to hurry the cow with calf. Here, we need more wine." Ramos rose to go inside but stopped, looking down the canyon. "Speak of the devil," he muttered, "and he appears on your doorstep."

Lundberg rose from his chair and followed the old man's gaze. Down the valley he could see Dickman's Jeep making its way toward the house. "I suppose I need to talk to him sooner or later," he said. Then he turned to Ramos. "I did not intend to bring trouble to your doorstep. I'll tell him I'm still thinking about it and send him on his way."

Lundberg walked down the steps and crossed the lawn to the place his truck was parked. "No need," Ramos called after him. "Better to meet him on familiar ground."

"All right," said the younger man, "but we'll talk down here. I don't want him smelling up your porch." Ramos laughed and went into the house. Lundberg leaned against the fender of his truck and watched the Jeep come up the drive.

Dickman parked next to the pickup and got out. "Heidey, Marty," he said. "How you been?" He continued without waiting for an answer. "Where have you been? I've been trying to get hold of you for a week. Feller I talked to in town said he seen you driving out this way."

"I've been attending to some business," said Lundberg noncommittally.

"Hey, you got a new pickup! You must be planning to settle around here somewheres." Dickman laughed and gave Lundberg a huge wink. He looked toward the house. "Heidey, Ramos. Rheumatiz got you down?" Lundberg looked up and saw Ramos coming down the walk supporting himself with an ornate walking cane. Dickman went on. "Say, why don't we go on up to the porch and talk. It's cooler there."

"We can talk here," said Lundberg. "What can I do for you?"

"Huh? Oh, I was wondering what you'd decided to do?"

"I've decided to buy the place," the young man answered.

"Well, good. You're getting yourself a good deal." There was no mistaking Dickman's pleasure.

"I think so." Lundberg was still noncommittal and Dickman was surprised. At this point most buyers were eager and terribly excited, and the young man was showing none of the anxiety most buyers show. He decided the young man was covering with a very good poker face.

"Well," Dickman said. "I better get back to town and set up the paperwork."

"That won't be necessary, Mr. Dickman," Lundberg told him.

"What do you mean?" the realtor asked.

"I have decided to deal directly with the principals and let our lawyers handle the details. The deal's set."

"What? You can't do that!" Dickman was indignant.

"Sure I can. The Gerrards were more than happy to deal with me. They have had their place on the market two years now and you haven't moved it. Your contract with them stipulated you had six months to sell the property, after which they could sell it themselves and that is exactly what they are doing."

Dickman was getting angry. "That contract also says they got to find their own prospects. I was the one who brought you out here and showed you around! By God I'll sue you both if you go behind my back like that!"

Lundberg shrugged. "Don't worry, Mr. Dickman. You'll get your six per cent as the contract stipulates. You don't really deserve it but you'll get it. My lawyer will mail you the check."

"You damned right he will. Tell that lawyer the fee's six hundred."

"Six hundred is six per cent of ten thousand, Dickman, but the selling price is half that. Your fee will be three hundred. Not bad for an afternoon's work."

Dickman was livid. "Three hundred? My minimum's five hundred."

Lundberg shrugged. "Three hundred. Hobson's choice, take it or leave it. Not a penny more."

"You goddamned cheat!" Dickman's face was flushed and veins stood out on each side of his throat.

"No, Dickman," Lundberg said, more patiently than he felt. "I'm not the cheat. You thought you had a patsy with more money than sense, even after I told you I know the business. You should have listened. If you'd been honest with me I'd have been glad to have you handle the deal. As it was you tried to cheat me and you jacked up the price so you could swindle your clients. I think you planned to sell it to me for eight thousand, tell the Gerrards you sold for four, and then pocket the difference plus your commission. I've talked to them and to the Real Estate

Board in Santa Fe. We could push it and probably nail you for fraud. At the very least we could have your license."

Dickman's face evolved from anger to fear and back to anger as Lundberg spoke. "You cheat!" he said. "You goddamned filthy Yankee cheat!"

Lundberg ignored his words. "That being the case, I'd advise you to get back in your Jeep and get out of here while I'm still in an agreeable mood. You might talk yourself out of three hundred dollars and into a criminal complaint."

"You ... Meskin-lover!" Dickman spat at him.

Lundberg's reply was deathly quiet. "That's quite enough, Dickman. Keep your filthy bigotry to yourself."

Dickman mistook the soft reply for fear. "I'll tell you something, Yankee boy! You think you can come down here with your money and your high school Spanish and walk all over us, but by God that ain't the way it's going to be. You try it and we'll by God show you how it is. You better get your butt back up north where it belongs with your other Meskin-loving friends."

"For your information, Mister Dickman, my mother was named Delgado before she married. I suppose that makes me a 'Meskin' in your eyes. Good! I'd rather be a 'Meskin' than poor white trash like you!"

"You can't talk to me like that!" Dickman yelled.

"Can't I? Well, it seems I just did. Now what the fuck are you going to do about it?" Lundberg moved forward, pressed the attack. His face was hard with angry determination and there was a certain recklessness in his manner that was unmistakable. For the first time Dickman was afraid.

"What's the matter, asshole?" Lundberg taunted. "Can't you take what you dish out? Who the fuck do you think you are?" He reached out and shoved the other back.

For a moment Dickman wavered. He was angry enough to attack, but he could clearly see the younger man was ready to fight, wanted it. Something in the young man's eyes burned with the deep glow of ancient rage, a dreadful beast which begged to be unleashed and allowed to run wild. Suddenly Dickman shuddered. He knew he would lose. There was nothing he could grab to even the advantage. He took a step back but Lundberg followed. When Lundberg spoke his voice was like a whip.

"You had better get out while you can, Dickman. And you'd better apologize to Mr. Ramos for being such a jackass."

"Now wait a minute! I ain't...."

"Yes, you will! If you don't I am going to beat you to a bloody pulp and there's nothing on God's green earth that's going to stop me. Now DO IT!"

"Jesus! All right! I'll do it. Sorry, Ramos," the realtor muttered.

"You're sorry Mister Ramos," Lundberg corrected.

"All right. I'm sorry, Mr. Ramos."

Lundberg stepped back and Dickman hurriedly climbed into the Jeep. As he did so he remembered the loaded pistol he kept in the glove compartment. His hand was on the weapon when he heard a door open behind him and felt a sharp prick at the back of his neck. He heard the soft voice of Ramos say, "I would not do that, *senór*."

Dickman slowly moved his hand away from the pistol and turned his head cautiously. The old man was holding a sharply pointed blade a half inch from his neck. The blade ended in the handle of the ornate walking stick and Ramos' face held an odd smile. "Get the pistol," he said to Lundberg in Spanish.

Lundberg opened the other door and retrieved the weapon. It was an expensive Colt revolver with a short barrel, the kind firearms manufacturers describe as an "undercover" model. Lundberg opened the cylinder and removed the cartridges. He found the soft lead noses deeply scored in an "X" pattern. He drew back his arm to throw the weapon down hill into the fish pond but Dickman shouted, "Hey, wait! That cost ninety dollars."

Lundberg smiled and shrugged. "It wasn't my ninety dollars," He answered, throwing the bullets into the pond.

"Hey, I didn't mean no harm," whined Dickman. "I was just going to throw a scare into you. Come on, Marty. My son give me that pistol for Christmas."

"Ah, so it's all his fault. I see. And if I'd been shot that would have been a terrible accident." Lundberg smiled and shrugged. "Well, I suppose since it's got sentimental value...." Dickman smiled back weakly but the younger man was far from done. He walked to his truck and rummaged around in the back, producing a gunny sack and a heavy hammer.

Suddenly Dickman understood what Lundberg intended to do and started to protest, but the young man's glance silenced him. As Dickman watched with horror Lundberg laid the revolver carefully on the sacking, wrapped it tight and laid the bundle on a flat rock. Then he struck it twice with the hammer.

"There," Lundberg said, unwrapping the sacking. "Look, I didn't even scratch the finish." He handed the ruined weapon to Dickman, who looked as if he might cry. The cylinder of the pistol was warped and the barrel slightly bent. Lundberg went on. "I really wouldn't try shooting it. Might blow your hand off. That's the way it goes sometimes."

A very subdued Dickman started his Jeep and drove off down the canyon. Lundberg and Ramos watched until he was out of sight. "You were very hard on him, my son," said the old man.

"Not half so much as he deserved, grandfather," an equally subdued Lundberg replied. Then he sighed. "You're right, of course. That was rather foolish. I'm afraid I've brought you trouble."

"Life is trouble," said Ramos, pleased with Lundberg's use of a familiar mode of address. "I am more concerned for you than I am for me."

"You know what I hate so much about people like him?" the younger man asked. "They bring out the worst in me. And I let it happen."

The old man nodded and sheathed his sword. For a moment he looked incredibly sad. "Yes," he said, almost to himself. "Sometimes they force you to kill them." Then he shook himself. "Hey!" he shouted. "Are we going to let a stinking *gringo* ruin our whole afternoon? Let's have some more wine and talk about your new house."

"Sounds good to me," replied Lundberg. "Where in the world did you get that pig sticker?"

"Where else, from a priest? He gave it to me. It was made in Spain."

"You know some of the strangest priests," Lundberg said, laughing.

"Ah yes! I know some of the strangest people, too," the old man replied. They both laughed as they walked back up the steps to the house.

3. Christmas with los Ramos

Autumn 1962. The sun was high in the deep blue sky but the November air tempered its power to a gentle warmth. Even so, Martin Lundberg was sweating heavily by the time he carefully placed the last heavy stone in the wall and sat down to smoke and inspect his work. He was pleased by what he saw. The fallen rubble was once again in place and formed a broad wall surrounding the house. The yard was clear of the last inhabitants' trash and all the cactus had been rooted up except for an large clump in one corner of the fence. A narrow walk of flat paving stones ran through the yard from the house, ending in a wide gate framed of light cedar logs, and the hard ground on either side of the walk was soft now from hours of backbreaking spade work where manure from within the house had been carefully worked in. Here and there sprigs of lawn held a foothold, and green from the small pines Lundberg had transplanted along the fence remained bright despite the late season.

Beyond the gate the purple truck sat with its wheels blocked against the incline, while a pair of new ruts wound down the slope to the valley where they joined the main road. As Lundberg looked down the valley, an ancient grey Chevrolet coupe came into sight and turned up his drive. It was Luiz Gallegos, Ramos' nephew, come to bring supplies and the weekly mail.

Lundberg crossed the yard and watched until the grey coupe, engine complaining and belching oil fumes, shuddered to a stop behind the pickup. "Come in, Luiz," he shouted over the last coughs of the engine. "We missed you last week. What happened?"

"Hello, Martin." Luiz pronounced it Lundberg's name in the Spanish manner, making it sound like "HO-nas." "Ah, this *chingada de puta* threw a rod and when I got that fixed the goddamned water pump went out. I had to go all the way to Santa Fe to find another one!"

41

Lundberg laughed. "When are you going to get rid of that thing and get yourself a decent car?"

"I told you already. When you decide to trade me for the purple burro!" They both laughed at their ritual. Luiz looked around and whistled. "Man, you got this place looking good," he said. "Hey, you painted the house."

Lundberg was pleased Luiz noticed. "Yeah, it makes it look a lot different, doesn't it. Come on in. I've got some beer cold."

The two men unloaded the supplies and carried them into the house. Lundberg opened two cans of beer, and as they sat on the porch to drink them Luiz produced a package of 'tailor-made' cigarettes, offering one to Lundberg. Lundberg accepted, grateful at the change from his usual hand rolled wonders, and for a while they sat and talked as they sipped the cold beer. A new baby, the third now, was immanent in Luiz's household, and Lundberg laughed at the descriptions Luiz gave of the chaos that reigned. For some reason, not entirely clear, all three of his wife's aunts had come to assist her with the new baby, and Luiz found himself in the position of being a tolerated nuisance in his own home. Naturally, each of the aunts came with the intention of taking charge of the family and there were frequent conflicts of authority. Luiz was caught too often in the middle of these rivalries.

"Man," said Luiz, "you wouldn't believe some of the things that have happened. Aunt Luz came first, and naturally I had to give up my own bed so she could be close to my wife. Then the other two came and I even had to give up the couch and sleep on the floor. Then, when I suggested that I should stay at a friend's house my wife had hysterics and accused me of deserting her. Of course, the other three had to give me hell about it, too. Jesus!"

"Be glad you aren't an Arab," said Lundberg.

"How come?" asked Luiz.

"Well, some of them have several wives. Think how it must be with them," Lundberg laughed. "You think you have problems now! What if you had three wives?"

"Aiee! I'd rather not. One wife is bad enough, let alone the aunts. You know what they did?" Lundberg shook his head, "When they all got there they had a big fight about who was going to cook. First Aunt Luz said she was, then Aunt Estrella said no, she was. Then Aunt Carmen got mad and said she was the best cook, so she should. For an hour they argued about that. Finally, they all got mad and none of them would cook. When I got home from work they were all sitting in the living room glaring at each other and not speaking a word. I didn't know what was happening so I asked when supper would be ready. *Hijo*! I should have poked a hornets' nest instead." Luiz shook his head sadly.

"So what happened?"

"Man, they all took after me. From what they said you would have thought I was an ungrateful slave driver that got my wife pregnant so I could abuse her for not having my supper ready whenever I demanded it. That was the kindest thing they said. Finally I got mad and threatened to throw them all out in the street if they didn't shut up." Luiz smiled ruefully. "I shouldn't have said that. My wife came in just then and naturally she had to go into hysterics over that. Of course, that got them started all over again, and I finally left and went to my friend's house, anyway. They haven't let me forget that, either."

"Who ended up doing the cooking?" Lundberg asked.

"Who do you think? Me!" Luiz answered, jabbing himself with a forefinger. "Now they complain and say the food isn't fit to eat. Aiee, women!"

Lundberg laughed at Luiz's plight. "You make me glad I'm still a bachelor," he said.

"Enjoy it while you can," answered Luiz. "Hey, I almost forgot." He reached in a jacket pocket and extracted two letters, one of which was addressed in an elegant, feminine hand. "Maybe you're not a bachelor too long, after all," he teased. "Very pretty handwriting. Nice smell, too."

Lundberg glanced at the letters and smiled. "Forget it, Luiz. It's from my mother."

Luiz was disappointed. "Too bad," he said. "Don't you have a girl friend from where you came?

"No, not any more. I used to have several."

Luiz sighed. "Hey, a real heart breaker. I wish sometimes I was one again, too."

"Not always? Or is it only when the aunts come?" Lundberg asked.

Luiz laughed and shook his head. "Definitely when the aunts are here. But no, not any more. I'm too old and fat now, but sometimes in the spring when a pretty girl walks by...." He shrugged and finished the sentence by emptying his can of beer. "Old and fat like the old grey mare."

Lundberg crumpled his beer can and tossed it at a garbage can in the yard. The beer can bounced off the rim of the can, flew straight up, then tumbled in. "Good shot," said Luiz and tried the toss himself. He missed. "So much for the pros," he laughed.

"You want another?" asked Lundberg, retrieving the can Luiz had thrown and dropping it in the bin.

"No, I've got to get up to Uncle Mano's" Luiz answered. "You want to ride along?"

"Sure," Lundberg replied, crossing to the house and fetching a sweater from a peg behind the door. He joined Luiz in the grey coupe and they rolled backwards toward the creek. Luiz switched on the ignition and popped the clutch, causing the whole car to lurch and the engine to cough reluctantly to life. "Speaking of old grey mares," Martin said, "I think maybe I should walk. Riding in this thing is taking your life in your hands."

"Quit insulting my fine car," Luiz grinned. "It might get mad and quit before I get back to town. Then I might have to ride in your purple contraption." Luiz laughed. "Besides, I don't talk about your pickup that way. I don't even mention the horrible orange wheels."

"That's because you're jealous. If I had a car this decrepit I'd be jealous, too," Lundberg answered.

"And if I had a pickup like yours my wife would leave me and my children would throw rocks at it."

"Maybe the aunts would leave, too, if you drove it home." Luiz laughed, then and began another story about the tyranny of the three aunts, and how he had ended up washing the dishes as well as doing the cooking. The story took them all the way up the canyon to Ramos' place where Luiz announced their arrival with a loud blast of his car horn.

Old and decrepit as the car might be, Luiz was proud of the horns. They were a combination put together from a wrecked semi-tractor and a Model A Luiz had found in the local wrecking yard. To these he added something called the Wild Horse Whinny from a mail order catalogue, and the resulting cacophony was terrifying to livestock. As Luiz sounded the horns a second time, Lundberg saw a flock of chickens scatter, wildly flapping their winds and cackling as the milk cow ran for the woods at the edge of the pasture and the heard of goats scattered. Only Ramos' huge house cat remained sitting high on the front porch, viewing the proceedings with bored disdain.

Ramos appeared from behind the house, waving a hoe in mock anger. "Hey, you *pendejo* nephew," he shouted. "Quit scaring the animals and come inside. Where were you last week, getting drunk?"

"No, Tio. I was in jail for being your nephew!" Luiz opened the trunk and he and Lundberg quickly emptied it and carried Ramos' supplies into the house. Inside there was the delicate smell of cooking beans and Luiz sniffed the air appreciatively. He winked at Lundberg, "Hey, the old man must have got himself a woman," he said. "Something smells awfully good for a change."

"*Ai, Dios!*" cried Ramos, throwing up his hands in supplication. "That a man should be blessed with such relatives in his old age. A week late getting him food for his belly and they insult his table. I shall probably have to feed him, too."

"He should trade places with me," Luiz remarked to Lundberg, who laughed as Luiz spun out a long, involved explanation of the advent of the aunts and his car problems. The old man set the table while he listened, and then put out an enormous bowl of beans and a plate piled high with flour tortillas. Beside each plate he placed a water tumbler and in the middle of the table he carefully set down a gallon jug of his own wine. The jug was made of dark glass, which Ramos once told Lundberg preserved the delicate taste of the wine, and his care was to keep from disturbing the sediment at the bottom of the jug. The wine turned out to be a light red, full bodied, but delicate and fruity, with no harsh aftertaste. Looking around the table, Ramos nodded satisfaction to himself and waved them to sit down.

Luiz was still speaking when they sat down to sit down and eat, pausing only to observe the moment of silence and short blessing which was custom of the house. Lundberg had wondered about the custom, one familiar from his own family but not one he followed himself, but he had never asked the old man about this apparent contradiction with his often irreligious point of view. Yet Ramos had seen his question and answered without his having to ask. "You wonder why this sacrilegious old *pendejo* always says grace, aren't you?" he asked.

"Since you mention it, yes," Lundberg agreed.

"You're far too polite to ask directly," the old man grinned. Lundberg nodded. "Well, first of all, there are no stupid questions, *sabes?*" He pointed back and forth. "Not between us, eh?" Lundberg nodded, glad Ramos had chosen to use the familiar form of address.

"There are stupid people but not stupid questions," the old man continued. "They are the real fools. *Tantos* is the polite name, but I prefer *pendejos*. All a person's questions reflect is ignorance, not stupidity. The real stupidity is not to ask when one needs to know something."

"I don't really need to know," Lundberg answered. "I was simply curious. I didn't want to pry."

Ramos nodded. "I know, but I am telling you not to be afraid to ask, anything."

Lundberg gave him a knowing look. "One might assume that gives you the right to do the same."

The old man cackled. "Our Rosa didn't raise a *pendejo*, did she? Touche. I'm a nosy old *brujo*."

Lundberg considered a short moment. "I really don't mind, I guess, so I'll ask. How come you say grace?"

"For the same reason I pray the hours," Ramos replied. At Lundberg's raised eyebrows he nodded. "Oh, yes, I do. Not the way I used to, but I do." He raised an instructing finger. "While I have very little use for the Church, things of the spirit are quite another matter."

"Aren't they the same?" Lundberg was truly puzzled.

"Not at all, although the Church would have one think so," Ramos nodded. "Church is about power and prestige and position. It preaches religion, which means its doctrines and rules. Yet if one looks at the sacred stories, its Master never spoke of such things."

"That's not what I was told," Lundberg replied.

"No, because those in power do not want you to be free," the old man told him. "They are desperately afraid of the very freedom the one whom they call their God bought them with his life. They confuse freedom with licentiousness."

"What are you saying?"

"Simply this. What the Nazarene taught was a way of life, a way of life so radical few dare follow it. What the Church he founded preaches now is exactly what he preached against when he walked this earth in human feet! Power, possessions and prestige."

Ramos eyes blazed with an intensity Lundberg had never before seen there. "No wonder they kicked you out," he said. "You must have been way too radical, even for a Jesuit."

"Yes." The old man's laughter washed away the harsh intensity of the moment before. "Even for the Jesuits. I read once, 'Scratch a Jesuit, find a rebel.' And it's true. They tend to foster different points of view. Yet even they have their limits and those were far too narrow for me."

"Yet you still pray."

"Oh, yes," Ramos smiled. "Several times each day. I still use their book of the offices, too. I find the discipline very cleansing." He looked at the younger man. "You still don't understand, do you?"

"Not really," Lundberg confessed.

"Well, let me put it another way," Ramos said. "After a long while I came to understand my quarrel was not with God but with the Church. That was after I stopped blaming God for the evils done in the name of God by the Church."

Lundberg's face suddenly lit up. "You sound like one of the professors I had. Comparative religion." He thought a moment. "I'm trying to remember a story he told. Something about someone being black-balled from church membership."

Ramos chuckled. "Well, if it's the same story I heard, God consoles the man by telling him He's been black-balled there, too."

"That's it!" Lundberg said, excitedly. "The professor's point was that it is possible God has more trouble with Church rules and doctrines than we do."

"Exactly," Ramos observed dryly, "which is why this old *pendejo* is sitting here now rather than in some posh rectory." He shrugged, holding up his glass. "I think the wine tastes better here, too."

Crossing himself quickly, Luiz continued the tale of his woes. "So, between the *chingada* car and the old aunts I couldn't get away and there was no way to send word."

"Those old *brujas*!" muttered Ramos, with an unusual lack of charity. "They've been terrorizing the family for years. You should throw them all out."

47

"I would if they weren't relatives," said Luiz, shrugging. "But what can I do but hope the baby comes soon?"

"Then they'll want to stay and help until your wife is well," Ramos pointed out. "You'll never get rid of them."

"If they do, I'm going to move up here with you," Luiz replied.

Ramos laughed. "And eat me out of house and home!" He pushed the bowl of beans and plate of tortillas toward his nephew. "Have some more," he said. "There's too much here for me to keep."

The two men fell to talking about recent things which had happened in town. Since Lundberg did not know most of the people they were talking about, he excused himself and went out to the front porch to read the letters Luiz brought. Taking out the letter from his mother he opened it and began to read, taking out the makings and rolling a cigarette as he did. Casually touching the flame to the end of the lumpy tube of paper he held between two fingers, Lundberg blew the match out with his first exhalation of smoke, and carefully placed the now dead stick back in the match box, tail first. He was careful to make sure it was out. He'd failed to do so only once.

There was little news from his mother that Martin Lundberg did not know already. Two of his friends were getting married and a couple he knew well were in the final stages of divorce. An epidemic of exotic influenza had laid the town low, although the family had been fortunate in escaping infection. The exception was an elderly aunt with heart problems and everyone was gravely concerned for her.

Quickly Lundberg skimmed through these items until he came to something which caught his interest. A distant cousin just back from a military tour in Thailand had asked for his address. The cousin, John Thompson, would soon be out of the service and wished to see Lundberg. Lundberg was pleased. He had not seen Jack for several years, although they grew up together and were once quite close. He glanced at the return address on the other letter and deciphered the broad scrawl enough to see it was from Thompson. Yet he decided to wait to open it until he finished his mother's letter.

Halfway through her letter, his mother's normally cheerful tone changed to melancholy. The snows had come early, bringing with them gray cloudy skies and cold north winds, and already she was dreading the months of forced confinement until spring. Things were going well enough for the family, but she had just passed a cheerless Thanksgiving in the company of her husband and eldest son, and could take little pleasure from the business successes they spoke of constantly. She said they hoped he might come for Thanksgiving, although he knew well it was she, not his father and brother who wanted to see him, and were disappointed he hadn't been there. She hoped he would come home at Christmas, so the family could be together again.

Lundberg found the letter horribly depressing, and for the first time since leaving home, his conscience began to torment him. He'd written regularly, at least once a month, but it was eight months now since he'd seen his family and six since he called. The thought of his mother alone with an irascible husband and a whining son made him feel like a traitor for a moment.

Yet when he thought of the possibility of moving home, he dismissed it out of hand. The estrangement from his father was as complete for him as it was for his mother, and while he felt something resembling fraternal fondness for his brother, he could not stomach the man's company for long.

A move back could well be as disastrous for his mother as for himself. The results were all too predictable. The family would soon be torn apart by old disagreements, by the old rituals of anger and resentment and recrimination which would never be abandoned. Within a week of his return the family would be once more battlefield torn by the armed camps of his father and brother aligned against his mother and himself. Even a short visit would be painfully disruptive, for his father would hound him from the moment he walked in the door and his mother would fly to his defense. Far better to remain alone.

Lundberg's reverie was interrupted by the departure of Luiz, who left saying if he stayed any longer his wife's aunts would flay him. Lundberg paid him for the supplies and thanked him for bringing his mail, then returned to his dilemma while Ramos walked Luiz to the car. After a few moments he heard the gray coupe drive off and looked up to see Ramos regarding him gravely. "Bad news?" asked the old man.

"No, not really," he answered. "Just a letter from home. Winter's come and my mother's feeling low."

"Ah, she misses her favorite son?" Ramos murmured.

"What makes you think I'm her favorite?" Lundberg asked.

Ramos shrugged and sighed. "Sometimes, Martin, you are terribly obtuse. What else makes sense? You say very little about your family, except for your mother. One might say your silences are most eloquent."

"I didn't realize it was so obvious," Lundberg answered softly. "You're right, though. I am her favorite. My brother was the eldest and my father made him over in his own image, so to speak. That left me to be the mama's boy."

While Martin Lundberg smiled, the old man could see a lot of pain behind the effort. Ramos started to push the issue, then changed his mind. "I suppose she spoiled you rotten," he said, honoring Lundberg's privacy.

"Yes, she did, but there wasn't much I could get away with, at least not with her. My father was another matter. I usually could outwit him by simply staying out of his way. He never paid me much mind."

Ramos sighed. "Yes, that happens so often, especially when there are many children. Someone always seems to get ignored. Usually the ones in the middle. The oldest gets the scolding and the youngest, the affection."

"There wasn't much affection from my father," Lundberg answered, anger masking his pain. "He never could understand why my mother spent so much time with me. Stupid bastard."

"Gently, Martin. Do not be too quick to condemn him," Ramos cautioned.

"Why shouldn't I?" the young man snarled. "He was so wrapped up in his own thing he never knew how lonely my mother was. If she hadn't been such a good Catholic she would have divorced him years ago."

"Are you so sure of that?" Ramos inquired lightly.

"Yes!" Lundberg answered. "I don't see what you're driving at."

"It's quite simple, my friend. Many people use the Church as an excuse, a scapegoat in the classical sense. They pile their own sins on it and drive it off into the wilderness like the Jews did the real goat. They blame the Church for their own choices and the Church gladly absolves them of responsibility for making hard decisions. The Church takes the burden and strikes a devil's bargain with them. In exchange for power over their lives it absolves them of responsibility for making any decisions." The old man grinned. "The irony ... No, let's call it by its proper name. The hypocrisy is that what the Church tells them to do is what they want to do, anyway. At least most of the time. For other occasions there is the confessional. One finds out pretty quickly who the easy confessors are."

Lundberg nodded, "Yes, I know, but what's that got to do with my mother?"

"Just this. You say the Church kept her in her marriage, but what does she say? I think maybe she might have stayed even if she hadn't been a good Catholic. I think perhaps she stayed because of a sense of loyalty to your father and because she has strength of character to live with her decisions. No?"

Lundberg nodded. "I never thought of it that way, but it does make sense. She's been the one who has held us together." He thought for a moment. "Even so, it seems to me a lot of that living with decisions must be pure habit."

"Of course. Yet, what's wrong with good habits?"

Lundberg laughed. "Don't you know? They rob us of any claim to virtue. Like seeking Truth rather than Wisdom."

Ramos laughed with him. "All right, I take the hint. Very well." He went into the house and returned with two glasses and the bottle of wine they opened at lunch. The bottle was almost full. Ramos poured and handed a glass to the younger man. "What shall we toast?" he asked. "Another afternoon lost in wine while we both should be working?"

"Why not? I don't know about you, but my work's done for the day. I finished the wall this morning."

"Since yesterday?" Ramos was impressed. "*Hijo*! You must have been to bed with the moon and up with the roosters."

"I was. It was almost eleven when I quit last night and I've been at it since five this morning."

Ramos shook his head sadly. "I wish I were still young enough to work like that. How does it look now?"

"A thousand times better than it did," Lundberg said. "I'm beginning to see what you meant when you told me how beautiful it once was. I wish my mother could see it. She'd like it."

"Why don't you ask her to visit?" Ramos inquired.

"That would solve the problem," Lundberg answered, looking down.

"The problem?" Ramos asked. "What problem?"

"Oh, I'm sorry," Lundberg answered. "The Christmas problem."

Ramos still was puzzled, so Lundberg explained the situation with his family and why he was reluctant to go back even for a short visit. "Besides that," he added, "my finances really can't stand it. The house has set me back more than I thought, and that week's visit could cost me four month's living expenses." He laughed. "It's amazing how little a person can live on, isn't it? A month's expenses for me wouldn't begin to cover my father's coffee breaks."

Ramos nodded gravely, "You're probably right not to go back there, but it will hurt your mother not having you home."

"I thought of inviting her here for Christmas, but she wouldn't come. She wouldn't consider being gone then. It's a pretty important family thing for her."

"That's as it should be, but why don't you have two Christmases? Let her have one there and have another one here?"

It wouldn't be the same for her," Lundberg said. "Christmas is family and lots of people being together." He shrugged. "What would be good for her would be toxic for me."

"Well, you could invite her to have Christmas with us," Ramos suggested. "We celebrate the old Christmas here."

"The old Christmas?" asked Lundberg.

Ramos laughed. "Forgive me, Martin. Sometimes I forget you were not raised here. The *gringos* celebrate Christmas in December, but *chicanos* always celebrate it on the sixth of January. Your mother will know about it, I'm sure."

Lundberg thought it over a moment. "She might like that," he said, nodding. "Maybe she could come after New Year's and stay for a while. I know she'd like to get away from the cold." He frowned. "But I couldn't invite her without inviting the whole family, and then would be just the same as if I went back."

"So invite her to stay a month or two," the old man laughed. "How likely is it your father and brother would leave their precious business for so long?"

Lundberg laughed. "Not very likely, at all. It's very unlikely that they'd even come. They don't think anything south of Iowa is civilized."

"Good then," the old man smiled. "We'll plan on having you both. If you like, I'll even write her a special invitation myself."

"She'd like that very much," Lundberg said. "You'll write it in Spanish, won't you?"

"Of course. What else?"

"Good. That will pretty much insure that my father won't come. He may even refuse to let my mother come. A lot of good that will do him." He smiled.

Ramos cackled. "*Hijo*! What a couple of old women we are today, sitting here gossiping and plotting."

"Here's to gossiping old *brujas*!" said Lundberg, pouring them each another drink glass of wine.

"Just old ones?" Ramos asked slyly.

"No. To young ones, too." Lundberg took a long gulp of wine and added. "And to tall ones and short ones and blonde ones and fat ones and skinny ones and ..." He ran out of words.

"And to many afternoons lost in good company," Ramos replied.

"Amen, alleluia!" the other saluted, pouring himself another glass of fine red wine.

When Martin Lundberg woke the next morning the sun was high and he had a splitting headache. For a while he remained in bed trying to piece together the previous evening, but the details were slow coming. Vaguely he remembered finishing the gallon of wine, three quarters full at lunch time, and doing a great deal of talking. About what he wasn't certain, and he couldn't remember getting home or into bed. Thinking seemed to add to the dull pain in his head, so he gave it up and reached for the tobacco pouch in the pocket of his shirt hanging by the bed. Touching it was like grabbing a frog. The fabric was cold and wet to his touch, and the contents of the tobacco pouch were sodden. Only then did he remember tumbling into stream, and the memory reminded him how drunk he'd been.

Lundberg laid back and let the memory invade his mind. When he left the Ramos place, the moon was just coming up through the mouth of the canyon, a waning globe which almost filled the gap between the ridges. Ramos was dozing in his chair but woke when Lundberg brushed the empty jug with his foot and knocked it over. The old man urged him to stay the night, but Lundberg felt a little nauseous and wanted to walk it off going home. For some reason known only to God, if at all, he decided to follow the steep south bank of the stream and cross over just before getting to the vertical face. The safer route lay down the road, but it was longer and he was in a hurry to get to bed. Full of wine, he missed the crossing and suddenly found himself on a goat path up the face, ten feet above a broad, shallow pool. Trying to turn around, he misplaced a foot in the vague light and plunged into the icy stream. Yet, even the fall and the chill of the water failed to dispel the effects of the wine completely, and he stood for several minutes hip deep in the shallow pool before regaining his bearings and stumbling home. Luckily he had taken off the sodden clothing before collapsing into bed.

A distended bladder finally goaded Lundberg into throwing back the covers and climbing out of bed. The house was cold and he hastily threw on a bath robe on his way out the back door. At first the bright morning light stung his eyes, and he squinted fiercely against it as he relieved himself, steadied against the wall of the house with one hand. Miserable as he felt, the sharp morning air was a tonic clearing the fog from his senses, and when he was done, Lundberg felt remotely human. He stripped off his bathrobe, broke the thin skim of ice from a bucket of wash water beside the back door. Then he upended it over his head, emitting an involuntary whoop as the water sluiced down his naked back, and dancing and crow hopping about the back yard, he quickly dried himself with a rough towel. Within a minute he was back in the robe again, teeth chattering from the shock of the cold water.

Back inside, Lundberg built a fire in the wood cook stove, and with hands still shaking either from the cold or from the horrible hangover he'd cultivated, he put on a pot of coffee to boil. For a moment he huddled by the fire but he found very little warmth there and padded back into the bedroom to dress. His work boots were soaked through so he slipped on a pair of comfortable camp moccasins, a pair of dry pants, and a soft, warm flannel shirt. Fortunately his wallet was not on him the night before, but the notebook he carried in his breast pocket was quite damp, so he laid this and his pocket knife on a sunny window ledge to dry.

Sorting through the wet clothing he found the letters from his mother and John Thompson Luiz had brought. The ink on his mother's letter was badly run, staining his shirt, and the writing was almost illegible. The other letter was just as soaked, and Lundberg was afraid it was ruined, too. Between talking to Ramos and getting drunk last night, he'd forgotten to read it. He could imagine what his cousin, Jack, might have to say about that.

Setting his mother's letter beside his knife and notebook, Lundberg took the letter from Thompson with him into the kitchen. Since the kitchen still held the night's chill and the aftermath of wine left him with little taste for food, he decided to forego his usual hearty breakfast and make do with coffee laced with sugar and cream. Pouring himself a large mug, he went out onto a front porch warm with winter sun. Comfortably settled with tobacco and coffee within easy reach, and shades to protect his tender eyes, he picked up Thompson's letter and gently pried up the rear flap. While the ink of the address had run, the letter itself was written in pencil and still quite legible, although Jack's awkward hand was difficult to decipher.

Once he had mastered Jack's difficult hand, Lundberg was struck by the change of character in his cousin, and by the pain behind his words. The letter was dated ten days before and read:

Dear Martin,

Your mother gave me your address and I thought I'd write. It's been quite a while since I've seen you. I was home on leave several times but you were always out of town. I should be out of the service in March if the bastards don't freeze me in and I'd like to come by and see you there in New Mexico. Your mother told me what you're doing and it sounds great. I wish now I'd done something like that instead of going into the Army. I don't know why I did. It's about to drive me bananas. I guess I was a gung-ho bastard then. It sounded like fun and games. Real John Wayne stuff. You know the drill the recruiters give you. It's nothing but bullshit, Join the Army and learn a trade. All they do is fuck up your mind and teach you how to kill people. Then you get out that's all you know how to do. I wonder if the mob is looking for button men?

I'm really not that bitter. It was my own damned fault and I should have known better. I could have gone for pilot's school or into radar so I could do something useful when I got out, but I had to go into Special Forces. Now I'm scared shitless they'll freeze me in. Thailand wasn't bad, but this Vietnam thing is going to blow sky high. I was there three months as a special "adviser" to the South Vietnamese Army. That means you can get

your ass shot off but aren't supposed to shoot back, and they're doing a lot of shooting back there now. You wouldn't believe some of the things I've seen back in the villages. Most of the villagers don't really give a shit one way or the other. They look at the Viet Cong and the Saigon people the same way - just another bunch of war lords. Maybe they are. This shit's been going on now for almost a thousand years here, and I don't know why we're sticking our noses in. The South Vietnamese are as bad as the VC and the people really don't trust the government. I could probably get a court martial for saying so, but right now I really don't care. All I want is out. I've given them four years and that's all they get.

I don't mean to bother you with my problems - you've probably got enough of your own. But I would like to come down and see you. I'd like to be around sane people for a while and the folks at home don't know what I'm talking about. Some days I'm not sure I do either. I'm going to buy a Jeep when I get out and maybe you and I could bum around up in the mountains. I hear there are some good trout streams around there. I've got a good bit saved up so I could help with the groceries. How about it?

Jack

PS If it's all right, I might bring a friend along. He got screwed royally by Uncle Sugar and is almost as screwed up as I am. But he's a good guy and I think you'd like him. His name is Max and he plays a mean guitar.

Lundberg's first impulse was to write back and discourage the visit. He enjoyed the solitude he found in the canyon and was reluctant to give it up. Yet he was deeply touched by Jack's letter and oddly anxious to see him again. Jack Bear was a year ahead of him in school, and as they grew up Lundberg found in him the elder brother he never knew in his father's son. Through high school and college they were constant companions, dating the same girls, joining the same fraternity, and playing football together. Only when Lundberg graduated and decided on law school rather than military service had they grown apart.

For a while after that they wrote, but every time there was less common ground and finally they quit writing completely. Lundberg couldn't remember the last time he'd sent a letter to Jack or received one. Maybe two years before.

Lundberg read the letter again, confirming his earlier impression. The man who wrote it was a far different Jack from the one he'd known. Yet he could understand why Jack had chosen Special Forces over one of the more subdued services. Jack was the family Olympian, the best athlete, the golden boy most likely to succeed. Somewhere he had picked up the nickname of Bear, partly for his size, but more for his enormous vitality coupled with a casual manner. He became known not as John Thompson, but as Jack Bear, and the name had followed him through college.

Jack Bear drifted through school with the rest of them, casually accepting the best of things and never questioning that these were other than a birthright. All through high school and college he was always the one sought after by the fairest of the fair, the one whose name was always first suggested for honorary positions, the person with whom people liked to associate themselves in hope some of Bear's popularity might rub off. With teachers and professors Jack was a favorite, and although he did not graduate at the very top of his class, his grades were always quite high. Several companies vied for his services, but Jack Bear became caught up in the spell of the recruiters and set off to find glory with the United States Army. The last letter Lundberg got from him indicated he had found it, but that must have been two years before, at least. Maybe three.

Lundberg laid the letter aside and poured himself another cup of coffee. Jack's letter intrigued him, and he sat and considered what had happened to bring about such profound changes in his cousin. He was lost in thought when Ramos' head suddenly appeared over the stone fence. "Good morning!" Ramos said pleasantly. "I thought I better come down to see if you're still alive." Though the old man spoke in a normal voice, it thundered in Lundberg's head.

"Go away!" whispered Lundberg. "If you've got another jug leave it outside the gate. We're not in the market today."

Ramos laughed. "How do you feel?"

"Like hammered shit!" Lundberg replied. "Come in and have some coffee."

Ramos opened the gate and held up a bottle of dull red liquid. "I've got something even better," he said, walking up to the porch and taking a seat. "An old Indian cure for hangovers."

"I suppose you got it from a priest," Lundberg snorted.

Ramos laughed. "No, but it works. I invented it myself."

"I hope it works as good as your wine," Lundberg muttered as he poured out his coffee and held the empty cup out for Ramos to fill. "Lord, I haven't been that drunk in a long time."

Lundberg started to take a sip, but wrinkled his nose at the smell of pepper and Ramos stopped him. "Wait a moment," Ramos rummaged in the brown bag and produced a jar of butter and a half loaf of bread. Breaking the bread into two halves, he spread a thick layer of butter on each. "You need something solid to go with it. The butter will ease the burn."

Lundberg took the bread but looked doubtful. "I don't think my stomach is ready for solids yet." He sniffed the brew again and wrinkled his nose. "Smells hot. What's in it?"

"Mostly tomato juice and chiles. There's also a little *tequila* and some very special herbs. It's very hot, but in a half hour you'll feel like new."

Lundberg grinned. "I'm not afraid of a little chile pepper, Emil."

Ramos shrugged. "Very well. I warned you. Now, the best way is to drink as much at once as you can. It might help to hold your nose."

Lundberg was amused by the peculiar directions but decided to humor the old man. He pinched his nose with his left hand and raised the cup to his lips. He managed three enormous gulps and part of a fourth before the effects of the chiles hit him. He was out of his chair like a shot, spewing out the last mouthful and coughing and gasping for breath. He started toward the kitchen for water to quench the fire that was consuming his mouth and throat, but Ramos reached out and stopped him.

"No water!" commanded the old man. "Eat the bread. It will help."

Frantically, Lundberg tore into the bread and crammed as much as he could into his mouth. Tears were streaming down his face and heavy beads of sweat stood out on his forehead. Quickly he gorged the rest of his bread and beat his fists against the wall as he chewed. "More!" he croaked when he was done, and Ramos quickly buttered the remainder of the loaf and handed it to him. It was quickly consumed.

After a few minutes Lundberg sat down weakly and rubbed the tears from his eyes. "Jesus Christ!" he gasped. "I thought I was going to die."

"And afraid you wouldn't," Ramos chuckled. "You'll feel much better very shortly. After a while you can drink some water, but not too much.

It will make you drunk again if you drink too much."

Lundberg was still gasping for breath and didn't answer. Ramos smiled. "I'm proud of you," he said. "All I can usually manage is two swallows." He patted Lundberg on the shoulder. "You're *muy macho, hombre.*"

"I'm half dead, too," whispered Lundberg. "If I'd known how hot that is I wouldn't have even taken the first swallow."

"It will pass," Ramos answered. "In another half hour you'll feel like doing a day's work." Lundberg eyed him balefully. "It will. You'll see. It's a rough cure but it does work."

"If it doesn't kill the patient," Lundberg replied weakly.

Ramos laughed. "Just sit still for a while. I'm going to fix us breakfast." Lundberg grimaced at the mention of food, but said nothing. Ramos disappeared into the house and Lundberg could hear him humming cheerfully as he cooked. Not long after that he discovered the burning sensation was gone and when the smell of food reached his nostrils, he found himself strangely hungry. Going into the house, he discovered a huge breakfast waiting, and after a few minutes of furious eating, Lundberg leaned back and uttered a loud, appreciative belch.

Ramos smiled. "So you feel better, eh?" he asked.

"Much," admitted Lundberg. "I almost feel like doing something." He smiled a Ramos' nod. "I'll learn to believe you when you tell me something. What makes it work?"

"I don't know," the older man responded. "Maybe the *tequila,* maybe the herbs. The important thing is to eat something and get your system back in order." He looked around. "I haven't been up here since you painted. It looks nice." His eye fell on a chair standing by the wall. "That's a good chair. Where did you get it?"

"I found it down by where the cars were. It was in the trunk of one of them. The bottom and back were out, but the frame was good, so I fixed it up. It turned out pretty good."

"I thought I recognized it," Ramos nodded. "It used to sit on my porch."

Lundberg did not know quite what to say. "I didn't know it was yours or I'd have brought it back."

"No matter," said Ramos, shrugging it off.

Lundberg was still uncomfortable. "No," he said, "it's yours. I'll bring it back up this afternoon."

Ramos laughed and waved Lundberg's protest aside. "*Hijo*, it is yours. It was ruined when you found it, anyway. I've replaced it already and besides, you need a chair there."

"Well, at least let me give you something for it," Lundberg said.

"You already have," Ramos replied, smiling. Lundberg was perplexed and the old man nodded. "You have," he said. "More than you know. Among other things, someone to get drunk with!"

Lundberg moaned. "Never again," he said. "Absolutely never again."

"Eh? Well, that's too bad," said Ramos with mock gravity.

"Don't take me at my word," Lundberg smiled weakly. "I always say that."

"Yes, so do I. But it never lasts. I always forget after a while."

"I know what you mean. The strange thing is, I never start out to get drunk. It just sort of happens, and by the time I realize it, it's always two drinks too late."

Ramos laughed and stood up. "Show me around," he said. "I haven't seen everything you've done."

Lundberg gave him a quick tour of the house and then they went out back where and he showed Ramos what he had done so far and outlined what he planned to do later on. Ramos nodded with appreciation and asked a number of questions. It had been a month since he had last visited, although Lundberg came up to see him several times a week, and he was pleased with what the young man had done. Their walk took them up to the spring house and they sat in the shade of an evergreen to talk.

"You've done very well," said the old man. "It's hard now to believe how it was when you first came."

"I have some pictures. I'll show you when we go back to the house. I spent almost a day doing nothing but photographing the mess. I'm going to show them to my mother after she's been here a while."

"I'm looking forward to seeing her again. Do you think she'll come?"

"I think so. It will be a good excuse for her to get away from the weather. And the family, too, although she probably wouldn't admit it. I think I'll go into town and call tonight." Lundberg laughed and pointed toward the newly rebuilt outhouse. "I don't know how long she'll stay. I don't think she'll particularly care for my facilities."

"You may be underestimating her. She grew up in Terlingua and she knows more about outhouses than you might imagine. I can't remember anyone who had indoor plumbing in those days."

"I suppose you're right, but I'd better warn her when I write."

"Don't make it sound too bad or she might not come," said Ramos. He glanced up at the sun. "Hey, I'd better be going. I need to get some wood in before the snows. If you'll stop by on your way to town I'll send my list for Luiz in with you."

"Let me give you a hand with the wood," said Lundberg, rising from his seat and reaching for a cap and jacket. "I need some, too."

The two men spent most of the rest of the day gathering windfall and sawing it into lengths to fit their stoves. By late afternoon they had gathered three truckloads, cut it up, and stored it away in Ramos' wood shed. It was not nearly enough, and they decided to go out again the next day.

After a simple, but satisfying meal of beans, tortillas, and fresh milk, Lundberg took leave of the old man and went home to wash before going to town. As he walked in the house the letter from Jack caught his eye. On impulse he sat down and drafted a quick reply.

Dear Jack Bear,

Good to hear from you. Let me know when you're coming. I know what you mean about sane people. No time now for a full letter - we can catch up when you get here. The Jeep isn't necessary but it could be useful. One of the best trout streams in the state goes through my front yard.

About the friend, if he's the sort that wears well and is willing to carry his share of the load, bring him along. You know what I mean, so use your own judgment. There's still a lot of work to be done and I could really use the help. Hang tough until March and don't let the bastards get you down. If you can't make it until then take French leave and we'll be mountain bandits.

Martin

When he got to town Lundberg mailed the letters and then called home. He was both grateful and surprised to find his mother alone on a Sunday evening, but she told him his father and brother were at a church board meeting trying to settle some commotion which was tearing the congregation apart. Even though he did not entirely understand the issue, he was not really interested and didn't press for details. He and his brother had been raised Roman Catholics, as custom and Church law demanded, but his brother had long since left Rome and joined their father's Lutheran congregation. The religious question was one of many issues which split the family and brought Martin Lundberg and his mother even closer. For her benefit, and only for that, he remained a nominal Catholic, although it had been years since he seriously practiced the faith.

On the phone, Lundberg tried to avoid the subject of Christmas, hoping to broach it in a letter, but his mother asked directly if he would be coming home. Cursing himself for a fool he answered directly. "No, I won't. I really don't think it would work."

There was silence at the other end of the line as his mother absorbed this news. "No, I suppose not," she answered sadly. "You know how I feel about it, though. I can't help that."

"Yes, I do," he replied gently. "I really do, mother. But I really don't want to get into another scene like the one last spring. What I've found here has only confirmed my decision to leave and I don't imagine Dad and Matt have changed their minds, either. Not that my choices are any of their business," he added.

"No, they haven't, Martin. If anything, they're set more than ever."

"You understand I can't live my life for them?" he asked.

"Yes, son, I do," she said gently. "With me it's different, but I understand you need to find your own way. I just wish it could be different."

"Don't we all?" Lundberg replied. Then he decided to change the subject. "Hey, let's forget about that for a while. You ought to see my house. I painted it inside and out last week. It really looks nice."

Rosa was immediately caught up in her son's excitement and responded in kind. "Oh! What color did you paint it?"

"All white inside, with dark brown around the *vigas*. Outside it's adobe tan with blue window frames."

"Oh, you!" his mother laughed. "Have ghosts been bothering you?"

"No," he responded, "but I wanted to be sure." They visited for a while longer before he suggested that she visit him to celebrate the old Christmas with the Ramos family. At first his mother was reluctant, not knowing the people and feeling self conscious, yet after a while he began to hear excitement in her voice as she talked about the Christmases of her childhood and the traditional customs she grew up knowing. She asked him many questions about the Ramos family, and though she remembered an Emiliano who was a friend of her grandfather, she didn't believe it could be the same man. Surely the man she knew must be dead by now. And while she didn't promise to come, neither did she decline. By the end of their conversation, Lundberg thought there was a good chance she would actually pay them a visit.

After he hung up Lundberg felt vaguely despondent and decided to see what was showing at the movie in town. Though it was months since he'd seen a film, this one looked like a poor grade western and he decided to return home and read a good book, instead. On the way back through town he spotted Luiz's grey coupe and stopped to drop off Ramos' list and to see if the baby had come.

A weary Luiz opened the door when he knocked, but his face brightened when he saw Lundberg. "Hey!" Luiz said, shaking his hand. "Come in, *cunado*. What brings you to town?"

"I had to mail some letters and make a phone call," Lundberg answered. "I thought I'd stop by."

"Ah, so it was a girl friend after all?" Luiz's face was expectant.

For a moment Lundberg looked at Luiz oddly before he remembered his remarks about his mother's letter. He laughed. "Sorry to disappoint you. Just my mother. I haven't talked to her for a while."

"Ah, too bad," Luiz answered, ushering him into the tiny living room and offering him a chair. "How about a beer?"

"No thanks," said Lundberg, taking his seat. "Your uncle and I finished the jug last night. I'm still getting over it. I came by to see if the baby's come."

"I just got back from the hospital!" said Luiz, proudly. "It's a big baby boy."

"Hey, that's all right," Lundberg responded. "Congratulations. What are you going to name him?"

"I wanted to name him after Uncle Mano, but my wife doesn't like that and naturally the aunts agree with her."

"So where are they?" Lundberg asked, looking around.

"Still at the hospital, I guess," Luiz shrugged. "I hope so. Sure you won't have a drink to celebrate?"

Lundberg groaned, "OK, but just one." He looked around. "Where are the rest of your kids?"

"They are with my cousin," Luiz nodded happily as he produced a quart of good whiskey and two short glasses. "You've met her, haven't you?"

Before Lundberg could answer there was a knock at the door, and loud shouts of glee when Luiz opened it. Four men Lundberg had never met came into the room, their laughter quickly falling silent at the sight of a stranger. "Hey, *amigos!*" Luiz said loudly in Spanish. "This man is my friend Martin. He's the one who lives up near my Uncle Mano."

The men turned out to be neighbors and two cousins, and their reserve vanished completely with the first drink. One of them disappeared after a while and came back with a guitar and a violin, and soon four of them were singing drinking songs while the other two played.

The bottle was soon emptied but someone else arrived with a case of beer and the celebration began to gain momentum. Still others dropped in, neighbors attracted by the sounds of the party and at one point Lundberg thought there must be at least fifty people in the tiny house. Despite his good intentions he found himself drunk again, and for a moment, dreaded the morning to come. Then someone opened another bottle of red wine and all thought of anything soon vanished.

An hour later Luiz and Lundberg were singing a duet, an infamous ballad about foolish young virgins, when the door suddenly swung open and the three aunts appeared, shattering the noisy laughter. For a moment there was a frosty silence as they stared around the room in haughty disapproval. Then the men began to quietly leave, some of them saying goodbye to Luiz, but most fleeing the almost palpable wrath of the aunts as fast as they could.

The aunts watched, eyebrows raised and their faces masks of scorn until the last of the other men had left, but Lundberg refused to abandon his friend and stayed. He was given the full force of their frosty stare and understood full well why Luiz felt so intimidated by the three harridans. They eyed him like an eagle might eye a fat mouse caught in the open, pitiless and with a strange fascination with the fear of their victim.

Standing there, they indeed looked like birds of prey or fierce carrion eaters, grotesque in their combination of beak-like noses, sharp and hooked enough to rend flesh, and fine dark plumage. Proud and haughty, their sharp noses perched between hard, coal black eyes, each was dressed in the deep black of severe mourning relieved only by the trace of black lace around neck and wrist. This was made even more severe by the grey mounds of hair stacked in piles atop their heads. The lace, hair and sallow color of their complexions reminded Lundberg of vultures and he shivered inwardly, wondering what stayed their attack.

After a moment of confusion, Luiz stammered out an introduction and the aunts responded by nodding their heads a curt fraction of an inch in dismissal. Lundberg responded in kind, making his nod a fraction less than theirs and coldly refusing the hint. Luiz looked at him in supplication, but Lundberg was suddenly angry and rebellious and poured the full power of suppressed rage into his gaze, knowing even as he did so he might be making trouble for his friend.

The aunts tried to stare him down and for a long moment the room was filled with an almost electric hostility. Then, fearful of this angry stranger, the aunts turned their rage on Luiz, all talking at once and cutting him to shreds with their tongues.

"*Callate!*" Lundberg roared, slamming the flat of his hand onto a table so hard an empty wine bottle fell to the floor. "Shut up!" he shouted at the aunts, who fell silent, shocked. "How dare you! How dare you enter a man's house and talk to him like that! And on the day his son is born! For shame!"

Aunt Luz started to argue but Lundberg was having none of it. "Shut up!" he roared so loud Luiz covered his ears. "Get out! Get out and don't come back until you can be civil!" His arm and finger extended toward the door left no doubt of his intent. Another of the aunts started to say something, but Lundberg roared, "Now!" and stamped his foot. The aunts quailed and fled.

"Jesus, Mary and Joseph," murmured Luiz in quiet admiration. "How in the world did you do that?"

Lundberg looked at him sadly, now completely sober. "I'm sorry, my friend. I let my temper get the best of me."

"Hey!" said Luiz grinning. "Any time, man. You just did me a big favor."

"I hope so," said Lundberg quietly. "I'm afraid I may have caused you more grief."

"No way, man," Luiz protested. "They give me any *caca* and I'll tell them you're coming to see them. *El lobo enojado.*" He held up a clenched fist. "Us men got to stick together. Right?"

"What about your wife?" Lundberg asked. "What's she going to say?"

"Who cares?" said Luiz. "She's not here." He shook his head. "No, my friend, you helped me tonight." Seeing the question in Lundberg's eyes Luiz nodded. "Yes, you did. You helped me to remember I am *un hombre*, a man. If they try that stuff with me again they will find I can be *un lobo enojado*, too." He bared his teeth and growled.

Lundberg thought it was probably the liquor speaking for Luiz, but nodded and said nothing more. "Well," he said, looking around at the mess from the impromptu party. "I seem to have scared off the char ladies, so I better help you clean up."

Luiz laughed but didn't refuse the help. An hour later the house was spotless, and as the two of them sat drinking coffee, a soft knock sounded at the door. Luiz opened it, and from where he sat, Lundberg could see a very scared Aunt Luz talking softly to Luiz. What amazed him, however, was the change in his friend. "No," said Luiz firmly. "You better find other accommodations tonight. My friend is staying over."

Lundberg had no intention of doing so, but he said nothing. For a moment Luz tried to argue, saying, "But our things are here!"

"I'll send them to you in the morning," Luiz countered. "Good night." He shut the door in a speechless Luz's face.

"You didn't have to do that," Lundberg said quietly once the door was closed. "I intend to go home tonight."

Luiz shrugged. "Whatever you wish. I've got plenty of room now and you can have the bed."

Lundberg reflected a moment. "No," he answered. "I think it might be wise for me to stay over but I'll take the couch."

"No, man. I don't mind the couch, really." Luiz laughed. "After all, it's much softer than the floor."

"I know," Lundberg said. "I appreciate the offer. I think tonight *el jeffe de la casa* should sleep in his own bed."

Luiz grinned. "'*El jeffe de la casa.*' The master of the house. Hey, I really like that."

4. El Paso Por Aquí

Somewhere in the desert. I am surprised to find myself sitting in a cafe alongside the road. I am seated at a table on a long enclosed porch looking out across the two lanes of narrow asphalt toward the high dunes which roll to the blue mountains far in the distance. The scene is familiar, yet it isn't, like the scene in a movie, perhaps, a movie seen long ago in another life, which is dim to memory. The table is strange, too. It isn't a table, exactly. It is more like a pew or deacon's bench and the waitress has taken away my food. While I can still hear sounds from the cafe behind me, sounds of dishes clattering and cheerful laughter, I wake up to the fact I am standing in a corridor outside an emergency room. No, I am not standing. I am lying on a metal Gurney. The doctor has just pronounced me dead. I see her put away her stereoscope and tell the aides standing to one side to take me to the morgue.

Somehow I can see the aides, too. For some reason they are not dressed in white, but in street clothes. They are dark, not Negroid, but like peoples from the Mediterranean, with long straight black hair and deep olive complexions. They look like American Indians and I realize maybe I am in Arizona somewhere, or maybe New Mexico. The attendants are dressed in denim jeans and cowboy boots and plain western shirts, and they are tall and lanky. One seems taller than the other, but not much.

Someone comes and tells me it is time to go. Is it the doctor or a nurse? I can't tell for some reason, but I feel her touch my arm. I am standing now, close to the wall, and I am standing because it is more comfortable than lying on the Gurney. I can also see more this way, and when I feel the touch on my arm, it is a very feminine touch. Suddenly I realize I am in a waiting area, a holding area for corpses waiting to be transported. I wonder what happened to the cafe?

I look at one of the attendants, who nods. Both men cross over to me, or do they? Now the people beside me are nurses. (What have I been drinking?

69

What am I on?) Someone tells me it's OK for me to ride the Gurney now. Since I'm dead I have the right to do so, but I smile at one of the nurses and tell her I'd rather walk. I'll save them the trouble. I feel very light on my feet. The nurse I speak to is pretty and blonde and dressed in baby blue. She is on my right, the dexter nurse. For some reason I cannot see the nurse sinister, the one on my left.

As we approach the doors leading outside they open. I see they are the wide glass automatic doors used in emergency rooms and we are walking on a wide rubber mat placed there to keep people's feet from slipping. Now I see the dark attendants again. They are standing just to the left of the doors next an old green pickup which they use to haul corpses. (Corpsii?, I wonder. My mind plays with the word, saying, Corpse eye? No, corpse sigh.)

The two attendants let down the tailgate of the truck and help me get on. They get into the cab and we pull off down the road headed to the left, which I think is west. They take off with a roar and as the driver makes the turn into the proper lane, I start rolling off the tail gate. I fall onto the road and roll into the ditch, which is now deep, but the attendants don't see me fall out and continue driving wherever they are going.

I pick myself up, pissed at their carelessness, and dust myself off. The long, wide burial cloths in which they wrapped me have come loose and I strip these off. My intent is to go back across the road to the cafe or hospital and wait for another ride, but when I start to cross the road, the cafe has disappeared. This really pisses me off. I'm stranded in the middle of nowhere without any food or water or provisions to get me through. Somehow I forget the fact I'm dead and don't need these any more. Yet as I stand there a ghostly figure takes form before me and without speech I am made aware I have just two choices: stay here and become a dry corpse, or set out across the wilderness. "Shit!" I tell the vague form. "Not that again!" Yet the ghostly figure is gone.

I look back down the road in either direction. There is nothing but miles and miles of empty road whichever way I choose, although the road to the west disappears through a pass between two dry hills. I think, These roads lead to Nowhere. I decide to follow neither way.

Across the road to the south are rolling dunes and dry hills, with very dry, sparse vegetation. That looks too much like where I have been, where I grew up, and somehow I know there is nothing there for me. So I turn north and cross the ditch heading north, yet that seems even more barren, if anything. Yet the sense is strong within me that this is the direction I need to travel.

I begin to walk to the north, cursing constantly. Far in the distance I see just the suggestion of what may be a house or barn and a windmill. I head toward that, but it is so far away. I keep walking endlessly until I am so tired I drop face forward into the sand. I am almost beyond caring, and when the Voice says, "You must get up and go on or you will die here," all I can do is raise my head. Yet as I do something happens. What is rolling desert sand now becomes lush green fields watered by springs and running streams. I am so startled I blink, and then the greenery is gone and I am staring at parched sand. "Get up!" the Voice insists. "Get up! You must get up and go on."

I rise and begin walking again, but this time I am encouraged because the distant building seems much closer and I can definitely see a windmill and, perhaps, trees. As I walk onward, I see green flashes from time to time and the scene changes from dry desert to lush, almost tropical, land. Then I spy something in the dry sand. I brush the sand away with my walking stick and I see it is a rubber tip like those used on crutches. Again I am made aware of something without being told. Someone has walked this way long before me. (Martin Quinn's Journal)

December 1962. Martin Lundberg awoke drenched with sweat. He lay still for a while, not sure where he was, or when. The familiar sights of his bedroom looked strange in the early morning light, almost alien, as if something had subtly changed with the passing of the night, or someone had shifted things and turned them around. Then he moved, shifting the covers off his leg and something attacked, fastening itself painfully to his naked foot. He heard himself scream like a banshee as he jerked upright to defend himself, and he wakened to find himself crouched stark naked in attack stance in the middle of his bed. Against the far wall, staring at him with eyes wide in terror, was the black and white form of Tonto, the kitten Ramos had given him the week before.

For a moment Lundberg glared at the kitten. Then he chuckled, and then laughed. "You dumb-ass *gato*", he said taking a seat on the edge of the bed. "I should have named you *pendejo*, instead." He reached a hand toward the kitten, but it was still afraid and wouldn't come. "Come on, Tonto, I'm not going to hurt you." He picked up a string they had used the night before and trailed it across the floor. Tonto was interested, but not buying.

"I know what will get you," Lundberg said, drawing on a pair of shorts and a sweatshirt. He slipped his feet into sheepskin slippers, the wool turned in, and padded into the kitchen. "Kitty, kitty, kitty!" he said, opening the refrigerator door and taking out a pitcher of fresh milk. By the time he shut the door and crossed to the cupboard to get a saucer, Tonto was purring and rubbing himself against Lundberg's legs. "Don't give me any of that crap," he told the kitten. "I know cupboard love when I see it."

Cupboard love. The phrase reminded him of his mother, who coined it as far as he knew. Kindling the stove from last night's fire he thought of her, of the phone conversation early last week. A letter came yesterday, a reply written the morning after their talk telling him she was coming and would be arriving at the Albuquerque airport two days after Christmas. She said the booking for her return flight was left open, although she could not get space before January 8 and tentative reservations were made for a week later. They could be confirmed at any time or she could fly space available standby. And while it was a long way to drive, would he consider taking her down to Terlingua for a few days? She'd never been back since the family moved when she was ten, and while no one she knew might live there any more, she wanted to see it again and to show him the marvelous country where she grew up. Nor was Martin to worry about expenses for the trip. His father's business did incredibly well during the last year and it had been a long time since she'd been away. Perhaps they could explore El Paso on their way south and make it a real adventure like the ones they used to have before everyone got so busy.

Putting water on to boil for coffee to boil, Lundberg found his mother's letter and read it again while he waited. As he did he absently rolled a couple of cigarettes, his hands automatically falling into familiar rhythm, and set them beside his mug on the table. Most mornings it was a personal rule for him never to smoke before coffee, but reading the letter, he took one of the cigarettes and lit it. He was immediately sorry he did, for his head began to swim and he became aware of a terrible taste in his mouth. After carefully placing the lit butt in an ashtray so it couldn't fall out and scar the table, he walked to the sink and brushed his teeth. The cold water tasted good and he splashed some into the wash basin, noticing a skim of ice was beginning to form in the water bucket. Looking out the kitchen window, he saw the thermometer on the north side of the house stood at twenty-six. The temperature was still in the mid fifties in the house, he judged, even though the fire had burned out hours ago. *That's one thing Dickman was right about*, he thought. *Adobe really holds the heat.*

Not wasting any time, Lundberg washed himself in the icy water, making a solemn vow he would heat water for a decent bath before the week was out. One thing he'd discovered was how to shower with very little water, and a large metal tub hung on the wall out back just for that purpose. Beside it hung the empty gallon can, carefully cleaned of all remnants of paint and punctured with ten or twelve small nail holes in the bottom. Standing in the metal tub he could dip water from the large kettle on the stove and quickly sluice himself off. The first two dips were to get wet for soaping and shampoo, and the second two were for rinsing. While it was crude, it was effective, and more than once had he treated himself to the luxury of three more dips, almost scalding, before drying off.

As he toweled himself, he wondered how he could rig something a little more civilized for his mother. One of her personal luxuries he remembered growing up was taking long baths, but considering what he knew now about his family, he thought perhaps they were more than luxury. Perhaps they were one of the ways she remained sane in a crazy household, and he decided to make the investment in a bigger, longer tub the next time he went into town. And not just for her visit, either. Spit showers were all right, but he often paid a visit to Ramos' place so he could soak in the long tub the old man kept in his sauna. Nothing was better for muscles sore from hard work, or a psyche weary from the exhausting dreams which troubled his night. There seemed to be a lot of those lately, and he wished they would just go away.

The coffee was done by the time he finished his ablutions, and Lundberg poured himself a cup full, gentled with sugar and a little milk. He relit the dead cigarette and picked up his mother's letter again, settling himself comfortably to read it. This time he managed get through the first page before intense pain in his left leg claimed his attention. Bending down quickly he made a grab and came up with a black and white handful of fur hanging by the scruff of its neck. The kitten's eyes were wide in innocence. "Hey, *gato*," he said, thrusting his face into the kitten's. "Enough is enough, already. *Sabe?*" Tonto simply stared back at him, unimpressed. Laughing, Lundberg placed the kitten over his shoulder and began stroking it gently. Tonto struggled against confinement for just a moment before relaxing and beginning to purr loudly.

"Doesn't take much to please you, does it?" Lundberg said, leaning back in his chair and picking up the letter again. This time he only got three-quarters of the way through the second page before he heard his gate bell ring. Jumping to his feet he almost unhorsed Tonto, who dug in his claws for safety, eliciting a yelp from Lundberg. Gently disengaging himself from the kitten, the young man cradled it in the crook of his arm and went to see who was at the door. It was old man Ramos.

"*Buenas dias!*" the old man said cheerfully. "I see *el gato* has taken over the house already."

"*El gato pendejo,*" Lundberg answered, motioning for his guest to come in. "He's just like a little kid, always getting into everything he shouldn't. His teeth are like needles. So are his claws." The old man grinned. "You want some coffee? It's fresh."

The old man nodded and Lundberg brought him a cup full, sweetened with a little sugar and no milk. Ramos took a sip and nodded, "*Bueno,*" he said. "Very good." He looked at Lundberg directly. "So how are you this morning?"

"All right, I guess," the young man answered, shaking his head. "I'm still waking up. I had a helluva dream this morning and I'm having trouble shaking it off."

Ramos muttered something in Latin, but Lundberg had trouble following what he was saying. "What was that?" he asked. "It was out of my range."

"Only a quotation I used to like," Ramos answered. "It comes from the Old Testament. What it says it, 'Your old men shall dream dreams and your young men shall see visions.'"

Lundberg laughed and began to quote from memory. "'In those days I shall pour out my Spirit on all flesh and all your sons and daughters shall prophesy; your old men shall dream dreams and your young men shall see visions.'" He shrugged. "I never heard it in Latin before."

Ramos looked at him in surprise. "I didn't know you were such a scholar," he said. "I better watch what I say."

"No, not really," Lundberg responded. "There used to be a television show with a shot of that carved in stone over a doorway. I liked it so much I looked it up and memorized the reference."

"I'm impressed," said Ramos, nodding soberly. "One of my favorites is this: 'I will restore to you all the years the destroyer has eaten, the locust and hopper and grub.' Do you recognize that?"

"No," Lundberg answered. "It sounds sort of ominous."

"Oh, it is," Ramos answered. "It comes from the same source as yours, only a little earlier in the book." He looked at the younger man shrewdly. "I think maybe the dream bothered you. Do you want to tell me about it?"

At first Lundberg started to refuse, then decided to go ahead. The fact remained the dream was troubling him, the more so since he had no idea what it might mean or why it would disturb to him. It made no sense. Yet he told it as best he could remember, filling in details from time to time as the old man asked for them. When he was done he looked at Ramos for some response, but the old man simply sat and nodded, frowning to himself. Feeling a little impatient Martin asked, "So what does that tell you?"

Ramos shook his head. "What it tells me is not the question," he replied. "The question is what it tells you."

"It doesn't tell me doodley squat," Lundberg answered a little tersely. "That's why I asked you."

"Would you ask me to exercise for you if you wanted to build your body?" Ramos asked, taking a sip from his cup.

"Of course not," said Lundberg. "That wouldn't make any sense."

"Well, with spiritual things the same principle applies. You need to do your own work to develop your spirit," Ramos answered. "The dream suggests many things to me but I can only suggest what it might mean. I might miss the mark by the whole width of heaven. The final determination must be yours and I am hesitant to say anything which might mislead you."

Lundberg thought a moment. Impatient as he felt, Ramos had rarely been wrong about matters of the mind and soul, and he'd come to respect the older man's wisdom and counsel. "The trouble is, it's like wandering around in a fog," he told Ramos. "I don't even know where to start. Right now I'm tempted to blow it off as a bad experience, but I'd like to know why it bothered me so much."

Ramos shrugged. "You can blow it off it you want to, but I don't think that will help. With me ignoring such things means they come back again and again, always getting worse and worse until I face them." He looked at Lundberg directly. "Haven't you ever had a recurring dream you didn't like?" he asked.

Lundberg shuddered, remembering. "Yes," he replied quietly. "The prison dream." Ramos sat quietly, waiting. After a minute Lundberg continued. "It is always pretty much the same. There's a prisoner behind heavy bars and he's yelling at me. No, not yelling, screaming. What he screams is always the same. 'See me? I'm you! I'm the part of you that's locked up in here, doing hard time. And when I get out I'm going to kill you! You understand? I'm going to kill you!'" He shook his head. "I wish I could get rid of it."

"I can imagine you do," Ramos answered softly. "How often have you had it?"

"Maybe three or four times over the last ten years," Lundberg answered.

Ramos nodded. "And you have no idea of what it means?" The younger man shook his head. Ramos sighed and rubbed his eyes. "Aiee! What a dream. How do you feel when you waken?"

"Scared shitless," Lundberg stated in simple candor. "I usually get up after I've dreamed it because it's so hard to get back to sleep."

"I think it would be," said Ramos. He looked very thoughtful. "You know, I can make some suggestions, my friend," he said. "But I don't want you to take them as more than suggestions."

"I wish you would," said Lundberg. "I'd like to get rid of it."

"What the prison dream suggests to me is some questions," Ramos said. "I don't have answers for you, but maybe my questions would help."

"Fair enough," Lundberg grinned. "However, to ask a question one must know at least half the answer."

"Exactly, which is why I hesitate to even ask my questions. They aren't even your questions. They may point to answers which may not be yours, either. I want to be clear about that."

Lundberg wondered why Ramos was being so scrupulous. Normally their give and take was carefree. "All right," he said. "I'll keep that in mind. But whatever else they are, your questions are more than I have right now."

Ramos nodded. "Very well. The first question I have is who is the prisoner? The second is who is his jailer?"

"How am I supposed to know that?" Lundberg asked, exasperated.

"How would you find out in real life?" Ramos replied.

"I'd look at his records," the young man replied. "Or call the sheriff. But there isn't any sheriff to call. Or any courthouse, either."

"I wouldn't be so sure of that," Ramos said. "But what else could you do to find out? Suppose the sheriff wouldn't tell you. What would you do then?"

"Ask around, I guess," Lundberg said, puzzled. "I don't see what you're driving at."

"Very simple," said the old man. "You're overlooking your most obvious source of information."

"What?" Lundberg was confused and beginning to get angry.

"The man himself," Ramos replied sternly. "Why don't you ask him?"

"He's a criminal," Lundberg protested. "Even if I could ask him how do I know he's telling me the truth?"

"How do you know the sheriff would tell you the truth, or even the judge?" Ramos grinned, then added. "You could ask the prosecutor, I suppose, but he'd be just as biased as the prisoner."

"Fine, then. I'll ask the prisoner the next time he comes around, two or four years from now." Lundberg was distinctly annoyed.

"You don't have to wait that long, Martin," the old man answered gently. "You can start today if you wish. Just don't be too impatient for an answer. It will come, but like birth, it will have its own time."

Lundberg regarded him closely. "All right," he said, sighing. "What to I have to do?"

"There are several ways, but let's try the simplest first. You have some work laid out today, don't you?" Lundberg nodded and the old man continued. "Is it hard physical work that won't take too much concentration?"

Martin nodded again, this time smiling. "That's most of what I have around here, Emil. I like it because it gives me time to think."

"Good. That's exactly what I want you to do. As you work, think about the man in prison. Think about what he looks like, what he smells like, how he's dressed, how it feels to be around him. Look at his cell and pay attention to the smallest detail. Then, when you have the clear picture in your mind, ask him who he is and who is keeping him in prison. He'll tell you."

"Just that simple?" Lundberg asked in disbelief.

"Yes, but the answer may take a while coming or you may not be aware of it for a while. That's all right. Just keep the picture in your mind as you work and sooner or later you'll get an answer." The old man grinned. "Just keep your wits about you so you don't pick up a *culebra de casca* thinking it's a stick."

Lundberg laughed. "Our rattlesnakes are in hibernation now," he said, "but I take your point. It's a long way to the doctor."

"Precisely, and you're too much for me to carry," Ramos cackled. "And if I had to drive *El Morado*.... Aiee! I'd kill us all."

Lundberg rose and poured them more coffee. He wondered why Ramos had come down to see him, but was too polite to ask. The old man would tell him in his own time. "Are you hungry?" Martin asked. "I have some fresh eggs and could cook some *fedeos* to go with them."

The old man glanced at the sun. "Sure," he said. "Why not? I haven't eaten yet today. And if you go with me this afternoon it may be late before we get anything else."

"Go with you?" asked Lundberg, crossing to the counter and beginning to prepare their food. "Where are you going?"

"*Posadas*," Ramos answered. "That is, if you can give me a ride to town." He grinned at the transparency of his own game.

"*Posadas*?" asked Lundberg. "Hotels?" This last he said in English.

Ramos laughed. "Yes! Hotels. That's what it means. Hotels." He laughed again. "What it means is a Christmas celebration."

Lundberg nodded. "I think I remember hearing my mother mention it. Something about Mary and Joseph's journey to Bethlehem."

"Yes, and the *posadas* are the inns where they try to find lodging," Ramos told him. We do it just before Christmas and tonight's the first night."

"The first night?" Lundberg was surprised. "You mean it's like mardi gras? How long does it last?"

"Around here just four nights. We do things simply. I hear there are places in Mexico it lasts for as long as nine days and is as big as mardi gras in New Orleans." Then Ramos added, smiling, "Of course, that's only what one hears."

Lundberg was intrigued. "So what happens at *Posadas*?"

"Well, everyone gathers at the church tonight and *el nino* is taken from his place with the Holy Family to a place where he will stay for the next three nights. Then everyone comes back to the church and Mary and Joseph are taken from house to house looking for a place to stay. People sing Christmas songs while *los peregrinos*, the 'pilgrims', are carried from house to house. At the last house each night they find a place to stay, and that is where we meet to start the next part of the journey tomorrow night." Ramos grinned. "Then a fiesta starts. Wine and fire crackers and dancing." He reflected a moment. "That comes at the end. What I like is listening to the music while we walk and the candles people carry. It is beautiful."

"It sounds like it," Lundberg agreed. "The closest thing to it I've heard of is Christmas caroling, but this sounds even better."

"I thought you might like it," Ramos said. He smiled again. "I know it's the last minute and your social calendar is full, but I thought I'd ask."

"I'm glad you did," Lundberg said. "As it just so happens, I had a cancellation for tonight, so I'm free."

"Good," said the old man, sniffing the *fedeos* Lundberg set on the table in front of him. "My goodness, Rosa did a good job teaching you to cook." Lundberg set out the rest of the food and the two men kept silence a few moments before starting to eat.

"Oh, gracious," Ramos murmured, taking his first bite. "This tastes every bit as good as it smells."

"I suppose I'll make somebody a good wife someday," Lundberg observed dryly.

"Not hanging around up here like *un lobo solo*," Ramos said. "There are a lot of pretty girls in town, and most of them have heard of you." He stopped eating to spread some *picante* sauce on his eggs. Lundberg had scrambled these with bits of corn and crushed hard tortilla for texture.

"They have?" Martin was surprised.

"Of course!" Ramos laughed. He sprinkled some brown sugar on a hot flour tortilla spread with butter and rolled it up. "Heavenly!" he murmured, taking his first bite.

Lundberg had stopped eating and was staring at him. "What do you mean, 'of course.' Nobody's ever heard of me."

"No?" Ramos said, his mouth so full he could scarcely talk. He chewed and swallowed. "Think about it. Someone buys the old Vasques place, which is said to carry a curse. Some *estupido* from up north who is too ignorant to know such things are real. Only this *estupido* speaks the tongue of *la raza* like it is his mother language and keeps to himself. So he becomes a mystery man, and it is said he associates with *el brujo* who lives at the top of the canyon, which makes him all the more mysterious. Then he comes into town and exorcises Luiz's house of three demon aunts, and the neighbors not only hear every word, but the aunts are seen fleeing the house." Ramos shrugged. "So everyone had heard of you and *las senioritas* are all curious, for it is rumored you are as handsome as the Devil himself." Ramos shrugged and turned to attack his food again. "Twice as charming, too."

Lundberg was very still. "Damn!" he said. "I've been trying to keep a low profile around here. Maybe I better not go, after all. I'll take you into town and bring you back, but maybe I better not go to *posadas.*"

Ramos was surprised. "Why not?" he said. "Those old chickens are going to cluck, no matter what you do."

"I don't know. It just feels odd knowing how they've been gossiping. Especially after the thing with Luiz's aunts."

"Luiz's wife's aunts," Ramos corrected. "There is a difference. They are not his own flesh and blood or he would have had to challenge you. As it was, you gave him his *cojones* back." He grinned. "I hear his wife has been very, ah, gentle since your visit. I think she's afraid you might come back."

"I was pretty drunk that night," Lundberg answered sheepishly. "I guess a side of me got loose I don't want to let out. That's why I don't want to go tonight. I don't want to be someone people use to scare women and children."

Ramos said nothing for a long while. Finishing his lunch he pushed back his plate and reached for his tobacco pouch, but Lundberg stopped him. "Just a minute," the young man said, going to the refrigerator and taking something out. When he returned he held out a fresh pack of Pell Mell cigarettes. "Luiz brought me these from town last week," he said, opening the pack. "I thought they'd be nice for us to have over Christmas."

"*Gracias,*" said Ramos, helping himself to one of the long white tubes. He lighted it and sighed with content. "The small pleasures of life." Looking at the young man he added, "So you got a little drunk, eh? So *el lobo enojado* slipped out and howled, so what? You think you're the first man who got drunk and a little angry in town? All that proves is that you're a man." Ramos held up a hand and began to count off on his fingers. "Number one, you didn't kill anyone. Two, you didn't wreck anything. Three, and most disappointing to them, you didn't get anyone pregnant. This time next week they'll have forgotten all about you, if they haven't already." He shrugged and took another drink of coffee.

"Even if they forget, I won't," said Lundberg.

For the first time Ramos looked indignant. "What's the matter with you, man?" he asked, testily. "Can't you learn from your mistakes? How long are you going to crucify yourself for slipping up and getting a little drunk?"

"You weren't there," Lundberg argued. "You didn't see what happened. Besides, that was the second day in a row I was drunk."

"No, I wasn't there," Ramos admitted. "Yet I see the result and it's pretty damn good. Luiz gets his life back and you learn something about yourself." He shrugged. "Or maybe not. Today I don't know. Anyway, I think you're a real *pendejo* if you let that keep you from having a good time." He looked at the younger man. "You worried about getting drunk again?"

"No!" Lundberg snapped, then changed his mind. "Well, yes, maybe I am. I don't start out to get drunk, but it just slips up on me. The first thing I know I'm drunk again, and I don't like myself very much when that happens." His face was filled with grief.

Ramos became very still. "I am very sorry, Martin," he said softly. "I didn't know there was a problem or I would never have offered you a drink."

"It's not like I'm an alcoholic," Lundberg said. "I mean, I don't have to have it. I go for weeks without anything to drink and I do fine. And as long as I watch it and only have a few it's all right. Sometimes I just seem to forget."

"Maybe sometimes you want to forget," Ramos suggested kindly. "Maybe sometimes the remembering gets too painful."

Lundberg nodded. "Yeah, maybe that's it. I've been remembering a lot of painful things lately. Things I thought were done."

"Perhaps they still need finishing," the old man suggested. "Maybe that is what your dream is about."

"What do you mean?" Lundberg asked.

"Nothing in particular," Ramos assured him. "Yet when I get sad without knowing why, there is usually something from the past I'm not done with yet. Or not done grieving. Or maybe something I haven't forgiven, either myself or another." He sighed. "It's always worst when I don't know exactly what it is."

"So how do you deal with it when you don't know what it is?" Lundberg wanted to know. He looked close to tears.

The old man was silent a long while. Finally he shook his head sadly and said, "To answer that, my friend, I have to speak in a way which may put you off. Perhaps it won't, but I think it may. That is why I hesitate."

Lundberg looked at Ramos oddly. "I can't imagine what that might be," he said. "We've talked about everything under the sun."

The old man held up a warning finger. "Except things of the spirit," he said. "We have walked very carefully there."

"But we have spoken of such things," Lundberg said. "And without getting into a bind over it."

"Only because we've talked in general,' Ramos replied. "To answer your question fully I must become very personal and very specific, and I'm afraid you may not like what I have to say. You're a very good friend and I don't want to offend you."

"Well, if you do, I won't take it personally," Lundberg responded. "I won't hold a grudge. I promise."

"Very well," sighed Ramos. "Though you may think me a superstitious old fool when I'm done." He paused just a moment and then went on. "When I am disturbed and do not know why, I to two things. First, I ask the One who is the source of all being to enlighten my heart and mind to what I need to know, and to lead me to the truth I need to face as gently as possible." He looked at the younger man, seeing doubt in his eyes. "The second thing I do is to wait as patiently as I can for the answer to come. While I wait I ask the grace to not be blind to whatever the answer may be."

"That's it?" Lundberg asked. The old man nodded and the young man grinned in relief. "That's not so bad. I thought you were going to tell me I had to come to Jesus," he said.

Ramos smiled back. "Well, that is one way of putting it," he answered. "I prefer to say all roads lead Home, sooner or later. *El Camino Nazareno* is just one among many. Some find it helpful, others do not and find another way. The point is they all lead to the same end. Or, perhaps, to the same beginning." He nodded, more to himself than the other, and rose to his feet. "So how about *posadas*," he asked. "Are you coming?"

Lundberg was still distracted by Ramos' answer and wanted to pursue it, but the old man was headed for the door. "Sure," he said. "Why not? Maybe I'll meet one of those pretty senoritas you've been talking about."

"Excellent!" said the old man. "Why don't you pick me up an hour after noon and we'll save Luiz a trip out tomorrow."

The sun was standing half way between zenith and setting when Ramos and Lundberg set out for town in *El Morado*. The younger man spent a hard two hours working in his garden before washing himself for going to town, and he tried Ramos' suggestion. The only result at first was a sense of frustration. While he felt better having talked with Ramos, he found the anger of the man in prison distasteful and it was difficult to keep him in mind at first. Then, as he worked, he imagined he was in prison himself, that the stone walls of his garden were high granite with guard towers at the corners. As imagination took over the ground before him became the prison truck garden, and a deep sense of rage and injustice came over him. He found himself stabbing violently at the ground with his turning fork, and was surprised to suddenly discover he was done.

The strangest thing, however, was how good Lundberg felt, and he wanted to talk to Ramos about it. Yet every time he approached the subject on the way into town, the old man turned the conversation another way. Finally, he said, "Why don't you want to talk about it?"

Ramos favored him with a smile and an impassive gaze. "Why don't I want to talk about what, Martin?"

"You know. What happened after you left this morning."

Ramos nodded and was silent a long while. When he spoke it was with a question, "Do you remember what I said about being patient?" The young man nodded back and Ramos smiled. "I knew something happened the minute you drove up. What I suspected was you tried what I said and it worked, and you were bursting to tell me." Lundberg murmured agreement. "When the wine first comes off fermentation, Martin, it is not finished," Ramos explained. "One has to carefully siphon it off and let it settle without being disturbed for a while. When this is done properly it becomes very clear and it matures. Only then is it ready and fit to drink."

"So let it rest?" Lundberg asked.

"Precisely," said the older man. "I am curious to know what happened, but I am more curious to know how it matures without being disturbed. There is no rush. You and I have plenty of time to talk about it when the moment is right." He murmured something else Lundberg did not quite catch. "I beg your pardon," he responded when the younger man asked. "What I said was, 'in the fullness of time.' It's something I learned studying Hebrew."

"Hebrew?" Lundberg asked. "I didn't know you knew Hebrew."

Ramos nodded. "I'm no scholar, and it's been many years, but I still read from original texts from time to time. It's more earthy and robust than Greek."

"Greek, too?" Lundberg observed, giving Ramos an odd look. "How many languages do you know?"

"Fluently, seven, including Latin. I can get by with a dictionary in two or three others." He chuckled at Lundberg's look of amazement. "Hey, I was a hard tailed Jesuit once. Language is no virtue for me. I seem to have a talent for it."

"You must," said Lundberg. "Is there anything you can't do?"

"Sing," Ramos answered quickly. "I believe I was the only person in the history of my seminary who the choir master exempted from rehearsals." He laughed at the memory. "My talent there was for confusing trained voices."

"So are you going to sing tonight?" Lundberg asked playfully.

Ramos looked at him in horror. "Why do you think they make me live up here by myself? I have to promise not to sing to even come to *posadas*." The old man looked at him. "How about you?"

Lundberg responded by breaking into song. Ramos was surprised at the clarity of his rich baritone as he sang the opening lines of the original Silent Night, "*Stille nacht, hoh heilege nacht, alles schlaft, einsam wacht....*" Caught up in the tune, Lundberg sang a second verse, then repeated the first. When he was done he fell silent, concentrating a bit too hard on negotiating a particularly bad stretch of road.

"Marvelous," murmured Ramos in classic high German. "Thank you. I've always liked that better in the original German. I had no idea you had a voice so well disciplined."

"Well, it should be," Lundberg replied, answering in the same tongue. "After twelve years of choir and six of private voice lessons." To the question in Ramos' eyes he added, "At first it was a way to get out of being an altar boy. Then I discovered I really enjoy it."

"You still sing don't you?" Lundberg nodded and the old man laughed. "I thought I heard something a couple of times. Almost like opera. I thought you were just playing your radio loud."

Lundberg laughed and said, "I don't have a radio." He laughed again at Ramos' consternation with himself, then he broke into the haunting, lilting lines of *Cielito Lindo.*

Despite himself Ramos soon joined in until he caught a strange look from the younger man. "Sorry," he said. "I'll just hum softly."

"You weren't kidding, were you?" Lundberg asked.

"No," Ramos said so sadly the younger man regretted his question. "That is one thing I always wanted to do. Yet no matter how hard I tried I could never get the music I hear inside to come out the way I hear it," he said, pointing to his breast. "So I play my *flauta,* and somehow that connects."

"I've never heard you play," said Lundberg. "I'd like to sometime."

Ramos gave him an odd look. You may not know what you are asking," he pointed out. "I only play what I hear inside, and usually it is when I am very sad. I know a few other tunes I'll play for you sometime soon, but I warn you. My playing is not so good as your singing."

"That remains to be seen," Lundberg answered. "This is one of my mother's favorites." To Ramos' surprise, he began to sing the Magnificat to a drifting plainsong tune, first in Latin and then in English.

"Ah, my choir master would have loved to get his hands on you," Ramos said, then chuckled wickedly. "In more ways than one. You better be careful tonight. You sing like that at *posadas* and half the women in town will be in love with you."

"Only half?" Lundberg snorted, clearly pleased.

"The other half are too old or too deaf to care," Ramos replied. "Do you take requests?"

"Only if I know them," Lundberg answered, and he was still singing when they drove into the outskirts of town.

Parking beside Luiz' beat up old car, Martin waited for Ramos to join him before going to the door. The old man could tell he was nervous, but the door opened before he could say anything to help.

"Tio Emil!" Luiz cried as he flung open the massive oak planking and grabbed his uncle in a bear hug. While Luiz wasn't drunk, Martin could see he was far from feeling much pain. His face was flushed and it was apparent he had already begun the night's celebration. "Hey, and you brought Martin with you, too! Come in. Come on in!" Releasing Lundberg's hand, which he'd almost crushed, Luiz took their coats and hung them on a rack beside the door.

Coming into the living room Lundberg was surprised to see almost the whole neighborhood gathered in the tiny house. Several of the men he met on his last trip to town rose to greet him warmly, which also surprised him, and also helped him feel at home. The reserve these gentle folk could put up to strangers, and particularly toward *gringos*, was so strong as almost to be tangible. Now the warmth of their acceptance was just as overpowering.

At first Martin thought it was his friendship with Ramos which paved the way, but then he remembered how much they feared the old man. Perhaps it was his friendship with Luiz. During a quiet moment a few minutes later, when the two were alone, he asked Luiz. Ramos' nephew laughed. "No, man," he said. "They liked you because you were my friend and respectful of the ways of *la raza*. They respect you because you are *muy macho*. Because you have big *cojones*!" He held out his hands as if he were holding a full grown cantaloupe in each.

Lundberg laughed, embarrassed but pleased. "How do they know that?" he asked.

"Because of the *brujas*, man." Luiz laughed. "They heard how you chased the *brujas* out of my house."

"Oh, Jesus!" Lundberg said, cupping his head with a hand. "How did they find out about that?"

"They were here, man," Luiz said. "Don't you remember? They were here until *las brujas* came."

"Yeah, but they left," Martin replied.

"Shit, man," Luiz answered. "They could hear you all over this end of town. You yelled so loud it hurt my ears! Then they saw the *brujas* leaving."

"I see," said Martin, nodding. That explained the cool response from Luiz's wife when he came in, standing to one side, her mouth hard in tight disapproval, but saying not a word. "I guess I better apologize."

Luiz was shocked. "Oh, no, man! No way. You must not do that. They'll lose respect if you do."

"They will, indeed," said Ramos, who had slipped up behind them, unseen. "To apologize is to be weak in their eyes, especially when one is in the right. And you were very much in the right defending your friend." Lundberg still looked doubtful, but the old man insisted. "Trust me on this for the moment," Ramos said, taking his arm and leading him toward another room. "Right now there is someone I want you to meet."

"One of your beautiful senoritas?" Lundberg teased.

"No," the old man replied calmly, "not one of beautiful, but the most beautiful of all."

As they crossed into the dining room, Lundberg's eyes met those of a young woman standing by the deep window seat. She was tall, standing perhaps two inches shorter than himself, and slender. Yet she had a magnificent figure accented by the simple blouse she wore above her bright pueblo dress. Her hair was light brown, hanging in two long braids across each shoulder, and her eyes were a deep, luminous blue, a blue so dark they seemed almost black against the light brown of her skin.

As their eyes met, they locked, and Lundberg felt an incredible surge of power, of raw emotional current arc between them like millions of volts hurling itself from heaven to earth and back. Something moved, something shifted deep within him, and he felt his barriers of reserve falling down like dominoes standing in a line, crashing one after the other in lines of mad confusion. He felt naked to the depths of his soul before this woman, and he could see clearly the same was true for her. A deep flush crept up her cheeks and he was aware of an answering response from himself. Only when the tightness in his chest become acute did he remember to breathe.

"Ah," said Ramos, smiling as he took this in. "Just so. Perhaps introductions are superfluous here. Still, Martin, let me present my niece, Stephania Ramos. Stephania, this is my good friend Martin Lundberg."

"Stephanie," she murmured quietly, correcting the old man automatically. "Or just 'Stef,' please. How do you do?" She offered her hand.

Martin was almost speechless. "You're beautiful!" he stammered, taking her hand in his, then flushed, realizing how openly he'd spoken his intimate thoughts to this breath-taking stranger.

"Thank you," she replied, flushing even more deeply. "You're very handsome, too, Martin." She looked down at his hand, still holding hers.

"Oh!" he exclaimed, letting go her hand as quickly as if he had been holding a red hot piece of iron. "Excuse me."

Stephanie was amused. "Would you like some punch?" she asked, smiling. Lundberg nodded, unable to speak, and flushed when she said, "You will have to let me by." Realizing his mistake he backed up so suddenly he collided with Luiz, who was carrying a fresh jug of wine. "Aiee!", Luiz yelled as the jug flew out of his hands, plunging for the floor, but Martin, tumbling beside it, managed to get a hand out to catch it, just in time.

Conversation stopped suddenly as people turned to see what Luiz was yelling about, and Lundberg found himself lying back down on his host's dining room floor holding up a gallon of wine.

"Nice catch," said Stephanie, trying not to titter and the whole room exploded with laughter. "Here, let me help you up," she offered, holding out a hand. Yet even as she did so, her own foot slipped on the tile floor, and when Martin pulled to get up, she tumbled face down on top of him.

The jug of wine flew out of his hand, but was caught by Luiz, who was now laughing so hard he backed into the dining room table, knocking a plate of cookies to the floor. By this time, everyone was laughing, even Luiz's wife, who was gasping so hard she backed into a side table on the other side of the room, upsetting it and spilling Christmas candies all over the floor.

"I'm pleased to meet you," said Martin Lundberg, looking into Stephanie's eyes from a distance of two inches. Through the thin fabric of her festive dress he could feel the firm outline of her breasts and legs pressed against his own, and the delicate warmth of her body. He felt himself begin to respond.

"Do you always make such a strong impression?" she asked, lingering a moment longer than necessary before getting up, smiling at her own play on words as she felt her own response to his lean presence.

"Only on fifth Tuesdays," he answered, helping her to her feet. "Or when I meet someone as beautiful as you. Excuse me," he added, turning to help Luiz and his wife gather up the scattered candies. Stephanie bent down to assist, but slipped again and landed on his back. Again the crowd roared. "Do you always throw yourself at strange men?" he teased as they untangled themselves.

"Only at *posadas*," she assured him. "And then only on the very first night. After that...." She smiled, leaving him to finish the thought.

"So, I'd do well to seize the moment," he asked lightly, helping her to her feet and smiling broadly.

"Or something," she said, flushing deeply as the meaning of her words came home and turning to help clean up to cover her embarrassment. "You'll never know unless you do," she challenged, looking back at him directly.

"Well," he asked, "may I be your escort tonight? Or has someone else been honored with that privilege?"

Stephanie looked at him sharply, was glad to see he was not mocking her. "Only a ten year old," she answered. "And he's my brother."

"He can be our *duena*," Martin suggested. "Our chaperone."

"Don't tell him that," Stephanie laughed. "He's very much all boy and would be terribly insulted."

"Our *caballero*, then," he suggested. "I don't want to offend him."

Stephanie looked at him oddly, then came to him and whispered so softly no one else could hear. "Whose honor would he be defending, Martin? Mine or yours. I'm no blushing maiden."

"Neither am I," he answered simply, feeling the raw emotions pass once more between them. "I wasn't thinking of you or of me. I was thinking of his feelings. I didn't want for him to feel left out."

Seeing the truth deep within his eyes, she smiled. "Good. We'll take him with us and then you and I can go for a walk. I'll give you the Cook's tour of town, most of which you've probably seen."

"I would be honored," he replied, smiling gently. "Now introduce me to our *macho caballero*. Us hairy types have got to stick together."

"He's dying to meet you," she laughed. "Tio Emiliano speaks well of you and Juanito thinks *El Morado* is the living end." She nodded toward the kitchen and said, "Now I need to go help Tina."

For the next hour Martin made the rounds, being introduced to a number of people from town he'd never met. Several times something curious happened, when he greeted those he was meeting in Spanish and they responded in perfect English. During a lull in introductions he asked Ramos about it, "Why don't they speak Spanish back to me? Why do they insist on speaking English?"

"They don't know you," said the old man. "You have a *gringo* name and you look a little like a *gringo*, so they may think you're trying to patronize them." The Hispanic term for North Americans sounded rather strange against the high German they were speaking just then.

"Ah," said Lundberg, nodding. "Maybe you should use the formal way the next time you introduce me."

The old man nodded and the stratagem worked. As it turned out, the next couple he was introduced to was the banker and his wife, both of whom were very correct and markedly reserved. Yet when Ramos introduced him as Martin Lundberg de Delgado, the banker smiled and shook his hand warmly. "Ah," he said, continuing in Spanish. "It is good to meet you. Welcome to our town. I believe you have an account at the bank but I didn't know you were one of us."

"The name is a little misleading," Martin acknowledged, in Spanish. "Being from Minnesota I probably talk funny."

"It's quite charming, actually," the banker's wife said. "You speak very classic Spanish with only a very subtle touch of something else."

"Norwegian, probably," Martin laughed. "It's sort of like fine flour in the bakery. You can't be around it without picking some up."

At that moment the parish priest arrived and Luiz rang a large handbell. The room fell silent as the padre called them to order with prayer, after which three acolytes began handing out candles and song booklets. Four musicians appeared out of nowhere, one carrying a classic guitar, another a home made fiddle, the third with something which looked like a pan flute carved from pieces of cane or bamboo, and the last with a primitive drum. This was decorated with beads and feathers suspended from the crisscrossed lacing which held raw skin heads in place across a hollow length of cottonwood.

Hearing the bell, the musicians began playing at once, a wild pagan melody Martin guessed was subdued only slightly by the presence of the padre, and he felt his blood begin to quicken. He looked for Stephanie, but she was nowhere in sight.

When the wild melody was done, the padre baptized it with holy water and a prayer and the musicians struck up the tune of the first hymn of *posadas*. After a few moments the people began to sing, some of them looking at the song books, but most singing by heart. The tune was simple and Martin found himself singing along with the men in the second refrain:

> Come, O Mary, my blessed
>
> Come, O Mary, my bride
>
> We must be off to Bethlehem
>
> The time has come to go.

The men fell silent and the women took up the song, singing in response. Martin heard a high, clear contralto rising above the rest and looked to his right to see Stephanie coming toward him across the room, a young boy following her. Her eyes met his and she held his gaze, singing as if to him alone.

> O gentle Joseph, my husband
>
> So strong and so good by my side
>
> I cannot travel to Bethlehem
>
> For I am heavy with child.

The men answered again, their gentle voices carrying a strain of urgency which was not there before:

> Come, O Mary, my beloved
> Heavy with God's own child
>
> Though the night is cold and snowy
>
> We must travel to Bethlehem

As the people sang, they lighted their candles, one from another, and Martin waited until Stephanie reached him to light his candle from hers. She was surprised by this and blushed shyly as a titter of laughter rippled around the room. Martin looked up to see several of the older women smiling and giving him knowing looks, and he wondered what he'd just done. *Probably just got myself engaged*, he thought, surprised to find himself not at all displeased with the thought.

Then Stephanie took his arm, and, as if it had been so arranged from the beginning of time, they followed their *caballero* into the street as he led them to the first station. "I hope he knows where we're supposed to go," Martin said softly as they walked out the front door. The feel of her hand on his arm was warm and good, and he found himself walking straighter, taller, almost strutting like a rooster. *Primate display*, a cynical side of himself whispered in his ear, but before he could frame an answer, a stronger, more ancient voice spoke up in stern rebuke. *Be quiet, Cynic!* the voice of an ancient warrior said. *Bridle your tongue. You're standing on holy ground.*

"He does," Stephanie whispered, calling Martin back to the moment. He wondered if she was experiencing the resonance he could feel surging between them. He glanced her way. Her eyes met his yet again, and there was no doubt left in his mind she could and did.

Will you marry me? he thought, wondering how she might respond, and even more startled the thought should occur to him at all.

"Yes," she whispered softly, looking at him in alarm as she felt his surprise tighten the muscles of his arm. For a moment he wondered if he had whispered the thought or if she'd read his mind. "What's wrong?" she whispered urgently.

"You surprised me, that's all. I didn't expect an answer that soon," he blurted, kicking himself as soon as he said it, realizing his mistake.

"I just told you he knew the way," Stephanie said, nodding toward their escort. Then she gave him a strange look. "Why? What did you think I said?"

"I'm crazy," he answered, trying to avoid a direct lie. "I thought you just read my mind." He tried to shrug it off.

Stephanie nodded sagely. "I see. So what did I say yes to?" she asked, a trace too casually.

"I was being foolish," he answered. "I just thought of you and me like... well sort of like Mary and Joseph."

"So I agreed to be your bride," she said solemnly, nodding. "I could do a lot worse, Martin," she murmured softly. "So could you."

Martin was saved an answer by the priest announcing their arrival at the first *posada*, or inn, along their night's journey. Stephanie detached herself from his arm for the moment, moving to join a group of women singers, and Ramos took Martin' arm, leading him firmly up onto the porch. "Sing the inn keeper's part," the old man whispered hoarsely, pointing to a page in the booklet as the women began to sing.

> Oh, let me in, let me in
>
> I'm heavy with child tonight
>
> The snow is deep upon the ground
>
> And I need a place to stay.

Again, Stephanie's clear contralto soared above the others, carrying the chorus and so capturing his attention he almost missed the beginning of the man's response. Hastily reading the lines, Martin joined the chorus who sang the inn keeper's harsh reply.

> There is no room, not a single one
>
> For you to have tonight
>
> Many travelers have come this way
>
> And my simple inn is full.

To this the women answered,

> Oh, please, kind sir, have pity on me,
>
> For I am heavy with God's child
>
> If not for me then for God's love
>
> Let us spend this night.

And the men responded

> Go away, you miserable wretch,
>
> Have you no shame or pride?
>
> To claim your child is God's very own
>
> What a horrible thing to say.

The men moved off the porch to rejoin the women, and Stephanie took Martin' arm again as the procession moved on, singing Christmas carols in Spanish. For a long time she said nothing, singing softly, blending her voice with his as they sang. Yet more than once she looked at him, sometimes rather oddly, sometimes rather sadly, and he wondered what she was thinking.

Cursing himself for a fool for putting his foot in his mouth and ruining the best opportunity he'd had even before it began to develop, Martin started to prepare himself for the let down he knew was sure to come. Yet Stephanie continued to hold his arm and to look at him, not with disdain but with something akin to wonder, and perhaps a little awe.

It was only when they reached her door, long after the *posadas* was done, that she told him what was on her mind. "Martin," she said, after coming into his arms with a kiss which rocked the foundations of his soul. "I won't lie to you. Though it's tempting to try. To put it in a nutshell, you scare me."

"Stephanie!" he protested. "I would never knowingly hurt you. I am not that kind of man."

"I know," she answered quietly, gently stroking his cheek. "You would scare me less if you were. Then I could tell you to buzz off."

"I don't understand," he said huskily.

"I don't either," she replied. "What scares me is I have no defenses against you. Right now you can come in and spend the night if you wish and I'll welcome you gladly to my bed. Or you can walk away right now and break my heart. That might even be best, you know." She met his gaze and he knew she was telling the truth, standing naked to the core of her soul before him.

"How could it be best?" he asked gently, taking her into his arms, kissing her again. She responded eagerly. "I know how I feel and you seem to feel the same way."

"Just this," she whispered in his ear. "It's too strong. If we let it go on much longer, I'm afraid I'm going to end up loving you too much. Someone's going to get hurt. I'm afraid it might be you."

His answer was a kiss which left no doubt of his intentions.

5. Paseo Por Los Chisos

S outhwest Texas. *The Spaniards called this place* los sierra chisos, *the Ghost Mountains. Was it the wind, whispering and sighing among the tall ponderosa pine? Or was it the same wind softly playing the many holes in the rock, caused by sulfurous volcanic bubbles, like ghostly organ pipes? Or was it the doves, singing their mournful vesper song which echoes up and down the canyons? Or was it all of these things? Perhaps they simply gave the place the name by which it was known by the natives.*

While the answers are lost in time, they can still be found here. For this is very much a place where spirits move, and their presence can be felt by those who will listen. Standing now high in the Chisos Basin looking west at the desert floor through the magnificent view of what is called The Window, one can sense them very near, whispering of things forgotten, of mysteries lost to the ages. "There is gold here," they say, tempting the greedy to destruction in the vain search for the Lost Dutchman mine. "This is the Devil's land," they tell others, tempting them to find the presence of evil behind every thorny bush, spinning out tales of betrayal and massacre and murder whose victims' voices can still be heard crying out from the bloody earth for justice so they can rest. Yet to those attuned to hear it, these spirits sing a different song and they speak a simple truth: that this harsh and mysterious land, so marked by sharp stone and spiny growth across its vast empty reaches, yet holds within itself an austere beauty found nowhere else on earth.

(Martin Quinn's Journal)

January 1963. They were somewhere south of Pine Springs, Texas. The reason for the name of the town was fairly obvious, for the land they were now traveling was dry and desolate, with vegetation so sparse most of the earth lay bare beneath the merciless sun. Here and there cattle grazed, nibbling at God knows what yet looking surprisingly fit and in good condition. Windmills seemed to be the only source of water in this barren land. The gullies were cut deep by wind and flash floods, and natural reservoirs dried up quickly. Yet every few miles there was a windmill next to a large round steel tank, low to the ground and open on top so cattle could drink, and around each watering tank grew a thin band of thick grass, kept nibbled close by the stock which came to water. How far the cattle had to walk to quench their thirst was anyone's guess, but from the spacing of the windmills, it must be several miles.

The sun was past zenith when they left Pine Springs, and as they drove south along Texas 54, it cast a strange light against the looming purple height of the Sierra Diabolo range to their right. Who so named them, he did not know. Yet it was easy to imagine why, seeing the unsoftened edges of the newly volcanic rock surrounded by occasional clumps of spiny desert plants. Too, the natives seemed to take perverse pride in the stark, harsh nature of the land. What was it the attendant at the gas station at the junction said? "This must be God's country because the Devil wouldn't have it!" Then his crony, huddled by the open gas heater in the station house, added, "Yeah. Everything south of here either sticks, stings, or stinks!" How many times had they said the same to travelers headed for Van Horn?

Despite the work his place still needed, Martin Lundberg was glad to accept his mother's invitation to make this trip. To be honest, he had to admit he was getting a little tired of the endless work of restoration. Though he did enjoy it, he found himself sometimes restless. This was made more acute now Stephanie was gone, returning to school for her final semester, leaving him at once lonely yet grateful for time to reflect on all which had passed between them.

So it was good getting away now. It was good seeing different country and doing things outside his routine, and Rosa was an excellent traveling companion. Silence did not bother her, nor did the desolation of the countryside or the minor inconveniences of travel. From the canyon their route took them first to Las Vegas, where they left the mountains and headed south across rolling plains toward Vaughn. There, in the long stretches between Vaughn and Roswell and Artesia, and finally Carlsbad, where they spent the night before, there was plenty of time for earnest talk and gentle remembering. Somewhere along one of those desolate stretches yesterday, though he couldn't remember exactly where, he'd discovered again how much a trooper Rosa Lundberg could be.

"I need to stop at the next rest room," she said in the middle of one of the long stretches between towns. "I'm afraid my system isn't used to much chile any more." She explained, embarrassed to have to ask, and more embarrassed for her reason for asking.

"I think we must still be forty miles from the next town," he answered, looking at the odometer. "The only thing closer is that bridge up ahead," he added, grinning as he teased her.

"That will do fine," his mother answered urgently, surprising him.

"Are you sure?" he replied, taking his foot off the gas pedal and looking to see if she were serious. "I was only kidding."

"I'm not," she answered, unsmiling, and he began to brake as he pulled the big car to the side of the road. Once they were stopped, Rosa grabbed a box of tissues and ran quickly to the near end of the bridge where she disappeared around the side of the safety railing.

Martin started to call after her, then thought better of it. His mother was a very private person when it came to such things and she would ask if she needed assistance. *That is, she would if there were no way she could avoid assistance*, he thought. Then he laughed at himself, too, thinking how well he'd learned this from her.

Taking advantage of the stop, he got out of the car and walked back the way they came to stretch his legs. The air was much colder than when they started that morning, even at that much lower elevation, and he thought a front must be moving through. Shivering he walked quickly back to the car, where he turned up the heater as he waited for his mother.

"Goodness!" Rosa said when she climbed back in the car, smiling as she pulled her jacket closer around her. "I forget what a blessing indoor plumbing is. Especially in January with a sharp north wind."

Martin laughed and nodded. "I don't suppose there's much shelter under a bridge, is there?" he asked. "I almost froze walking twenty yards, but at least it isn't snowing." Then he laughed. "I take that back," he said, pointing to the first flakes drifting across the wind shield. "Good timing!"

That was the first snow they'd seen on the trip, and the last so far, though the air was still quite brisk earlier that morning when they left Carlsbad to explore the caverns south of there. This was something neither of them had done and exploring El Paso was left to the return trip, if there was time and if they were still in the mood. Both of them had seen the city before and he was glad they made the decision they did, for on their way to the caverns Rosa was excited as a small child, anticipating a buried treasure she'd heard about all her life.

Despite occasional twinges of claustrophobia when he allowed himself to dwell on how far they were underground and how many tons of stone lay overhead, Martin found he enjoyed the guided tour. Due to threatening weather and the season, their group was small and cheerful and the ranger leading them was very enthusiastic about the caves. So even when the lights were turned out for a few moments to let them experience total darkness, he was surprisingly undisturbed, although he found himself relieved when they came back on. He was even more relieved to be back on the surface when the tour was done.

"That was wonderful," his mother sighed as they walked across the lot to their rental car. "I've always wondered what it was like to be so far underground. My father would never allow me to go into the mines."

"Much more cramped there," Martin said, feeling his palms grow wet at the thought, despite the cold.

Rosa caught the edge of panic in his voice. "Thank you for going with me, Martin," she said, hugging his arm. "I hope you didn't think you had to do so, but I really do appreciate it."

Martin took a deep breath, shook off his panic. "Strange," he said. "It didn't bother me until just now when you said something about the mines." He laughed as the panic passed away. "Then my imagination ran wild, but before that I enjoyed it."

"I'm glad," she said, yawning as she got into the car. This cold air is making me so drowsy." Settling into the seat she rested her head on the back of the soft cushions and was sound asleep, snoring softly, before they reached the main road.

Now, driving along far to the south of Pine Springs, he found himself growing ever more drowsy, too. The deep murmur of the Buick's powerful engine scarcely audible over the soft hiss of the tires was seductive and the road stretched on and on, mile after mile without turning. Suddenly he became aware he was no longer in control. He sensed his mind detach strangely from his body, and even the panic he could feel rising within himself knowing this could not seem to break the hypnotic spell of the road. Then he watched, as if from far away, a sudden dip in the road approach, growing deeper and more treacherous as they grew ever near. Even knowing he needed to take his foot off the accelerator, even feeling fear rising within him, he discovered himself strangely unable to act.

The rise of his stomach as the car settled into the shallow dip startled him out of his reverie, and though the solid suspension of the big Road-master took the dip in stride, making it barely perceptible, Rosa was startled awake, too, her eyes wide and fearful. "Goodness," she said. "I must have really slept. I think I remember you stopping for gas, or was I dreaming?"

Martin was grateful she was not wide enough awake to see his own fright. There was no need to worry her with what might have happened and to cover his sheepishness he spun a tale. "Don't you remember?" he asked, feigning surprise. "You made such an awful fuss over the dirty rest room. I thought you were going to chew the poor man's head off. He was terribly embarrassed."

"I didn't, either!" she said, indignant. "You're just making that up." Even so, she gave him a questioning look. "I didn't did I?"

"No," he said, relenting. "I was just giving you a bad time. We stopped in Pine Springs but you only woke up for a moment. We're about thirty-five miles from Van Horn if you need a pit stop."

She nodded and yawned. "I can wait," she said, looking out the window at the passing country side and shivering. "You know, I've forgotten just how desolate this country can be. Especially in the winter time."

"Well, at least it's cold now," he answered. "I bet it gets unbearably hot in the summer and even more desolate." She nodded, still waking up. "It's a lot different from the Midwest, isn't it?" he asked, thinking of the winters growing up near St. Cloud, Minnesota. "How much snow was on the ground when you left home?"

"There was surprisingly little there," Rosa answered. "So far we haven't had more than ten or twelve inches all year." She laughed. "I got out just in time, too. I read in the paper the Twin Cities got almost that much the day I left."

Martin chuckled. "I can almost hear Dad *gevitching*. I don't suppose he broke down and got a new snow blower this year?"

"Of course no," Rosa smiled. "He's too fond of cursing the old one."

They both laughed at the memory, then lapsed into a comfortable silence as they drove on. Though the sun was still high, the relatively high elevation of the valley they were traveling and the deep shadows cast by the mountains kept the earth from giving much warmth to the valley air. Where it did, the little heat generated in protected low places was quickly striped away by a raw north wind. High cirrus clouds streaked a hazy sky in the crystal clarity of the air in this land still unmarked by pollution, and sun dogs shone bright far to either side of the earth's mellow star.

As they passed an isolated homestead not far off the road, Rosa pointed to a group of children playing in the barren yard in front of a lonely frame house standing some distance from several large barns. "Gracious!" she said. "How can they stand it? They look like they could freeze."

Martin followed the direction of her gaze and nodded his agreement. The children were poorly dressed by northern standards, wearing only light jackets and thin caps, and one of the larger boys seemed to be clad only in jeans and a long sleeved tee shirt. Yet the children seemed oblivious to the cold as they ran in and out among the ten or twelve cars and trucks parked in front of the house, kicking what looked like a basket ball toward some undetermined goal. "Makes me cold just watching them," he responded.

"What in the world is their mother thinking?" Rosa demanded, now quite indignant. "They'll all catch their death of cold."

"Well, I guess as long as they keep running they're all right," Martin said, and as he spoke, two of the smaller children dropped out of the game, ducking quickly into the cab of a pickup. He laughed, seeing the bright flurry of a red blanket being quickly drawn around their small bodies. "See?" he said, pointing. "They're doing all right."

His mother snorted but did not argue. After a moment she smiled as the memories warmed her features. "You're right, of course," she admitted. "I seem to remember doing exactly the same thing. We used blankets because it was never cold long enough to buy all of us winter coats. She was silent another long moment, then continued. "I remember my father and mother buying my sister and me our first winter coats when we were eight. They were wool on one side with cotton twill on the other, and we could wear them inside out so it looked like we had two coats." She smiled again. "Mine was white with a black stripe and a red stripe around the bottom. How proud I was!"

Martin nodded, smiling. "What about the boys? Didn't any of them get wool coats, too?"

"Some of them did, of course," Rosa replied. "But the boys were always very macho about their clothes. It was considered unmanly to admit one was cold, or so my brother told me. All the boys wore were jean jackets most of the time. I think some of those were lined with cotton or wool, but mostly they weren't. I do remember one of the Rivera boys had a leather jacket. His uncle was an aviator and gave it to him. It was leather on the outside and wool inside, and it must have been too warm to wear most of the year. But he was proud of it. It had a patch on the shoulder and straps and clips and all sorts of pockets, and he wore it even when the weather turned warm. How the other boys envied him."

"I can imagine," Martin said. "A lot of people these days are wearing those green military field jackets. Cloth ones, not leather. Remember how I used to wear Dad's old leather bush pilot's jacket?"

"Before you outgrew it," his mother laughed. "It's always been hard to imagine how someone as small as your father had two sons so tall. My people weren't small, but they weren't the size of you two."

"Must be a wild Viking gene in the line somewhere," Martin teased. "Or some tall caballero from Spain. Wasn't your father a tall man?"

"He was for the times, yes. He was about a head taller than most of the other men, but he wasn't as tall as either of you." Rosa frowned and shook her head. "I think part of your father's being so small was that his family was so very poor when he was growing up. He was the youngest of seven and all his brothers and sisters were always much bigger than he was." She looked at him seriously. "He took a lot of abuse for being the 'runt of the litter', as he calls it. He was always the last in line."

"You think not having enough food stunted his growth?" Martin asked, suddenly realizing what Rosa was telling him. He was shocked. "I knew they were poor, but I didn't realize they were that poor."

"They were," his mother answered simply. "They were always poor and the year before he was born was a particularly hard one for them. His father had trouble finding enough work and his mother was very sick. She once told me he cried all the time his first two years, only because he was always hungry."

Martin could not begin to imagine the reality of what she was describing, or what it might be like to live that way. Not to have enough food to feed one's children was something that happened in other places, to other people. There was something which felt almost immoral about it, and to learn it happened not only in his own family, but to one of his parents, was overwhelming. He found himself filled with an unfamiliar feeling of compassion for his father. "You mean...?" he asked, leaving the question unfinished.

"Yes," she said sadly. "He must have been like one of those poor little African children we see in the papers. Only it was here, in this country." She looked at her son, caught his eye for a moment. "I've never told you this, but I think that's why your father is the way he gets sometimes. He's still hungry, so hungry he can't be filled."

"Or maybe he's afraid it could happen again," Martin suggested. Rosa nodded and he started to say something more but stopped for a moment, reflecting. "Do you think that's why he drinks the way he drinks, too?" he asked, finally uttering the thought which lay unspoken between them.

"Maybe," Rosa nodded. "I think it's more that he learned it at home. His father was a terrible alcoholic, just like one of his two uncles and his grandfather. One of the reasons there was not enough to eat was because his father drank his pay up. Then he would come home and give them terrible beatings. Once he beat your father with a piece of wire until he bled." Rosa shuddered, remembering the face of her husband as he told her this in a moment of rare intimacy. Not that he was angry, nor that he was bitter or even hurt. Rather it was his disconnected lack of passion as he spoke which disturbed her far more than rage could ever.

"So he passed it along to us," Martin said, somewhat bitterly, biting back his rage. The sight of his mother's face twisted in pain made him wish he'd kept his mouth shut. "I'm sorry," he said. "But it's true."

"I tried to protect you, Martin," Rosa said, crying. "For some reason he always got more angry with you than with your brother. Maybe because you are so much like him. I couldn't always be there to protect you. When I did he beat me, too." Her tears turned into racking sobs.

Martin pulled the big Buick to the side of the road. Reaching for his mother, he cradled her in his arms until her weeping finally stopped. Sniffling and embarrassed, she wiped her nose with a tissue, keeping her gaze fixed on her hands. "I didn't mean to do that," she whispered. "Let's talk about something happy." When she looked up her eyes were pleading.

"Sure," said Martin, more than a little ascerbic. "So we talk about something happy and we ignore it one more time. Then, when it comes up again and again, we do the same thing all over. Do you know what I wish, mother? I wish we could just talk it through for once."

"What's there to talk about?" his mother asked. "We both know what happened. Talking about it only makes it worse, Martin."

"That's what you've always said," Martin answered in a level voice. "What happens is that things just get worse, anyway. I don't see what talking about it will hurt. What do we have to lose?"

"Yes," his mother answered. "You're right. What do we have to lose? Yet what will it help? It won't change things. You know that as well as I do."

"I know that's what you believe," her son said, calm now. "I'm not sure it's true. After all, we've never tried. When I talk to Ramos about things which trouble me, I feel better. Even when nothing changes, I feel better."

Rosa Lundberg sighed. "I used to talk to your Aunt Rita before they left for to California," she said, nodding and touching his face lightly. "You're right. It made me feel better."

"So why can't we talk, then, you and me, about Dad and Brother?" he asked. "Maybe it will help us get through the bad times, just having talked. Even if it doesn't change much, maybe it will help the two of us get through."

His mother looked at Martin, her dark eyes almost black, even in the bright noonday light. "I have always tried to be a good mother, son, but I am a wife first. My first loyalty is to your father."

"I'm not asking you to betray that loyalty," he pointed out. "Not at all, even though I don't know why you've stayed with him. I know how he's treated you and I know what he's put you through. He doesn't deserve your loyalty and your kids are grown now. You don't have to put up with it any more. You don't even have to worry about money. Half of what he's got is yours, anyway."

"I've stayed because I vowed to stay," his mother replied, simply. "When I married it was for better or for worse, and it was for life." She shrugged. "So I've just tried to make the best of it, and it hasn't been all bad, either, Martin."

"What I've seen hasn't been what you deserve," he argued. "Not by a long shot. He's treated you like..." He stopped short, respecting his mother's normal aversion to earthy language.

"Like what, Martin?" Rosa inquired gently. "You're a man now, and I know all the words. So speak your mind. I learned to use them all fluently long before you were born." She giggled. "I learned them from Rita."

Martin flushed, but was not about to be put off. "He treats you like trash," he asserted. While he enjoyed the freedom of earthy language among his peers, he found himself inhibited despite his mother's candor. Somehow he could not even say "*caca*", much less "shit". The early conditioning was simply too strong. "I started to say like a dog," he lied, without conviction. "He'd never treat his dog the way he treats you."

"Or you," she pointed out. "Even so, he is your father and he is my husband. That cannot be changed."

"Not according to him," Martin replied. "He threatens to disown me ever time he sees me. I think all he's waiting for is a good excuse."

"He'll never do that, Martin," his mother said, alarmed. "That's just talk, the drink talking."

"Or the drunk," he said. "I'm not so sure you're right. I think he would have done it already if it weren't for you."

"No!" Rosa exclaimed. "He loves you, Martin," she protested.

"He has a funny way of showing it," he responded sharply. Then, seeing the look on her face, he relented. "Look, I know how much you would like to believe that," he continued earnestly. "All right? At the same time, I think you're dead wrong. I think he hates me because he can't control me the way he can his first born." He shook his head angrily. "All that's beside the point, anyway. We were talking about you and him, not me and him, and I think the way he treats you is awful."

Once again Rosa Lundberg said nothing. Tears began to form in her eyes once again, tracking down her face. Martin had to strain to hear what she said next, "I know, Martin, but it wasn't always like that. There was a time he treated me very well, like a princess."

"So what happened?" he asked gently. He could not remember the last time he had heard his mother speak so openly.

"I don't know," she said. "At first it wasn't much. He was working very hard to get his business going and while I was keeping the office it was very good. Then your brother was born and we hired a young woman to be our part time bookkeeper. She needed the job very badly.

She was also very competent and it was easy to let her handle more and more things. Then you were born and by the time both of you were in school, she was running the whole office." Her voice turned bitter, "Among other things."

Martin did not know what to say. Yet, as much as he feared the answer he might get, he felt he had to know. "What do you mean?" he asked, trying hard to keep his voice as neutral as he could.

"The office was not enough for her," Rosa said in a deathly quiet voice. Martin had never seen her so angry, and he could feel the rage revealed in her eyes flare like the like the open door of a blast furnace. "I never said anything to you before, but the day you were born your father went home and took her into his bed." She shrugged. "I was not sure at first why he lost interest in me. Never was there a time he did not want me physically until then. Nor I, him. Yet, when it happened he made no bones about it, either." Her eyes were bleak. "He told me about it almost as soon as it happened. As if it were my fault and he could rub my nose in it and make me run away!"

"That son-of-a-bitch!" Martin snarled. His knuckles gripping the steering wheel were white. "That dirty rotten son-of-a-bitch!"

Rosa's answer was a wry smile. Though it still burned fiercely, her rage had been restrained, vanishing as quickly as it flared, shoved back firmly by habit into its customary cage. "No, Martin, I knew his mother well and I loved her. She was an angel. It was his father who was *un diablo*. Again she put a restraining hand on his arm. "You mustn't judge him too harshly. He was only being a man."

"No!" he almost shouted. "Damnit, no! I'm a man and I'm not like that. Neither is Ramos. I'll never let myself be like that. I'll shoot myself first!"

Rosa Lundberg nodded, smiling. "No need to buy a *pistola* just yet, Martin," she answered. "As much as you are alike in the good ways, you are different, too. Mostly you remind me of your grandfather, my father. He was a real man, too. You seem to have a lot of his strengths." She smiled. "Some of his faults, too. One of which is a passionate nature. That is why you were named for him." She laughed. "He was so proud when I told him."

"Why did he never use his first name? Why did everyone call him Ignacio and not Martin?"

Rosa shook her head sadly. "His father called him that. I don't know why, but he insisted his son be called by his second name, Ignacio."

Martin sighed, knowing the subject of his father and mother's marriage was firmly closed. While he would liked to pursue it more, they had come a long way farther than ever before and he knew from experience his mother had said all she was going to say for the moment. "I'll be right back," he said, pulling on a stocking cap and getting out of the car. "I need to run some steam off. Start the engine if you get cold."

Turning to face the wind Martin began to run along the side of the road, slowly at first until his muscles began to relax, then faster and faster until he'd gone about a mile from the car. Circling a mailbox beside a gravel road leading off into nowhere, he slowed his pace, feeling the tension of his anger drain from his body through his legs and feet, like lightening going to ground. By the time he reached the car his mind was clear and his breathing was almost normal. Only his cheeks and his nose, unprotected from the wind, were worse for wear, showing stark white against two patches of bright red.

Jumping into the car, Martin started it up again, turning on the defroster to clear the steam from his breath on the windshield. Rosa smiled and handed him a cup of cocoa from a thermos. It was warm, not hot, but it felt almost scalding against his cold lips. "Goodness, that tastes good!" he said, balancing the cup on the transmission hump and looking back up the road before turning the car out onto the highway. While it was a good habit, it was wasted effort. No one was coming. Nor had anyone passed since he pulled over a half hour before.

"So how old was I when he died?" he asked once the Roadmaster was up to speed. "Was I ten, or eleven?"

"Your grandfather?" Rosa asked. He nodded and she thought a few moments. "I think you must have been nine," she said.

"No, I think I was ten when he gave me my first pocket knife," he responded. "So it must have been after that."

"You're right," she said. "Yes," she added, correcting herself and counting on her fingers, "you must have been almost eleven, I think. It's written down in the family book at home but I think that's right. What I do remember is how upset you were when it happened."

He nodded. "I remember the day very clearly. The people sitting around talking and all the food. I don't remember much about the funeral. I think someone sang the Ave Maria during the requiem. A cousin of ours?"

"That was Alberto," his mother smiled. "He's still singing. We got a nice card from him for Christmas and he said he's a grandfather again."

"What?" Martin asked, surprised. "I remember him being a very young man at the funeral. Maybe twenty at the most."

Rosa laughed. "Everyone thinks that. He's actually two years older than me. Of course, I was only thirty-three when Papa died." Her eyes clouded with memory. "I was very concerned about you for a long time because you didn't cry. You just seemed to go way, far away inside yourself like you sometimes do."

Martin' face became very still. "Well, mother," he said dryly. "That's what your husband taught me to do. 'Real men don't cry.' I don't remember how many times I heard him say that. If I cried, he beat me until I stopped."

"My husband," she insisted softly, "and your father. There's no changing that, Martin. That's who he is."

"No?" he asked in an ominously quiet voice. "Well, if he can disown me I can disavow him. Not that he'd care," he added bitterly, "unless I did it first. That would really get his goat."

"Oh, Martin, he would," Rosa protested. "Please believe me. There's a whole side of him you don't know. You would have liked him if you knew him at your age. He was very much like you are now."

"That's not very reassuring," he said, almost to himself. "It causes me to wonder if I should ever have children."

"You didn't turn out so bad," she pointed out.

"I'll have to take your word for that," he grinned. "You couldn't prove it by me." Sobering, he added. "About Dad, I find it's easier not to think of him at all. As if he died a long time ago."

"Perhaps he did, Martin," Rosa added softly. "Yet sometimes I still get glimpses of the man I came to love with all my soul. As if he is locked inside himself somewhere, trying desperately to find a way out."

Sudden insight flooded his mind. "So that's why you've stayed all these years?" he asked gently. "You keep hoping that man will come home." Rosa nodded and said nothing more, fixing her attention on the passing countryside. From time to time she dabbed her eyes with a corner of her handkerchief, but gave no other sign of her grief.

Martin drove in silence, respecting his mother's want for privacy in her grief. As he drove, it occurred to him she was not only mourning the hurts of her marriage, but also the loss of the way of life she'd known as a child and the people who lived there. No wonder she'd been so enthusiastic about coming down, or in sharing the Old Christmas celebration with *los* Ramos. It was her connection to a time in which she belonged and a place she knew as home.

A deep sense of loss washed over Martin thinking of this, the loss of something he'd never had nor ever known he'd really wanted, the loss of roots, of belonging, of being cherished for who he was. The times he could remember feeling this way were those spent at his grandfather's house, when his grandfather was alive and living with the beautiful woman he still called his bride after fifty years. Yet that house, that place, held no real attachment for the old man or his wife. It was out here in the barren wastes of western Texas the family memories gathered, for Rosa was the second generation born in *el Presidio del Norte* in the state of Chihuahua. It was here, in the harsh land in which they were traveling, the old man made the place he called home.

Passing through Van Horn, they drove on south and east in silence through the wide valley between the Wylie Mountains to their left and the Sierra Vieja ten to twenty miles, and perhaps more, to their right. Vast cattle ranges ran along both sides of the road with cross fences spaced far apart and ranch gates identified with multi-digit numbers. Other than the highway and the fences, the land was empty of civilization, the only signs being occasional buildings widely scattered in the distance and the railroad which ran parallel to the highway on their left. Somehow the cattle they saw from time to time sprinkled across the endless landscape looked as if they really belonged here, as if brought forth by a whim of nature and not human intention.

The road ran on, flat and straight as an arrow and Martin felt himself nod again, beginning to really tire. Stopping in Valentine to top the big Buick's tank, and more to break the monotony of the road than for need of fuel, he consulted the map and then looked at the sun, which was moving far over into the western sky. "It looks like we have a choice," he said to Rosa, speaking Spanish as they often did between themselves. "It's about forty miles to Marfa and then we either turn south for Presidio or go on to Alpine before heading south It looks to me about the same distance to Terlingua either way."

"Excuse me, sir," the attendant said in Spanish. "I overheard what you were telling your wife...." He stopped when Rosa and Martin both broke out laughing.

"Please pardon us," Rosa smiled to the confused young man. "Thank you for the compliment. I'm his mother."

"Surely not!" the attendant lied gallantly. "You look like his younger sister." Rosa rewarded his gallantry with another smile, which he acknowledged with a nod, almost a bow. "I think you might want to go on to Alpine if you're trying to get to Terlingua," the attendant said. "The road along the Rio Grande is very bad now I hear." He shrugged. "With a jeep or pickup, no problem. What's a few more dents? But with this new car..."

"You mean the car won't make it?" Martin asked. "It must really be a rough road, then."

"No, your car would make it all right, I think. Just it will scratch the paint for sure, I think, maybe."

"What if we take it easy?" Martin asked, finding himself intrigued by this mysterious road at the end of nowhere. "You think we can make it?"

"I think you'll do all right," the man answered, "but who knows? Take plenty of water and a rope and shovel in case you get stuck."

Rosa paid for the gasoline, adding a sweet tip and being rewarded with another flash of bright, even teeth from the young man. "What do you think?" Martin asked after they were on the way. "Presidio or Alpine."

His mother gave him a shy smile. "There's something I've always wanted to do," she said. "Ever since I was a little girl."

"What's that?" he asked, wondering at the sudden alteration in her manner, in the advent of this shy child he beheld in her mature face.

"Do you promise not to laugh?" she replied. He nodded and she went on. "Ever since I was a little girl I have wanted to see the Marfa lights," she said. "My father wouldn't allow it. He called it superstition."

"You mean the town lights?" he asked. He could not imagine what the attraction might be seeing the lights of any of the small cities they'd passed on their way. "Sure. There ought to be someplace we can stay there."

"No, silly," his mother laughed. "Not the city lights, the ghost lights. We'll stay at the Paisano Hotel. The food at the restaurant there used to be the best in this country and tonight we can go see the lights."

The Paisano turned out to have rooms for them that night, but since it was midweek in an off season, the restaurant was closed for repairs. The clerk suggested a local restaurant known for its excellent chicken tacos, and which was right on their way. So after checking into their rooms and changing to warmer clothes, they were on the way again.

The restaurant was distinguishable from other houses along the highway only by its neatly lettered sign which read, "The Old Barunda". As a matter of fact, it was a house converted to restaurant use and they could see living quarters to the back of the building. "I wonder how that translates," Martin asked as they were shown to their table.

"I don't know..." his mother started to say, then stopped halfway down into her chair and stared. "Carolina?" she asked in a soft voice, looking at the woman who could be seen cooking through the kitchen door.

The woman turned to look, then dropped her spoon and wiped her hands with her apron. "Rosa?" she said, coming toward them. Both women shrieked as they embraced, suddenly grey headed teens speaking a rapid, excited Spanish which Martin had a hard time following.

Remembering her manners, Rosa turned and introduced Martin to the other woman, who nodded gravely and smiled brightly as she shook his hand. "So pleased to meet you," she said in heavily accented English. Rosa began to explain to him who she was, but the exact connection escaped Martin. All he could gather from their staccato Spanish in the peculiar dialect he'd never heard before was that they had known one another growing up. Apparently they had not seen or heard of one another since Rosa's family left Terlingua some years before. Extracting from them a promise to stop by the next morning before leaving town, Caroline returned to her cooking.

When their meal came, it was nothing like Martin expected. Rather than the hard yellow folded tacos he was used to getting in Mexican restaurants, these were made with grayish blue corn meal tortillas rolled tightly around chicken filling and were served with refried beans and a shredded salad. Not caring for the waitress' suggestion of a strawberry soda, which was quite popular locally, Martin asked for coffee and drank water with his meal. Despite their ordinary appearance, the chicken *flau-*

tas were incredible, so delicious he asked for a second helping, provoking a laugh from Caroline in the kitchen. She said something to Rosa, who laughed in turn and fired back a rejoinder, but the only phrase Martin could catch ended in *gordo*.

"*Yo no soy un gordo,*" he protested. I'm no fatty, causing both women to break into more laughter. Several other patrons looked around trying to see what so funny.

"No, Martin," his mother said, gasping for breath, but speaking in a more deliberate Spanish. "She didn't say you're a fatty." Rosa laughed again. "She said that as fast as you were eating the *flautas*, you would choke if they were as fat as regular tacos."

"Well, I don't eat as fast as you two talk," he teased back, and both Rosa and Caroline laughed again. "It's hard to believe you're speaking Spanish."

"True," Rosa said. "We're not." Then she added, "One of the men in the mine was from Brazil and taught several of us a little Portuguese. Caroline and I used to mix it in when we didn't want anyone else to understand, and we even made up our own words." Martin could see Caroline nodding from the kitchen. Then Caroline said something in a rapid burst to Rosa, who laughed again before translating. "She said if you eat like this all the time you'll soon be *un gordo*."

"*Viva los gordos!*" he declared, diving into his second helping and drawing a round of laughter from the whole restaurant, which was following every word. Someone on the other side of the room gave a Jalisco yelp and Martin held up his fork in a clenched fist, grinning.

Later, as they sat huddled in the front seat of the Buick watching for the ghost lights to appear, if, indeed, they would that evening, he wished he'd exercised a little more discretion at table. He'd taken two bites too many, he decided. While they were worth every bit of the slight discomfort he was feeling, perhaps he should have gone easier on the refried *frijoles*. "I think I need to stretch my legs," he told Rosa, patting his stomach as he opened the door. "Walk a little of this off."

He was not a moment too soon. As he closed the car door with a solid "chunk!" a burst of methane presented itself to the world. Glad it was dark enough to hide his embarrassment, and hoping she hadn't heard, Martin jogged to the west about a hundred yards. After about fifty yards every stride seemed to carry with it a gift of gas and he was grateful for the opportunity to work it out of his system. Why it was embarrassing to fart in front of a lady who had changed his diapers, he didn't know, but it was, and he knew it would embarrass Rosa, as well. *Or maybe not*, he thought. He was discovering a lot of things about her on this trip which overturned much of what he once believed, deflating many of his childhood preconceptions.

Jogging back toward the Buick he noticed what looked like car lights far to the south and east, and high up on what looked like a mountain. He decided these must be lights from the road to Presido or some other road, although the cars were either moving at very high speed or were much closer than they appeared. Another car had parked by the Buick and Rosa was talking to the family gathered in front of the vehicle. "Did you see them, Martin?" she asked, excited, pointing to the lights he'd been watching.

"Those are car lights, aren't they," he answered. "Up on the mountain or out on the road to Presido."

The man standing next to him chuckled. "That's what the Army thought back during World War II when they had an air base out here," he said. "Then when they set up two observation posts and triangulated the distance, they found out the lights were too far away to be cars. They also calculated they'd have to be moving about Mach 6 to Mach 12 to cover the distance. That's faster than anything we have right now."

"I expected something different," Martin admitted. "For ghost lights they look pretty ordinary."

The man nodded. "Yeah, me too. But you have to remember the Indians used to see them long before there was anything around that could make a light that bright." He laughed. "The Army spent a lot of time and money driving themselves crazy looking for German saboteurs before they gave up. They found when you approach the lights directly they disappear before you can get to them."

"Why did your father think the light were just superstition?" Martin asked Rosa. "There they are for anyone to see."

"Not always," she replied. The man standing with them nodded. "They only shine at certain times there are many times they do not appear at all."

"My dad says the same thing," said another man standing to one side. "He's traveled all through this country since 1947, and he's never seen them. So he thinks they don't exist."

"But you've seen them," Rosa protested. "You're his son."

"That makes me as crazy as the rest of you in his eyes," the man said, laughing. "You've got to understand, my dad's rather, um, opinionated."

"You're rather diplomatic," Rosa answered, introducing herself and Martin to the young man, now in his late teens. He was tall and thin and wore heavy lenses carried in horn rim frames. The young man introduced the young woman who was with him. Where he was very gregarious, she seemed reluctant to join in the conversation and stood shivering beneath the folds of his warm football jacket. A large, embroidered A in purple and gold covered the left breast of the jacket, and cream leather arms complimented the gold wool of the body. "You must be from Alpine," Rosa said, pointing to the jacket.

The young woman smiled and nodded back. "I'm cold," she told the young man, who nodded but made no move back toward their car. Rolling her eyes at Rosa she said, "Excuse me, please. I'm freezing!" and quickly climbed back into the large white Chrysler convertible they were driving. A moment later they heard its engine start as she turned up the heater.

There will be hell to pay later, Martin thought, not envying the young man his ride home. *On the other hand, maybe he's right. He is the way he is and there is nothing wrong with it. So if she can't live with it, better to find out now than later, when there may be children.* He could imagine their conversation and almost wished he could be a mouse in the corner to hear it.

Then he wondered what there was about himself which might similarly offend Stephanie. He felt a sharp pang of loneliness remembering their last parting, the tenderness of their touch, the sweeping fire of their passion and the gentle urgency of their loving. *Where are you tonight, my love?* he asked the starry sky. *Do you miss me as much as I miss you? And is this the real thing? Or will it end like all the others have for me?* Then the thoughts began to play back and forth in his mind, turning into a poem,

> Where are you tonight, my love?
>
> Does your heart yearn as mine,
>
> Or feel the emptiness of this night
>
> Full of stars and moon

And mysteries we cannot share?

How do you bear this lonely time

We must now be apart

That tears my soul?

Will you love me so tomorrow

As I know you do this day?

Or will our love turn cold with time,

The bright fire dying day by day

As each ember turns to ash?

"Martin, what's wrong?" Rosa's voice pulled him back to the present. He looked up to see the young man staring at him oddly, became aware of tears frozen on his cheeks.

"Sorry," he answered, trying to laugh it off. "I was just thinking. It's a dangerous habit." He gave them a wry grin.

Rosa started to ask something more, then stopped. The young man chuckled awkwardly, and after a moment bid them good night and made his way back to his own car. Martin caught sight of the young man's companion in the courtesy light as he opened the door of the Chrysler and decided he might not like to be a mouse in the corner, after all. It would be like standing a half mile from ground zero at the testing range he guessed.

"Was it thinking of your grandfather?" Rosa asked as they drove back to the hotel.

"No," he answered simply. "It was Stephanie."

"You miss her, terribly." Rosa nodded.

"Yes, it's never been like this before," he told her.

"Then let your mother give you some advice," she answered softly. "Don't think I'm just an old woman butting in. Think about your love every day. Do not let a day go by without nurturing it. It's too beautiful to be allowed to die." Her eyes were bleak when she uttered her last thought.

Martin waited, expecting more. "That's it?" he asked.

"Oh, there's always more any woman could say about love," she said, almost smiling at herself, he thought. "We probably talk it to death, but it's the only thing that ultimately matters. At least to a woman."

"You may be ahead of men there," he said. "You know, until the first night of *posadas* I was happy with my place up the mountain. Ever since then it feels so different," he added, searching for words. "It feels... almost empty."

"There's only one thing which will fill that part of your soul," Rosa replied. "You are very fortunate to have found it."

"But it hurts," he said. "It's so beautiful it hurts. I don't understand that. I feel like I'm lifted up and thrown down at the same time."

"So does having a baby, Martin, but it is well worth it. At least I think so," she smiled. "Especially when he turns out like you." Rosa paused, then added, "Of course, it hurts. Every human relationship hurts, even our casual friendships. I find the beauty overcomes the pain, and I think perhaps that is why they are given to us."

"I don't follow," he replied.

"They teach us that love conquers all, just like the Good Book says," she answered, almost primly. "They teach us that in the end all that matters is love." As she spoke her eyes took on a far away look, as if she were talking mostly to herself, calling back to mind something she knew well, but which she had forgotten.

Martin was surprised at Rosa's words, for he had never considered her a deep thinker even though he knew she was full of wisdom. Like many children of wise parents, he assumed she was simply born that way, although as an adult he clearly knew better. It was something he'd never thought about. Now it reminded him of a conversation he had with Ramos late in the fall, another conversation in which the subject was love.

"I think the drunks are right," the old man said, lifting his coffee cup in what looked like a toast.

"Right about what?" Lundberg asked. While they were on the same wavelength most of the time, sometimes the things Ramos said were inscrutable, like the sayings of a Zen master. This time, however, his sense was that the old man was inviting the question and he decided to play long.

"About motivation," Ramos answered, interrupting himself with a deep sip of coffee. Lundberg waited patiently, using the time to roll them each a cigarette. Ramos watched him solemnly, as if he were an ancient acolyte beholding the celebration of great mysteries.

"*Gracias*," the old man said, striking a kitchen match with his thumb nail and offering Lundberg the first light. "Ah," he said, drawing the smoke deep into his lungs and holding up the cigarette. "I think it would be harder to give this up than to give up wine."

"Is that what the drunks say?" Martin teased, being deliberately obtuse and ignoring his own earlier question.

"Yes, as a matter of fact, it is," Ramos nodded, joining the game. "Any of them will tell you it is harder to quit these *chingadas* than to stop drinking." He took another deep drag. "Of course, that isn't what I was talking about." He fell silent.

Lundberg nodded and blew a perfect smoke ring. They watched as it rolled out in the still kitchen air, growing as it traveled until it perfectly circled an unlit candle. Ramos rewarded his efforts with a Jalisco yelp. "Aiee!" he said. "You're getting good at that."

"Lots of practice," the young man acknowledged, shrugging as he chuckled. "It sure beats television." Aside from the fact reception in their area was blocked by the high canyon walls, the only set either of them owned was an ancient thing stripped of its electronic guts and used in Ramos' barn for a chick brooder.

Ramos looked at Lundberg, then nodded to himself and sat quietly, waiting patiently for the question he knew would come. He took another deep drag from his cigarette, closed his eyes, and blew the smoke out his nose with a deep sigh of pleasure. "Ah!" He could almost feel the intensity of the young man's controlled agitation shaking the room.

"All right, I'll bite," Lundberg finally grumped, acknowledging the older man's tenacity. He blew another smoke ring, this time at the candle burning in the middle of the table. It was a perfect shot, though the candle's flame cut through the top of the ring as it wrapped itself around the stick.

"You'll bite what?" Ramos asked, his eyes wide in innocence.

"I'll bite your head off if you don't tell me what you meant," Lundberg grinned. "And don't ask me what I'm talking about, either. You win."

"Ah," Ramos answered, making an imaginary mark on an imaginary chalk board. "About motivation." He waited until Lundberg nodded, then continued. "My friends the *borachones* tell me that while human beings do things for a number of reasons, there are just two basic motives for human acts. One of these is love."

"The other is hate, I suppose," Lundberg snorted, feeling let down after going to so much trouble to get the answer.

"No, although that's what many people think," the old man said. "Yet hate is only a twisted form of love, a distorted form of love. It has too much desire, too much passion for what it aims toward to be the opposite of love." He waited for a moment before going on, watching intently as Lundberg digested this. He could almost see the pieces falling into place in the young man's mind.

After a long moment the other nodded. "I think I see what you mean," he said. "They're too much alike to be opposites." He looked at Ramos with interest. "So what's the opposite of love, apathy? That's lack of passion."

"Fear," Ramos answered simply. "Or so the drunks I know say," he added, nodding again, almost as if to himself. "I tend to think they are right. Apathy seems more a lack of something even more basic."

"Fear has passion," Martin objected. "Whenever I'm afraid, I have a lot of passion." He grinned, remembering his first ever fight with a childhood bully who had gotten him down in a closet. Not having sought the fight, not being able to defend himself any other way, he had planted his teeth firmly in the bully's thumb and bitten down with all his might. The bully screamed, losing all interest in pursuing the conflict and backing away in abject fear. "That's not fair," his adversary had shouted. "You bit me!"

"Next time I'll bite your fucking ear off!" Lundberg snarled, baring his teeth and advancing on the bully, who departed the room in haste. Laughing, Lundberg told the old man about the incident. "Fear gave me a lot more strength than I knew I had," he said.

The old man laughed. "That's happened to me, too!" Then he sobered. "Fear has lots of raw power," he said, nodding. "Yet the power fear has isn't the same as passion, at least not for me. Passion is for something I think lies outside myself. Fear is for me, for my own safety. It gives me power to save my own *cojones*. Passion gives me power to use them."

"I could get kind of passionate about that, myself," Lundberg snorted, crossing to the wood cook stove to refill his coffee cup. "About both, as a matter of fact."

"Even an old man can," Ramos cackled. "Though the *cojones* don't seem to do me much good these days. Of course, they don't get me in trouble the way they used to do, either." He shrugged. "It's sad, but they don't."

Lundberg laughed and started to change the subject, but Ramos broke in. "No, wait. There is something very important I need to say. Call it passion, if you like, but fear is like a mirror that gives energy that is pointed at me. Passion is like a lens pointed toward something or someone else."

The young man nodded, but said, "Still, when I love something, isn't it because I want to possess it?"

"No," Ramos answered simply. "People die for their country. They die defending friends or family. Yourself, wouldn't you die defending your mother's honor? Or her life? That's love, Martin, not fear."

"What about the love between man and woman? Isn't that a little possessive?" the young man asked.

Ramos nodded. "Sometimes it is, but when that happens, what is being expressed is fear not love." Seeing the other did not understand, he went on. "I think when a man or woman is possessive what one sees is fear not love. It is fear of losing their beloved, maybe, or fear of something else. On the other hand, when someone loves another enough to die for them, that is love overcoming fear for one's own safety."

Lundberg shook his head. "I don't understand. I guess I've never been in love, at least, not that way. I don't understand why you say it's fear."

"When love is possessive, the fear is fear of being alone," Ramos answered. "Or perhaps, fear of being discarded or abandoned." He thought a moment. "As if one is not worth keeping."

"The measure of one's worth," Lundberg whispered, suddenly aware of strong tensions at war within himself. "Jesus!" he said, leaping to his feet and pacing the room like a caged tiger. "That's it."

"That's what, Martin?" Ramos asked gently.

"The whole thing with my dad. Nothing I do is ever good enough for him." His eyes were filled with pain mixed with rage. "Nothing!"

"Tell me, Martin," Ramos urged him quietly.

"I busted my butt in school. I was salutatorian of my high school class. Second out of four hundred. You what the bastard said? He asked me why I wasn't first, why I was two hundredths of a grade point behind the person in front. So he didn't even come to the commencement!" He shook his head. "It didn't matter to him the girl who was first scored the highest ever on the achievement tests, or that she turned Stanford down for a full ride scholarship at MIT. He was ashamed of me being beaten by a woman."

Ramos nodded and the young man continued. "The same thing happened when I was captain of our team, our football team. We almost made it to state that year. Do you think he came to a single game? Hell no! Screw the fact I was the best halfback in the district and made all state. I wasn't the quarterback, so it didn't count." He looked at his feet. "So I busted my butt again and made it all the way to the top of my class in college. So what? Even though it was one of the best schools in the state it wasn't the University. It wasn't where he wanted me to go." He shook his head angrily. "So after that I said, 'screw it' as far as he's concerned. It didn't matter any more."

"No?" Ramos looked at him and nodded sadly. "I think it still matters very much to you, my friend. Regardless of the fact that's sometimes how it is with fathers and sons," he said. "Or fathers and daughters, too. It happened to my eldest." When he looked up the grief in his eyes was unmistakable.

"Well, can't you do something now?" Martin asked. "Can't you tell her it doesn't matter now?"

"No, it's too late," Ramos said softly, ancient grief haunting every line of his face. "She's dead. She ran her car into a canyon when she was drunk." He sighed, shook his head vigorously, like a dog drying itself. "Those are some of my ghosts, Martin," he said, closing the subject. "Perhaps we need to let them rest."

Ramos got to his feet and went outside. Lundberg could hear him clucking as he scattered grain for the chickens. Getting to his own feet he rinsed his cup and washed out the pot and Ramos' cup. Drying his hands he put on his hat and made ready to leave, but the old man walked back in. "You have to go already?" he asked, clearly disappointed.

"No," said Martin. "I thought maybe you needed to be alone."

"Alone with my ghosts?" Ramos laughed. "Heavens, no! I spend enough time alone with them already." Despite his good humor, the old man's laughter held a large measure of sadness Lundberg could not help hearing. Shrugging, he sat back down, watching the old man put a pot of pinto beans on to boil. "*Viva los frivolo frijoles!*" Ramos cried.

"*Frivolo?*" the young man asked. "I'm afraid you lost me there."

Ramos roared with laughter. "I guess it's not something Rosa would teach you. Or maybe she used *futil* or *caduco*."

Lundberg shook his head. "No, none of those, either."

"*No sabes flatulencia?*" Ramos asked with a wicked grin, sticking out his tongue to make a rude noise.

"*Si, ahora yo lo se*," Martin answered, laughing. I understand now. "Long live flatulent *frijoles*. You're right, that's not something Mother would teach us."

"So what were we talking about before *los malos* came to haunt me?" the old man asked, setting out dishes and taking his place at the table. "There was something else I wanted to say."

"Love," Lundberg answered simply. "Or maybe passion."

"Ah, yes, passion," Ramos nodded. "I remember now. What I wanted to point out is that passion between a man and a woman is often a passion for the other side of ourselves, the side we do not, or cannot, love for some reason."

"That sounds familiar," Martin replied, "but I don't know why."

"You probably read it in class," Ramos answered. "The man I learned it from was a famous psychologist, although I didn't know it at the time I met him." He smiled, remembering. "To me he was just another old Swiss man talking to a couple of know-it-all seminarians hiking around the Alps. We stopped in a certain village to eat and have a glass of wine and got into a conversation with him. We even argued with him. When we got back and found out who he was we felt like a pair of *pendejos*."

"You mean, you actually met...?" Lundberg could not remember the name, but a face from his psychology text came to mind.

"The man himself," Ramos nodded, beaming. "Carl Gustav Jung. In pictures he comes across so austere and reserved, but he was quite the contrary with us, very warm and accepting. Later, when I knew who he was, I wondered why he would waste so much time on two *pendejos*. I think he was planting seeds for the future. And enjoying himself." The old man shrugged. "For times like now, for instance. His work was controversial, not so well received in the field of medicine, so perhaps he was simply spreading his ideas to anyone who would listen. Even *pendejos* like me."

"Sort of a Carlos Appleseed?" Martin asked, intrigued. "Is there any-one you haven't met?"

"Dwight Eisenhower and the Pope," Ramos laughed, and the con-versation moved in a different direction. Remembering it now, Martin Lundberg wished they had pursued the matter to the end, or at least taken it farther. For he found himself very much in love, in love with a woman as different from himself in some ways as night is from the day. It was at once as fearful as it was consuming, and he wondered whether he could survive in the crucible of such passion without losing his soul. Or now, having known such passion, if he even cared. *What a way to die,* he thought, as he remembered their last hours together and what the French call *le petit noir,* the little death. *What a way to go out of this world, consumed totally within the ultimate act of love.*

6. Requiem for a Small Town

Somewhere in West Texas. Six-thirty. The bank clock chimes, the town is closed. The sidewalks are carefully swept, the doors locked tight. A lonely truck with a flat tire guards the empty buildings and dust hangs in a shroud of silence along the main street.

Six-thirty. Ghosts gather in the dusty shadows, whisper secrets to those who listen. It was not like this, they say. Not before. There were people here, real people. Men and women, children with dogs. You could hear them laugh, smell them sweat, see them smile. You could feel their sorrow. And not even death could silence the soft voices of life that spread like ripples in the evening dust.

Now it is six-thirty. The clock chimes a silent requiem. A deserted tavern whispers an echo of a better time and a faded revival poster in its cracked and dusty window shrieks an epitaph. It's been a long time, so very long since life graced these empty streets, these empty people. Fear has made them hollow shells waiting for death in a dying town. And their children, their children are sacrificed to fear. They grow old at five and their laughter is lost in the silence of six-thirty dust. (Martin Quinn's Journal)

Late January, 1963. Terlingua was a disappointment for Rosa. Though she said very little about it, Lundberg could tell the ghost town affected his mother deeply. Where it showed most was when they came to the graveyard with its fallen-down fence and leaning grave markers. Some of these were tombstones and others were once white boards, now bleached by the sun and deeply etched by dust carried on the constant wind. Though he tried, he could not imagine what it must be like to return to a place one knew well and find nothing left of the people one knew but ancient tombstones whose lettering was scarcely legible now. *It must be tough being a survivor*, he thought. *The dead don't hurt. The dead don't mourn. That's for those of us left behind to do.*

Even though Rosa was subdued by what they discovered, Martin was fascinated with the old town. The old hotel was still standing, and though it was in great disrepair, much of the tin roof remained. The windows were long gone, as was the floor planking, but the joists remained in surprisingly good shape and he gingerly made his way over the porch and into what had been the main room. Looking out the window he appreciated why this site was selected for the hotel, for it commanded one of the best views of the town and the countryside. Down the hill to one side, near a gully, he could see the cemetery with its bleached markers, and to the other side he could see the ruins of the small church and a number of houses. What caught his attention was the view immediately before him of rolling desert hills covered with greasewood interspersed with occasional *ocotilla* and thick clumps of *lechegia*. Far in the distance he could see the Chisos mountains rising from the desert floor in their many shades of blue and purple and, closer in, reds and browns. Bright fluffy clouds drifted across a sky startling in the depth of it's deep turquoise, and the light of the afternoon sun reminded him of what he'd read of sunlight around the Mediterranean. Were it anything like this he could understand why the artists seemed to love it so.

While it was warm in sheltered areas outside in the sun, the thick stone walls of the building retained the chill of the night before, and Martin pulled his jacket close around himself. A gentle breeze coming up the watercourse found its way through the open windows, and he realized the building must have been set there to catch any breeze on days when the sun would turn the stone building into an oven. So lost was he in his reflections he did not hear Rosa come up to the porch until she called. "Martin?"

Right here," he answered, sticking his head out and looking around the thick wall. She was standing by the porch eyeing the weathered joists and looking worried. "What is it?" he asked, seeing her concern.

"That looks dangerous," she replied. Martin knew she wanted to say more, to ask him to be careful, but she did not. He appreciated her restraint.

"The joists are pretty solid," he told her. "Probably better quality than the ones Dad can get now." He pointed down. "I don't see any rotted flooring, and I think someone must have salvaged it for something else."

"Why didn't they take the beams, too?" Rosa wondered.

Martin laughed. "They probably didn't need them," he said, pointing to the rusty, but intact galvanized iron roof. "That's probably why only part of the tin is gone. That's all that they needed."

Rosa nodded. "You're right, I think. I can remember your grandfather doing the same. They needed some tin for a new building at the mine and he took me with him when his crew scavenged some from a couple of abandoned houses in a little settlement down the road."

"Why didn't the mine just buy new stuff?" Martin asked. "Couldn't they afford it?"

Rosa laughed for the first time since coming to town. "Yes, they could and I remember my grandfather telling someone salvaging wasn't really saving them any money. The problem was getting it here. I think they had to order it from San Antonio or maybe El Paso. And that would take weeks." She smiled at her son. "Your grandfather was a very patient man, mostly, but sometimes he got a bee in his bonnet. And over the smallest things, too." She laughed in earnest. "I remember one time he couldn't find a collar button. He had plenty of them but there was one missing and that was the one he wanted to wear. He tore the house apart trying to find it and even moved all the furniture out of the bedroom looking." She shook her head, still laughing. "He was like a washing machine that wouldn't stop. Your grandmother tried to help him find the button until he started moving furniture, then she went into the kitchen and sat down until he was done. Then she told him he could expect his next meal when the bedroom was back in order."

"Did he find it?" Martin asked.

Rosa looked at him and smiled. "You are like him," she said. "But, yes, he found it but it wasn't in the bedroom. He found a crack in the floor near where he kept his small things so he changed his clothes and crawled under the house." Again she laughed. "He found the button but he also found a snake under the house. I never saw him move so fast as when he came out from under the front porch, but he had the button." Her face softened. "I still have it. I've kept it for you. I meant to bring it when I came but I'll send it when I'm home."

"I'd like that," Martin replied, reaching in his pocket and taking out an old pen knife. The mother of pearl handle was cracked and the metal worn from the caress of many pockets. "I still carry the knife he gave me. I think it was very old even then."

Rosa nodded, taking the knife from his hand and looking at it carefully. "I think this was the one his mother gave him," she answered. "He carried it even though it wasn't really a man's knife."

"That's what he told me," Martin laughed. "He said not to use it for wood carving or throwing or anything but cutting paper and cleaning my nails. He said it was a good luck knife and if I ever broke it or lost it bad things would happen. But he said I could give it to someone special."

"Someone like Stephania?" his mother asked, coy.

"I think he was thinking of someone more like a son," Martin replied, a bit stuffily. He wished Rosa would let the subject of Stephanie lie.

"Well," his mother answered lightly, "the obvious way to get yourself a son is to find yourself a wife."

Despite himself, Martin laughed. "I walked into that one, didn't I? Why do I think someone wants a grandchild?"

"I wouldn't know," she replied, smiling.

"Brother's a lot better bet than I am," Martin observed. "At least he's married." Rosa's smile was replaced with a troubled look. "What is it?" he asked.

His mother was silent for a moment. "Melissa told me last week that she and Jeremy are having problems," she told him. "She told me she's thinking about moving out."

What?" Martin asked, incredulous. While he and his brother were ever more distant the older they were, Martin had always felt an unspoken kinship with the spirited bride his brother brought home from Italy. "What did he do?" he asked. Suddenly he was furious. "Did he hit her?"

"No, Martin," his mother replied sadly. "It would almost be better if he had. Then she would know he at least cared. The problem is not what he's done but what he hasn't." Rosa looked embarrassed.

"I'm sorry," he replied. "I don't follow you. I know he neglects her but I never knew it was that bad. Even though he spends all his time at work, just like dad." Sudden insight flooded his mind. "Is it his drinking?" he asked.

"Among other things," his mother responded. She was carefully studying the ground, avoiding his eyes.

"You mean Jerry's got another woman?" Martin replied, indignant.

"When does he find the time? I though the business was his mistress."

"Another woman she could fight," Rosa said. Still she would not look up until he reached out, touched her arm. When she did, her eyes were bleak, full of shame. She seemed to be having trouble gathering words. "It's not another woman, Martin," she started, then stopped. "It's another man. Several other men."

Memories hit him like a wall of water breaking through the dam of his own denial, through the barrier of family secrets never uttered. "Jesus!" he said, feeling his stomach lurch as if the ground had fallen open beneath him. A hand went to his forehead, covered his eyes. Everything fell into place, the odd looks, the inside jokes Jerry's friends were always telling, laughing at things no one else found funny. There were also several incidents when it felt to him like Jerry had crossed the boundaries of comfort, perhaps even propriety, with him but always subtly and never overtly enough to be challenged. "I don't understand," he said. "Is he..." The word caught in his throat, the dispassionate clinical term which is so easy to use of strangers, so hard of one's own. Desperately he sought for an alternative, any alternative. "Is he bisexual?"

"No, Martin," Rosa said gently, stepping out of her own grief for a moment to stand with him in his. "Melissa was very clear on that. Never once in the year they've married has anything happened. It's never been consummated. The reason is Jeremy doesn't like women. That's what he told her."

"Then why did he marry at all?" Martin wanted to know.

"The term she used was 'window dressing'," Rosa replied sadly. "He did it to appear normal to his customers."

"That bastard!" he growled, then realized to whom he was speaking. "I'm sorry, mother. I didn't mean it that way."

She nodded. "I know you didn't."

"I know he's my brother, but he's being a complete jerk using her like that. For business, like some piece of equipment. To protect himself."

She looked down. "Mostly from your father."

"Dad doesn't know?" Martin asked, aghast. Despite himself he began to chuckle, then laugh.

"Martin!" Rosa snapped. "It isn't funny."

"I'm sorry," he answered, unrepentant. "I'm not making fun of it.

The irony of the whole thing is just too much. It's so painful I can't cry," he said soberly. "The son he's made into his own image is queer, which is something which Dad hates with all his soul."

"I don't think it's hate, Martin," Rosa said softly. "I think it's fear."

"Fear of what?" he asked. "Jerry's not going to grope him. Dad would kill him."

"I think it's fear of the same thing inside himself," Rosa replied. "I talked to a doctor about it once, thinking it must be me." Seeing his look of surprise, she explained. "His office manager was not the first," she said. "There were others before her, many others. I thought perhaps I was not adequate or that it must be some glandular thing." She shook her head. "But it wasn't. The doctor sent me to another doctor who explained it very clearly. He told me your father's behavior was not normal, that it was an obsession which masked his fear of his own feelings of being physically attracted to other men. He called it a Don Juan syndrome."

Martin took a deep breath, let it out slowly. Then another. "Are you all right?" Rosa asked, worried.

"Yeah," he replied. "I am. It's just a lot to take in at once. I'm having trouble getting my mind around it."

She nodded. "I know you must be, I've lived with it a long time. It doesn't make any difference in how I feel about Jeremy or your father. He's still my son. And Dad's still my husband."

Again Martin sighed. "You know, it's funny. I don't like the way either of them are acting right now." He touched his chest. "But somehow it's hard to be mad at them, too, knowing this."

Rosa nodded. "I know, Martin. I know."

"Think of the hell they must live in," he said. "Always afraid of someone finding out. With everything always at risk."

"Especially us, Martin, and we already know." Rosa was solemn.

"I wish we could bring it out in the open, at least in the family, and just accept it," he said. "But I can't see either of them doing that."

"No," Rosa replied. "I can't either."

"Meanwhile you and I have to play the pretend game, as if nothing is wrong." He looked at her sadly. "I think that's why I can't come home any more, mother. I just can't take it any longer. They act as if their diapers don't stink, and then they get all over my case for being the way I am. It isn't fair."

"I know, Martin, it isn't."

Suddenly he was defiant. "So why don't we just bring it out. Me and you at the dinner table." He switched to a comic voice. "Hey, Dad, I've been meaning to ask you something...." Rosa's look of horror stopped him cold. "I'm not going to really do that," he reassured her. "I'm just imagining what it would be like to have the tables turned on them for once."

"Please don't," she begged him. "Don't even think about it. It would be a disaster." She shook her head in horror. "I can't imagine!"

"On the other hand, Mother," he said gently, using a form of address he only used with her when he was in dead earnest. "What do we have to lose? It's not as if things are that good now."

"They could be worse," Rosa asserted. "They could be much worse."

Martin shrugged, then sighed. "All right, I'll take your word for it. But it's hard for me to imagine how."

She nodded, grateful. "Come on," she said, closing the subject and taking his arm, pointing with her head. "I found some grave stones I want you to see. Do you have your camera?"

"Right here," he said, bringing an ancient Argus out from under his coat where he was keeping it warm. While it was designed to work in any weather, the Argus was at times affected by the cold, like an older man or woman whose joints predict the weather. "I just put in a fresh roll of film."

"So what did he tell you?" Rosa Lundberg demanded. They were once again in their own car headed north from Presidio to Marfa. Compared to Terlingua, the cities of Presidio and Ojinaga, facing each other across the Rio Grande, were booming centers of trade and commerce. The rickety bridge connecting the two had been washed away and rebuild more than once, and at the advice of another filling station Samaritan, Rosa and Martin opted to travel by taxi to the other side rather than risk their own driving. The Samaritan, of course, had a cousin who ran a taxi and who strongly reminded Martin of Luiz, the major difference being that the taxi was an even more ancient rattletrap than Luiz's car. After negotiating a set price for the day, which surprised Martin,

Rosa had the driver show them all around the city, ending at the main Market where Martin was again surprised when the gentle Rosa turned into a fish-market harridan, yelling and gesturing wildly as she haggled over every purchase. At first he was a little embarrassed until the taxi driver expressed his genuine admiration for Rosa's bargaining skills.

"I don't understand," he said to her while they were taking a break having a Coca-cola in a small cafe at the edge of the market. "When you buy something it sounds like you're about to carve the shopkeeper up with a paring knife. Even their asking prices aren't that high. Why haggle?"

Rosa looked at him as if he'd suggested desecrating a cathedral. "And miss all the fun?" she asked. "Besides, it would be very rude."

"Rude? What do you call what you're doing?"

Rosa laughed. "Poor city boy, you didn't grow up here, did you? If you did you'd understand. They expect haggling and enjoy it. To refuse would to be very ill mannered, a *yanqui*. It would be a sign of contempt for the shopkeeper."

"Well, I'll take your word for it," he said, shaking his head. "You won't catch me doing it."

Rosa laughed. "Why not, it's fun? Come on, don't be an old stodgy. See that red scarf over there?" He followed her gaze to a shop just across the road. The shopkeeper caught her interest like radar sweeping for aircraft and smiled. "I would like you to buy that for me I wait here."

"No," he refused, self conscious. "Please."

"Just don't insult him personally by calling him names," Rosa advised, ignoring his refusal. "Tell him he's taking the food out of your children's mouth."

"I don't have children," Martin said.

"He doesn't know that," Rosa answered. "Tell him your poor old mother over here just can't do without it and she won't listen to reason. That will be the truth." She looked at him, eyes pleading.

"Don't do this to me, mother," he said. The shopkeeper was crossing the street to them. "Please."

"*Buenas, dias,*" the shopkeeper greeted them in Spanish. "The red scarf is very beautiful, lady. It would look lovely with your dress."

"I'm sorry," Rosa answered in German. "I don't speak Spanish."

Martin was sure the merchant knew she was lying but decided to play along for the fun of it. "My older sister is visiting from Germany," he said. His mother smiled. "The poor dear isn't very bright but she's very sweet and I'm afraid our mother spoils her terribly." The shopkeeper nodded sympathy. He was facing Martin and could not see the sudden frost in Rosa's smile. "She likes the red scarf, but I'm afraid we really can't afford it."

"For you, my friend," the tradesman said, "it's not so much. Even though it's pure silk I could let you have it for...." The man twisted his face in a grimace, as if a nail had suddenly gone through his shoe. "A hundred and fifty pesos."

Twelve dollars, thought Martin, *not bad if it's silk.* "A hundred and fifty pesos," he shouted. "Why don't you ask for my first born child? I could buy the whole *chingada* market for a hundred and fifty pesos." Martin' voice carried down the street to other vendors, who smiled in anticipation. Casi Sanches had a live one.

The vendor gave Rosa an anxious look, who, to her credit, did not even blink at Martin' use of the foul term. Rather, she smiled idiotically at the shop keeper and pointed to the scarf. Inwardly she smiled to herself, proud of her son. *Good*, she thought. *He thinks he's rubbing my nose in it. That's one word I taught Rita.*

The merchant put on his most wounded look and began his litany of the merits of the silk and the color. Martin listened patiently, then pointed out he thought he'd seen the same scarf for a tenth the price on the other side of the marketplace. The merchant denied it, saying no one in the market had better prices and he would beat the price of any competitor. "No, he added, "not even that. I'll sell it to you for the ridiculous price of a hundred pesos, even though it will cost me my whole profit for the day."

Martin shrugged and suggested that since he was losing his profit anyway, he might as well sell it for twenty-five, and the haggling began in earnest. Ten minutes later they settled for fifty-five pesos, or five dollars, American, the merchant offered, drawing a chuckle from Lundberg. He paid the man in pesos, and offered him a beer. The vendor thanked him but took a Coke instead, and they stood and visited for a few moments before another American tourist arrived to look at the goods. She was well dressed, as was her companion, a tall man who stood off to one side looking bored.

Holding up an index finger Martin winked at the vendor and smiled at the tourists, pretending to be the shop owner. The lady asked the price of a scarf almost identical to the one Martin had just bought, but not so lovely, and without turning a hair he answered in heavily accented English, "Three hundred pesos, lady, but since you are such a lovely lady, two seventy-five." The merchant turned away and rolled his eyes to the heavens. Other merchants, seeing what was happening, stopped to watch what this crazy *norteamericano* was doing.

The lady took out her billfold and held up two hundred pesos. Martin shrugged and looked apologetic. "I can't take the food out of my children's mouths, lady. As pretty as you are, I can't do that."

The woman looked guilty and added fifty pesos to the two hundred she was holding. Sighing, Martin, took the money and put the scarf in a brown paper bag. "Thank you, lady," he said humbly. "I don't make much this way but I make something and my kids can eat." Nodding she handed him a tip and rushed off into the market, trailing her companion behind. Looking down he grinned. It was twenty-five pesos.

Grinning, the vendor clapped him on the arm, reaching for the money he still held. "Just a minute," Martin answered in Spanish, pulling away and extracting a hundred pesos before handing the shop keeper the rest.

The man started to protest, then laughed. After all, he'd gotten twenty-five pesos more than he'd asked Lundberg for a better scarf. "Thank you," he said, smiling at Rosa, too. "I'm glad you don't live here. You'd put the rest of us out of business." A crafty look came over his countenance. "Unless, of course, you want to work for me..."

"Thank you, but I have a good job," Martin answered, pulling out Rosa's chair and walking her back to their cab. Their cab driver, who had watched the whole incident, looked at him appraisingly. This was no typical *yanqui*.

"I could have gotten it for ten pesos less," said Rosa as he settled himself into the back seat beside her.

"You could have gotten it for free and made sixty pesos, too?" he responded.

"*Touché,*" she answered, smiling. "Do you have anything else you want to do here?" Martin shook his head and Rosa asked their driver to take them back to the American side. On their way out of Ojinaga she noticed a group of single story houses off to the right some distance from the road. "What's that over there?" she inquired of their driver.

The driver glanced in the direction she was pointing and gave her a strange look. "I don't know, lady," he said in English. "I don't go there. I think some bad people live over there."

Rosa thought he was lying, and later, while they were waiting for the US Border Patrol to inspect their purchases, she saw the driver talking quietly with Martin. The driver nodded toward the clump of houses she'd asked about and said something to her son, who shook his head. Now, back in their own car, she wanted to know what the driver said. "So what did he tell you?" she demanded.

"What did who tell me about what?" he replied.

"Don't play dumb with me, buster," she snorted. "What did the driver tell you when you were standing there on the bridge?"

"He told me that part of town you were looking at was called Boy's Town," he answered, seeming a bit embarrassed.

Rosa nodded. "That's why he said bad people live over there." She was silent for a while. "I don't understand. Why was he embarrassed about telling us there was a reform school there? That's nothing to be ashamed of."

Martin said nothing, hoping she would let it drop. She glanced his way, saw he was paying a great deal of attention to the road and to his driving, more than seemed necessary. "What are you trying not to tell me, Martin?" she asked.

He sighed. "Boys Town is not a reform school," he said, not looking at her as he answered. "Quite the contrary. It's what they call their red light district."

"Oh," said Rosa, surprised. "I saw you shake your head and I wondered what he was asking you," she blurted without thinking what she was saying.

Martin mistook her statement for a question. "Well, mother, if you must know," he replied tersely, "he was asking me whether I wanted to drop you off on the American side and pay them a visit."

Rosa replied in a small voice, blushing. "I'm sorry, Martin. I didn't mean to embarrass you or intrude."

He looked at her directly. "Then perhaps there are some things you should not ask me," he said, somewhat huffily.

Rosa started to reply, but the set of his face told her there was little use trying to sort things out with Martin. She nodded and withdrew into herself and her on thoughts as they drove on in silence for several miles. Then suddenly she giggled, surprising them both.

"What's so funny," Martin asked, still a bit testy.

"Oh, I was just thinking," she answered, shaking her head and turning to look out the window at the unchanging desert landscape. "I didn't mean to laugh out loud but I thought of something funny. It was nothing, really." She pointed. "Look at that!" she said, trying to change the subject. "They haven't had rain in weeks and weeks. Isn't this desolate?"

Something perverse within Martin made him dig in his heels. "Come on, tell me," he insisted, knowing even as he saw the look on her face he had gone too far and was making a mistake. "Quit trying to change the subject."

"Well, Martin, if you must know, I was thinking it's too bad you didn't tell me at the time so I could have gone with you. I've always wondered what one of those places looked like." She looked at him archly. "Perhaps there are some things you shouldn't ask me."

They drove in silence until he pulled the Roadmaster off the pavement so they could visit the ruins at Shafter. Leaning back to retrieve the Argus his eyes caught hers and he smiled a wry smile. She giggled and he snorted, and then the both of them began laughing, finally so hard the tears came. "Goodness," Rosa said, gasping for breath. "We're silly, aren't we?"

Returning to Marfa that night they ate supper at Caroline's. And even though Martin looked at the menu, he found himself ordering the chicken tacos once more. They were nothing like anything he'd eaten before, and he ordered a second helping again, much to the delight of Caroline. Business was slow so she joined them when they were done eating, bringing out a special treat of wedding cookies. Someone had ordered several dozen for a wedding and Caroline baked an extra two dozen for Rosa and Martin to take on their travels. "Maybe I should have made four more dozen," she observed, watching with pleasure as Martin demolished a half dozen. "I don't think these are going to last until you get out of town."

Rosa laughed. "He's still a growing boy," she said.

"He's going to be growing the wrong way, if he doesn't watch out," Caroline responded and the two women laughed like school girls.

Martin was glad when the conversation turned to other things, but he had a hard time following what was being said, even though Rosa and Caroline were using standard Spanish. The accent and syntax were as different from that of New Mexico as the drawl of rural Georgia is from the patios of blue collar Bronx, and by the time he figured something he did not understand out, the flow of the conversation was two sentences down the pike. So as soon as he decently could, he excused himself. "I think I'd like to stretch my legs," he told Rosa, handing her the car keys. "I'm going to walk back to the hotel and look the city over."

"All the way back there?" Rosa asked, surprised. "That's all the way to the middle of town."

"It's just over a mile and a half," Martin answered. "I clocked it when we came. I walk almost that far to get to Ramos' and back." To Caroline he added. "That's Emiliano Ramos. He's my nearest neighbor."

"I knew someone by that name once," said Caroline. She turned to Rosa. "Remember that nice young man who used to work for your grandfather?"

"It's the same man," Rosa said. "I just saw him at Christmas." Caroline shrieked her pleasure and the two were off and running again, talking about Emil Ramos and memories of the courtly young man every girl in town adored.

Martin waved goodbye, pulling on his jacket, but neither of the women noticed him leave. He paid the tab, earning a flash of bright, even teeth from Caroline's granddaughter by adding a generous tip, and, pulling his jacket tight around himself, stepped out into the chill of early darkness. He sensed that Caroline's granddaughter would have been receptive to an invitation to walk with him, but there were enough women in his life as it was. Perhaps too many. To take the edge of any disappointment, he turned and smiled to the young lady through the door window. She waved back.

The streets were poorly lighted, at least by urban standards, but the city was quiet and there was no challenge to his passage except for one dog, who followed him half a block, barking hoarsely. Taking his time, Martin walked for the better part of an hour, covering much of the town north of the railroad tracks. Nor was it lost on him that the railroad did more than divide the town physically. North of the tracks was clearly *gringo* territory. The houses were better, the cars were newer, and the yards seemed more remote and forbidding.

Coming back to the hotel, he discovered Rosa was not in. Concerned, he phoned Caroline's, having some difficulty finding the listing, but the grand daughter assured him they were still at table, laughing and talking. Again, he sensed unspoken invitation in her manner, but he politely ignored it, being deliberately obtuse.

Asking her not to ruin the ladies' fun, Martin went to his room, intending to read himself to sleep. Yet nothing in the outdated magazine he'd picked up in the lobby held his interest. In desperation for something, anything, to read, he rummaged through the dresser drawers, coming up with an out of date phone directory and a black Gideon Bible. The phone directory told him about half the telephone subscribers in Marfa had Spanish surnames, but he felt sure a large part of the Hispanic population did not have service. From the outhouses behind many of the homes south of the track, a good many of them did not have indoor plumbing, either.

Bored of the directory, Martin picked up the Gideon Bible and began to casually thumb through it. The name Ruth caught his eye and he stopped. Ruth was Stephanie's middle name and, while he was aware it was a biblical name, he really could not remember who Ruth was or why a whole book in the Bible was named after her. Turning back to the beginning, he began to read.

At first the meaning of the Middle English was difficult to follow, although Martin was moved, as always he was, by the rolling majesty of the language itself. Reading aloud he became so caught up in the melody and cadence of the words he discovered himself deep into the first chapter with only a vague sense of the content of all he'd read. Laughing at himself, he turned back to the very beginning, starting over and taking the text phrase by phrase, allowing time to savor the meaning. "Now it came to pass in the days when the judges ruled," he read, "that there was a famine in the land."

Nice, he thought. *Modern English lost a lot in the transition.* He went on, reading slowly until he came to Ruth's response to Naomi, admonishing Ruth to return to her people.

....and Orpha kissed her mother in law; but Ruth clave unto her. And

she said, Behold, thy sister in law is gone back unto her people, and unto her gods: return thou after thy sister in law.

And Ruth said, Entreat me not to leave thee, or to return from following after thee: for whither thou goest, I will go; and where thou lodgest, I will lodge: thy people shall be my people, and thy God, my God: Where thou diest, will I die, and there will I be buried....

Martin felt his eyes burning strangely as tears blurred the page. Closing the Gideon's and setting it aside, he thought of Stephanie, thought of himself standing facing her in some sacred place and uttering those self same words. Then he saw himself taking her gently by the hand and leading her into their home, which he had built with his own hands.

His reverie was broken by a soft knock at the door. "Yes," he answered, rising from the bed to slip on some jeans.

"Don't get up," came the muffled voice of his mother from the other side of the door. "I just wanted to let you know I was in. I'll see you in the morning."

"Good night," he replied, sticking his head out the door, but Rosa was already going into her own room. Blowing him a sleepy kiss, she shut the door.

Returning to his own bed, Martin slipped off his jeans and crawled under the covers. He closed his eyes, sighing as his weary body hit the, bed, but tired as he was, sleep would not come. Too many things intruded, things he could not get out of his mind. Crossing to this luggage, he got out a spiral steno's notebook and a pencil and laid them on the table by the bed, intending to write things down as they drifted into consciousness so he could let them go, promising to take care of them the next day. This was something a coach had taught him. "Write it down," the man said. "Make an appointment with it. Whatever is bugging you, make a promise you'll worry with it plenty when the time comes. Then be sure you keep the promise, too."

The technique normally worked, the only times he found it didn't being those when he failed to keep the promise. Or else when something was eating at him he was trying to avoid. Emil Ramos had pointed that out during one of their many conversations. "Remember your dream about the man in prison, the one you've had so many times?" Martin nodded. "Things we try to avoid are like that dream. They stay after us until we give them what they need."

"So what does the bastard need?" Martin growled in exasperation.

Ramos smiled. "Exactly what you are so reluctant to give him. Attention is one thing. Acceptance of him as he is, is another. He needs you to honor him."

"Give honor to a devil?" Martin retorted.

"Yes," Ramos insisted. "So he doesn't have to stay a devil. Honor him by accepting himself as a part of yourself, and you will be surprised what happens. I think that will allow him to be the angel he is."

"He's a pretty fallen angel, " Martin observed. "I don't know why he's there, but he's not in prison for nothing."

"Then rehabilitate him," Ramos urged. "Or allow him to be rehabilitated by Whomever you consider your God."

"Maybe I consider myself my God," the younger man replied.

Ramos rolled his eyes and muttered something Lundberg missed. "What?" he asked. "I didn't catch that."

"Good," Ramos answered dryly. "It wasn't kind and I don't have to apologize."

"You don't think much of the idea, do you?" Martin asked, grinning. "I may need to apologize. I only said it to get your goat."

"Well, you know where it's tied," Ramos answered, a little testily. "What I said was that you're too smart to believe that *caca*."

"Yes, but I'm not ready to 'come to Jesus' just yet," Martin replied, his grin suddenly turning pensive. "That reminds me. Do you remember a conversation we had just before *posadas*?"

Ramos smiled. "*Hijo!*" he responded. "That's been a while."

"I know," Lundberg agreed. "It was the first time we spoke of spiritual things in a personal way. Remember?"

"I think so," the old man said. "But remind me. We have had many talks and sometimes it's hard to remember one and not the others."

"You said that all roads lead Home, and the way you said it I knew it was a specific place to you. Remember now?"

"The mist is clearing," the old man said, making a turning motion with his hand. "I think I remember the time but keep telling me."

"I asked you what you did when something inside was not quite right and you could not figure out what it was. You said you were concerned that your answer might offend me." Lundberg smiled.

Ramos nodded. "Yes, I remember now. I told you that I do two things. One is that I ask the One who is the source of all things to enlighten my heart and mind to what I need to know. I think I said to lead me to the truth I need to face as gently as possible." He looked at the younger man, who nodded. "The second thing I said is my part is to wait as patiently as I can for the answer to come, and while I wait I ask for grace to see the answer no matter what form it may or may not take."

"That's the conversation," Lundberg said. "It was the next thing you said I wanted to ask you about. Do you remember that?"

"Quite well now," the old man smiled. "You said were relieved because you thought I was going to tell you to 'come to Jesus' like the fundamentalists."

"Yes, and you told me that was one way of putting it."

Ramos looked at him in awe. "You have an incredible memory, you know" the old man said. "I think those are pretty much our exact words."

Lundberg agreed. "They are. And I do. That's one of the positive things I inherited from my father." Ramos nodded and started to reply but Martin waved him off. "Just a minute. I've wanted to ask you this several times, but every time I remember we were talking about something else and I forgot to get back to it. What I want to know is what you meant by that. When you said 'that is one way of putting it.'"

"Ah," said Ramos. "I remember wondering at the time how long it would take you to come back to that and I'm sorry we got sidetracked. I was sure you would. That's why I remember the conversation." He smiled.

"So what did you mean?" Lundberg's grey eyes were intense.

Ramos thought a moment, rocking himself back and forth as if to massage his thoughts. "How to put it best? At some point almost every man understands just how weak and fragile he is. Sometimes this happens early, sometimes very late. I think it is better the earlier this happens, because this is the beginning of his discovery of his real strength."

Ramos eyes held a far away look and his speech had moved into an almost pedantic style. Suddenly he was so intensely present Lundberg was startled. "No! I can speak only for me. I came to understand just how weak and vulnerable I was. I came to understand just how little control I had over the external circumstances of my life. And when I did so, I then realized any real happiness I could find lay within me, not outside in material things or with events, even though these are pleasant, or even in my relationship with other people, who can be even more pleasant." He chuckled. "Especially *las lindas*, no?"

Lundberg smiled his affirmation. "Yes, but how do you discover it within yourself? How do you find this happiness?"

"Ah, that's the point. I discovered just how blind I was in my selfishness. I was so full of myself I could not begin to see anything else. I lived in the not so happy delusion I could control my life, and, as you would say, it was going to shit in a hat basket."

"To hell in a hand basket," Lundberg corrected gently, smiling.

"What did I say?" Ramos asked, then cackled as he remembered. "Yes, my life was going to *caca* in a *caja de sombrero*. Hey, I like that."

Lundberg held his head with his hands. "Play on words in one language is bad enough," he said.

"Forgive me," Ramos replied, unrepentant. "Where was I? Oh, yes, the *caja de caca* my life had become. To put it in a *piñon* shell, things had become hopeless and I was in despair. I even considered killing myself, but things were so bad I was afraid I might fail there, too. And be maimed or worse." He paused for a moment. "I considered myself an atheist then, but in my desperation I very clearly remember crying out for help. And it came. Immediately." The old man stopped, seeing the doubt in the young man's eyes. "Are you sure you want to hear this Martin?" he asked. "It's very personal."

Lundberg nodded and Ramos continued. "What happened was something so extraordinary I thought I was going crazy. For the briefest moment it seemed as if the little finger of God brushed me ever so lightly and I was filled with joy. There in the middle of despair I was filled with joy and peace."

"And all the *caca* went away?" Lundberg asked, his voice full of reservation.

"No, not at all. That was the strangest part of it all. The same problems were still there. Some of them even got worse. What changed was how I came to see them and how I began to respond differently." He looked at Lundberg directly and said. "I was very suspicious at first, but after a while I had to admit to the changes which were obvious to everyone around me. There was a reality which went far beyond anything I could imagine and it had been opened to me as a gift. There was nothing I had done to deserve it. Nor could it be earned. The gift was just there and the choice I had was to accept it or not, and this *pendejo* even considered refusing it! Can you imagine that!"

"So you came to Jesus," Lundberg said. Despite his intentions there was a cynical edge to his voice even his own ears could not deny.

"You are not that foolish, Martin," the old man snapped.

"I'm sorry," the young man said instantly. "That was unkind. It just slipped out." His eyes were full of remorse. "I don't know where it came from."

"I suspect from your father, but perhaps I'm wrong," Ramos said, not unkindly. "Perhaps I do him an injustice."

"No, that sounds just like him. Tone of voice and all. God, I'm sorry," he said again. "I'm so ashamed of myself." Tears began to form in his eyes.

"Hey, friend," the old man said, patting him on the shoulder. "You just discovered, maybe, how human you are, eh?"

"I swore I'd never be like him," Lundberg continued. "Then there he is." The tears flowed over and began to run down his cheeks.

"Martin!" Ramos said sharply. "Stop it!"

Lundberg was startled out of his mood. His eyes flared in anger, but he said nothing. "Good!" said Ramos. "You're angry. Throw it at me if you need to throw it somewhere, but stop flogging yourself!"

Lundberg opened his mouth but nothing came out. Ramos was looking at him not in anger, but with eyes filled with concern and compassion. For a long while they sat looking at one another, saying nothing. Then the moment passed. The young man sighed and nodded. "I hate it when I do that."

"I know," Ramos answered gently. "I've have lived there, too. I hate it when I do that, too. My point is that things like that are not altogether within our control, either. They just happen."

"Are you saying it's hopeless?" Lundberg asked.

"Of course, not! Not at all," Ramos answered. "Life is hopeless only when I try to stay in control. When I seek the help of the One I call God, for lack of a better word, I find such things like that happen much less often. When I do step on my own *chora*, as I still do now and then, it is only when I fall back into the habits of self will."

"That sounds strange," the young man said. "It doesn't make any sense."

"I know," Ramos answered gently. "At first it sounds contradictory, but it is still true. It's a paradox, but whether you read St. Frances or the Zen masters, you will find them saying the same thing. When we give we receive. When we pardon we find pardon. When we surrender we find victory. Pain is the teacher which often brings us to our senses."

Ramos could see Lundberg still did not comprehend. He sighed. "You may not have come to the place where you can do this," he said. "People don't often do so until they are absolutely desperate. Yet once they do, they wonder why it took so long." He chuckled wryly. "When your pain is greater than your fear and you have no where else to turn, it is then you will either destroy yourself or learn the truth of what I've just said." He shrugged. "You may not have experienced enough pain to understand the price of hubris yet. Or caused enough pain."

Lundberg was shocked by his friend's suggestion. "What do you mean?" he demanded. But the oracle had closed his doors for the day, and Ramos only shook his head sadly as he gazed into the far distance to another time, another place, and another young man so confident, so full of himself he could not see the pain his willfulness brought forth in the life of others. "I'm sorry," he said. "We will talk of this again, my friend. Right now I need to be alone, I think. To talk with my *flauta* to some of my own grief for a while."

The old man rose and started for the door, then stopped. "Please don't think you caused this," he said, pointing to his own breast. "What's heavy on my soul are some things I have not yet forgiven myself." He turned and walked out his kitchen door, and as he walked home Martin could hear the tragic lilt of the old man's wooden flute drifting in and out among deep shadows cast by the silver light of the full moon.

Now, lying alone in his hotel room five hundred miles south by southwest of the Canyon, Martin Lundberg was haunted by the voice of the old man's flute as he tried to sleep. *Martin*, it called him across the miles. *Martin, my son.* And then he remembered one of the many odd things the old man said, that the sins we regret the most are those we leave uncommitted. Or to put it another way, as Ramos had pointed out, it is far better to have to ask forgiveness for acts done with passion than to eat the dry ashes of love lost to fear.

Throwing off the covers and jumping from bed, Martin pulled on jeans and a sweat shirt, and soft moccasins to keep his feet warm, and crossed to the small writing table on the other side of the room. Turning on the lamp and taking pen and paper from the desk drawer, he sat down and began to write. *My Dearest Stephanie*, his letter began, *I miss you terribly.* A bit self conscious at his own candor, he crumpled the sheet and took up another, but found himself writing the exact same words. All right, he thought, that's the way I feel. So let it be, friend. Let it be. Pushing on, he continued in the same vein,

> **Tonight when I got back to the hotel my room seemed so very empty, much like my life alone seems now, even though it was filled with things I thought I loved. Without you, these things turn so drab now, and I feel like I am walking through life like a zombie, one step in front of another with only my body present. As if my soul is somewhere else.....**

The loud racking stutter of a car with glass-pack mufflers broke into his thoughts, even though the hotel windows were shut tight against the cold, and Martin reached out and switched on the radio sitting on the table to drown out further noise from the street. He found himself listening to station KVLF, Alpine, which styled itself "the voice of the last frontier", and he smiled at the conceit. Then his smile disappeared as the opening lines from the next record came softly over the air waves. It was Henry Belafonte, singing a love song only too familiar to him. Martin listened to the end of the song, then, feeling as if he'd been turned inside out, took up his pen and began to write.

> **The strangest thing just happened, Stef. I just turned on the radio and what did I hear but Henry Belafonte singing Unchained Melody. And the words he sang echo how I feel. I miss your touch, I miss your smell. I hunger to see you, to rest in your arms and look deep in your eyes and tell you how terribly much I love you, and how scary this is to me.**

> **What makes it scary? Thinking you might not feel the same way is one thing. Another is feeling so lifted up and so cast down at the same time. I am fearful for where this may lead, for I could come to love you so much I could not bear to live without you. This may have already happened and there's not anything I can do about it.**

I hope this doesn't put you off. It's scary to think it might. Yet it is the truth of how I feel about you. Without you I feel incomplete, as if someone has shown me an image of myself, the image of half a man standing in front of a mirror, with the best half of himself missing....

Martin stopped, read what he'd written, then sat looking at the letter for a long while. Adding a few lines in closing, he signed and sealed it in an envelope. Taking a stamp from his wallet he addressed the letter and then picked up his room key. Like a diver going off a ten-meter platform for the very first time, he forced his feet out the door and down the hall to the mail drop. He hesitated for a moment, standing there on the edge of the deep plunge, almost returning to his room and waiting until morning to mail the letter. Yet he knew if he did he might well never send it, and with Ramos' words in mind he practically crammed the envelope down the slot.

Turning to go back to his room he saw Rosa standing behind him, smiling. She handed him several post cards. "Would you mind?" she asked and he dropped them into the slot.

Martin knew Rosa was curious, yet would not ask. He felt embarrassed, like a junior high adolescent caught staring at the object of his infatuation. Not knowing what to else to say, he shrugged. "Just doing what my mother told me," he said, somewhat lamely. At her questioning look he grinned, despite his flush. "Not letting a day go by without nurturing it."

"Ah," she murmured, nodding. "Good." She hesitated, then said. "She seems a very intelligent young woman. I think she'll understand what a gift she is being offered." Kissing him on the cheek, Rosa let herself back into her room. "Good night, Martin," she said, adding something he'd not heard her say in many years. "Sweet dreams."

7. Our Winter Of Distant Lent

*S*omewhere over enemy territory. The open hatch of the cargo plane yawns before me. There is nothing to see but darkness and I wonder what I am doing here. We are over enemy territory and I must jump into the darkness to achieve my mission.

I remember nothing of the jump. There is no jump-master urging me out of the plane, no rush of wind on my face, no terror falling through the darkness, no jerk of the harness snatching me to safety. There is no memory even of the plane itself except for myself standing, waiting to jump. Yet now I am standing on the ground gathering my chute to bury it, to hide it from the enemies who seek me on every side.

I look around. All I can see in the deep gloom is low rolling hills cut by dry river beds. The land is desolate and without greenery, yet where I am is at the foot of a hill and there are a few trees here, tall stately pines looking over the simple frame camp cabin I have been told to find. There I am to wait for the one whom I am to meet.

I look at the cabin again. It is simple, built along the lines of a World War II military barracks and there is a single light burning on the porch. This is also as I have been told to expect, the single light shining in deep darkness. I am to go there and I am to wait, yet I am afraid. This is the only light burning in this dark and desolate land and I am afraid it will attract enemies, too, and that they will attack. The ones I fear most are the Russian troops, I think, and I am afraid the light which is my beacon to refuge may be their beacon for attack. I am unarmed.

Even so I walk into the cabin. There is no switch to turn off the light burning on the porch and I am reluctant to stay here with it burning so brightly. And there is no one else here. I think about unscrewing the light bulb, but this is not my cabin. I go into one of the bedrooms and lie down to rest, hoping the person I am to meet will arrive soon. Without intending to do so I fall asleep and suddenly awake, aware someone else is in the cabin. I

145

lie there quietly hoping it is the owner of the cabin end not an enemy.

As I lie there I see a tall thin man dressed in a tee shirt and boxer shorts look into the doorway at me and then move on. I cry out a greeting, not getting up and feeling awkward as can be. The man replies without reappearing at the door. He says he has been expecting me for a long time and to get some rest since we have a long way to go tomorrow. Somehow I feel safe with him there and fall off to sleep again.... (From Martin Quinn's journal)

March, 1963. The letter lay open on the kitchen table. Beside it lay a canary second sheet covered with writing in a strong, precise long hand, and a heavy brown craft paper envelope reinforced with packing tape. The letter and canary sheet came in a standard envelope which bore first class postage and was attached to the outside of the larger package.

Martin Lundberg sat silent for a long time looking at the letter. At last he sighed and rolled himself a cigarette. Lighting it he picked up the letter and began to read it for the third time. "Dear Mr. Lundberg," the letter began, then it continued,

> Enclosed is the novel manuscript you sent us for reading. Your story is interesting and reads quite well, and it demonstrates a talent for writing, which I encourage you to pursue. However, in its present form the manuscript is not usable and a detailed critique is enclosed. Should you agree to the changes we suggest and make them, I would be happy to read the manuscript again.

> I hope you do understand what we have to say is a vote of confidence, not an outright rejection. Nor are we being critical of your style or content. Simply put, we know fairly well what will sell and what will not, and the changes we suggest will improve the chances of success for your novel. Normally we would not even do a detailed critique, but I felt this manuscript deserved it. I think the summary our other reader attached is quite accurate. To be fair to you I put off reading the critique until I was done reading the manuscript, but I was not surprised by what Jan had to say.

> Keep up the good work. You're on the right track and sooner or later it all will come together. With best wishes....

The letter ended with the scrawl of one Jerome Samuels of the firm of Samuels & Pickering, Literary Agents. Setting the letter down Martin picked up the yellow second sheet. He admired the bold, precise script. *I wonder what she's like in person,* he thought, wondering what her hand and her choice of crimson ink revealed about the writer's character. *Maybe someday I'll get a chance to find out.* The lady certainly pulled no punches when it came to her notions of good writing. *I bet the manuscript looks like it's been flayed if she used the same pen,* he grinned to himself as he began to read,

Your manuscript troubled me and it took two readings for me to pinpoint just what it was. Your plot is good, the story moves well and the resolution of the conflict is excellent. You also have a natural flair for descriptive material and your dialogue is crisp and clean. Normally, given all this, the manuscript would be salable, particularly if it were not a first novel. Perhaps it already is, but I think you would be doing yourself a real disservice trying to market it in its present form.

Where the major weakness lies, in my opinion, is in your characters. They feel a bit flat, two-dimensional, and not altogether believable. To put it another way, I could not get into their skins, could not establish the rapport between reader and character which is so terribly important. Once I understood this, and with your manuscript it's very subtle, I could see the trouble. I don't know what makes them tick, what motivated them to do what they did and some of their actions are not consistent with my conception of them. While it is true that art follows life and people are inconsistent, their inconsistencies follow patterns. So their contradictions of themselves should appear consistent to the reader as he knows them, i.e. as you have presented them. To put it in a nutshell, it's almost as if these are caricatures of real people rather than flesh and blood folk. Well done, yes, but still caricatures.

I know this is discouraging because you obviously have put a great deal of yourself into the work. Don't let it get you down. To be quite blunt, we get hundreds of manuscripts a year, too many to give one full reading much less two, and as a rule we don't take time to make up a critique sheet like this. So rest assured your manuscript is far superior to ninety-eight percent of those we receive.

I don't know precisely what to suggest you do to make your people more real. You may be too close to your characters. It does happen, even with the most experienced writers, and it might help to put this aside for a few months, or even a year or so, and take up people watching. Try to watch them without any preconceptions, as if you were an anthropologist trying to figure out their customs. Make character notes and keep a journal of these for future use. If memory serves me, it took Mark Twain several years to finish Huck Finn and he did a lot of other writing in the interim. Maybe you could try short stories for a change, or character sketches, or even some nonfiction articles. Perhaps you can even do news writing. The point is, keep writing and keep the faith and it will come together. I assure you I have seen it happen with writers whose first work was not near the quality of yours.

At the top of the yellow sheet a single line was printed, stating the note had come from the desk of Janis L. Pickering. *I bet you tell all the boys that, Jan,* he thought, irreverent. Yet the fact both partners in the agency would take so much trouble answering his inquiry impressed him.

Despite his initial sharp disappointment, Martin Lundberg now found his feelings confused, as if he were somehow caught on a high wire between hope and despair. *Slap me down and build me up.* He shook his head, thinking, His mind wandered to a man he knew as a particularly obnoxious bore, someone, it was once said, who once had a great deal of potential. What made the man such a bore was his constant talk of all he could have been if the breaks had gone his way. Yet the Great American Novel he claimed was already written was never available for anyone else to see, and Martin suspected that it either had never been written or, even worse, had been written and did not measure up to literary standards. The thought of having to face that after repeated revisions was overwhelming. *Maybe I better stick to my last,* he thought, *and just be a simple farmer. Write my poems for my own pleasure.* The one thing he resolved never to become was a bore like the man he knew. Yet even as he thought this, it occurred to him the man himself never set out to be a bore. This thought was even more chilling.

Rolling himself another cigarette, Lundberg went to the kitchen sink and took out the sealed bottle of Canadian whiskey he was keeping hidden there for a special occasion. *I'm not going to get drunk*, he told himself. *That's the chicken shit way out. I'm just going to have one or two to calm my nerves. Then I'll talk to Ramos.*

Four hours later when Emil Ramos came to invite him to supper, Martin Lundberg was slumped to the floor. At first the old man was alarmed, then he saw the half empty bottle on the table beside the open letter, and nodded to himself. He bent over and straightened his young friend out on the floor, rolling him over on his side so he could not aspirate his own vomit. Then he sat down at the kitchen table and poured himself a glass of whiskey.

For a while Ramos hesitated, first building himself a cigarette and smoking it while he sipped the liquor and considered the possibilities, listening to Lundberg's heavy snoring. Then he came to a decision. *Sin boldly*, he thought, making himself another smoke and lighting it. That done he picked up the letter and read it first then the yellow second sheet. Done with those, he poured himself another glass of the water of life and looked at the package. He could see it had been opened, so he picked it up, impressed by its heft. Glancing at Lundberg he came to a second decision and slipped the manuscript out of the heavy envelope. Pausing only to refill his glass from time to time, and to check on his friend, Emil Ramos began to read, all thought of supper now gone.

"So you found it so boring it put you to sleep?" Emil Ramos was jarred awake by the harsh note in the young man's voice. Light from the full moon was pouring through the window at the back of the house, spilling across the kitchen where he sat. The whisky bottle lay empty beside him on a small side table and the manuscript he had half read lay open on his lap.

"Ah! No, the whiskey did that!" Ramos answered, rubbing the sleep out of his eyes. He looked at the bottle in shock. "That was half full when I found it," he said in wonder. Nothing remained of the Canadian except a half-inch of amber in the bottom of a water tumbler beside the bottle.

Lundberg nodded. "It was full when I started." He moved to the kitchen sink, filling a porcelain teakettle and preparing a pot of coffee. Stirring up the embers in the stove, he added a bit of kindling and some sticks of firewood, and even as he replaced the cast iron covers a wisp of smoke was rising from the kindling. Then he went to the sink, emptying a bucket if icy water over his head and letting out a whoop as some of the water hit his bare back. At the whoop, Ramos held his temples, feeling as if someone had pushed an ice pick through them and Lundberg laughed at him as he dried his hair with a rough towel. Reaching across the old man he picked up the tumbler and drained half before handing it to his friend. "Hair of the dog?" he asked.

Ramos nodded, tossing down the remaining whiskey. It burned like fire going down, but soon a comfortable glow filled his belly and his head stopped pounding so hard. "*Hijo!*" he said, "I didn't mean to do that. It's been a long time since something like that happened."

"I didn't either," said Lundberg, taking out a frying pan and preparing to scramble some eggs. "You want something to eat?"

"No," said the old man, "but I think I better. I don't think that last shot is going to last very long." He looked down at the manuscript lying open in his lap. "I hope you don't take offense. You told me you wanted me to read it when you were done, so when I saw it...." He shrugged.

The young man nodded. "Yeah, I did. I meant to get you my copy to look at but I forgot." After a moment he added. "Did you read the letter, too?"

Ramos nodded. "It was lying open on the table. You were passed out and I thought it might be bad news from home. I hope you don't mind."

"A little late for that, isn't it?" Lundberg said lightly, but at the sight of Ramos' face he relented. "No, it's all right, really. I was going to bring it up to you to see today anyway."

Ramos looked at him levelly. "I should have waited," he said. "It will not happen again, I assure you. I feel very strongly about that."

Martin turned and looked at him levelly. "Hey, it's my book, my letter, not yours, so stop beating yourself. What do you think?"

"I think it's my sin. And it's terrible using an old man's own words against him." Ramos complained. Lundberg rolled his eyes and shrugged to the heavens, spatula in one hand. Ramos laughed. "Actually, I think I'm glad they read it first," he said. "I think the lady is right, but I don't think I would have seen it. I'm too close to you to give good criticism."

"That's never slowed you down before," Martin observed dryly.

"With this it's different. So when I read it I can't tell the difference between the characters talking and my good friend speaking."

"They are me. At least, they are part of me. I created them." The young man was confused.

Ramos shook his head. "No, I don't think so. I think maybe you think that and sometimes put words in their mouths when you should listen to what they are trying to say. They need to speak for themselves."

"Come on, they're characters, not people," Lundberg protested.

"Precisely!" the other responded. "That's exactly what the lady is telling you. They sound like characters. To be people they must speak for themselves. They must tell their own story." Seeing he was not getting through very well, Ramos changed directions. "Look, suppose you were telling me about something Luiz did. Do you think I would want you to tell me what you wanted him to do or say, or about what he really did and said?"

"What he really did, of course. You're always very emphatic about that."

"And what would you, Martin, call it if you told me either what you think I wanted to hear or what you wanted him to do?" The old man's was watching him closely, his gaze, very intense.

"I'd call that a lie," Lundberg answered simply.

"Exactly! And caricatures are lies! They are lies which contain some very basic truth, but they are still lies."

"That's what fiction is," the young man protested. "People make up yarns and write them down. But everybody knows it, so it's not a lie."

"Maybe the run-of-the-mill writers," Ramos answered. "Great writers tell us the truth while making it appear they are lying." He laughed. "I think it was Pablo Picasso who said something about that."

"Wait a minute, he's a painter. Is he a writer, too?" Lundberg was getting a bit impatient with the way the conversation was going.

"Not that I know," Ramos told him. "What he said applies to both."

"So what did he say, already," Lundberg wanted to know.

Ramos gave him a hard look but answered, "He said something like this: 'Art is the lie that shows us the truth, at least that part of the truth we are given to understand.'" The old man grinned.

"That sounds like a Zen koan," Lundberg observed. "Did he really say that art is a lie?"

"No, he said art is *the* lie that shows us the truth. Much like the crooked line helps us understand what straight means, helps us see the straight lines." The old man looked at him fondly. "He also said we all know this, so maybe don't try to push the river understanding it," the old man told him gently. "Just try to remember it from time to time and the meaning will come. Trust me."

"God, I hope so," said Martin, completely confused. "I don't understand what all that has to do with my book."

"Maybe what you need to do is to set it aside a while, like the lady says," Ramos told him. "Read it again in six months or a year, maybe more, and I think you'll see what she means."

"Six months to a year!" yelped Lundberg. "I could be dead by then. I want to get it published so I have the money to really fix up this place."

"You've already fixed it up quite a bit," the old man said. "So what's your hurry? You have years to do this."

"I don't think so," said Martin. "I've always had the feeling I wouldn't live very long. Maybe to age fifty if I'm lucky."

"Fifty?" said Ramos almost shouting. "I passed fifty a dozen years ago, maybe more. Fifty is very young."

"My mother would love to hear you say that," Lundberg laughed. "She told me you make her feel young."

"Why not?" Ramos asserted. "I'm just a young man myself! I plan to live a long time yet. Don't you?"

"The way I feel at the moment, I'm not sure I want to," Martin replied. Shaking his head he turned back to making breakfast, muttering something else to himself as he tossed four flour tortillas out to warm on the cooler side of the wood cook stove and began to scramble eggs in a dished skillet on the other. The older man sat quietly a moment, trying to decipher what Martin had said. His mouth was open to ask when he suddenly realized what he'd heard was in Latin, not Spanish. His heart went down to his feet as he realized that while Martin was passing it off as an ironic joke, beneath his light tone lay a deep well of pain and grief. *Perhaps I am reading to much into it*, he thought, but it still seemed to him the words were uttered not in defiance or even mild blasphemy, but as the cry of a soul near despair.

"*Ave Domini,*" the young man had said. "*Moraturi te salutamos.*" It was a transliteration of the ancient gladiator's greeting to Caesar before the opening of the deadly circus games, now uttered as a mild reproach with all the melancholy of Job. "Hail to the Most High King," it cried out. "We who must die salute you.

They were awakened that afternoon by the loud blast of Luiz's diesel horns. Not wanting to leave him alone, Ramos had asked Martin to help him with a chore which might well have waited. Some seasoned firewood needed to be moved from near the barn up to the back porch before the next snow came and the young man accompanied him back up the canyon to his place. For two hours they worked together as the sun came up, moving slowly at first, then faster as the clean, crisp air of the winter morning cleared their heads and the exercise sweated the poison of the previous night from their bodies. "There," the old man said at last. "That should hold me through the very worst. *Gracias.*"

Going in to the house, Ramos fixed them a pot of tea and some sweet breads while Martin tended the embers buried in the ashes of the fireplace. Soon they were seated, comfortably full, watching the crackling pinon burn. Neither felt like talking and they sat in comfortable silence, staring into the hypnotic flicker of the burning wood. Martin was the first to nod off, lying back into the deep cushions of the easy chair and murmuring his thanks when Ramos covered him with a blanket. The old man covered his own legs with another as he sat in the other stuffed chair and was soon keeping tenor accompaniment to the soft deep snores of his friend.

When the sharp blast of air horns jarred them from their nap, Martin at first stared around in confusion, not sure what had wakened him. "It's Luiz," the old man reassured him. "He's come with the mail."

"Strange," said Martin, nodding and still half asleep. "I was just dreaming of him a while ago." He was still confused. "And after that I was dreaming about Stephania. We were up on the mesa and we were..." He broke off, flushing furiously as he realized suddenly what he was saying.

"Sounds like a most pleasant dream," the old man laughed. Then, at a second blast of the horns, Ramos got to his feet and walked to the door. "*Callate, tanto!*" he hollered in mock indignation out the open door. Shut up you fool! Then he laughed as Luiz pumped out "shave-and-a-haircut, six-bits" on the horns. The old man turned to Martin and said. "Hey, he's got someone with him."

Martin rose and looked over his shoulder. Parked behind Luiz's old car was a bright blue Jeep with a rag top, and a tall, familiar figure was following Luiz up the path toward the house. "Jack," he shouted, almost knocking the old man down as he pushed past him to dash down the walk. He collided with the tall figure and the two grappled with one another like Sumo wrestlers starting a bout. "Damn, it's good to see you," he exclaimed, looking closely at his cousin.

Except for being a bit thinner and appearing a bit lankier as a result, Jack looked much the same as always. Yet there was something in Jack Bear's face Martin had never, ever seen there before. Part of it was the lines on either side of his nose and mouth, once shallow wrinkles but now cut deep as lines of something akin to sorrow. Yet it was Jack's eyes which troubled him, for they were haunted, full of pain too long borne and withdrawn far into themselves, as if the man behind them were watching the world from a great distance across an deep chasm no one would dare to cross. Suddenly Martin remembered where he'd seen eyes like this before. It was in a book of photos taken during the Korean war, photos of American soldiers just back from the front lines, their eyes hollow from fatigue and haunted by the horrors of war their too young eyes had seen. "You look different, Jack," he said tentatively.

Suddenly his cousin was present, as if he'd leapt the chasm and was standing nearby. "You're a helluva lot stronger than the last time I saw you," Jack replied, trying a quick fake and throw which Martin countered easily, stopped cold. "What the hell you been doing, cuz, lifting weights?"

"You might say that," Martin laughed. "Every damned one of them went into building my garden wall."

"I saw that," Jack said. "Pretty impressive if you did all that, yourself. We stopped by on the way up. Place looks good."

"So this big fellow is the famous Jack-Bear?" Ramos asked in Spanish, reminding Martin of his manners. "He looks like you, poor man."

"God help us!" Jack Bear answered fluently in the mother tongue, offering a hand. "My sisters got the good looks in the family. You must be the famous Emiliano Ramos he wrote me about. I'm very pleased to meet you. May I present my friend, Maximillian Shapiro?"

"Very pleased to meet you, sir," the young man who was with Jack answered in English. "Jack's cousin speaks well of you."

154

Ramos extended his hand. "Please pardon our poor manners," he answered in the same tongue. "We'll speak English, of course."

"Please do not the trouble me for to make," Max answered in broken Spanish. His accent was atrocious, grated on the ear. "I understanding can in the Spanish most times, but trying to improve am the speaking."

"You've been learning from a Cuban, I bet," Ramos answered.

Max's face lit up. "Yes, but how did you know?" he asked in English.

"The Cuban accent is very distinct," Ramos said diplomatically. "No one else speaks the mother tongue quite like Cubans."

"What he means and is too nice to say, Max," laughed Jack, "is that it's atrocious. Not you, just the way Cubans talk. Guatemalans say it is doubtful that Cubans really speak Spanish."

They all laughed. "Martin, this is Max," Jack said. "The fellow I wrote you about. Max this is cousin Martin, also known as...."

"Don't you dare!" Martin replied, extending his hand to Max.. "Just remember I've got as many goods on you as you do on me." They shook hands. "I'm pleased to meet you, Max. Jack speaks well of you and I told him you both are welcome to stay a while. There's plenty to do but I'm afraid I can't pay you except in groceries." He looked at the other man. Max was thin and wiry with the dark good looks many women loved. Soft curly black hair grew long over his shirt collar coming to a stop high over delicate brows and the darkest, most liquid brown eyes Lundberg had ever seen.

Damn, Martin thought, *I bet those eyes melt the ladies.* Yet there was something in Max's manner which let him know the regard would flow only one way. For Martin found himself strangely, almost physically attracted to the man's handsome, almost pretty features, and deep within the other's eyes he saw recognition of this awareness. Within the confusion which followed in the wake of this realization, his mind, caught between this strange attraction and a deeply conditioned revulsion, he simply stopped, staring into the other's face, his clear and certain knowledge written on his own.

"Yes," Max murmured, as if answering Martin' thoughts. "I am."

"Max..." Jack started to say. The other silenced him with a motion.

"No, Jack, I'm tired of hiding who I am," Max said, almost sighing as he did. "If it's going to be a problem, let's find out now so we can be on our way. All right?"

"My friend, you are most welcome in my poor house," Ramos said, trying to smooth things over quickly. "Please, do me the honor of coming into my house and having some refreshment." He looked pointedly at Luiz, who was staring back and forth from one of the men to another trying to figure out what was going on. Then Ramos turned and walked back up to the porch where he stood waiting with the door held open.

"Sure," said Martin, taking the cue and reaching out and patting Max on the back. "Come on in, Max. I'll stoke up the fire and we can get acquainted. Maybe Jack can give Luiz a hand with the supplies." He exchanged a look with his cousin and Jack nodded and walked back to the Jeep, leaving a confused Luiz to follow, still wondering what was going on to cause the strange tension he sensed.

Walking Max up to the porch Martin murmured, "We can talk when Luiz leaves after supper. He's a little, um, small town in his was of looking at things."

"So there's not a problem?" Max asked directly. "For you?"

"Not with me, although I don't, um, swing that way," Martin answered. "I am sorry for my response. You surprised me. I mean you and Jack. I didn't know."

To his surprise Max laughed. "Sorry, I didn't think. Jack and I have hung around together so long I forget not everyone knows we're just very close friends, Martin. That's all, I assure you." He glanced toward the kitchen where Ramos had disappeared. They could hear him preparing the stove. "What about the old man?" Max asked.

"Well, I can't speak for him but I don't think there's a problem with Ramos either," Martin smiled. "He's pretty sharp and very tolerant, and very little gets by him. The only thing that really bothers him is dishonesty."

Max sighed deeply, his eyes suddenly filling with tears. "Thanks, man," he said. "You have no idea what a gift you've just given me. You really don't."

"Hey, I meant what I said in my letter to Jack," Lundberg answered, trying to make a joke. "You may not thank me so much when you see the work I've got lined out."

"You might be surprised," Max laughed again, truly relaxing for the first time. "Did Jack tell you I'm an engineer?"

"No shit?" Martin asked, excited by the possibilities this presented. "What kind of engineer?"

"He's a rambling wreck from Georgia Tech," Jack answered, coming in the door followed by Luiz. Jack had a box of groceries under one arm and a guitar case under the other, and each hand held a sack. "Honest to God, and an honest to God Seabee, too. He's one of the best sappers you'll ever meet."

"Well, I don't have much to blow up," Martin laughed. "Except maybe one of the local realtors, but Ramos and I have been talking about a water project we want to try with our stream higher up the canyon. You know anything about irrigation and drainage and that kind of thing?"

Max flashed a grin of bright, even teeth. "Are you talking rice patties, farmer, or just a well irrigated orchard?" he challenged. "I'm a civil engineer, which means bridges, earthworks, and that stuff. Seabees can be pretty specialized, but I'm not."

"Civil means you don't bite, either, right?" Martin laughed.

"Dear God, what have I gotten myself into?" Max said, rolling his eyes toward the ceiling. "Jack's bad enough. Now I find it runs in the family."

"Even his mother," Ramos added, sticking his head into the living room. "Why don't you come in here and we'll have something to eat. I always feed Luiz before I send him back to town. Even though it triples my grocery bill." They laughed followed him into the room, took seats at the kitchen table.

"I don't tell her, but Tio Emil cooks better than my wife," said Luiz, who had just come in with the last load. "Who plays the guitar, anyway?" he wanted to know. It was obvious he'd been wanting to ask ever since he'd spotted the case in the Jeep when they left town.

"Don't look at me," Jack said, coming into the kitchen and sitting at the table. "That's Max's department. I just provide the pretty face."

"What kind is it, man?" asked Luiz, who supplemented his income playing lead guitar with a local band called Del Rio Enojado. So far, the highlight of the group's career was a single they had produced on their own and two last minute gigs for major events in Albuquerque. One of these gave Del Rio the dubious distinction of being the replacement band for Cat Stevens.

"I don't think you'd recognize the maker's name," Max answered. "It was made in Spain and I traded a pretty good Gibson for it. I've only seen a couple of others like it.'"

"You traded a Gibson?" Luiz asked. There was lust in his eyes. "Man, I'd love to have a Gibson. That would be like driving a Cadillac compared to the thing I play."

"Luiz is the musician in the family," Ramos explained. "He's even got his own band now and plays in clubs."

"Would you like to see it?" Max asked. Luiz's eyes lit up like those of a child in a candy store and he nodded. "All right," Max added. "After we eat we'll take it out and you can give it a try."

"You mean play it?" Luiz asked, scarcely believing his good fortune.

"Sure," said Max. "Driving out here I heard something on the radio I never heard before. Maybe you could show me how it's done."

Lunch was *chile con frijoles* from the large pot Ramos kept filled for just such occasions, served with corn tortillas, fresh milk, and what remained of the sweetbreads for dessert. Martin noted Ramos had not brought out any of his wine and was quietly thankful he had not. Somehow it was hard to stop at just one glass, and while his hangover was mostly gone, he thought it was probably best to give his system time to get over last night's excess. *Not that we didn't have reason to drink*, he told himself, remembering the editor's letter. *At least I did.* Why Ramos had finished the bottle remained a mystery, but he knew what the old man would say. "Because it was there."

After lunch Max and Jack insisted on cleaning up, much to Ramos' delight, and Luiz fetched the guitar case, setting it almost reverently on the best chair for Max. Martin stirred up the fire with new wood and poured himself a cup of coffee before he moved the large porcelain pot closer to the coals. "So how's the family?" he asked, and he and Luiz visited until the others joined them.

Jack and Max were not long. Jack took a chair near the fire and sighed contentedly, sipping his coffee. Max opened the case and took out what looked like an ordinary guitar to Martin' eyes, but he could see Luiz was looking at it with great interest. He wondered what Luiz saw. Max quickly tuned the instrument and then played a chord and Luiz's eyes grew wide with appreciation. "Aiee!" yelped Ramos coming into the room. "I haven't heard anything like that since I was in Spain. Do you know flamenco?"

Max grinned and his fingers began to move over the strings like liquid, filling the living room with the strong, wild sound of Spanish music. To everyone's surprise, Ramos jumped to his feet and began to clap and shuffle slowly to the music, from time to time breaking into a wild song none of them could understand. Shutting his eyes Martin listened closely to the interplay of guitar and voice, and found himself drifting, an incredible lightness filing his whole being. Suddenly he was aware he was in another time, in another place separated from the canyon by thousands of miles and scores upon scores of years. It was a time filled more with joy than sorrow, a time gentle in his remembering, and he found himself surprised to be back in Ramos' house when the music came to an end. Yet seeing the look in Jack's eyes, Martin realized he was not the only one deeply affected by the music. He resolved to talk to Jack about it later when they were alone.

"Aieee," sighed Ramos, speaking for all of them. "You play very well, Max, very well, indeed, for someone not from Spain."

"I had a good teacher," Max demurred, handing the instrument to Luiz, who looked at it as if it were the Holy Grail.

"I can't begin to play that good," Luiz responded quietly, taking the guitar gently as if it were made of delicate crystal.

"I can't either," Max assured him. "Try it and you'll see what I mean."

Luiz strummed two or three chords and a look of pure pleasure spread across his face. "Aiee," he said, in wonder. "It's like making love."

"Now you know why I paid more than four Gibsons would cost," Max laughed. "Go ahead, try it out. Play something you really like."

Luiz nodded and closed his eyes. His fingers began to run lightly over the frets and strings, tentatively at first, then bolder as the instrument responded to his caress, playing the gentle strains of Cielito Linda. Then, having taken them through the traditional tune twice, Luiz began to improvise, at once playing the melody and an intricate counter point, his pace growing faster and faster until his fingers were almost a blur, ending in a magnificent crescendo.

"Ole!" Max cried when Luiz was done. "You underestimate your talent, man. That was marvelous."

"How much you want for this?" Luiz asked, looking at the guitar. "My car, my house, my wife, my kids?"

While they all laughed, it was clear Luiz was at least half serious. "Not for sale," Max said, "but I can tell you where you can get one like it. There's a six month waiting list, but you can play this one anytime you like. When you're up here," Max added, clarifying his offer.

"You pay him that way and maybe I won't have to feed him so much," Ramos said, laughing. "Every time he comes up he almost eats me into the poor house."

"Hey, Tio, is it my fault you're such a good cook?" Luiz answered. Then turning to Max he said, "Any time you want to play with a band, man, you let me know."

"Thanks," Max demurred. "I appreciate the offer, but I only play for my friends and for my own pleasure these days. I don't like crowds." He shuddered.

"Amen to that," Martin agreed heartily. "You came to the right place if you don't want to be around crowds. This is the biggest gathering we've had since Christmas. And most of the crowds around here are relatives."

"Who can sometimes be worse than strangers," the old man murmured.

Lundberg saw Luiz nod his agreement, apparently remembering the tyranny of his wife's aunts. "Oh, I don't know," he smiled, thinking of Stephanie. "Some of them are not so bad, you know."

Ramos cackled, slipping his hand under his shirt and fluttering it over his heart. "Poor Martin is moonstruck over my niece, Stephania," he explained to Jack and Max. "I think she's pretty fond of him, too, from what I see." He turned to his nephew. "Quit tormenting him, Luiz. You know he's too proud to ask."

"Damn, I almost forgot," said Luiz, taking two letters out of his jacket pocket and handing them to Martin. The stationery was light blue and inscribed with strong, clear strokes. A delicate scent of rose water followed their passage to Martin' hand. "I left the rest of your mail up at the house," Luiz apologized. "I thought you'd want me to bring these on up here." He shrugged. "Damn, I'm glad you remembered, Tio."

"I am, too," Ramos laughed, nodding agreement. "I'm used to having you around, nephew. We'd both miss you, Martin and I, I think."

Martin smiled and slipped the envelopes into his jacket. "Was there something from my mother?" he asked. "I've been expecting a letter from her for the last week."

"There was one from Minnesota," Luiz said, frowning, "but it didn't look like her writing. Hey, you want me to run up and get it right quick? I will."

"No," Martin answered. "It will keep. I can drive in tomorrow if I need to call." Then, seeing the look on Ramos' face he asked, "What?"

The old man shrugged. "Only a feeling my friend, but maybe you should let Luiz go get it. Or take you while we visit." He smiled at Max. "I'm curious who taught you to play like that. There was a time I knew many of the masters in Spain."

Lundberg laughed as he got to his feet. "It's incredible who he knows," he told Max. "He probably changed the diapers on the master who taught you." Ramos waved him off. "Tell you what, why don't you and Jack come on up the place when you're done. And take your time. I need a little time to swamp the place out and get ready." Over the last few months he had come to respect the old man's intuitions, or "feelings", as he called them. Far more often than not they were unerringly accurate.

"Someone's welcome to stay up here if you're too crowded down there," Ramos volunteered. "I'll kick the goats out of the back room."

Five minutes later Martin was reading the letter from St. Cloud. Luiz had been right. It was not from Rosa, but from Helen Stearnes, her very best friend, and was dated four days before. The message was direct and to the point, and as he read it, Martin' face grew solemn.

Dear Martin,

I am writing even though Rosa has told me explicitly not to. She has been in the hospital and I think you need to know that. And why. I hope she'll forgive me for telling you but I hope even more she doesn't find out I have written. I'm putting our friend-ship on the line even writing.

Rosa came in for a routine annual check but they found two masses in her intestinal area that looked suspicious. I happened to be visiting with Rosa when the attending physician gave her the news. (He's new in town and didn't know I'm the radiolo-gist who interprets most of his group's film, but to be fair, I was on my way out of the clinic and dressed in street clothes.) I could not help seeing some other things on Rosa's x-rays which

trouble me greatly. They point to earlier trauma, some of it very severe and some of it fairly recent, and when I asked about it, Rosa became very evasive.

Martin, I don't know how else to say it, but I fear for Rosa's physical safety. I don't think there's much to worry about with the masses, even if they prove malignant. They're not in that dangerous a spot so long as they are taken care of right away. What frightens me is what I read from the trauma signs. I treat a lot of battered women and the marks are all too familiar. I would appreciate your calling me at home as soon as you get this, and please reverse the charges. I'm usually there after ten o'clock (I guess nine, your time) but don't worry about the hour....

"Jesus," Martin said, shaking his head angrily.

"Bad news, man?" Luiz asked.

"Yeah," Martin said, pushing the anger back. "My mother's in the hospital and I need to go into town tonight and call." He looked at his friend, outwardly calm. "They found something the doctors say might be cancer but it's not for sure. I need to call and see how she's doing."

"I don't know," Luiz responded. "That cancer's bad shit, man. Rosa looked OK when she was here."

"Yeah," Lundberg responded. "She hasn't been sick or anything, so they must have caught it pretty quick. Her friend who wrote is a doctor and isn't too worried about it but she wants me to call. Mostly I need to call and cheer my mother up."

"You could call from my place," Luiz said. He looked doubtful.

"Thanks, " Martin told him. "And don't worry, they said to call collect." He saw a look of relief cross Luiz's face. "Besides, I've always been good for it, haven't I, Luiz?"

"Yes, Martin, you have," Luiz protested. "Always. That's not it." He shrugged. "I had to have the long distance cut off because of my wife calling her damned aunts, that's all. I just hope you can make the call."

Despite his concern for Rosa, Lundberg laughed. "Well, if I can't, there are other phones in town, my friend. There's a booth at the hotel and maybe I'll just try that first." He chuckled. "Besides, I'm not exactly on your wife's top ten these days." He looked around. "Let me gather up a couple of things and take me back up to Emil's."

"All right, I'll wait for you in the car," Luiz answered. As he walked out to the car he puzzled over the strange things he'd seen and heard that day, not least of which was Martin' quickly concealed anger after reading the letter from Minnesota. Luiz shrugged. *I guess that's his business*, he thought. There were many things he did not understand, and, if the truth be known, most of these he did not care to understand. Yet there was one thing Luiz understood very well. Strange as he might be, Martin Lundberg was a good friend to him. With Luiz that covered a multitude of sins.

When they arrived back at the old man's place, Ramos knew something was wrong the minute Martin walked in the door. Stopping in mid sentence he asked, "Is it Rosa, Martin?"

Martin nodded, not trusting himself to say more. He handed the old man the letter and turned to the others. "My mother's in the hospital being checked out for cancer," he said. "One of her friends is a doctor and wrote me. I need to go into town and call her and find out what's going on."

"We can drive you in," Jack volunteered.

"No need for everyone to make the trip," Martin said. "Max, would you mind staying the night here with Ramos? You can stay at my place but it will be probably late when we get back."

Max looked doubtful but the old man cut in, handing the letter back to Martin as he did. Knowing him as he did, Martin knew Ramos was probably as enraged as he, although none of it showed. "That would be marvelous," the old man said. "I would appreciate it if you wouldn't mind, Max. I don't get many opportunities to talk with people about the Old World."

So that was the way it worked out, though Martin had a little trouble convincing Luiz to let them go first. "You drive too damned slow," he said bluntly, "babying that damned heap of yours, and I'm in a hurry to get into town. Give us ten minutes start and you won't even see our dust."

Luiz finally agreed and Martin asked to drive, handing Jack the letter as he got behind the wheel. Jack read the letter twice, once quickly to gather the gist, and once slowly for the details. When he was done he sat a long time looking out the windshield as Martin drove. "Shit!" he finally said. "I know he's your dad, Martin, but Jeremy Lundberg can be a real asshole. I'm sorry if it offends you but right now I think I'd shoot the son-of-a-bitch on sight! God damn!" he roared, pounding his thigh with a fist.

"Don't apologize, Jack," Martin replied. "I feel the same way." He drove on for a few moments in silence, obviously struggling within himself. Then he stopped the Jeep, laying his head in his arms on the steering wheel and weeping bitterly, great sobs racking his whole body.

After a few moments Martin felt Jack's strong arm encircling his shoulder. "Let it out man," he heard his cousin say. "Let it all out. Don't try to keep it inside. It's too big, man. It's too fucking big."

The old man was still up, reading a well worn book in front of the fire when Martin Lundberg stuck his head in the door late that night. "I saw the light so I came on up," the younger man said.

"I'm glad you did," Ramos answered, waving him into a chair beside his. "There is some fresh tea in the pot," he said, pointing to a cup beside a thermos on the table between the chairs. He waited until Lundberg had settled himself comfortably, then asked, "So how is our Rosa?"

"She's fine," Martin replied. "As a matter of fact, she's in very good spirits. The lab results came back this morning and they were negative. So at least she doesn't have to worry about cancer."

"*Gracias a Dios!*" the old man declared. "A prayer answered. What did her friend, the doctor, have to say?"

"Nothing more than she said in the letter," the other answered. "She didn't seem too surprised when I confirmed what she saw on the x-rays. I guess it's pretty obvious if you know what to look for." He sighed deeply.

"So, what is troubling you, Martin?" Ramos asked lightly. "You have not learned anything new."

"No," Lundberg admitted. "It's just that down here I'm able to forget about it for days at a time. This just brought it up again." The old man waited patiently. "There are two things eating at me, really," Martin continued after a short silence. "Maybe three. One is that she won't do anything about it." He stopped.

"That distresses you deeply because you have," Ramos replied. He shrugged. "We've talked about this before. Our Rosa is loyal to a fault, and there is nothing this side of heaven which will change that. Assuming one would want to change it."

Martin gave him a lopsided grin and nodded. "That's a trait I'm afraid I learned from her. Some times it seems more like a curse than a virtue." Ramos nodded, waiting.

"The other thing is that I had to lie to protect Helen, and I don't like to do that," Martin went on. "Especially not to Mother."

"You never lied about cookies, I suppose," Ramos said dryly.

Lundberg chuckled and shrugged. "Come on, now. That was when I was a little kid," he answered. "This is different."

"Not really," said the old man, nodding to himself. "To our mothers we are always little children, and for most of us they always seem to have the ability to put us there when we are with them. Or maybe we put ourselves there." He fell silent, waited for some time, but Lundberg was lost in contemplation of the coals in the fire place. "You said three things," Ramos reminded him finally.

Lundberg nodded. "It's the same old, same old thing. I'm down here and she's up there where I can't do much to support her." He nodded his head before Ramos could speak. "I know what you're thinking," the younger man said. "I'm her son and not her husband. Taking care of her is his responsibility and staying with him even when he doesn't is her choice. Yet, even knowing all that, it bothers me."

"Of course it does!" Ramos replied, almost fiercely. "As you say, you get your sense of loyalty from her. And taking care of Rosa is Rosa's business, just like taking care of Martin is yours." He looked at Lundberg sternly. "Martin, one of the most painful things we have to do is separate from our parents, particularly when we love them as you do Rosa." He nodded. "I do know, my friend. I was every bit as close to my own mother. That's why I almost became a priest, because I thought that's what I needed to do for her. Then a wise old monk asked me for whom I was living my life and pointed out my mother had become my god. Aiee! I was angry at him for many years for pointing that out."

Martin started to flare. "Are you telling me that's what you think?"

"No, my friend, I'm not. I value your friendship too much to even begin to suggest that." He shook his head. "You are the only one who can make that determination. Still, I am not so sure I am being as loving to you in my silence as the old monk was to me by speaking the truth, however much it distressed me at the moment." He stopped speaking and they were silent a long while. When he spoke again it was so quietly Martin barely heard him.

"I'm sorry," the younger man told him. "I didn't quite hear what you said."

Ramos nodded. "I didn't realize I was speaking aloud. I said I think there is a fourth thing troubling you." He looked at Martin, his gaze quite level. "I think it will cause you grief until you come to terms with it."

What is that?" Martin asked, almost breathless, suddenly aware of being terribly afraid of what he was about to hear.

"You are afraid you will become a man exactly like your father," Ramos said gently. "Until you come to love him even as the man he is, there is a very good chance you will."

The long silence which followed was broken by the sound of Ramos' toilet flushing. A few minutes a very sleepy Max wandered in dressed in a long night shirt and soft deerskin moccasins. He had a blanket wrapped around his shoulders. "Is this a private conversation?" he asked, sensing the tension in the room.

Martin looked up, relieved at the interruption. "No, Max," he said. "Come on in. We were just talking about my mother. She's in the clear. It isn't cancer."

"Thank God for that," Max yawned. "Excuse me." He looked at Lundberg closely. "Tell me if I'm intruding, but you don't seem very happy about it. Is something else wrong?"

Martin looked down at the floor and for a long moment it seemed as if he were going to ignore the question. Ramos sat quietly, studying the dying fire. Max nodded. "Sorry," he said, getting. "I'm really not being nosy. Good night."

"Wait!" said Martin, taking Helen's letter from a pocket and holding it out to Max.

"You sure, man?" Max asked gently. "It's none of my business."

"Jack tells me you've been family to him," Martin forced a weak smile. "So I guess we're adopted cousins."

Max nodded gravely and sat down. Reading the letter his face grew very still, very sad. "Jesus, man, I'm sorry," Max said softly when he was done, his eyes filled with compassion. "I know how it is. That's the way it was in my family, too."

Emiliano Ramos said nothing. He sat listening as the two young men shared their common history of grief. Then, taking his coffee cup with him as if going for a refill, the old man got up and left the room, quietly as a mouse, not even saying good night. Yet as he shut the door to his own room and prepared for bed he was nodding and smiling, silently giving thanks to the Most High for grace given in answer to his prayers.

8. Fiesta De San Juan

A Tewa Pueblo, New Mexico. The earth trembles beneath my feet at the rolling thunder, as if a thousand bison are running wild across the plain, their feet churning the dust and their hooves drumming the ground. My shirt sticks to my back, the smell of dust is heavy on the hot dry air and just above the rolling thunder my ears are filled the resonance of many deep voices singing the ancient song of the herd. Only my eyes tell me all this is but the song of perhaps a dozen men pounding eight huge cottonwood drums as they chant the song their people have sung exactly the same way for a thousand years. And as they drum, three others, two young men and a young woman, perform an ancient ritual dance in exact time to the drums.

Even so, my eyes themselves tell me this is far more than the simple enactment of an ancient ritual. For the buffalo dance comes from before the time this people was converted at gunpoint to Catholicism by Spaniards, and even more, it is celebrated with a vitality rarely seen within the canon of the Mass. For as they sing, the singers sing with all their hearts. As they drum, their rhythm joins the heartbeat of the earth itself. And the dancers, as they weave and turn, their ritual movements so well known they are now second nature, they become the buffalo, calling their brothers and sisters to the hunters. As the young men pound the earth with their feet and toss their heads, heavy with hides and horns and sacred feathers, they are bulls of the herd courting their mates to renew their numbers. (Martin Quinn's journal)

June, 1963. The dust from the dancer's feet hung lightly on the still air of the dirt plaza, even then, an hour after the ceremonial ended, left in place by absence of a breeze and teased by errant rays of the late afternoon sun. Within the stillness, Martin and Stephanie stood in the shade of the outer wall of the great kiva waiting for Ignacio. They were quiet, reflective, sharing the mood of the plaza itself and only the smoke of Martin' cigarette, rising lazily and lifted by its own heat, moved in the quiet air. Even the normal sounds of people going about the business of everyday life were muted, stilled in the hush. As she stood reflecting on all she had seen that day, Stephanie would have sworn she could hear the silence.

"So," said a quiet voice behind them. "How was it?"

Startled, they turned to see Ignacio, small smears of white paint still clinging to the corners of his face, now dressed in street clothes and grinning. "You white folk better be careful," he snickered, imitating the voice of a famous cowboy actor. "Some wild Indian is likely to slip up on you and lift your scalps."

"I don't have words," Martin said, shaking his head in wonder. "It was incredible. I've never seen anything quite like it." Stephanie nodded. "You actually were the buffalo," he added. "The way you moved and tossed your heads I could almost see you trotting across the plain."

Ignacio smiled, obviously pleased. "Good," he said, nodding. "That's the way it's supposed to be. That's how we bring the buffalo." Then he patted his well rounded stomach and grinned. "I think this buffalo is hungry, especially after running after cows all day. Let's go to Uncle Pedro's and see what Aunt Maria has to eat." He turned and led them out of the plaza and down one of the dusty streets. As they walked he pointed out different things and waved to other people along the way. "Man, I love this," he said. "Most everyone who can comes home for the fiesta and it's good to see them."

As they walked, Martin Lundberg thought about their guide, Ignacio Trujillo, who they'd met last Christmas before *posadas* in town. He was not sure exactly why Ignacio had been there, he seemed to remember something about him visiting the family of a schoolmate, one of Stephanie's cousins, on his way home to the pueblo for Christmas. Then Ignacio showed up with Luiz and the mail one afternoon after Martin and Rosa returned from their trip to Texas. For some reason the young Indian was not returning to school that term and wanted to talk to Ramos. Martin could not remember exactly why, but what he did remember very clearly was the time he and Ignacio spent discussing their Christmas celebrations. What captured his interest was Ignacio's description of the blending of Catholicism with the ancient way in the pueblo, and how Christmas and the celebration of the pueblo's patron saint coincided with two most significant days in the Indian cycle of annual celebration. "It's funny how that worked out, "Ignacio said. "I've always wondered about that." He shrugged. "I guess it's the way God wanted it."

Ramos cleared his throat discretely. To Martin it was a sign the old man found himself forced to disagree. "Perhaps so. Yet I think it was more the Church bending to necessity," he suggested politely. "It would be that was why the place was named by the Spanish for that particular saint."

Ignacio laughed. "I never thought of that," he answered.

"That's because you're a good Catholic," Ramos said gently. "And a kind hearted man." He smiled at Ignacio.

With his European view of the Church, Martin was surprised it tolerated this blending of ways and said as much. "I don't understand. Why did they allow it here? They don't anywhere else. At least, not from what I understand. They tended to force their ways on people at gun point."

Ignacio seemed embarrassed by Lundberg's question, but the old man snorted. "The Church has been very wise in such things, Martin. At least some of the time. I think it's mostly because they realize they have little choice. They can force the people to go to Mass and accept baptism and all the rest, but there was no way they could police their personal spirituality."

Ignacio nodded. "Especially in my home," he said, almost proudly. "We were where the Pueblo Revolt began in 1680."

"A hundred years before the American Revolution?" Martin asked.

Ramos nodded. "Yes, and they drove the Spanish completely out of New Mexico," he said, shaking his head sadly. "They kept them out, too, for a dozen years."

"What happened?" Martin wanted to know. "Why did they let them back in?"

Ramos shrugged and looked at Ignacio who shrugged in turn. An outsider's point of view is all I can give," Ramos said. "From what I have read there were two things the Spaniards had the Pueblos lacked. One was firepower, although that might have been overcome, but for how long, who knows? The other thing was lack of unity among the various pueblos. They were not able to act as a single people." He looked at Ignacio and raised an eyebrow.

The young Indian nodded. "I think that's pretty fair," he said. Then he grinned. "Martin, if you ever attended an Inter-tribal Council you'd see what he means in action. All chiefs and no warriors. Literally."

"Sounds like the Minnesota legislature to me," Lundberg laughed. "I went once while it was in session. I couldn't believe what I saw."

"Considering their constituency, they were probably pretty well behaved," Ramos observed dryly. "Scandinavians tend to be reserved."

"Not these clowns," Lundberg countered. "One man was asleep with his feet up on his desk and another was making paper airplanes. All the time a debate was going on."

Ignacio laughed. "I've never seen paper airplanes, but a lot of them are asleep through Council. Some of them seem to do it with their eyes open."

"Many go through life without ever awakening," Ramos murmured, nodding. "Their eyes may be open but their souls are asleep."

"I wonder how they do it," Lundberg replied. "Doesn't sound so bad."

"No it doesn't," Ramos chuckled, stretching and yawning, and leaning back into the cushions of his easy chair. "Excuse me. I think it must be time for a nap." He shut his eyes and was snoring softly within seconds.

"How does he do that?" Ignacio asked in a subdued whisper.

"I don't know," said Martin in a normal voice. "Don't worry about waking him. I've seen him doze through a thunder storm. He'll be back in ten minutes, rip, raring and ready to go, but not much will wake him before that." He rose to his feet, winked at Ignacio. "Come on into the kitchen and let's finish the pie."

The old man's nose twitched. "Save me some," he breathed, resuming his snoring without missing a beat.

"Don't try to figure it out," Martin laughed, leading the way. "That's why they call him a *brujo*," he told Ignacio, pouring them fresh coffee and fetching the half finished pie from the safe. "That's why he doesn't need a watch dog around here." Neither could see the old man's lips draw back into a smile in the other room, yet even if they had, they had no way of knowing if it was in response to Martin' statement or simply a pleasant dream.

A sudden turn called Martin back to the moment. Ignacio was leading them to a single story adobe house. He stuck his head in the back door, speaking softly in Tewa. A moment later two people appeared in the doorway, a very short and plump grey headed woman in a long dress, and a grey headed man with a flat top hair cut dressed in denim and a flannel shirt. "This is my Aunt Maria and Uncle Pedro," Ignacio said in Spanish. "These are my friends Martin and Stephania from the other side of the mountains."

Tia Maria smiled, looking as if her eyes had been squeezed shut by her cheeks and the elder Trujillo solemnly held out a hand and nodded his head in welcome. Martin was not surprised when the man did not grip his hand but simply touched it lightly, shaking it up and down and withdrawing his own hand immediately. He had experienced this several times earlier, being introduced to other relatives and friends, and Ignacio had explained when he asked about it. "Shaking hands not a native custom," he said. "It's something we learned from the Europeans."

"Really?" asked Martin. "I've seen people here doing it all day."

Ignacio nodded. "Yes, but if you watch closely you'll see it's always done the way it was with you. Very formal." He grinned. "I had to learn how to do it your way when I came to school, and I have to remember not to when I come home."

"Really?" asked Stephanie. "Is it impolite?"

"Not so much impolite as, um, alien or maybe foreign." Ignacio had to search for the right word. "To be known as an Indian I have to remember to shake hands like an Indian."

"Sort of like a fraternity handshake," Lundberg observed.

"Yeah, but not quite so..." Ignacio paused trying to find the exact word he wanted.

"Exclusive?" Martin suggested.

"Intentional is a better word, I think, Martin," Stephanie interjected, coming to Ignacio's rescue. "I don't think it's meant to be exclusive so much as a way of identifying countrymen in a foreign land."

Entering the Trujillo's house, Martin and Stephanie found themselves in the kitchen. A wooden table stood to one side of the spacious room and a cast iron cook stove dominated the other. Two large pots stood on the wood stove, more as a matter of convenience than anything else. The stove was not heated, it being summer, and Martin thought the food had probably been prepared in one of the many open air kitchens he'd seen beside the houses. Most of these were shaded with what looked like cottonwood and willow branches, and many even had tables where the families could eat. Yet here in the Trujillo kitchen the air was cool, conditioned by the thick adobe walls, and filled with a delicious aroma unlike any he'd ever smelled.

Their arrival was apparently expected, for several places were set at the table and there were two baskets set out containing round moons of baked bread. The sight and smell of the food made Martin' mouth water and Tia Maria said something in Tewa, drawing a polite titter of laughter. "She said you look as hungry as a winter wolf," Ignacio translated and Lundberg nodded vigorously, drawing another round of humor. Then Ignacio's Tio Pedro said something in Tewa which sounded like a formal blessing, after which plates were passed around and the lids lifted from the huge cooking pots. The intensity of the aroma increased tenfold.

"This is chile, pueblo style," Ignacio told them, pointing to a pot filled with a deep red sauce covering small cubes of some kind of meat. "It's pretty hot, so you may want to take it easy."

"What's this?" asked Stephanie quietly, dipping a ladle from the pot containing some sort of white stew. What looked like chunks of potato and meat in cream sauce swirled around the bottom of her bowl.

"We call that *sende-po*," Ignacio laughed, speaking English. "Mostly it's potatoes and some seasoning. That's what makes up the *sende*, and *po* is simply water. So when you've got a lot of company and don't have quite enough *sende*, all you have to do is to add a little more *po*." Both Tia Maria and his Tio Pedro laughed at what Martin guessed was a family joke of long standing. He suddenly realized that while they had not spoken it, the Trujillos were at least tri-lingual and understood English, too.

Even so, Tia Maria and Tio Pedro were quite reserved, almost shy, and seemed to prefer speak their mother tongue. Yet when they spoke, even in their native Tewa, their voices were so soft Martin could barely hear them. While they were eating conversation lapsed, and Tia Maria beamed at the gusto with which Martin attacked the *sende-po*. "This is marvelous," he said in Spanish. "I've never tasted anything so good!"

"It's heavenly," Stephanie agreed. "Is it a family secret how it's made?"

Tia Maria laughed and began to speak rapidly to Stephanie in Spanish, almost too rapidly and quietly for Martin to follow. She was describing in detail exactly how the *sende-po* was made, and how it varied with the season depending on what was coming fresh in their garden. Right now the first corn was just coming ready and the next batch she made would contain corn, but for this batch she had used other things which might have gone to waste first. When she was done, Martin started to ask her something, then spoke to Tio Pedro instead. "I have a garden at home, too," he said, still speaking Spanish. "I would like to see yours if there's time after supper."

"Sure," Tio Pedro answered in English. "I show you after we eat. My Maria raise good garden."

"Maybe I can learn something from you," Martin replied, wondering why Tio Pedro seemed to prefer broken English to fluent Spanish. "I'm from Minnesota and gardening is different down here."

There was a short exchange between Tia Maria and Ignacio, and the young man laughed. Tia smiled, looking at Martin and Stephanie and nodding. "Are you talking about us, Ignacio?" Stephanie asked. He nodded. "What did she say?" Stephanie wanted to know.

"She asked me why Martin' new wife didn't tend his garden," Ignacio replied, chuckling.

"We're not married," Stephanie said, looking down, the color rising in her neck. Tio Pedro chuckled, too.

"That's what I told her," Ignacio said. "She was surprised. She said you would be soon."

"Martin is willing," Lundberg said, joining in. "I just have not been able to talk her into it. Yet," he added, looking at Stephanie and smiling. The Trujillos all laughed softly.

Tia Maria said something to Ignacio, who translated. "She told me to tell you she will make your wedding jug if you like," he said, adding, "She is pretty famous for her pottery."

"I would be honored," Lundberg replied, "but I don't know what a wedding jug is."

Tia Maria smiled and went into the other room. She came back carrying a black ceramic jug, big enough to hold perhaps a liter of liquid, maybe more, and handed it to Martin. What was unusual about the jug, apart from the beauty of it's design and glazing, was that it had a double spout at the top. She said something to her nephew who explained.

"When a couple gets married in the pueblo, they are given a pot like this at their formal engagement. When the marriage ceremony takes place, the jug is filled with water, and sometimes wine, and the couple drink from it. The man drinks from one side and the woman from the other." Tia Maria said something else and he continued. "When one of the partners dies the jug is saved and given to someone else. It is never thrown away or broken."

"How beautiful," Stephanie breathed. There were tears in her eyes.

Tia Maria smiled and crossed around to Stephanie, handing her the jug. "For you," she said in perfect schoolbook English. "For your marriage to keep it strong."

"Oh, I can't," Stephanie started to refuse, saw the disappointment rise in Tia Maria's eyes and took the jug. Setting the jug gently on the table she rose to her feet and took Tia Maria's hands. "Thank you," she said, gently hugging the tiny woman. "No one has ever given me anything so beautiful."

"Your husband will," Maria answered softly, nodding toward Martin. "He will give you the gift of children."

"I take it we're now engaged?" Martin asked, taking advantage of the moment. After the barest hesitation Stephanie nodded." Super!" Martin almost shouted, first hugging Stephanie and then Tia Maria, startling the old man, although he laughed. "Thank you," Martin said beaming at Maria. "Thank you for the pot, too."

"I only did what I knew she wanted," Tia Maria shrugged, smiling.

"So how soon is the wedding?" Ignacio laughed.

"As soon as I can get a license and find a priest," Martin answered, but Stephanie held up her hands.

"Please, Martin," she answered, imploring. "Not so fast. Let me get used to being engaged first. I still have some school left to finish, too," she reminded him. "This is all rather sudden."

Tia Maria came to her rescue, leading her into the other room where the men could hear them murmuring. After a few moments they came out, giggling like school girls and carrying a chocolate cake. "Ignacio thought we forgot," Tia Maria told Martin, laughing, "But we fooled him. Today is his birthday."

"I wish I'd known," Martin said. "I'd have brought you a present." Stephanie nodded her agreement.

"You already did by coming all the way here to visit," Ignacio told him. "Especially bringing Stephanie."

"Wait a minute," Martin said, rising and fetching his satchel. After rummaging around for a minute he produced a small cardboard box. "It isn't wrapped, but happy birthday, Ignacio."

Ignacio took the box and opened it. "Wow," he said, taking out a flat pocket knife. "Thank you." As he held it in his hand they could all see the white cross set in the red handle, marking it as a Swiss Army knife. "Look," he said, opening it up. "A can opener, a bottle opener, and an awl, as well as the cutting blade."

"Turn it over," Martin told him.

Ignacio did as he said, opening a tool set in the back of the knife. It was a tiny pair of scissors. "I really appreciate this, Martin," he said. "This will really come in handy with my crafts. Thank you." Shutting the knife he secured it in his pocket and nothing more was said.

"That was a *beau geste*," Stephanie murmured in his ear a while later when they were driving home across the mountains. Even though it was a little late when they left the pueblo they chose to travel the more direct dirt road over the mountains rather than the roundabout way following the pavement. The unspoken agreement was they would spend the night at Martin' place. "You're a very generous man, Martin," she added. "That's one of the things I love about you. I know you've been wanting that knife a long time and you scrimped to be able to buy it."

"I can order myself another one," he replied, trying to shrug it off. "Compared to their hospitality it was nothing."

"Horse hockey!" Stephanie replied sternly. "You can be such a hard-headed mule sometimes! I know you can order another one, but will you?" she asked. "I think not, even knowing you the little time I have. You're very generous with everyone but yourself."

"Other people's needs seem greater," he replied, feeling apologetic but wondering why he felt that way. "As the Good Book says, it's far better to give than to receive." He grinned. "At least, that's what I think it says. It's been a while since I read it."

"It does say that," Stephanie assured him. "But I'm not going to let you change the subject, bub." She looked at him levelly.

"Hey," he complained. "What gives? I didn't do anything wrong."

"No, you didn't," Stephanie told him. "It was a very generous thing to do, but if you don't get yourself another knife you'll wrong yourself." She grinned. "And when anyone wrongs my man, they got to deal with me, bub. That means you, too."

"Oh," said Martin, smiling his relief. "I thought you were serious there for a moment."

"I am, Martin," she answered, kissing him lightly on the lips. "Very serious. Mostly about you. But Rome wasn't built in a day and time's on my side. I'm taking you just the way you are, but that's one thing I'm warning you now I'll never stop trying to change my mind about this. I want you to be kinder to Martin."

"You sound like your uncle," Martin gripped.

"Then maybe he's right, too," Stephanie rejoined. "So put that in your pipe and smoke it, kemo sabe" she laughed, relenting. "Look, dear heart, I really don't want to spend the night I get engaged arguing over something dumb we can talk about later," she said. Then, pointing ahead of them, she added. "Not with a moon like that coming up. So pull over, buster, and show me how much you love me."

"Right here?" Martin asked, feigning shock as he pulled to the side of the dirt road and set the parking brake.

"No, over there in the grass by the pond," she answered, jumping out of the car and running across the broad meadow toward a beaver dam across the creek. "Bring the blanket from the back," she shouted, kicking off her shoes and wading into the pond, her skirt held high.

The next morning Martin Lundberg awakened in his own room to the smell of fresh hot coffee. For a moment he was disoriented, not knowing where he was. He'd been dreaming, dreaming he was in his aunt's house, his father's youngest sister. Yet even though her house was in Minnesota, and looked like houses look there, in his dream it appeared like Pedro and Maria Trujillo's home in the pueblo, and not at all unlike his own bedroom in his house in the canyon.

He lay there for a few moments trying to focus his mind. Someone was moving around in another room, making what sounded like soft noises in the kitchen, and he heard snatches of low conversation and laughter. Then the door opened, and when a beautiful dark skinned woman stuck her head in the room she looked familiar, although he did not recognize her at first. He stared at her, almost rudely, trying desperately to clear his head, knowing he should know her name.

The woman's smile disappeared, replaced with a look of concern. "Martin?" she asked, coming to the side of the bed and touching his cheek. "Are you all right?"

"Where's the dog?" he asked, bewildered. "Where's Penny? She was just right here a minute ago."

"Penny?" the young woman asked. Shaking him gently by the shoulder she said, "Martin, wake up. You're still dreaming. You don't have a dog."

"I don't?" he asked. Then coming fully awake he added, "No, of course I don't. Penny's been dead for years. Sorry, Stephanie. I was dreaming but it seemed so real."

"It's all right, dear, the best ones and the worst ones do," Stephanie told him, handing him a cup of black coffee she'd set on a dresser. "Here. This will help, but watch out. It's very hot."

Martin thanked her and took a sip, scalding his upper lip. "Ouch!" he said. "You weren't kidding." Taking another, more cautious sip he asked, "Did I hear someone else?" he asked, frowning. "Or was I dreaming that, too? I thought Jack and Max were going hiking all week."

"They're still gone," Stephanie smiled, assuring him. "Tio Emil came down early. He needs a ride into town as soon as you can give him one."

"Did he say why he's in such a hurry?" Martin asked, concerned.

"I don't think he's in any hurry," Stephanie answered. "I think he just wanted to be sure and catch you before you got away. He wants to go in sometime today. Some business he needs to take care of."

Martin nodded, looked at her with loving eyes. "Did I tell you today you're the most beautiful woman in the world?" he asked reaching out and pulling her to himself. "Or that I love you with all my heart and all my soul?" He kissed her deeply.

"I love you, Martin," she replied when they were done. "I'm glad I said 'yes' when Maria offered me the pot." She reached out and took the marriage jug from the deep window shelf by the bed. "I've never been given anything so beautiful," she murmured, caressing the smooth black surface and tracing the design with her fingers.

"Hey! That's right," he said, grinning and jumping from the bed and hastily pulling on a pair of jeans and a tee shirt. "You did. Hey, Ramos!" he shouted. "We have some good news to tell you!"

The old man yelled something back, but the thick walls and heavy door muffled his response so Martin could not make out his words. Taking Stephanie by the hand, Martin led her into the kitchen where they found the old man seated at the table drinking coffee and eating a sweet bread. "Good morning, Martin," Ramos said raising his coffee cup in a salute. "That's what our princess told me but she wouldn't say what it was. Looking at her face I bet I can guess." His eyes fell to the marriage pot clutched in her hand. He nodded, smiling.

"No bet," laughed Martin. "She finally agreed to marry me. It was in a moment of weakness, but I'm holding her to it."

"Good," Ramos chuckled, getting to his feet and giving his niece a hug. "How marvelous. Two of my favorite people getting married. When is the celebration?"

"We're still working that out," Stephanie answered quickly, changing the subject. "Look at what Ignacio's aunt gave us," she said, holding out the marriage jug. "Isn't it beautiful?"

"Indeed," murmured Ramos, looking intently at Stephanie, then at his young friend. A slight frown crossed his face, then quickly disappeared. "Did you say Maria gave you this?" he asked.

"Yes," Martin answered, oblivious to the undercurrents Ramos felt in the conversation. "That's what made Stephanie finally agree to marry me."

"Ah," the old man murmured, looking intently at the jug for the very first time with a practiced eye. "The rightness between you must have really impressed her," he added. "This is how she makes a very good living, making pottery and selling it. She's famous for it and this is one of the very best pieces of her work I've seen. They're all excellent, but this one is beyond excellence." He stroked the lines of the pot reverently.

Martin did not know what to say to this. Refilling his coffee he said, "Stephanie tells me you need to go to town today." The old man nodded absently, still looking at the pot. "Any particular time you need to be there?" Martin added.

"No," said Ramos, handing the pot back to Stephanie and giving his young friend his full attention. "I have to have some things notarized, so it doesn't matter when I go so long as it's before the bank closes. I think they're open late today."

"I think so, too, but why don't we go in early, anyway? I need to take

Stephanie in to pick up some things from home and I could use some more groceries. Jack and Max will be back in before I get in again." The old man nodded and started to get up from the table.

"Wouldn't you like something more for breakfast, Tio Emil?" asked Stephanie. Martin looked up in surprise and she laughed. "He's a terrible host, tio," she said to her uncle. "He invites people home and then he makes them cook his meals."

"Makes them?" Martin yelped. "I'm not twisting your arm."

"He's too subtle for that, tio," she said, not answering Martin directly. "He just starves them into it."

"Here," Martin answered in mock disgust and reaching for the skillet. "I'll cook, then."

"Sit down, buster," Stephanie answered, ducking out of his reach. "Never send a man to do a girl's job."

"If you haven't noticed already," Ramos murmured to Lundberg, "our sweet Stephania has sharp teeth."

"Oh, I've got the fang marks to prove it," Martin laughed, drawing a stern look from his beloved. "Right here," he said smoothly, touching his breast over his heart.

"He says such romantic things, doesn't he?" Stephanie said to Ramos, still full of devilment. "Like, 'Did you want that nose hair sticking out like that, or did you forget to look in the mirror this morning?' Or, 'Gee, you don't sweat much for a fat girl.' Things I love to hear."

The old man shook his head at Martin' growing consternation. "See what I mean? I think maybe you've only seen her milk teeth, my friend," he chuckled. "You have an interesting life ahead," he added. "Never boring."

"Has she always been like this?" Martin asked, responding in kind to Stephanie's jibes. "Or are these her company manners?"

"Aiee," said the old man rising from the table and crossing to the door. "I think maybe it's time to go home now. You love birds pick me up when you're ready."

"We'll be up in an hour," Lundberg answered. Then catching a look from Stephanie he added, "Maybe an hour and a half." Ramos laughed and waved good bye.

"Did I say something to set you off?" Martin asked carefully when the old man was gone.

"No," smiled his lover. "I'm just being a bitch. He's right, you know."

"He's right about what?"

"I do have sharp teeth, sweetheart. As a matter of fact, that's why I'm not married. I've run a lot of men off."

"They were fools," he declared, "but I'm glad you did."

"No, Martin," she disagreed gently. "I have little time for fools. Most of them were very nice young men. Too nice, perhaps," she added, giving him a long look. "Sometimes I think you may be, too."

"Oh, I can be a real bastard," he rejoined. "I just don't enjoy it much. I end up feeling bad about it. Rotten."

"That's what I mean, my love," she answered, lightly. "I hope with all my heart I never drive you away, but I know I am capable of being mean spirited enough to do just that." She looked at him gravely. "Martin, we've got to talk," she said, her tone serious. "I did say 'yes' and I mean it with all my heart, but I don't want to marry right away. I want to finish school first."

"Sure, sweetheart," he answered. "That's what? Another semester?"

"No, dear," she answered. "I'll finish my master's next semester, but I want to go all the way. I want to go after my doctorate. That means three more years, maybe more." She looked at him, torment in her eyes. "Please don't ask me why I need to do this. I just do. For me. Then I'll be ready to marry and have your children."

Martin framed his response cautiously, choosing his words with care. He remembered another conversation about marriage, a conversation in which they were suddenly in the middle of an argument. He couldn't seem to remember just how they had gotten there, where there conversation had led them. Yet it was if they suddenly found themselves in the middle of a mine field, one they'd no idea was there. He felt as any move he made could be fatal, for there was no going back. Not now. They were too far in to back out gracefully, and safety, as well as grave danger, lay directly ahead.

As he remembered later, their conversation began innocently enough. Martin was telling Stephanie some of the things his mother said on their trip south to the Big Bend country of western Texas. "She told me some things I'd never heard before," he said, still troubled by the poverty which shaped and so marked his father's character. "Terrible things about our family."

"Like what, Martin?" she answered, gently urging him on.

He gave her a strange look, then laughed. "I don't know if I should even tell you," he answered. "You might not want to have anything to do with me any more."

Stephanie started to give him a smart reply, like, "You may be right, I might not." Yet some tone in his voice, some sense it would not be right to do so stopped her. Rather, she looked at him gravely. "Martin," she said, "I love you with all my soul. I don't think there is anything you could tell me to make me love you any less. But if we're going to spend the rest of our lives together, then I need to know what you're dealing with."

So he told her. She was right, he realized. Who more had a need to know the demons who plagued his family? No, who had more of a right to know? So he told her. He told her with fear and trembling, holding nothing back. He told her how it was growing up in a house dominated by a man he was convinced was a raging alcoholic.

Yet as he spoke of the verbal abuse, of the shaming and blaming and mind games his father played with the whole family, his face was devoid of feeling or emotion as if he were speaking of something as ordinary as an afternoon rain. Saving that his face was too quiet, too controlled, too detached, almost frightfully still. Suddenly Stephanie realized Martin was talking like the survivors she'd seen on television, the survivors of things like airplane crashes. Only the tears streaming down Martin' cheeks gave silent witness to the turmoil and pain which was tearing at his soul. It was only when he came to the abuse of his mother, to the savage beatings this gentle woman took to draw the fury of his father's rage from her children, did he stop, unable to continue for the great sobs racking his body. And then, looking at her with eyes at once ancient and innocent as those of a child, he revealed his greatest fear.

"You know what scares me?" he asked. Stephanie shook her head, caressing him with her eyes, afraid to even touch him lest the spell be broken and he retreat into that distant place he did at times. "What scares me is what she tells me about him when they were first married, that I am so much like how he was at this age."

"Martin," she answered softly. "That doesn't mean you are him. It doesn't mean you have to make the same mistakes."

"God, I hope not," he replied fervently. "There's no way I want to turn out like him, but I'm scared I might. What's really scary is I remember him telling me the same thing about his father, that he swore he would never be like him. Yet my mother tells me that's exactly what happened. At least with his drinking and the abuse."

"How can she be so sure, Martin?" she asked. The look on his face told her she was walking on thin ice coming even this close to challenging the saintliness of his mother. "No, Martin," she assured him. "I'm not saying anything against Rosa. I love her and respect her far too much for that, but she's human, too. There's no question in my mind she believes what she tells you, but what if she's wrong? I mean, how could she know? Did she know your grandfather, your father's father, as a child?"

Even though Stephanie's point was well taken, and quite to the point, Martin was reluctant to accept the idea Rosa might be mistaken. "I don't know," he said. "The point is they both turned out the same. I asked a physician about it once and he told me these things often go down through families from generation to generation, like hemophilia."

"So you're saying you have no power over this and that it's hopeless?" Stephanie asked, a bit sharply. "That doesn't sound like you, Martin."

"Not completely," he answered, a bit stung by her tone. "What I'm telling you is that my dad is all right to be around when he's not drinking. The only thing is, that's all he seems to do when he's not working. It's funny, you know. Not humorous, but odd. He doesn't drink all day long, even though anyone can see things really bother him. Then come six o'clock, and you can set your watch by it, don't stand between him and the nearest bottle or you'll get run over." He shook his head sadly. "Once he starts drinking it's like Dr. Jeckyll and Mr. Hyde. He's not the same person."

Stephanie nodded. "So what are you telling me, Martin? Are you telling me you've changed your mind? That you don't want to marry me?"

"No," he said, "not at all. I want to marry you. I want to share the rest of my life with you. What I am saying is I'm scared to have children. I'm afraid I'll treat them the way my father treated us."

"Then why marry at all, Martin?" Stephanie asked. "I'm willing to live with you and be your woman any way you want me as long as you want. But if we marry, I want children. I'm not willing to marry without at least letting it happen when it's time." She shrugged. "If we can't, we can't, but that's another thing. We can cross that bridge later. And at least two children. I don't want more than three or four, but I want at least two."

That was when the argument began in earnest, their first painful clash, and it went on for days. Miserable days, he remembered now, choosing his words with care. Nor could he remember exactly how they had overcome the rift, except they both agreed it needed discussion and not argument. What he did remember was their making up, the sweetness which made the pain of their estrangement almost worth while.

"All right, sweetheart," he said gently. "I'm sorry if it seems like I'm pushing you. I want you to go to school. I want you to follow your heart's desire, but I don't want to lose what we have in the process."

"Do you think we might?" Stephanie responded. "I think it's stronger than that, Martin."

"I do, too, Steph," he told her gently. "I'm just afraid. This is the most precious thing I've ever had."

"Me, too," she answered seriously. Then she grinned. "Martin?" she asked, an interesting look in her eye.

"Yes, my dear?" he responded, knowing what was coming.

"Why are we standing here talking on such a beautiful morning for making love?" she wanted to know.

"I was just wondering that myself," he replied, taking her in his arms and kissing her thoroughly, feeling her legs lock around his hips.

Late that afternoon Martin was sitting on a bench with Emil Ramos in the plaza in Old Town while they waited for Stephanie to finish her errands there. As was their custom they sat in silence, watching the people there go about their business, occasionally sharing a chuckle when one of them saw something very human taking place. Once it was a mother with two toddlers, who reminded Martin of films he'd seen of a mother bear with two playful cubs. One of the toddlers was perhaps a year older than the other, but his brother seemed determined not only to keep up with his elder, but to best him at whatever they could see to get into. "Reminds me of me and Jeremy," Martin told the old man. "Our mother had her hands full with two rowdy boys." He laughed as one of the toddlers, seeing his brother get attention he was not, looked around and pushed over a trash can. Fortunately, it was light weight and almost empty, but it brought the wrath of the child's mother like an avenging angel.

"Poor Rosa," Ramos nodded. "Which one were you like? The one who just pushed over the trash?"

"Me?" Martin disclaimed. "I was like both of them at once."

Ramos chuckled and they sat for a long while in silence. Martin sighed and Ramos glanced over at him. Martin caught the glance and looked back. There was a troubled look in his eyes but the young man said nothing, so the old man simply waited. His young friend would tell him when it was time. Something else caught his attention and he was in the middle of a pleasant reverie when Martin spoke.

"Tio Emil?" the young man asked. Most of the time Martin simply called him Emil or by the patriarchal, Ramos. The exception was when he wanted the counsel of an older man. Then he used the familial Stephanie and Luiz used. Ramos looked his way and Martin continued. "You know me better than anyone else," the young man said. "Even better sometimes than I know myself. "

"That's only because I've made some of the same mistakes."

"You seem to see things I cannot see in myself," Martin responded. "You see them a long time before I do."

The old man shrugged. "The same is true of you, my friend. I am sure you see things in me to which I'm blind." He chuckled. "As a matter of fact, you are like a mirror, showing me many things about myself as a young man that I had forgotten."

"The sins of your youth, eh?" Martin grinned. "Maybe that's what makes you such a good confessor."

Ramos laughed. "If I am a good confessor, it is only because I have left very few sins uncommitted." He shook his head. "But no, you remind me mostly of good things in myself I could not see when I was younger."

"Really?" Martin was surprised. "I don't lay claim to much virtue."

"That's exactly what I mean," Ramos said. "You see the faults in yourself very clearly, just as I did as a young man. You don't see the basic goodness I see in you."

"That touches on what I want to talk to you about," Martin said, looking around the plaza for Stephanie. She was nowhere in sight.

"She's talking to her cousin, Carmelita," Ramos told him. "I'm sure they're talking about your romance. So we have at least another half hour to wait."

Martin glanced at the clock in the square, noted the time. "I'll bet you are right within two minutes," he said, laughing.

"No bet," said Ramos. "I'm far enough behind at cribbage as it is."

"Two million, five?" Martin said, deprecating the loss. "You won twice that last month at chess."

"That was last month!" the old man laughed. "So, what is it you want to ask your mirror on the wall?" he inquired, sobering.

Martin told him about giving the knife he'd bought for himself to Ignacio and what Stephanie said on their way home. As he did so, Martin did something which always amazed Emil Ramos, for the younger man fell almost into a trance, repeating the conversation with Stephanie verbatim and with precise inflection. As he spoke Ramos could literally hear his niece speaking the same words, and he wondered were she aware of this uncanny ability in his friend. He expected it might not be an altogether welcome gift in the marriage. "So what is your question?" he asked when Martin was done. "Are you asking me if she is right?" Martin nodded.

"Are you planning to buy yourself another knife?" the old man asked.

Martin shrugged. "To tell you the truth, I wasn't completely happy I'd bought the first one. I mean, it's not like I really need it. I have other pocket knives and it was just an impulse."

"I think not," Ramos answered. "I remember your looking at the catalogue for months before you ordered it. I remember how excited you were the day Luiz brought it." He looked at Martin levelly. "I would be willing to make this bet. Double or nothing. You've had it over a month now but I bet it was still in the original box when you gave it to Ignacio."

"No bet," Martin laughed. "You must have seen me take it out of my possible bag recently."

"I did," the old man said slyly. "Why do you think I was willing to bet?" He sobered. "Do you know why you never took the knife out and used it, Martin?"

"Yeah!" the younger man protested. "I wanted to keep it nice. I didn't want it to get all bunged up."

"Ah, like your shovels?" Martin had worn out three in the first four months he was in the canyon. "Or, maybe, like your new axe?" Ramos had gone down to Lundberg's place some months back and found Martin in the back yard splitting firewood with an old axe with a taped handle and a chipped blade. "Why aren't you using that one?" he asked, pointing to a brand new double bit leaning against a wall.

"It's too easy," Martin laughed, throwing aside the old axe and picking up the new one. "And I don't deserve it. I'm working off some sins of the flesh." With the new axe he made short work of the rest of the job. "Damn, that works well," he added, picking up the split wood and stacking it under a piece of tin next to the shed.

"That's the way they're made," Ramos had observed dryly. Now he looked at Martin as if he were examining a bug with a magnifying glass. "I think it's like that, isn't it? It's like your new axe. That knife was too nice. You didn't deserve it so you wouldn't let yourself really have it by taking it out of the box and using it." He shrugged. "So now it's gone and it's not a problem for you any more." He looked at Martin sternly. "Put it in the worst light and what do you see?"

Lundberg sighed. "Shit!" he said. "I didn't give him a gift at all, did I? I got rid of a problem for me!"

"No! Stop that!" said the old man rudely, shocking Martin silent. The mother with her toddlers was crossing the plaza, looked their way to see what was going on. Ramos smiled at her and tipped his hat. "I beg your pardon," he told Martin quietly, his voice still quivering with anger. "You can be such a *pendejo* at times, just like me!" He took a deep breath, let it out. "You touched a nerve," he explained. "I was saying that more to myself than I was to you. Give me a moment." He took another deep breath and exhaled.

Martin' face had moved from shock to anger to sullen wariness. He shrugged. "Never mind," he said. "We can talk later."

"Please indulge me," said the old man gently. "And if you can find it in your heart, forgive me for my outburst." There was no question of his utter contrition.

"Don't take it so seriously," said Martin. "*Se hace nada.*" It's nothing. "Water under the bridge."

"It was rude and I thank you for your graciousness," the old man said. "I do want to have my say, however. I think it was a generous gift to Ignacio, especially in light of Maria's gift to you. There is a spiritual axiom which says we can never really possess something until we can give it freely away. So you truly own the knife now. The question I have is, why did you give it to Ignacio?"

"Because I thought he would like it and it seems he did," Martin said. "But it didn't seem to please him as much as I imagined. He didn't say much."

Ramos nodded. "Different cultures. Knowing Ignacio, he loved it. But it is not the Indian way to do much more than say thank you."

"Why is that?" Martin wanted to know.

"I'm not sure, but I think it has something to do with manners, with not putting other people in an awkward position. Still, I'm not sure." He looked at Martin closely. "My friend, I'm not suggesting you did this with Ignacio, but I used to give people things so they would like me." He shrugged. "I still do when I can't help myself," he added. "Yet I do see it as trying to manage my own fear, not as altruism." He grinned. "I tend to trust basic goodness, but I distrust too much altruism. I have found it often self serving."

Martin nodded. "One of the reasons I hate to take gifts is that I hate to be beholden to anyone."

"I, too. That brings me to the real point I wanted to make. When one is a giver, one is in control of the relationship. When I am a recipient, I am not. I give control to another by accepting a gift."

Martin sighed. "You got me pegged."

The old man laughed. "You spot it means you got it," he replied. "That's what a good friend of mine says. But what does he know, anyway? He's a *borachon*."

"*Borachon*? You mean a drunk?" Martin asked.

"Well, yes, he was. Now he's an alcoholic."

"What's the difference?"

"What's the difference with what?" asked Stephanie. They looked up to see her crossing toward them with a young woman Martin had never seen in tow. "Martin, this is my cousin, Carmelita." Stephanie said. "Carmelita, this is my friend—fiancee—Martin Lundberg," she corrected herself, laughing. "I'm still having to get used to the idea," she added, almost giddy.

"I am, too," Martin answered, "but I like it." Taking the petite hand

Carmelita offered he bowed deep and kissed it. "Goodness," he said. "I see why Stephanie's been keeping you out of sight."

"Did not!" Stephanie protested indignantly. Carmelita flushed and laughed nervously, not knowing what to make of this.

The old man chuckled. "Aiee! 'Til I kissed her little sister...'" he teased. Stephanie glowered at him. Martin looked from one to the other, feeling vaguely guilty but not quite sure why.

"Hello, Carmelita," Ramos interjected smoothly, taking her hand and kissing it himself. "It's been so long since I've seen you I didn't know what a lovely lady you've grown up to be. I didn't recognize you at first. Tell me, how is your dear mother?"

Carmelita beamed at the compliment, relieved to have the attention drawn away from herself. She and the old man exchanged family news for a few moments while Stephanie studied Martin with a critical eye. "Why don't we have a treat?" Ramos suggested, pointing toward the ice cream shop on the corner. He offered his arm to Carmelita and led the way.

Martin and Stephanie fell into line a few places behind. "Sorry," Martin whispered, shrugging. "I was just being gallant."

"Well, just don't be too gallant, Charley," she answered dryly. "Or you'll find yourself singing alto."

"Steph!" he protested, stopping and turning toward her. "She's just a kid, a teeny-bopper. You don't have any reason to be jealous."

"I wasn't aware jealousy required a reason," she responded. "She's no kid, buster. She's seventeen, almost eighteen now, and by then half the girls in this town have babies."

"Sweetheart, I'm not about to go after a seventeen year old child," he argued. "She's not a woman yet. Not in my eyes. Even if she were, I certainly wouldn't be trying to get her pregnant."

Stephanie looked at Martin levelly. "None of them are conceived on purpose." She shook her head. "Look, sweetheart, I know how men and women are, and especially men and young women. You're here and I'm there and I know what can happen when people get lonely."

"Are you talking about me as a man or are you talking about yourself as a woman?" he asked quietly.

"About you as a man," she answered, looking down. "You don't seem to understand how attractive you are. You could have Carmelita in your bed tonight if you tried."

"I don't want her in my bed!" Martin whispered fiercely. While he spoke his words too softly to be distinct, several people looked their way at the growl of his voice. "Listen," he whispered urgently. "You are the most beautiful woman in the world to me. You're the only one I want in my bed."

"When?" she said, her voice suddenly choked with passion.

"Right now!" he murmured, passion burning bright in his eyes. "I'd take you right here and right now if I didn't think we'd get arrested," he said, glancing around the square. "Maybe we can find a deserted alley."

"Or maybe I need to go back to my room for something I forgot," she suggested, grinning.

"Maybe I'll meet you there in three minutes," he answered. "Go ahead. I'll tell them and meet you there." He started to turn away, then turned back. "God, you're beautiful!" he murmured, and for a moment Stephanie thought she might swoon.

"Hurry!" she urged him. "I'll be waiting."

Some time later they were lying together quietly on Stephanie's narrow bed. "Martin?" she said. I don't want to beat a dead horse, dear..."

"Then don't, sweetheart," he murmured, sleepy, kissing her lightly on the lips.

"I really need to say something," she countered, rising to an elbow.

"All right," he answered, caressing her gently.

"Remember what I said about men and women?" she asked. He nodded. "Well, it's true of us, too, dear."

He frowned, trying to understand what she meant. "How's that?"

"Neither of us took any precautions, dear," she told him. "I'm not sure about the timing, but we may have just conceived our first child."

"Really?" he asked, confused. "I thought you...."

"That's just what I mean. I didn't think about it until after we started and it was too late to stop."

He sat up in bed and looked at her gravely. "Well, if we did, we did. All that means is that we'll marry sooner, sweetheart. You know how I feel about bringing children into this world, but if one's on the way, we'll deal with it as best we can." He looked at her thoughtfully. "You said you weren't sure of the timing?"

"I think it's still three or four days early for me to conceive, but I'm not completely sure. I'll have to look in my calendar." She looked down, the color high along her neck.

"You keep track?" he asked.

"Ever since we met," she said. "I'm normally as regular as a clock, but we can't count on that."

"No," he nodded, grinning. "You know what they call people who rely on the rhythm method, don't you?"

"Parents," she chuckled. "So you're not angry with me?" she asked.

"How can I be angry with you and not be angry at myself, too?" he answered. "I seem to remember we were both in a rush." He looked at her with an enigmatic smile and asked. "So we're already at risk?" She nodded. "Well," he said with a shrug, "If that's the case, another exposure wouldn't hurt, would it?"

"Oh, no, you don't, buster," she laughed, pushing him off the bed. "We've been gone over thirty minutes as it is. If we're gone much longer they'll get suspicious."

"You think Tio Emil doesn't know?" Martin asked, incredulous.

"Of course he does," Stephanie answered. "He's no fool. Who I am thinking of is Carmelita."

"Right," he said. "But after all, she's just a child," he added, laughing at the withering glare this drew from his beloved.

9. Rites Of Spring

Ecce homo. *Behold the man. He does not look like a Savior. For his clothing is torn, soaked with his own blood, and from the bruises on his face and neck, it is surprising he can see at all. Blood flows into his eyes from a crown of thorns they have crammed on his head and when they strip him for hanging high on the barren tree, one can see why his garments are soaked. He is bleeding from dozens of small wounds as he stands naked before the crowd. To the men assembled there he does not look like a King, or like a Messiah at all.*

Behold the man. Those are the words of a Roman governor stationed in a remote province of the Empire at the beginning of the Common Era. He utters them not long before the expedient execution of a notorious rabbi who is accused by his own people of sedition against the Empire and blasphemy against the local deity, and both are capital crimes. Yet the man is innocent under the law of the land, just as the man standing naked in his own blood before this crowd is innocent under the laws governing his native land. For this is not Palestine in the year 33 AD, and the men acting as executioners are not Roman soldiers. Nor is the condemned a rabbi nor a rabble rouser, nor has he been accused of blasphemy, although the charge would hold in light of what is about to pass. For this is Rio Arriba County, New Mexico, in the year of our Common Era, 1965, and the man's tormentors are not his enemies but his relatives and his friends. (Martin Quinn's Journal)

September 1964. The old man was seated on his front porch when Martin Lundberg drove up and parked his ancient truck. Dropping himself into the other chair Martin stretched out his legs and sighed. "Damn, it's good to be home," he said throwing back his head and running his fingers through his hair. Throwing out his arms he arched his back and yawned so wide it seemed as if he might dislocate his jaw. "*Hijo!*" he declared loudly.

The old man nodded. "Yes, it always is for me, too. How was your trip?" he asked. "I presume you got Stephanie on the train to Boston all right." Martin nodded glumly and the old man laughed. "Did her baggage take up a whole freight car as you thought?"

"No," Martin smiled wryly. "She was traveling surprisingly light for such a long stay. Only two suitcases and one big trunk."

"She always travels very light," Ramos told him. "Not like her cousin, Carmelita. Man, when she comes up to stay overnight Carmelita brings half the house with her."

"Our sweet Carmelita?" Martin asked, smiling. "Come on now, she's not that bad. We were gone five days and all she took was a small suitcase and her overnight kit."

"You took Carmelita with you?" The old man was clearly surprised.

"Yes," Martin answered, wondering at his friend's look of concern. "I ran into her in town, in the library as a matter of fact. When she found I was going to Albuquerque she hitched a ride with me."

"I see," Ramos answered carefully, nodding. "That's interesting. Did she enjoy her visit?"

Martin's smile brightened. "The kid had a marvelous time," he replied. "She wanted to see everything, all at once, of course, and she drove us crazy until their cousin came and showed her around." He chuckled. "I think by then Stephanie was about ready to choke her."

"I don't blame her," the old man told him. "Stephanie's going away for a long time and having to say goodbye to her young man and her little cousin intrudes? I'm surprised she didn't throw her out right away."

"Carmelita really didn't intrude," Martin countered. "I mean, yes, she drove us crazy, but I was the one who offered her a ride to Albuquerque." The old man raised an eyebrow and Martin shrugged. "Well, the kid wanted to say 'goodbye' to Stephanie and see the University, and I was going that way. What else could I do?"

"You could have done many things," Ramos told him. "Among them, offer to take her there another time." He looked at Martin directly. "You don't seem to understand Carmelita is half in love with you."

"No, she isn't," Martin argued. "Or if she is it's just a teenage crush and she'll grow out of it. After all, I'm ten years older than her."

Ramos nodded. "Exactly the same as the age difference between Rosa and your father, I believe," he said dryly. "I think if you looked into your heart of hearts you'd find some feelings there for Carmelita."

"Of course, there are!" the younger man rejoined. "She's cute as a bug and she's a good kid. And I love her for it. But she is a kid, Emil. I mean, she hasn't even been to school yet."

"I didn't realize school was required for such things," the old man replied archly. "Several of Carmelita's friends seem to have started families without it, thank you kindly."

"Emil, I'm not a cradle robber," Martin protested with some heat. "I thought you knew me better than that."

The old man shrugged and waved it away. "Of course," he replied softly. "Please forgive me." His eyes turned inward and Martin knew the subject was closed, at least for the time being. He nodded his thanks and settled back into his chair, lighting a cigarette and tossing the pack to Ramos before he slowly began to rock.

For a long while they sat like that in silence, rocking back and forth, each lost in his own thoughts. The acrimony lying between them was not pleasant, but there was little they could do about it. They'd come to places like this before and both knew it was simply best to let things be. Ramos knew his younger friend was perturbed and wanted to talk more about other things, but he also knew it was better to let Martin find his own time, his own words, his own understanding.

When Martin did begin, it was with a sigh. "I don't understand, Emil," he said. "Why does she have to do this?" There was no hiding the anguish in his voice. "Why does she have to go to Boston? This last year her being in Albuquerque was bad enough. Now she's changed her major and is looking at four more years of graduate school."

The old man sat for a while as if he'd not heard. When he spoke the younger man could barely hear him. "I have been concerned about you for a long while," he said. "For both of you. Forgive me if what I have to say troubles you, but I believe I must speak from the heart. You are too dear to me not to, both of you." He looked at Martin, his eyes filled with concern and compassion. "I know you well, my friend. You have given me the gift of knowing you and your lady grew up coming to me in her times of trouble and confusion, more than to her own mother. So I know you both very well and I would not have made a match between you."

Martin was clearly surprised. "You wouldn't?" he asked.

"No, even though our dear Rosa would. She and I have talked about it at length in our letters." He smiled. "I tell her that her desire for grandchildren clouds her better judgment and she tells me I'm a stubborn old man."

Martin was not surprised to hear of their correspondence, for he knew his mother wrote his friend from time to time. Yet he was surprised to learn he was apparently more than a casual subject of discussion between them. "Why not?" he asked. "We really connect."

"Yes, you do. Yet my opinion is that you are too much alike in some ways and not enough alike in others," Ramos told him.

"How do you mean?"

"Well, you both are very reluctant to let others make decisions for you, even those you love." Ramos grinned. "Even decisions you would come to for yourself."

"Well, yes, we both know what we want," Martin said. "But there's nothing wrong with that."

Ramos thought for a moment. "No, there isn't. Let me put it another way. Your strengths are not complimentary. They don't fit together like the pieces in a puzzle. They bump up against one another like those that don't fit together."

He could see his young companion did not quite grasp what he was saying. Spreading his fingers evenly the old man brought them together and clasped his hands tight. "I think your qualities do not come together like this, making a bond and leaving no voids." Touching just his fingertips together he continued. "I think it is more like this. You and Stephanie connect in many places but there are voids between them and no bond except attraction to your own likeness. I think you will soon discover the voids and will be bitterly disappointed. Both of you."

Martin shrugged, shook his head. "You may be right. I guess I just can't see it right now. We seem to get along so well when we're together."

Ramos nodded. "You get along well because you're both on your best behavior when you're together. You don't have to live with one another's shortcomings and eccentricities."

"I love her eccentricities," Martin protested.

The old man nodded. "You do now because you find them amusing and even endearing, as she does yours. Will they be so ten years from now? Will yours be so for her?"

There was no answer for this. Martin sighed and stretched, changing the subject. "That drive gets longer every time I take it. I'm glad I had company on the trip back." Realizing what he'd said he added, "Carmelita helped me keep awake."

"I bet she did," the old man laughed. "If you want to really stay awake, let her drive."

"I did let her drive," Martin admitted. "*Hijo*! She almost had me saying the Rosary!"

"You let her drive?" Ramos covered his face with a hand. "I was just teasing. Carmelita doesn't have a license yet. Her mother wouldn't let her learn to drive and Luiz is afraid to teach her."

"No wonder she got so scared when we saw the highway patrol," Martin laughed. "Well, I guess the joke's on me. Maybe I can teach her how before she leaves for school next spring."

"Just be careful, my friend," Ramos laughed. Lundberg looked up sharply but the old man's face was bland innocence. "Did you find what you were looking for in the library?"

"Yeah, but I had to go all the way to Albuquerque to find it," Martin told him. "You're not going to believe this, but the library at Highlands has no references. Not one."

Ramos nodded noncommittally. "No, that doesn't surprise me at all. I suspected that's what you might find."

"I didn't know that's what you meant," Martin told him. "I thought you meant it would be hard to find because the library is so limited." He shook his head. "I can't believe anyone actually did it. It doesn't make any sense."

"One man's craziness is another's sanity," Ramos answered. "What did you find? Anything?"

"There are plenty of references in the card index and in the periodicals index, but there's nothing on the shelves. The one book which listed a whole chapter was lost and never reordered, and someone cut entire pages out of several of the reference journals." He shook his head. "There have been two masters thesis projects in the last fifteen years, but neither one of those could be found. So Highlands was a washout."

"But you did get what you were after?" the old man asked.

"Yeah, I lucked out," Martin replied. "One of the people who did the research I was after teaches in Las Cruces. I ran into him by accident in the library at the University. He was there doing research and he's sending me a copy of his thesis. He told me where to find the journals I was looking for in the University library. Even then, someone had cut the article out of one of those." He paused and looked at the old man. "I don't understand. What's the big deal, anyway? All it did was make me have to look harder."

"Are you familiar with the Masons?" Ramos asked him.

Lundberg nodded. "Yes, my father was one."

"Did he ever explain to you what that was about?" the old man continued. "Or tell you his lodge secrets?"

"No, but then, he never told me doodley squat," Martin answered. "I came across a little lodge book one time. It was called the Monitor and I read it our of curiosity. Most of it was mumbo jumbo and there was some of it that was left out."

Ramos nodded. "Certain secret things were to be uttered," he went on. "With *los penitentes* it's like that, a brotherhood lodge. Even though it appears to be very religious, it's a secret society like any other secret society. There is us and there is them and knowing the secrets is what makes a man one of us rather than one of them. Around here that's very important."

"That's very important anywhere," Martin responded. "Why keep it secret? That's what I don't understand."

"There is great power in secrecy," Ramos told him. "So long as the secrets aren't known, they are fearful." He shrugged. "Once they are known, they lose their power."

"How do they lose their power?" Martin asked. "Just knowing them doesn't change anything."

"Ah, but it does," Ramos argued softly. "When something is known it can be held up to ridicule and that robs it of its power to instill fear." He smiled. "As you said, most of it is mumbo jumbo to anyone else."

Martin nodded. "From what I was able to find out, some of the things they do are ridiculous, especially some of the stuff the guy told me he didn't include in this thesis. Some it is probably illegal, even though they use volunteers." He changed his mind. "No, a lot of it is illegal, which must be why they try to keep it secret."

Ramos nodded. "I'm sure it must be one reason, but being illegal does not stop it. Some say it goes all the way back to the Aztecs, but I think that's reaching. The rituals are different, even though the general purpose may be the same." His voice became almost pedantic as he explained Aztec public worship in detail.

"Do they really leave the guy up there three days?" Martin asked a bit impatient. At the moment he could care less about Aztec piety. The old man nodded. "That's longer than Christ was on the cross," Martin protested.

Ramos shrugged. "Well, they don't stab them with a spear these days," he said. "That's something. They take them down sooner if they die. Just like Christ."

Martin could tell the whole conversation was very uncomfortable for his friend. He wondered why. "What happens if they live?" he asked.

"Then they never have to worry about anything as long as they live," the old man answered. "Their scars are marks of honor and everyone thinks they have God's favor." He shrugged. "So they always have a job and their families always have what they need. So who knows, maybe they do have God's favor. A severe mercy."

"Scars? You mean on their hands and feet? I thought they tied them to the cross these days. Do they still nail them?"

"The ropes leave scars, my friend, believe me. They are scourged, too. Just like the Good Book says. That leaves horrible scars." Though his face remained still and expressionless, there was pain etched in each of the old man's words.

"You've seen the scars?" Martin was fascinated. The old man looked at him for a long while. Then nodding and sighing, he rolled up his pants leg and pulled down his sock. Encircling his ankles were ancient light marks, as if a long time ago the skin had been ripped away and replaced by scar tissue.

"You?" the young man asked. Ramos nodded and rolled up his sleeve to show him scars just like the ones around the old man's ankles. "You told me those were rope burns, and I guess they are," Lundberg said, pointing to the marks on the old man's wrists, "but I had no idea."

"Why do you think they let you go when I showed up?" Ramos asked him. "Because of the sweetness of my disposition? No, it was because I survived their torture and now they're scared of me. *Sabes?*"

"Jesus," murmured the young man. The way he said it was almost like a prayer. "You?"

"Yes," Ramos answered dryly. "To both. Precisely."

Martin looked at the old man with awe. He clearly remembered the night the old man came to his rescue early last spring. He could not now remember why he went out into the forest that night except he was restless and it was a beautiful clear night illuminated by a moon only a few days past full. The feel of spring was in the cool dry air and after the hard winter he was looking forward to the change. Somehow, though he knew Easter was the following Sunday and he and the old man intended to go into town to Mass, more to get away from their routine in the canyon than for any pious intent. It slipped his mind that it was Holy Week and that night was Maunday Thursday. Not that it would have made much difference in his decision to explore the woods, but he might have been more prepared for what he found.

Slipping on a warm jacket and a knit cap, he'd taken a flashlight and wrapped his wooden flute carefully, placing it in his satchel with a loaf of bread and a half bottle of wine, intending to pay a visit to Ramos later that evening. Then he walked up the hill behind his house to a flat place he often sat. Had the old man been with him a campfire would have been built and perhaps good talk would have distracted them so he never would have seen the line of torches following the goat trail up the sheer face opposite his spot. As it was, he lit a candle instead of a fire and blew gently through his flute, warming it to play. Then touching it to his lips and reaching to the depths of his soul, he began to softly play a lilting, haunting tune never heard before under sun or moon.

Twenty minutes later when the tune came to an end, he laid the flute aside and warmed his hands over the candle. Then, as he bent to light a cigarette he saw the lights going up the face, and reaching into his rucksack he pulled out a pair of light-weight field glasses he always carried. Focusing them he was surprised to see a line of men carrying wooden torches up the steep path. Then he saw something even more surprising, even shocking. For at the head of the line, following two men with torches, the naked figure of another man could be seen in the dim light, stripped of his clothing and carrying what looked like a large wooden beam over his shoulders. Even as Martin watched, another man came up from behind, shoving the naked man and kicking him on the buttocks, causing him to fall. Yet another man, this one with a whip, came up and struck the naked man until he struggled back to his feet. Then the man with the whip slashed another man and pointed with his whip to the huge beam. Two others helped him pick up the huge beam, set it on his shoulders and followed along as the naked man climbed the goat trail.

The procession crossed over the lip of the face and disappeared from view. Sick to his stomach Martin lighted another cigarette and opened his satchel, taking out the bottle of wine. Setting the bread aside he took a deep drink of the wine and sat there quietly, thinking of what he'd just seen. There were rumors, always rumors of strange doings in these mountains, but this was no rumor. This was like a nightmare come to life and he wondered if he were dreaming or hallucinating. Picking up the field glasses again he looked at the other side of the canyon, but all he could see was what he thought might be a the dim reflection of a campfire beyond the lip of the face. Yet it was too vague to be certain and he set the glasses down. The old man would know and Martin decided to go ahead and pay him a visit.

Carefully wrapping the flute and placing it in his satchel, Martin was about to blow out the candle when he saw them. Two men stood at the edge of his clearing, their clothing and faces dark against the moonlight. He could see they were both armed. Leaving the candle lighted Martin sat back and nodded to them. "*Buenos noches*," he told them, good evening.

Neither of the men responded. One of them motioned with his head and the other circled around behind Lundberg, keeping what looked like a shot gun raised but not pointed directly at him. The leader pointed to the candle and the satchel, signaling Martin to empty them and he did. Seeing the field glasses the leader gave Lundberg a hard look and half raised his own weapon. "Pack it!" he said, almost spitting out the words. Lundberg blew out the candle and repacked his bag. "Come!" the leader commanded, leading the way down the hill toward Martin's house. Martin could hear the second man following close behind.

They were across his yard and through the front gate when the leader stopped abruptly. Someone was coming up Lundberg's drive and the leader raised his gun. A moment later they could see it was the old man coming toward them, a candle lantern in his hand.

Seeing the three young men Ramos nodded and walked up to Martin. He nodded and then looked at the leader, motioning with his head for them to leave. The leader opened his mouth to argue but the old man cut him off with a chopping motion of his hand. Then the man shrugged, nodded to his companion, and the two drifted away into the shadows. "You have some wine in there?" Ramos asked him. Martin nodded and the old man said, "Good. Let's go to my place and drink it. You can stay there tonight so you don't get into any more trouble."

That night he'd been confused and the old man had not said a word by way of explanation, refusing all questions and telling him there were simply a few things he might be better served avoiding. Now as he looked at his old friend in awe Martin asked, "But why?"

Ramos looked at him uncertainly. "I'm not sure what you are asking, my friend," he said. "Why did I do that? Or why is it done?"

"I guess both," Martin replied. "I don't understand."

"The answer is probably the same, anyway," the old man spoke almost to himself. "I was seeking something. I was fresh out of the seminary and I was looking for a way to atone for what I thought were horrible sins, sins against God but not the Church. The Church had failed me, or so I thought. I believed it was supposed to be more perfect than other human institutions, and I found it more corrupt than most. So blaming God for the Church's failures, I did some very terrible things." He shook his head sadly, sighed. "Those are things which still trouble me," he added, murmuring something to himself.

"I didn't quite catch that," Martin said.

"I was quoting the English Prayerbook," Ramos answered. "One of the most sublime passages in the language. It says, 'The remembrance of these things is grievous unto us; the burden of them is intolerable.' I like that way of saying it."

Martin nodded. "Are those your unforgivable sins?" he asked.

"Unforgivable? Not to God," Ramos answered. "I am sure I was forgiven by God long before I forgave myself."

"So that was your act of contrition?" Lundberg asked quietly. "Going through all that?"

The old man nodded. "That and many other things. I tried to kill myself using piety and I almost succeeded. Only later did I understand that to refuse forgiveness is the only sin which cannot be forgiven."

"Why is that unforgivable?" Martin asked. "It seems fairly minor."

"Yes, that is the way we think," Ramos told him. "Yet think about it. What I said is that it cannot be forgiven, not that it is unforgivable."

"So what's the difference?"

The old man reached in his pocket and took out a silver dollar. Martin could see it was so worn the date could barely be made out and Liberty's face was almost featureless. Yet the inscription "In God We Trust" could still be read fairly easily. "I've carried this a long time," Ramos said. "It was given to me by the man who answered for me the same question you just asked." He pulled out another silver dollar, this one much less worn. "He gave me two, one to use and one to keep as a reminder."

Handing both coins to Martin he continued. "Suppose for a moment I am God and I give you these. I tell you they are tokens of forgiveness. One you are supposed to use for yourself and the other you are to keep for others. Are you with me?"

Martin nodded, puzzled where the old man was going. "Suppose you keep both," Ramos continued. "That means my forgiveness to you has not done you any good. You have not accepted it and used it as I wished. Or to put it another way, you have not received my forgiveness."

Martin nodded but asked, "And you can't forgive that, too?"

"Oh, no," said the old man. "I can give you billions of tokens of my forgiveness. I have a universe full of them. There is no limit. Yet there is no difference between one and a billion billions if you will not spend it. So it is not that your refusal is unforgivable, but that I, God, am not able to forgive you since you will not receive it. I cannot force you to do so. I can only mercifully put you out of your misery."

"No hellfire and damnation for pissing you off?" Martin asked.

"No, my friend, only an infinite sadness because with you I have failed in my love." As he said this, the old man's eyes filled with tears. "Because without you, my universe will be less than full in its perfection."

"No wonder they kicked you out," Martin replied. "Take away the threat of hell fire and the Church loses control."

"I find love a far more powerful mover than fear," the old man replied. "You, my friend, are a case in point. I don't think anyone could ever scare you into loving them. Not even Rosa."

"Scare me into loving them?" Martin asked. "You lost me there. That doesn't make any sense."

"Precisely!" the old man pounced. "It does not make sense. It's absurd to believe God uses that tactic. Give him some credit. God is not that stupid. Love does not foster fear, it drives fear away." He shrugged, added, "At least that's what San Juan said and I think he's right."

"The voice of one crying in the wilderness," Martin murmured.

"Yes and no," Ramos told him. "The San Juan who said that was another San Juan, but love often is a voice crying in the wilderness." He looked at the younger man intently. "Your mother is an example."

Martin nodded examining the coins. Then he grinned mischievously. "What if I give both away?" he asked. "Or spend them?"

"Then you're two dollars poorer and a thousand times more stupid," Ramos declared. "Don't you see, that's the same as keeping both?"

"You mean, both are ways of refusing to do what you intended?" His friend nodded. "And both...." He could not quite finish the thought.

"And both are equally arrogant," Ramos pointed out. "Both place one's own judgment in place of that of God." He shrugged. "That is what the theologians call 'original sin'."

"The sin of being original?" Lundberg quipped.

"No, the sin is in not being original," the old man laughed. "A good friend who is also a priest told me once that the most terrible part of his job is the confessional, and only because it is so boring. As he pointed out, most people make wretched sinners. They are not very good at it."

Later that afternoon, as they sat eating supper at Ramos' table, Martin asked if the old man had seen his cousin or Max. "No one was around when I came by their place this afternoon."

"Ah, yes," the old man told him. "I have a message for you. Jack asked me to tell you they have gone looking at some ruins near Chaco Canyon. Jack asked you to be sure his mail gets into the house. He's looking for something important."

Martin nodded. Earlier that year Jack bought a place further in toward town, paid for out of his poker winnings during his tour of duty in Southeast Asia. The place was even more run down than the old Vasques place and for the first two months Jackbear and Max stayed with Martin while they made the place livable. There was still a great deal left to do, as any place in the country always has left to do, but a couple of weeks before Jack mentioned the trip to Chaco Canyon as their reward to themselves for the hard work of getting the place in shape. "Why don't you come with us?" he asked Martin. "We'll be there after the tourists and before the snow flies."

"Maybe I will," said Martin. "I've never been there." While his tone was noncommittal, Jack recognized a reluctance in his cousin's voice. Martin was a loner when it came to exploring new country, and to him even three close friends was too much of a crowd after a few hours. So Jack did not think to mention it again before they left.

Now Martin found himself with confused feelings. While he knew all this, and had come to love Max as a friend, he found himself resenting the bond Max had with Jack, resenting that it was Max and not himself exploring Chaco Canyon with his cousin. Had he chosen to go he knew the other two men would have been glad to have him along, and would have included him in their conversation and company gladly. Yet with the two of them he felt like an outsider, always a fifth wheel or the girl without a date who's been asked to dance out of pity.

Covering his feelings Martin nodded, then got up and quickly and efficiently dispatched their supper dishes, washing them in the sink and placing them carefully on the wooden rack to dry. While he was doing this the old man rolled them a couple of cigarettes apiece in a hand-held machine and lit one of his. "I like this tobacco you brought," he said. "It's much lighter than the stuff we get at the store in town. It also has a very distinctive flavor and aroma."

"Oh, that's the wildwood weed I laced it with," Martin teased. "Max found some up the canyon last week."

"Left over from the world war," Ramos nodded, laughing. "He told me. Everyone grew hemp for rope back then, but this doesn't taste like any hemp I ever burned."

"Actually it's mild pipe tobacco," Martin confessed. "I found a pipe shop in Albuquerque and the guy there said this was good for cigarettes, too." The old man nodded and laid out a checkerboard on the kitchen table. He raised an eyebrow but Lundberg declined. "Thanks, but I better get down to the place. I have some things I want to get down on paper." Ramos nodded and, as he left, began setting up a chess problem from a paperback whose cover was worn and soiled.

Back at his own place Martin unloaded his truck and unpacked. Then, after taking care of several chores, he still felt restless, so he packed his flute into his rucksack and set off up the rise behind the house. Arriving at his spot he kindled a small fire and began playing the flute, starting with a simple tune he knew as a small child. Soon he was playing from the heart, staring into the coals of the fire and pouring out his joy and his pain through the wooden instrument in a long, wandering tune that drifted lightly across the pinones caressing the night air.

When he was done Martin sat quietly. Suddenly he was aware he was not alone. Looking up he saw the same two young men who had accosted him the spring before. This time, however, they were not armed and simply stood standing, looking at him. "*Buenos noches,*" Martin greeted them quietly, good evening. "Would you care to join me?" he added in Spanish, pointing to the other side of the fire. The men looked at one another, then quickly took seats on the other side of the fire.

Martin rolled himself a cigarette, handing the makings across the fire to the men when he was done. The leader shook his head, "Thank you, I don't smoke." But the other man nodded rolled himself one, lighting it from a splinter held in the fire.

Martin waited patiently, wondering what they wanted. When he was done with his cigarette he picked up the flute again and began to play a folk song he'd learned from Luiz, one he was sure was familiar to most Spanish speaking people in the area. Both men smiled and the leader got up and went off into the darkness. After a moment he came back carrying a large flat drum and looking toward Martin he raised his eyebrows in question. When Martin smiled and nodded, he began softly playing the drum to a wild, pagan beat which fitted the lilt of the flute like a key to its lock.

Caught up in the beat, Martin began to improvise, his fingers flying over the wooden tube while the beat of the drum carried the tune higher and faster until Martin knew he was playing far beyond his ability. Suddenly, without warning, it came to an end, and both stopped playing simultaneously. "Aie!" cried the second man, clapping his hands bringing things to a close. Then, for a while they said nothing as they sat, each staring into the fire.

Looking up Martin said, "*Yo soy Martin.*" I am Martin.

The leader nodded and replied in Spanish. "I know. You are Luiz's San Martin, *el lobo de navidad pasada.*" The wolf of Christmas past. He laughed. "I am Jimmy. This is Pedro. We didn't know who you were the other day when we came up here. We thought you were spying on us."

"No," said Martin. "I really wasn't. I was just up here and happened to see you. I come here often."

"Yes," said Jimmy. "We hear you often. A lot of the people think you are Kokopelli. They are scared."

"Scared of me?" Martin laughed." I only eat human flesh in Lent."

Pedro's eyes grew wide, but Jimmy laughed. "Be careful what you say, man. There are people around here who would believe you."

"Seriously?" Martin asked. "That's incredible."

"I know," Jimmy nodded. "Ask *el viejo*, the old man. Some of them never made it to the twentieth century."

"You understand I was just joking, don't you?" Martin asked Pedro. The other nodded but Lundberg could tell Pedro was far from convinced he didn't have horns under his hat. Slipping off his moccasins he held up his bare feet. "See, man," he said to Pedro. "I don't have cloven feet."

Jimmy laughed and patted Pedro on the shoulder. "Hey, man, he's right. Would *el viejo* have vouched for him if he was a devil?"

Martin suddenly realized that Pedro was not the only one who had failed to make it to the current century. *I better be careful with these two,* he thought. *They don't have much sense of humor when it comes to religious things.* "Does my flute playing really scare them?" he asked. Jimmy nodded and shrugged.

"The old man plays a flute," Martin pointed out.

Jimmy nodded again. "Yes, but he's *El Viejo*. People are scared of him, too. Because he has God's favor and can curse people."

"Curse people? I can't imagine him doing that," Martin protested. "He's been nothing but kind to me."

"You've never really made him angry, then," Jimmy told him. "The last man who did died of slow cancer."

"People think Ramos did that?" Martin asked, not quite able to believe what he was hearing.

Both other men nodded, fervently as if Martin had asked if the Virgin was really God's mother. *Jesus!* he thought to himself. *This is even worse than I imagined.* "Well, thank you for telling me," he said to Jimmy seriously. "I'll be very careful not to make him angry." Changing the subject he asked, "Do you fellows live around here?"

"No," Jimmy told him. "We're from Mora."

"Mora?" Martin said, surprised. "I hear that is a rough place."

"Only for *gringos*," Jimmy assured him. "You won't have any trouble there, not if people know who you are."

"You mean people in Mora have heard of me?" Martin was startled at the thought. "Man, it's a smaller world than I imagined."

"Oh, yes," Jimmy told him. "Luiz is one of my cousins and has told us all about you."

Martin nodded, was about to ask what brought them to the canyon, then thought better of it. They would tell him if they wanted him to know. He rolled another cigarette and picked up his flute. "*Otra vez?*" he asked. Want to do it again? Jimmy grinned and picked up his drum. "You start it this time" Martin told him, "and we'll see what the flute has to say."

Jimmy nodded and started playing his drum, beginning with a slow, almost lazy beat. Pedro closed his eyes and begin to clap softly, then began singing what sounded like a melancholy folk song. Martin waited until Pedro fell silent and picked up the mood, drifting high and falling low. Jumping to his feet Martin began to shuffle around the fire, playing his flute while Pedro followed, clapping his hands with the beat of the drum and occasionally giving out a melancholy cry. Then, as Jimmy picked up the pace with the drum, Martin followed close after with the flute, and an image began to form in his mind as his spirit took flight.

"*Yo soy el lobo de navidad!*" he cried, suddenly aware he was running fast, his nose close to the ground, the scent of his prey heavy in his nostrils. "Aieeeeeeeeeee!" he howled. "Aieeeeeeeeeee!" With his flute he took up the primordial cry, "Aieeeeeeeeeee!" the instrument cried, calling his brothers and sisters to join him in the hung. "Aieeeeeeeeeee!"

"*El es un lobo de navidad!*" Jimmy shouted, joining his cry with that of the pack. "*Yo soy un lobo!* Aieeeeeeeeeee!"

Martin could never remember how long this went on, the drumming, the singing, the cry of the pack. Time slipped away and he was never sure if they danced for hours or only moments. There were times it seemed it only began when the drum suddenly stopped in mid beat, yet while it was beating it seemed as if they were running forever.

When he opened his eyes, Martin saw the reason why the drum stopped. Standing there just at the edge of the light from the fire, its eyes glowing with the flames' reflection, stood a large black wolf. Pedro gasped and Jimmy scrambled to his feet, but the wolf never moved. It stood staring directly into the eyes of Martin.

"*Buenos noches, mi hermano,*" Martin whispered. "Good evening, my brother. How goes it with you?" Then, not knowing quite what else to do, he put his flute to his lips and began to play a high plaintive series of notes, almost like a cry. Putting back its head, the wolf joined him, its howl echoing from the stony faces along the canyon.

This went on for several long moments. Then the wolf stopped at looked at Martin as if he were smiling, and disappeared into the darkness.

"Jesus, Mary, and Joseph," breathed Jimmy, crossing himself. Pedro simply stood and stared, terrified. Then he cried out as a human shape took form, coming out of the shadows. The figure stopped at his cry and stood looking on from the edge of the light. It was Max.

Trouble! thought Lundberg, and he acted quickly. Crossing to Max he gave him a big hug and turned back to the other two men, smiling. "This is my true brother, Maximilliano. He is from Spain and we call him *el lobo cantando.*" The singing wolf.

Pedro looked as if he might die from fright and Jimmy crossed himself again. Max nodded solemnly and slowly made the sign of the cross over the two men. "*In nomine patri et filie et spiritu santo,*" he murmured. "Go with God in peace." Then, seating himself at one side of the fire he picked up the makings and rolled himself a cigarette. Martin sat down on the other side of the fire. "Is this a private affair or may I join you?" Max asked Martin, but looking directly at Jimmy.

"Oh, no, sir!" Jimmy added hastily. "Please do join us."

"Thank you," Max said, nodding at Martin and smiling. "We came in from Chaco Canyon about an hour ago."

Martin nodded. "Did you and the Bear have good hunting?" he asked, knowing the effect his words would have on Jimmy and Pedro.

Max picked up on the game afoot and answered, "Yes, indeed. Very good hunting. With the Bear, one always eats well."

"All is well with the Bear?" Martin inquired.

"Yes. The Bear needed to hibernate for a while and stayed down below." He nodded at the flute. "I heard you call so I came."

Martin nodded casually, as if they were discussing the weather. The other men looked frightened enough to wet their pants and Martin decided to bring the game to an end. "Are you hungry, my friends?" he asked the two of them, rubbing his own belly. "Would you come to my house for supper?"

Jimmy looked at him as if he'd been offered strychnine. "Oh, no, sir, thank you," he said politely. "We really need to get going."

"I'm, sorry to hear that," Martin responded sadly. "I was enjoying your company. I hope we haven't kept you from something important?"

"Well, you know, I told my aunt we'd be back by now and I don't want her to worry," Jimmy improvised. Pedro nodded solemnly.

"Of course not," Martin replied. "Well, good night. Please, come back any time."

The two fled into the darkness but Max and Martin could hear them scrambling all the way down the hill. When the sounds had faded away Max looked at Martin and asked, "What was that all about?"

"A new legend just got started in the Sangre Christo mountains," his friend laughed, telling him what had transpired. "Thanks for playing along. I couldn't help having a little fun with them."

Max nodded. "I just hope it doesn't backfire," he said. "These people could burn you for being a witch."

"I agree," said a voice out of the darkness. Both men jumped, then smiled as Ramos made his way to the fire. "But I don't think they will. The boys were off base coming back up here and they know it."

"Damn, Emil, you gave us a start!" Martin greeted his old friend with a grin. "I hope I didn't scare them off for good. We were just beginning to break the ice and be friends."

The old man looked at him gravely. "Those two *ladrones* you don't need for friends," he said harshly. "They were probably coming up here to rob you. They are part of the family who used to live here."

"They told me they were cousins of Luiz," Martin told him.

"It's not a kinship Luiz or I care to claim," Ramos declared. "They are cousins, distant cousins, by marriage. But only that. What happened? I only heard the last part."

So Martin told him of the events earlier this evening. When he came to the part about the wolf, the old man nodded and grinned. "Well, I can't think of anyone less predatory than our friend, Max," he said, shrugging and smiling. "Well, as the Good Book says, it's the wicked who flee when no one pursues."

"Thanks," said Max. "I can't, either."

"So what was it?" Martin asked the old man. "Were we just seeing things or was the wolf really here?"

"Where was the wolf standing?" Ramos asked, taking a flashlight from his pocket. Martin pointed to a gap between two bushes just to the right of the trail leading into the fire circle. Ramos got up and shone his light on the ground. "Come here," he said and both Max and Martin joined him. "Look," he said, pointing to a set of deep canine tracks in the dust near the bush. "Visions don't make those."

"Couldn't it be a dog?" Martin asked, not wanting to believe what his eyes were telling him. "Those tracks aren't all that clear."

The old man nodded. "It could be, I suppose, but I've never seen a dog that big anywhere around here. On the other hand, I've never lost a single goat except to coyotes. With a wolf that large around I think surely I would."

"So what are you saying?"

"I'm saying I don't know, but I'm going to keep close watch on my herd for the next few weeks," Ramos answered. "Even though I don't think it's a normal wolf. The tracks are too big."

"I didn't think wolves have been around here for years," Martin added. "I asked the game warden once when he was up."

"At least not the four legged variety," the old man snorted. "I better get back and check my goats."

"Maybe we better come with you," Martin suggested. Max nodded.

"That might be wise," the old man replied, and gathering up their stuff they followed him into the night.

Early the next morning Martin Lundberg rose before daybreak and when the sun rose he was already at his sitting spot, examining the tracks. Taking a coffee can from his rucksack he mixed a small box of plaster to make castings of the deepest tracks and sat smoking and reflecting as the plaster hardened. Then he decided to return later for the castings. Covering them with a light layer of dust he shouldered his satchel and picked up a thin oaken walking cane and began following the tracks leading away.

The tracks led downhill a few yards, then turned abruptly to the right where the wolf had changed its direction to avoid the old man coming up the path. Curiously enough, they circled around, approaching the fire site from the opposite side, but never getting closer than about fifty feet. Martin could see where the beast had stood for a while, as if listening to their conversation before continuing its trek up the slope.

Following the tracks Martin suddenly topped over the lip of a hidden coulee he never suspected was there. Over the lip of the coulee the tracks turned downhill and Martin followed quietly and cautiously. This was wild country, Forest Service land, and he did not want to provoke an attack by startling the wolf in its lair.

The coulee led downhill to a larger coulee which turned in the general direction of the road leading up the canyon. The tracks led across the sand of the bottom until they turned to the left and crossed over the bank of the gully. From where he stood at the bottom Martin could see the road crossing about a hundred yards farther down and smiled. He knew the road wound around getting to his place, but he never knew of this short cut. While it would be difficult to make in a sedan, and impossible in any vehicle in high water, his truck could probably make it and Jack's jeep could, for sure.

Twenty minutes later Martin was standing at the back of Jack's place. Again the wolf stopped as it had at the campfire the night before, apparently watching the house for a while before moving on. Then the tracks turned away, following a brush line which skirted the place, and led straight as a beeline into the desert plain. Looking at the sun Martin decided to follow the tracks for a while before stopping at his cousin's. It was still quite early and he could not see any smoke rising from the chimney in the front room or from the kitchen flue.

As he followed the tracks Martin noticed the wolf often stopped and turned back a pace or two, as if checking his trail for followers. This was a wise fellow, he decided, one who had been hunted before, and he doubled his own watchfulness as he followed the tracks. At one point he saw where they stopped, then started again, the stride lengthening threefold. Not far away he discovered the reason for this, the remains of what might have been a jack rabbit or perhaps a cotton tail. For a while he studied the scene, trying to figure why the rabbit had not run. Then he laughed, spotting a brown spotted feather blown under the scattered branches of a small bush. The wolf had surprised an owl, stealing his prey. Not far beyond were signs the beast had taken a nap afterwards.

Beyond the meager breakfast remains the tracks continued straight into the heart of the desert. After following them about a mile Martin was about to give up when they suddenly turned in the direction of the prevailing wind, running straight and true as an arrow. Curious what had distracted the wolf from his course, Martin followed quietly behind for about another mile to a point where a second, smaller set of tracks joined those of the singer. *Ah*, Martin thought, amused, *our singer has found a lady friend.*

However, the pattern of the tracks made little sense until he came to the lip of a deep gully and spotted his lupine friend caught up in the act of mounting a beautiful grey companion, a German shepherd. Though Martin was making no sound, the big black wolf seemed to sense his presence and without pausing his amorous activity turned his head to look at him, as if to say, "Do you mind?"

"*Perdoname, amigo*," Martin whispered, causing the bitch to start as she turned to look at him, as well. Then saluting the pair with a wave and a benediction, he turned back along his way.

When Martin came to Jack's place there were more signs of life, so he stopped to cadge breakfast. Max was in the kitchen when he stuck his head in the door and raised his spatula in greeting, nodding toward their wooden table where Martin could see three places set. "I saw you go by earlier and thought you might stop back," Max told him. "Tracking the wolf?"

Martin nodded and helped himself to a cup of coffee. Jack came in with a load of fire wood and greeted him. "Hey, medicine man!" he said, laughing. "Max told me you've been scaring the locals by calling up wolves."

"Ramos tells me these locals needed it," Martin laughed and told his cousin about the night before, some of which was new to Max, too. Then he told them about tracking the big wolf and his discovery of the short cut to his place going the back way. "Your jeep could make it easily," he said, "but I don't want to get a road started there. At least, not one that can be seen from the main track."

Jack nodded. "There's a way we can go there from the back of the house here. I discovered it a few weeks ago but I didn't realize it led up to your place." He thought a moment. "I bet that's the way those guys slipped up there last night."

Martin nodded. "It probably is. I spotted what looked like their tracks when I was following the wolf this morning." He laughed. "After last night, I don't think they'll be trying that again."

"From what Ramos said, it's probably a good thing," Max observed, serving their breakfast. "He has no use for them."

"He's probably right," Martin said. "You could have fooled me. They seemed like pleasant people."

"Yeah," said Jack. "They probably are very nice people. I bet they're still smiling when they shove the knife in your back." He nodded to Max. "We ran into a lot of folk like that in Southeast Asia."

"Not all of them locals," Max added, taking his seat. "Can we be silent a moment for grace?"

The other two fell silent and after a long moment of silence Max went on, "How blessed art Thou, Creator and Ruler of the heavens and the earth, of the mountains and the valleys and of all who dwell therein; how blessed art Thou who givest us this day and makest our hearts glad with the gifts of the harvest. How blessed art Thou, Creator and Ruler of the heavens and the earth for the gift of this food and this day."

Though it was not his custom to offer thanks, Martin was struck by the simple beauty of the blessing and joined the Bear with a heart felt, "Amen." Silence descended again as the men ate, broken only by the sounds of their utensils against the ceramic plates and occasional moans of culinary ecstasy. When he was done Jack sat back and rubbed his belly. "Damn, Max, you're going to make some fellow a fine wife some day."

"I hope so," Max laughed, delighted by their compliment. "Not much chance of that stuck out here in the mountains," he added softly and Martin would never forget the momentary flash of grief in the man's eyes. Yet it was gone as quickly as it came and Max said, "Well, you two can show your gratitude by doing the dishes."

"Hey, Max," Martin said as he was carefully putting away the plates he had just dried. "What did you mean by 'not all of them local'?"

"A lot of them were our own people," Jack answered bitterly, picking up the dish pan and going to the door to toss it out on the lawn.

"Our military people?" Martin wanted to know.

Max nodded. "Yes, although the civilians were worse. They looked at us like we were expendable equipment put there for their use."

214

"Fucking spooks," the Bear growled. "We'd have done the country a greater service by shooting those assholes."

Martin had rarely seen his cousin so angry outside of an immediate situation. "Hey, Jack," he said. "We don't have to talk about it. I was just curious what Max meant."

His cousin shook his head. "Don't worry," Max told him. "We talk about it all the time. That seems to help, somehow."

"It must have been awful," Martin replied.

"It was," Jack Bear said, much more calmly. "Believe me, you don't ever want to find out if you can help it." He shook his head. "I'm sorry, man. It still pisses me off. The way I usually handle it is to work it out on the wood pile."

"I wondered why you had so much," Martin observed carefully. To his relief Jack laughed.

"Yes, it does come in handy," Max added.

"Well, I haven't been what you've been through, but when I get pissed, I work it out on the ground," Martin responded, telling them about what the told man suggested when he was first cleaning up his place and about what happened when he did it. "You know, it was strange," he told them. "It was almost a mystical experience."

Jack laughed. "I'm not surprised. You and the old man are mystics." Max nodded his agreement.

"Oh, come on, Jack," Martin argued. "Quit pulling my leg. I'm the practical type and you know it."

"This is the guy who calls up wolves with his flute and talks to them like brothers?" Jack said to Max. "And he claims he's no mystic? Jesus, they'd have burned him at the stake three hundred years ago."

Max nodded. "They would in Europe. Here they'd have made him their shaman."

"All right, guys," Martin protested, raising his hands. "I can take a joke as well as anyone, but enough is enough, already."

Jack looked at Max, out of long friendship communicating without speaking. *He really doesn't know, does he?* his look said and Max's nod spoke agreement. *No, he really doesn't.*

"Well, old buddy," Jack Bear said quite serious. "We won't tease you about it any more." Max nodded and Jack continued, "But if we were

Indians I think we might call you whatever their name is for wolf."

"Black Wolf," Martin laughed. "Hey, I like that."

"No, Martin," said Jack Bear solemnly, shaking his head. "Not Black Wolf. No, we'd call you Fucking Wolf."

"Fucking wolf!" Martin howled, encircling his arms and moving his pelvis to mimic the wolf hard at work. He and Jack began to laugh.

"Honestly!" Max snorted, grinning. "You heterosexuals can be so gross. Personally, I'd call you Schtuppin' Wolf."

10. El Lobo De San Juan

Indian Country, New Mexico. Searing heat. Air so dry my lungs feel like cracked leather. My body screams for moisture, screams for me to give in, to swallow the precious ounces of water I carry in my mouth even though it will give only a passing instant's relief. My legs ache beyond belief, go numb, my knees buckling constantly, making me stumble from side to side like a drunkard, drunk with fatigue.

"Why am I doing this?" my soul screams. "O God, if there is a God, tell me this," I demand. Yet no answer comes from the burning sand beneath my feet, no answer from the cloudless sky, no answer from the bright yellow star searing the earth at mid day, no answer from the God Unknown. There is only a mocking answer from deep within me, an insane sing-song answer chanted out to the pounding cadence of my blistered feet,

> *flower child walks down the street*
>
> *where only hostile faces greet*
>
> *the weary pounding of his feet*
>
> *who runs a thousand miles a week*
>
> *to find a cross that he must meet*
>
> *take all the shit that he can eat*
>
> *tomorrow...*

I try to shake off this pounding chant, to focus my mind far away, to another time, another place, to fly with the condor high above the torment, to shut out the drumming insanity of my personal devil's song,

> *a silent moon face, cold hard grin*
>
> *fills the sky, looks down at him*
>
> *you're such a fool to love all men*
>
> *for don't you know they'll do you in*
>
> *and never know they've done a sin*

217

> *then do it to you once again*
>
> *tomorrow .....*

Yet I cannot shake it, and the insane sing-song grows ever more loud, ever more insistent, ever more powerful, driving me down and down with its yammering words crying,

> *then when you finally learn to hate*
>
> *you find you learned it all too late*
>
> *they changed the rules and locked the gate*
>
> *and tell you now that you must wait*
>
> *to see what is to be your fate*
>
> *before you meet with death your date*
>
> *tomorrow....*

"Why am I doing this?" my soul screams once more. "Why am I doing this? Why am I running across this God forsaken desert? O God, if there is a God, deliver me from this insanity!"

Although it is unexpected, this time there's an answer. At first it seems mysterious, unreal, as if to protect itself my mind has gone around the bend, and perhaps it has, I think. For what I hear at first is the soft low song of a flute drifting softly over the desert plain. Surely my mind is gone now, yet the song of the flute grows ever louder, lightening my heart, my steps. What I feel is the melody falling upon me like ocean mist bathing my soul, washing away the torment, the pain, the shame that weighs me down, then drifting down over my aching legs like soft light giving radiant power.

Then, as in a vision, far off I see way in the distance the Indian, the runner from my dream, now standing high on the hill by the emerald pool, playing his flute, calling me home. From my tortured brain a memory comes to surface, the memory of an old man standing at a graveside softly singing the refrain from an ancient hymn,

> *...come home, come home, come home,*
>
> *ye who are weary come home...*

Then the flute joins itself to the voice of the old man and they become as one, lifting my soul from my body, giving it wings to fly along the ground like a hawk in full hunt. Far and away across the plain I hear the drums, the eternal drums, the heartbeat of Earth Mother calling me, singing to me, "RUN! run! RUN! run! RUN! run! RUN!...." I look up and see my brother, the black wolf, running wild and free just ahead of me, and a cry of exultant *joy rises in my throat as I scream my hunting call, "AIEEEEEEE!"*

Suddenly I am aware of others, other men clad as I am in breach cloth and moccasins, other men running beside me holding me up by my arms to keep me from falling on my face. They bring me to an old man, wrinkled and dwarfed below the massive buffalo head rising from his own. He comes and holds a gourd to my lips. "Spit!" he tells me, and I look at him without comprehension. "The water in your mouth," he tells me. "Spit it into the gourd." I look to the other men. They stare back, then one of them nods and I do as the old man commands me, spit my mouthful of water into the gourd. A snaggle tooth grin bathes his face as the old man lets out a whoop of triumph and pours the water I have spat out over my head for the others to see. They yell in acclamation and someone hands me a bucket of water, dipping the gourd for me to drink and pouring the rest over my head. Then I hear my own voice, cracked but deep with joy as it joins the song of the others to the deep thunder of the drums.... (Martin Quinn's journal)

"I think he's all right." The voice of the old man came from far away, as if he were standing down the hall. Yet Martin could smell him, smell the pleasant mixture of tobacco and *piñon* smoke and chiles on his breath as he bent over the cot where he was lying. Yet he was puzzled at the anger he could hear in the man's voice.

"Daddy!" he tried to say. "I did it!" But only a indistinct mumble escaped his lips and he heard another voice, surely the voice of an angel expressing concern.

"Are you sure?" the angel asked the man. "He looks awful. Look at his feet. They are bleeding!"

"The bleeding has stopped," the voice of the ancient one assured the angel. "The blisters will heal." A dry chuckle followed the words. "He certainly won't be chasing around much for a few days."

Again Martin tried to speak, to open his eyes to learn who it was who spoke, but a blinding sheet of pain across his back tore at his consciousness, causing him to twitch and moan. "Lie still, Martin," said the voice of the angel. "Lie still and rest. Let yourself heal." He felt a pleasant coolness as a wet wash rag wiped his forehead, bathed his pain-filled chest.

Who is she? he wondered. "Mother?" he managed to whisper, his voice hoarse and husky as if he had been shouting.

"He's asking for Rosa," the angel said, her voice full of fear. Martin wondered why she was so afraid, especially of his mother.

"*Yo soy aqui, Martin*," said the strong voice of the ancient, the Voice he seemed to recognize from before his birth, and he understood. He finally understood. *I must have died running across the desert, died of heat stroke or dehydration,* he thought. *Now I'm standing before the Throne, face to face with the Ancient of Days.* Summoning all the strength he could muster, Martin began to whisper the Act of Contrition, but the Voice interrupted.

"*Te absolve*," came the muttered response, speaking Latin. "*In nomine patri, et filie, et spiritu santo....*" I absolve you. A strong, gentle hand made the sign of the Cross on his brow. "Rest now, my son, rest and heal."

So I'm not dead after all, he thought, surprised. *Unless Purgatory has confessors. Which makes sense. But who is the priest? I know his voice from somewhere.* Then another wave of pain across his back washed over him like sheet lightening, carrying him over the threshold of pain into the comforting balm of darkness. Yet even through the darkness he could hear what he thought was a drum playing softly, and the high, soft voice of a flute or perhaps a singer, lifting him like a child, holding him gently, carrying him safe in its melody through the darkness of night.

A soft light was filtering in the open window when Martin awoke just before dawn. For a while he lay still, trying to figure out where he was. The *vigas* and the closely laid cane of the ceiling reminded him of his own home, but the room was somehow different. Looking to his right he saw a smooth white plaster wall hung with a bright Navajo rug. Then looking to his left, he saw a young woman sitting next to his bed asleep in a rocking chair. She was beautiful, her dark brown hair gathered in braids falling across a well developed breast of ample proportion, now accentuated by a traditional white fiesta blouse and a simple silver pendant hanging from a leather thong. A wash basin sat on the table beside her chair and her hands held a crumpled wash cloth. He looked at the pendant, then smiled. Etched deep into the silver shell was the dark figure of Kokopelli, the mysterious flute player still said to roam the wastelands of Indian country.

Hearing a soft snore Martin lifted his head to look across his feet and another wave of pain washed across his back, this time less intense. Shutting his eyes against the pain, he waited for it to pass, propping himself up on his elbows. When he opened his eyes again he saw a young Indian man sitting slumped in a straight chair, a small round drum loosely clutched in his hands. Puzzled, Martin looked at the young woman again and recognized her as someone he knew well. Yet he could not remember who she was or recall her name.

As if feeling his gaze, the young woman's eyes opened and met his. A radiant smile lit up the room like the morning sun as she leaned forward to clutch his hands. "Martin!" she said softly. "Oh, Martin! You're awake. Thank God."

Stephanie! he thought, starting to call her name, then stopped. This is not Stephanie, he told himself, wondering who Stephanie was. *Stephanie is in Africa*, he remembered. Then he knew. "Carmelita," he said, surprised how glad he was to see her, and then, surprising himself as well as her, he raised himself and kissed her lightly on the lips. Carmelita was startled but did not pull away, kissing him back, instead. Realizing what he had done he flushed. "I beg your pardon," he said. "I didn't realize what I was doing." Then realizing how those words could be mistaken he mumbled, "I mean ... well ... I'm not really sorry, but...."

"Oh, that's all right," Carmelita answered without thinking. "I don't mind." Then she realized what she had just admitted and blushed, dropping her eyes to her lap.

A dry chuckle from the other side of the room called them away from one another. "You're amazing, my friend," said Ignacio, crossing to the foot of bed and smiling at Martin. "You almost ran your feet off yesterday and here you are today, courting the girls before sunrise."

"Carmelita's not the girls," Martin protested, his head still not quite clear. "She's an angel."

"I would have to agree with that," came another voice from the door, laughing. "At least most of the time." Martin looked up to see the old man come into the room, followed by Max.

"Emil!" Martin said, surprised. "Max! When did you get here?"

"Last night after the angel called Luiz and sent him for me," Ramos chuckled, crossing to his bedside. Max took a chair beside Ignacio. "She thought you were going to die." He looked at the young Indian sternly. "I understand some of the people in the kiva did, too."

Ignacio nodded, his face grave. "They gave him the hardest run," he said. "No one has ever completed it before. I didn't know or I would have said something to him." He nodded at Martin.

"Just as well you didn't," Martin said, sitting up. "If I'd known it was impossible I doubt I could have done it," he added dryly. He looked at the flute. "As it was, your flute saved me, Ignacio. You were playing, weren't you? He whistled part of a tune which clearly startled Ignacio.

"I was playing in the kiva," Ignacio responded. "Deep down at one of the lowest levels. There is no way you could have heard me."

"Except he did," the old man pointed out. "Have you ever played that tune before? Or heard it?"

Ignacio shook his head. "No," he said. "Never. It was strange to me. For some reason I was thinking about a deep pool of water in a sacred place my father told me about a long time ago, and it just came to me as I played." He shook his head in wonder.

The old man nodded. "I thought so," he muttered. He looked at Martin. "Was that it?" he asked. "Just the voice of the flute?"

"No," Martin answered. "There were the drums and the black wolf. And the old man standing by the grave singing." He told them all which had happened as he ran, how the call of the flute and the beat of the drums and the running wolf brought him home. "For a while there I thought I died," he concluded. "I thought my soul was leaving my body for parts unknown." He sighed. "I'm a little sad it didn't. I have never, ever experienced joy like that before. Not ever. It was like God touched me with his little finger, like you described. There was nothing more I wanted."

"Perhaps he did, my friend," the old man told him. "Perhaps you died and came back to us, anyway." He looked at Ignacio. "I gather the Council knows nothing of this?"

Ignacio nodded. "They know something very deep happened. No one has ever done what he did, and no one has ever been led back to the kiva by a black wolf and a raven. They are just not sure what it means."

"You mean the wolf was really there?" Martin asked, troubled by the thought. "I thought I was just dreaming him."

"No," Ignacio said. "They told me the black wolf was running right in front of you and the raven was flying right above." He laughed. "It scared the crap out of them. At least it did some of them." Then he looked at Martin. "You need to tell them what you told us." The old man snorted and looked fierce, as if he were about to object, but Ignacio was adamant. "No, it is a gift of the Powers to the People. Despite those who thought evil of him. I think they will punish themselves."

The old man nodded. "I hope they choke on their envy!"

"That would be too swift," Ignacio remarked with a wicked grimace. Turning to Martin he said, "When you are ready I will take you to them."

"Let them come here," Ramos growled. "The medicine is his."

"I know, but these things are best done in the kiva," Ignacio responded, his face an unreadable mask.

"He's right," Martin said, tossing back his covers. Trying to sit up, he almost fell, and would have had Carmelita not caught him.

"Martin!" she said, pushing him back onto the bed. "What do you think you're doing? You're hurt."

"She's right," Ignacio told him. "It doesn't have to be now."

"All right," Martin said. "I'll rest through the day. Tell them I will be there at sundown. Ramos will be coming with me. Max, too."

"They are not allowed in the kiva," Ignacio reminded him, clearly not liking what he had to say. "No one is who has not been initiated."

"Then I will not be there, either," Martin said. He placed his hand on the old man's shoulder. "This is my father in the spirit world. Tell them that and tell them Max is my spirit brother, Singing Wolf. It is a matter of personal integrity."

Ignacio was obviously disturbed being the messenger of such news to the elders of his people. Yet he nodded and smiled. "They're too damned stiff necked," he said. "He's my spirit father, too. I'll tell them that. Maybe the evil thinkers will choke."

Three days later they were driving home together in an old carry-all owned by Ellen Hayes, the primary teacher at the pueblo, while Max drove Martin' truck. Hearing what happened Ellen insisted on driving them back to the canyon, and only a promise to Ignacio kept her from peppering them with questions. "I don't want to intrude," she said, "but I am curious what happened. One of the reasons I teach for BIA is so I can collect folk stories from the pueblos. From what the kids at school told me, another legend just got started."

Martin sighed. He was tired of the story now, tired of the celebrity he never sought and anxious only to get home. Reaching in his satchel he pulled out a spiral notebook. "I wrote it down," he said, handing her the notebook. "You're welcome to read it if you wish." Ignacio frowned at him, but Martin said, "No, Ignacio, it's only my story. There's nothing in it about ceremonial secrets." Turning back to Ellen he added, "The only thing I ask is that you ask my permission before publishing it."

The temptation was too much. Ellen agreed readily. Pulling over to the side of the road, she asked Ignacio to drive and even before the young Indian was back on the pavement, she was pouring over Martin' cramped writing, stopping only to ask him to decipher an occasional word she could not read. When she was done she sat silent a long while. "Goodness," she said, looking at Martin with something bordering on awe. "Wolf and Raven both. I'm not sure what that is for the Tewa, but for the Plains people that's powerful medicine." She thought a moment more. "I bet that's what they name you, Martin, Wolf Raven."

"Raven Wolf," he corrected, nodding. Ignacio looked at him askance. "I didn't say it in Tewa," Martin argued, "so it doesn't count. Besides, it's my name to use now. I can give it to whom I please, can't I?" Shrugging, Ignacio nodded and turning to Ellen Martin asked, "What's the meaning of those for the plains Indians?"

"It varies," Ellen told him. "There's been so much intermingling of traditions it's hard to sort out. The raven is considered a very sacred bird for most native Americans, and the wolf is a very powerful symbol, too. What is incredible is for them to both be a person's totem."

"Like totem pole?" Carmelita asked.

"Yes," Ellen replied. "Animals are known for their special powers and generally speaking, when the animal appears during initiation, its powers are given to the person being initiated." She looked at Martin. "I hear they were really rough with you," she said, "so having both the wolf and the raven come to your aid is a very powerful message to them. Especially when it's a black wolf."

"What's the significance of a black wolf?" Ramos asked.

"I'm not sure, exactly, but they are relatively rare. More so in some places than white wolves. So it's like an exclamation point at the end of a very powerful message from the Universe." Ellen looked at Ignacio, who was clearly uncomfortable with this discussion of sacred things, yet nodded confirmation and shrugged. "The Tewas are very reluctant to talk about their spiritual and ceremonial things," Ellen added.

"That's how we protect them," Ignacio told her. "Especially from the Spanish, who tried to rob us of our whole way of life."

"In exchange for their brand of Catholicism," Martin remarked. "A very poor trade for your people."

Ignacio smiled at him. "Your people now, too, Martin. You've been initiated into the kiva. You're one of us."

"I'll have to take your word for that," Martin laughed. "I don't even understand the language."

"Several of our sisters told me they'd be very glad to teach you," the young Indian laughed, drawing a sharp look from Carmelita. "Although it would be more proper for you to learn from the men. The women have their own ways and their own tongue."

Ellen nodded. "That makes it very confusing for an outsider."

"Well, it's confusing to this insider, too," Martin said. "Tell me more about the wolf and the raven totems."

"Wolves are very intuitive creatures," Ellen said. "They seem to know without knowing, and they travel freely back and forth into sacred territory. I would guess this is particularly true of the black wolf. Black is the color of the inner way, the introspective world of dream time for the plains people, and I would suspect a black wolf would be considered to travel very easily between this world and the spirit world of dream time."

Martin nodded. "That sounds strange but somehow it feels right," he said. "I don't understand it, but it does."

"Knowing without knowing," Ramos murmured, chuckling. "That's you, my friend. The intuitive wolf."

"Come on, Emil," Martin protested. "I'm no mystic." There was a stunned silence, then everyone broke out laughing.

"You continually surprise me that way," the old man said. "What is so delightful is that you are so unaware of it." Ignacio nodded. "Who is it who sits for hours and hours in his own sacred place playing his flute and staring into the fire?" Ramos asked.

"That's not mystic," Martin argued. "I do that to relax."

"Who calls the black wolf with his flute and talks to him like his brother? Wouldn't you call that mysterious?"

"What's this?" Ellen wanted to know, and Martin hesitatingly told her the story of the black wolf who had come to the fire.

When he was done Ellen looked at him disbelieving. "You say you're no mystic?" she laughed. "There are people who would kill to have that kind of experience."

"It was just coincidence," Martin responded.

"Right, and the wolf and raven just happened to show up wen you were making your initiation run," she retorted, grinning. "It happens all the time. Like once maybe in a thousand years, if that."

"So tell me about the raven," Martin asked, trying to shift their talk in a safer direction. "What's the meaning of the raven?"

"I almost hate to tell you," Ellen laughed. "The raven is the shaman's bird. It flies into the Great Unknown which lies at the center of the Universe and returns with special knowledge of the sacred Mysteries." She looked at him with something bordering compassion. "I'm afraid you're stuck with it, Martin," she told him gently. "This is a message from the Universe, so to speak. It says very clearly who you are, who you were created to be, and maybe who you were in previous lives. For sure it is an indication of who you are now and you can either accept this or fight it." She shook her head almost sadly, as if she'd just told him his cancer was terminal.

"What are you telling me?" Martin asked, aware of the others, yet not willing to wait until they were alone for an answer.

"Well, I'm no shaman," Ellen said. "I am a trained anthropologist, and I've studied the shamanic tradition. From what I can tell, you're in for a very interesting life, one with a lot of pain, although most of that may be behind you. I don't know. I'm no clairvoyant."

Ramos nodded and asked, "What makes you say that, Ellen?"

She shrugged. "I was thinking about the death experience shamanic traditions talk about. Somehow I was thinking that's what Martin' run was about. Shamanic death. Maybe an NDE."

"An Indy?" Carmelita asked. "What's that?"

"Sorry. N-D-E. That's medical short hand for near death experience. Sometimes people go through them in the emergency room or surgery. It's an out-of-body experience as if the person is standing off to one side watching things happen, seeing themselves lying there dead. As rough as Martin' initiation was I think it's possible he may have had a near death experience. It would fit with shamanic initiation in most traditions, coming close to death and returning from it's gates."

"I thought I was dead," Martin told them. He smiled at Carmelita. "I thought Ramos was God and Carmelita was an angel."

"I think you were dead," Ramos corrected him, not allowing him to divert the conversation with a joke. "I think Ellen's right."

"What's the connection between that and the shaman?" Martin asked. "I'm not a medicine man and I wasn't trying to become one."

"It's the Universe that chooses the shaman," Ellen replied. "Not the other way around. This is the process the shaman often goes through to gain his power to do what he does."

Martin shook his head. "I still don't understand."

"Don't or won't?" Ramos muttered softly, too softly for Martin to hear. Carmelita did and jabbed the old man in the ribs with an elbow. He grunted and looked at her sharply, but Carmelita glared right back.

Ellen heard, too, but chose to ignore the old man's jibe. "Well, there is an old Siberian legend about the wounded healer," she explained to Martin. "Siberia is where the word 'shaman' comes from. The legend says that before he or she can become a healer, the young man or woman is led out into the wilderness by a shaman and left there over night. During the night the earth opens up and the demons responsible for human disease and sorrow come out. They literally tear the young shaman to pieces, killing him and devouring his flesh before they return to the underworld and the earth closes. Yet when dawn comes, the earth opens again and the shaman comes forth, reborn and fully restored to health. From that time on, he has power over every demon who tasted his flesh. This is what gives a shaman the personal power to heal."

There was silence for a long while after Ellen stopped taking. The first to speak was Martin. "Jesus," he said, as if breathing a prayer.

"Exactly," Ramos answered dryly. "Consider what that says about the Mass, my friend. 'Hoc est corpus meus....' That literally means, 'eat my flesh and give me power to heal you.'"

"It's too much," Martin said. "No one in their right mind would want it." Both Ellen and Ignacio nodded their agreement. Carmelita looked very puzzled but kept silent. Only Ramos smiled, somewhat sadly and nodding.

"That doesn't seem to matter," the old man told him gently. "At least, it never did with anyone I know." He held up both forearms so the scars on his wrists showed plainly to Martin but not to Ignacio or Ellen. Carmelita, now seated between them frowned, but again she said nothing.

"You mean...?" Martin nodded toward the old man's scars but left the thought unfinished. He was aware of the others listening, uncomprehending, but neither he nor Ramos enlightened them. There is no explaining to those who do not understand at least the questions. The conversation was between the two of them and it was as if they were speaking soul to soul within their own milieu in another universe.

"The rest of your life is your resurrection," Ramos concurred. "There is no way of avoiding it and fighting it will only bring you more pain." Slipping into an ancient tongue, the old man said something else, something Martin was surprised to find he understood where the others did not. "Thy destiny is to be shaman, my brother. Thy work is to heal and thy name be Raven Wolf." The words hung in the air like dust in the stillness of a vast cavern, as if the old man were speaking *ex cathedra* on Mount Zion. Not understanding what had passed between the two men, the others looked at one another uneasily within the silence as it gathered, and for many miles the passage of the carry-all was marked only by the sounds of the engine's deep murmur and the hiss of the tires along the rough surface of the road leading home.

Martin and the old man found Max waiting for them patiently when they arrived at the canyon. Over her strong objections that Martin needed further nursing and from her, Carmelita had been dropped off at her mother's house in town, and Ellen, sensing the men wanted to talk took her leave with Ignacio soon after they arrived. "I'd like to come back and talk to you both," she said in leaving. The old man nodded and Martin gave her a hug, looking deep into her eyes and smiling as he spoke a blessing for her in the ancient tongue. Ellen looked startled but seemed oddly reassured as Ignacio drove them down the dusty drive, looking back twice once as they crossed the stream to the main road.

Max looked at Martin with wry amusement. "I think you just claimed another heart," he said.

Ramos nodded and said to the younger men. "I don't know how it is for you, but this kind of thing makes me hungry." They both nodded. "Let me see what I have for us to eat," Ramos added, turning toward the house.

"I hope you don't mind," Max told him, following after. "I was a couple of hours ahead so I took the liberty of bringing lunch." He nodded toward the old man's house. "It's warming on the stove."

"Gracious!" declared Ramos. "Mind? I wish I could afford to hire you for a housekeeper."

Max laughed. "I'll remember that," he said. "I may need a job some day when Jack kicks me out."

"Jack's not going to kick you out!" Martin argued.

Max shrugged. "Well, some day he may decide to get married."

"Then you can live at my place as long as you like," Martin told him. "And if I'm married we'll mix some mud and build you your own place."

"Not if I can talk him into living up here," Ramos declared.

Martin was surprised to see the look of gratitude that flooded Max's face. "Thanks," he told the others. "I really appreciate it."

"*De nada*," Ramos murmured. It is nothing. "You are one of us. Now let's eat."

After lunch Martin cleaned up the dishes while Max and the old man took seats on the front porch. When he came out a few minutes later, Max rose from his chair and told them he needed to head home. "Let me drive you," Martin said, patting his jeans for keys.

Max laughed and handed them to him. "I almost forgot. Thanks, but no. I need to walk the kinks out after the long drive this morning. You need to talk, and I'm about ready for a nap."

"And so?" said Ramos as they watched him walk down the drive to the stream crossing. "There are still a couple of things I want to know." He fell silent, waiting.

"Well, I can guess what one of them is," Martin replied, a little testily. The old man make no response. "One is why Carmelita was there in the first place, right?"

"No," the other told him, shaking his head. "I know why Carmelita was there. She was there because you were. That is very evident."

"Come on, Emil, give it a rest," Martin complained. "There's nothing going on there as far as I'm concerned." Ramos replied with silence. "So what did you want to know?" Martin asked.

Well, if you care to tell me, I want to know what else happened out there," the old man responded. "When you were telling it there seemed to be some things you left out. Maybe not, but that's what I thought."

"You don't miss much, do you?" Martin laughed. "I give up, Emil. How did you know?"

"Because I think I have been there, too," Ramos said. "I think what I experienced with *los penitentes* was like what you just experienced with *los indios*. For me there were lots of strange things which happened."

"Like in The Last Temptation of Christ?" Martin asked.

"Yes," Ramos replied. "I'm surprised to hear you've read it. It's not that well known."

Martin shrugged. "A friend recommended it and I came across a copy by accident in the library at the University."

"Surely you don't think it was accidental," Ramos admonished.

"I did at the time, but now I don't know. Maybe reading it set me up to experience what I did out there." He looked troubled at the thought.

"Or maybe reading it helped get through it," the old man countered. "Have you thought of that?" Martin shook his head, and Emil Ramos waited patiently for him to speak. That his young friend would speak was not in doubt, but the silence lasted so long Ramos wondered whether he were mistaken.

Finally Martin broke silence. "It was very strange," he said. "It was as if every bad dream, every nightmare I ever had happened all over again at once." The memory made him shudder. "If I'd known about that, I would not have gone."

"Yes," Ramos agreed. "Yet you would have missed the greater blessing that goes with it."

"You keep saying that but I don't know what you mean."

"You will, my friend," Ramos assured him. "You will, but for now just tell me what happened."

"I don't know how else to describe it," Martin said apologetically. "It was as if out there I met the Devil face to face and discovered he was in me."

Ramos nodded enthusiastically. "Excellent!" he said. "You've got it exactly right!"

"Excellent?" Martin was surprised. "It didn't seem very excellent to me. It was awful. Almost overwhelming."

The old man bobbed his head. "Yes, I know it was. I'm not denying that, but some people make the mistake of thinking evil is outside themselves. Their Devil is someone else."

"That's what the Church teaches," Martin observed dryly. "It's also stated that way pretty clearly in the Bible."

"That is precisely where the Church is wrong," Ramos said, quite emphatic. "None of the great mystics really agree with that teaching. They knew the evil in their lives stemmed mostly from within themselves."

"Mostly, but not entirely."

"Of course not. The evil in me is distinct from that in you. So in that sense there is evil outside ourselves. What I am saying is that the Devil lies within each of us. In both senses of the word." Ramos looked at Martin gravely. "I think most people cannot stand the idea. It makes them too responsible for their choices. So they make up a mythological figure to act like the scapegoat did for pious Jews on the Day of Atonement. They pile all their soiled clothing on their Devil and drive him out into the wilderness. That way they don't have to do the work of cleansing their garments. The psychologists have a name for this but I cannot remember what it is."

"The objectification of self?" Martin suggested. "Or transference?"

"You are a storehouse of information today," Ramos laughed. "Yes, to both, and they call the process 'scapegoating'. That's what the story of the Fall is all about. The man blamed the woman and the woman blamed the snake, and underneath their objections is the strong suggestion God is responsible because this is how he chose to make the universe in the first place." The old man shook his head. "And we wonder why things don't change."

"'The Devil made me do it?'" Martin laughed, quoting a contemporary comedian. "I like that."

"I imagine you do, but its more like 'your Devil made me do it' said when one is talking to God," Ramos answered. "It's like asking what God expected when he gave us free will."

Martin nodded and thought a while. "So all that stuff I experienced is in here?" he said, touching his chest. Ramos nodded. "So how do I change it?" Martin wanted to know. "How do I control it?"

Ramos looked at him sadly. "So long as you think you can control it you will fail," he said. "The truth is that human beings cannot control these things very well or for very long. The only source of help for us is something much greater than ourselves."

"You mean God?" Martin asked bluntly.

Ramos nodded. "That is one way of putting it, but there are many others."

Martin shook his head. "I'm sorry, but I can't accept that right now."

"You don't have to apologize," the old man told him. "It is something you must do for yourself, not others. Yet I think when you have experienced enough pain at your own hands, and seen what pain your best efforts causes for others, you will. Not until then, but you will."

"What makes you so damned sure?" Martin demanded, a bit testy.

Ramos shook his head. "Because you are so much like me!" he said as sharply as Martin had spoken. "Like me, you're full of yourself and blind to it!"

"Well pardon me all to hell!" Martin declared, jumping to his feet and stalking off down the drive to his truck.

"Martin, please!" the old man shouted after him but he got no answer. Slamming the door to the ancient truck, the younger man started it with a roar and slammed it into gear, popping the clutch and spewing gravel from the spinning tires as he sped off down the road to his own place.

"Aiee, *Dios!*" Emiliano Ramos cried, covering his face with a hand. "I have done it again." Too clearly he remembered another time, saying exactly the same words in the same tone to his only son just before the young man left for war, the war from which he would never return. "Dear God, forgive me," the old man wept. "Forgive me for going too fast, trying too hard and thinking I could keep him from repeating my mistakes. Do not let him suffer from my poor judgment. Please, help him forgive me, too."

That evening, when Martin came to bridge the estrangement, he found the old man in bed with a high fever. Nor did his friend recognize him, at first calling him Chico, a name he'd never heard mentioned in all their talks over the years. Taking a basin of cool water he began to bathe his friend, trying to break the fever, but the old man became chilled, and even though he was sweating profusely, shivered violently under two quilts. Becoming alarmed, Martin ran back to his place to get the truck, intending to take the old man to the hospital in town, but when he returned, Emiliano was sitting in front of the fireplace, wrapped in a quilt and in his right mind. "Hey," he said as Martin rushed in the door. "I'm feeling a little sick."

"A little?" said Martin. "I came to take you to the doctor."

"Were you here before?" the other asked.

"Up until ten minutes ago when I went to get the truck to take you to town," Martin answered. "You were sort of out of it."

Emiliano Ramos nodded. "I thought you were someone else. Then when I woke up and no one was here, I thought I dreamed it."

"No, you called me Chico," Martin answered.

Ramos nodded. A look of infinite sadness came over his face at the mention of the name. "Ah," he said. "Did you and I have an argument, or did I dream that, too?"

"No," Martin said. "We had an argument. I came up to apologize for having such a short fuse."

"Would you mind telling me what it was about?" Ramos looked at him sadly. "Unless it is too...." He shrugged.

Martin nodded. His face went flat and he repeated verbatim what had been said. "That's what I think was said, but I'm very tired and apparently very touchy, too."

"It's close enough," Ramos told him. "I had almost the same argument with Chico the day he left for Korea." Shaking his head sadly, the old man told Martin about his son. Tears formed in his eyes as he spoke, ran down his cheeks unnoticed.

Silently Martin rose from his seat and put his arms around the old man. For a moment Ramos tried to resist, but he was far too sick to keep down his grief any longer. Clinging to Martin like a child he began to weep with deep, racking sobs, repeating his son's name over and over again. After a while his sobs began to abate, and he pulled back and looked at his young friend. "At the risk of pissing you off once again, my friend," he said in English, "you have a very healing presence. I have never wept like that before for my only son."

"Perhaps the only son of your loins," Martin told him, "but I meant what I said at the pueblo. With anything that matters, you are my father." He smiled as he looked at the old man. "You know what made me so angry? What I suspect really pissed Chico off, too?"

Ramos nodded. "I was pushing the river," he replied. "Not to mention minding your business rather than mine. You had every right to be angry."

Martin shook his head. "Maybe so, but what got my goat was that you were probably telling me a truth I didn't want to hear. Maybe I can't accept it now, but I suspect you may be right."

"I shouldn't have pushed," Ramos replied. "It looked like you were about to make some of the same mistakes I've made and I wanted to save you from that pain. That is something I am not able to do." He risked a grin. "Not even God, assuming for a just a moment there is one, can do that. All anyone else can do is help pick up the pieces if you need us."

"I will always need you," Martin assured him. "You're not allowed to die until after I stop needing you."

"Thank you, I think," Ramos laughed. Then he grew somber again. "I feel like another attack is coming on, and I want to say this while I am still a little clear headed. You are everything this man could ever want in a son. I am proud you consider me your father in spirit."

It was Martin' turn to have trouble seeing for his tears. "Thank you," he said. "Now is there anything I can get you?"

"Kidney medicine," Ramos told him. "There should be some in the medicine chest over the sink." Martin was gone a moment, then came back with two plastic pill bottles. "That one," Ramos said, pointing to the larger.

Martin read the label and opened the bottle. "There's only one pill in here," he said. "Do you have more?"

"No," Ramos answered. "Give me the one now and that should last me for a few hours. Could you go to town and get more?"

"Of course," Martin said. "What do I do, call Dr......" he read the label. "Dr. Cosmo? Is that his name?"

"No," Ramos told him. "He retired a couple of years ago and moved away. I don't know where he is. Maybe Luiz knows who took his place. "He shuddered violently and drew the quilt close around his shoulders.

Martin helped him back to the bed, then had Ramos wait until he got fresh sheets. "These are wringing wet," he said, bundling up the old one. Having helped the old man into bed, he went to get a glass of water.

The old man swallowed the pill and nodded. "Thank you," he said, his voice sounding as if he were speaking from far away on the other side of a wide river.

"Are you sure you'll be all right while I'm gone?" Martin asked. The old man nodded, his eyes closing sleepily. "I'll stop on the way in and ask Max to come up," Martin told him, but there was no reply. Anxious, Martin checked his friend's pulse, but it was strong and regular, if a bit fast. After setting a pitcher of water and a glass within easy reach, Martin checked his friend again, then took off for town.

"Our old friend's going to be all right," the doctor said, coming into the kitchen and setting his black bag on the table.

"Thanks for coming up," Martin told him. "I'm glad you were in town and still make house calls."

"Emil and I have been friends a long time," said the good doctor. "I'm glad I happened to be in town." Helping himself to a cup of coffee from the pot on the stove he grinned. "Actually, I'd have come for this. Can't beat coffee made on a wood stove."

The doctor took an appreciative sip from his mug, then looked at the four others sitting at the kitchen table. "Who will be taking care of him?" he asked, looking at Martin.

"I will," Carmelita answered before Martin or the others could speak. "I'm his niece, doctor."

The doctor looked at her and frowned. "You look familiar but I can't quite place you, miss. What's your name?" Carmelita told him and the doctor laughed. "Now I know why. You look a lot like your mother did forty years ago. Matter of fact, I just saw her today. She's still a beautiful woman, and I think maybe more so now."

"She'll be glad to hear that, doctor," Carmelita said. "I think you were the one who delivered me."

"You would have been one of the last ones," Cosmo answered. "It was almost twenty years ago when I let the young Turks take over that end." He chuckled. "So to speak."

Martin grimaced and Carmelita laughed. "He's as bad as you are," she told Martin. Max nodded his vote of agreement. "What do I need to do?" she asked the doctor.

"Be sure he takes his medicine," the doctor smiled. "And be sure he takes it all but four pills. Those are for him to have on hand if this happens again. It was good he had one left from the last bout. I'll leave a prescription and Luiz can bring it up the next time he comes."

"That will be Thursday," Martin told him. "Is that soon enough?"

Cosmo nodded. "I've left enough for a week, so it should. Be sure he takes enough water," he added to Carmelita. "No coffee or tea, and it would be better if he didn't smoke too much." He grinned again. "At our age that doesn't leave much, but alcohol is out of the question, too."

"Any idea how long this will last?" Max asked.

"He should be feeling better within twenty-four hours," the doctor told him, draining his coffee. "Come and get me if he doesn't start doing better by day after tomorrow. I'll be in town the rest of the week." Looking at Martin the doctor said, "Anytime you're ready. I don't dare have another cup or I'll be awake all night."

"What about decaffeinated coffee?" Carmelita asked. "Can Tio Emil have that?"

The doctor laughed as he rose from his chair. "If you can get him to drink it, that's fine. The last time I suggested it he told me coffee without caffeine is like deco art and elevator music, good taste but no soul."

"I'll check in when I get back from town," Martin told Carmelita. To Max he added, "You need a ride to your place?"

Max nodded. "Why don't you let me drive the doctor to town?" he asked. "You've been through a lot today already."

The doctor nodded. "If you were my patient I'd tell you to stay," he smiled, adding, "You look pretty peaked."

Martin nodded, rubbing his neck. "Thanks, Max. I'd really appreciate it. I'll take a nap here on the couch until you get back."

"Why don't you go on home?" the doctor said gently. "Emil will be all right. Trust me. He's been through a lot worse than this."

"What we're saying is you look like road kill, bubba," Jack told him. "So give it a rest. Do what the doctor says."

"You have such a gentle way of putting it, Bear," Martin told him with a tired grin. "I like it when you talk nice."

His cousin shrugged. "You've got to get the mule's attention first," he answered. "Then you can talk nice."

Carmelita giggled and the doctor laughed. "That's what my nurses used to tell me," he declared, leading the way out of the kitchen.

The next morning Martin was back at the Ramos place not long after the sun rose. He startled Carmelita when he walked into the back door to get a bucket of grain to feed the chickens and a sack of oats for the old man's goats. She was standing at the stove, dressed only in slippers and a very thin shift that revealed more than it hid, and she gasped as he walked in. "I'm sorry," he told her, having a hard time taking his eyes from the shift. "I'm still asleep and didn't think. I forgot you were here."

"That's all right," she said, flushing and acutely aware of the tips of her breasts growing taut against the fabric of the shift. Turning away shyly, she walked out of the kitchen, not realizing she was giving him an even more stunning view. "Let me get a robe," she said.

"I'll be in when I've tended the stock," Martin called to her, glad of the opportunity to busy himself with something else. Stephanie had been away a long time and this morning his feelings for her younger cousin were anything but Platonic. *Jesus, Mary and Joseph*, he thought to himself. *Cool it, man. She's kinfolk.* Even so, he was acutely aware of the tightness in his jeans and found it difficult to concentrate on what he was doing. It must be tied to the survival instinct, he reasoned. Come close to death and the old boy wants to make sure the race goes on. So when he was done feeding, he went to the stream to wash his feet in the icy water and chill his ardor. Stepping into the water up to his ankles, he gasped as the chill shot up his legs and lodged in his groin, stunning him for a moment. Yet it worked. The shock completely drove any erotic thoughts from his mind as his testicles screamed for him to quit this madness and flee from the icy stream. Stepping out onto the dry rocks his feet immediately felt warmer, even in the mountain morning air.

"What were you doing at the stream?" Carmelita asked when Martin returned to the kitchen. "Wasn't it cold?"

"I was trying to wake up a little," he replied smoothly, telling himself it was not altogether a lie. After all, he was trying to wake up to the reality of the consequences of indulging his feelings, and the stream helped. At least, until he walked back into the house and saw Carmelita dressed in a robe which accentuated her figure. Then he found himself fully aroused once more. "Yes, it was cold," he added. "But not cold enough."

Carmelita looked at him puzzled. "You're strange," she said. "That must be why Tio Emil likes you so much."

"How is he this morning?" Martin asked, glad to get to a safer topic.

"He slept well last night," Carmelita said with a huge yawn. "I got up to look in on him but he rested well." She smiled sleepily. "Better than me. Maybe I need to go wade in the stream, too."

Martin laughed. "That wouldn't be a bad idea." Then he realized she had no idea what he was laughing at. "I'm glad to hear that," he said. "About your uncle."

"Did I do something to offend you, Martin?" Carmelita asked him.

"No," he told her. "It's just me. After all the excitement of the last few days I'm in a weird mood. That's all." He shook his head and smiled at her. "I'm glad you're here." He crossed the room and hugged her very carefully, trying to avoid touching much more than her shoulders, but finding himself becoming even more aroused. "I am going to look in on your uncle," he said, hurrying from the kitchen. "Then I'll be on my way."

"Aren't you going to stay for breakfast?" Carmelita asked, puzzled.

"No," he told her, sticking his head back in the door. "I really do need to get going this morning."

"Well, maybe we'll see you for supper," Carmelita responded.

"Let me take a rain check," he said. "I'm going to be working late and I won't want to stop."

"Martin," Carmelita insisted. "Are you sure I didn't offend you?"

"No," he replied earnestly. "Really. I'm in a strange place today and need to sort things out. Hard physical work helps me do that."

Carmelita nodded. "That's what you've said. Talking is what helps me. So if you want to talk...." She looked at him directly.

"Maybe later," he promised. "Tell you what. I'll check in when I take care of the stock this evening." Then he added. "Maybe I can come to supper tomorrow evening. Emil should be better by then."

"Luiz will be here," Carmelita told him. "He's coming to get me but I think I may stay a few more days."

"Think your uncle can stand that much nursing?" Martin teased.

"He may just have to put up with it," she laughed back saucily. "I'm not easy to get rid of when I think someone needs me."

Martin made no answer to this but a smile and a wave as he went into the front bedroom to see how his friend was doing. Yet he bumped into the door frame on his way out of the kitchen. He glanced back into the kitchen to see Carmelita smiling strangely.

The old man was still asleep, his fever seemingly gone, and Martin let himself quietly out of the front door. Glancing back as he walked across the stream he saw Carmelita standing on the front porch watching him. Seeing his glance she waved and he waved back. *Damn*, he thought. *If I weren't engaged to Stephanie....* Yet he pushed the thought down. *But I am engaged to Stephanie! he told himself severely. That's the point. So cool your jets, friend. That's the quickest way to screw up your marriage. Literally.*

Resolute, Martin spent the morning engaged in the brutal work of several projects he'd let slide. *Damn it! he* thought, wrestling a huge stone from its primal resting place. *Get a grip on yourself!* Then he laughed aloud at what he'd just thought. There was no question Carmelita had grown up into a beautiful, desirable woman, and as he worked, he found his mind going back again and again to her laugh and her smile, and to the image of her standing in sleepy innocence in her night shift by the sink.

When he returned to check on the old man that evening, Martin could no longer deny his attraction to Carmelita. Nor had the joys of an onanistic workout more than temporarily blunted the sharpness of his desire. The fact was, when he tried to remember Stephanie's face, he had a hard time doing so and when he tried remembering how it was making love to her, his thoughts kept shifting disturbingly to Carmelita. *I love Stephanie*, he said to himself. *She's my fiancee and we're to be married soon.* Yet another side of himself answered harshly, *Then why isn't she here, dummy? Why isn't she getting ready for the wedding? Why isn't she celebrating like any other woman. Carmelita would be.*

Shutting out the thoughts did not work. Nor did the brutal exercise he put himself through, as it once did, for he was in excellent physical condition now and his body took the work in stride. After a few minutes rest, he was ready to go again. *Damn!* he smiled to himself as he realized this. *What a way for my body to betray me.* He thought of how weak he'd been when he first came to New Mexico and how exhausting himself with hard work gave him an alternative to brooding. Then he felt a moment of panic. *What am I going to do when it doesn't do the trick any more? What am I going to do when I can't sweat out my problems?*

At the thought, he drove himself into a frenzy of activity until he fell gasping on the ground. Yet even as he lay gasping for breath, the image returned, the image of Stephanie's younger cousin standing in Ramos' kitchen. *Jesus!* he said to himself, with reverence and almost as a prayer. *Jesus, what a mess!*

Then a strange thing happened. From far off and away Martin could hear the clear, mellow voice of a flute singing the strange, haunting melody Ignacio played in the kiva as Martin ran. Once again Martin felt a warm radiant light seeming to surround and engulf him, bathing his tortured body in its healing radiance and soothing the terror howling in his soul.

Hearing the mellow voice of the flute, words of an ancient mystic came to mind, words he once read which had haunted him for years with their simplicity and assurance. "All shall be well," the mystic Julian had written in Norwich at the height of the Black Death in fourteenth century England, meaning, "God is in the heavens and all manner of things shall be well, indeed." With these words the tears came, tears released with a flood of grief for the loss of all that had ever been for him and all which would never be again. Yet mostly for those things Martin knew in his heart of hearts would never, ever come to be.

11. Leaving Cheyenne

May, 1966. The old man was sitting on his porch when Martin arrived back in the canyon. Still too weak to rise easily, he watched as Martin got out of his truck and walked up the path. The answer to his most important question was written all over the younger man's posture and bearing. He looked whipped, defeated, like a dog that's been in one fight too many.

"No luck, eh?" Ramos asked, his eyes full of concern.

"No," Martin answered him. "Luiz told me she left for Albuquerque yesterday. When I asked him where I could reach her, he became evasive. I think he knows but was asked not to tell me." He shrugged. "I went there, too, to Albuquerque, and asked around everywhere I could think, but nobody could or would tell me where I could find her. So after a while I just came on back." He sighed dejectedly.

The old man absently scratched his ear, frowning. "She was pretty upset when she left with Luiz Tuesday morning. I knew something was up when he decided to stay over night. They had their heads together a lot but they wouldn't tell me, either." He looked at Martin searchingly. "As a matter of fact, you haven't told me much yourself."

"I'm not sure what's wrong, exactly. I was pretty drunk." He reached in a pocket of his shirt and pulled out an envelope. It was powder blue with red and white air mail stripes running around the borders, and was addressed to Martin in Stephanie's sure hand. The postage stamp was foreign, but the old man could not quite make out the cancellation mark. South Africa it seemed, but he was not sure. "Please, go ahead and read it," Martin asked. "It pretty much says it all."

Emil Ramos sat looking at the envelope a long while before he opened it and took out the two sheets of matching paper folded inside. Reading very quickly, he sighed when he was done. "I am sorry, my friend," he said. "I know the pain this must cause you. It is not pleasant to be..." He searched for a word.

"Dumped?" Martin suggested.

"Refused is better," the old man replied. "I think perhaps she has been trying to tell you this for a long while."

"Why didn't she tell me to my face?" Martin demanded. "Why did she have to do it this way? Dear fucking John!"

The old man nodded. "I do understand your being angry. It may seem sneaky or underhanded to you."

"You damned right it does," Martin retorted, indignant.

"What you don't understand is how persuasive you are, my friend," his companion told him. "You are a very hard man to refuse once you've made up your mind. It may have seemed impossible to her to do this in person. I don't know for sure, but it may have been that. I truly doubt Stephanie was trying to hurt you. Whatever else she may be, Stephanie is not mean."

"Well, she did a damned good job of it anyway," Martin said, his voice almost breaking. "Shit!" Tears formed in his eyes and Ramos could see his young friend's anger yield to hurt. "Shit! Shit! Shit!"

The old man opened his mouth to say something, then stopped and waited. After a few moments he continued. "So what does this have to do with Carmelita?" he asked softly, knowing the answer even before he asked.

Martin looked miserable. "As I said, I was pretty drunk. After I read that I hit the bottle pretty hard. Then when Carmelita came by...." he stopped and shrugged. "I'm not sure, but I think...." He shook his head.

The old man nodded, the ghost of a smile touching the corners of his mouth. "She took advantage of the situation?" Martin looked up sharply but there was no malice in the old man's eyes, only compassion. He nodded and the old man shrugged. "Well, that's not the end of the world, my friend, even if it was the first time for her."

"It was, but you don't understand," Martin told him. "I was still out of it when I woke up later. I think it was early morning. I was as hung over and very confused. I think I called her Stephanie." He hung his head, stared at the porch decking.

"Aiee, yi, yi, yi, yi!" Emiliano Ramos said, squinting as if someone just poked him with a needle. "Now I understand. *Hijo*, what a *chinga de puta.*"

"Yeah, I really put my foot in it, didn't I?" Martin agreed.

The old man could see Martin' anger begin to turn from Stephanie and toward himself. "No!" he almost shouted, shocking Martin out of his brood.

"Our little Carmelita was volunteer, my friend. Don't forget that. She set out to seduce her cousin's fiancée and she succeeded." He shrugged. "I know you think of her as a child, but she is a woman. When a woman decides it is time for a man to be in her bed, no man is safe."

"Seems to me I was a player, too," Martin observed dryly.

The old man nodded. "Of course, you were! You're not some wilting violet, either. Yet I know you and your temptation is to take all the blame. If there is fault to be found in anything that happened, it's not yours alone." He shrugged. "Now I know how it was with Stephanie, I'm not sure there is any fault at all. Things happen at times. They just happen and they often happen without us knowing exactly why at the moment. I have found I feel better if I don't judge a thing like this until I know the fruit it bears."

Martin nodded and shrugged, but Ramos was not content. "Forgive me if I go too far again, my friend, but think of what could happen if you and Stephanie married and this came about later on. I think it would be far more devastating then."

"I'll have to take your word for that," Martin answered. "I don't see how I could feel worse."

"There are no children involved now," Ramos pointed out. "It would be much worse later on when there were."

Martin agreed, "I guess you're right. No, I know you're right. I just don't want to admit it right now." Shaking his head he took some papers out of his hip pocket. "Driving down to Albuquerque and back I had lots of time to think," he said, handing them to the old man. "When I was there I had these drawn up." Ramos glanced at the papers. They were legal forms. "I've set up a trust for taxes and repairs on the place and the other instrument is a durable power of attorney naming you, or Max in your place, to do whatever needs to be done and to draw against the trust to do it. I need to get away and I may be gone a good while."

The old man nodded. "I've been expecting this for some time now, my friend," he said gently. "You've been very restless for the last few months and I didn't think it had much to do with Stephanie."

Martin nodded. "Yeah. Somehow I thought coming here and doing what I've done with the place was what I wanted. And it was," he continued, almost as if to himself. "Then I thought getting married and starting a family was what I wanted to do. Now that's out and I'm right back where I started."

The old man held up the letter. "So you're not altogether disappointed this happened?" he asked.

Martin shook his head. "No, I'm not, completely. I hate to admit it but I was also relieved. I thought that was what I wanted, but now I don't know."

Ramos nodded. "I think perhaps you may have been trying to do what you thought you were supposed to do. Perhaps in part to please Rosa and give her the grandchildren she wants." Martin nodded his agreement. "I think perhaps Stephanie may know this in her heart of hearts, too, and that is why she did what she did. It took a lot of courage. She really loves you."

"Maybe so, but I'm not sure I know how to love someone back the way I should," Martin told him.

"No, that's the point," Ramos interjected. "What you have been trying to do is what you thought you *should* do. In my experience, love is a matter of the heart, not a matter of shoulds or oughts or duty. It is something which simply exists and the only choice we have is how we respond to it. I know nothing which will kill it quicker than a sense of duty, or being coerced."

Martin nodded and touched his temple. "What you say makes sense up here. What I seem to be lacking is something down here." He touched his breast. "Assuming you're right about Stephanie loving me, I don't seem to know how to respond the right way."

"Not to beat a dead horse, but your father didn't either. That's why he never taught you." The old man smiled. "But Rosa does and she taught you better than you may know."

The younger man was puzzled. "What mother has done is stick by my father even though he treats her like shit. If loving means treating a woman like shit, then I need to find a monastery."

Ramos laughed. "I do beg your pardon, my friend. I'm not laughing at you. It's a misconception that cloisters and monasteries are where one goes to get away from things like sex and love." He chuckled. "I labored under the same misconception when I sought refuge there. What I didn't know is that monastic communities are probably the places in the world where one is most directly confronted with the issue of sex and the mystery of loving. That is why I had to leave. It was too intense."

"You've got to be kidding!" Martin protested.

The old man nodded and said, "Let me show you. Over the fireplace on the second shelf, there is a brown book. I believe it is the fourth from the left. Would you bring it to me? Bring the Bible, too."

Martin frowned, but went to do as his friend asked. When he returned the old man took the larger volume first, turned to a well worn place, and began to read aloud,

> I am my beloved's and his desire is for me alone,
>
> as mine is for him.
>
> Come, my beloved, let us walk out into the fields
>
> To lie among the henna shrubs;
>
> Let us rise early to go to the vineyards to see if the
>
> vine is blossoming or the buds have come out,
>
> and if the pomegranate is with flower.
>
> There will I give you my love when the mandrakes
>
> give out their fragrance,
>
> and all the exotic fruits are laid at our door,
>
> The new, the old, which I have for you, my love.

When he was done, the old man sighed softly. "That is one of the very favorite passages among the brothers in the monastery where I stayed. It is from the Song of Songs, which is also known as Canticle of Canticles or the Song of Solomon." He looked at Martin. "There's probably no more erotic literature in the world than what I have just read."

"I've read it, too," Martin told him. "It's about romance, being in love and getting married."

"No," Ramos told him. "English translations tend to be romantic but the Hebrew is very earthy. It's about sex and about physically making love with the person you love most in the world." He grinned. "That's not something your average parish priest would tell you in Catechism."

"All right, but what does that have to do with monasteries? So the monks like it. That doesn't prove anything."

"Are you familiar with St. John of the Cross?" Ramos asked him.

"The Spanish mystic?" Martin asked. The old man nodded. "Yes, but not much."

"I will read this directly from the Spanish he wrote," the old man told him. "You be the judge. When I'm done you tell me. Is this about lyrical romance or about down to earth swiving?"

"Swiving?" Martin asked. "I don't think I've heard the term before."

"A polite English term for fucking," Ramos grinned as he opened the smaller volume and began to read in Spanish, his face becoming gentle and still as he spoke the words as if to a lover,

> On one dark night
> With desires inflamed by love
> - Oh, the happy venture! -
> I went out without being seen
> My dwelling now being quiet
>
> In darkness, and safe
> By way of the secret ladder disguised
> - Oh, joyful venture! -
> By darkness and concealed
> My dwelling now being quiet
>
> On that happy night
> In secrecy, so that no one saw me
> Nor I looking very much at things
> Without any other light or guide
> Other than she who burned
> passionately in my heart
>
> That one guided me
> more certainly than the light of midday
> To the place he awaited

- to him who I have known so well! -
Within a place where no one appeared.

Oh, night that guided me!
Oh, night more lovely than first dawn!
Oh night that joined together
The lover with the beloved
The beloved in the Lover transformed

On my flowering bosom
Which entirely for him alone I kept guarded
There he lay sleeping
And I caressed him
And the fanning cedars gave a breeze

The breeze from the battlement
When then it scattered his hair
With his serene hand
He wounded my neck
And suspended all my senses

I left myself wanting and forgotten
Reclining my face on my beloved
Everything ceased, and I left myself
Leaving my caution
Among the white lilies forgotten

The old man was silent a moment when he stopped reading. Then he sighed. "I can never read that unmoved," he said.

"It is beautiful," Martin agreed. "It was written by a monk?"

"Yes, and there is very little metaphoric about it," Ramos answered. "Or perhaps I should say, it's not just metaphoric, as it is usually taken. It is also very earthy and very sensuous. It's about physical love, too."

Martin nodded. "There's not much getting around that, is there? But

I don't understand. What's your point."

The old man laughed. "I'm not sure I remember now." He thought a moment. "Oh, yes. The point is that monastic communities are the last place one wants to go to get away from problems with sex and love."

Martin nodded again, growing impatient, his attention shifting. "I thought about staying here and doing my thing, but there are a couple of problems with that. One is money. I could hang on about another year, but that would about wipe me out. I hoped the writing would be bringing in enough by now that I could keep on doing what I'm doing by selling a couple of things a year."

Ramos shrugged. "You could do that getting a part time job in town," he pointed out. "Or you could practice law if you cared to. You're well known in the Hispanic community, well enough known to make a living as an honest lawyer if you wished pass the bar and do that. However, I don't think money is the problem for you, is it?"

Martin shook his head. "No, I've always been able to shake money loose when I needed it. The problem is there's something missing in this way of life. It's not quite enough for me. Do you understand what I mean?"

Ramos smiled. "Perhaps better than you might think. This is a very pleasant life for an old man or for someone like Max who wants nothing more than a time and a place to perfect his music," he said. "For you I think it is a dead end, at least for now. The world has not experienced you yet."

Despite his preoccupation, Martin smiled. "That's an interesting way of putting it, Emil," he said. "Most would have said it the other way around, though it can be taken at least two ways."

"Most would have not been talking about you," the old man answered. "You have a place in this world to fill, I think. Some people do and others do not, at least not in the same way. There is a purpose, a mission, or whatever you wish to call it for you, and you alone, and you will not be content until you first find it and then engage with it."

"I thought that was being a writer," the other answered. "Now I'm not sure what it is." He grinned. "I wonder if there's a need for a wolf caller?"

"Always, my friend," the old man answered. "You are a healer and I think that's part of your purpose." Martin shrugged impatiently but Ramos ignored it and continued. "You are also a very fine writer," Ramos pointed out. "You have done nothing but improve since you first came here. Yet there is something more you may need to be a great writer which you cannot find here, and anything less than greatness will never satisfy you. So you must go out and find it."

"I wish I knew where to look," Martin told him.

"That I can answer," Ramos smiled. "Look within yourself. I have found the answers are always there, no matter what I would prefer."

The younger man was puzzled. "I could do that here," he pointed out. "That's what I came here to do. It didn't work."

"Perhaps this place is too friendly, too accepting, to show you what you need to know," the old man said. "Perhaps you need to see yourself reflected in ways that are not possible here." He nodded thoughtfully. "On the other hand, perhaps it has worked, at least in part."

"What do you mean?" Martin was completely baffled.

"I was thinking of *el lobo de navidad*," Ramos answered. He held up the blue envelope. "And this. Perhaps in her decision Stephanie is reflecting something about yourself that is painful to behold."

The stress of the last week finally caught up with Martin. "Damn it, that's about her, too, not just me!" he declared. "I've owned up to my feelings but I'm also committed. Maybe I'm relieved, but I made a promise and I'll keep it, come hell or high water. It's as simple at that."

Ramos held up his hands in supplication. "Please, pardon me. I did not mean to suggest it was you alone. It is about her, too, of course. You are quite right."

"Of course, I'm right!" Martin snapped, furious. Then hearing himself, his tone, he stopped cold. "I beg your pardon, Emil. You didn't deserve that. I'm just having a hard time accepting things. Do you think she'd change her mind?" The old man looked at him sadly. "No, I guess not," the younger man admitted to himself. "I'm not so sure I'd want her to, either. Damn, why does it have to be so hard?"

"For me, it was because I was so hard headed," Ramos answered. "I wouldn't presume to speak for you."

"Horse hockey!" Martin snorted.

The old man chuckled. "Would you mind making us some tea? I'm thinking that would taste good. With lemon and honey. Luiz brought up some sweet breads if you care for one of them."

Ten minutes later Martin brought him a tray and for a while they sat and sipped hot tea, smoking from a pack of cigarettes Martin purchased on his trip. After a time the old man looked at Martin and asked, "So, what have you decided, my friend? What are you going to do?"

Martin shook his head. "I'm not sure. I know some people who own a newspaper up north, not far south of Chicago. Maybe I'll try to get on there. It's a large enough city, but not too large."

The old man nodded. "It will seem strange after living out here, what? Five years now?"

"Four," Martin answered. "Almost to the month. I came here for the first time in April and I'm leaving in May."

"So you're going right away, then?" While his voice was neutral, there was no mistaking the old man's sadness.

"As soon as I get the place closed up. There's not much I need to take with me." He looked at the old man. "I thought I'd store the stuff that might walk away up here if you don't mind. You've got a key to the house if you need it."

Ramos nodded. "Of course! I'll look in whenever I'm down that way." He looked at his young friend. "I don't wish to burden you, Martin, but I hope you'll write from time to time. To let me know how it is with you."

"Of course, I will," Martin said. Then he frowned. "I do think I want to make a complete break, though. It would be better if people didn't know I'm gone. I'd like you to promise to keep what I write to yourself, or between you and mother."

Ramos nodded. "And if Stephanie or Carmelita wants to know? Or if Luiz or someone else asks?"

Martin gave him a wicked grin. "Feed them some of their own stuff. Tell them you're not sure and let me know. If I feel like getting in touch with them I'll write."

"I hope you never get this angry with me," the old man told him. There was no trace of humor in his words.

"I don't think I will be," Martin told him. "You play things pretty straight with me. Even when I don't think you are."

"Remember that last statement," Ramos laughed. "I may have to remind you of it one day." He sighed and got to his feet unsteadily. "Very well, I'll keep your confidence. Now I think I need to lie down a while."

"I'll look in on you later this evening," Martin told him, holding the door open and making sure his friend was comfortably settled before going down to his own place and beginning to pack. Yet easing his ancient truck down the drive he had a terrible moment of doubt, and he almost turned back to tell the old man he was staying. For as he drove he thought for a moment he heard the voice of the flute playing. As before, it was interweaving itself with the voice of an old man standing at the side of a grave quietly singing the tune of what was now an all too familiar hymn,

> Come home, come home, come home,
>
> ye who are weary come home.
>
> Softly and tenderly Jesus is calling,
>
> calling, 'oh, sinner, come home.'

Then Martin Lundberg, known as Raven Wolf among the People of the Tewa, found tears again streaming down his face under a tidal wave of grief washing down, pulling him under. Yet even as he was pulled under, he heard the voice of the flute again, or was it the old man singing? Yes, it was the old man and the lines he sang were familiar, something he'd read somewhere but now could not recall,

> **My soul is heavy within me,**
>
> **therefore will I remember Thee from the land of Jordan,**
>
> **from the peak of Mizar among the heights of Hermon.**
>
> **Deep calls to deep in the thunder of Thy cataracts,**
>
> **Thy waves and billows have rolled over me....**

To which he heard the soft, gentle voice of the flute answering,

> **Why art thou so full of heaviness, o my soul,**
>
> **and why art thou so disquieted within me?**
>
> **Put thy trust in the Holy One,**
>
> **for thou shalt yet give thanks**
>
> **unto him who is the help of thy countenance**
>
> **and thy Vindicator...**

Vindicator, he thought as he parked in his driveway and walked into his house. What an odd thing for me to think. *Why do I need a vindicator? I'm not seeking revenge. Justification, sometimes, but not revenge.* Taking his well worn dictionary from its place on the bookshelf he looked up the word, then nodded at what he read. At an earlier time the primary meaning of the word 'vindicator' was to set free from bondage. *So what the Psalm is saying,* he told himself, *is something like this: put your trust in the one who dries your tears and makes you smile, the one who sets you free.* Shaking his head he replaced the book on the shelf. *Whistling in the dark,* he thought. *All that church stuff is like kids walking past a graveyard at night, whistling in the dark.* Shrugging off the mood, he began thinking which books he wanted to take with him, which he would leave with Max and the old man, and which he would give away.

Yet later that night, Martin was again unable to sleep, haunted by the song of the old man and the flute. It kept going through his mind and he rose to find its source. Not knowing why, he went to the small pile of books he planned to take with him. There he dug out an old Book Of Common Prayer the old man had given him for its translation of the psalms. He was sure that was there he had read the words going through his head and it was there he finally found it. Yet, not before reading through a dozen or two of the songs of David. As he read them, he was struck, as he almost always was, by the beauty of the traditional Coverdale translation. *I bet these are even more beautiful in Hebrew,* he thought as he read. This thought was followed by another, one which surprised him in its truth. *I think I could be a good Jew. I really do. None of this horse shit about people rising from the dead. Just a good, clean reverence for all creation and a strong code of how to live with others.* Then he smiled at a random thought which flitted across his mind. *I really don't like pork anyway.*

The next few days were filled with activity as Martin began to close down the home it had taken him four years to make. Many times he found himself wondering why he was doing this, and often he found himself in the evening at his special place above the house, playing his flute softly as he stared into the fire. Once he thought he caught a glimpse of the black wolf out of the corner of his eye, but when he turned to look he saw nothing and the next day he could find no tracks. At other times he thought he heard a deep croaking and looked out to see whether the raven was visiting, but there was nothing there when he looked. Almost afraid to do so, he spoke of these things to the old man. "It's crazy," he said one evening when he came up to drop off some books and bring supper. "It's driving me crazy."

Emil Ramos nodded his sympathy. "You are between the hammer and the anvil," he said cryptically.

"What do you mean?" Martin wanted to know.

"When I was a young man," Ramos told him, "I was fascinated by the art of our blacksmith. What fascinated me was how iron was formed and how it was jointed together. To form it, the blacksmith heated it red hot and beat it into shape. You've probably seen that before." Martin nodded and the old man continued. "What you may not have seen is the process of joining two pieces of iron together, welding the old way." Martin shook his head. "It is fascinating. Both are heated up red hot, or even hotter. Then they are laid together on the anvil and flux is put on them to made the metal flow, and as the smith pounds them, they become inseparably one. With a good smith it is almost impossible to tell where the weld took place." He stopped.

"All right," Martin replied after a long moment. "But I'm not too sure what you're getting at."

"The process is called welding and I am told that is where the English word 'wedding' is derived," the old man laughed. "Two people, heated as hot as they can be, given love to bond them and pounded between the anvil of heaven and the hammer of life." Ramos jammed his hands together, fingers intertwined, and clasped them tightly. "The two become one!"

Martin nodded. "All right. I get your point. The only trouble is, I'm not getting married," he said dryly.

"Ah, but you are," the old man contradicted. "You may not be getting married to Stephanie, but you are being formed by fire to the purpose for which you were created. You are being wedded to your purpose in the scheme of things. That is why the raven and the wolf are coming to you. To give you power to do what you were created to do."

"Jesus Christ!" muttered the young man.

"Exactly!" Ramos pounced. "This is precisely the same sort of process he went through, too. It's called the Way of Holiness."

Martin looked at him askance. "No sale, kemo sabe. I didn't exactly ask for this," he said. "I'm not making any messianic claims."

The old man shrugged. "Neither did he. No one asks for what happens to them in this life, Martin," he said. "What matters is how we respond."

"Why me?" Martin almost shouted, indignant.

"Why not you? Why someone else?" the old man looked at him levelly. "How can you be so sure you're not here for a purpose?"

"I'd like to have a little choice in the matter," Martin argued.

The old man sighed. "I know," he said. "I really do. I used to curse the gift of intelligence, of being able to see things others don't. Then two things happened. One was when I came to the place I realized I would not trade the gift for even ten times the pain. Even at it's great cost, I realized how much I loved it, how much a part of me it was and is." He sighed and fell silent, nodding to himself as if to remember something he sometimes forgot and needed to remember often.

"And the second thing?" Martin asked.

"I ran into a man whose intelligence I respect," Ramos answered. "In those days that was a rare person, indeed. That was before I realized that for all my learning and intelligence I don't know beans." He nodded. "That was very humbling to realize, by the way, but very useful." Again he stopped.

"Well, what about the man?" Martin wanted to know.

"He told me something which shook the ground beneath my feet," the old man replied. "It was something which touched the core of my being as the utter truth, yet it was something I did not want to believe. I still don't want to believe it, but it feels as certain and true to me as the rising and setting of the sun." He shook his head.

"Damn it, Emil! Are you going to make me drag it out of you?" Martin inquired more than a little impatient.

"No, my friend. I beg your pardon," the old man said. "Truly, I'm not playing a game with you. My mind still shrinks away from this truth so much I hesitate to even utter it. The man who told me this was a Druid, I think, in the best sense of being a seeker of wisdom and knowledge. What he told me is that when we come into this world, we do so having agreed ahead of time that, for the sake of the universe itself, we will accept all the wounds we receive here."

Martin started to say something. Then he closed his mouth and sat quietly, looking stunned. Ramos nodded. "That was my response, too," he said. "Even though it's been years now, it still moves me that way." He fell silent again. Taking out the makings, he rolled himself a cigarette and sat quietly watching the smoke rise.

After a long while Martin rose, shaking his head. "Good night," he said to Ramos. "I'm going to bed." The old man could see there were tears in his young friend's eyes as he made his way down the path.

"Good night, Martin," the old man called after him, but there was no response, and for a long while the old man sat rocking, asking the One whom he loved best if he were right in revealing what he'd just said. Then asking once again that if he were not right, for his folly to be redeemed.

Part II. The Odyssey

Hear my prayer, Adonai, give ear to my cry; hold not
your peace at my tears.
For I am but a sojourner with You, a wayfarer, as all
my forebearers before me.
Psalms of David 39

By the waters of Babylon we sat down and wept,
when we remembered you, O Zion.
As for our harps, we hung them up on the trees
 in the midst of that land....
How shall we sing the songs of Adonai upon an
 alien soil?
Psalms of David 137

1. First Edition

*S*omewhere in Cloud Nanaland. *My career in journalism began almost by accident. At least, I believe neither I nor anyone else could foresee the chain of events which has led me to where I am here and now. Nor do I believe any human agency could have set them in motion. Yet looking back, each step along the way led inevitably to the next, as surely and certainly as if my course had been laid out like a railroad track, or as if Something or Someone were messing around in my life.*

This is a troubling thought, one I have mulled over for years. Nor has the mulling led to any conclusion, only to more and more questions. Were I able to believe human life is a matter of random chance combined with human caprice and ends with death, these questions would all be laid to rest with the mortal remains of every friend I bury. Perhaps it would not be comfortable solace, but I could accept the whole human drama for its humor and absurdity and lay them to rest. Yet all which I have seen, and all I have read, and all I have heard points beyond human existence to a silent Partner whose acts of involvement can only be witnessed in their consequences. The sum of all these consequences taken as a whole fits too well together to have occurred by chance.

Nor do I appreciate where such conclusions leave me. For I seem to be left with both feet planted firmly in midair, rooted in the fertile soil of imagination in a place called Cuckoo Land. And while this is never a dull place to dwell, neither is it very comfortable, for there are no certainties but two: 1) that I don't know jack shit, and 2) that Someone Else is messing around in human affairs. Nor is this Someone a celestial puppet master pulling a million billion strings, for the messing around is far more subtle than this. Rather this Someone seems like a benevolent prankster who cheerfully plays things the way we leave them lie, and human life as we know it seems to be like playing a game of celestial billiards with a cosmic Hustler who is much too genteel to cheat, far too polite to take the first shot, and who never misses unintentionally.... (From the Journal of Martin Quinn)

May 1966. The editor looked at the young man with a degree of compassion mixed with skepticism. "So you want to be a writer," he said laughing quietly to himself. "Well, I tell you, kid, this may not be the place you want to be. He reached into a little used desk drawer and took out a cardboard stationery box, one made to hold a full ream of inexpensive paper. Martin could see from the height of the cover that the box held far more than a half thousand pages, perhaps half again as much more. It was enough more that the two halves of the box had to be secured with packing string to stay together. The editor laid the package gently, almost reverently, on one of the few clear spaces left on top of his desk. "See that?" he asked. "You know what it is?"

"No, sir," Martin replied, shaking his head. "I've no idea. I'd hate to have to guess." He examined the box carefully without picking it up. It was made out of cheap blue pasteboard and there was nothing remarkable about it.

"Good way of putting it, son," the editor grinned. "You may do all right around here after all."

"I hope so," Martin smiled back. "So what is it?" he asked, knowing the editor wanted him to ask.

"That is the work of fifteen years, maybe more," the man said sadly. "That is a Great American Novel which will never be published." He sighed, then laughed as he replaced the box in its drawer.

"Why not?" Martin wanted to know.

"Oh, a number of reasons, kid," the other answered. *That's good*, he thought. *The kid goes after the story.* "One is I've never been able to finish it. It's all there but the last part, the resolution. I can't for the life of me figure out how it needs to end." He stopped abruptly, nodding to himself, then shaking his head.

"I can appreciate that," Lundberg responded. "I've never written as much as that but I have two manuscripts pretty far along that seemed to peter out for one reason or another." He nodded. "That's a good reason, but you said there are others. I'd like to know what they are. Assuming you finish it, what else would keep it from being published?"

Again the editor was pleased, although he was careful to let none of this show. *The kid's far too polite*, he thought, *but six months in this busi-*

ness should cure that. What impressed him was Martin' curiosity. The kid knew how to follow up, and even more, how to frame his questions to elicit a response. "Well, assuming I did finish," he said, "and that I was satisfied with the result, the next hurdle would be marketing the thing. Competition is pretty stiff and it's hard to get a publisher interested, no matter how good it might be. It's got to sell and that's what they look at first, potential sales."

Martin nodded, then frowned. "I don't understand," he said. "You're in the publishing industry and, I would imagine, pretty well established. Don't you have some contacts in some of the publishing houses? Wouldn't one of them at least give you a reading?"

The editor nodded and smiled. *The kid has a sense for what lies under the surface,* he noted. "One thing you don't understand is that a lot of my contacts aren't necessarily friendly. There's been some pretty stinky water under the bridge with some of them, and some of those bridges I burned, too. You've got to realize newspapering can get rough, kid." He saw a flash of irritation in Martin' eyes, although none of it reached the young man's face. The older man grinned. "Nobody likes to be called 'kid', son. But you're a rookie and you better get used to it. It's nothing personal and it doesn't mean a damned thing if you don't let it."

Martin nodded back and smiled. "Yes, sir, I couldn't agree more. The fact is, nothing means much if I don't let it, sir. To get my goat the bastards have to know where it's tied. I'm the only one who can tell them."

The editor laughed and nodded. "That's the attitude, kid. We could all do well keeping it in mind. You'll do well if you don't let the horse shit in this business get too personal. Always consider the source."

"Horse shit, sir?" Martin quipped. "Actually, I was thinking more of the source, to tell you the truth."

Again the editor laughed. "The sources are horses, all right, kid, more often than not." He thought a moment. "I think you might work out here, son. You're a little long in the tooth for a cub but we'll give you six months and see. Bust your butt and it will pay off big with me. Don't and you're out on your ass, no matter how good you think you are. Fair enough, Lundberg?"

"Fair enough, sir," Martin answered promptly. "Although, if you don't mind, I'd rather write under a pen name."

"You get good enough to deserve a byline, kid, and you can write under whatever name you damned well please," the older man growled. "Now get out of here and let me get some work done. McLeod will fill you in ." It was a clear dismissal.

"One more question, if I may, sir?" Lundberg didn't move, but neither his tone nor his face was belligerent.

Damn! the editor thought. *This kid's better than I thought. Persistent cuss, too.* "All right," he growled. "But only one, and make it quick."

"Yes, sir, thank you." Lundberg replied. "What did you mean when you said this is not the place I might want to be if I want to be a writer?"

"Three reasons," the editor said. "One is the work, itself. There's nothing literary about the way we write. It's quick and dirty and it has to be. News doesn't wait for us to pick our words." He looked at the younger man, who nodded. "Second is the miserable hours we keep. It doesn't leave much time or emotional energy to invest in your own work. That probably nails more would-be writers than anything else."

Martin nodded. "Yet there are those who do it anyway," he pointed out. "Robert Ruark comes to mind."

"Bob's a writing fool, son," the editor grinned. "I personally don't think the man stops writing long enough to crap. All he takes time out for is to shoot a lion or maybe, and only maybe, have sex. But I think he probably scribbles notes while he's doing that." He nodded. "But that brings up the third reason. Not many writers remain journalists these days. Not in the style of Mark Twain, anyway."

The man paused, looked uncomfortable. Lundberg waited patiently for the answer he knew would come, impressing the editor even more. "The third reason is human nature, myself included." There was no mistaking the grief in the man's eyes. "The fact is, even though most journalists have a novel they've started, most don't finish them. It's not a matter of talent but of character. Since most don't, there's a strong, but subtle pressure to conform to mediocrity."

Martin' surprise showed itself on his face and the older man chuckled. "That one surprised you, didn't it?" Lundberg nodded. "You think this old fart's as full of shit as a Christmas turkey, too," the editor chuckled. There was no escaping his gaze. Lundberg answered with a laugh and a shrug.

"I thought so," the older man continued. "At least you're honest about it, and despite what you may hear, honesty still goes a long way in this business." He fished out a cigarette and lit it, then pressed a button on his desk intercom. "Margie, send McLeod in to rescue me from this pup," he ordered. Martin heard her laugh on the other end and say something back. While he couldn't understand the words, her tone was saucy.

The editor grinned. "No respect," he grumbled. Then he turned and looked hard at Lundberg, pinning him to his chair with his gaze. "Like it or not, son," he said, taking a deep drag from his cigarette and blowing it out without breaking eye contact, "when you succeed you stop being a brown monkey and become a grey monkey. The brown monkeys will attack you for it, mostly out of fear. The third reason is success has its price and not everyone is willing to pay it. Not even me. I'm afraid of losing what I already have."

After a long, uncomfortable moment the door opened and a handsome ebony face peered in. "Yassa, boss!" the man screeched in a Kingfish voice. "You called?"

The editor grinned. "McLeod, quit being a shuck and jive darkie and show Kid Lundberg the ropes around here. He's taking up my whole damned afternoon and I've got a paper to get out." His voice was plaintive.

"Thy merest wish is my command, illustrious master," the man replied in perfect Oxford English. Switching to a normal voice he held out a hand to Lundberg. "You must be Martin. Othello McLeod. Good to meet you."

"Go on, get out of here!" grinned the editor as they shook hands. Grabbing his coat Martin followed McLeod out the door. As he closed the door behind them he saw the editor grinning and he sorted through a pile of paper on his desk. "No respect," the man said, winking. "I get no respect around here."

Pausing at the door Lundberg stuck his head back in. "May I ask a personal favor, sir?" he said quietly.

"A personal favor?" the editor was surprised. "Already? What is it?"

"May I read it, sir?"

The editor looked at him hard but Martin was not kidding. "You mean the manuscript?" the older man asked. Lundberg nodded. "I'll think about it. Now get the hell out of here." Lundberg nodded his thanks and gently closed the door.

"So what do we call you?" McLeod asked as they walked across the cluttered news room. "Martin, Martin, or what?"

"Orewhut sounds good," Martin laughed. "But to save confusion we better stick to Martin. I really don't care for Martin that much."

"I know what you mean!" McLeod declared. "I don't care for the name, Mac, but people are too lazy to say McLeod."

"Why don't you use Othello?" Martin asked, surprised.

"I don't care to be called 'O' or 'Thell' or even 'Oth'," the other answered. Moving the conversation away from himself he asked, "So how long did he say?"

"I'm not sure I follow you," Lundberg replied.

"How long did he give you to work out?" Othello asked.

"Not that long," Lundberg admitted. "I don't have any background in journalism so he only gave me six months to make it or break it."

"Six months" McLeod asked. Martin nodded and the other laughed. "Man, you must have impressed the shit of him. He usually says six weeks." He chuckled again. "He gives you six months he must think you're going to make it big. Of course, he's almost never fired anybody. Either they quit or someone steals them away from him." He looked at Martin soberly. "I don't want to swell your head, but you won't make it running scared, either. So he thinks you've got what it takes and if it's there, he'll bring it out." McLeod gave him a wry smile. "You may or may not like him for it, but he'll bust ass to bring it out. Yours and his both. You can rest assured of that. But if you do what he tells you, you'll be all right, for sure. He knows his business, which is more than I can say for some of the management around here."

"Make it or break it is how he put it," Martin replied. "That must be why he doesn't have to fire people. Most of them must quit before they're fired."

"You'll do," Mac answered, grinning. "You're a fast study and that's what it takes. What's your background?"

"History and the law, but I've never practiced," Lundberg replied.

"Ah, the mystery is revealed. What was your class standing?" McLeod was looking at Martin with an interest Lundberg did not understand.

"Top of my class in law," Martin admitted, obviously embarrassed.

"Summa cum laude in history." He shrugged. "No big deal."

"No big deal?" McLeod was aghast. "Man, I was glad to graduate 'thank you, Lawdy' with a B-plus average."

Lundberg laughed. "Actually, me, too. I mostly lucked out. Got good grades my first couple of semesters and that's what they expected to give me after than."

"Horse shit!" Mac said loudly, pronouncing each word separately and distinctly, and causing several people in the crowded news room to look up. One woman frowned her disapproval and opened her mouth to say something. "That's a direct quotation from Harry Truman," McLeod assured her solemnly before she could speak. She glared at Martin as if it were his fault for encouraging the fool and he simply shrugged.

"Harry Truman's one of my favorite people," McLeod confided once they were out of earshot. "You can attribute almost anything outrageous to him and people will never question it."

"I believe Ike's just as earthy," Martin laughed. "He's just more political than Truman and never shows it. Personally I prefer Truman's direct approach. You know where he stands." He chortled. You know, someone once asked Bess Truman if she couldn't get Harry to exercise a little more restraint in saying, 'horse manure.' Supposedly she laughed and told them it took her a lot of years to get him to say 'manure.'"

"Oh, no you don't," said McLeod, laughing. "You aren't getting off that easily, dude. I was calling what you said 'horse shit' and it was. You don't get to the top of your class by luck. You must be a real ball buster." Martin said nothing but McLeod demanded an answer. "Well?" he asked.

Lundberg sighed. "I'm afraid you're right," he said, looking all the world as if he'd just confessed to some secret character fault. "A total drudge. It's a vice I picked up at my daddy's knee." He looked at McLeod imploringly." I prefer people not know."

"Why?" McLeod demanded. "If you got it, man, flaunt it!"

"I don't like braggarts," Lundberg said. "I don't want to come across as one."

"If it's true, it's not bragging," McLeod asserted, laughing. "It's telling the gospel truth." He grinned sheepishly. "Actually I'm the same way. Magna cum laude." He shrugged. "But I don't advertise it, either."

"What school?" Martin demanded, his eyes boring into McLeod's.

McLeod winced and his face folded into a grimace. "Harvard?" he said softly.

Lundberg laughed loudly, causing several heads to turn their way. "That's the best one I've heard in a long time," he said. Bored, the heads turned away. "Talk about the pot calling the kettle black!" he said in a much lower voice. Then, realizing what he'd just said, he started to apologize.

"Apt metaphor," McLeod smiled, waving his apology away. "That's exactly what was happening." They'd stopped in front of an empty desk. "Why don't you set up shop here?" McLeod suggested. "It ain't the best but that way I can keep an eye on you so you don't wander into the ladies' john unintentionally." He pointed to a desk not a dozen feet away. "That's where I hang out when I'm around. That's not much."

"Out pounding the pavement chasing news," Martin murmured.

McLeod looked up sharply but saw Lundberg was not being sarcastic. "Yeah," he said, relaxing. "That's what they pay us for. Most of the time it's chasing rabbits or chasing our own tails. That's when we could just as well stay here shooting the shit and making up the stories from what we get off the phone. Mostly it's the same old shit with different names and places. Mary or Sue or Betty Jones or Smith or Brown died in a car accident or residential fire or domestic shooting last night or this morning, *et cetera, et cetera, ad nauseum.* But every once in a while," he said, raising an index finger almost to his eyebrow, "every once in a while you hit a hot trail and big game. Even if it's a only tempest in a teapot like the Payola scam, that's when it gets good. That's what makes it worth it for me, worth every bit of penny ante rabbit chasing. When it happens, you've got to be there to get it, on the spot. Because it sure as hell ain't going to come to you."

As McLeod talked, his whole being changed, came alive with an intensity Martin Lundberg would later experience for himself. At the moment, however, it was almost frightening to behold, and he was glad the intensity was not focused on him. Yet there was also something very compelling about it, something which touched something else deep within him. Martin found himself getting strangely excited, too, caught up in story lust, the almost sexual passion to be there first, to get the story before anyone else, to possess it and hold it to oneself for a magic, ecstatic moment before reporting in and releasing it to the thrashing of the thundering herd.

McLeod saw this excitement in Lundberg's eyes and knew he saw a kindred soul. While such passion is similar to the passion involved in the quest for excellence and perfection in any profession, with news people it is different. Their arena is not the quiet office in high, cloistered towers where corporate gladiators contend, working in quiet and concealment, hiding their moves and their wounds behind the curtains of legal fiction. The arena for news people is the street, filled with its raw humanity and its dramas unfolding in the harsh, exacting light of full public view. Within this milieu, the measure of true greatness in a journalist is being in exactly the right place at the right time and reporting exactly what is there, no more, no less.

While some might think this is a matter of accident or coincidence or pure luck, it is not. Rather it is a developed intuitive sense for what is about to happen before it does. This, coupled with the ingenuity to get wherever one needs to be at the moment one needs to be there, is the true measure of greatness. Others can be found to write the copy and do research, but it takes greatness in a newsman to understand what is news, and then, despite the worst of obstacles, to bring it in.

There was an awkward silence when McLeod finished speaking, as if he were embarrassed for having revealed his passion, and Lundberg, too, for being the unintentional voyeur. "So," said the latter, trying to break the mood. "What are these ropes you're supposed to show me?"

"Come on," McLeod answered, gesturing with his head. "I'll show you around, starting with a pit stop at the john."

"Sounds good to me," Martin replied. "You ever wondered why they're called that?"

"No," McLeod answered. "Can't say I've ever lost any sleep worrying about it. Why do you ask?"

"Well, it would make a lot more sense to me to call them 'tommies' or 'the tom,' you know," Lundberg replied.

McLeod looked at him suspiciously, then decided to play along. "All right, Martin," he said, nodding slowly. "I'll bite. Why does 'tommie' make more sense than 'john' for the loo?"

"That's the first name of the man who invented the flush toilet," Lundberg answered. "Thomas Crapper."

"You're shittin' me," Mac laughed. "Literally."

"No, really. That's why they're also called 'crappers'. Look it up." He grinned. "I thought it was bullshit, too. I was wrong."

"Well, here it is," McLeod laughed, "whatever you want to call it. The W.C., johnny, loo, or tommy. See you back out here in a minute."

When Lundberg came out of the men's room he found McLeod waiting for him impatiently, looking at a scrap of paper in his own hand. Come on," he said to Lundberg. "All hell's busting loose down in the projects and they're sending us to cover it. Our photographer will meet us there."

All right!" Martin said. "That's what I'm here for."

"Don't get too excited, brother," McLeod replied thrusting a pencil and spiral pad toward the other. "The reason they're sending us is the people down there are madder than hell and it looks like a race riot may be going down." He gave Martin a wry grin. "You may find yourself an instant minority, white man, but maybe this will keep you safe." He penned a bright yellow badge on Lundberg's jacket pocket which said, "PRESS."

"Just remember, keep cool, no matter what happens. All we're there for is to get the news and all we need to know to know is who, what, when, where, and how. The rest we can fill in later. But keep cool. It may keep you alive."

Oddly enough, Martin found himself remembering Othello's words months later as he faced the angry young black man in the dark shadows of the alley. The man's face was hidden in the shadows but he was clearly armed. Light from a street lamp at the head of the alley cast a band of light across an automatic pistol gripped in a dark hand, and the hole in the end of the gun's barrel looked big enough to put his fist in. Not that Martin thought he'd try just at the moment. At the moment he had his hands up and spread, almost in the attitude of humble supplication used by a priest at the high altar. "I'm not armed," he said, gently opening the lapels of his sport jacket so the man could see there was no hidden weapon under his arms.

"You ain't Othello McLeod, either, honky!" the man snarled. He accented his words by jabbing the pistol toward Martin.

"No, I'm his swamper," Martin replied. "I cover for him when he can't make it."

"How come he didn't come," the black man demanded. There was something familiar about his voice, but Martin couldn't place it.

"We got two calls about the same time," he answered. "Both callers wanted to meet him right now, claimed they had a story for him. So he took the other one and asked me to take yours."

"Shit! I asked for him and he said he'd be here." The man's face was still hidden in the shadows but there was no mistaking the rage in his voice. Martin wondered if now was his hour of death. "Shit! Can't even trust a fuckin' black man these days!"

"He asked me to offer his apologies," Martin said. "And to tell you he'll be happy to see you another time if you don't want to talk to me."

"I asked for him!" the man insisted. "Tonight!"

Martin decided if he was going to die he was going to die. "Well God damn it, baby, you got *me*. So either shoot me, or talk to me, or tell me to get the hell out of here!"

Oh, shit! he thought in the ominous silence which followed. *Me and my big mouth. Why in the hell did I do that?* "Excuse me," he said, and crossed himself the way he'd been taught in parochial school, whispering what he could remember of the Act of Contrition.

The man's dry chuckle surprised him more than a gunshot. "You got balls, man!" said the other, moving forward so his face became visible in the dim light from the street. "Old Othello's really coming up in the world these days getting a white-ass swamper like you. I guess he's too good to talk to black brothers any more."

A shock of recognition flashed across Martin' face, drawing another chuckle. The face was one every American knew as belonging to one of the most eloquent voices of the Black Power movement. "Yeah, it's me, baby," said the man. "T. Floyd Newman at your service. Who are you?"

"Martin," he replied. "My name is Martin Lundberg. I write under the name of Martin Quinn."

"Martin Quinn," Newman mused. "Oh yeah, I remember you, now," he said. "You're the one who wrote about the little sister whose house and mama burned." Martin nodded. "Yeah, I remember now. Three, four months ago. Damned good article. How's the little sister doing?"

Quinn nodded. "Better than she might, I guess. Nothing will ever replace her parents and brothers, but at least she doesn't have to worry about things until she gets out of college. The response from the community was very gratifying, white and black. You'll read about it a week from Sunday." He grinned and shrugged. "Assuming I'm still alive to write the story." He nodded at the pistol. "Mind if I take my hands down?"

"There is that," Newman said, nodding as he put away the pistol. "Assuming I'm still alive to read it."

"You sound as if there's a chance you won't be," Quinn observed, his professional persona falling into place. "Are things that bad?"

Newman nodded. "Yeah, they that bad, all right. Half the cops in this town would nail my ass in a minute if they could get away with it and most of the white people would cheer. But the real trouble is with some of the other brothers. They're power mad."

"I need my notebook," Quinn said, reaching very carefully into his jacket pocket. While Newman didn't retrieve the gun, he watched carefully until he was sure what Martin was taking out. "Now," Martin added, flipping to a fresh page, "Care to name any names?"

"Oh, baby, you want to get me in trouble for sure," T. Floyd Newman laughed. "How about I just tell you what I was about to tell Mr. Bigshot McLeod and then we go from there?"

"All right, but no bullshit, either." Martin' manner was brisk and professional. "Do you mind me reporting you feel as threatened by some of the people within the movement as you do from the white majority? I won't if you prefer not, but it is the truth."

"I don't want to do anything to hurt the movement," Newman said.

"Can't see how it would," Martin replied. "Especially so long as you don't name names. Gets it out on the table."

"Where everyone can smell it stink!" Newman laughed. "All right Mr. Martin Quinn, you tell it like it is, but just remember." Newman opened his jacket and nodded toward the butt of the automatic sticking from his belt. "I can find you easier than you can find me, so tell it straight."

"I always do," Quinn answered. "It's a matter of principle."

"Ah, a man of principle," murmured T. Floyd Newman. "A white man of principle. Talk about a pearl without price."

When Quinn returned to the office and reported in three hours later, Othello McLeod was outraged. "No, damn it!" he shouted. "It's my story! I'm the one he called, and it's mine!"

"I couldn't agree with you more, Othello," Martin Quinn replied.

"The fact remains that I did make a promise to the man and I've got to keep it or lose credibility."

"What exactly did you promise him, kid?" asked the editor, not unkindly.

"He told me I could print the story under my own name but specifically not under Othello's. Not even as co-author." Quinn shrugged. "I tried to talk him out of it but that was his only condition and I agreed. The only concession I could get was that it could be published without a byline so long as that was an editorial decision." He shrugged. "That's all right with me, too. After all, he did call Othello first."

"Well, it's not all right by me," Othello asserted angrily. "That's my story and it needs to be published under my byline."

"Would it have been your ass getting shot off?" the editor asked. "No, Martin' life was on the line and if there's a byline it will be his." He turned to Quinn. "Why did he insist on that?"

"He was pissed because Othello took the other call and couldn't make it," Quinn answered. "I also think he feels betrayed by some of the other black leaders and may be down on them right now." He shrugged. "Hell, I don't know. We hit it off pretty good. The man's got a sense of humor."

"You've got the rapport with him," he editor said, pointing at Martin. "So he's your source, at least for now." He turned to McLeod. "I'm going to recommend publishing the story under Quinn's byline like the man wants," he said. "I'm not thinking about today alone. Newman's going to be a newsmaker until they shoot him and he's too good a source to burn."

There was unmistakable finality in the editor's voice, and no question the final decision had been reached. Ripping his jacket from the coat rack and slamming the door behind him, Othello McLeod stormed out of the office and stomped across the news room swearing every step of the way. A number of heads turned to watch him go. One man said something to another and they both laughed. Martin made a mental note of who they were.

"I wish you hadn't done that," Martin told the editor. "I don't suppose there's anything I can do to change your mind."

"No, son, there isn't," the older man said softly. "It's your story because you earned it. Your skin was on the line and, by damn, your name is going on it. It's a matter of principle."

"I hate to lose a friend over a story," Martin replied. "No story is worth that."

"Blasphemy!" the editor declared. "If that's the only friend you ever lose over a story, you'll be damned lucky."

"One is too many," Quinn insisted.

"Ah, hell, don't worry about Othello," the editor said. "You can make it up to him later." He shrugged. "He'll get over it even if you don't. Blame it on me if you have to, son. That, he'll believe."

"I hope so," said Martin Quinn sadly. "He's a good friend."

"Well, he's got a better one in you, kid," the old man growled. "I hope the damned fool realizes it."

Martin Quinn was startled awake by the loud rasp of the steel lock being opened. "Lundberg!" the huge jailer sang out cheerfully, banging the steel door against the wall and causing Martin to wince. "Front and center, sweet thing. Someone made your bail." He stood waiting patiently for Martin to get up.

Quinn stared at the jailer uncomprehending for a moment. Only the uniform on the tall black man made any sense. *He's a policeman,* he thought. *What's a policeman doing in my apartment?* Then he realized, *I must be in jail.* He wondered how he got there. "Come on, man," the guard told him pleasantly. "You can do it. One foot at a time. Just reach it out and plant it on the floor."

Quinn swung his feet off the steel bunk, groaning and reaching for his head as he brought it up too fast. The jailer laughed. "Must have been some party, baby. Hope it was worth it."

The guard closed the door behind them and led him out through the cell block. Quinn noticed that there were only a few empty cells. "We had us a busy shift last night," the guard said, catching his glance. "All kinds of new guests when I came to work this morning."

"What time is it?" Quinn asked. His watch seemed to be missing.

"Damned near nine o'clock by now," the guard said. "You slept through breakfast," he added grinning. "I tried to wake you but you were still out like a light."

Quinn groaned at the mention of food. The guard opened another steel door with a massive key and pointed to the left. Turning the corner

Quinn could see they were passing the women's section. For some reason there seemed to be more women crowded in each cell than was true for the men, and despite the hangover he wondered why.

"Hey, sweetie," said the rich voice of a tall, husky woman from one of the cells. "You spare Alice a smoke?"

Quinn stopped and fished in his jacket pocket. Taking out a crumpled cigarette pack he started to hand it to the woman. The guard smoothly caught the pack out of his hand and looked at it carefully and smelled it before he handed it on to the woman. "Just checking," he smiled. "Sheriff don't like prisoners getting stoned before court."

"Thanks, dear," the woman said to Quinn. "If you're ever down on Front Street just ask for Alice. I remember favors."

Nodding Quinn waved and stumbled on down the corridor. "He's sweet, ain't he?" another woman's voice observed. "Cute, too."

"You keep your sneaky hands to yourself, Twyla," Alice warned. "I saw him first."

"Good thing he didn't see you first!" Twyla snapped back. Alice's rejoinder was lost when the jailer closed the heavy corridor door behind him and led Quinn down the long hallway beyond. "Those girls!" he laughed. "Wouldn't know they're the best of friends, would you? One gets busted, the other goes bail. They're up a creek today with both of them in the can." He chuckled. "Up the creek without a paddle because they're both broke."

They came into a long room dominated by a police sergeant's high desk. Martin was surprised to see Othello McLeod already standing there with their editor, his left arm in a sling. Against the soft ebony of his friend's face Martin could see a nasty bruise forming over one of Othello's eyes, and his lip was badly cut. "Damn, Othello," Quinn said, stopping in front of him. "What in the hell happened to you?"

McLeod stared at him in disbelief. "You're shitting me," he said. The editor looked every bit as skeptical as McLeod sounded.

"No, I'm not," Quinn answered, earnestly. "Why? Was I there when it happened?" Hung over as he was, they could see he was truly surprised.

"You could say that," the editor interjected dryly. "We can sort this out later." Turning to the desk he asked, "What's the fine, sergeant?"

"Fifty dollar bond on each of them," the officer at the desk answered.

His voice was flat, his manner, bored, as if he'd said the same words at least a thousand times before. "They have to come back to see the judge within ten days or forfeit the bond. But if they forfeit, a warrant will be issued and it gets more serious." He looked at McLeod and Quinn sternly. "So be sure and show up, you hear? We have to come get you, you'll do time in the can."

Both men nodded solemnly. McLeod looked at the editor, worried. "Can you cover it until payday, Jack? I'm a little short right now."

"I've got it," Quinn said. "You got my stuff?" The sergeant nodded and handed him an envelope, and he retrieved his wallet. "You can pay me back then," he added, signing a hundred dollar traveler's cheque and handing it to the officer. "Good thing I keep one of these for emergencies," he added, grinning. "Never know when you might need it."

The sergeant gave Quinn a receipt and Martin started to place it in his wallet. Seeing a couple of large bills there he asked, "How much is bail on Alice and her friend? Twyla, I think."

"Twenty-five apiece," the sergeant answered, frowning. "You a friend of theirs?" he asked casually, looking at Quinn with new interest.

"No, but they need one," Quinn said, handing across another fifty. "I understand they're in a jam both being in at the same time." The sergeant smiled and nodded. "Maybe they'll help me with a story later on. Who knows? Helps to have friends in low places."

"It's your money," said the sergeant, grinning and handing him another receipt, "but I wouldn't count on it. You may find they have short memories at payback time." He nodded to the jailer, who grinned and returned to the cell block, whistling.

Quinn handed him a card. "So Alice will know who I am," he said. Turning to McLeod and the editor he said. "Let's get out of here. I could use a seltzer and a snooze."

"You could use a shave and a bath, too," the editor snarled, leading them out the main doors. "I've got to get to work. You two bums get cleaned up and come on in. I want you there in an hour, flat." He stalked to his car and drove off.

"The man's really pissed," McLeod observed.

"So what happened?" Quinn asked McLeod.

"You really don't remember, do you?" Othello asked, incredulous.

Martin shook his head. "All I remember is running into you at a bar downtown. I think I was looking for you for some reason. Everything after that is really fuzzy."

They were interrupted by a woman's voice calling Quinn's name. They turned to see Alice and Twyla approaching from the station house. They looked like salt and pepper, Alice as dark as Twyla was fair. "Mr. Quinn!" said Alice. "I wanted to thank you, honey. That was sweet of you to go our bail. I can pay you back later today." She looked at him suggestively. "Or you can take it in trade, if you want, sugar." She winked at Othello. "Bring your friend."

Quinn laughed. "Thanks, Alice, but the way I feel right now it's going to be all I can do to get to work. Why don't you put it on account? I may need a favor back some day."

"Sure, honey," Twyla cut in, "but if you change your mind, you know where we are."

"He knows where I am, sister," Alice interjected and the two walked away arguing in a good humored way.

Othello laughed. "Well, you made a couple of friends there." Then he frowned. "Maybe I should warn them how rough you can be on friends."

"What do you mean?" Quinn asked. Then it dawned on him. "Oh, shit!" he said nodding toward McLeod's injured arm. "I didn't do that, did I?"

"Afraid so," Othello told him. "Among other things. Do you want to hear my side of it?"

"I guess that's the only side there is," Quinn answered. "I simply don't remember a thing after meeting you. Not even being thrown in jail."

"I'm not surprised," McLeod laughed. "You took on quite a load last night. Tried to kill the creature swallowing it whole as some might say." He gave Quinn a baleful look.

"I've got to do something about this, man," Quinn said. "It's getting out of hand. Maybe I can limit myself to two drinks. More than that and I seem to go off the deep end."

"Come on, Martin, everyone gets drunk once in a while," Othello told him. "You had every right to be pissed. I was being a total asshole about the Newman story."

"Those are your words, not mine," Quinn protested. "But I seem to remember you were." He thought a moment. "As a matter of fact, I think I went looking for you to set things square."

"As a matter of record, they're your exact words, too," McLeod laughed. "Hey, I like this. You can't remember shit so you have to take my word for it."

"Just remember we're friends," Quinn reminded him. "That's why I came looking for you. I must have checked out half the bars down town."

"I won't forget it for a few days," McLeod promised, rubbing his jaw. He laughed. "Although it ain't all bad, friend. Someone in my tank asked me if I got this from Cassius Clay last week. After I told them it was George Foreman they left me alone."

"Well, come to think, you do look like the other guy," Martin replied. "You know, what's his name. Especially now." He grinned, then grabbed his temples. "Ooh, damn, it hurts to smile." Squinting in pain he asked his friend, "You want to come up to my place and clean up? It's a lot closer and you don't look in much shape to drive."

"Borrow me some clothes and you're on," McLeod said. "Then we can face the music together. If there's blood it will be on your clothes."

"Think it will be that bad?" Quinn asked, concerned. He had worked very hard to keep on the good side of management.

"After that story we just got them?" McLeod grinned. "Hell, no." He shrugged. "All right, the story you got, but the man called for me."

As things turned out, however, it was bad. The publisher wanted to fire them both out of hand and it was only the editor who saved their jobs. Even then it was a close call and only the paper's long established liberal tradition saved them. For the publisher did not want come under fire from his friends for sacking a black man. Since he did not want to fire Othello, the publisher found himself forced to keep Quinn on, too, out of his own sense of justice. "This simply will not do, gentlemen," he said with quiet heat. "And I use the word loosely. Public brawling like this is quite unacceptable."

"With all respect, sir," Quinn interjected, "it was all my fault."

"No way!" McLeod said. "That redneck called me a nigger." At Quinn's surprise he added. "I guess I forgot to tell you. You only hit me because the bastard ducked."

"That will do, gentlemen!" the publisher said severely. Behind him they could see the editor hiding a smile behind a hand. Then looking at McLeod sternly he asked, "Is that true? The city judge called you that?"

McLeod nodded. "Yes, sir, he did. That was the exact word he used and that was why Martin went after him. Too bad he missed."

The publisher glared at him and the smile disappeared. "Do you have any witnesses?" he asked austerely. "If you do we'll take it to press. I simply won't tolerate that in a city official."

"The only witness I have to that is Martin, sir, and he doesn't seem to remember much," McLeod told him.

The publisher glared at Quinn, who shrugged. "My memory seems to be coming back, sir," the young man suggested hopefully. "I'm sure I could swear to it by this evening."

"No," the publisher said. "That will not do, either. We simply do not do things that way. Were there no other witnesses?"

"Maybe the bartender?" Quinn asked. "I think the other guys were the judge's drinking buddies."

"I rather suspect that means they'll back him," the publisher observed dryly.

The editor responded. "The judge's brother-in-law owns the bar, kid. I don't think you'll get much help there."

"So we're left holding the bag," the publisher said. "What are the exact charges, Thomas?"

"Disturbing the peace," the editor answered. "The judge was talking about assault but I reminded him of a couple of things he'd rather forget." Seeing the publisher's glance he responded, "No, Jack. I don't have any hard evidence there, either. Nothing that would stand up in court. If I did we'd run it, believe me."

"I've heard on good authority the bastard's a so called knight of the Ku Klux Klan here," the publisher said. "Surely we can come up with something on him we can print."

"Knowing it and having reasonable corroboration are two very different things, Jack," the editor said. "As you know. I'd like to nail him, too, but he's kept his act publicly clean so far."

"Well, we're getting pretty far afield," the publisher said. "You two gentlemen understand you're on indefinite probation, do you not? Regardless of the provocation, there's no excuse for public brawling." Both men nodded. "Then get out of here," he said. "I have some things to discuss with Jack and you've taken up too much of my day as it is."

"Yes, sir," they both answered and left.

After they were gone the publisher looked at the editor and grinned. "Think I did much good?" he asked.

"You were pretty convincing," laughed the editor. "But with those two hot shots, I don't think so. It's in their blood."

"Young Turks that were once me and thee," the publisher remembered fondly. "Although they seem a bit tamer than we were."

"I wouldn't bet on it, Jack," his long time friend said. "We probably don't hear the half of it. You do know we're probably going to lose both of them soon, don't you?"

"I imagine so," the other answered. "I hear Mike Smith is in town and I think he's here to recruit Othello for his wire service if he hasn't already. As for Quinn, we'll be lucky to hold onto him another year." He shook his head. "I don't know, Thomas. Maybe we'd be doing him a good turn firing him. I think news will eventually eat him alive."

"You may be right," said the editor. "But right now he's worth a whole lot more than we're paying him." He laughed at the look on his friend's face. "Don't worry, Jack. I won't be the one to tell him."

Thomas Perry remembered the conversation six months later when Martin Quinn knocked on the door of his office. "Yes?" The editor said, looking up. Then he smiled. "Oh, hello, Martin, come on in. I've been wanting to talk with you about the housing story." Seeing the younger man's face he asked, "Is something wrong, son?"

Martin nodded. "Yes and no, sir," he answered. "I have a personal dilemma and it's a little embarrassing."

The editor grinned. "Sounds like woman troubles to me. Someone rushing you to the altar, son?"

"Woman troubles would be simple compared to this," Quinn replied, laughing despite himself at the look of skepticism which crossed the older man's face.

"Then it must really be troublesome," the editor said. "I didn't think there was anything less simple. You want to tell me about it, Martin?"

"Yes, sir," the other started, then hesitated. "I don't know where to start, sir. You've been very good to me here. You've been very good for me...." He shrugged, struggling for words.

"You impress me son," the editor said. "You impress the hell out of me and you always have. You might be surprised to know why. Do you?"

"No, sir," Quinn answered glumly. *Damn it*, he thought. The man was making it even harder.

"Well, it's not your professional skills, even though they are superb," the editor answered. "You're a quick study and you brought some very well developed writing talent to the job. You are probably one of the few who can be a journalist and a writer, too, and I think you're one who can handle success gracefully." He shook his head. "As impressive as all that may be, that's not what impresses me most."

"Then what does?" Martin asked, intrigued.

"Your integrity, son." Martin was clearly surprised and it showed. The editor chuckled. "I tell you what. I'll make it easier for you. Othello called me yesterday to tell me what he was up to. Even before he talked to you. When did he call you?"

"Last night, after I got home." Martin was dumfounded.

"Another man of integrity," the editor smiled. "He wouldn't call you to offer you another job during working hours." He nodded. "You always manage to amaze me, son. I figured you'd wrestle with it at least over the weekend before you came to tell me you're going to leave."

"Oh, no, sir. That's not why I came to see you." Martin shook his head. "Not at all."

The editor's was completely taken aback. "What?" he asked, frowning. "It's not?"

Martin laughed at the look on the other's face. "No, sir. What I came for was to ask your advice. I wanted to do it without poisoning the well here."

"All right,' the editor answered, confused. "So what's the problem?"

"The problem is, how do I tell Othello I'm not coming?" Martin asked.

"You're what?" the older man exclaimed.

"I'm not going, sir," Martin replied. "I'm staying right here and working for you."

"Are you crazy?" the editor cried. "This is the chance of a lifetime," he argued. "Believe me, Martin, opportunities like this don't come up every day. Who knows how long it may be before another one comes along?"

"Well, I guess I'll just have to wait," the younger man rejoined. There was a stubborn set to his face.

"Why, for God's sake? This is a good career move for you. It's coming at a very good time, too." He smiled. "There hasn't been a news environment like this since the Korean war and you're in a position to take advantage of that, son."

"We haven't finished our contract, sir," Martin replied, sounding rather offended he had to explain. "Our six months isn't up and I'm not going to leave you in the lurch."

The older man looked at Quinn as if he were an idiot. "Martin, go check your calendar," he said. "Our six months were up a long time ago."

The younger man shook his head. "It doesn't matter. I'm not going to leave you in the lurch like the others have."

The editor studied Quinn a long time, so long the silence grew heavy. Nodding, he said, "This is just what I was talking about, son. Your integrity is a gift, but not when you let it make you stiff necked." He sighed, looking down. "I guess you leave me no choice, then. You're fired."

"I don't understand, sir," Martin said, stung by this unexpected response. "I'm doing all I can to be very up front with you. What do you mean, fired?"

"What I mean," the older man growled good naturedly, "is that you have a choice, my friend. You can quit or I can fire you." His eyes were level. "I may get fired for doing it, son, but that's the way it is and that's the way it's going to be. I'm not going to let you use this dump as an excuse. You can take the wire service job or not, but after today you're not working here any more." He grinned wickedly. "Like it or lump it," he said, glancing at his watch. "I want your resignation on my desk in fifteen minutes. Then I hope you'll let me buy you lunch."

"Seriously, sir?" Martin asked. The older man nodded and Quinn grinned. "Then what you see is what you get," he laughed. "I quit!" He grabbed the editor's outstretched hand. "Thank you, sir. I appreciate it very much. More than you know."

"Ah, go on!" the editor growled. "You wouldn't have been worth a damn around here after turning them down, anyway. You'd always wonder where that might have led, and that would eat at your soul." His eyes grew bleak as he spoke and Quinn knew the man was talking about himself. "So grab for the brass ring, son. Always grab for the brass ring. You may get your ass in a crack from time to time over reaching, but I think you'll never regret it. Not in the end."

"Yes, sir," said Martin Quinn, wondering what the older man was talking about but deciding not to intrude. "Is two weeks sufficient, or do you need a month?"

"Finish the story you're on and we'll call it square," Perry growled. "You've got at least a couple of week's vacation coming. Now get out of here and let me get to work, Quinn. I've got a paper to publish."

"Yes, sir," Martin said, smiling to himself as he gently shut the door at the rose he'd just been given. It was the first time the old man had called him by his professional name.

2. Feast Of Lights

*S*omewhere near Jerusalem. A shell bursts off to the right. The flash shows *people, buildings, pieces of trucks and tanks, all frozen in the instant eternity before the shock hits. There is too much to see, but I see it. I see sharp shadows cast by soldiers crouched by the ruins of a tank. Their faces are terrible gaunt caricatures of humanity in this cruel light. A fleeting image comes, is now gone, the image of baby chicks huddled by a dead brood hen. The eye moves on beyond the tank, to the crumbled wall, smeared with dark stains by a playful child's hand. There is no color, very little texture to the stark black and white images. Yet I know. I know the stain is red and the hand which smeared it lies dead in the street.*

I know, but there is no time for reflecting. The shock wave comes. The broken body of the brood hen rears, rises on a pillar of fire. The tiny chicks leap a dozen feet in the air, six of them in grotesque death dance. Yet there is no sound, only a terrible pressure. The eye sees a human leg fly past and there is pain. There is awful pain and the sense of death close at hand. A face appears, a face shining in the gathering darkness. It is the Madonna, the one who touches my brow and brings merciful darkness....

So the script is written. So the actors perform, each doing his or her small act, which taken together, builds the scene, and then the story. It is pure Hollywood with a cast of thousands, done on location. The soldiers I see blown to bits are dummies, so artfully made the eye cannot tell them from real people. The wall has been carefully crumbled with hammers, laid out just so and the stain I see is red paint. The red soaked bundle I see below it is only rags set to look like the crumpled body of a child. For this is not real. This is a make believe war where the audience is given the God's eye, the view to the hero dying so heroically, moving them to tears. They 'ooh' and 'ahh' and when it is done they leave, pleased with the director's brilliance, with the virtuosity of the entire cast. Thus pleased, they come to worship war for the noble thing it is. They praise their generals, their politicians for the opportunities given their sons to die heroically. They pay their taxes to provide ever bigger and better props, and the divine comedy goes on and on and on.

For this is not Hollywood. This is Palestine and there are no cameras here except the cameras of news people and the human eye. Hundreds of thousands of human eyes recording the horror of each scene on the filament of the human mind. There are no retakes, no directors shouting 'cut!' at the end of a scene, only officers screaming orders. There are no prop men, no grips to remove the dummies or arrange them artfully for the next take. There are only medics who desperately try to save the wounded. There are no contracts, no unions to protect these human actors. They are simply here. They had little choice but to come, to see, to fear, to feel ungodly pain until the final curtain goes down for each one. For this is Jerusalem, and this is war.... (Martin Quinn's journal)

June, 1967. The sergeant hurriedly bent over the prone form lying by the wall. There were no obvious wounds and he reached out and shook the man's shoulder. "Quinn?" he asked urgently. "Quinn! Are you hurt?"

There was no answer and the sergeant felt the man's neck, trying to find a pulse, but an arm moved, spastically jerking up and falling back. The sergeant flagged a passing medic. "Medic! Over here. Concussion. Shock."

The medic stooped and checked the downed man's pulse and eyes. The man groaned. The medic reached for his satchel, but his patient suddenly sat straight up, fighting for balance. "Easy, man," said the medic. "You're alive, so lie back down." He gently pushed at the man's shoulder until he complied. "Feel any pain?" he asked. His question was interrupted by a burst of machine gun fire raking what was left of the street behind them and showering them with debris from a buckled wall. Grabbing Quinn they quickly pulled him into a nearby blast crater.

Quinn blinked and stared at the medic dully. "I don't think he can hear you," the sergeant said, pointing to his own ear. He reached in his jacket and took out a grenade which he lobbed in the direction of the hostile fire. The explosion of the grenade was quite loud and showered them with debris. "Shit," said the sergeant. "I got a bad bounce."

"Not in my opinion," said the medic. "It could have rolled back in here with us." He looked around the blast crater. "He's damned lucky to be alive so close to this," he observed, finishing his careful examination of Quinn and picking up his satchel. "No visible wounds," he shrugged.

"Not much more I can do for him. Stay with him as long as you can and I'll send a stretcher team."

"Never mind," said the sergeant. "Take care of the others. I'll scout up a stretcher and get him back."

The medic gave him an odd look. "Shouldn't you get back to your own unit?" he asked. "Or have you been hit, too?"

"No, I'm not hit," the sergeant replied as he shook his head in disgust. "The captain told me to stay with him and look after him," he answered. "He's some hot shot American journalist." He grinned. "He's not a bad sort, but it's a pain in the ass playing nursemaid."

The medic was impatient to leave but his curiosity held him there. "How the hell did he get in? I didn't think they were supposed to be here."

"They're not," the sergeant nodded. "He just showed up here this morning and there was no way to send him back."

The medic smiled and took a colored tag out of his satchel. He attached it to Quinn's jacket. "Well, there is now," he grinned. "He's going to the rear, COD." He laughed at his own joke and started to get up but quickly ducked when another machine gun burst struck the wall behind them and sent ricochets howling down the street. "That guy's getting to be a pain in the butt," he observed dryly. "Good thing Arabs are such poor shots."

"Yeah, he's probably going to jail, too," the sergeant replied, his cheek pressed to the dusty surface of the crater. "These frigging American journalists are crazy!"

"No," the medic grinned, cautiously surveying the street. "Americans are crazy, all of them. I know. I'm from Chicago."

"Chicago?" the sergeant said, flabbergasted, pointing in the direction of the wrecked tank. "You traded Chicago for this? Why, for God's sake?"

The medic laughed and jumped to his feet. "I told you," he shouted over his shoulder as he ran for the cover of the next rubble pile. "Americans are all crazy. Shalom!" He leapt to his feet again and danced his way across to another blast crater just ahead of the machine gun stitching the path behind him.

"They must be," yelled the sergeant, an expatriate from Eyrie, thinking Americans were really not that different from people in his native

Belfast. *Maybe because so many of them are Irish*, he thought. "Shalom," he added, heaving a grenade toward the hidden gunner, but the medic had vanished from sight. This time the grenade blast was muffled and the silence told him it had found it's mark.

"Shalom!" the medic shouted from the other blast crater, careful to keep his head down. "Good throw. The Sox could use you after the war."

The sergeant laughed and took a note pad and pencil from his pocket, scribbling a note he showed Quinn. The man started to sit up and protest but the sergeant gently pushed him back, shaking his head and pointing over the lip of the blast crater, making hand motions like a gunner. Quinn nodded and laid back. *Well, it really wasn't a lie*, the sergeant told himself in the Irish way. *After all, there was a gunner there a moment ago, and it's keeping the damned fool down.*

Quinn's visitor stood up to leave. He was an unremarkable man except for a faint, but very distinct, air of authority. His normally mild face showed weariness and dissatisfaction, and a marked degree of impatience. The interview had been long and not terribly productive in his opinion. "Very well, Mr. Quinn," he said in public school English. "I see no reason why we should take action against you. It would only take up resources better given to other things. However, the final determination lies with my superiors, you understand. They may not agree."

"I'm sure they will, colonel," Quinn answered, offering the officer a hand. "I'm sure they respect your competence. After all, I didn't do anything too terribly wrong."

"That's entirely a matter of opinion," said the Colonel, remaining civil and shaking the offered hand. "More to the point, however, is whether you're worth prosecuting. Believe it or not, there are more pressing concerns at the moment."

"I know, colonel," Quinn said more contritely than he felt. "I broke the rules. But I was on the spot and the news was breaking. Can you really blame me too much for trying?"

The colonel allowed him a sardonic grin. "I suppose not, really. In your place I might do the same. I do wish, however, you would be more specific about how you got there from Beth-el."

Quinn shrugged apologetically. "Like I said, Colonel, I mostly lucked out. I ran into a truck load of your soldiers and they gave me a lift."

"Well, they shouldn't have. Their officer should have stopped you."

"To be just, their officer didn't know I was coming along. I ran into one of your other officers who told me to turn myself into the proper authorities right away. I didn't know who that was so I surrendered to the troops in the truck. It just happened they were on their way to the front." Quinn shook his head. I'm not even sure exactly where we finally ended up."

"That's stretching the point," the colonel said dryly, "but I'll concede it. I do wish you remembered who they were. It's bad for discipline to let such things slide." He looked at Quinn closely.

"I honestly don't remember, colonel," Quinn answered. "Things are still a bit confused. I think the sergeant's name was Zev, but I couldn't swear to it." He stopped, but the colonel sensed Quinn had something more to say and waited. "Even if I did, sir, I'd really hate to tell you. It's hard to resist a determined news man if he wants to interview you. Particularly if he offers a flask."

"Really, Mr. Quinn," the colonel replied, suddenly very official. "You didn't mention that before. This is a very serious matter. I'm afraid we really cannot release you until we clear it up. Drinking on duty is a grave offense."

"Pardon me, colonel, but I said 'offered', and I did so not knowing it was against your regulations. None of the men accepted, although some wanted to. They really are a well disciplined group."

The colonel looked at Quinn seriously for a few moments, then decided he was telling the truth. "Tell me, Mr. Quinn. Are you sure you actually offered the flask? If you did, of course, this thing could drag on for weeks and take up all kinds of official time. I really wonder if that is necessary."

Quinn smiled. "As I said, colonel, the blast really scrambled my circuits. I am not sure I even remember getting on the truck. I think I did but I'm not sure. I'm not even sure I had a flask to offer. I want to cooperate, but I simply can't remember details well at all."

"Very well," the colonel answered. "We'll leave it at that. You've been very fair and supportive of our cause in your reporting, and that is very much appreciated in the right quarters. I'll let you know what my superiors decide."

"Thank you, colonel. When do you think I might be released? That is, assuming they agree with your recommendation."

"Oh, perhaps two days, or three, at most."

"I don't suppose there's much chance of my getting back to the front, is there, sir? I'd really like to cover the fighting."

The colonel stiffened. "Under the circumstances, Mr. Quinn..." he started to say, then stopped. He gave the journalist an odd look. "To cover the fighting, did you say? Didn't anyone tell you?"

"Nobody has told me anything," Quinn answered. "I have to practically beg to get the time of day around here."

The colonel laughed. "Well, we did tell them you were a security problem. Remarkable. They didn't tell you. Most efficient."

"What didn't they tell me, sir?" Quinn exercised a great deal of restraint keeping his tone neutral.

"The fighting is over, at least for now."

"Over?" Quinn asked in disbelief. "It just started."

"It's over," the colonel smiled, smug as a Cheshire cat. "We won and it only took us six days."

"Won?" Quinn had a dozen questions, but the colonel waved them aside. "I'll tell the nurse to fill you in," he said. "I really need to be going."

"On all fronts?" The colonel nodded happily and waved good-bye. "I owe your people an apology, colonel," Quinn said. The colonel stopped. "I underestimated your army completely."

"So did the Arabs," the colonel replied, softly shutting the door behind him. "So did the Arabs." *Thank God for that*, he thought as he walked down the hall to the nurse's station. It had been a close thing, much closer than the world knew.

The nurse the Colonel sent in to brief him was someone new. As he soon found out, she was not a regular nurse, but a lieutenant in the Israeli Army assigned to help care for the sick while she recovered from her own wounds. One arm was in a sling and a bandage covered the left side of her neck. Yet there was no indication in her manner that these troubled her at all, although he knew they must. When he asked she told him her wounds were second degree burns sustained from the exploding fuel tank of the supply truck she'd been driving to the front.

Her name was Tovah Sharon and she was a sabra, born to a mother sent to Jerusalem by Tovah's grandparents shortly after the Munich riots left the patriotic Jewish community stunned. Raised in a kibbutz after her mother died at the front in the war for independence, Tovah was trained as a school teacher. Her assignment was the age group Americans call senior high, and from her calm self assurance, Quinn had little doubt Tovah experienced no discipline problems in her class. What surprised him most was her candor about herself and her history despite a deep reserve he sensed lay behind her apparent openness. "So what's to hide?" she asked when he expressed his surprise. "There are thousands of others like me here. I'm hardly unique," she added, shrugging in a way he would always remember as uniquely her.

"There is no one like you, Tovah," he declared more vehemently than he intended, causing color to rise in her neck. "I couldn't disagree more," he insisted, trying to get to safer ground. "People I grew up with have no idea of some of the things you've been through."

"I assure you it wasn't by choice," she laughed, trying to turn the attention from herself. "There are a lot of people here with stranger stories than mine. So what is it you wanted to know?"

The question to Quinn was like the red cape to a bull, and being the reporter he was, he went after the story. "Everything," he said. "The last thing I remember was the general mobilization."

"Here," Tovah replied, laughing as she handed him a stack of news papers and current copies of two weekly news magazines. "I thought you might want specifics, so I brought these. They'll give you most of what you want and I'll drop in later to fill in what I can."

"Where did you learn English?" he asked, piqued by her broad nasal accent.

"From two Americans," she replied. "Immigrants. Why? Did I say something incorrectly?"

"Not at all," Quinn laughed. "But I bet they were from west Texas."

"Amarillo, but how in the world did you know?" she asked. "Most Americans sound pretty much alike to me."

"But different from the British, right?"

"Everybody sounds different from them," Tovah agreed, smiling as she ducked out the door. "I'll be back to see you this evening."

Taking the news magazines first for a quick summary, Quinn was startled to see the face of an official he knew smiling at him from the pages of Time magazine. *Damn*, he thought, chuckling to himself. *I've got to learn to read Israeli Army insignia. Leave it to me to cross swords with the head honcho.* Quickly he scanned an article about the Israeli defense minister whose face was now known around the world as the military mind which defeated overwhelming Arab forces. *Dyan is not a man to be fooled with,* Quinn decided. *He sees more with his one good eye than most people ever will with two.* Then another thought struck him. *I better keep a low profile until I get out of the country.* After all, there was more than an outside chance the man might remember seeing him at Beth-el and ordering him to turn himself in, and there was no question in Quinn's mind he'd be harder to convince than the colonel.

Martin Quinn spent most of the afternoon pouring over the news accounts between frequent naps. While he was aware how close he'd come to being numbered among the war's fatalities, he was surprised how much the injury had sapped his strength. Or perhaps it was the medication they were giving him. *I wouldn't put it past the colonel to tell them to keep me sedated,* he thought. It would certainly be more effective than taking someone away from urgent tasks to guard him. Yet even as he thought this, he knew he was wrong, very wrong. The Angel of Death had brushed him with its wings.

The thought sobered him. It was not so much the thought of dying which did so, but rather the question of who would miss him, who would mourn aside from his mother and perhaps Ramos if the man were still alive. There was no one whose life would be significantly changed because of his passing, except perhaps Rosa. The insurance money and his estate would surely buy her freedom from his father if she desired, but he doubted she would. Maybe Jack Bear and Stephanie would feel sad for a few days, but they had their own lives and he'd pretty well burned that bridge. Maybe someone would raise a glass to him in a bar where news people gather, and maybe others would respond, but that would be about it. There would be nothing left, nothing marking the passage of one Martin Lundberg, a.k.a. Martin Quinn, through this transitory life except those things he'd written. Even those would soon be forgotten. A wave of grief washed over him and he found himself craving a drink, no, a bottle, in which to drown this ghost of Christmas future. Then he smiled to himself. *Why not?* he thought as he took a pencil and pad from the table beside his bed and began to write. *Why not?* Words began to flow from his hand as if of their own accord.

"Somewhere near Bethlehem. The ghost of Christmas present rides hard among the Horsemen of the Apocalypse who sweep across this ancient and war torn land...."

Not bad, he thought, reading back over this beginning. *The language is a little purple but I'll clean that up later.* Reading it aloud to himself he continued the thought and was writing furiously an hour later when Tovah returned to the room. Hesitating at the door, she waited patiently for a break in his intense concentration. It was a long time coming and as she watched him, Tovah became aware of feelings in herself left long denied. Whether it was because of the war or her own close brush with death or some other reason, she found herself responding to him as a woman to a man. Nor would she have indulged this luxury of feelings had Quinn been aware of her presence. Caught up in his work as he was, it was like spying on at him through a one way mirror, and without realizing it Tovah became as intent on the mystery of Martin Quinn as he was in the passion of his work. There was something almost sensuous about the way his hand drew the pencil quickly across the paper, like a lover stroking the breast of his beloved. There was something gentle about his mouth, even clamped tight in thought, and the way the hair curled along the base of his neck sent a quiver of pure delight through the core of her being. She began to imagine the strong arms holding her close, his quick sure hands stroking her back, running themselves down her sides and lightly across her full bottom. She could feel him growing firm against her, slowly, achingly moving up and up to possess her...

Suddenly Tovah was aware Martin had turned, looked up to see her standing there, and that his eyes were locked to hers. At once it felt as if a lightning bolt of raw power surged, leaping the chasm of years and cultures and the bare fourteen feet which lay between them, sweeping them away in the flood of its fiery passing, fusing them, melding them, welding them flesh to flesh and bone to bone for all time and forever. Beholding the fullness of his response mirrored in hers, she knew full well that if he leapt from the bed and took her right there on the hospital floor, she would gladly respond with all her mind and with all her body and with all her soul.

Then the moment passed, leaving her confused, uncertain. "I brought you some more newspapers," she stammered, grasping the doorway for support. She did not seem to be able to move her legs, which tingled and felt strangely heavy.

"Are you all right, Tovah?" asked a nurse passing around her to check Martin' vital signs. "Maybe you better sit down," she added, pushing a chair across the room and waiting to make sure Tovah could seat herself without help.

"Thanks," said Tovah, slumping into the chair. The deep flush of her neck stood in bright contrast to the jet black of her long hair. "I'm all right. I just felt a little light headed for a moment. It will pass."

"Sure," smiled the nurse, wondering why people bothered to lie about things so obvious to others. *Saving face*, she thought, turning back to Martin. *Why do we even try?* "Ah, your blood pressure's up just a bit," she noted dryly, recording the reading into his chart along with the fact he had a pretty visitor at the time it was taken. "I wonder what that's about," she murmured to herself, loud enough for them both to hear her teasing. "Well, it's still normal," she smiled, taking the thermometer from Quinn's mouth. "You're disgustingly healthy," she told him, writing her figures in the chart.

Three days later Martin Quinn was standing at the discharge desk when Tovah Sharon walked by pushing a cart of magazines and paperbacks for the other patients on their floor. Seeing him she stopped and smiled. "Hi, Martin," she said, surprised. "Are you getting out today?"

"Yes, thank God," he answered. "I'm about to go stir crazy."

"Stir crazy?" Tovah asked, puzzled. She make a circling motion with her hand, as if stirring a pot.

"American slang," he explained. "It means being in prison and going crazy from being confined. Sort of like cabin fever in the winter up north back home."

"Cabin fever?" she asked. "Goodness, you Americans have a strange way of using English."

"That's what they say in London," Martin laughed. "How about you? Will you be released soon?"

Tovah made a face. "Next week at the earliest," she said. "I told the doctor I'm perfectly capable of light duty right now, but he insisted I stay." She smiled. "Actually, I think it's because we're short of orderlies."

Martin laughed. "Maybe I ought to volunteer," he suggested.

"Are you serious?" asked another voice behind them. Turning around Martin saw a short grey headed lady in a long lab coat. Glancing at her name badge Martin realized he was talking with the chief surgeon of the hospital.

"Why not?" he said. "I won't be allowed to leave the country for a few days yet and I'd like to talk to some of your people here about the work you're doing here. Rehabilitation of people wounded in the war. Would you let me write about it?"

"Subject to the standard military censorship and protecting the privacy of my patients, yes," the doctor said, nodding. "Is that agreeable?"

"One more thing," Quinn said. "Can you arrange an evening pass for Tovah so I can take her to dinner?"

"Only if she's willing," the doctor smiled. "But from what I see now that shouldn't be a problem." Switching to German she spoke rapidly to Tovah. "He's a nice looking man, *liebschen*," the elder woman said gently, smiling. "Even if he thinks too much of himself," she added, giving Martin a sweet, wry grin.

"I think he's handsome, too," Tovah answered in kind, smiling shyly at the doctor.

"Thank you, gentle lady." Martin spoke to the doctor in high German, snapping his heels and kissing her hand before the doctor could recover from her surprise. Then turning to Tovah, he raised her hand to his lips.

"You've got to watch this one," the doctor told Tovah in precise public school English. "There's more to him than meets the eye."

"I hope so," Martin told her, laughing. Squeezing Tovah's hand lightly he asked, "Is seven this evening all right?"

The harsh ringing of the telephone awakened them from a deep sleep, and it rang four times before Tovah picked up the receiver. "It's for you," she said, poking Martin with the receiver. "Someone named Othello."

Martin took the phone and Tovah went into the kitchen to start their morning coffee. The clock on the wall said five, too late to go back to sleep and too early to rise either. Over the sound of the percolator Tovah could hear the murmur of Martin' voice in the other room, explaining the time difference to Othello. After a few moments he followed her into the kitchen. "Sorry about that," he told her. "He thought it was later here than it is. I'm going to call him back a little later when I'm more awake."

Yawning, Tovah asked, "Othello, is he a Moor?" She giggled.

Martin laughed. "No, sweetheart, although he's dark enough to be. His mother was a romantic who liked the name. I think they're some kind of black Catholics or Orthodox or something."

Extending her arms over her head Tovah stretched. "Mmm," she said, bringing them down to encircle his neck as he nuzzled her breasts. "How soon do you have to call him back?"

An hour later, showered, shaved, and well loved, Martin picked up the telephone to call Othello. As he waited to be connected he looked at Tovah, lying naked across the bed, smiling back at him. She seemed almost like a cat lying there purring, stretching sensuously and blowing him a kiss. Even though they'd just made love, Martin found himself becoming aroused and it was with difficulty he turned his attention to the phone again.

When he was done, he sat there a long time, thinking. Worried, Tovah rolled over and touched his arm. "What is it, Martin?" she asked.

"Othello wants me back in the States," he told her, sighing. "There's a race problem building in Detroit and he wants me to cover it."

"Detroit?" she asked. "Where's that?"

"Michigan," he told her. "Mid continent, northern edge. It surprises me he wants me to go there, that's all. I can't figure whether it's a good story or a red herring."

"Why does it surprise you?" she wanted to know.

"Well, from what I've seen, Chicago is pretty bad, but Detroit is the All American City. Motown is what the blacks call it. Good music, good wages, high employment. It's a party town from what I hear. I can't imagine blacks there being discontent enough to even march, much less riot."

"Riot?" she asked. "You mean like the one in Los Angeles?"

He nodded. "That's what Othello thinks is going down. I think he's crazy as hell, but I guess I've got to go there and check it out." He looked at her sadly.

"You mean you've got to leave right away?" she asked. He nodded. "How soon?" she wanted to know.

"Othello wants me there the day before yesterday, but I told him it would be at least a week. We compromised on three days." He shrugged, looked at her. "Tovah...." he started to say but she shushed him with a finger to his lips.

"No," she said. "It's all right. I'm not going anywhere. You go ahead and do what you need to do. Then come back to me."

"I'm tempted to quit," he said. "I don't want to leave. I just found you and I don't want to lose you."

"Try it and I'll track you down, buster," Tovah laughed. "I have friends in the Mossad."

"You don't mind?" he said, not quite believing her.

"Of course, I mind, silly," she said kissing him. "I want to make love to you every day at least once. But just think of the warm welcome you'll get at your coming home."

"Home coming," he laughed, correcting her with a pun. "Seriously, it may be two to four months before I can get back."

"Maybe I can come see your All American City," she said lightly. "I have some leave coming and I've never been to America." Then she laughed. "I know! My brother goes there all the time raising funds. Maybe if I come with him I won't have to use my vacation." Her eyes twinkled. "We can use that later. Have you ever seen Beirut?"

He nodded. "It's beautiful there. A real vacation city." He looked at her. "All right, then, I'll go. Will you marry me when I come back?"

"I would love to marry you, Martin," she answered gravely. "But I'm Jewish and very much a Zionist. Could you live with that?"

"I was raised a good Catholic," he said. "I guess I could convert. Is that allowed?"

"Yes," Tovah answered. "But I would never ask that, Martin. Should you convert I want it to be for the love of God, not for the love of me."

Martin sighed. "Tovah, I admire those who believe in God. Especially those who live out their faith. I'm afraid I've lost what little of that I may have once had."

"Oh, no, Martin," she answered. "You're a very spiritual man. You may not know it, but you are. That's one of the things which attracted me to you in the first place."

"I wouldn't say that about myself," he protested. "I respect things of a religious nature and I participate in the rituals of the community in which I find myself, but I do it for the sake of others, not myself."

Tovah smiled. "I seem to remember a certain rabbi who wandered this part of the world a long time ago. I believe he was the one who said, 'It is more blessed to give than to receive.' Do you remember?"

"Yes, of course I do. That was drummed into us in Catechism. I am surprised to hear you quoting the Nazarene," he told her. "Is that kosher?"

"I don't know it it's clean or not," Tovah smiled, "but it is true. I believe all truth comes from God."

"Can you put up with my skepticism?" he asked. "I'd love to study the Torah in Israel with an honest to God rabbi, but would my lack of real faith bother you?" His face was very serious.

"Martin," she told him gently. "You may not know it, but you are a man of faith. You believe the truth exists and that it can be found, and that is faith in something greater than yourself."

Martin smiled. "Are you sure you're not a Jewish lawyer?" he asked. "You sure argue like one."

"No, I don't," Tovah protested. "Am I not right, though?"

"I can't argue the point," Martin said. "But I've never really thought about it that way. You may be right."

"Now you sound like the lawyer," she teased.

"I am one," he told her. "At least, that's how I was trained. First the Jesuits and then the University. My best professors were all Jews."

She smiled. "It runs in the blood," she said lightly. Then she looked at him gravely. "There's a lot about you I don't know and I want to know it all." Her look was the kind no one could fail to understand.

Martin chuckled. "Some of it you may not," he said, taking her in his arms and kissing her gently on the neck and shoulders. "I've done quite a few irresponsible things I'm not proud of at all."

"I can't imagine you as irresponsible," Tovah told him, snuggling as close as she could. "Quite the contrary. I think you carry the weight of the world on your shoulders most of the time."

"I'll carry your weight on my shoulders any time," he responded, his voice husky. Slowly he began kissing the other side of her neck, working his way down her shoulder. Tovah shuddered with pleasure.

"We have three days, Martin," she said, running her hands through his hair and down his back. "Three days is a life time here. Let's not waste any of it talking too much."

Seventy-five hours later, as the passenger plane carried him over the Middle Earth Sea, Martin Quinn began a letter to his mother he'd mail from New York. The message was simple and it began,

...Here in what people call the Holy land I have found the woman I want to share my life. This will mean moving here, for she is Jewish, an ardent Zionist who is devoted to the cause of her nation's independence, and she wants her children raised on her ancestral soil. While she insists I need not convert to her faith, I do intend to take instruction from the best rabbi I can find, for there is something about these people and the way they look at the world I find very deep, very attractive. This is where it began for us Catholics, too, isn't it? With a wandering rabbi who refused to be corrupted or compromised, and whose execution we still revere. These days I am not sure whether the man was a cosmic fool or really the Messiah for us all, but I do know there is something different about this place, this people, who formed his character and his thinking. I'd like to know more about it.

I started to write you about the lady of my life, and here I am talking like a mystic about the land and the people. Yet this is not inappropriate. Tovah reflects both the land and its folk in her character. In this she is very much like you, who for me have always reflected the soul of *la raza*. Only here *la raza* is Jewish and damned proud of it, and I see a great many similarities between the two peoples and the way they choose to live.

Like many of her cohorts, Tovah is a sabra, which means she was born here in Palestine, and a kibbutzim, which means she was raised on one of the rural settlements where orphans were sent after the Holocaust. Her parents were refugees from the war in Europe who made it here safely, but both were killed in the 1948 war for independence after the British pulled out. So she is an orphan, too, and the members of her 'family' are other people who grew up in the same kibbutz as she did. I have met a number of them, and they are as impressive as she is. In many ways they remind me of the people I knew when I lived in the canyon.

While Tovah has not completely agreed to marry me yet, we are very much in love and she is giving it much thought. I know she is afraid to commit at this point, yet she tells me she wants to do so with all her heart. I am not sure what is in the way other than my career as an journalist, but I have assured her where my heart is in this matter. No career is more important than the woman I love. That priority is very clear to me and it also tells me the degree of my certainty. I can always write and I really don't care what I do for a living as long as it is clean. Tovah is my soul mate and my place is at her side. I have told her this and I know we may need to be separated from time to time if I pursue this career. Yet I have also told her that when I finish this next assignment in Detroit and clean up some other details, I will return to Zion no later than Hanukkah to ask her hand...

December, 1967. A raw wind whipped across the international airport in Tel Aviv, chilling passengers dashing for the protection of cabs or busses and bringing tears to unprotected eyes. Martin Quinn pulled his hat down and shielded his eyes with a gloved hand as he followed Tovah across the parking lot to her car. When he left New York he thought the tightly woven trench coat he was wearing would be too warm for Palestine, but now he was glad he'd worn it, zippered lining and all. Tovah was wearing a heavy duty military field jacket with a naval watch cap pulled down over her ears. She looked as cold as he felt.

Throwing his luggage in the back of Tovah's ancient Morris, Martin dashed around to the right hand side of the vehicle, expecting to be in the passenger seat. Tovah laughed when he slid in behind the wheel and handed him the keys, but he said, "No, you better drive. You know where you're going and I'm not used to local traffic." Sliding into the other seat he blew on his hands, then sat on them trying to get warm. "I never thought I'd need gloves," he told her.

Tovah laughed again, reaching over to kiss him quickly before starting the car. Running his hand under her jacket he was startled by the fullness of her breasts. "Goodness," he said, joking. "I forgot what a handful you are." Tovah looked at him strangely, then pulled away and started the car. "What did I say?" Martin asked, surprised at her response.

"Nothing," she said shyly. "There's just a little more of me now than there was. I hope you don't mind."

He nodded. "I don't mind," he told her, grinning. "That means more of you for me to love. I wondered if you'd gained weight but I thought it was just the jacket."

"No," she told him. "I have gained weight. This jacket was the only warm thing I had that fit me." She turned back to her driving.

"What is it, Tovah?" he asked. "What's wrong?"

"Nothing's wrong," she said, beginning to cry. "Damn, I didn't want it to be this way."

"You didn't want what to be this way?" Martin asked, alarmed.

Tovah pulled the Morris to the side of the pavement and turned to look at him. Opening her jacket she took his hand and pressed it against her belly. He was surprised how firm and round it was. "I'm pregnant, Martin," she told him quietly. "We conceived a child."

"Are you sure?" he asked, shocked.

"Am I sure?" she snapped angrily. "Am I sure it's yours? Is that what you're asking?"

"Of course not," he snapped back. "Are you sure you're pregnant?"

Tovah's anger vanished as quickly as it came. "I'm sorry," she said. "I seem so moody these days." She smiled. "But, yes, I'm sure I'm pregnant. I've been sure for some time. I'm five months along."

"That's wonderful!" Martin said. "Why didn't you let me know?"

"I thought you'd be back before this and I didn't want to just write you or tell you over the phone," Tovah answered. "Then you told me you were coming so I just waited."

"Marvelous," he told her. "So how soon can we get married here?"

"Martin," she protested. "As much as I love you, this is not a reason to get married."

"No," he pointed out. "But we were talking marriage before this ever happened." He grinned. "Or maybe while it was happening. Remember? We talked about it in June and I told you I'd be back now at the latest for a decision. You said I didn't need to convert and I told you I am willing to do so. The only thing I ask is we find a rabbi who's, ah, very skillful with his, ah, pruning knife."

Tovah laughed at the look on his face. "We can't use pinking shears?" she teased, then grew serious. "Martin, you don't have to convert for me. Or for our child, either. We don't even have to marry. The wars have made us very tolerant of such things. All I would ask is for you to acknowledge him, mostly for his sake."

"Him?" Martin asked lightly. "Are you sure it's not a her?"

Tovah shook her head. "No, I'm not. It's just a way of speaking."

"Please believe me, Tovah," Martin spoke earnestly. "I would never knowingly abandon a child of mine. Or you, either."

"Do you believe me when I tell you this child is yours?" she asked. "In your place I'd understand if you had questions."

"Of course, I do," he responded urgently. "Why would you lie?"

"It happens, Martin," she said. "It happens all the time."

"Not with you," he told her. "I think you're the kind of person who would tell me if you were carrying another man's child. That's why I want to marry you, because I love you and that's the kind of person you are."

Tovah said nothing, but clutched him around the neck and began to cry softly. Martin held her for a long while, then pulled back. "Sweetheart," he said. "I love you with all my heart, but I'm about to freeze to death. Could we find someplace a little warmer to talk?"

Half an hour later they were snuggled happily under a blanket on the sofa of Tovah's tiny efficiency apartment, their feet pointed toward the glow of a small, ancient electric space heater. A pot of fresh tea sat steeping on a table beside the sofa and two large mugs kept wait beside a plate of cookies. Huddled under their blanket Martin sighed contentedly. "I don't know what's the matter with me," he said. "I normally don't get this cold."

"You didn't have much on," Tovah answered from under his chin. "I thought you grew up where it was cold."

"I did," Martin complained. "But I've never been this cold. I must be coming down with a cold or something."

"Or something, I'd say," Tovah giggled, stroking a vital place under the blanket. "Or maybe up with something."

"Let me warm up a little more and we'll see," he promised, shifting to a more comfortable position. "So, how long have you known?"

"Not for a long time," Tovah admitted. "I missed a couple of cycles, but I thought that was due to being burned. When I missed the third one I was pretty sure but went to the doctor to find out."

"So you've only really known for a couple of months, then?" Martin asked. Tovah nodded and he continued. "How do you feel about it?"

"Very happy and scared all at once," she said. "It's very strange having someone else living in your body."

"I imagine it is," he answered. "Have you thought about names."

"Yes. I want to name him after his father and my father. Martin Isaac. Is that all right?" Tovah looked up at him, searching.

"Of course," he nodded. "I'd like that. However, you're assuming it's a him, but what if it's a her? Have you thought of a name in case it's a girl?"

"No, not really," she said. "There are lots of girl's names I like but not any special one. Do you have something in mind?"

"Rose," he answered promptly. "Or Rosa. That's my mother's name." He smiled down at Tovah. "On the other hand, you may not want to name her after your mother-in-law."

"Does she know about me?" she asked. "Rosa?"

"Yes," Martin answered. "I told her about you in my first letter after I left last June. I told her I'd met the woman of my dreams. She wants to meet you and was ready to fly out then, whether I was along or not. I had a hard time convincing her it wasn't a good time to travel in this part of the world."

"She'd be fine!" Tovah protested. "You should have told her to come on out. I'd like to meet her, too."

"Even right now?" he asked, teasing.

"Yes, unless she'd be put off by my condition," Tovah answered, "But from what you've told me about her, I don't think she would."

"No, if anything, she'd be excited. She's wanted a grand child so long now I don't think she'd give it a second thought."

Suddenly Tovah was excited. "She could be here for Hanukkah. We could see it in Jerusalem!" she said. "I have friends there we could stay with. They've already asked me to come."

"I don't think that's a good idea," Martin responded. "They invited you, not me and my mother. Besides, I don't know if she'd leave this close to Christmas. She's big on family holidays."

"I bet she would if she knew she had a grandchild on the way," Tovah told him. "I certainly would."

"Well, let me talk to her about it first," Martin answered, a bit reluctant to change the plans he'd made for exploring Palestine.

"Don't you want her to come?" Tovah asked.

"Yes, but I don't want anything to cut into our time together," he told her. "I've been looking forward to spending this time with you and looking around the country."

"She won't interfere," Tovah protested. "I promise. I'd really love to meet her. She could help me plan the wedding." Suddenly her eyes were filled with tears. "You don't understand," she said. "It would be good for me. What I remember of my own mother is very good, but..." She left the thought unfinished.

"All right," he said gently. "I will call. I do understand. It was the same for me. I never had anyone for a father until I met Emil Ramos. At least, not the kind of father I wanted." He looked at his watch and thought a moment. "I better wait another couple of hours before I call. I don't think they're up yet."

Tovah looked at him and smiled. "They're not up and we haven't been to bed yet. We've got some catching up to do, sailor."

"I thought you'd never ask," he whispered as he kissed her, gently at first, then more urgently as they moved into the ancient dance of love.

Four days later they met Rosa's plane at the airport. Unlike her son, she was dressed for cold weather and remarked how much warmer it seemed there than in Minnesota as they passed through customs. Nor had there been any problem with travel documents. Rosa had traveled with Martin' father on a construction project in Central America the summer before and her passport and vaccinations were up to date. As a matter of fact, both her husband and her other son were on site there and would be until late January, leaving her with the prospect of spending Christmas alone with Jeremy's whining wife. Nor was there hiding her excitement at meeting her future daughter-in-law. Yet when Martin brought Rosa into the restaurant where Tovah was waiting, she gasped as they approached the table. "Martin!" Rosa said in a voice full of awe. "Is this her?"

Martin nodded happily. "This is Tovah, mother." Tovah rose but hesitated, unsure what Rosa's response meant.

"Gracious, dear," Rosa said, looking at her intently, then hugging her gently. "You look just like my sister Rita when we were your age."

"You mean Raunchy Rita?" Martin teased happily.

"Martin!" Rosa scolded mildly. "Mind your manners."

"I haven't been able to get him to do that either," Tovah laughed. "I think it must be gender related."

"I'm sure it is, dear," Rosa said, taking Tovah's arm and leading the way out of the airport, handing Martin her baggage checks and leaving him to find her luggage and follow along. "So tell me, dear," he heard Rosa saying as they walked toward the exit, "when is the baby due?"

The next three weeks were the happiest time Martin could remember in any of his twenty-seven years. As Tovah predicted, Rosa was no trouble at all and fit in as easily as if they'd been family for years. At first Martin was a bit uneasy about lodging arrangements when they traveled, but Rosa settled the issue before it ever arose. Taking the key to the single room and leaving them the double when they checked into the hotel, she smiled at her son and Tovah and said, "Well, I'm going to my room for a quick nap and change for dinner. Why don't we meet down here in an hour?" Smiling and taking her bell boy in tow, Rosa crossed to the elevators, leaving Martin and Tovah gawking in her wake.

"So you were right," Martin said in answer to Tovah's raised eyebrow. "I don't understand it, but it's great."

"It's a woman thing," Tovah responded, drawing close and kissing him lightly on the cheek. "You hairy types don't stand a chance."

That evening, as they walked through the streets of the archaic city, it was apparent the quickly won peace was still uneasy. Uniformed soldiers walked the streets in pairs, their automatic weapons slung casually barrel down over their shoulders, but ready for instant use. Even so, the city was festive in the clear night air with an atmosphere of celebration, and they could hear people laughing as they walked along. Suddenly Rosa stopped and pointed. "I've always wondered what those were," she said.

Looking where she was pointing Martin answered. "They are called menorah" he told her, referring to the candelabra set on the sill of a window with two of its eight candles burning.

"Why are only two candles burning?" Rosa asked Tovah. She pointed on up the street where they could see a number of other menorah sitting in the windows of houses and apartments facing the street. Each held eight candles, but only two were lit.

"Let's let Mr. Smart Pants tell us," Tovah challenged, looking at Martin with a jaundiced eye.

"It's only the second night of Hanukkah," he answered grinning. "The Feast Of Lights. One candle is lit each night for the eight days of celebration. It's sort of like we used to do with the Advent wreath at home." He looked at Tovah and winked.

"And what's the meaning of the celebration?" Tovah asked, a catechist to his performance.

"I thought you'd never ask," Martin responded, grinning even wider.

Rosa frowned at him but Tovah laughed. "He wants to show off," she told her future mother-in-law. "He's been reading up."

"So you've learned already what we've been putting up with all these years?" Rosa asked her, nodding. "It's terrible."

"Yes," Tovah said, looking at Martin as if he were a horse she were considering buying. "But he seems to have some redeeming qualities, too."

"Yes, he does at that," Rosa grudgingly admitted. "But it's best not to let him get too puffed up with himself."

"Absolutely," Martin agreed, continuing as nothing had been said. "I understand the festival is not one of the big ones of Judaism, but it has really become popular among the people. It's the celebration of the rededication of the Temple after the Macabeeans threw the Greeks out of Palestine in about 167 BC." Rosa looked interested so he continued. "When the Greeks conquered the country they desecrated the Temple by making a sacrifice to Zeus of Olympus in the sanctuary—in the holy of holies. So when the Jews defeated them and took Jerusalem back, the Temple was ritually cleansed and rededicated to Jewish usage. An annual celebration was commanded by the king and the current customs grew up around that."

"Why is it called the Feast of Lights?" Rosa wanted to know.

"There's a medieval legend that right after the rededication they ran low of holy oil to burn in the lamps. Supposedly there was only enough for one day and not time enough to consecrate more, but the oil lasted all eight days."

Rosa nodded. "I always thought it was just an alternative the Jewish people had for Christmas. The people I know give gifts at Hanukkah. Children get those little tops."

Martin nodded. "I know, but apparently that's a fairly new custom. It grew up mostly in Europe, I think, during the medieval period."

"Yes, it was mostly from Europe we got those customs," a cultured voice responded from behind them. Turning they saw a short bearded man standing on the street dressed in a heavy coat and a flat brimmed black hat. "Good evening, Tovah. I thought I recognized you," he said, smiling.

"Reb Cohen!" Tovah cried as she hugged the small man. "Can you guess how much I've been thinking about you? Here are some people I want you to meet." She introduced Martin and his mother.

"Good thoughts, I hope," the rabbi smiled, shaking hands with Martin and bowing deeply to Rosa without offering his hand.

"Always, rabbi," Tovah told him. Looking down she added, "Martin and I will be marrying soon."

The rabbi looked at Martin gravely. "You're not Jewish, are you?" he asked, his bright eyes missing nothing.

"No, sir, I'm not," Martin responded. "But I want to take instruction. I was raised a good Catholic."

The rabbi nodded, looking at Rosa. "So how does your family feel about this?" he asked gently.

"Martin must find his own way," Rosa said. "We've talked about it at length and I respect his decision."

"Are you not afraid for the souls of your grandchildren?" Rabbi Cohen insisted. "Most Catholics would be."

"That's not the God I know," Rosa told him, holding his gaze. "The priests are simply wrong about that, the ones who would say they will go to hell. The God I believe in would never do that to innocent children. Or to a good man like yourself."

"Ah," said the rabbi, nodding. "Thank you. You are very kind, but I'm afraid you don't know my sins. Would you like instruction, too?"

"Thank you, no," Rosa responded politely. "I had quite enough of that to last a lifetime when I was a girl. I study on my own, but...."

The rabbi chuckled. "A free soul," he declared. "You are a rarity these days, Mrs. Quinn."

"Mrs. Lundberg," Martin explained. "I write under a pen name. My birth name is Martin Lundberg."

"You write well," the rabbi said. "I thought I recognized your name. I really appreciated your series on the wounded from the war. You look below the surface."

"Would you care to join us?" Rosa asked. "We've had supper but we were going for a glass of wine and perhaps some dessert."

"Ordinarily I would be delighted," the rabbi told them. "Tonight I have duties I must attend. May I take a..." he said something in Yiddish to Tovah.

"Rain check," she told him.

"Rainy check," he finished, frowning. "Curious term."

"Rain check," Martin corrected. "I hope you will. Mother will be here for another couple of weeks. We're going to see as much of the country as we can."

"Marvelous," said the rabbi, handing them a business card. Seeing Martin' puzzled look he laughed. "It's printed in Hebrew, of course, but Tovah can read it. Or any school child if she's not with you. Shalom," he added, offering Martin his hand.

"*Shalom, alecheim!*" Martin responded, taking the offered hand and shaking it warmly.

"I see you've begun your instruction already," the rabbi laughed as he walked away. "Look me up!"

Ten days later, when they put Rosa on the flight to Rome and then to the United States, the wedding had been set for late June. Martin had wanted it much earlier, but ran into a united front with the two women. Both agreed they should wait until after the birth of the child so there would never be any question of its Israeli citizenship. "You're married already," Rosa told her son. "You feel it and Tovah feels it. What we're talking about now is not your union but the celebration of your marriage, so there's no rush."

"I want the child to be known as mine," Martin argued.

"I talked to Reb Cohen about that," Rosa informed him. "Everything here is decided by the rabbis. He agreed that waiting will guard your baby's citizenship, and it will not affect your being the child's father. They trace a child's lineage by maternal ancestry," Rosa added, smiling. "Which makes a lot of sense if you think of it."

"What makes you say that?" Martin asked.

"Well," Rosa answered primly, "there's no denying who's the mother." Martin laughed and Rosa added. "Reb Cohen also agrees with me that in the eyes of God you and Tovah are already husband and wife, too."

"See why I like these people, mother?" Martin smiled.

"Well, if one is not going to be Catholic, it's the next best thing," Rosa said, surprising him. "After all," she continued, "the greatest man the world has ever known was Jewish."

"So was his mother," Martin laughed. "So was his mother."

3. Deep Water Blues

S omewhere in Nanaland. Unaware I am not awake, I dream I am float-ing along at sea in a small boat on a beautiful bright day. Off in the distance I can see sail boats sailing away and they seem to be running with the wind. Suddenly I am aware I am not on a sail boat, but am in a life raft propelled awkwardly by a paddle, and the sea seems to be running ever higher. Then I realize what I am on is not a life raft, at all, but a queen sized air mattress floating along on the sea and I become very afraid, for the sea is deep and I cannot swim very well. I look toward the sail boats, hoping to hail someone to help, but they are now so far away all I can see is their sails above the horizon. As I do this, I become aware that the mattress is growing ever smaller, leaking air from a pin hole in the bottom. I realize I am sinking and I awake in sheer terror, soaked with sweat. (Martin Quinn's journal)

March 1969. The old man did not look like a monk, or even a priest, for that matter. As he hobbled across the stone floor of the chapel to where Martin sat he reminded Quinn somehow of Santa Claus, a some-what disabled Santa Claus, one forced to use a cane and dressed in the rough white robes of the monastic order. As the old man drew closer, his face reinforced the image. His white hair, worn in boyish style, was long and curly, with rosy cheeks rising above an equally curly white beard, worn full. Yet it was the man's eyes, bright blue and cheerful behind their quaint rimless octagon lenses, which told the world this surely must be St. Nick himself. The smile which played around the corners of the man's mouth, even when he was solemn, confirmed this.

"Hello, father," Martin said, getting to his feet. "Thank you for see-ing me today. I really appreciate it."

"The pleasure is mine, young fellow, believe me," the padre told him. "In a moment of madness I agreed to forty days of Trappist silence for Lent this year, and it is a pleasure to have a good excuse to talk to someone." He sighed, the smile never leaving his lips, yet somehow under-scoring the serious regard with which he looked at Quinn. "You must be desperate, my friend, desperate, indeed, driving all the way out here seeking a priest."

Martin nodded. "I am desperate. I need to talk to someone, father, but I was already out here, anyway, and I just happened to see the sign by the road. So I thought I'd ring the bell and ask." He looked down, shook his head. "I feel like a hypocrite being here. I'm not a believer any more. Even though I suppose I need to make confession, I'm not sure how sincere it would be. I haven't been to Mass in years."

"Well, let's let God worry about your sincerity," the old priest told him. "Tell me, are you Roman Catholic?" Martin nodded and the priest continued. "Are you aware that this is an ecumenical community?"

Martin shook his head. "No, father, but that's all the better. I happen to think all the divisions in Christianity are wrong, so it doesn't matter. You are a priest, aren't you? I guess it doesn't really matter, but I would feel better talking to a priest. As I said, it's hypocritical, but I would."

"Oh yes," said the good father. "I am a priest, indeed, which is one of God's little jokes on all concerned. And if you're a hypocrite, there's always room for more in this man's church. Which is all living proof that our Lord God has a good sense of humor. What you need to know, however, is I am not in Roman orders. I am an Anglican priest."

"Church of England?" Martin asked. The old priest nodded. "What's the difference, father?"

"Well, it depends on who you talk to," the padre chuckled. "To me it is pretty much the same, especially since Vatican II. Same seven sac-raments, same three orders of clergy, same Mass in the language of the people, and we follow the same cycle of celebration of the Church year. Our main difference is the vanities we affect, at least in my opinion, and for me, the fact our clergy are allowed to marry." He chuckled. "I would have flunked celibacy." Then he added, "As far as anything you say to me, I will treat it as confessional, if you wish, and the same seal of silence will apply."

"Are you married, father?" Martin asked, surprised.

"Oh, yes," said the good padre. "Just about forever now. I enjoy all the comforts of domestic life. I'm only up here on retreat."

"I apologize for intruding..." Martin started to say, but the aging cleric interrupted, waving it away.

"Good heavens, man," the padre said. "After two weeks up here with the brothers, and three to go, I'm delighted to be interrupted. As a matter of fact, you are the answer to a very specific prayer."

Martin was even more surprised. "I am? How is that?"

The cleric chuckled. "I was doing my usual whining to the Lord God this morning at Mass, assuring him that, while I was very happy on this very useful retreat, and delighted in His company, I really would like to talk with a normal human being. An hour later, you rang."

Martin nodded. "I don't know what claim I can make to being normal, but I'm glad to know this is a happy coincidence. I feel better about barging in."

"Oh, no," the padre corrected him gently. "It is no coincidence. That is simply a word scientists use to tell us they're confused. Coincidence is Him or Herself being anonymous. You are here for a reason, just as I am. Not to take our vanities too seriously, I think this meeting may have been the reason we both are in this desolate place." Seeing the look on Martin' face, the padre rushed on. "Forgive me, please. You needed to see a priest and here I am prattling on and on like an old fool. What is troubling you?"

"It's my wife," he said. "Or rather the woman I was to marry and our child. We weren't married yet." He stopped.

"You called her your wife," the priest said. "And you had a child by her. Did she consider you her husband?"

Martin nodded. "Yes, she did. She used to call me, 'my husband' in private when we were together. The child was mine. I'm sure of that."

"You were also to celebrate the marriage ritually," the padre said. "I think in the eyes of God we can say she was your wife. What happened to keep you from carrying through with the celebration?"

"A bomb," Martin said. "A fucking Arab bomb!" A deep moan, like the howl of a wounded animal escaped him, and covering his face with his hands, he began to weep, deep, racking sobs shaking his frame.

"Jesus," said the old man, reverently, reaching out and putting an arm around Martin' shoulder. Martin came to him like a small child, burying his head in the old cleric's shoulder and crying so hard his breath came in gasps between howls. When they begin to subside the padre said gently, "We have all the time in the world, my friend. When you feel like it, tell me about it. It will help to talk, believe me." He waited patiently.

"I'm a newsman, father," Martin told him a few minutes later. "I work for one of the wire services and I met Tovah covering the Six Day War." As he spoke, Martin' face grew more and more open, and he told the old priest not only of his meeting of Tovah, but of his mother's trip to meet her and their plans to marry once the child was born. He also spoke at length about his arranging for instruction for conversion to Judaism and his plans to settle in Israel and raise a family.

Although his grief was deep, overshadowing all he said, there was no mistaking the joy the prospect of marrying Tovah brought him, and that of raising his child in Israel. When he was done talking, he fell silent for a time, looking far into the middle distance. Then he said, "I can't get it out of my mind, father. I don't understand. Why did God, if there is a God, allow this to happen? Why me? Why Tovah?"

"I've asked him that many times, my friend," the priest assured him. "All I got in reply was celestial silence, and I grew quite angry about it, so I did some very destructive things. Then I was given an answer that I didn't particularly like, but it was satisfactory." He reached in the pocket of his cassock and pulled out a small black book with a gold cross on the front. Seeing it, Martin was reminded of the Anglican Prayerbook Ramos had once given him, but this one seemed much thicker. The old padre turned to a well worn page near the middle and began to read softly, his deep voice gentle and solemn, mixed with equal measures of sorrow and joy,

> I am the man who has known affliction,
>
> I have felt the rod of his wrath.
>
> It was I whom he led away and left to walk
>
> in darkness, where no light shines.
>
> Against me alone he has turned his hand and
>
> thus it is so all the day long
>
> He has wasted away my flesh and my skin
>
> and has broken all my bones;
>
> he has built up wall around me, ahead and behind
>
> and has cast me into a place of darkness
>
> like a man who is long dead....

The old man looked up, his eyes full of tears of remembrance. "It goes on and on," he said gravely. "The low point comes with these lines a little further down." Focusing on the book again, he resumed his reading,

> He has broken my teeth on gravel; fed on ashes
>
> I am wracked with pain;
>
> peace has gone out of my life and I have forgotten
>
> what prosperity means.
>
> Then I cry that my strength is gone and so has my
>
> hope in the Lord.

The good padre stopped reading and looked up at Martin. "I imagine that may sound familiar to you, doesn't it? The feelings of desolation and being without hope?" Martin nodded. "I lived there for many years," the old man told him. "It's an awful place to be. Yet, looking back, I think perhaps I lived there so long primarily because of my own stubborn, pig-headed self. I simply could not believe faith was anything but a bucket of shit people used to deceive themselves. Does that strike a chord with you?"

Martin was shocked to hear a priest speak so directly and bluntly. He nodded. "I could claim that verbatim, father," he answered. "When I read Marx's description of religion as the opiate of the masses I thought the man was right on."

The other nodded. "Poor old Karl Marx. No one deserves the kind of disciples he gained for his troubles. Yet I, too, understood exactly what he meant when he wrote that. Mostly because it is true. Religion, as it is practiced and exploited by some of its more virulent heretics, has indeed become an opiate for the great masses of the uninformed American public." He grinned and added, "Many of whom would undoubtedly consider me the devil incarnate for what I happen to believe, and would gladly see me burn at the stake." He shook his head. "But that's another story. As for how I felt, I could well have written that passage of the *Lamentations of Israel*."

"You no longer feel that way?" Martin asked.

"No," said the priest. "I don't. Grace finally got through in the good offices of an innocent soul, and I began to realize my thinking was rather clouded by my attitude of self importance." He chuckled. "After a little deflation I began to realize I was the bucket which was full of *le caca*." Turning to another place in the book, he resumed reading.

When my heart became embittered,

I was sorely wounded in my heart.

I was stupid and had no understanding;

I was like a brute beast in your presence.

Yet I am always with you;

you hold me by my right hand.

You will guide me by your counsel,

And afterwards receive me with glory.

Martin waited a moment, reflecting, then asked, "I don't understand, father. That's a nice sentiment, but what was the answer you were given? I don't hear an answer there."

The cleric nodded, as if speaking to himself. "That was only the first part, the realization I was becoming rather bitter and cynical. Then I was told I was asking the wrong questions. I was asking the Lord God 'why' questions rather than 'how' questions, and there is quite a difference."

"I still don't understand," Martin told him. "You have to know why to know how something happened."

"I didn't understand either, at first," the padre admitted. "Until the Lord God chose a very simple soul to tell me this, one of the six pure in heart I am convinced uphold the Universe with their daily prayers." He nodded as he remembered. "She did not realize she was giving me my answer." A smile came to his lips and he chuckled. "She came to me telling me about this theophany she had during one of my sermons. Can you imagine the irony of that? I thought it was rather shameless of God to do that, to convict me with my own hypocrisy."

He chuckled again, laughing at himself, then continued, "Anyway, her theophany was the realization that asking questions why is like spinning our spiritual wheels. There really aren't any answers to the why questions that can satisfy us, and insisting on knowing why can drive us crazy. Those were her very words. 'Asking why can drive you crazy, father.' What we've got to ask, she told me, is 'how' questions. Like, how do I respond to what has happened? I didn't like it at the time, but I had to admit she was right. She always was. I think she has a direct line to the Highest of Heavens and doesn't know it."

Martin said nothing and the old priest nodded. "I believe the question you need to ask...." He paused, surprised, and said, "I'm sorry, my friend. I just realized I don't even know your name. We just jumped right into our conversation. Not that names are necessary, but I am Thomas McAlpin." He laughed. "One of the doubting variety."

"Martin," Quinn answered. "Martin Quinn."

"Quinn?" the old man mused. "A journalist." Then recognition came to the startling blue eyes. "Yes, I remember now. I think you did an article on Floyd Newman some time ago. An excellent piece of work." Then he abruptly shook his head. "Forgive this old man, Martin. Galloping senility seems to have set in. What was I saying before I rudely interrupted myself?"

"Something about not asking why," Martin responded.

"Why questions, oh, yes," the padre smiled. "What I was going to suggest is that you ask the how questions. Start with how you responded to Tovah's death and the death of your child. How did you respond?"

Martin shrugged. "I got very drunk, for damned near two weeks. It was the longest bender I've ever done. I wanted to die and I didn't."

The old man nodded. "I can imagine. I've never lost a wife but I did lose a daughter several years ago. It was devastating." He thought. "Getting drunk is human, Martin, but staying drunk that long is a very self destructive response. One how question is how you might respond to your grief without destroying yourself in the process."

"I didn't want to live," Martin told him. "I still don't. I thought about suicide but I am still too much a Catholic to pull the trigger. Or maybe too much of a coward," he added bitterly.

"Oh, my friend," the padre said gently. "Don't be so hard on yourself, not about this. Wanting to die when we lose someone is normal. One of the most difficult things which can happen to us is being the one who survives. I wanted to die after my daughter's death, but I couldn't abandon my son or my other daughter. Or my wife, for that matter."

"I deserve to die, father. If I had been there it wouldn't have happened. She was on the way to mail me a letter." Again Martin buried his face in his hands and began to weep. "I got the letter just an hour before I heard about her death."

"You weren't notified right away?" the old man asked, puzzled.

"No, she didn't have any family except people in her kibbutz. The one who was handling her affairs didn't know Tovah was getting married and did not know to call me. I heard about it off the wire."

"Off the wire?" McAlpin did not comprehend.

Martin nodded. "Teletype. The Israeli authorities suppressed the story for a few days. My supervisor picked up a rumor there had been a bombing in Jerusalem and gave me a call. When the story came out, we queried for a list of the dead, and it took a while to get, but her name was on it. I called to be sure, gave them her address, and they told me it was her." He shrugged. "By then she was buried, so I never went back. I've not been to Israel since."

The padre nodded. "So you never got to say *keddish* for them, to say a proper good-bye. That's why you think it's your fault, is it?" He asked. "Because she was going to mail you a letter?"

Martin nodded. "What if she had been going out to buy groceries? Or anything else? Would you feel any different about it?" The old man's voice was very gentle.

Martin shook his head. "I couldn't feel any worse, but at least I'd know it wasn't my fault."

"Forgive me for being blunt, Martin, but did you set up that bombing?" The padre's eyes were grave. "Were you involved somehow?"

"Of course not!" Martin snapped. "How could I?"

"I didn't think so," the priest said, "but it occurred to me that it might be what you were confessing. Stranger things I've heard and I had to be very clear what we are dealing with." He nodded. "So even though you know in your mind that you were not directly responsible, in your heart you do feel in some way responsible." Martin nodded, even though the priest said it as a statement and not a question. "Your problem, then, is one of the heart," McAlpin nodded. "All right, Martin, given what happened, how might you respond in a more healthy way? What are your options?"

"Killing fucking Arabs!" Quinn snarled, his teeth bared like a wolf. "They're the assholes who did it."

The priest nodded. "That's one option," he said. "Very tempting, too, I imagine. You could seek vengeance, blood on the floor. However, the problem with vengeance is that it is as self destructive as direct suicide. No, worse, I think. Vengeance kills the soul, the spirit, a little bit at a time, like a cancer eating away from within. What other options do you have? Creative options, not self destructive ones," he added. "How can some good be brought out of this?"

"I thought about going after them in print," Martin told him. "But I'm not sure what you mean by a creative options."

McAlpin shook his head. "So long as you're going after them it won't work," he pointed out. "On the other hand, if you used your position to try to prevent future bombings by going after us, holding us all responsible for what happened, that would be a creative response, indeed. The difference, I think, is that creative responses are life giving, for you and for others, too."

"That sounds like damned hard work," Martin told him.

"Ask any contractor," the old priest smiled. "Demolition is much easier than construction. That seems to be a principle of life. We can destroy in seconds what it takes years to build. Nor does destruction take much in the way of resources. All it takes is anger and self will, and boom! It's done." He shook his head sadly.

A bell rang in the distance. "It's time for None," the padre told Martin. "Noonday prayers. You are welcome to join us in the chapel and to stay for lunch, too, if you wish. I have to go now because I am preaching."

Martin looked uncertain. "That would really be intruding," he said.

"Not at all," McAlpin informed him. "All kinds of people seem to show up from time to time, and sometimes none of us know who they are. Of course, you don't have to come to chapel if you prefer to wait here. We'll only be about twenty minutes. I'm not going to be long winded. But the singing alone is worth coming for, even if you don't participate in the prayers."

"Twenty minutes?" Martin asked. "And you're preaching?"

"That only accounts for about five to six minutes," the padre laughed. "I believe if I can't say it in five minutes I haven't thought it through."

"I know a lot of priests who would do well adopting your philosophy," Martin told him. "If you don't think it's intruding, I think I will come. I like Gregorian chant."

"It's Celtic chant today," the padre told him, getting to his feet, leading the way. "I think you may like that, even better. It's gorgeous. As are some of our hymns." Turning to walk up the stone pavement, he began to hum a beautiful haunting tune.

Martin was startled, shocked, and watched wide-eyed as the old cleric walked up the path humming the same tune as the flute played with the old man keening at the grave in his running vision of raven and wolf. An ever growing sense of familiarity suddenly became crystal clear, and Martin was thunder struck at the realization that what he'd seen in the vision was Thomas McAlpin keening at the grave of his daughter. "Jesus!" he said reverently, almost crossing himself. Then he jerked, looking around as if he'd heard an answer, but he decided it was only the wind playing across the garden.

When they arrived at the chapel, Martin was surprised at what he saw. The chapel was laid out like a basilica, the chairs arranged in a large single circle around the front of a simple stone altar set on a platform perhaps a third of the way across the room from the east wall. Bright light filtered in through windows set high in the walls and colored with large panels of what looked like chunks of stained glass bound together like stones with something similar to mortar. The walls themselves were smooth white plaster, and the vaulted ceiling was Carolina blue, held in place by large columns set at four corners of the central part of the building. Yet what struck Martin most was the air of quiet and peace, even in the confusion of people taking their seats. *God lives here,* Martin thought. *If there is a God,* another voice within him started to answer, chiding him for his foolishness. Yet even this voice of his critic was silenced by the stillness and peace in this place. Then, when the abbot took his place in the circle, now filled but for a single empty chair, his opening words affirmed all that Martin sensed. "The Lord is in his holy temple; let all the earth keep silence before him," the abbe said, reading from the prayer book, to which the brothers responded, "Amen."

The singing turned out to be even better than Martin anticipated. The acoustics of the basilica were incredible, as if it had been built tuned for the frequency of the brothers' voices. Even though there was a small tracker on one wall of the basilica, the monks sang *a cappella*, led by a younger man of their number, and hearing the incredible harmony of the monks' voices echo through the stillness of the basilica, Martin was given a deeper appreciation of the original meaning of the term. *This must be the way angels sound,* the thought came unbidden, together with a response Martin believed he heard, but was never quite sure, quietly in the background. *Indeed they do.* With the thought tears came again, this time quietly, washing away his pain and gently bathing his wounded spirit.

At the appropriate time Thomas McAlpin rose and went to the ambo to deliver his homily. It was a meditation on the words of Job in response to his comforters, and Martin was struck by how it sounded as if McAlpin wrote it for him, even though they never met until that morning. *There are no chance meetings,* the thought flickered across his mind. *Fr. McAlpin seems to be right about that.* But this raised more questions than it answered and Martin set them aside firmly to listen to the singing of the prayers which followed the homily. Again he was struck by how the monk's voices blended into one, reverberating through the basilica, and as he listened, watching the monks as they sang, a strange thing happened. Time folded in on itself, drawing the congregation with it, and suddenly they were no longer on the American continent in the middle twentieth century. Suddenly it seemed they had been transported to the holy isle, Lindisfarne, where they sat in the chapel singing on a fine, clear October day in the year 1053, *anno domini.*

With the realization, Martin started, looked out one of the few clear windows high on the basilica wall. The sky was grey, heavy with late winter rain, and the sun was gone. *What was that?* he wondered, looking around at the others, but no one else seemed to have notice, nor was anyone disturbed, if they did. *This is a very strange place,* he told himself, but strange as it might be, it was neither a scary oddity, nor even really very extraordinary, as if things like this happened there every day. When he asked the old priest about it later on as they walked the gardens, Fr. McAlpin smiled. "I do understand what you mean, Martin. Here, they are common. Outside these walls it would be a very unusual, and perhaps a frightening thing. Yet here it seems to be such a normal thing to happen at chapel."

"Then you noticed it, too?" Martin asked.

"Not exactly the way you did, my friend," the padre said. "For me it was a very beautiful time of peace, but I did notice others seemed unusual recollected after chapel."

"Recollected?" Martin inquired.

"Yes, brought back together," McAlpin answered. "Within our normal life pursuits we are often like the bug which hits the windshield, splattered all over the landscape. One of the reasons for places like this is for us to be put back together and healed." He looked at Martin over the top of his glasses. "At least, that is how I experience it. Tell me, you are something of a mystic, aren't you?"

"I've been told that," Martin smiled. "Although I'm not sure exactly what that is. I'm certainly not very religious."

"One doesn't have to be religious to be a mystic," the padre said. "Just very attuned to things of the spirit. The word *mystikos* derives from the root *mystos* in Greek, which means keeping silence. A mystic is simply someone who is aware of mysteries and the mysterious in the midst of normal life."

Martin began to chuckle, then the chuckle turned into a laugh, and that turned into laughter he couldn't control, though he was gasping for breath. Two of the brothers passing by looked at him with concern, but Fr. McAlpin shook his head and simply waited until the hysteria left Martin gasping on a bench. "I don't know why that struck me as so funny," Martin said when he was able to speak. "It isn't, not really."

"I think it was pain coming out, not humor," the old cleric told him. "I apparently touched a nerve with my question."

Martin shook his head. "I was laughing at myself," he said. "I just then realized how stupid I've been. I have many names, Father, and one of them is Raven Wolf, which was given to me by the Tewa. If you have time I'd like to tell you about it."

"It would be my care and delight to hear, Martin," Fr. McAlpin assured him gravely. "We can sit here or we can continue our walk."

"Let's walk," Martin said, rising to his feet. "Somehow walking seems to get my mind going better."

"It does that for me," the priest replied. "If I remember, Tewa are in New Mexico and keep very much to themselves. Tell me how they happened to give you the name Raven Wolf. That sounds like a very mystical name."

"Oh, it is," Martin said. "It's also a long story, so please bear with me. I'll make it as concise as I can." Choosing his words carefully, Martin told Father McAlpin of his brush with the *penitentes*, of calling the black wolf and of his initiation run, and of his vision of the old man singing by the grave, his voice blended with that of the flute.

When he was done, the old priest was thoughtful for a long while. "Do you remember the melody?" he asked and Martin. "Could you hum it for me, do you think?"

"I'll do better than that," Martin told him, reaching into an inner pocket of his jacket and pulling out a simple brass flute.

"Gracious," said the padre. "A penny whistle. I haven't seen one of those since I was in England."

"Amazing what you can do with them," Martin answered, rubbing the pipe gently to warm it up before playing. Sitting down on a large rock near the path he began to play the simple tune the old man always sang as he stood at the grave. Then his fingers began to move over the slender pipe as of their own volition, and the strange eerie melody filled the garden, drifting across the wet grass like a sun beam caressing all it touched. Three of the monks came into the garden, following the call of the flute, and sat listening at a respectful distance away. As Martin played on, the old padre began to sing, or maybe it was a chant, in a high, keening voice in a tongue Martin had never heard.

"Gaelic," the old priest told him when they were done. "It is one of the oldest prayers we have from the mystic isles. Maybe seventh century."

"You mean what I've been hearing all these years is a Celtic prayer?" Martin asked, not believing what he was hearing.

"Indeed," Father McAlpin smiled, and started to say something else. Yet he was interrupted by a harsh croak from high above, and looking up they say a huge raven circling against the leaden sky. Seeing them look up, the raven cried again, turning to the north and flying off into the low hanging clouds. "Jesus," McAlpin said reverently. "If I were more superstitious, I'd cross myself, Martin." He glanced toward the three brothers who had also seen the raven and were obviously discussing it among themselves quietly. "If they weren't here, I would, anyway." Then he laughed. "Herself is having some fun, apparently."

"I wish I could be a believer, father," Martin told him. "Truly I do."

"I suppose you'd say the raven just now is another coincidence?" the old priest asked dryly.

"What else could it be?" Martin asked. "Unless, of course, ravens like flute music," he added, smiling.

McAlpin snorted. "Quoth the raven, 'play some more.'"

That evening after Compline, Martin found himself being shown to the room where he would spend the night by one of the brothers, "Is someone from the community gone?" he asked the monk.

"No," said Brother Raphael, who was in charge of the commissary. "We have two extra people here with you and Father Thomas, but everyone in our community is here. This is one of our guest rooms. Why do you ask?"

"I noticed the empty chair at chapel both times today," Martin said. "I wondered if someone were missing."

Raphael smiled. "That's what we call the Elija chair," he explained. "As the Jews at Passover do, we keep it for the stranger at the gate or the messenger from God who may show up at any time." He nodded. "It also reminds us of the real presence of God with us in the Sacrament and when we pray." Then he smiled. "The more irreverent among our novices call it our bishop's chair, because he's almost never here. They say it is a reminder of his real absence."

Quinn laughed. "Well, it's good to know your novices are irreverent. At least about the Bishop."

To his surprise Raphael nodded. "Yes, they keep the rest of us from becoming too stodgy. Taking ourselves too seriously is something we can fall into very easily. They keep us in touch."

"How do the older men take that?" Quinn wanted to know. "I would imagine it would really bother some of them."

The monk nodded. "Some of them it does. Oddly enough, it is the brothers in middle years it seems to bother the most. Our older brothers seem much more tolerant." Raphael grinned. "I'm no exception." Quinn judged he would be in his mid forties.

"Maybe they can't hear as well or see as clearly," Martin suggested.

Raphael nodded. "That may be part of it. Not being able to hear would cover a multitude of sins, I'd think. Particularly singing off key."

Martin chuckled. "I better let you go, brother. I'm sure you have other things you need to do."

"Not really," Raphael told him. "Hospitality is a large measure of my work here. We don't get visitors that often, but when we do, I'm the one who talks to them and answers questions. Of course, that's within the framework of the hours of the community."

Martin sat on the edge of his bed and waved Brother Raphael into the room's single chair. "I've heard someone use that expression before. What are these 'hours' you mentioned?"

"It's an archaic term," the brother explained. "Everything in the life of the community centers around the traditional hours of prayer. Every day we gather at certain times for community prayer, and those are called the hours." He smiled. "That doesn't mean we are not in prayer at other times, but only that our community prays as a body then."

"So you spend most of your life talking to God?" Martin asked.

"No," Raphael said, surprising him. "Prayer is not talking. It is a very intimate relationship." He gave Martin a shy smile and added, "It's like the most passionate love affair you can imagine." Martin blinked and Raphael chuckled. "I wasn't always a monk, my friend. Before I came here I was an attorney, and I was even married for a number of years. I became quite well acquainted with the ways of the world and the flesh."

"Not the devil, too?" Martin asked.

"No, that's why I came here," Raphael answered simply, touching his breast lightly. "To learn about the devil, the devil within, which was robbing me of joy."

Martin covered his head with his hands. "I feel like my mind wants to explode in eight different directions. There must be two dozen questions I want to ask you."

Brother Raphael shrugged. "That's what I'm here for and we have all the time you need." He looked thoughtful. "Let me explain the schedule of the community first and then take on your questions. I take it you are going to be here for a few days at least."

Martin frowned, then nodded. "Yes," he sighed. "I hadn't planned on it, but I would really like it, I think. I don't know what it costs, but I've got plenty of cash, at least enough for a few days."

Raphael smiled. "There is no specific charge, Martin. We ask people to contribute whatever they can afford." He grinned and added, "Being a former lawyer I tell people to pay what they think it's worth. Our revenues have gone up a great deal since I started doing that."

Martin looked at him appraisingly. "There's a lot more than meets the eye to you, brother," he observed.

"I hope so," the monk laughed, holding up his skinny arms. Then he said, "Back to business. We ask that you come to chapel at least once per day unless you have taken on a special discipline. The rule is that you can always seek out your spiritual guide at any time, but that conversation is limited to the Talking Room in the library or by invitation to private cell, like we are doing now. Or walking together in the garden as you did with Father McAlpin. Other than that, we assume everyone wants to remain in silence, especially during Lent, and we respect that."

Martin nodded, and Brother Raphael went on. "Except during Advent and Lent, we also can talk at meals, but we're still in Lent for the next three weeks. The hours of community prayer we keep are based on the traditional hours kept since about the eighth century. They begin with Matins at four in the morning, which is followed by a time of personal prayer and reflection. Then, at six, we observe Prime, which is followed by Mass and breakfast and a period of physical activity." Raphael smiled. "We don't require our guests to work, but if you would care to do so, we can surely accommodate you."

"I think I'd like that," Martin said. "I used to grow some big gardens. It's been a long time since I've had my hands in the dirt."

"Brother Augustine will be glad to have the help," Raphael said. "We have a short break mid-morning to observe Terce with fifteen minutes of silence, wherever we are on the grounds. A number of our brothers use the time for their Rosary, but what we ask is simply being still until the second Terce bell rings. At noon we have a short service, followed by a light meal in the refectory, and then a free period for reading or napping until half past two, when we're called to our community study period. The next bell calls us to Evensong, followed by supper about six. After supper we are free to write letters or read until nine o'clock, when we end the day with Compline and go to bed." He shrugged. "It actually sounds more complicated than it is, but just ask one of us if you are not sure. That's the only real exception to our rule of silence."

Martin nodded. "Good. I don't know how long I'll be staying, but I imagine only for a couple of days." Raphael nodded and Quinn asked, "Just out of curiosity, how long do you allow guest to stay?"

Raphael chuckled. "As long as they wish to stay or as long as they need. After six months we do consider them members of the community, whether this has been formalized or not."

Quinn nodded. "Whatever happened to Lazarus?" he suddenly blurted, startling himself, as well as the good brother.

"Lazarus?" Brother Raphael asked, then laughed. "You must have just read A Canticle for Liebowitz," he said. Any other reply he might have made was just then interrupted by the chapel bell. "There's our call to Compline," he told Martin. "Let me tackle your question tomorrow. Will it wait?"

Quinn nodded and followed as Brother Raphael led the way to chapel. As he followed he was amazed to see the brother wore sandals, despite the early spring chill, although rough wool socks covered his feet and calves. Nor did the monks seem to have much on except their simple woolen robes and perhaps cotton underwear. Martin wondered what they did when the weather really got bad, then smiled to himself. Even up here his reporter's training was hard at work, seeking the story in its details. He'd have to carry a notebook to remember all the questions he wanted to ask.

"Brother Raphael is right," Father McAlpin told Martin the next afternoon when they were walking around the gardens. "Prayer is a relationship more than even a dialogue. I like the way our new Catechism talks about it." He pulled out a worn paperback and quickly turned to the right place. "What it says is, 'Prayer is responding to God, by thought and by deeds, with or without words.'" He looked at Martin. "That pretty much sums it up, I think. Covers all the bases."

"The part I couldn't understand was Raphael saying it is a passionate relationship," Martin said. "Like the kind between men and women. I don't see how...." He struggled for the right words. "I mean, that doesn't seem very spiritual to me. It seems rather earthy."

The old padre nodded gravely. "The Greeks really did a number on us splitting body and spirit, didn't they?"

"The Greeks? You mean the Orthodox?" Martin inquired.

"No, the philosophers," McAlpin told him. "As much as they admired the human body, it also disappointed them terribly. It gets sick and doesn't work right. Then it dies and rots. I guess they found that unacceptable."

"I do, too," Martin told him.

"I know," the old padre said. "You're a child of the western world, and the western world was shaped by Greek thought." He looked at Martin over his glasses. "Nor is that the only way to look at things. Not the best way, either, at least as far as I'm concerned."

"You're way out of my depth now," Martin admitted. "I don't know what you're talking about."

"Well, the Greeks had this idea of an eternal divine spark caught in the earthy, corruptible stuff of the human body. Somehow when a child was born, or maybe when it was conceived, a spark from the divine was stuck in this mud and trapped there until death, when it was free to ascend to the spirit realm from whence it came." He sighed. "That's a beautiful fantasy, but it doesn't have much congruence with our contemporary understanding of life. Our scientific understanding."

"How else would you look at it?" Martin asked. "What you said makes a lot of sense to me."

Father McAlpin nodded. "Try this one. Before anything came into being, there was a Prime Mover. 'God' is simply a shorthand word for that. This Prime Mover was so full of goodness and love, He or She was like a little child who is so excited they can't contain themselves. So in a moment of pure ecstasy, the PM says 'Let It Rip!' and the universe as we know it comes into being with a Celestial Bang." The old man gave him an earthy smile. "I like to think it was much like an ultimate orgasm that's still going on. At some point the PM scoops up a handful of mud and breaths the PM's very own spirit into it, so it's created in the image and likeness of the PM. Which is the traditional Hebrew way of looking at human beings. We are a mystery made of mud and the divine spirit inseparably bound together!" As he spoke, Thomas McAlpin's voice grew more and more animated, and when he was done he sighed happily. "Now ain't that a grand way of looking at it?" he asked.

"I envy you," Martin told him earnestly. "I wish I could believe that, too. But I can't, father. I just can't."

To Martin' surprise the old man nodded and said, "It doesn't matter, Martin. Despite what some of the more stupid preachers say, we are never beyond the grace of God. There is nothing that can overcome that grace, either, so it doesn't matter much what we do or do not believe in our rather dim minds. What matters is the reality that I call God, and the fact that this is a very good and benevolent universe despite appearances to the contrary."

"I wish I could believe that, father," Martin said.

The good padre looked at him and asked, "Tell me, do you like science fiction, Martin?"

"Does the sun rise in the east?" Martin smiled, nodding. "I don't just like it, father. I love it."

"Well then, suppose you were raised on the surface of the planet Venus like one of Heinlein's 'fog-eaters'. Suppose you'd never seen the sun blazing in a noonday sky. It might be a little hard for you to believe in it's existence, might it not?" The old priest smiled. "Yet your lack of belief would not have much to do with whether the sun warmed your planet or not."

"Not so fast, padre," Quinn laughed. I saw you tuck that card up your sleeve. I'd know the sun had to exist because I could observe the effect it had on my world. For one thing, without it, my Venus would be solid ice. For another, nothing would grow without a source of energy."

"Ah," said McAlpin slyly, like a fencing master drawing a star student into a terrible blunder. "But there could be other explanations, Martin. One is geothermal activity. Another is radioactive breakdown. Either of those could serve to explain conditions on your home."

"Occam's razor, father," Quinn told him, parrying easily. "The simplest explanation is the most likely."

"Exactly!" McAlpin almost shouted, slipping past Martin' guard and piercing his argument with his own words. "A Prime Mover is the very simplest explanation, isn't it?"

"*Touché!*" Martin grumbled. "You set me up for that!"

"With your help," the padre assured him. "Yet am I not right?"

"You may well be," Martin nodded. "Yet I am not able to accept that right now. I wish I could but I can't."

"Forgive me for pushing, Martin, but can you at least accept the least possibility I may be right?"

"Of course, I can," Martin declared. "I can admit almost anyone might be right, even the Mormons. But it will take a lot of proving to me," he said.

"Good," Father. McAlpin told him. "The toughest nuts make the very best rabbis, the apostle Paul being a case in point. So long as you're open, even the least bit, grace can get through." He smiled and shrugged. "After all, the PM's got all the time in the world."

"Assuming you're right, that would pretty much have to be the case, wouldn't it?" Martin laughed, enjoying their play on words. "Literally. But I am afraid I'm not cut out to be a rabbi."

"Literally? You're not cut out?" the padre laughed, making his own play on Martin' words. "That could be arranged."

Suddenly the grief flooded back like a tidal wave, crushing Martin' mood. You know, I was considering it," he said, his face growing somber. "Not being a rabbi, but converting to Judaism."

"So you told me," Thomas McAlpin responded gently. "Forgive me if I have stirred up something painful. However, I find it less painful to grasp the nettle firmly and laugh when we can."

Martin nodded and they walked a while in silence. Then, when they came to a stopping place, Martin sat down on the wet grass, took out his flute and began to play. At first he played quite softly, almost hesitantly. Yet then he grew more and more bold as he faced the tidal wave and released more and more of his anguish to whatever tender mercies might be. When he was done, Martin lay back, closed his eyes, and fell into a deep sleep. Smiling at him, as if Martin were a child given to his care, his companion covered him with a heavy wool cloak. Then, as Martin slept, the old priest sat quietly, an ancient dark warrior of the human spirit serving his king and guarding his charge, a Rosary clutched in one hand, and his cane, like a mighty sword of wrath, in the other.

The two weeks Martin remained at the monastery were two of the most peaceful weeks of his life. When it came time to leave, he was surprised how reluctant he was to do so, and put it off for three days, not understanding why he was so torn. Nor did his ambivalence go unnoticed. All the brothers were aware of his restlessness long before he was, of course, but they said nothing to Martin, respecting his need to bring himself to terms with his own spiritual dilemma. It was only on the third day, as Martin sat playing his flute quietly in the garden, that Raphael came and sat down, waiting patiently.

It was some time before Martin, lost in a sad, drifting melody, became aware of the brother's presence. When he did he brought the tune to an end somewhat abruptly and set aside his penny whistle. "The flute is distracted today," he told Rafael. "It seems to be wandering rather aimlessly, doesn't it?"

Raphael smiled and nodded, but said nothing. Martin would find his own way in his own time and the purpose of his presence was simply to give his younger friend someone to talk with if he wished. Looking at him Martin chuckled. "You're not going to say it are you?" The brother smiled and shook his head. "Well, you're right, you don't have to. The flute's fine. It's me who is distracted, at loose ends."

Brother Raphael smiled and nodded again. "There is a spiritual axiom a recovered alcoholic once shared with me. It says that when we find we are out of sorts, no matter what the reason might seem to be, the source of the disturbance lies within us." He nodded seriously. "It took me a long time, but I came to agree with that. At least, it's true for me."

"Well, in this case, it's true for me," Martin admitted. "I feel restless, Rafe. No, torn would be a better way of putting it. I find the life of the community here is very attractive. You don't ask me to even pretend to be a believer, and you accept me just as I am. I like the balance you practice with work and study and quiet time, and even in Lent, I sense a deep sense of joy in almost everyone here. I don't understand it, but I recognize it is real." He looked at the good brother intently.

"For some reason it always seems greater during Advent and Lent," the brother told him, nodding. He held up a restraining hand. "Not to sway you in your decision, as if anyone really could," Martin smiled, "but if you remain here you will find that joy. I suspect it will cost you a great deal of pain any way you go, whether you are here or somewhere else. I suspect you will have to cross a desolate wilderness before you find your promised land." His eyes were full of compassion. "As a matter of fact, you are already on the journey and I suspect this time here is simply an oasis for you before you go back into the wilderness."

Martin' looked at his companion, his eyes wide with surprise. The monk returned his look with curiosity, but said nothing. "You don't know just how strange this conversation is," Martin told him. "Since I've been here I've dreamed about that exact thing, twice, and it reminded me of another dream I had a long time ago. It was about running in the desert." Quickly he told Raphael about his dream of the desert runner leading him to the emerald pool, and then on into the desert.

As he listened to Martin, Brother Raphael nodded emphatically, and when Martin was done, he smiled and observed, "That seems to be a rather direct message. Someone seems to be trying to tell you something."

"Do you really think that's what these dreams are?" Martin asked. "I know the Old Testament is full of people having dreams they thought came from God, but that's always seemed strange to me."

"The ways of the Kingdom are strange," Raphael said. "But to answer your question, yes, I believe dreams are often 'angelic' messages. Yours certainly have a numinous air about them."

"Numinous?" Martin asked.

"Sorry," Raphael said, searching for other words. "When something is numinous it has mysterious qualities, spiritual qualities, that seem to go way beyond the material world. 'Transcendent' is another word I could have used. The details seem to point to a larger reality."

"God?" Martin asked dryly.

"Holiness," Raphael nodded. "Not just God as a separate person, but a whole different reality."

"A Separate Reality," Martin mused.

"No," Raphael asserted, more strongly than Martin had ever heard him speak. "I'm not talking about the way of the Yaki. What I'm talking about is a different reality but one which is connected to this reality as solidly as the sky is connected to the earth. The best word I know for it is Emannu-el."

"God-with-us?" Martin asked, remembering the little Hebrew he knew.

The good brother nodded. "God incarnate among us is another way of talking about it." He held up his hands. "I know, Martin. The whole idea is scandalous, but that is the center of the Catholic witness, and the whole idea is God becoming somehow incarnate in each of us." He shook his head. "I am no theologian, as you know. But wherever undemanding love grows," he asserted, touching his breast, "there must surely be something present which is much larger and much more powerful than human fear and our normal self centered concern." He looked at Martin levelly. "That is what I have come to experience in myself, and it literally startled the hell out of me." He gave Martin a shy grin.

"I see that in you very clearly," Martin affirmed. "That's certainly been my experience of the community here, too. I wish I could find it for myself."

Brother Raphael smiled gently. "Having seen this in myself, I seem to have also been given the gift of seeing it in others. I see a great deal of this in you, Martin. Yours is a very healing presence."

"I've been told that before," Martin sighed, shaking his head. "I just don't see it."

"That doesn't surprise me," the monk told him. "We tend to be blind to our real virtues as well as to our very worst vices. That seems to be how we are made. Without it we would not need others to be our mirrors." He was quiet a moment, then said, "No," as if to himself.

"No what?" Martin wanted to know.

"There are a number of places what I've said really connects," Raphael replied. "I was going to recommend meditating on a couple of things, but on second thought, I don't think that's appropriate at the moment. When it's time you will find your own way, your own sources."

Martin was intrigued by the man's self restraint. "I don't think it would do any harm to suggest them," he shrugged. "I can take them or leave them."

"All right," Raphael agreed. "On that basis. The one which came to me first was from Isaiah." He smiled. "I suppose because you're sort of an Old Testament person, or that's the way you feel to me."

"You mean like Moses?" Martin asked, amused. "I think Charlton Heston's already been cast for that."

"Elija was actually who I had in mind," the monk told him. "Or even John the Baptist, maybe, the voice of one crying in the wilderness."

"I can identify with that!" Martin declared.

"Sort of romantic, isn't it?" Raphael agreed. "A flower child of the first century, bearding the lion in his den."

"And losing his head over it, if I remember the story," Martin nodded. "Or was that someone else?"

"That was John," the other assured him. "But what came to my mind was a passage from Isaiah which seems to describe you, at least from what I have known of you. I don't remember exactly how it goes, but it is close to this." Closing his eyes, Brother Raphael began to speak from memory,

> The spirit of the Lord is upon me,
>
> because he has anointed me
>
> to bring good news to all those who are afflicted.
>
> He has sent me to bind up their broken hearts,
>
> and proclaim freedom to those who are captives,
>
> to comfort those who mourn and to give them oil
>
> oil of gladness for their fainting spirits,
>
> and to proclaim to them the Lord's favor.

Opening his eyes, Raphael looked at Martin. "To me that describes who you are, my friend," he said. "If you wish to look it up, it comes from the sixty-first chapter of the prophet. There is more than what I have told you, and I may have the verses out of order, but that is the essence."

"I wish I could believe that," Martin replied, tears in his eyes. "I wish I could believe in the God you do, brother, and I wish I dared to believe what you have told me about myself. I'm not saying you're wrong, but it's hard to square that with what I know about myself."

"You really don't understand, do you?" Raphael asked gently. "Those of us who have eyes to see know far more about you than you can suspect, Martin, both of the good and of the unredeemed. We see it because it is in us, too, just as the same goodness is, as well." He nodded. "Well, everything in its time. Just remember that wherever you go, all of us here will be lifting you up in our prayers every day. Never doubt that."

Martin was overcome with emotion. He had no idea how to respond. Yet before he could even begin, Brother Raphael smiled, clasped his shoulder in farewell, and walked away, leaving him stunned. Then, out of nowhere, Martin thought he heard the call of a wolf, and looking upward without quite knowing why, he was stunned to see the huge dark form of a raven winging its way toward the sacred mountains to the north.

4. Old Glory

Kent, Ohio. Yes, old friend, our national flag is a sacred symbol. I understand this. My dad was on Iwo Jima the day they raised the flag, and he was not the only one of our family who paid our dues. My cousin was a Sea Bee who died in Korea and his brother was in for twenty years. I, too, volunteered in the fall of 1965. I did so to keep from being drafted, but while Canada was a real option, it was one which never occurred to me to take. And if you must know why I volunteered, in my family, the prospect of having to confess to being an Army grunt, and a draftee to boot, was as bad as owning up to nose picking or solitary vice. The point is that I understand quite well why Old Glory is a holy symbol for many. I simply wish pious Christians who wave the flag would give such unquestioned obedience and awesome reverence to the one they confess as Lord and Master.

For I am also painfully aware of the other side of the coin. Some of my people came across the Bering strait twenty thousand years before the Vikings came to Vinland or Christopher Columbus was a gleam in his mother's eye. To this other side of my ancestry, Old Glory is a symbol of desecration and shame tied to the memory of Wounded Knee and Mai Lai, to the internment of thousands of Nipponese cousins who were loyal American citizens, to the bombing of Dresden and, yes, even Kent State and the 1968 Police Riot in Chicago. To our black brothers it is a sacred symbol of men who hide their faces behind white sheets and leave crosses - can you imagine crosses! - burning in the yards of people who dare differ, a symbol of rapists who leave strange fruit hanging from live oak trees. We understand quite clearly the words of John the Divine speaking of the abomination of desecration erected on holy ground, and when others begin getting tears in their eyes over the red, white, and blue, we begin to be afraid. For we are not that distant in time or space from Germany in 1934 and we remember quite clearly what happened in the name of the Fatherland there. Six million Jews dead, forty million Russians and God only knows how many Germans and Chinese and Swedes and British and Japanese and Italians and Melanesians. We wonder *why you do not see this and why you think this flag is so holy. For to us it is Old as sin and it is just as Gory.....* (Martin Quinn's journal)

July, 1970. The publisher finished reading the fresh edition the editor brought and tossed the paper down on his desk. "Damn, the man writes good copy," he said, shaking his head sadly. "But he's a loose cannon on deck."

The editor nodded. "I think so, too. You want me to let him go?"

"We really don't have cause," the publisher replied. "At the moment. I talked to Greg down in our legal department and he said it could backfire if we go ahead. The man's been here longer than our normal probation period and stepping on the political toes of our advertisers isn't enough. We can't even fire him for selling it to the competition. He offered it to us first and we turned him down. Under his contract he has the right to sell it elsewhere. So Greg suggested we try something else."

The editor looked at his old friend and grinned. "I can see you have something in mind," he said, shifting his cigar from one side of his mouth to the other. "I think I'd hate to be in his shoes."

"Ah, John, you know me too well," the publisher almost purred. "Yes, I think I have just the thing to make our redoubtable Mr. Quinn either quit or seek employment elsewhere." He chuckled to himself. "We'll promote him."

"Promote him?" the editor asked.

"Yes, promote him. Tell him we appreciate his way with words and would like him to join our editorial staff."

"You're making him an editor!" John could not believe his ears.

"Relax, old friend, that's just the bait," the publisher grinned. "I'm not quite around the bend yet. We offer him an editor's contract and when he takes it we put him to editing copy. For our greenest writers. What we don't give him is the right to hire and fire them."

The editor thought a moment. "Yeah, that could work. I can see only one possible problem with it. What if he turns us down?"

The publisher rubbed his thumb back and forth rapidly over his first two fingers. "I doubt he will considering the generous terms we'll offer."

The editor shook his head. "I don't know," he said. "Offer him too much and I'm sure he'll smell a rat."

"I'm not entirely senile, John" the publisher said with some asperity.

"No, you're not," growled the editor. "On the other hand, you don't work with the man every day and I don't think you know him as well as I do. You know he's turned down better offers from other papers? Money doesn't seem to mean that much to him."

"No, I didn't know that," said the other. "Well, there's always the good old journalistic standby if he doesn't rise to the bait."

"That actually might work better," the editor observed.

"Then do it," the publisher grinned. "Tell him he's the best we've got and give him everything you can come up with."

"What?" screamed Martin Quinn. "No way, John! Send one of your cubs fresh out of school. That's not a real story."

"Martin, the man asked specifically for you to cover it," the editor replied. "I told him you'd scream but he says you're the best we have and he thinks there's a real story there somewhere."

"That's not a story, that's human interest horse shit!" Quinn argued. "He can't do this to me."

"He's not doing anything to you, man," the editor asserted. "I think it's just a passing thing but he wants us to do more good news stories."

"Then let him send Simpson!" Quinn replied. Roger Simpson was the religion editor. "He's just full of all kinds of Pollyanna Anna shit."

"Our illustrious publisher doesn't want Pollyanna stuff, Quinn," the editor growled. "He wants good writing. Simpson isn't in your class by a long shot. He'd be the first to admit it."

"Well, damn it, tell him to get someone else!"

"Are you refusing the assignment, Quinn?" the editor asked, his voice deadly quiet. "You haven't given me good cause for turning it down and if you refuse he can fire you."

"He can or you can, John?" Quinn snapped.

"He can tell me to," the editor snapped back. "With your attitude the way it is right now, it would be a pleasure!"

"So it's a setup," Quinn said. "It's a setup to get rid of me. Well, it ain't going to work. So tell him to take his little setup and shove it. I have a contract and that clearly states what he can and cannot do."

"It's not a setup, Quinn. It's legitimate journalistic research and story development. Just because you don't like it doesn't mean it isn't news."

"Retirement age women selling real estate?" Quinn asked. "What are they supposed to be, some kind of communist front organization?"

"If they are, I'm sure you'll find out," the editor said softly, changing tactics. "Look, Martin, just give it a week. All right? I'll try to talk him into something else. In the mean time, treat it like a working vacation. Man, we all should be so lucky."

Quinn nodded. "This is about the flag essay, isn't it? Some of his advertisers raised hell and he's taking it out on me. Right?"

The editor shook his head. "Anything that increases circulation for our competitors he doesn't like," he grinned. "I happen to know it torqued his nose, too. But we didn't run it, they did."

"But I'm on his payroll," Quinn pointed out. "Regardless of where I publish. And they're trying to muzzle me." He shook his head. "I simply won't have it, John. There is a First Amendment of the Constitution that protects my right to publish the views I hold."

"The First Amendment doesn't require them to advertise with us," the editor answered. "Or for us to retain writers who slant their stories toward a point of view we abhor."

"That's what this is all about, isn't it?" Martin asked. "Tell me, John. Why did you all hire me in the first place?"

"What this is about is covering the news," the editor said, ignoring the question. "It's Hobson's choice and end of discussion. Take it or leave it."

"Oh, I'll take it," Martin warned. "I'll find a story there. You may not like it but I'll find it."

"What the hell is this?" the publisher roared, slamming the copy down on his littered desk. "God damn it, John, I told you to run his ass off, not give him ammunition."

"I did exactly what you told me and you agreed," the editor snarled back. "So get off your damned high horse. The bastard outsmarted us." Even upside down he could read the text of the article under the headline in all caps banner.

BLUE-HAIR BETTIES BLAMED

Denver, Colorado. State Real Estate Board President Lucas R. John today said elderly agents in the local real estate industry are making the market soft in all areas of the state. According to John, the principal cause is what he called "Betty Bluehairs" becoming licensed under lax standards and "undermining the standards of the profession." John went on to say "everyone and his grandmother is selling real estate now" and that the mark of the local real estate agent has changed from the utility station wagon to 'flat, slip-on tennis shoes and a dime store hand bag...."

The editor chuckled. "You know," he said, "if it weren't so damned outrageous it would be funny."

"What's so damned funny about it?" the publisher snapped. "Lucas John is a personal friend of mine and I assure you he would fail to see the humor, too."

The editor sighed. "Give the devil his due," he told the publisher. "He outsmarted us and that's what's pissing you off. Wouldn't you think it was funny if it happened to Hervey instead of us?" Hervey was the owner of the competition. "Besides, it's not in print."

"Well, it will be," the publisher pointed out. "He can sell it to Hervey and the bastard would publish it, too. The man has no standards."

"Not for a year," the editor pointed out. "We can tell him we're going to use it next spring just before school's out. Then we can change our minds and by the time Hervey prints it, the story will be old news." He shrugged. "Our thorn in the flesh may not be around by then, either. If he's not on staff, we can sit on it for five years."

"You mean we can sit on everything he writes for five years if he's not on our payroll?" the publisher asked, not daring believe his ears. "When did you find this out?"

"This morning. I asked Greg to go over the contract with a fine tooth comb and spell it out to me in terms a third grader could understand. He's the one who found this wrinkle." The editor grinned. "I thought you'd like to know about it."

"So all we have to do is tell him we plan to use whatever he writes within the next year and we can end up sitting on it for five?" The editor nodded. "Does he know this?"

"No," John told him. "I've set up an appointment this afternoon with Greg and he'll explain it to Quinn." He looked at his employer. "I thought you'd like to be in on the kill," he said.

You're damned right!" the other declared. "I want to see the bastard's blood all over the floor."

"You need to promise me one thing," the editor said. "We don't want to step on our own feet. So we let Greg do all, and I do mean *all*, the talking."

"Our Greg is a good man, John," the publisher said. "You think it might be time to promote him?"

"We're going to lose him if we don't," the editor told him.

The publisher nodded. "We'll use it as a reward for taking care of our personal pain in the ass, Mr. Quinn."

"You can't do this," Quinn said. "I have a right to sell if you refuse my copy. What you're doing amounts to refusal."

"Not legally, Mr. Quinn," Greg replied calmly. "Legally we have a right to hold anything for up to a year for publication, and if you are with us no longer, you may not sell it for publication for five years after you have left. That's very clear."

Quinn sighed. "I thought something was going on. So I had my own lawyer look over it. His opinion is that what you're doing is de facto refusal, but he also told me it would require litigation to prove my case and that would be expensive. Even then there is an outside chance we might not win."

"You seem to have chosen a very good attorney," Greg observed. "I agree completely with his assessment of the situation. David and Goliath is good in children's stories, but it doesn't often work that way in real life."

"Yes, he is quite good," Quinn agreed. His calm was unsettling. "He also pointed out another provision of the contract. I turned in copy just this morning ." He took a piece of paper out of his pocket. "Carol was surprised when I asked for a receipt for it, but she gave it to me." He grinned.

"What is he driving at?" the publisher demanded.

Greg shrugged and Quinn answered. "He doesn't want to tell me if I don't know about it already. Right Greggy, baby?" He looked at the publisher and grinned. "I have to submit copy or a report at least every three weeks, but it doesn't have to meet any particular standards. You cannot dismiss me for a full year for not producing something you care to print. Ask your lawyer. Am I right, Greg?"

"Something along those lines," Greg admitted. "But it has to be news. Anything you write in that year belongs to us."

"Small correction," Quinn grinned. "Anything you can prove I wrote during that year belongs to you. But as my lawyer pointed out, litigation as a plaintiff, especially a corporation against an individual, is risky and expensive. So for the next year, you will receive installments of this story. This is a copy of what I gave Carol." He handed the publisher three type-written pages. Across the top of the first page was the title, "BEHIND THE INK: How The Times Cheats You Out Of Your Right To Know, a series by Martin Quinn."

The publisher glared at Quinn but the editor laid a restraining hand on his arm. "You publish this and we'll sue," Greg told Quinn. "This is libel and we will have no problem proving malice."

"Oh, I'm not going to publish it," Quinn said. "Even though I will be able to document everything I say. I'm a journalist. I'm submitting it to you for publication. You have up to a year to use it." He grinned. "If you try to fire me, it will become a matter of public record at the trial." He got up and walked to the door. "I've got to get to work, gentlemen. So have a nice day." He closed the door firmly behind him.

"Shit!" said the publisher. The editor withheld a grin. Despite all that happened, he found he admired the bastard for his guts bearding the lion in his own den. He thought, *One of these days, I'd like to do the same.* While the publisher was his friend, he was a royal pain in the ass as a boss.

Two days later Othello McLeod ran into Quinn in *El Nido*, a quiet bar a number of older journalists seemed to favor near the center of the city. "I've been looking for you," McLeod told him, taking the stool next to his and ordering single malt with spring water on the side. "I hear things aren't going too well at the office. As a matter of fact, I hear they're looking for a way to get rid of you."

Quinn looked at him feigning shock. "Me? Why, Othello, where in the world did you hear that? You know me. I'm too much of an ass kisser for that to happen."

McLeod rolled his eyes. "Right, and the Pope just got married." He took a sip of his single malt, sighed with pleasure. "Water of life," he murmured.

Quinn laughed, nodding. "Yeah, you're right. They are trying to get rid of me, as a matter of fact. Things were right tense the last time I was in." He looked at Othello. "I guess it's a good thing I don't have to punch a time clock."

McLeod nodded. "Damned good thing or you'd be pounding the street by now. What happened?"

Quinn told him, giving the background of the last few of weeks and a brief summary of his conversation with the editor and the publisher. "You know, I think John was on my side, actually," he added. "I got the distinct impression he'd like to tell the old fart off, too."

"Yeah, but he ain't doing it," McLeod responded, shaking his head. "He likes his job too well. You need to be careful, man. You don't want to be pissing in your own well. Word gets around in this business."

"Word gets around when you deliver, too," Quinn snapped back. "One asshole firing you can be a recommendation to another."

"Not if you go in thinking of them all as assholes," his friend told him. "The word I have is you're hitting the sauce pretty hard these days and a lot of people think you're a loose canon on deck."

"Those bastards!" Quinn said, loud enough to cause a couple of people down the bar to look their way. Dropping his voice he said, "That's character assassination, Othello. Pure and simple. I won't let them get away with it."

"Give me some credit, man," Othello replied. "I know sour grapes when I see it. I didn't get that from them. Or from a single source, for that matter. The word is out and has been for quite a while."

"Well, where did you get it?" Quinn's tone was surly.

Othello looked at his friend with concern. "Like I say, all over. The first I heard was six months ago in Cairo. The guys I was talking to treated it like it was common knowledge. That's what bothered me. It wasn't jealousy talking, either. The people who were talking are all friends of yours and are very concerned about you. You're getting a reputation for being a souse."

"Horse hockey! I can quit anytime I want." Quinn was indignant. "I just don't care to do so."

"Then do it, man! I mean it. You're too good to let yourself go down the tubes this way."

"Damn," Quinn laughed. "All this time I thought it was because you liked me. Because you were my friend."

"I do, baby, and I am your friend," Othello said urgently "I wouldn't be here talking if I wasn't. Now come on, let's get something to eat."

"All right," Quinn said expansively. "I'll even buy. Just let me finish my drink." He lifted his half full glass to McLeod.

Othello's reply stopped Quinn's arm half way to his mouth. "Leave it, man! Just set it down and leave it!"

"Are you crazy?" Quinn asked, tossing his drink down in a gulp. "It's single malt just like yours and I paid for it."

McLeod looked down at his drink. About half of it remained. "No, baby," he said sadly. "You just think you did. I think you haven't begun to pay for it yet."

"What do you mean?" Quinn snarled, but McLeod was half way out of the bar. Quinn jumped to his feet to run after him, but stumbled and almost fell. "You need to get that floor fixed," he snarled at the bar keep. The man bent over the bar and looked at the place where Quinn stumbled. The floor was bare, dry and level. The bartender started to say something, but Quinn, too, was gone.

"So what are you going to do this next year?" Othello asked, snagging the last dinner roll. The remains of a huge meal lay before them on the table of their booth, and at his insistence there had been no more liquor with their feast. Quinn was noticeably more sober, and noticeably more dour. He ordered a seltzer from the waiter, made a face as he drank it. "I can't picture you sitting around twiddling your thumbs," McLeod added.

Quinn nodded. "No, neither can I. So I think what I'll do is block out the outline for my Great American Novel and do some basic research. I've got something in mind I've wanted to do for quite a while."

"Well, be careful," McLeod advised. "I don't know how your contract reads but anything you produce may be theirs. You may want to buy out your contract before you get too far along."

Again Quinn nodded. "I thought about that and I think you're right. My lawyer says I'll be all right either way, but I wouldn't put it past them to hassle me about it. However, our old friend the publisher is pissed and won't talk settlement."

Othello nodded. "Yeah, he will, if you give him good enough terms. What did you offer?"

"Ten per cent and he wouldn't even talk to me," Quinn complained.

"I don't blame him," McLeod said, laughing. "He could get that and more loaning the money out short term to contractors. Why not offer them more? Say fifteen per cent for a starter?"

"No," Quinn declared emphatically. "It's a matter of principle."

Othello sighed. "It's also a matter of principle to not cut your nose off to spite your face. Or step on your own pecker. How long would it take you to write it? Six months?"

Quinn nodded. "I think I could do it in that, easily. At the rate I work, nine at the most. That even allows a couple of months for research."

"All right, say it takes you nine months and at the end you go back to work at the same salary as now." McLeod thought. "You probably could get a little more, but let's say you got the same pay. That means you can settle for eighty per cent for the nine months and be five per cent ahead."

"I don't know," Quinn replied dubiously. "Assuming what you tell me is true, I may have trouble getting another job."

"No, it shouldn't take you long at all. What's going around now is just scuttlebutt. Keep your act clean and I think you'll see management has a very short memory. Especially when they need someone who isn't afraid to get in and get the story." He grinned at his friend. "Like you."

Quinn said nothing. Suddenly McLeod understood what was going on with the other man. "That's not it, is it?" he asked.

"What do you mean?"

"You could settle for half and still make out like a bandit, couldn't you? I've never seen you spend much except on hooch and I know the old man would settle for twenty to twenty-five." McLeod shook his head. "That is not the problem, is it? The problem is your pride. You're pissed, aren't you?"

"So what if I am?" Quinn demanded, immediately defensive. "I have every reason to be mad."

"Yeah, but people get over being pissed, baby," McLeod answered. "I don't think that's the problem."

"So what is my problem, Dr. Freud?" Quinn answered.

"Your problem is you like it. You enjoy this kind of shit." Quinn would not meet his gaze. "That's it, isn't it. You enjoy being pissed and you like to fight."

Quinn tried to dismiss this with a wave. "Hell, Othello. Everybody likes a good fight now and then. Even you."

"Yeah, but not like you, baby. You don't just like to fight, you love it! Don't you?" McLeod's eyes were dark as anthracite, and about as soft. "At heart you're still a lawyer, even though you never practiced, and you love it. You goddamighty love it!"

"You're the one who's picking a fight here!" Quinn retorted. "Not me."

"No, my friend, I'm not." Othello sighed, shook his head. "I grew up thinking I had to fight everyone and everything just to survive." His eyes grew bleak. "The projects do that to people. I survived and I fought my way out, but I never liked it. I found a different way to get what I want."

"Yeah," Quinn said, his voice heavy with sarcasm. "Shuck and jive."

Othello's ebony face became very still and Quinn knew he'd gone way too far. "Don't knock it if you ain't tried it," he replied softly.

"I'm sorry, man," Quinn apologized. "You don't deserve that."

"You damned right I don't," McLeod said, unrelenting. "You can call it shuck and jive if you want but I call it learning to be a team player. It's served me very well."

"All right, it's worked for you," Quinn admitted. Touching his own chest he said, "I'm not cut out that way, man. I'm cut out to be a lone wolf."

"Yes," McLeod replied softly. "I think you really believe that. I think you really see yourself as *der Steppenwolf*, the tragic figure who just can't fit in. I bet you even have the poem by Robert Service memorized, 'The

Men Who Never Fit In'."

Quinn blinked in surprise. "As a matter of fact, I do. It's one of my very favorites."

"I thought so," McLeod nodded. "As long as you believe that about yourself, you won't fit in. Never."

"I'm not like other people, Othello!" Quinn protested.

"Have you honestly ever tried to be?" McLeod's features were like a stone mask, unyielding. His dark eyes were obsidian.

Despite the harsh nature of his countenance, Quinn knew Othello was not attacking. "Yeah," he said quietly. "Ever since I was a kid. I really tried but people seemed to hate me for being as good as I am."

"Or maybe it was for having their noses rubbed in it?" Othello smiled, a hard, brittle smile.

His friend shrugged. "Yeah, I guess I did some of that, too." He shook his head. "I hate to admit it, but you're right. How did you know?"

McLeod eased up, chuckled. "Well, friend, if we spot it we got it. I know only because I used to play that game. I still catch myself doing it every once in a while. Helps keep me humble." Quinn snorted and McLeod quickly added, "All right, more humble. Humility is not a vice I've courted."

"Nice way of putting it," Quinn said dryly. "Neither have I."

"I thought you'd like it," Othello grinned. "Most writers like to be quoted."

Quinn sat quietly for a long while, thinking. McLeod said nothing but sipped his coffee and smoked one of his wretched long black cigars, waiting. "So tell me about this great American novel you want to write," he said, finally. "I bet it's about a writer. Or maybe a history teacher."

"Those are numbers three and two, respectively," Quinn laughed. "The one I want to do first is about a lawyer."

Othello laughed. "Why am I not surprised? I bet it's about a lawyer who has never practiced law."

Quinn glanced at him sharply. "How did you know?" he asked.

"A lot of first novels tend to be autobiographical," the other answered, shrugging. "They unfortunately tend to be boring, too."

Martin laughed. "Most lawyers are boring."

"I was talking about first novels," Othello reminded him.

"All right, but what would you expect from an autobiographical novel by a lawyer who never practiced?" Quinn grinned.

"Even more boring!" McLeod insisted. "Boring squared."

"Who also happened to be a newspaper reporter?" Quinn laughed.

"Hackingly dull!" Othello cried. "God, you've got me doing it!"

"I bet you tell all the girls that," Martin told him.

"Only those I'm trying to bed," Othello retorted. "Are you for hire, Martin?"

"As a girl or as a writer?" Quinn wanted to know.

McLeod looked him up and down critically. "How about we say as a reporter?" he asked. "You'd never make it on the street. Too skinny."

"'The closer the bone...'" Quinn quoted.

" I know, 'The sweeter the meat!'" Othello finished. "Well? What do you say?"

"Depends on what you got," Martin answered. "Sometime in the next year I do want to get the first one written."

"Give me six months," McLeod said. He mentioned a figure, drawing a whistle from the other. "That will give you six months off to write."

"Who do you want me to kill?" Quinn asked. "With the right person I might pay for the privilege."

"It's as snaky as skunk shit," McLeod told him seriously. "You could get killed without ever knowing what hit you. But I think it's worth doing." He outlined the project he had in mind.

"How much life insurance are you taking out on your sucker?" Quinn asked him. "That's not dangerous. It's suicide."

"Not if it's done right," McLeod said. "At least, that's what I figure." He sketched out a strategy.

"Well, it's not your ass on the firing line," Quinn told him. "Still, it just might work." He looked at his companion. "We're supposed to be friends, good buddy. So why do you want me?"

McLeod shrugged. "I think you have a better chance than anyone to pull it off." At Quinn's raised eyebrow he nodded. "All right, straight talk. What I said is true, but I also think you're trying to kill yourself, anyway. It might as well be put to use."

"What?" Quinn demanded. "When have I ever talked suicide?"

"Never, ever," McLeod answered him. "You just take ungodly risks, Martin. Like the way you're trying to jerk your publisher around only more so. Like the way you live. What's your monthly liquor bill. How many DWI's have you had in the last nine months?"

"None of your goddamned business!" Martin snapped.

"You've had two I know of," McLeod bored in. "It's a matter of public record. I happen to know of two others you sweet talked your way out of. If you get one more you are going to be doing the wrong kind of research on the state penal system."

"What the hell's it to you?" Quinn demanded belligerently.

"I happen to be your friend, asshole," McLeod said. "Believe it or not I do care what happens to your sorry ass. I'm offering you a way to get out of town and go straight for a while until the dust settles. It's not forever."

"They don't even have booze there!" Quinn complained. "And I hate fucking Arabs."

"I thought about that," McLeod admitted. "Your reasons for hating them are pretty damned good. I thought about that and decided it didn't matter. We can send you in straight, without cover."

"Without cover?" Quinn almost shouted. "Shit, man, that could get my throat cut in a hurry!"

"I don't think so," McLeod said. "Most of the bastards are on real ego trips and they crave press coverage, even unfavorable coverage. That makes them martyrs of a sort, martyrs to the cause. It makes us minions of the Great Satan for them. They win either way, and the bastards know it." He shrugged. "It's investigative reporting."

"So I go in as myself?" Martin asked. "Surely they must know my sympathies are with the Zionists. I've certainly written enough about it."

"Maybe you could go in saying you want to see the other side," his friend suggested. "Offering to be open minded. They will go a long way for a possible convert of your stature in the West."

"What happens if I don't convert?" Quinn wanted to know.

Othello shrugged. "As I said, it's slippery as snake shit, but it is a very good story. I could get someone else to go in but I don't think they would have the same chance of success you would." He shrugged. On the other hand, if you don't want to do that one, I have some other things on the back burner you could check out. None of them are as interesting, and none of them pay as good, but all of them are a helluva lot less risky."

"Hemmingway was right," Quinn observed.

"What was he right about?" Othello asked.

"We're only truly alive when we are an inch from the bull's horns," his friend answered. "Everything else is boredom."

"Yeah," McLeod retorted. "He was literally bored to death. So to speak." He looked at his friend. "He also had a drinking problem, a very serious one. Did you know that?"

"Who didn't?" Quinn asked. "We certainly made enough of it." He returned his friend's look. "Has it ever occurred to you, Othello, that we're like a pack of dogs? Even when one of our own gets hit, and there might be a little sympathy, there isn't. We all go after his blood like flies on shit."

"Hyenas," McLeod answered softly.

"What?" Quinn asked. "I didn't hear you."

"Hyenas," Othello said more loudly. "Us news people remind me of a pack of hyenas. They're much worse than dogs. Yet sometimes they bring down a lion."

"Good thing our personal lives are not fair game like those of the folk we cover," Martin observed. "We'd be up shit creek."

"So how about it?" Othello asked. "Are you in or not?"

"How soon do you need me?"

"How soon can you get your situation settled with your publisher?" McLeod asked. "Two weeks enough? It will take at least that long to get things set up in Palestine. Can do?"

"Can do!" Quinn said. "I'll tell my lawyer to get it settled. And to look over your contract, too."

"Standard contract," McLeod insisted. "Either you trust me or you don't. If you don't it won't work."

Quinn looked at him and smiled. "All right. With a thirty day notice for both sides and residuals to me. You get first rights to anything I write or research in that time but that's all."

"Fair enough," Othello said. "It's a deal."

"One more thing," Quinn said. Othello glanced up suspiciously. "You all take out a full million of term insurance on me. I'll name the beneficiary."

"Who did you have in mind?" McLeod wanted to know.

"The American Jewish Fund," Quinn grinned.

"You have a strange sense of humor, Martin," Othello told him.

"No, this time I'm not making a joke," Quinn said seriously. "Maybe it wouldn't make any difference in the heat of the moment, but it might keep me alive if some fanatic knows killing me will net the Zionists a cool mil."

"Not bad," McLeod said. "But we better keep it quiet. For that much money the Mossad might make the hit and blame it on the Arabs."

"We live in a cynical world, don't we, friend?" Quinn observed.

"I'll drink to that," McLeod nodded, raising his tea glass.

"I do drink to that, Othello," Martin told him, sadly looking at his own tea glass. "All the fucking time."

As it turned out, the settlement with the publisher went quickly, netting Quinn seventy per cent. Even though his lawyer wanted to push for more, Martin was anxious to settle so he could get on with his assignment. Yet the assignment to Palestine did not materialize. The Arabs were suspicious and negotiations dragged on interminably. Then on August 7, 1970, Jonathan Jackson raided the San Rafael courthouse in Marin County, California, and Othello wanted Quinn back in the states. "I want you to find Angela Davis," he told Martin. "I want you to get an exclusive with her."

"You and every other editor in the world," Quinn answered. "I'll give it a shot, but what makes you think I can do it?"

"Your old friend Floyd is still in circulation," McLeod told him. "He just happens to be a close friend of hers, too. He trusts you and if anyone can get it out of him, you can."

Quinn thought briefly. "All right," he said. "But if you know this, so will J. Edgar. I'm liable to be ass deep in FBI agents. They tend to take killing a judge seriously."

"So do I," McLeod answered. "What I want to know is the extent of Angela's involvement."

Quinn picked up something in his friend's voice. "This isn't just an assignment, is it, Othello? This personal for you, isn't it?"

McLeod sighed. "Yeah, it is. I know the lady, too. I respect her and what she's trying to do with prisoner's rights. I think this whole frigging thing is as political as it can be. It stinks to high heaven and I'd like to expose it for what it is. More political bullshit."

"Sponsored by J. Edgar, Tricky Dicky, and the boys in their little Nazi band," the other quipped. "Not to mention friend Ronnie Rayguns and his Death Valley Dudes. So, hell, yes, I'll do it."

"I want the truth, Martin," Othello warned. "This is a rough crowd we're going after and we need confirmation of what we publish."

"Seems I heard you mention that once before," Quinn laughed. "At least they won't blow me away like the Arabs might."

"I wouldn't be too sure of that," McLeod warned. "I'd advise you to file every single thing immediately so we can go after them if they set you up."

"You're serious, aren't you?" Martin asked, surprised.

"We're dealing with scared people," Othello pointed out. "Maybe even desperate people. Desperate people do desperate things. So watch your ass, friend I like having you around to argue with."

"Oh, Othello, I didn't know you cared," Quinn teased, grinning. "You say such sweet things!"

"I mean it, Martin," McLeod told him. "Watch out."

Relenting, Quinn became serious, reassuring his friend, "Believe me, I will. I really will. I am not quite as flaky as you think and I'd like to nail the bastards, too."

"Why should I talk to you?" Floyd Newman asked.

Quinn sighed. "Because you know me, Floyd. You know I respect the truth and you can trust me to write it."

"I know you're a honky," Newman corrected him. "You're a white man and white men have been screwing us brothers from the start."

Quinn looked at his source puzzled. "I find it hard to believe what I'm hearing," he said. "Floyd, this is Martin, Martin Quinn, not some red neck cracker from Georgia. You trusted me before and I didn't let you down. I'm your friend."

"There's a first time for everything," Newman responded. "And don't call me your friend. I don't need honky friends."

Martin sighed. "I'm really surprised, Floyd. That's a very racist thing to say and I thought you were a bigger man than that."

"You ain't going to get what you want with that horseshit!" Newman responded angrily. "I'm not the racist here. You are!"

"Right," Quinn responded. "I'm the one who's throwing around racist terms like 'honky' and 'nigger'."

"You may not be saying it but you're thinking it!" Newman declared.

"How would you know?" Quinn asked, beginning to anger. "Are you some kind of mind reader now, too? What have I ever done to betray your trust, Floyd? What have I, Martin, ever done to you, Floyd? Tell me that!"

"White men have been betraying my trust since I was a baby," Floyd insisted doggedly. "And you're a white man."

"So you've decided to become just like them," Quinn sneered. "That's great. That's just great, Floyd. That's really swift." He folded up his notes and crammed them into a pocket. "I really am disappointed," he said, sadly shaking his head. "I really thought better of you. I really did"

"Where you going?" Newman demanded.

"I'm going to try to find somebody who will level with me," Martin told him. "I need someone who won't waste my time with this shit. Somebody who's not afraid to look at the truth."

"I am looking at the truth!" Newman flared. "Truth is, white men been exploiting black people for three hundred years in this country."

"That's right," Quinn agreed quietly. "Just like white men have been exploiting other white men, and black men have been exploiting other black people. It's called the human condition, Floyd, and it may not be pretty, but it cuts across every line of race and culture there is." Floyd Newman made no reply, looked at him sullenly. Again Quinn sighed. "Do you know what the real tragedy in this is, Floyd? The real tragedy is what it does to men of good will like you and me, so we can't trust each other."

"So you admit you don't trust me?" Newman said.

"You've just told me not to, man," Quinn explained. "You've just said that what matters to you is the color of my skin, not what's in my heart. So how can I trust you? Anything I do or say is suspect."

"How am I supposed to know what's in your heart?" Newman wanted to know. "I ain't no fucking mind reader." Though his words were still belligerent, Newman's tone had softened, and there was an aching loneliness in his voice.

Quinn nodded. "I guess in your place I wouldn't, either," Martin told him. He shrugged. "I don't know any way out of this, man. We are at an impasse and I can't see any way out. I appreciate your seeing me at all." He looked at Newman and offered his hand. "If I said something today that offended you, I hope you'll blow it off."

Newman looked at his hand a moment, then took it. "Shit, baby," he said. "You don't know what it's like being a nigger in this country."

"No, I don't," Martin said. "I can imagine, but that's about it. I will listen any time you want to tell me what it's like, and I'll write exactly what you say. Your exact words. No more, no less. Just like I always have."

Newman looked at him levelly and was about to say some thing when a voice from behind them harshly cried out, "Freeze, asshole!" Looking around they saw three white policemen approaching them menacingly, weapons drawn and leveled at them. Raising his hands Newman looked at Quinn. "Nice setup, baby," he spat. "Trust me."

"I didn't have anything to do with this!" Quinn told him, his own hands in the air.

"Shut up!" Snarled one of the police, pointing his pistol back and forth between them, while another circled to their rear, quickly cuffing Newman.

"Are we under arrest, sergeant?" Quinn quietly asked one of the police, an officer with stripes on his sleeves. His hands were still raised.

"Shut up, I told you!" the policeman repeated, jamming his pistol into Quinn's side, doubling him over with pain.

"Lindquist!" snapped the sergeant. Not shifting his eyes for a moment, the officer who hurt Quinn backed off a step. "Who are you?" he asked Quinn, who told him, gasping. "You have anything that proves that?" the sergeant wanted to know.

"My identification is in my jacket pocket," Quinn told him.

"Then let's see it," the sergeant demanded.

Quinn started to lower his hands, then saw Newman's eyes narrow and stopped. "With all due respect, sergeant, Lindquist has already hurt me. I don't want to give him any excuse to pull the trigger." He nodded toward Lindquist who was standing stiffly, his pistol still pointing at Quinn's chest. There was a wild look in the man's eyes, and hatred.

"Call us in, Lindquist," the sergeant said. "Call off the backup."

"But, sergeant...." Lindquist started to argue.

"Do it!" roared the sergeant. For a moment Lindquist wavered, then he holstered his revolver and stalked off. "Now," the sergeant reminded Quinn, "some identification, please sir." The third officer continued to cover them but his gun was pointing between them, not at them, and the sergeant was very careful to keep out of his line of fire.

Carefully Quinn removed his press credentials from his jacket pocket and handed them to the policeman. The sergeant examined them closely, then tossed them back to him. "All right, Mr. Quinn, you can go."

"Not until I have your name and badge number," Quinn insisted, taking out his notebook. "I need those of the other two officers, too."

"You're skating on thin ice, Mr. Quinn," the sergeant said quietly.

"I'm well within the law in this matter," Quinn told him. "If you refuse to give me the information the public will want to know why."

"Oh, a lawyer, are we?" the sergeant said, turning aggressively toward Quinn. "I'll show you some law."

"As a matter of fact I am," Quinn said, raising his hands in a gesture of surrender. "I happen to be a member of the bar in this state. I also happen to be Mr. Newman's attorney of record."

The sergeant glanced at Floyd Newman, who was clearly surprised. "Sure you are," he said.

"He is, "Newman told him. "I hired him just before you busted us."

"We were talking about whether he could trust a white lawyer or not," Quinn added dryly, knowing the officers had overheard at least part of their conversation. "Check with the bar association, sergeant. I'm registered with the state bar of Minnesota as Martin Lundberg of St. Cloud, and this state is one which happens to have full reciprocity."

The sergeant was immediately suspicious. "Your press ID says your name is Quinn," he said, his features hardening.

"That's the name I write under, officer," Quinn smiled, "but my name as a lawyer is Lundberg." He shrugged. "Check it out. My birth certificate names me as Lundberg, too."

"I intend to, Mr. Quinn, or whoever you are," the sergeant told him. "You better come with us to the station."

"Gladly, officer, since I'm instructing my client to say absolutely nothing to you without me present." He looked at the sergeant blandly. "I assume you have heard of Miranda vs. Arizona," he added dryly. "What about my car?"

"You can follow us to the station," the sergeant said tersely, taking a card out of his pocket and reading from it rapidly. "There," he said to Quinn when he was done. "That satisfies Miranda."

"Could you understand what the man said?" Quinn asked Newman.

"Naw, sir, ah coun't," Newman said in a rural Alabama black patios, playing along with Quinn's lead. He grinned. "Who be Miranda?"

Quinn shrugged and looked at the officer." So much for Miranda. I'll follow you to the station, but I warn you, Mr. Newman better not be harmed in any way."

"Then he better not resist," the sergeant growled.

"I'm formally instructing him not to," Quinn replied. Looking at his companion he said, "Mr. Newman, you must go with these officers since you are under arrest. Please do not do anything to provoke them in any way or give them any excuse to harm you. Just don't answer any of their questions, either. Will you do that, sir?"

"Yassuh!" Newman nodded, all trace of anger wiped from his face.

"I'll see you at the station," Quinn replied. Turning to the sergeant he said, "My car is on the other side of the park."

"We'll drop you there," the sergeant said gruffly. "Come on."

The police lieutenant was even more skeptical than his sergeant. Yet their captain was a careful man and not one prone to take unnecessary risks. This was a character trait which accelerated the advancement of his career. Nor had his friendship with the press hurt, a fact which Quinn later learned had greased the skids considerably.

"Well, Mr. Quinn, or Mr. Lundberg, as the case may be, you are indeed a bona fide attorney licensed to practice law in Minnesota."

"And here, too," Quinn reminded him, smiling.

"So long as you are associated with a local attorney," the captain responded, raising his eyebrows in question.

"Certainly, I am," Quinn nodded. "I think you probably know my local associate." He mentioned the name of a well known local lawyer, one known in legal circles as a legal "rambo".

The captain made a face. "I see," he replied. "Well, I am just making sure we're following the proper procedures. No offense intended."

"Of course not," Quinn murmured. "None is taken, captain. Now, when can I see my client?"

"Right away," the captain told him. "Just as soon as we finish booking him in. In the meantime, there is a small point on which I'd like clarification, if you don't mind." He smiled a beaming politician's grin, but Quinn noticed the smile never reached his eyes. They were like archer's slits in a turret and there was no doubt in Quinn's mind he was being watched for the smallest sign of weakness. Rather than answer, Quinn smiled back the same way and simply waited. After a heavy silence the captain went on. "Are you here as a lawyer or as a member of the press?"

"I am representing Floyd Newman as his attorney," Quinn answered. "I beg your pardon. I thought I made that clear."

"That was why he approached you?" the captain bore in.

Quinn shrugged. "Captain, Floyd and I have known each other a long while, which I'm sure you know. The purpose of our meeting night was lawful private business and I'm sure you know that as his lawyer I am not at liberty to divulge the nature of our conversation." He smiled. "No offense intended, but that's the way it is."

"None taken," the captain said rotely. "Yet you publish what he tells you, Mr. Quinn. Doesn't that violate your relationship?"

"Of course not, captain," Quinn replied quietly. "What Mr. Newman gives me from time to time is human interest information I can publish. In return for this I perform any legal services he may need. The point is that it is Mr. Newman, and not me, who determines what I can and cannot publish."

"Interesting," the captain nodded, but Quinn sensed his patience was getting thin. "Is there anything else, captain?" he asked.

"Nothing that can't wait, Mr. Quinn," the captain told him flatly. "One of the things police work has taught me is how to wait. Sooner or later those who skate too close to thin ice go too far, and when they do in this town, they find me standing there with a big net."

"I'm sure you're most efficient, captain," Quinn murmured. "With men like Officer Lindquist I'm sure the streets are much quieter."

"Officer Lindquist has won three letters of commendation in the last two years," the captain stated. "He has an excellent record."

"I'm sure he must," Quinn replied. "I am sure you were proud to sign all three. That will make it all the worse if he ever falls into the net and you have to arrest him. I don't envy you." He shrugged. "You can imagine what the press would do with that."

For a moment Quinn thought he'd gone too far, pushed too hard. Then the captain laughed it off. "I wish I had his energy," he replied smoothly. "Lindquist will settle down in a couple of years. He's a good officer."

Unless he kills someone, Quinn thought. Yet he did not say it. He was already on thin ice, as the captain might say, and the important thing was to get Floyd Newman out of jail as quickly as possible. "What charge are you booking Floyd on?" he asked.

"Material witness," the captain shrugged. "The FBI wants to talk to him. That's why we picked him up."

"Material witness to what?" Quinn wanted to know.

"The whereabouts of one Angela Davis, suspected of conspiracy to do murder in California," the captain said dryly.

"Are you charging Floyd Newman with conspiracy, too?"

The captain smiled. "I honestly don't know. That's up to the FBI. If they do, of course, it will be a federal charge." There was no mistaking his amusement about this.

Quinn nodded. "I'm licensed for federal court, too, captain. Perhaps I'll see you there. On the stand." He grinned as the captain's smile set into a grimace. "Now, when can I see my client?"

An hour later Quinn was on the phone with Othello McLeod, calling from a pay phone near the airport. "So that is where things stand now," he told his friend. "The people from the ACLU showed up about an hour later and I turned things over to them. Floyd is in good hands."

"What about the other matter?" McLeod asked, not referring to Angela Davis by name. "Any luck there?"

"I don't think Floyd can help us with that project," Quinn told him. "He doesn't have access to the information we need. Quite frankly, I don't know where else to look."

"What about some of your other contacts," McLeod asked.

"With the fat boys involved I'm not sure I'd be doing them any favors by calling," Quinn answered, knowing McLeod would know he was referring to the FBI. "I don't want to burn them."

There was silence on the line. Quinn could almost see his friend as he stood in the news bureau thinking. "How secure is this line?" he asked.

"We need to talk in person," Othello answered. "I don't think there's much hurry about it so I'd like you to check something else out on the way. I know it's not part of our agreement, but you're the closest man I've got and I'd consider it a personal favor."

"No sweat," Quinn told him. "It won't even cost you a marker."

"You'd better hear what it is first," Othello laughed. "I'll be sending you out to the reservation. There's a situation heating up with AIM I want you to check out. It may not pan out, but it may be the next big push in civil rights."

"The American Indian people?" Quinn asked, taken off guard. "I don't mind going, Othello, but I don't know Dooley squat about AIM."

"When has that ever slowed you down?" McLeod snorted. "Who is it who once told me too much information was a handicap for a good reporter."

"I must have been three sheets to the wind," Quinn replied, laughing. "I think it was in Cairo, wasn't it?" He thought a moment. "All right, Othello, I'll do it, but can you get me a file on it?"

"It's on the way," McLeod told him. "I can send a photographer and she'll bring it along to you."

"She?" Quinn protested. "Come on, Othello. Things could get rough. I don't want to have to be looking after some woman."

There was a deep laugh on the other end of the line. "If things get rough you are liable to be the one who needs looking after, Quinn," Othello told him. "Believe me, our Rosalind is just the person you want on your side in a brawl." He laughed again. "I'll tell you what. If you don't think Rosalind measures up, you can be the one to tell her."

"I smell a setup, Othello," Quinn said suspiciously.

"No, no setup, Martin. What you don't know, however, is that Ros stands six three in her stocking feet and could whip the shit out of both of us together with her right hand tied behind her back."

"Sounds like I better be careful," Quinn muttered. *That's all I need,* he thought, *another fragile ego I have to tender.*

"Not at all," Othello answered, as if reading Quinn's thoughts. "All I am suggesting is professionalism. Rosalind responds very well to common courtesy, and gallantry works wonders."

"This Rosalind sounds like a publisher's daughter," Quinn grumped. "Just how gallant do I have to be?"

"As much as you're man enough to be, Martin," McLeod laughed as he broke the connection. "Call me back in an hour with your flight schedule."

5. Pauwau

Looking back now from the safety of a decade later, I would have to say one of my lowest periods came during the mid 'Seventies. I think that was when the drinking started to become a real problem. It was during that time I experimented with other things. Up to that time what I was doing was mostly recreational. I did it to ease the pain within the hole in my soul and it seemed to work for a while. Now I know it didn't work at all, but only made the problem worse. The other day I came across a poem I wrote in 1975 or maybe 1976 that confirms this. It is pretty clear to me now that I was going down then, and going down fast.

> *The vision's lost, the mountain's high*
> *The birds are gone, the winter sky*
> *Grows dark with rain and winter night*
> *Sets in your soul*
>
> *Lost and blind and all alone*
> *Time hangs heavy, is a stone*
> *That grinds to bits the dreams of Home*
> *And crushes hope to dust*
>
> *Then from the night a raven's cry*
> *Bespeaks the vain and mindless lie*
> *I live each day until I die*
> *A bleak and pointless death....*

(*Poems & Recollection*, Martin Quinn)

Summer, 1975. The loud voice kept pounding at his ears, shattering the lovely purple sky with its thundering insistence, scattering the shards of his vision. Desperately Martin tried to ignore the voice, to gather the pieces of beauty slipping like quicksilver between his frantic fingers into the ocean of darkness. Yet as each word exploded on his ears, a piece of the universe shattered, disappeared into nothingness, leaving him in a harsh landscape of sharp edges and blinding light.

"Quinn!" the voice sounded, blasting into his world like rolling thunder of heavy artillery. "Quinn! Goddam it, Quinn, wake up! Wake up!" There was a shrill edge to the voice and someone was shaking him violently, or was it an earthquake? Sudden terror accomplished what the voice could not and Martin Quinn bolted awake, eyes wide and hands clutching the mattress.

"Jesus, Quinn, you scared us!" He looked uncomprehending into the face bent over his. It was familiar, someone he should know. He tried to ask the face its name but all that escaped his lips was a deep groan.

"That's it, baby," said another voice, and Quinn turned his head to see another familiar face staring at him with what looked like concern. "Stay with us, man. The ambulance will be here in just a minute."

Quinn laughed, his own voice sounding as if it were coming from deep in a chasm. This world wasn't so bad, either. The light was harsh, but he loved the way the black man's words floated on the air, like musical notes dancing up and down the scale, gently beating their wings like big Canadian geese in full flight. He watched them circle, form their flying formation and, following the leader, head north through a picture on the wall. "Wow! " he said. "Did...you...see...that?" He began to giggle.

"He's stoned out of his gourd," the first voice said. Unlike the voice from the black face of God, the words of the first voice shot across the room like Chinese rockets, shooting off sparks and smoke and angry flame.

The Adversary! Quinn thought, his eyes growing wild. "Get... thee... behind... me... Satan!" He shouted, seeing his words hurling through the air like comets toward the volcano on which the Devil was standing.

"Martin!" the voice of God said urgently, but gently. "Martin, it's me, Othello and Rosalind. We're your friends."

"Thou...art...God!" he heard his voice grating like a rusty gate.

"Sometimes I'd like to be," Othello chuckled. "But most of the time it's lucky for me I ain't." Gently he shook Quinn's shoulder. "Stay with us, man. Don't go away. We'll have you at the hospital in no time." Glancing across the room he asked someone, "Any idea what he's on?"

"Cassius!" Quinn cried. "Cassius Cactus. I am the Greatest."

"Whatever it is, it's hallucinogenic," the first voice said. This time the rockets were gone and her words floated like bright balloons across the room and a corona of light surrounded her face.

This can't be Satan, he thought, confused. *This is an angel.* Then he remembered Satan was the name of an angel, an angel of darkness who didn't like human beings. Yet behind the angel's anger he thought he heard concern for him, and lifting his head, Quinn peered in her direction. "Ros?" he asked. "Is that you, Ros?"

"He's coming out of it!" Rosalind said, excited. There were tears in her eyes.

Quinn could not grasp why she seemed to worried. "What's wrong?" he asked. "What's going on? Did someone die?" Somehow he felt heavy and strangely weak, as if he'd walked a thousand miles.

"You've been tripping out on some heavy duty shit," Othello told him. "Any idea what you took?"

"Cassius," Quinn murmured, then shook his head and tried again, but his tongue was not in synch. "Cassius! No! Caseous!" he tried.

"Cactus?" Othello asked and Quinn nodded. "You mean peyote?" Quinn nodded again. "He'll be all right, then," Othello said to Rosalind, relaxing for the first time. "You have been doing a little first hand research on the peyote cult, haven't you?" he asked her, and Quinn nodded with a silly laugh.

"Yeah," Rosalind told him. "He was supposed to meet with some sort of medicine man last night. The guy was spooky and he would only talk to Martin by himself. He said absolutely no photos. So I went out and took some pix for background. This was how I found him when I knocked on his door a little while ago. The manager let me in."

Othello McLeod nodded. Turning to Martin he said, "You're going to be all right, buddy. We're going to take you to the hospital just to make sure but it should pass pretty quick from what I've heard." Quinn nodded and McLeod shook his head. "You're a lucky bastard," he told

Quinn, shaking his head. "I also hear peyote contains an alkaloid similar to strychnine. Maybe arsenic, too. If you want to kill yourself, rat poison is quicker."

"Rat poison, hell," muttered Rosalind, almost growling. "I feel like strangling the dumb shit, myself."

Othello looked at her closely, saw symptoms he knew well. Not for the first time he regretted assigning her to cover Quinn's stories. Yet the two of them worked well together, scrapping and bitching with one another like brother and sister. There was caring there, and not just from Rosalind's side. Martin seemed to appreciate his photographer, and while there was no physical relationship between them, or rather, no signs Othello could see, McLeod suspected this was only for the lack of Martin asking. Rosalind obviously loved him deeply, nor did her love appear limited to sibling affection. As a matter of fact, he'd once indirectly asked his friend about it, teasing about the size of his expense account. "Why the hell don't you and Rosalind get married?" he asked him. "Or at least shack up and share a room? It would save us a helluva lot of money."

Quinn laughed. "We might as well, I guess. We could certainly pass for married. We've been together almost five years now and there's not many secrets between us, or many idiosyncrasies we don't know. She even bosses the hell out of me, at least as much as I'll let her."

"So why don't you?" Othello challenged, only partially kidding.

"Fear," Quinn told him. "Naked fear, literally." He grinned. "Can you imagine what a wedding night with Rosalind would be like?"

McLeod chuckled. "I see what you mean, but what a way to go."

"Man, it would be like setting off dynamite on top of a volcano. Talk about going out with a bang!"

"Well, if it happens, I'll send flowers," McLeod responded, turning back to their work. Remembering the conversation now, he smiled.

"What?" asked Rosalind suspiciously, as if she'd read his thoughts from his face.

"I was just remembering something funny he told me once," McLeod said, shaking his head. "It's really not funny out of context." He changed the subject. "How far along are you with the project?"

Rosalind's answer was delayed by the arrival of the ambulance. The attendant shook his head and made a note in a spiral notebook when

McLeod told him what they suspected was wrong. "Why can't they just go to church like everybody else?" he asked peevishly. "I swear, we haul more frigging Indians than anybody else. Most are drunk, but we've had our share of peyote overdoses, too." He shook his head. "A waste of our time, and the taxpayer's dollar."

"What do mean?" Othello wanted to know.

"Well, like him," the attendant said, pointing at Martin. "Since he's coming out of it pretty good, most likely all they'll do is put him in a bed for observation until tomorrow morning and the county will end up picking up the bill for feeding him."

"Not on your life!" McLeod snapped. "He's a reporter on assignment and our wire service will take care of his hospital stay."

"No offense," the attendant said hastily. "Looking at him I thought he was an Indian. You know how Indians are."

"As a matter of fact, I don't," Othello told him quietly. "Why don't you just tell me how they are? Buddy."

"Hey, we got to get this guy to the hospital," the other attendant said. "He didn't mean nothing, sir."

Othello was disgruntled, but let it ride. The man was right. Martin' care came first. "All right," he growled, "we'll meet you there. Where are you taking him? And how do we get there?"

"County Memorial," the second attendant told him. "Just follow the main street west and it will be a couple of miles down to the right." Quickly they lifted Quinn onto their stretcher and left.

"It will be a while before they get him into a room," Othello said to Rosalind when they were gone. "Grab what you have so far and we'll go over it while we wait at the hospital. I'll meet you in the lobby."

The doctor was kinder, but no less direct than the ambulance attendant. "Is your friend trying to kill himself?" he asked pointedly.

"Not really," Othello answered quietly. "Why do you ask?"

"Well, he's obviously not taking care of himself very well," the physician answered. "He seems to have a good constitution but there are signs of malnutrition and anemia. Does he have a drinking problem?"

"I wouldn't call it a problem," McLeod said, coming to Martin' defense. "He is a heavy drinker, but not that bad."

"I'd have to disagree, Othello," Rosalind told him. "You don't see him day after day like I do."

"Mrs. Quinn?" the doctor asked. "I don't like being so blunt, but how long has his drinking been a problem?"

Rosalind flushed. "I'm not his wife," she said. "I'm his photographer."

The doctor was confused. "We're news people," McLeod explained. "Quinn has been on assignment looking at the peyote cult and Rosalind is his photographer. They work together all the time."

"Ah," the doctor nodded. "Then you probably see more of him than his wife." Rosalind flushed again and the doctor added, "Well, that's what my wife tells me about my scrub nurse."

"What's the immediate danger, doctor?" Othello wanted to know Are there any side effects we need to watch for?"

The doctor shook his head. "After a few days he should be back pretty much to normal. I understand there are some residual hallucinations and he may experience what are called flashbacks, but the peyote itself will wear off. My real concern is his drinking." He looked at them gravely. "Are you his supervisor?" Othello nodded. "Have you suggested AA?"

"He's not a bum," doctor, McLeod responded, indignant. "He's a very competent professional who has trouble holding his liquor."

The doctor shook his head and sighed. "That's part of the problem, Mr. McLeod. People have the idea that alcoholics are Bowery bums. That's where any alcoholic might end up, but the truth is that most of us are very bright, competent people. Unfortunately, that hides the disease."

"Us?" McLeod responded, his whole face a question mark.

"Yes, us," the doctor told him. "I'm in recovery, myself. What a lot of people don't know is that the Program was started by a physician and a stock broker, neither of whom ever reached the streets." He nodded. "At least not for good. I've been in recovery now almost twelve years, one day at a time. I may get drunk tomorrow, but by the grace of God I'll get through today without having a drink. I've learned to trust God to take care of tomorrow." He shrugged. "That's how it works." Rosalind nodded.

"I didn't know it was a religious program," Othello replied.

"It's not," Rosalind interjected. The doctor looked at her with new interest. "My dad is in AA," she told them. "He has been for years and years and it's really made a difference. In all of our lives."

"What she's saying," the doctor explained, "is that alcoholism is a spiritual disease requiring a spiritual cure. The Fellowship is not allied with any religion or denomination, but it is spiritual. Who each of us learns to rely on is not ourselves or other people, but a God of our own understanding and experience. There's no dogma or doctrine or creed. There's just a sound method that works in almost any religious setting. So you're likely to find Baptists and Buddhists and Jews and Catholics and agnostics all attending the same meeting and enjoying the same fellowship. It's marvelous."

"So how do we get him there?" Othello asked.

"Well, I prefer direct hard line," the doctor said. "As his employer you can insist he attempt recovery as a condition of employment."

"That wouldn't work with Martin." McLeod answered. "He's too good at what he does, and he's financially independent. He doesn't have to work. He saves most of his salary and he lives on very little. I imagine his biggest expense is his bar bill."

"That's tough," the doctor said, shaking his head. "Usually it takes some leverage to get us in recovery. How about family?"

McLeod looked at Rosalind, who shrugged. "Aside from his mother, we're about it, I think. Apparently he's cut off from his family except for her. There were some people in New Mexico he talks about, but it's been years since he's been in touch with them."

"No wife or children?" the doctor was surprised. "Or is he divorced?"

"They were killed in a car bomb in Jerusalem," Othello told him. "Six or seven years ago now."

"Damn!" the physician said, wincing. "No wonder the poor bastard drinks so much. Doesn't seem have much to live for, does he?"

"His work is about it," Othello told him.

"Well, I'll talk to him in the morning when he's a little more clear headed," the doctor said, bringing their conversation to a close. "I don't expect it will do much good, but I'll give it a shot." He grinned. "One thing about it, I know most of the lies we tell ourselves. But it's really not up to me, either. Your friend's drinking is God's problem. And his."

Walking Rosalind back to the car, McLeod confronted her. "So it's been getting pretty bad then?" She nodded. "Why didn't you tell me?"

Rosalind shrugged. "Up until lately it's not been all that bad. He goes for long periods without drinking anything. Then something happens and he ends up drunk. Usually it's only for the night." She made a face. "It's disgusting how chipper he is when he wakes up."

"Up until lately?" McLeod stopped, turned and looked at her directly. "I think it's time to let our hair down, Ros," he said. "This time the ship hit the sand, but Quinn was lucky. I don't want it to happen again. The next time it may be fatal. I don't want to lose a good friend."

Rosalind nodded. "Honest, Othello, it's only been in the last couple of months his drinking's been anything like out of control. Even then it's only at times. I don't think it will happen for a while after this."

"I don't want it to happen at all," McLeod insisted. "But I don't know how to make it stop."

"Martin is the only one who can do that," Rosalind told him. "At least, that's what my dad says. Until he understands it's a problem, he won't do anything about it. No, until he sees it as a problem, he can't." She sighed. "I'll talk to him, too, but I don't know how much good it will do. Nagging doesn't work."

"So, Mr. Quinn," the doctor said, washing his hands carefully and putting away his stereoscope. "It looks like you're back in the land of the living again. Is this the first time you've experimented with peyote?"

Martin nodded. "Yeah, and I didn't have that much. Only one or two buttons at the most."

"More like three or four," the doctor corrected him. "Judging from the depth of your stupor. Of course, you probably wouldn't remember much after eating the first one or two." He nodded. "That's the danger, you see. The people who eat peyote regularly build up a tolerance that you don't have and the stuff does contain poison. So you could easily overdose without your knowing it. That's my concern."

Quinn nodded. "Yeah, I know what you mean. I feel like shit."

"That is not entirely due to your peyote experience," the doctor replied. "There are other factors involved, as well."

Quinn wondered why the doctor was taking so much time with him.

366

Most of them were in a rush to see as many patients as possible, but this fellow must be paid by the hour. "Am I keeping you, doctor?" he asked.

The doctor gave him a wry smile. "I understand your not wanting to talk about it," he replied, "but we need to, and I wouldn't be doing my job if I let things slide. The point is, your experience with the cactus was made much worse by your general physical condition. You apparently have not been taking care of yourself very well. Your blood work indicates you have not been eating right and I suspect you have been drinking pretty heavily of late." He waited for confirmation, but Quinn said nothing. "A little drinking in moderation is good for most people in my opinion, and there is research that bears this out. However, beyond one or two drinks a day, or two or three glasses of wine spread over the whole day, it turns against us. One of the most serious effects is that it becomes a substitute for eating, which I suspect has been the case with you in the last few months."

Again Quinn said nothing and the doctor took another tack. "These things often have a precipitating event. What got you started this time?"

"The Fourth of July," Quinn replied in a monotone, wishing he had a cigarette. "Do you have a smoke, doctor?"

The doctor nodded and fished out a packet of Pall Malls. "Terrible habit," he confessed, taking one and offering the pack to Quinn. "Almost impossible to break. At least for me." He lighted their cigarettes, passing an ashtray to Quinn. "Hootch was bad enough, but God help the person who stands between me and my next smoke."

Quinn laughed, decided the medic was all right, after all. "The Fourth of July?" the doctor asked. "Were you celebrating?"

Quinn's face became very grave. "No, doctor. I was trying to blot out the pain." When he looked up the good doctor was startled to see the depth of grief in the man's eyes. "Do you remember what happened on the Fourth of July this year?" Quinn asked.

"No," said the doctor. "I was on a hiking trip in the Bob Marshall wilderness area in Montana. We were out of touch for two weeks. What happened?"

"A fucking Arab decided to blow up as many innocent people as he could," Quinn told him. "The worst terrorist attack in the history of modern Israel and the bastards knew exactly what they were doing."

"I remember reading something about that in Newsweek," the doctor replied. "A market bombing, wasn't it?"

Quinn nodded. "They set it off in Zion Square at the worst possible time. People were shopping for the Sabbath and it was crowded. I know, I've been there doing that. Thirteen dead and seventy others wounded. It's very lucky it wasn't worse."

The doctor nodded. "I remember the story now. It was ghastly." He looked at Quinn, puzzled. "What I don't understand is what that had to do with you. How did that set off going on a bender?"

"That's how my wife and child died eight years ago, doctor." Quinn's eyes were bleak as a granite wall. "An Arab bomb going off on a crowded bus in Jerusalem. It killed them both."

"Damn!" muttered the physician.

"When it happened again this year, it all came back to me. All the pain. So I decided to get drunk." He looked at the doctor. "I'm a newsman, doctor, and this has been a really shitty year for news. As a matter of fact, it's been a really shitty decade. About the only good news this year is that we're out of Vietnam. With over fifty thousand of our people dead."

The doctor nodded, but refused to be deflected. "I'm sorry for you, my friend. I know how devastated I'd be. My wife and kids were who I was with in the Bob Marshall. We don't get to do that sort of thing enough."

"We don't get to do that sort of thing at all," Quinn murmured. At the look on the doctor's face he added, "Oh, I didn't intend that as a shot at you, doctor. What you were talking about is something I'll never have."

"Why not?" the doctor asked. "Don't you want it?"

"Nothing more," Quinn said. "I was the happiest man in the world when I was getting ready to get married. Then it was gone. Blown away by some fanatic asshole who probably couldn't even read. They died for no reason other than they happened to be in the wrong place at the wrong time. I have thought about trying again, but losing them was just too painful. To think of risking that again is just...." He shook his head. "No way."

The doctor thought a long moment. "I can't say how I'd respond in your shoes, Mr. Quinn. My time with my wife and kids are about the most precious thing I have. That's why I don't work the way some of my friends do. I know I'd be devastated if I lost them. Yet I think for me the risk would still be worth it. Even if I lost my family twice I think I'd still risk it again." He nodded. "That's how good it is for me."

"I'm glad for you, doctor," Quinn murmured. The physician looked up sharply, but there was no sarcasm in Quinn's expression. "I mean it. You're a man who appreciates what he's got and I really am glad for you. I wish I could have the same, but I don't think that's for me."

The doctor nodded. "I hope for your sake that you're wrong." He paused. "I'm curious about something. With the news as bad as it always is, why do you do what you do? Why don't you try another line of work? I guess what I'm asking is, what keeps you going, Mr. Quinn?"

Quinn looked down, almost as if embarrassed. "I ask myself that all the time," he confessed. He shrugged. "I'm an idealist, doctor. The tough, cynical newsman thing is just a mask I use to keep others from knowing how much I care. Maybe myself, too." He touched himself on the breast. "Down here I seem to believe there's something out there worth it all, worth all the pain and suffering. Some purpose to it all, some reason to keep on keeping on. So I do. Keep on looking for it." He laughed bitterly. "All my Jewish friends tell me I'm looking for the Messiah."

"I hope you find him, my friend," the doctor said gently, rising and walking to the door. There he turned back for a moment, looking at Martin with compassion. "Yes, I think your Jewish friends may be right. I hope for your sake you find him, and soon. I'll check by later." Then he was gone.

Martin sat thinking about what he'd just heard come out of his own mouth. There was no denying the truth of it, yet he had no idea of what to do about it. Reflecting on what the doctor suggested about another line of work, he grinned to himself. There was only one place he knew where the news of the world would not haunt him. "Maybe I ought to try being a monk," he murmured to himself.

A laugh from the doorway brought him out of his musings. "That will be the day," Rosalind said, walking into the room and crossing to his bed. He was glad to see that McLeod was not with her. "Although, from what I've seen you've got part of it down." Then, realizing what she'd said, Rosalind flushed. "I mean like a Christian brother...." she stammered. "You know."

"You mean like one of the Christian Brothers?" Martin asked with a wicked grin, exploiting his advantage while he could. It was not often he was able to get Rosalind off balance. "I'd have to admit the brothers most likely have a more active love life than I do, but at least I have the possibility."

"That's not what I meant," Rosalind retorted, defending herself. "I was talking about their wine and brandy."

"There's that," Martin said. "One of the compensations of life in the monastery." He laughed. "Rosalind, why don't you marry me?"

"No way, Kemo Sabe," she laughed, nervously, he thought.

"You might as well," he told her. "We've been together five years now and I've treated you right."

"Yes," Rosalind laughed again. "I have to admit you're benevolent at times, at least for a dictator."

"Come on, it's not that bad," Quinn protested. "Why not? You surely know me by now, better than my own mother."

Ros shook her head. "I'm sure I do, but not on your life, brother. If I married you I'd have to take care of you."

"What the hell?" Quinn asked. "You do that now, anyway." Reaching out he took her hand. "Seriously, Ros, thank you. I know you've been covering my ass for the last few months, and I really appreciate it. I'll try to fly straight, at least for a while."

"That's just the problem, Martin," she murmured, looking at him with a sadness that startled him. "You'll fly straight for a while. You won't touch the stuff for weeks and maybe months. You'll prove to yourself and to the world there's not a problem. Then something will happen and you'll be on a binge again. I know, I've seen it happen time after time."

"Is it really that bad?" he asked.

"No, and that's just the problem," she told him. "Up to a point you're fun to be with when you're drinking. You're funny and witty and it's a gas, but then you reach a point you turn sad. You turn mean, too. Remember that guy in San Antonio?"

"Hell, Ros," Quinn argued. "He was being obnoxious as hell. Not to me, but to you. He wouldn't take 'no' for an answer."

"That's just the point," she told him. "He was being obnoxious to me and I would have handled it without breaking his jaw if you'd let me. As it was, I had a hell of a time convincing the judge you were defending me when you jumped him. I mean look at me. I'm three inches taller and broader than you across the shoulders. That Hispanic prick thought I was a black hooker. No man's going to give me much shit if I don't want him to, Martin."

"I hope you never get that mad at me," he said, shifting the subject.

"You don't know, baby," Rosalind assured him. "You don't know."

"I don't know what?" Quinn asked.

"You don't know how close you've stood to the Angel of Death," she told him. While she said it lightly, he was left with little doubt she was very serious. "Or how far you've walked into the Valley of the Shadow with me."

"Do I owe you apologies?" he asked her.

"No," Rosalind told him. "You're very good with apologies. What you aren't good with, Mr. Quinn, is change."

Whenever Rosalind called him "mister", Quinn knew he was in trouble, but felt like shit and he'd had enough. He sighed. "Look, Rosalind...." he started to say.

Rosalind cut him off. "No!" she declared. "You always do that when you don't want to talk about something. You heave this big, heavy sigh and say, 'look, Rosalind,' and I'm tired of being cut off! This time you're going to listen, and listen good!"

Looking up at her Quinn was reminded of a painting of the ride of the Valkyries of legend. All Rosalind lacked was a Nordic helmet to look like a dark Celtic raider. "You have me at a disadvantage, Ros," he whined in a futile bid for sympathy. "I'm sick."

"You fuckin' bettcha, I do!" Rosalind declared with some heat. "And I'm here to tell you I'm not letting go until I'm good and fucking ready! Savvy 'coon-shit', white-ass?" she asked, punching his chest with an ebony finger.

"All right, already!" Quinn snapped. "So tell me or kill me! I don't give a shit which!"

"I know you don't," Rosalind told him. "That's what pisses me off. I have to bust my butt to accomplish half of what you do without thinking about it, and you don't appreciate what it is you have. You just piss it away."

"All right, Rosalind," he said, holding up both hands in surrender. "I'll listen. I really will."

To his surprise Rosalind burst into tears. "Some of us happen to love you, damnit, Quinn," she said, wiping her eyes with a handkerchief. He was surprised, as always, to note how lacy and feminine it was. Somehow that always seemed out of character for Rosalind. "Othello is one and I happen to be another," she said. "You've got more soul than any white man I've ever met, and with the exception of Arabs, you don't seem to hate anybody but other white people. That's rare." Rosalind fell silent.

"Thank you, Rosalind," Martin responded quietly. "I'm truly sorry if I have hurt you in any way. It was not intended."

"Shit, Quinn, don't you think I know that?" Rosalind told him. "I just hate to see you destroy yourself."

"You're beautiful, Rosalind. You know that?" he asked. "You are one of the most beautiful people I know."

It was her turn to be embarrassed. "You just trying to get in my pants, white boy," she snorted. Yet he could tell she was pleased and there was an awkward silence. Neither of them knew where to go from there. Finally, Rosalind retreated into the safety of work. "So what you want me to do while you're laying up here in bed?" she asked briskly.

"Hell, I don't know," Quinn told her. "What did you get when I went off to see the medicine man?" Thirty minutes later when Othello returned to the room, they were deep into a discussion of their next story. Seeing them back at work, Othello heaved a sigh of relief. Quinn should be good for a while now if he ran true to form, and, hopefully, Rosalind would tip McLeod off immediately when she saw another bender shaping up. Maybe they could catch it in time for once. McLeod hoped so. While he might never say it in so many words, he loved Quinn like a brother, warts and all.

"No, Quinn," Rosalind laughed. "That's not the way they say it. You got to make it three syllables, baby. You only used two."

"All right," Martin said, "how's this? Ghaaaaawd!"

"That's better," she told him, "but it's still not right. Try making each letter a syllable, like this." She demonstrated.

"All right, I've got it!" he declared, excited. "Gh!-AHHHH-duh!"

"That's it!" Rosalind told him. "Now you just practice that and the soft cover Bible snap, and you'll lay them in the isles."

"Whose bright idea was this , anyway?" Quinn bitched. "Othello must be getting senile already. Who gives a shit?"

"You'd be surprised," Rosalind answered, taking a quick look to her left and then putting the accelerator to the floor, pulling out to pass a large truck. "About umpteen jillion blue collar Americans, to tell you the truth," she added as the response of the sedan's huge engine pushed him back into the seat cushions.

"Tell me when it's safe to look!" Quinn told her, ducking down in mock panic and covering his face with his hands.

"Shit, baby," Rosalind laughed. "Ain't nobody coming for... Sheeut!" she cried out, swerving hard to the right. An angry blast of the diesel's air horn behind told them what the trucker thought, as did the angry raised fist of the driver in the other lane. "Hey, it's all right, man," she shouted, waving to the truck driver. "A miss is good as a mile."

"I hope he didn't think you were shooting him the bird," Martin said, amused by her indignation. "Some of those bastards carry guns."

"He pulls a gun and I slap the pee-waddin' out of his silly ass," she assured him.

"Gracious, Miss Rosalind, how you do talk, "Quinn answered in his best imitation of a Southern accent. "How was that?" he wanted to know.

"Another hundred years and you might have it down," she laughed. "I hope you don't plan to try it out on anyone down here. You'll likely get their goat if they don't die laughing first."

It doesn't sound that bad," Quinn protested. Rosalind simply shook her head and rolled her eyes. "Gh!AHHdh!" he declared. "See? What I can't figure is why Othello sent us on this wild goose chase," he added, changing the subject.

"What do you mean?" Rosalind asked, surprised. "You're the one who suggested it to him."

"I didn't mean for us," Martin said. "I get a new idea for a story every five minutes. I thought it might be something he could put some young Turk to work on."

"Well, apparently he thinks it's a bigger story than you do," Rosalind answered. "For what it's worth, I think he might be right."

"Really? How do you figure?"

"Look at the last fifteen years, Martin. Who's provided the leadership for change?" she challenged. "Not so much at the national level, but down at the grass roots where the people live?"

"I see your point. At least in the civil rights movement." He thought, then added. "Even in the peace movement, too, for that matter. Those who aren't preachers sound like them."

Rosalind nodded. "Who knows any better what the people are feeling? Your politicians? Shit, all they know is who butters their bread, and they're elected for specific terms. Most preachers I know survive week to week, and the way they do that is by keeping tabs on how their people feel and what they're thinking."

He gave her a cynical smile. "So you're saying their aim is to reinforce whatever their people are feeling? What's the difference between than and a political demagogue?"

Rosalind shot him a look of pure disgust. "You can be such a dumb shit when you set your mind to it, Martin" she observed acidly. "That's not what I was saying and you damned well know it."

"I really didn't mean to offend you," he replied evenly, refusing the bait. "What were you telling me?"

"Just that any preacher worth his salt knows how the people in his flock feel about things. He may not agree with them, and he may or may not be able to do much about it, but he knows how they feel. He also knows how to respond." She looked at him oddly. "You haven't been to church much, have you?"

"I went to Mass pretty often as a kid," he said. "Took all the CDC courses and that sort of stuff." He grinned. "Believe it or not, for a while I was even an altar boy."

"They must have been hard pressed for bodies," Rosalind laughed. How come you quit, or did they fire you?"

"How did you know?" he grinned. "Tommy Rossi and I got into an argument how to light the candles and managed to set the whole altar on fire. Poor Father Francis. He wasn't very mechanical and shot himself in the face once he found the fire extinguisher. I think he was willing to laugh it off and give us another chance, but the parish council was not. They had enough." He shrugged. "We were put on probation for a year and I never went back. I must have been fourteen then and I guess I just got out of the habit." Then he shook his head. "Goodness, I haven't thought about Tommy in years. I heard he ended up being a priest somewhere in the West. Seattle, I think."

"Well, that's my point, exactly," Rosalind told him. "Your padre did not agree with the lay folk, but he knew how they felt and he responded to it. That's what I'm talking about, man. That's grassroots power and that's why Othello thinks this story is so important. Not right now, maybe, but it won't be a long time coming, either." She looked at him oddly. "That's why he's so good at what he does. He's got a sense of what may be coming down the pike, what will turn out to be solid news and what won't."

Quinn nodded. "You're right, I know. Yet I can't seem to get rid of a feeling he's putting us on the shelf with this one. It looks more like human interest stuff to me, Ros, not hard news."

"Human interest is news, baby," Rosalind protested. "Didn't they teach you that in school?"

"I didn't take journalism," Quinn laughed. "I went to law school."

"How could I forget?" Rosalind said. "No wonder you have such a hard-assed world view. Not even undergrad?"

Quinn shook his head. "The closest I came was writing a series of stories for the school newspaper, but I did that for fun."

"How did you ever get to be such a flaming liberal, then?' Rosalind wanted to know. "You ain't no poor boy."

"I was raised by the most tight-assed Republican you ever met," he told her. "Only my mother was a genetic Democrat, being from southwest Texas, and I came down on her side, like I always did."

"I'm glad you did," Rosalind said. "You'd put William F. Buckley to shame if you were a Republican."

"The man knows how to use words."

"He's also got his head up his butt," Rosalind reminded him. "Though he doesn't have a monopoly on that."

"Are you trying to tell me something?" Quinn asked casually.

"Shoot no, baby," she grinned. "When you gots you head up you ass, I tells you, boss man. No messing around."

"Rosalind, you've got to marry me," he protested. "Save me from a fate worse than death."

"What fate? Yourself? Not on your life, sweet thing," she responded. "I don't need a Chinese burden." She laughed. "The black woman's burden. Now, that sounds like a story, Quinn."

"I'll tell Othello you suggested it. But why not?" he teased, trying to keep her off balance. "You take care of me, anyway."

"So far, dumb shit," she told him. "So far, but I have my limits."

"Oh, well," Martin remarked, continuing up what had become a ritual between them. "Any time you change your mind..."

"You'll be the first to know," she nodded. "I'll be sure to write it down in my suicide note." They laughed and ended their ritual by singing the theme song from the movie, "M*A*S*H". When they were done Rosalind looked at Quinn critically and said, "You got a nice voice, Martin."

"You ought to hear me sing love songs," he replied, breaking in to a crooning imitation of Elvis Presley's "Sweet Surrender" and looking at her with doleful eyes.

"The answer is 'no', Kemo Sabe," she said when he was done. Then she turned serious. "You know, we kid around a lot, Martin, but I don't want you trying to off yourself without talking to me first. I'd be really pissed."

"Off myself?" he asked. "Sugarpie, I do that all the time. That's how come I don't get mosquito bites."

"Damn it, Martin, I'm serious!" Rosalind snapped. "That peyote trip you took damned near turned sour, and that's not the first time I've seen you do something like that. You know what I think? I think you're trying to kill yourself a little bit at a time."

"Hey, Ros, I don't need the substance abuse lecture," Quinn replied lightly. "That bummer peyote trip was just an accident."

"That's what I mean, Martin," Rosalind told him soberly. "You seem to be getting into a lot of 'accidents' lately, especially when you're drinking." Her eyes began to tear. "Damn it, I care what happens to you."

Martin sighed. This was not the first time they'd had this kind of talk, and it seemed almost domestic by now. He rubbed a hand over his face. "I know you care," he told her, "but cut me some slack. I've got to work these things out the best way I can in my own time." Yet the determined line of her jaw told him it was no sale. "All right, I promise

I won't kill myself or do anything foolish without talking to you first. OK?" Reaching in the back seat he grabbed a pillow and plumped it. "Now how about letting me get a little sleep? I'll take a turn driving when I wake up."

Rosalind glanced at him, a sharp rejoinder on her lips, but bit it back. Quinn was already asleep. Shrugging, she turned her attention back to her driving and wondered, for at least the thousandth time, why she cared when Quinn obviously didn't. Yet there was no denying she did care, and as she drove she began to sing quietly, to sing an old lullaby her grandmother sang whenever she was upset as a young child. "Hush, sugar baby, don't you cry no more, grammie's right here to sing you a song. Bullfrog's a singing down by the tree, and sitting in my lap you're singing with me..."

An hour later Rosalind looked over at Quinn napping in the passenger seat. As if feeling her glance, his eyes opened and he looked confused, wild eyed for a minute. Then he shook his head vigorously. "Jesus," he moaned. "What a strange dream. Someone was chasing me."

"It was that awful cheeseburger you had for lunch," Rosalind assured him. "It damn near made me heave just smelling it. Eu de grease."

Quinn nodded and chewed a couple of antacid tablets, making a face when he was done. "That's almost worse," he muttered. "Tastes like pure chalk. Do we have anything to drink?"

"There's some cold coffee in the thermos from yesterday," Rosalind laughed. "You better chew a couple more of those before you drink it."

Quinn nodded, reaching behind the seat and opening the thermos. "It smells molded," he said, peering down the throat of the jug. "Are you sure it was just yesterday?"

"The other thermos," Rosalind reminded him, laughing. "Not that one. Where did you find it, anyway? I've been looking for it for weeks."

"I guess it rolled out from under my seat," he replied, replacing the red thermos and retrieving a blue one. Removing the top and smelling this one. "Hey, it's still a little warm!" he said happily.

"Yeah, just what the doctor ordered," Rosalind quipped. "Stale coffee, the perfect thing for your ulcers. I don't know about you, Quinn. Sometimes I think you sit on your taste buds."

Despite the way he felt, Martin laughed. "I bet you've been saving that one for a month," he said, "just waiting for the right moment."

"Shoot, honey, I heard that one in grade school," Rosalind lied boldly, fooling no one. "You just reminded me. How can you drink that stuff cold?"

Quinn laughed. "A habit from law school. Whenever I stayed up late studying I'd take a slug of cold coffee to wake up. I got to like it."

"I guess that proves a body can get to like anything," Rosalind snorted, sticking out her tongue. "I think it tastes bad enough hot."

Quinn pointed to a drive-in approaching on the right. "Why don't you pull in and we'll get a refill? I'll drive for a while."

"Sounds good, boss man," Rosalind smiled. "Let's live dangerously. I was getting to feel pretty bored, anyway."

After their pit stop Quinn took the wheel and headed south. He still felt sleepy so he tried the radio, and when he could not find a station he liked, he switched it off again. "You asleep?" he whispered softly to Rosalind, was sitting quietly, her eyes closed and her head back.

"Yeah," she mumbled and turned her head into the pillow. Quinn grinned at her answer and drove on, thinking about the assignment Othello had asked them to cover. Half an hour later Rosalind rubbed her eyes and glowered at him. "You going to do that, we may as well talk," she grumped.

"What?" he asked, wondering why she was so irate.

"That humming," she told him. "You got a nice voice, but more than three times is too much."

Quinn thought. "Hey, I was just singing to myself," he said. "You do the same thing all the time."

"Not fourteen times in a row," Rosalind replied. "I think I've heard 'Blue Eyes Crying in the Rain' more in the last thirty minutes than I have in the last six years. Give it a rest, man."

"I guess you're right," he said. "Sorry. I was thinking about Tovah. About Stephanie, too."

"Who's Stephanie?" Rosalind wanted to know.

I've never told you about her?" he asked. "I was engaged to her when I lived in New Mexico."

Oh, yeah," Rosalind nodded. "I remember her. I just didn't know her name. She's the one who ran off to Africa."

"Yeah," he said, sighing. "Se sure did. Sometimes I wonder if I was foolish not going after her."

"Then go after her," Rosalind said. "She's not dead yet, is she?"

"No," Martin told her. "She's not dead. My mother told me she had married my cousin Jack Bear."

Rosalind was lost in thought a moment. "Are you telling me you are an Indian, Kemo Sabe?" Rosalind asked. "Why didn't you say something when we were in South Dakota? It might have helped."

Martin laughed. "No, I'm not Indian. Any Indian blood I have comes from my mother. That side of the family are mestizos, Mexicans. What made you think that?"

"Your cousin's last name," she answered. "Or is it German?"

"Oh, that's just a pet name," Martin told her. "He was always so big growing up we called him Jack the Bear, and later, just Jack Bear." He sighed again. "I miss him. We used to be close."

"You all fell out over Stephanie?" Rosalind asked casually, interested but trying not to show too much interest. Martin always clammed up when she did.

"No, that part of it was clean. We broke up when she was in Africa. That was several years before she married Jack." He shook his head. "No, with Jack and me, I think we just went our separate ways. Even when we were doing the same thing there was a lot of distance there, and I think the main thing was what happened to him in Asia. He never seemed to let anyone in after that, except maybe Max."

"Who is Max?" Rosalind asked, and for the next half hour Quinn told her about his time in the Canyon and the people there. When he was done she said, "Man, that sounds like heaven on earth. Why did you leave?"

"That's another question I've asked myself a million times. The answer is, I don't know. I seemed to feel the need for something more."

Rosalind nodded. "I know what you mean. I think that's why I never settled down and raised a family, myself. I wanted something more, but I'm damned if I know what it is. What I do know is that the times I feel best are when I'm in the field doing my job. Then it's me and the camera and what's going down, and nothing else matters. Next to that is the time I spend in the printing room," she added.

"When I'm writing it's like that for me," Martin told her. "I have to make myself stop sometimes, just to go to the bathroom, and even then I take a pencil and pad along." He looked at her severely. "That stays between us, Rosalind," he said, and there was no doubt he meant it.

"Shit, baby, you got as much on me as I do on you," she protested. Then she grinned. My ex told me I like burning film better than sex," she laughed. "I told that sucker in comparison with him it was a *whole* lot better."

Martin laughed in return. "Writing's that way with me. Especially if I'm doing a steamy sex scene." He glanced at her. "I guess that's where my medium has it over yours. I can combine them. Unless, of course, you film sex, but I'm not sure it would be the same."

"You asking if I ever shot people doing it?" Rosalind responded, her eyebrow going up half way to her hairline.

"Oh, no," said Quinn. "I was just thinking that when I write about sex my imagination is involved, and so it's almost like being there. Sort of like acting out a fantasy, maybe. Making it real on paper. With film I'd think it must be the reverse. You're taking what's real and trying to capture it in a particular way on film. So it seems to me you would still be detached from whatever was going on."

Rosalind nodded. "You got it, baby. When the action's going down I can't be part of it, and it doesn't matter what it is. As a matter of fact, I have filmed people doing it. Single shots, not motion pictures. I was moving just about as fast as they were trying to get the right angles, and working even harder not to distract them." She grinned. "I didn't have time to get turned on until I was in the printing room. Then it hit me like a ton of bricks and I was about ready to grab the nearest man." She flushed with the memory. "Martin," she said in a small voice. "We need to talk about something else. Please."

Quinn was surprised but complied. "Sure," he said, thinking. "Why don't you tell me about these people we're supposed to meet. Are any of them people you know?"

"Not personally," she told him. "With one or two exceptions. I have met most of them at least once. What do you want to know?"

"Mostly background. Education. Family. Occupational history. That sort of thing." He smiled. "Any personal skeletons you know about."

"Know for sure or gossip?" Rosalind asked.

"Yes," he told her. "Either and both."

"Well, a lot of what I've heard can be put down to petty jealousy," she reminded him. These guys are competitive as they can be, even though they try to come across as being soul brothers. Fact is, there's only so much lime light and they're all after it. Real show boats."

"There's got to be more to them than that or Othello wouldn't have sent us," Martin observed. "He was pretty cryptic when I talked to him but he seemed to think there is an important story here."

"Oh, there is. There is more to most of them than that. It's just that most of them happen to piss me off. They think they are God's gift to women and a lot of the sisters let them get away with it. That's the main problem. The sisters let it slide."

"You mean womanizing?" Quinn asked, surprised.

"I mean anything they can get away with," Rosalind said. "Mostly it's the attitude that the universe revolves around themselves and the sisters encourage it." There was no mistaking the contempt in her voice, or her bitterness. "They make over the brothers like the sun shines out their ass, and they do it so they can get what they want. So they can be somebody. They deserve exactly what they get when they marry the preacher man."

Martin said nothing. Then Rosalind thought better. "No, I take that back, at least what I said about the brothers. Most of them are hard working men who aren't any better than the people in their congregations. Only thing is, they're supposed to be better, or so their people think. So they set them up on a pedestal, and they aren't very realistic in what they expect. Their people expect these men to rise above temptation, and when they come crashing down, everybody acts so shocked a preacher could do that sort of thing." She smiled. "Mostly it's sins of the flesh that bring them down, but some of them are on the take, too. Not many of them are into drugs or even heavy drinking. Power and status are what they want. Sex, too."

"Are we supposed to be after an expose?" Martin asked. "I thought McLeod had something else in mind."

"He does, sugar," Rosalind told him. "Only you asked for background and I'm giving it to you." She looked at him levelly. "I'm not lying, either. I think the same thing probably goes on in white churches, but people are just a lot more quiet about it." She grinned. "White brothers don't favor razors and white sisters don't scream and carry on."

"No, we prefer shotguns," he quipped, equally bitterly. "That and silent martyrdom, followed by passive vengeance. We kill with politeness."

"You all can afford shotguns, honey," Rosalind corrected gently, surprised by the rancor in Quinn's voice.

"Touché," he acknowledged, laughing. "Tell me more."

Rosalind thought a long moment before answering. When she did, her voice was flat and factual. "Well, the brothers are fairly well educated, for the most part. Most of them have been to college and a lot of those have seminary training. With a very few exceptions they are all married and have children. At least, that describes the younger ones. The older men are not as well educated, and not nearly as assertive, either. They tend to have larger families and less money." She thought a moment. "As a matter of fact, most of the older men come across as Uncle Toms, even though they really aren't."

"Sounds like most professions," Martin responded. "It's the young men who have the least to lose who tend to be the most aggressive when it comes to change." He gave her a wry smile. "They are also the ones with the most to gain from a new order and the most energy to hustle a buck. Tell me, are these full time pastors and preachers, or do they have to support themselves with outside jobs?"

"A lot of them are full time pastors," Rosalind answered, "though it doesn't pay much by most standards. I'd say at least a third to half of them have outside jobs, at least part of the time. Some even find work seasonally, following the harvest."

"I doubt many of their second jobs are professional positions," Martin nodded, "especially in the Old South."

"Yeah, you're right," Rosalind told him. "Yet, some of them are school teachers, although that's mostly the younger men, and a few of them in the larger cities are private business people. But not many are in professions like medicine or law. Out in the toolies, it's root-hog-or-die like it is for everyone else, except the deck is stacked against them." She frowned, lost in thought. "Those who become preachers are some of the best and brightest we have, Martin. Professionally, preaching is probably the one place where a black man can succeed without being considered uppity and pretending to be better than he is." There was no mistaking the bitterness in her voice. "So a lot of people who might do better as dentists or architects or company managers end up as preachers."

"Or else they become athletes or soldiers or entertainers," he suggested gently, nodding. "All of which are high risk occupations."

Rosalind smiled. "Or writers or photographers," she said dryly, looking at him with amusement. Then she frowned. "The trouble is, those of us who do make it as professionals leave and never come back. They marry white sisters or other oreos and live in the suburbs. Of course, who am I to talk? I don't live in the projects either."

"Other what?" Martin asked. "Oreos? You mean like cookies?"

Rosalind nodded, but said nothing. Then Martin said, "Oh, you mean like what AIM calls 'apple' Indians, those who are red outside but white to the core inside?"

"You got it, kemo sabe," Rosalind answered. "Chocolate covered white people, and they're worse in some ways than rednecks. At least with crackers you know where you stand. Oreos hate niggers as bad as George Wallace, but they won't admit it." She looked grim. "Thing is, you can do something with someone like George. With oreos it's like kicking at swamp gas. All you accomplish is stirring it up so it stinks more." She wrinkled her nose and stuck out her tongue.

Martin laughed. "That's not just oreos, Rosalind. I know a lot of other folk like that. Hispanics, American Indians, Asians, and even a lot of white folk. The common denominator isn't race, it's fear."

"Yeah," she agreed. "They're scared shitless, and they have reason to be, but who doesn't? Not everyone who's scared becomes a hypocrite. Not in the fullest sense of the word. There are other choices."

Martin looked at her, puzzled. "I'm not sure I follow you. What do you mean, 'in the fullest sense'?" he asked.

Rosalind grinned. "I don't believe it!" she declared. "You're telling me that you, Martin Quinn, don't know the root meaning of a word?"

"Rumors of my omniscience are exaggerated," he told her. "No, I don't, but if I had to guess, I'd guess it comes from Greek and means too much of something or other."

"Give the man a cigar!" Rosalind laughed. "Or at least, the butt. Not too much, but too little. 'Hyper' means too much. Hypo is diminutive."

"Give the lady fifty cents for the word," he laughed. "As in too little 'pottamus'? I'd have said it was the other way around."

"You're unreal," Rosalind told him, shaking her head. "Didn't your mother ever tell you puns were the lowest form of humor?"

"I've heard that," he replied, "but I think it's wrong. Think about what we laugh about for a moment. Play on words is the only form of humor I know which does not do violence to people in some way or another. All it violates is the language."

"Don't forget the hearer's mind," Rosalind snorted. "I don't know if you're right or not, Quinn. It sounds good, but then, most of your bullshit does. I know I'm in trouble when I start believing it." She smiled to take any sting out of her words.

"That makes two of us," he grinned back. "So what does it mean in the original sense, Ros?"

"What does...? Oh," Rosalind remembered. "It always startles me when you do that. Especially when it's a conversation we had a month ago. You just swoop back in like it was the last thing we were talking about."

"I guess I do," Martin admitted ruefully. "It's a bad habit I can't seem to break."

"No!" Rosalind declared, startling him. "I mean it. I thought it was a pain in the tush until I realized it means you are really listening. Don't stop listening, Martin, not ever," she implored.

"Thank you," he said awkwardly. "That's a compliment, Rosalind. I appreciate it very much."

"You're very welcome," she said. "Thank you for being someone who really listens." Then, seeing the look on his face, she asked, "What?"

"I was just thinking," he said, shaking his head.

"They tell me that's a dangerous habit," Rosalind responded, laughing. "My daddy used to say when he got to thinking, especially into brooding or what he called 'stinking thinking', that he was conspiring with the one person on earth who had consistently tried to kill him. Of course, he was a drunk, so what did he know." She gave him a stern look. "So come on now, baby, tell Mama Ros. 'Fess up."

"It really wasn't all that big a deal," he laughed. "I was thinking about what you said. That's the hardest thing in the world for me to do."

"Listening?" she asked, not believing what she was hearing. "Quinn, you're a natural when it comes to that. The only time you don't is...." She broke off suddenly, embarrassed.

"When I'm drinking?" he inquired. While the question was asked very casually, there was a raw edge to his voice.

"That sounds like a cheap shot, Martin, but it's not, "Rosalind told him. "If you thought so, I apologize, but that's not what I meant. It just sort of popped out." She looked at him anxiously.

"I know, Ros," he said quietly. "There's not a mean bone in your body. I think what slipped out was the truth, and that hurts sometimes." He smiled weakly. "You were giving me a compliment. Thank you."

"Well, it's true, kemo sabe, and you know it. That's one of the things that makes you so good in this business."

"Hey, that's another one," he laughed. "You better cut it out, Ros, or my hat won't fit." He frowned in concentration. "I must be getting senile already," he said. "What were we talking about? There was something I wanted to ask you."

"We were talking about puns," Rosalind suggested. "Something about a hippopotamus."

"I remember now," Martin declared, and rushed on, anxious to get the question asked before their conversation darted away along another path. "It was hypocrisy. You were going to tell me the original meaning of the word. Too little of something or other."

"Right," Rosalind responded. "Hypo-cracy. Too little 'chrasy', whatever that is. I looked it up once, but I can't remember what that part is. As a whole word, hypocrisy means someone who is an actor."

"An actor?" Quinn replied, intrigued. "Wow. Someone who is not real but who is playing a part. And like an actor, they have a public life and a private one, and the two don't match."

"You amaze me," Rosalind told him. "The way you take an idea and peel it like an onion is unreal. I've never seen such a quick study. Once something gets your attention," she added dryly.

"Ouch!" Martin laughed. "There is that. I seem to walk around in a fog most of the time."

"Not really," Rosalind reassured him. "You're pretty much in touch with reality until it comes to yourself. Like most of us." She grinned. "That is why you need me around, baby."

"That's what I keep telling you!" Martin complained. "That's why I keep asking you to marry me, Ros."

I know you're kidding, Martin," she said, giving him a droll look. "I do think, however, someday you're going to ask me once too many. When that day comes you're going to end having to put up or shut up." She looked at him seriously. "You really think you could take this big black gal home to momma?"

"I'd be honored to, Rosalind," he told her, using her full name as he rarely did. "I am kidding, but I'd have no trouble introducing you as my woman of choice to my mother. She would love you. Where I'd draw the line is inflicting my dad and brother on you."

Rosalind was suddenly very self conscious, something which Martin had rarely seen in all the years they worked together. "That's very nice of you to say, Martin," she said softly.

"Goodness, Rosalind Taylor," he told her. "You keep talking to me nice like that and I'm going to press my suit."

"It needs it, kemo sabe," she laughed. "Both of them do. The one you're wearing looks look like you picked it up at the Salvation Army charity store."

"So who's the pot calling the kettle a punster?" he asked.

"Comes from hanging around with you too much, baby," she told him. "You're introducing me to all kinds of bad habits."

"Rogue nuns?" he asked, wincing as Rosalind punched him in the arm.

6. The Pool Of Siloam

September 14, 1990. As I was going downhill personally in the mid 'Seventies, I clearly remember thinking the whole fabric of American life was coming apart at an ever more rapid rate. This was not just our social structures and public agencies, for it seemed the glue that held the social bond together was dissolving, and that nothing was evolving to replace it. Not only were our institutions literally dis-integrating before our very eyes, but our basic customs of relating to one another seemed to be up for grabs. The attitude seemed to be 'hooray for me and up yours!' in the words of a good friend, and basic human courtesy and decency seemed to be passing from the scene. I realize this perception had to do with my own attitudes more than with anything else, and that I tended to surround myself with people of similar opinions, but trapped in my own self centered view, it was easy to succumb to what people in the Program call 'ocular rectitis'. The one thing I remember quite clearly was there was no Higher Power we allowed ourselves to hope for which could straighten out the mess we made of things and restore our lives to sanity.... (Martin Quinn's journal)

Summer, 1975. Their meeting with the black clergy went much as Martin imagined it would. Both Rosalind and he were received with warm hospitality, but Martin sensed a deep reserve behind the good manners. Nor was he sure why the group had requested the meeting in the first place. When Othello mentioned it in passing before, Quinn had jokingly suggested it sounded like a story and was shocked when Othello took him seriously. "Hey, Othello," he told his friend, "I was only joking."

"I know," McLeod replied, "but I think you're right. They wouldn't call unless something big was up. They know better than cry 'wolf' with me."

"So why don't you send one of your new people?" Quinn wanted to know. "They can cover it just well as I can." He shrugged and grinned. "Maybe even better, although I'd hate to suggest it. Youth and enthusiasm covers a multitude of deficiencies. At least, it did for me."

Othello thought a moment before answering. "No, Martin, you're wrong," he said, shaking his head. "Maybe one of our new people could get the facts as well as you, and enthusiasm does make a difference, but there is more to it than that. It's a matter of respect. Sending a senior reporter will tell these folk I'm taking them seriously, and you're the only one available right now. Besides, Rosalind knows some of the people involved. She can be a good resource."

Martin started to argue the point, but gave it up. The set of McLeod's jaw told him it was no use trying to get him to change his mind. "All right," he said, "but you owe me one for this, Othello."

"Charge it against the dozen or so I have outstanding on you," McLeod replied dryly. "Your meeting with them is set three days from now, but we can extend that a bit if you need to."

"Might as well get on with it," Quinn told him. "Since I'm the man on the wire, what do you think they want?"

"I'm not at all sure," Othello said, frowning. "Most of what I'm going on is my sense of the conversation. It was all very circumspect and indirect, but when I told them you were available, they were very pleased." He shrugged. "Your guess is as good as mine, but I think it's safe to assume it has something to do with civil rights."

"Brilliant, Watson," Martin answered, looking over the list of names McLeod had given him. "Since most of these turkeys are active in the movement there's a very high probability you're right." Despite himself, Quinn found himself becoming interested in the prospects. "You're holding out, Othello," he told his friend. "Come on, give."

The other laughed. "No fooling you, is there, Quinn? But no dice. I want the story as you discover it. I have an idea what it's about, but I don't want to influence your objectivity. We'll talk when you get back."

"So you've heard rumors, then," Quinn answered, giving him an appraising look. "Rumors about the civil rights movement."

McLeod held up his hands. "No, Quinn, it won't work. All I want you to know going in is that there may be a major story. No more guessing games. Will three days give you enough time to get there with Ros?"

"Yeah," Quinn grumped. "She is supposed to be finishing up what she was working on today, so we're free. Damn, it, Othello, sending us in blind like this isn't fair," he whined.

"Since when was this chicken shit business fair, baby? Remember the deal with Floyd Newman?" McLeod grinned. "I'd cover this one myself if I could, but I can't. Now get the hell out of here and let me get to work."

Now, as he listened to the group talk about the civil rights movement, about the gains and losses experienced over the last months, Martin sensed McLeod was right. *There is a deeper agenda here*, he thought to himself, and despite his better judgment, he felt himself become excited. *Gently, man*, he cautioned himself. *Even if there is a deeper purpose here, they may not tell you what it is. There is a lot of distrust of whites in black circles these days.* Nor was he surprised when the conversation turned to exactly that problem. He did not know whether to be delighted or dismayed at the frank way in which the ministers talked with him about that growing issue.

"The truth is, Mr. Quinn," a man old enough to be his grandfather told him, "we don't know who we can trust among whites these days, especially among white liberals. Your bleeding hearts have left us hanging out alone to dry far too often for us to really believe they mean what they say."

The other members of the group nodded vigorously, and another man, a younger one, spoke up. "Seems like you all come down here full of righteous wrath over the way white folks treat us down here. Then, about the time things really get rolling, you go back north and leave us to deal with the consequences. Despite your fine intentions, the way some of us see it, you make the messes we end up having to clean up." Several heads nodded their agreement at this.

"So what you're telling me is that your road to hell is paved with our good intentions," Martin said, drawing a polite laugh from the group. "There ought to be a good story in that. That is, if anyone who needs to read it will."

Again members of the group chuckled and the conversation went on in this vein for more than an hour, moving from one concern to another. Yet Martin had the impression none of these things were the real issue, either, despite their importance to the black community. He wondered why the group was being so cautious, then suddenly he knew. *They're weighing me*, he decided. *They are sounding me out to see what I think, what I feel. They want to know how I'll respond to what they want to tell me, but what is it?* He could not imagine what it might possibly be.

Almost in answer to his silent question, the mood of the group changed and their conversation turned to lighter topics for a while, to their families and flocks, and amusing stories about these. Then to his dismay, the pastors began to excuse themselves, one by one, exchanging handshakes and hugs and promises to get together again soon.

Seeing this, Martin was disappointed. *I apparently failed whatever test they were giving me,* he thought, and there was little point staying longer. He looked over at Rosalind, using their private system to signal his desire to leave, but she frowned slightly and shook her head.

Damn, he thought, standing to mask his surprise. *We've been together so long we're just like any old married couple with their own private language. Hubby suggests it's time to go and wife lets him know she's having too much fun.* Then it struck him that anyone catching the signals would understand exactly what was going on and he smiled. *How foolish we are to think we deceive anyone but ourselves. We think other people can't see through us, like a child shutting its eyes to hide.*

Quinn crossed the room to refill his water glass at the side table and returned to his seat. He hoped they would break soon. His bladder was reminding him he needed a pit stop, rather urgently. He set the glass down on the table untouched.

The last two pastors were standing to say goodbye to one another as he approached the table, and when the older man left, the younger waved Quinn back to his seat. "So what do you think?" he asked. His name was Clarence Powers and he looked more like a college professor than a preacher.

"I was very impressed by members of the group," Quinn answered carefully. "You seem to have a strong group of leaders." He paused and then decided to take the plunge. "I'm sorry I couldn't earn their trust."

"Why do you say that, Martin?" Powers asked. "If we had any doubts about you we would have insisted Othello send someone else."

"Maybe I'm wrong," Quinn answered, "but my impression is we talked about everything under the sun except the real subject. Forgive me for being very blunt, but it seemed a consensus was reached not to mention what you really wanted."

Clarence Powers smiled and nodded. "I see how you could come to that conclusion," he said. "What the brothers were doing was reassuring themselves, and you passed with flying colors." He smiled. "So to speak."

"Oh, dear God, not another one!" Rosalind complained. "Excuse me, gentlemen," she added, rising to leave the room. "I'll be right back."

I don't understand," Martin told Powers when Rosalind disappeared through the door. "So why didn't we discuss whatever you wanted to talk about, then?"

Powers smiled. "Some things are better talked about between two people face to face, Mr. Quinn," he said, nodding toward the door. "Bear with me a bit longer and I promise it will be worth your while. Why don't we take a walk? There's a nice fountain I don't think you've seen."

"I think I better make a pit stop first," Quinn smiled. "Running water could be a disaster. Why don't you call me Martin, if you don't mind?" he added.

"Second door to the left," Powers told him. "I need to make a call, too. My friends call me Clare."

"That must have made for some interesting times growing up," Quinn observed. "Especially here in the South."

"You have no idea," the other told him. "It did teach me the art of defending myself verbally, at least with bigger kids."

"Let's step back in here a moment," Powers said when they returned to the hallway. Quinn was surprised to see the man take off his coat as he entered the room where the meeting had taken place. "Now, if you please, Martin, would you search my coat for a recorder, and then search me?"

"This isn't necessary," Quinn told him, complying with his request and laying Powers' coat over the table when he was done.

"Humor me a bit more," Powers asked, raising his arms. "Now make sure I'm not wired with a hidden microphone."

Nodding he understood, Quinn did so quickly. "Now it's your turn," he said, handing Powers his coat. "There is a recorder in my briefcase and Rosalind has one, too, but it hasn't been used today."

"You must have been in stir," the pastor chuckled as he carefully checked under Quinn's arms and the small of his back. "You did that well."

"Takes one to know one," Quinn laughed. "You're not bad, yourself."

"Oh, a lot of different people have showed me how," Clarence said sadly. "Some of them weren't so gentle, either." Pointing toward the door, he said. "Let me show you the fountain. You can leave your coat here if you want. It's pretty warm for a jacket."

Quinn nodded and followed Powers out of the building down a brick path leading into a grove of tall trees. At the back of the grove there was a fountain set against a stone wall, with brick pavement radiating out from the fountain. Seeing the fountain, Quinn was intrigued. Standing waist deep in the water at the center of a pool several feet wide was the figure of a black man, perhaps three feet tall and facing outward with his arms and head raised to the heavens. An expression of utter joy and profound peace was cast forever into the bronze of his features as rivulets of water frozen in bronze trailed down his neck and shoulders. Standing behind and above him was the figure of another man, this one with Semitic features and a wild, full beard, dressed in rough clothing and holding a large urn from which water poured into the fountain, splashing loudly into the pool just behind the other figure. Cast in a bronze plaque and centered in the brick pavement just before the pool was a single word in large block letters, "Siloam."

Seeing the word, Martin looked back at the figure as if seeing it for the first time. He was caught speechless by the expression on the face of the figure standing in the water and stood gazing for several minutes. Powers smiled and stood silent, looking from one figure to another as he waited patiently. Finally, Quinn roused himself. "Jesus!" he said, reverently, as he reached for a handkerchief to wipe his eyes. I've never seen anything like that, not ever."

"It takes a lot of people that way," Powers told him. "But which figure is which? And who are they? Some say this is Jesus being baptized by John the Baptist, but the sculptor deliberately named this pool of Siloam, which seems to say the one pouring water might be Jesus healing the paralytic, or even one of his disciples baptizing someone else. Maybe it's Philip baptizing the Ethiopian or maybe even the man born blind washing his eyes. Or Naaman washing away his sores."

"No," Quinn told him, his tone certain. "At least, not for me. That is John the Baptist anointing the Messiah."

"Martin, that took place at the River Jordan," Powers told him. "Not at the pool of Siloam."

Quinn looked at him and smiled. "Don't you understand? The artist is playing a trick to make a point. Remember what Picasso said, 'art is the lie which shows us the truth'? That is exactly what this sculptor did. In doing it he managed to catch all of us. That's why this is so great."

"I agree it's excellent," Powers told him. "But I don't understand what you're telling me."

"I spent a lot of time in Israel," Martin told him. "They speak Hebrew there and I managed to pick up a little of it. What other Hebrew word does 'Siloam' sound like?"

Clarence Powers thought a moment. "Shalom?" Then his features cleared. "I see. The pool of Siloam is the pool of shalom. Gracious!" he said as the full impact of the thought descended on him. "I never thought about it that way. The place of cleansing is the place of peace. What a beautiful thought. I wonder if that's what she meant."

"There's one way to find out," Quinn suggested.

"Ask her?" Powers said. "I'd like to, but that's not possible."

Quinn looked disappointed. "Is the sculptor dead?"

A deep look of grief came over Clarence Powers' face. "No," he said quietly. "She's not dead. Several years ago she had a stroke and she can't talk or even write. Somehow she can't use language and even has to be reminded to eat or she'd starve. All she can really do is sculpt. This is something she produced after the stroke."

"A black woman?" Quinn asked.

Powers nodded. "My mother's older sister," he replied. "She was my favorite aunt before it happened. Now she doesn't even seem to know who I am."

"Who is she?" Quinn asked. "I'm not familiar with her work. Has anything been written about her?"

"No," Powers said simply. "Who's going to write up a simple black woman in the South who had a stroke?"

"You're talking to him," Quinn replied. "I'm no art critic, but this is more moving than any sculpture I've ever seen. Anywhere."

"I don't know," Powers said. "I don't see how the notoriety could do her any good. It might do her harm."

"The rest of the world needs to know about her, Clare. Not for her sake, but for theirs," Quinn argued. "I've never seen anything quite like this."

Powers still looked doubtful. "I tell you what," Quinn urged him. "Let me talk to your mother, her sister, about it. I'll abide by whatever she says and you have my word on that. All right?" Powers shrugged and nodded. "Tell me, Clare, has Rosalind seen this?"

"No, not that I'm aware," the other replied. "But aren't we getting a little off track here? What about the story you came to get?"

Quinn grinned. "Clarence, if I am right, your aunt's work is on a level with that of any sculptor who ever lived, including Michael Angelo. I've seen everything he's done and I can't imagine any story bigger or more important than that. Can you?"

Powers nodded. "Assuming you're right, I would have to agree. We'll talk to my mother and I'll even help you if she thinks it's all right. But I still need to talk to you about the other thing. I promised the brothers I would."

"All right," Quinn replied, finding it hard to keep his impatience out of his voice, and his eyes off the figures in the fountain. "What do you have?"

"Nothing for certain, but a number of us have become aware we are being spied on. We know our phones are being tapped and we've spotted people with binoculars and cameras. Some of them don't even try to hide."

"I don't see what you can do about it," Quinn told him. "We know the FBI has been watching protest leaders. There's nothing illegal involved and at least they're being open about it."

"That's just it," Powers replied. "Some of them are obviously FBI but there are others not being open about it. We hired our own investigator, a brother who can pass for white anywhere. We wanted to know the names of the watchers and he only came across the others by accident. They threatened him with bodily harm if he didn't keep his mouth shut and they only let him go because he convinced them what he was doing was domestic surveillance on a cheating wife. After that he quit."

"That doesn't sound like the FBI," Quinn frowned. "They are pretty straight when it comes to stuff like that. They may try to intimidate but overt threats are not their style. Or it hasn't been," he corrected himself. "Everything seems to be up for grabs these days."

"Oh, the brother knew they weren't FBI," Powers told him. "He is well connected there and he's pretty sure it's not even one of their special operation teams."

"Then who could it be?" Quinn asked. "A private group? The Klan?"

"I guess it could be," Clarence said, "but we don't think so. Their equipment is state of the art according to our man and the Klan are poor folk like us. Who we think it might be is the CIA."

"The CIA?" Quinn was puzzled. "Their charter is for overseas stuff. They're not supposed to be involved in domestic surveillance."

"Exactly," Powers said. "It's illegal, and if they're the ones doing it, they're not going to take too kindly to anyone exposing them. Now do you see why we are being so careful, man? If they can overthrow an established government in South America, what do you think what they can get away with doing to a bunch of poor nigger preachers here at home in the South?"

"So what do you think?" Rosalind asked as they drove north toward home. For the three hours since they began their return trip Quinn remained quiet and reflective. Nor had he said much after the meeting with Clarence Powers, and the rest of their last three days was filled with a visit to Powers' family. Nothing would do but that Rosalind and Martin stay with them in the family home, and there had been no time for them to talk by themselves. Not that Martin showed much inclination to do so. After their walk in the garden by the fountain he had been subdued, thoughtful to the point of being distracted, and even the simplest interactions seemed beyond him.

"What?" Martin asked, startled. "Oh, I think Ruth Ann Matthews is one of the most incredible people I have ever met," he answered. "I have never seen anything like the work she does. I can't believe she hasn't been discovered by now. She's been at it almost fifteen years."

"Sometimes it takes a while," Rosalind nodded. "Actually what I was asking about was your private meeting with Clarence. When you and he took a walk by the fountain."

"That was an incredible experience," Quinn replied, enthusiastic for the first time in days. "The sculpture was striking when I first saw it, almost compelling. Then, when Clarance told me about Ruth Ann, the full meaning of what I was seeing came down on me like a ton of bricks."

"Oh?" asked Rosalind, looking at him curiously. He had not answered the question she asked, but she was intrigued by this side of the man she had never, ever seen. "How was that?"

"It's hard to put in words," he told her. "Were I religious I would probably call it a personal theophany. I don't know how to describe it except as a very mystical experience. Like what happens sometimes smoking hash or dropping psychedelics. Only it was even more intense and incredibly clear. There wasn't any haze like you get with dope." He lapsed into silence, remembering.

Rosalind drove in silence for a while. "I've heard of mystical visions," she told him. "Was it like that?"

Martin shook his head. "No, there wasn't anything like that. All I saw was what you caught on film. I guess I'd have to say what came over me was an incredible sense of knowing, as fully as a human being possibly can, the precise nature of what I was looking at." When he looked at her, his eyes were wide with wonder. "If I were a religious I'd say God touched my mind and heart at that very moment and gave me the gift of total sight. Sort of like a person who's color blind being made able to see colors for the first time." He looked at her. "Wasn't there a song about that? A hymn or something about being blind and seeing again?"

Rosalind laughed. "You could say that," she told him, and broke into a fervent rendition of the opening verse of 'Amazing Grace', sung in the black gospel style common to the South.

"That's it!" he laughed. "Rosalind, I knew you could sing, but I had no idea you could sing like that. That's beautiful!"

"Well, sugar, I cut my teeth on gospel music," she confessed. "The only thing I really miss about not going to church is music and singing. All the preaching and praying and carrying on leaves me cold, but, oh my, the music sends me." Taking a deep breath and throwing back her head, she began to sing again, this time finishing the popular old Anglican hymn. When she was done there were tears in her eyes. "Yeah," she said huskily. "That's what I miss."

"I wish I could be a believer," Martin told her. "I really envy people like Clarence and his mother who can. They seem to be in touch with some very beautiful thing I've missed. At least until I went into the garden." He fell silent again, lost in thought.

"Did you hear voices or anything like that?" Rosalind asked, almost afraid of the answer she might get. There was nothing wild or crazy about her friend, but as far as she was concerned, they'd left the borders of Cloud Cuckoo Land far behind already. Singing was one thing. This was another.

"No," he told her. "The closest I've ever come to anything like it is when I came over the rim of the Grand Canyon once just at sunset and the magnificence of that almost made my heart ache. It was the same way with Ruth Ann's sculpture, and when I saw the word 'Siloam', it hit me like a blow to my chest."

"That's something I didn't understand," Rosalind told him. "If Ruth Ann can't use words, how did they know what to name the thing?"

"I wondered the same thing and asked Clarence," Martin smiled. "He told me the original was simply Hebrew letters spelling it out. Someone else translated it into Siloam."

"How did she come to know Hebrew?" Rosalind asked.

"No one knows," Martin replied. "As a matter of fact, Clearance's mother says she didn't before the stroke. I don't think she's lying, but I don't see how that could be. That's one of the things that's been bothering me."

"You're wrong, you know," Rosalind told him.

"That doesn't surprise me," he laughed. "What are you talking about?"

"You," Rosalind answered. "We've been together now for five years almost, and I think you're fooling yourself. I think you're a deeply religious person. Not in the normal way, maybe, but you are."

"Rosalind Turner, how you talk!" Martin tried to deflect her attention, but with no success. "Come on, now!"

"Well, kemo sabe, you can deny it but it doesn't mean it's not true."

"Come on, Ros," he retorted, somewhat indignant. "When have you ever seen me in church? Except at a wedding or a funeral or on assignment?"

"Several times when you didn't know I was watching," she answered. "I've also seen you reading the Psalms." She looked at him levelly. "What struck me was not what you were reading, Martin, but how you were reading it. A lot of preachers I know don't read that well. It was coming from the heart."

"Oh, that," he exclaimed. "I like the Psalter, Ros. It's beautiful poetry and I like the way it sounds. I always have."

"I also remember several occasions when you've read kaddish," she reminded him. "Or are you going to claim that's poetry, too?"

"You know what that's about," he said quietly. "I do that to honor Tovah on the anniversary of her death."

"All right, have it your way, Martin," she sighed, her voice great with resignation. "There is no God for you. You're an atheist who reads kaddish a lot more than once a year and who carries a *Book Of Common Prayer* that's almost worn out. The thing with Ruth Ann is simply some kind of psychological phenomenon you'll get over when you take a shower and two aspirin and come to your senses. I was off base even suggesting it might be anything different. You have my apology, so please do forgive me." Rosalind's neck was rigid as her face as she concentrated on her driving.

"I've offended you, Ros," he observed, not quite sure why she seemed to be taking all this so personally. "I've offended you."

"How did you ever guess?" she snapped acidly.

"The thing is, I am not sure just how I did so," Martin told her. "So I don't know what to do to set things right. Please, tell me so I can."

Rosalind looked at him, shook her head. "You really don't know, do you, Martin? I'm not sure I can explain without hurting your feelings, and I'm not trying to do that. But it's like you're so totally blind to yourself you won't accept anyone else's evaluation if it doesn't jive with your own."

"So what's your evaluation?" he asked. When she didn't answer he added, "Please, Ros, I really do want to know."

"All right, but remember I am your friend," she said. When he nodded she went on. "It's like you have this either-or view of yourself. It's like you have to either be the very greatest there ever was, or the very worst. Either the sun shines out your ass or you're the sorriest piece of shit God ever made. That's your view, not mine. The way I look at it is, you're somewhere in the middle like all the rest of us. The good outweighs the bad ten to one like it does with most people."

Martin did not know how to respond. "Thank you," he finally said. "As I said before, I have a hard time accepting compliments, but thank you, Rosalind. Thanks for being a good friend and thanks for putting up with my crap. Believe it or not, I do appreciate it."

Rosalind nodded but said nothing and drove on in silence. After a while Martin looked at her and said, "I missed the point, didn't I?" She looked at him clearly puzzled. "About my meeting with Clarence. I thought you wanted to know about the sculpture and what you were asking was about what he want to see us for, right?"

Rosalind smiled. "That's one of your virtues, Martin. I've told you that before. You do listen and you think about things and you remember." Her smile broadened into a grin. "Sometimes it takes slapping a knot on your head to get your attention, white boy, but you do listen when I have it."

"My mother tells me it's a gender related trait," Martin laughed.

"So listen to you mama!" Rosalind responded in her broadest Southern accent. "She know what she talking about."

"This goes no further than you and me and Othello, all right? At least, for now." Rosalind nodded, all attention. "Clarence and some of the other pastors think they've been placed under governmental surveillance," he told her. "That's what they wanted to talk to me about and he was speaking for all of them."

"So what else is new?" Rosalind asked. "J. Edgar spies on everybody these days. That's common knowledge."

"This apparently is not the FBI," he told her. "It's far more serious. Who they think it may be is the CIA. Or some other spook agency."

"That's bad," Rosalind replied, "but I'm not surprised. Not after that thing with the Mafia. Trying to get them to do Castro."

"Yeah," said Quinn. "Whatever else you say about Bobby Kennedy, he apparently put a stop on the contract."

"What I wonder," Rosalind murmured, "is who shot Sam Giancana last month? Was it really a mob hit or was it the CIA?" She shook her head. "Or maybe the real question is how much overlap there is between the two organizations. Now that's a story that could get you killed."

"So is this one if it's true," Quinn replied. "That's why Clarence and the other pastors were so careful, and that's why they chose me. That's why we have to be just as cautious. I think the reason they asked for me is my history covering civil rights. And the story we're going to do on Ruth Ann is an excellent cover for our walk in the garden if anyone was watching."

"If anyone was watching," Rosalind murmured as understanding settled in. "Jesus, Martin, where does it ever end?"

"I know, Ros," he said, nodding. "I know. Tovah is not the only reason I read the psalms." He looked at her. "Do you mind if I read you something?"

Surprised by the shyness in his voice, Rosalind glanced at Quinn. It was evident he was feeling very vulnerable and her heart went out to him. "Yes, Martin" she said softly as if speaking to a frightened child. "Please do."

Reaching into his satchel he retrieved a small black leather prayer book and turned to a well worn passage. "This comes from the eighty-eighth Psalm of David," he told her. "The whole thing sort of says where I am, but the last few verses sum it up." He began to read, and glancing at him again, Rosalind saw tears gather in the corners of his eyes.

> Lord, why abhorest thou my soul, and hidest thy
> face from me?
> I am in misery and like unto him that is at the point
> to die; even from my youth up thy terrors
> I suffered with a troubled mind.
> Thy wrathful displeasure goeth over me, and the fear
> of thee hath undone me.
> They came around me daily like water, and compassed
> me together on every side.
> My lovers and friends thou hast put away from me,
> and hid mine acquaintance out of my sight.

When he was done, Quinn fell silent and Rosalind nodded. "That says it all," she agreed. "Enemies on every side like standing in water. That's what it's like growing up black in these Newnineted States."

Martin glanced at her and then looked back at the text. "I never thought of it quite that way," he told her. "I always assumed the 'they' who 'came around ... like water' was the terrors the writer suffered even when he was a young man. But enemies makes sense, too. Real live enemies."

"Especially when you're black," she agreed. She looked at him directly for a long moment, so long he was afraid she was going to drive off the road. "You and I have never ever talked about this in any depth," she said. "We've talked around it, but you've never asked me what it was like for me growing up black and a woman."

"There's a reason for that," he told her. "I'd like to know, but I don't want to be nosy." He grinned. "You know what I mean. Other news people are off limits. Honor among thieves."

"Or liars," she snorted.

"So what was it like, Rosalind?" he asked gently. "What was it like growing up in America, being black and being a woman?"

"Well, I'll tell you," she said, smiling and nodding when he held up his tape recorder, asking her permission to tape her answer. She paused until he finished clipping the microphone to her blouse, then resumed. "I cannot ever remember not being different. The first thing I remember learning was not to piss off papa. Women and kids were supposed to be seen and not heard, and he was quick with a slap if we needed reminding. So the first thing I learned was being a woman was different from being a man. Men were allowed to get away with stuff women and kids couldn't, but I also learned real quick I never could grow up to be a man. My brothers could, but not my sisters or me. We were women and even the preachers told us God made us this way because we were sources of temptation that needed men to control them.

"Where we grew up was mostly black, so while I knew I was a nigger like momma and daddy, it took a while for me to learn that being a nigger meant being different, too. I remember the day it happened, clearly. Daddy was late with the rent that month, the first time ever I later found out, and a white man showed up asking for it. He was a little shrimp, ugly and white, looking like the grubs we found digging up turnips. Yet my daddy seemed to be afraid of him. This was my daddy who didn't take no shit off no other man where we lived, and I saw him groveling, whining, promising to come and pay just as soon as he had the money and to never let it happen again. I was shocked. I tried to ask my momma how come, but she slapped me, my momma, who almost never raised a hand against us. That was the day when I learned about the power that goes with having pink skin, no matter what the man is like who wears it. I remember trying to wash the black off my arms and my daddy laughing at me when I told him I didn't want to be black any more. 'None of us does, sugar,' he told me, and it was one of the few times he was kind to me. He took me up in his lap and rocked me. 'None of us does,' he told me. 'But that's the way God made us and we got to live with it. We ain't got much choice.'

"That was another shock. The preacher was always telling us how good God was, and here my daddy was telling me God made us black. It didn't matter how good we were or anything, we had to live with it. I asked my daddy why and I remember him looking so sad. 'We Cain's children,' he told me. 'We carry the mark of Cain.' I asked him who Cain was and he told me about the man who murdered his brother. I told Daddy I didn't hit Able, and he smiled and said neither did he. 'We his children,' he told me. 'Just like the children in this world, we carry his sign and his name. Every nigger carry it, child, even you granny mama.'"

Rosalind sighed. "Martin, my grandmother was the gentlest, kindest person I ever knew. She was a saint, and while she may have had her faults, I don't know what they were. When someone died or was sick or had a child in trouble, she would always go visit, take them a pie or something else to help cheer them up. She never had much but she always shared whatever she did have, just like Clearance's family did with us. And here was my daddy telling me this good woman was born a nigger because she was the child of a murderer. I think it was right then and there I decided I would never have children. Not if they had to carry the mark of Cain."

"Jesus!" Martin breathed. "I thought I had it tough growing up but I had no idea it was like that for black people."

"It's not just blacks," Rosalind told him. "Up your way in Minnesota it's Indians. Down in southwest Texas it's Mexicans. In Chicago it's Poles or Italians. In New York it used to be Jews."

"I didn't mean to interrupt you," he said. "Please go on."

"Wild horses couldn't stop me, kemo sabe," she smiled. "But we are almost out of gas and I need a pit stop. That station up there looks nice enough that it will let me use the ladies' room."

"They'll play hell if they don't," Martin growled.

"Now, baby, don't you go to getting in a fight," Rosalind said, looking at him anxiously. "These plowboys down here carry sharp pig stickers and with you traveling with a black woman, old John Law will just look the other way when they gang up on you." She pulled over in front of an old house a couple of blocks from the station. "I bet the lady here will let me use hers," she laughed. "I'll tell her you're my boss man. Go on up to the station and fill us up with gas and I'll meet you there."

"Yes, boss," Martin replied, but Rosalind gave him a somber look.

"Listen, Martin," she said. "I know you're trying to lighten things up, but, please, don't tease me about this right now."

There was pain in Rosalind's eyes, pain he knew she would carry to her grave. Not for the first time, or for the last, Martin Quinn wondered how a God of goodness could allow someone as special as Rosalind to suffer the way she did. *The old problem of evil*, he thought. Then he shook his head. *No, damn it! 'Theodicy' is just a word preachers have for prettying up human pain. How the fuck can God justify it?* Turning his eyes to the heavens as he drove away he heard himself saying, "You hear that, you bastard? How the fuck can you claim to be good?" Only much later was he struck by the absurdity of an avowed atheist taking God to task. Even so, for better or for worse, the heavens stood silent.

As Quinn predicted, Othello was interested in the story of CIA surveillance more than in the religious art Ruth Ann produced. Over Quinn's protests, he assigned a junior staffer to look into the story behind Clearance's aunt, and so strong was Quinn's objection he threatened to quit and pursue the story on his own. Finally, Othello agreed to allow him to continue collaboration with the junior writer on Ruth Ann provided he would give most of his time to the CIA story.

"It's a devil's bargain," Quinn told McLeod, "but I'll take it. I don't seem to have much choice."

"You're right," McLeod assured him. "After all, we own all the pictures Rosalind took, too."

"What pictures?" asked Rosalind, and Quinn thought McLeod would stroke out. "Something was wrong with the film," she lied, shrugging. "A bad batch, I guess. Or maybe the technician who developed them screwed up. I guess I could have stood too close to an x-ray machine, but I can't think when it might have happened."

Struggling for control, McLeod said in a strangled voice "I'll pretend I didn't hear that, Rosalind. You were on my time."

Rosalind looked stubborn. "I'm on a free lance contract which covers such contingencies," she reminded him. "You sent us after a CIA story and I have plenty of pictures of the preachers. Any collateral stories I develop in the process are mine, and you did not send us after the story on Ruth Ann." She looked at Quinn dispassionately. "I seem to recall Martin has the same sort of language in his contract. I know because I checked it out the first time we worked together."

Seeing their boss' face, Rosalind shifted tactics. "Please, be reasonable, Othello. We're not trying to hold you up. There's a Pulitzer in this and Martin and I deserve it for discovering the story." While her tone was quiet and courteous, there was no mistaking her determination.

Suddenly McLeod laughed and threw up his hands. "I don't know what I did to deserve such a pair of jokers like you and Quinn," he said, rolling his eyes to the heavens. "One of you lies and the other swears to it, and God help the soul that gets in your way."

"You pissed Her off," Rosalind smiled. "And you know what I think I did? I may have sent Processing a bunch of outdated film I was intending to throw out. Let me check my case again."

"I am almost sure you did," Othello answered dryly. "All right, already. Use Ruth Ann as your cover and work on the CIA angle as you can. I'll send you a memo on the art story. Black awareness, maybe. We'll run the Ruth Ann story next week and hint you're looking for other undiscovered talent among blacks in the South. Will that do for a start?" he asked, making no attempt to cover his sarcasm.

"Othello, that's a brilliant idea," Martin told him enthusiastically. "It gives us and excuse to go South again and dig around."

"I know it's brilliant, Martin," his friend said. "That's why you suggested it in the first place. All right, you two got what you wanted. Now get your butts out of here and get to work."

True to his word, Othello gave the story about Ruth Ann Matthews a full Sunday supplement spread. Martin and Rosalind paid a visit to the Smithsonian, presumably to develop deep background from the staff there, but also to tap sources Quinn had developed in the intelligence community over the years. Six days later they were back in Atlanta and Martin was on the phone to McLeod. "There's a good story here," he said obliquely. "I have lots of leads but very little documentation at this point. That may be a problem because very few records are kept. A family Bible sort of thing."

Othello smiled and nodded to himself. Quinn was onto something big and people were willing to talk, but not for the record. Quinn was also telling him that any documentation they might bet would be highly subjective and hard to corroborate. "Well, get what you can," he forced himself to laugh. "Family Bibles are better than nothing, and we can at least report on that. I don't think anyone's going to sue us."

On the other end of the line Quinn nodded to Rosalind. What his boss was telling them is that they would go to print with whatever Quinn and Rosalind dug up. The CIA might issue a denial, but it was doubtful it would go farther than that. They had too much to lose making a more elaborate public response. Of course, what was in each of their minds was the kind of quiet response the agency might make against them. It was quite possible for gadflies to find themselves faced with compliance audits from the Internal Revenue Service. Nor was this the nastiest the government could get and the only protection people like themselves had lay in whatever information they gathered which was not made public. Some of the dirtier stuff had to be withheld for insurance.

Suddenly Quinn's attention was drawn back to the phone by the tone of his friend's voice. "Martin," he said, choosing his words carefully. "I've been thinking. We may be chasing a will o' the wisp here. I know you've put a lot of work into this, but I wonder if your talents might be better spent on another story. I don't have a good feeling for how this will develop."

Martin was quiet a moment. "All right," he said. "I don't, either, but why don't I talk to Ros and get back to you?"

"You onto anything hot at the moment?" McLeod asked casually.

"Not particularly, why?"

"Why don't you come on back in. I have another possible lead for you and coming here is on the way. I'll fill you in when you get here."

"Well, you're the boss," Quinn laughed, remembering their earlier talk and seeing in his mind's eye the sour look this would bring to Othello's face. "We'll be on the first flight we can get."

Hanging up the phone Quinn raised a finger to his lips. "Boss man's tired of starving artists," he said, forcing a laugh. "He wants us to get back. His bean counters must be screaming bloody murder."

Rosalind nodded. "They always do. Well, if we're going to get out of here first thing tomorrow, I'd better pack."

"I think I'm going for a walk," Quinn told her. "I need to get a lady a present. Want to come with?" The look he gave her communicated the answer he wanted.

"Sure," she said. "I could use some fresh air. With your taste, the lady would thank me for helping out."

Forty minutes later they were window shopping in one of the plazas which began to invade the American landscape in the early 'Fifties. Out of the fifty or so shops in this center, one was a music store, or, more accurately, a sound emporium, selling records and tapes, and it was here Martin stopped to look at the displays. One of the more popular groups was blaring forth its latest production over outside speakers and when Martin spoke, Rosalind could barely hear what he was saying over the wail of electric guitars. "Can you hear what I'm saying?" he asked, not turning his head in her direction.

"Yeah," she said, picking up the game and pointing toward a display in the window. "But not very well."

"Good," he said, looking casually to the left and right at other displays in the window. Out of the corner of his eye he could see no one else was close enough to hear in either direction and the reflection in the window told him no one was behind them. He scratched his nose while he was talking so no one with binoculars could read his lips in the reflection. "I think Othello's scared," he murmured. "Not for himself, but for us. That's why he wants to see us at the office."

Rosalind nodded and smiled, reaching out to touch Quinn lightly on the arm. "What did he say?" she asked, barely moving her lips.

"Not much. It was more how he said it. Have you ever known him to pull someone off an assignment without giving them specifics?"

"Not unless he was going to fire them," Rosalind laughed and glanced at him, as if he'd said something funny.

"There is that," he laughed back. "Let's go buy something." Another shop down the way caught his eye and he pointed. "There's a store I bet you'd like to check out."

Looking in the direction he was pointing, Rosalind smiled. The shop was tucked into a back corner of the plaza, barely visible from where they stood, and looked as if had been there a long while. It's specialty was photo equipment and cameras, new and used. A sign over the door proclaimed, "If We Don't Got It, We'll Get It! No Extra Charge!"

Seeing the name over the door, Rosalind's face brightened. "You bet your sweet grits," she told him. "This pilgrim has just come to Mecca."

"You know this place?" he asked, surprised.

"Oh, yeah, I've been dying to come here for years," she confessed. "You can find their ads in all the photo magazines, and they have about the best prices around. The stuff I've bought by mail order is good quality and they seem to have everything."

For the next thirty minutes Rosalind explored the store's inventory while Martin wandered around looking at various items, all of which were a mystery to him. The prices on the tags confirmed what he'd heard. Photography is an expensive undertaking, and he came to a conclusion that much of Rosalind's income must go into the tools of her trade. Were these good prices, as she told him, Martin shuddered to think what the same things might cost in an expensive place.

Rosalind picked out a few purchases, then seemed to get caught at a glass counter in the back. Joining her there, Martin found he was at one of the used equipment displays, and his jaw almost dropped when he looked at the price tags on some of the items there. "This is used equipment?" he asked the sales clerk, who nodded. "I don't know anything about it," he said, "but some of these cameras seem much more expensive than the new ones you have up front."

Rosalind laughed. "Ask her what the same equipment would cost new," she responded. "But you better get some heart medicine first."

The clerk nodded and Martin and moved on down the display counter, trying to see what make this equipment so special. One of the older cameras caught his attention, and, looking at it closely through the glass, he didn't notice Rosalind and the clerk move on to another area. "That's a classic," another voice said, startling him. Looking up he saw a seedy looking man standing behind the counter. His hair was long, partly balding on top, and a straggling grey mustache and beard covered what must have been a weak chin and plain features. Yet it was the man's eyes which caught Martin' attention, deep blue and very intense behind the rimless glasses.

Glancing at the man's name tag, Martin asked, "Are you Murphy, the owner?" The man smiled and nodded and Quinn introduced himself.

To his surprise, Murphy was familiar with his work. "Yes," the man told him. "I caught that article that just came out on Ruth Ann Matthews. Is that your photographer?" he asked, nodding to Rosalind.

"That's us," Quinn said. "She's apparently bought from you mail order but hasn't ever been in before."

"Yes," the man affirmed. "I thought I recognized the name. Are you all here on assignment?"

"Just some follow-up on the Matthews story," Quinn answered. "Tell me, is this used equipment that good?"

Murphy smiled. "It's good for that price," he said. "To me, personally, the answer is 'no'. The Germans still make the best optical equipment in the world, except for some specialty stuff the Swiss turn out, but the Japanese are crowding them hard. Their pricing is much better."

"Then why do people buy used equipment at higher prices than new?" Quinn wanted to know.

"Between us chickens, it's like a Rolls-Royce or a Rollex watch. Snob appeal, but if you quote me, I'll deny it," Murphy said.

"Even as a 'well informed source'?" Quinn laughed. "I imagine the other stuff is your bread and butter trade."

"You're right," Murphy said. "Although we do a lot of specialty item business. Photographers are like anyone else. When they get in the habit of using certain equipment, they don't like to change." He shrugged. "Regardless who makes it, it all wears out sooner or later."

"Does it take that long to learn how to use new equipment?" Martin asked, surprised. "I wouldn't think it would be all that different."

"No, it's not, but it's a pain in the neck," Rosalind answered. She was holding her purchases in a small bag. Quinn introduced her to Murphy and smiled as the man mentioned several of her photos he particularly admired. They lost him for a few minutes in technical talk and he returned his attention to the camera which had first caught his attention. After a moment Rosalind asked Murphy, "You trying to sell Quinn that Leica?"

Murphy shrugged and shook his head. "Not really. We were just talking. Passing the time of day."

"That's good," Rosalind snorted. "To him that's just an overpriced Brownie. He has no idea what he's looking at."

"Would you like to have one like it?" Quinn asked, ignoring her snort.

"I'd give my eye teeth," Rosalind declared. "That's probably one of the finest cameras ever made. It doesn't have a lot of the bells and whistles the Japanese market, but I don't know anything else that will hold up as well." She nodded to Murphy, who took the instrument out of the case. "This one is in incredible shape," she noted, examining it closely. "Almost no wear at all."

"Used by a little old lady from the suburbs who never took it over fifty miles an hour," Murphy quipped, and they all laughed. "Actually, it was the backup for an uncle of mine. He never used it much and when he died my cousin didn't want it." He shook his head in wonder, looking at the price tag. "I priced it up out of sentimentality, but I'll never use it." He frowned. "If you're interested I can make you a good buy."

Rosalind laughed, but there was no mistaking the desire in her eyes. "Man, don't tempt me. It would take me a year to save my pennies for that," she told him. "Right now I'm equipment poor."

"Aren't we all these days," Murphy murmured, starting to replace the camera in the case. "That's how I started this business."

"Just a minute," Quinn said, taking the camera from him and looking at the price. "This is a collector's item?" he asked Rosalind.

"Yeah," she nodded. "I doubt anyone would risk it outside the studio."

"Then it might be a good investment," Quinn said. "Just how good a price are you willing to make?" he asked Murphy.

What ensured was fifteen minutes of hard core bargaining, complete with the exchange of friendly insults and cries of mock outrage. "All right," Murphy eventually said. "I'll let you have it at that price, but I'll want ten photos with your endorsement of the shop, too."

Quinn was surprised. "Sure," he agreed. "I don't know why. I'm not that well known, particularly among photographers."

"Pure speculation," Murphy told him. "You might win a Pulitzer one of these days, and then it will be worth a great deal. A personal investment, like you said."

"Done!" said Quinn, taking out his wallet and laying out century bills enough to cover the purchase. Rosalind stared, goggle eyed. "Get me some film to fit this thing, would you?" he asked her, handing her a twenty. When she nodded dumbly and moved to the front of the store Quinn asked, "Can you sneak this in the back and put it in a nice case? And gift wrap it?"

"She your girlfriend?" Murphy asked casually, nodding.

"No, but she's saved my sorry ass any number of times," Quinn told him, "and I've never even given her a Christmas present. It's catch up time."

Murphy nodded and smiled. He shoved Quinn's money back across the counter. "Just get her to pose with you when I take the endorsements," he murmured. "I'd like to invest in her, too."

A few minutes later Murphy appeared at the front of the store and asked them to come into the studio. Rosalind followed behind the other two, hanging back until Quinn asked her to join him in the photos. "As a favor," he laughed. "In case you get famous before I do."

Rosalind laughed and struck a pose, holding up the Leica and looking at Quinn. "That's great," Murphy said, snapping the shot.

"Hey, we weren't ready!" said Quinn.

"I don't like posed shots," Murphy said. "They look fake."

"Yeah," Rosalind agreed, laughing at Quinn's expression. "They make you looked much more tight-assed than you are, baby."

Murphy roared with laughter, still managing to catch Quinn's surprise on film. "Tell him something else," he pleaded with Rosalind.

"What should I say?" she asked him, not turning her gaze from her partner.

"How about this?" Quinn murmured softly. "'I found my own Leica at Murphy's.'" He smiled.

"I can't do that," she frowned. Murphy continued shooting. "That's not true, Martin. You know how I feel about that."

"Oh, yes it is," he countered. "Happy birthday, Rosalind."

The best shot Murphy took that day, and one he used in advertising seven years later after Quinn did win his first Pulitzer, was one of Martin looking at Rosalind, a broad smile on his face, while she stood wide eyed and dumbfounded. The caption read simply, "Happy Birthday, Ros! From Quinn and Murphy's."

Not many hours later, after midnight as Rosalind and Martin caught the red-eye special home through the early morning sky, she was huddled next to him wrapped in a blanket. A stewardess walking by asked if he would like a pillow for himself and one for his wife. "She's not my wife," he complained to the attendant, speaking louder than necessary.

"I've asked her several times but she won't marry me."

"I'm sure she has her reasons, sir," the flight attendant replied, smiling as a throaty chuckle came from the mound of blankets that was Rosalind, and moving on down the aisle.

"Hey, Quinn, you want to know something?" Rosalind asked him a moment later, pulling the blanket down from over her head.

"Sure, Ros," he said, handing her a pillow and wiping his eyes as he yawned onto his own. "What's that?"

"You want to know the real reason why I won't marry you?"

Fully awake now, Quinn raised his head and looked at her strangely. "Sure, Ros. Why not?"

"You're too much fun to work with," she said, smiling. "I think getting married might change all that. Most men don't treat their wives this good."

A reply was on the tip of his tongue, protesting he was not like most other men, but Rosalind was not listening. She'd turned over and was fast asleep, breathing deeply. Switching off his reading light, Martin settled himself back into his own pillow. For ten or fifteen seconds he wondered what it would take to change Rosalind's mind. Then he, too, was fast asleep, as the giant silver bird carried them home.

7. Writing A Rag

New Year's Day. Tonight I bring in the New Year walking through the city. I am told this is dangerous to do, yet here I am, walking now until dawn, never approached, never accosted, greeted only by a stray dog hoping for a handout. I feed him the leftover sandwich I called supper and he follows me several blocks before trying his luck elsewhere. I think about tempting him with more treats, trading food for companionship, but a lady with a catering van stops to make a delivery, tosses him a leftover ham bone. As he trots off I can almost see the happy son-of-a-bitch smile. Unless a bigger dog comes along and steals it, he'll worry the bone for hours, maybe days, sucking the fat from the marrow.

I walk on alone, seeing people celebrate everywhere. Come midnight many of them are drunk. The church bells sound, the fireworks crackle, the sirens wail and the people gathered in the streets cheer. I wonder why. Is it because they've survived another year? Or because they have outlived some of their enemies? Or perhaps it's because it's a good day to be drunk, to be happy for a while and to forget the boring pointlessness of their lives.

I sense beneath their merriment the sure and certain knowledge tomorrow is coming, and the fear this brings. For what comes with the morrow? At best it's a mild hangover, and within its pain the forgetfulness that this year will probably be no better than the last. This year there will be more wars, more crimes of passion, more body bags and more people of every kind left maimed and hopeless.

There is a personal edge to the remembrance, too, for in the early morning light, reflected in flashing red and blue lights of an ambulance parked outside an apartment house, there is the sure and certain knowledge that come the next New Year celebration, I may not be here to see it.

Step by step I walk the city and with the dawn I find my steps have led me to the news room, the place I call my office. I walk in to hear the news, to discover what rape or murder or fire or accident brought in the New Year.

413

They are all here, those who chase the news. Some are drunk, others sober. None seem very happy. Very little is happening so far this year so they all go home, one by one.

I sit at my desk a long while, looking over reports of the night of celebration. The fire department has rescued a drunk from the top of a tree. Who knows how he got there? Caught in the insanity of drink he could have thought he was a cat and run from a dog carrying a ham bone. The police have made eighty-seven arrests, most of these for drunk and disorderly or drunken driving. We are lucky this year. No one died.

Suddenly I realize there is nothing new in this place. Fires, assaults, rape, robbery, pollution indexes, lots of events take place, but no news. All that is new is which building burned or who was beaten to death by whom. Novelty in this circus of tragedy lies in the form of a unique blunt instrument.

I wonder why we even bother, why we chase after catastrophe. Long before we get to the scene we know what we will find, give or take a few morbid details. That's all we need, the details, the bloody awful details, and we can fill in the blanks, file the story. Yet we go to see for the thousandth time the homeless children staring at the ashes of their parents and their home. Or to photograph the bloody corpse. Or we hear again the mindless platitudes of mediocre politicians. After a while, even the reformers sound stale. Even the missionaries go home for a beer and turn on the tube.

So why do we do this? Or, more to the point, why do I? Why do I go? Am I like the others who seem like flies attracted to human offal? Am I in the grip of some atavistic human instinct which compels me to witness disaster? Or am I, like the rest, really looking for something truly new, some miracle, some mystery, some Second Coming? Perhaps that's it. Like pious Jews, maybe those of us who hang around news rooms are waiting for the true Messiah. Maybe we are looking for the One who will come and make things all right, who will make some sense out of this mindless treadmill we run day after day, month after year. Perhaps we are looking for the One who will take away our sins.

No, to hell with redeeming our sins. It's the pain we want taken away, washed in whomsoever's blood it takes. The only trouble is we are so consumed in our pain, so conditioned to squalor, we may never see it when it happens. Or we may look in the wrong place, standing around the White House gates while the real miracle is the birth of a child in a garage in the slums. Perhaps the real tragedy is that as scavengers of the gleanings of disaster, we become blind to anything else. So it goes on and on, day after month after year after year.

So today is the first day of the newest year, and I sit here wondering why I don't get out. Money is no longer a problem and probably never will be. I have a place to go and friends who would welcome me, and a work of restoration worth doing. There is nothing here to keep me and I could be packed and gone in three hours, much less if I simply grabbed my papers and the travel bag I always keep packed.

What a nice commentary on fifteen years. What an eloquent epitaph for my grave: Here lie the mortal remains of one Martin Quinn, who after a lifetime here on earth could be packed and gone in three hours.

Despite my glum mood I must laugh at myself. I know I won't leave this city, this hell hole I call home. It is tempting but I won't. I am too much of a coward to face a life I would have to create for myself. Or maybe I'm just crazy. Maybe I really do think I'll find the Messiah somewhere in the gutters of this wilderness we call Denver.... (Martin Quinn's journal)

July 1981. The letter was lying on his desk when he returned from the scene of the accident, tired, harassed and totally disgusted. The whole assignment was a reporter's nightmare, something he'd done only on the insistence of the editor. Fighting the traffic took Martin Quinn almost an hour getting to the scene, and then the photographer wasn't there. He was running even later, not that it mattered. The body was gone by the time Quinn arrived and all that was left was a crumpled mass of burned steel being hauled up on a trailer by a winch truck. While the officer told him it was likely she'd been drinking from the physical evidence, and that the victim was the daughter of a very successful corporate attorney, the name was not one which the public would recognize. *So there isn't even celebrity value,* he thought. *There is just the tragic, stupid death of a nineteen year old woman who had more money and fewer constraints than may have good for her.* He considered writing it up that way, in just those words, but he knew the editor would send it back for a rewrite. "To hell with him," he decided, muttering to himself in a broad Texas twang. "If he don't like it he can stick it where the sun don't shine."

"What?" the police officer said sharply, glaring at him.

"Oh," said Quinn, embarrassed. "Sorry. I wasn't talking to you. I was thinking what I'd like to tell my editor. He's a real horse's ass."

"Oh," said the officer, grinning. "Sounds like my Captain." Then, aware of his indiscretion he glanced anxiously over his shoulder, but the other officers were too far away to hear.

"Don't worry. I won't tell," laughed Quinn. "Even though it would make a good headline. 'PATROLMAN CALLS CAPTAIN HORSE'S ASS: SPCA INVESTIGATES'. Can't you just see that in twenty point type?"

The officer laughed nervously and walked away. He decided the other guys were right about Quinn. For a news hound he wasn't a bad sort. He wondered what such an OK guy was doing in such a shitty profession. *Takes all types, I guess,* he thought. It was too bad he couldn't share the incident with some of the others, but it was too risky. The Captain had spies everywhere.

Quinn saw the letter as he was sitting down to write up the story, if it could be called that. He glanced at it, noting the return address and shrugged. There was no name, only a street number and city printed in discrete type on high quality paper. *No, I take that back. It's the very best quality paper*, he thought, picking up the envelope and testing the texture. Velum, almost like parchment. Elegant was the word which came to mind, elegant and expensive, giving the whole impression of money, old, dignified money. The address didn't mean anything. *Probably some foundation,* he thought. *Something like the Smithsonian wanting a donation, using expensive paper to pull in contributors from the high end.*

The phone on his desk rang and he answered it, "Quinn!" Tossing the envelope on a pile at the back of his desk, he promised himself to look at it later. He was curious only because the paper was a cut above the usual solicitation. The caller was the city editor, clamoring for details of the crash he sent Quinn to cover. "Shit, man," Quinn growled. "I just got in this second, just got to my desk. Give me a minute or two to get it together. All right?"

"I don't have all day!" rasped the angry growl of the editor. "You've been in the building ten minutes. We need the copy."

"All right, already," Quinn snapped back. "I stopped to piss! Ten minutes and you'll have it."

"Make it five," demanded the other. Then his voice softened just a bit. "While I have you on the line, congratulations. The old man will be pleased."

"Thanks, I guess," Quinn answered, puzzled. "What did I do to please the old fart? I'll make sure I don't next time."

There was a stunned silence at the other end of the line. This was the first time Martin Quinn could remember his editor being speechless. The silence was followed by a roar of harsh laughter. "Jesus!" rasped the editor. "You don't know! You really don't know, do you?"

"I really don't know what?" Quinn was becoming impatient to get the copy written before the details evaporated from memory. "Look, I don't have time for games or dip-shit assignments. Do you want the story or not? I doesn't matter to me."

"Yeah, I want it," the editor retorted. "Five minutes. When you're done, take five minutes more and read your frigging mail. You might find a story you like there."

Quinn could not imagine what the editor was talking about but the story came first, anyway. He quickly summarized the details on his work station and patched it on to the news desk, glancing at his watch. Four minutes had passed since he hung up. Smiling at himself and his editor and the games they played, he leaned back and propped his feet up on his desk, lighting a cigarette as he did. The envelope lying on top of the maybe-when-I-have-time pile caught his eye and he retrieved it, sliding a blade of his grandfather's pen knife under the flap. Scanning the text he was stunned at first, then suspicious this was an elaborate joke with him as the butt. There was a telephone number at the bottom and he picked up his extension and dialed. Three rings later the other end answered and he said, "This is Martin Quinn down at the Times. I got a letter today from a Mr. Smith on your letterhead."

"Oh, yes, Mr. Quinn, this is Ivan Smith," said the pleasant voice at the other end. "I hoped you might call. Congratulations."

"Wait a minute. You mean this is for real?" Quinn asked, flabbergasted.

"Of course," Smith was puzzled. "Why wouldn't it be?"

"You apparently don't know newspaper people, Mr. Smith. I could name six people who have pulled this kind of hoax, and I'm just trying to verify it."

Smith laughed. "I understand, Mr. Quinn. I commend your integrity and your caution. Why don't you check the wire services first, and then call me back? We released the information an hour ago. Could the hucksters go that far? Or would they?"

"They'd never write for another rag if they did," Quinn replied. "The wire service pretty sacred. I'll check and get right back to you."

"I'll be awaiting your call," Smith assured him pleasantly.

Quinn dropped the instrument back into its cradle and rushed down the hall to the Teletype. A couple of other people were reading the news as the machine spewed out information and one of them looked up and grinned. "Well, if it isn't the famous writer himself! Congratulations, Martin." It was Tom Evans, who Quinn had known for years as a square shooter. The man was prone to cutting sarcasm, but he was honest as the year was long.

"Thanks," said Quinn, "or are you guys in on the scam?"

"Scam? Right here it is, Martin," Sandy Johnson, the other person watching the Teletype. While he did not know her very well, Sandy was always friendly and had a reputation for fair play. "Look," she said, ripping off a sheet of printout and handing it to him. "If it's a scam, someone's got real clout."

"That or a bad case of the stupids," said Tom Evans, the other. "This is not the kind of thing you kid around about. Not if you want to keep working the news."

Quinn read the printout carefully, absorbing every word. "Jesus!" he said softly, shaking his head. "I don't believe it. The Steinbeck award for fiction."

"Well, you should," said Sandy Johnson. "As a matter of fact, I think you're long overdue. Which book did they award it for?"

"The second," said Quinn, chuckling. "I guess I shouldn't say so, but I never thought that one was as good as any of the rest."

"Neither did I," said Sandy, nodding. "Although it's a matter of degree. They're all good but my favorite was the last one."

"Well, personally, I agree with their choice," Evans argued. "I guess there's different strokes for different folks."

"Hey, that's good," Sandy said. "You ought to copyright it."

"Too late," laughed Evans. "I heard it on TV last week."

"Listen," Quinn said, beginning to get excited. "Why don't you guys come help me celebrate? It's on me."

"On you?" Sandy said. "Gracious, I thought you'd never ask."

Martin laughed. "How about it, Mike?"

Evans shook his head. "As much as I hate to miss a once-in-a-century event," he said, "I have to pass. Tonight is Indian Scouts and I promised my daughter I'd be sure and make it. Thanks, anyway." Slipping on his jacket he headed for the door. "I'll tell you what," he said, turning back to the other two. "You do the celebrating tonight and I'll take a rain check for when you win the Pulitzer." He grinned. "I'll even buy, food, drinks, cover charges, everything. On me." He laughed.

They could hear him laughing all the way down the hall. "You're my witness," Quinn told Sandy Johnson. "I'm going to make that bastard regret that crack."

"I don't want to rain on your parade, bubba," said Sandy. "Winning the Steinbeck's a real honor, but the Pulitzer? The competition's pretty stiff."

"I know," Quinn answered. "It may take me ten years, but I'm going to do it."

"That's a long time to wait for a bet to pay off," Sandy chuckled. "By then you'll probably have forgotten it."

"You're right," he said. "By then I won't even remember who Tom Evans was."

"Tom who?" Sandy answered, laughing. "Hey, I hope you remember me when you're rich and famous. I may need a loan. To put my baby sister through school."

"I didn't know you had a baby sister," Quinn quipped back. "Is she good looking? I might want a date."

"You already got a date, bubba," Sandy answered, grinning. "It's too late to stand her up tonight."

"You're on!" said Martin, looking at his watch. "It's too early for dinner. Why don't I make reservations at this new Chinese place I heard about and let's have a drunk at the Brown Palace bar while we wait." He heard his slip of tongue but ignored it.

Not so Sandy. "A drunk?" she asked. "A drink before dinner would be nice but if we're going to get drunk I'd rather eat first."

"Schlipp a m' tongue," Martin joked, slurring his words. "No, let's have a drink at the Brown and then get something to eat."

"Does it have to be Chinese?" Sandy asked, grimacing.

"Not at all," Quinn assured her. "As a matter of fact, I think I'd rather have a steak. That all right with you?"

"Yes, thank you," said Sandy. "I got a plate of bad food at a Chinese place six or seven years ago and, God, was I sick. Now even television ads for canned chicken chow mein make me queasy." She handed him her coat.

"Wouldn't want to do that," he replied, holding the coat for her to put on. "Tell me something...." he started to say.

"Tell you what, bubba?" she asked, giving him a sidelong look. "Why a nice girl like me's working in a place like this?"

"No," Quinn laughed, opening the door for her. "As a matter of fact, not, but I'm willing to listen if you want to tell me. What I want to know is, what's with the 'bubba' thing? You've called me that twice."

"That's what we call good old boys down in Arkansas were I come from," she answered, shrugging. "I guess it's the equivalent of saying 'buddy' or 'Mac', but it's quite the same, either. It's friendlier. It means 'somebody from around here,' maybe. Down home folks."

"That's me," Martin answered. "Friendlier by the moment." He followed her down the hall rapidly repeating, "Bubba-bubba-bubba-bubba-bubba..." softly in a deep chant. One of the editors stuck his head out the door and gave him a strange look. "Sound of a tire going flat," Quinn shrugged, repeating himself as if he and Sandy were in a serious discussion.

Sandy laughed and the editor went back into his office, shaking his head. *With some people success goes to their heads*, he thought, but he was surprised it happening to Quinn, who was pretty level headed most of the time. Of course, Quinn was leaving the building in the company of Sandy Johnson and that could account for it, all right. The editor smiled to himself. From his experience, just being in the same room with her was distracting. *No*, he thought. *It's more like sticking your finger in a light socket. She is one high voltage lady.*

One drink at the Brown turned into three or four, and by the time Martin and Sandy got to the restaurant, they were feeling flying high. At Sandy's insistence they left his car parked in the lot by the Brown and took a cab to the steak house. "You can get it after we eat," she said. "That will give you time to sober up. You don't need to get busted for drunk driving."

Quinn was too mellow to argue though it occurred to him some

420

prominent writers were as well known for their drinking as for their work, maybe more so. He paid off the cab, adding a good tip. "Thanks, mister," said the hack driver. "Have a good evening."

"Mister?" said Quinn. "Do I look like a Mister to you? Just call me bubba!" he added, drawing peal of laughter from Sandy. Then, again at the restaurant, when he was asked his name for the waiting list for a table, he said, "Mah name's Quinn," he told the hostess in a mock Georgia accent. "Bubba Quinn."

"Quit!" Sandy whispered in his ear, giggling. "You're about to make me pee in my panties." The hostess shook her head and turned away.

"Oh, miss!" Quinn called out loudly in the same accent, causing the hostess to turn in mid stride and stare. "Which away is the outhouse? Bubbette shere's gotta go real bayud, if ya know whut ah mean."

"Honestly," Sandy told him once they were seated at a table. "You surprise me."

"How so?" he asked, unable to think of a fast quip.

"Well, please don't take offense, but seeing you at the office, I always thought you were sort of a stuck-in-the-mud."

"Me? A stick-in-the-mud?" he asked, aghast. "Whatever made you think that?"

"Not a stick-in-the-mud, silly, a stuck-in-the-mud," Sandy laughed.

"What's the difference?" he asked. "Both sound equally bad."

"Oh, no," she answered with mock gravity. "There's hope for a stick-in-the-mud. A stuck-in-the-mud's infinitely worse. Sort of like they're set in concrete."

Quinn began to sing in a high nasal West Texas twang, "Well, he's a stuck-in-the-mud, a drinking his Bud, a real down home dud, so call him old Bub-ba the concrete truck driving man..."

Suddenly Sandy was no longer amused. "Don't make fun of me, Martin," she said. "I'm pretty tolerant, but I don't like sarcastic cracks about the South."

Quinn was surprised. "I'm sorry. I didn't mean any personal disrespect. It's just different and I was having fun with it." He broke into an accurate Scandinavian accent. "I do da the same ting wit Oly and Olga back home in Manyso-ta." He shrugged. "I won't do it if it bothers you."

She nodded. "Thank you. After a while it does. There's this redneck stereotype people up here have about Southerners. Not everyone down South is an ignorant asshole, Martin." She relented. "As a matter of fact, after people got over your talking funny, I think you'd fit right in down there."

"White sheet and all, huh? I don't know. Some of my best friends are Negroes."

"As are many of mine, Martin. That's one of the reasons I live up here, although the same thing exists here." Martin started to say something but Sandy held up a hand. "Let me finish the thought. Up here the discrimination is mostly focused against American Indians and Hispanics, but Negroes still catch a lot of it, too. It seems to be everywhere. You can't get away from it."

"Yeah," he nodded. "I used to run into it all the time in New Mexico. The Hispanics look down on the pueblo peoples, who will accept an Anglo but not a Hispanic into the kiva, and Anglos tend to look down on everybody, including the Irish and Poles." He shook his head. "It doesn't make a bit of sense to me."

"You don't have your own prejudices?" Sandy asked.

"Only against politicians and tight-assed Republicans," he laughed. "I grew up with so many tight-assed Republicans the burden of proof is on them."

Sandy grinned at him impishly. "What if I told you I was one of those tight-assed Republicans?"

"You're not, are you?" Martin looked shocked, as if Sandy had just admitted to having a social disease.

"No," Sandy laughed. "Growing up where I did I'm a genetic Democrat, although down there Democrats are every bit as conservative as Republicans, maybe more so. But what if I were? Would you still buy me a drink?" Her look was challenging.

"Well," he answered carefully. "I'm relieved you're not, but if you were I might have to change some of my thinking."

"Some of your preconceptions?" she responded lightly.

"No," he said, laughing at himself. "Some of my bedrock prejudices. Let's call them what they are. What about you? What are your prejudices?"

"Smart-assed Northerners," she answered promptly. "Pushy Northerners who get in your face and have no manners. Especially the men. No manners at all."

"I'm glad I'm from the Midwest," Martin said.

"That's still Yankee country," Sandy laughed. "Anything north of Tennessee and Virginia, and west of Arkansas and Texas is Yankee country in the South."

"Sounds like you're still fighting the Civil War down there," Martin laughed.

"You must be referring to the late war of Northern aggression," Sandy said, winking as she raised her glass. "Save your Dixie cups, brothers and sisters, the South shall rise again."

They both laughed, but Sandy was thoughtful. "Being from Minnesota I imagine you've been to Mankato?" She asked.

"Yes, but I'm surprised you've ever heard of Mankato," Quinn replied. "It's not exactly a well known place unless you're interested in fishing tackle."

"Not me, although fishing's a religious experience for some of my cousins," Sandy laughed. "I visited a friend at the state college there once when I was in school," she explained. "He was the editor of the school newspaper and finally got himself kicked out of school for a stunt he pulled."

"Oh?" Quinn said, unsure where she was going.

"Yeah, but that's another story. He was just a writer there when I visited and he took me downtown and showed me something I'll never forget." She shuddered as she remembered. "Right down town at the intersection of the two main streets where the road crossed the river there was a filing station. They had a metal rack outside the station with worn out tires hanging from it. Thirty-eight of them painted red. There was a big white sign below the rack painted in big block letters, professionally done. The sign said, 'ON THIS SPOT IN 1858 THIRTY-EIGHT REDSKINS WERE HANGED.'"

"Jesus," said Martin. "I'd forgotten that, the Sioux uprising of 1858. That's one of the blackest days in Minnesota history. As I remember, at least some of the Indians who were hanged didn't even take part in the uprising."

"That's right," said Sandy. "The year I saw that was 1964, and it may well be there now. So don't give me a hard time about Southerners still carrying grudges from the War Between the States."

"I concede the point," said Martin, taking a large bite of salad. He chewed for a minute, then frowned. Taking a sip of water he looked at Sandy thoughtfully and asked, "How did you know I was from Minnesota?"

Sandy grinned, shrugging. "That's simple. I must have seen it on the dust jacket of one of your books," she answered.

"No," he answered. "It wasn't there. I am very careful about that. You had to have found out somewhere else."

Sandy blushed. "You caught me, Mr. Lundberg." she confessed.

Quinn was shocked at her casual use of his father's name. "I keep that a very carefully guarded secret," he said.

"I really wasn't invading your privacy," Sandy pleaded. "Not the way it may look. It was purely personal. I found you attractive, and I didn't think you were married, but I wanted to make sure without asking. So I did a little journalistic research." She looked down. "I hope that doesn't put you off. Your secret's safe with me."

"You surprised me," he said, still recovering. "Not that it's all that big a secret any more. Especially now I'm a 'public figure' as far as the press is concerned. It's all there, a matter of public record for anyone who wants to dig." He smiled at her. "As you obviously did. Actually, I'm rather flattered you would."

"Do you mind my asking you why you used a pseudonym?" she wanted to know. "I know you changed your name, but I'm curious why. Most of us want to make it under our own names."

"You promise not to laugh?" he asked. "She nodded. "I was named for my grandfather, so I didn't want to change my first name. I started to take his full name but I didn't want to have to fight the battle of having an Hispanic surname. Now I'm not so sure about that. I think perhaps I should have."

"I know what you're saying," Sandy asked gently. "I don't blame you. But it's not as if you're pretending to be something you're not or denying your heritage. I don't think you'd have gotten this far as Martin Delgado de Ortega."

He looked at her in admiration. "You're thorough," he said. "Are there any of my family skeletons you haven't unearthed?"

Sandy laughed. "Being thorough pays off. I learned that early and that's the secret of an success I've had." She looked at him soberly. "You know, Hispanics aren't the only minority who have a hard row to hoe in this profession. Try being a woman."

Martin was at a loss for words. This was something new to him. I don't think I understand what you're saying," he said. "Women seem to do all right."

"From the point of men, they do," Sandy answered. "What about your mother?" she asked. "Does she have her own career? Does she have the final say at home?"

"You really did your research, didn't you?" Martin was feeling a little piqued.

"No, not really. I purposely stayed away from your family. What I know I came across accidentally in the morgue bios. All I really know is that your father is a building contractor from St. Cloud and you have one brother. Your mother wasn't mentioned at all in the morgue notes. I came across her through genealogy records. But that's my point. Nothing was said in our morgue file about your mother. From a woman's point of view, that means she wasn't considered important enough to mention."

Martin opened his mouth to answer, then shut it again. While he felt a need to defend his gender, he could not argue with Sandy's logic. "Damn," he said. "I hate to admit it, but I never thought about that."

"No reason you should, guy," Sandy said. "Until now. Now you know, but look, I didn't mean to rain on our parade. Or change the subject." She smiled, pulling him out of his line of thought. "Why did you pick Quinn? Is that a family name?"

"No," he said sheepishly. "That's what I wanted you to promise not to laugh at."

"All right," she agreed. "I'll give it my best shot. Why Quinn?"

"Well, you know Anthony Quinn, the actor?" Sandy nodded. "Well, most of his roles make a lot of sense to me, even though I don't always understand why. It's like I understand deep down but I can't call it to mind. Does this make sense?"

Sandy nodded and Quinn continued. "I started with Black, but that wasn't quite right and I considered Blackwolf, since I can legitimately claim that. Then I had the thought people would think I'm pretending to be American Indian, so I thought about making it Blackwolffe, you know, with the English style 'ffe', but that looked pretentious. So I tried different combinations until I came up with Martin Quinn. At the time I didn't realize that there was a televesion celebrity named Quinn Martin. He won an Emmy about the time I moved to New Mexico. " He paused. "Are you sure I'm not boring you to tears?"

"Not at all," Sandy answered. "This is fascinating. You said you can claim Black Wolf. Where does that come from?"

"Now that is a very long story," Quinn answered. "Let's save that for the second date."

"So you think there might be a second date, bubba?" Sandy observed. "Well, it depends on how you play your cards."

"So you don't think it's silly?""

"There's nothing silly about it at all, Martin," Sandy responded. "Quite the contrary. I think it's beautiful to honor your mother's father using his first name." She looked at him, smiling. "You do realize that there's another Martin Quinn who's an up and coming lawyer."

"I do now, but it's too late," Quinn answered. "Not many people are aware of that connection and, hopefully, I'll never have to paractice law again. Does being a former shiester count against me?"

"Not quite," Sandy assured him. Then she turned serious. "At the risk of your thinking I'm teasing," she said gently, "are you going to tell anyone any of this now you've become famous?"

"No," he said quickly. "At least not yet. Maybe after I win a couple of Pulitzers."

"And make doubting Thomas Evans pay for his quip," Sandy added.

"Tom who?" he asked, and they both laughed.

As things turned out, they were both surprised when the news came over the wire sixteen months later. Martin Quinn was selected for the Pulitzer Prize for a series of articles exposing a major crime syndicate and the United States Senator it had in its pocket. While Tom Evans groused when reminded of his promise, he made good. Yet Sandy Johnson did not go along. After living together a year, and almost marrying, Sandy moved out of Quinn's apartment a month before the award was announced. Both were cut to pieces over their estrangement, but neither could seem to make the first move to reconcile. So while Tom's wife, Marie, went along, and Martin invited a clerk from the typing pool, the evening was a bust. Quinn got drunk and became morose, ending the evening sobbing like a child in Marie's arms while Tom took Martin' date home.

"Poor bastard," Evans said to Marie as they drove home later.

"Poor Sandy, too, from what you tell me," Marie answered. "Mother called and I forgot to ask you. Did she take the job in Atlanta?"

Evans nodded. "Yeah. The management even released her so she could leave right away. I think they were relieved. Saved them having to let her go."

"So the woman gets the axe," Marie said severely.

"No," Tom said gently. "In this case, not. Sandy's a better asset than Quinn and they knew it. Or she was. Once he won the Pulitzer..." he shrugged. "You just don't let a Pulitzer winner go of you can help it. Not in the newspaper business."

"Yes, but in the newspaper business, most of the Pulitzer prizes go to men," Marie pointed out. Tom nodded and they drove home in silence, lost in their own thoughts.

Quinn was out for three days, drinking hard. Those who knew him shrugged, for that was just Quinn. This happened from time to time, maybe once or twice a year, and they covered for him. Mostly they covered because the liked the man, because he was kind and gentle and, with those he considered his friends, generous to a fault. This was particularly true when it came to bedrock information. Quinn protected his sources, even so far as going to jail twice to keep from revealing their identities, yet he did not hesitate to use them if a colleague needed information. So when it came to markers, Quinn was always ahead and covering for him during one of his periodic binges was a sure and certain way of winning one or more back. While the editors were well aware of what was going on, Quinn never embarrassed them publicly, and so long as they got what they wanted, they really did not care. At least, that was their approach up until now. Lately the periods between binges had been growing shorter and the time missed, greater, and most of the editorial staff were tired of dealing with Quinn's eccentricities.

The exception was Zakhar Levnikov, a tough little agnostic soul who served as Quinn's mentor. As a captured prisoner of war and survivor of the German extermination camp at Fort Breendonk in the Netherlands, the only survivor in several branches of his family, Levnikov made his way to New York where he spent six months teaching himself to speak English by driving a cab and waiting tables in a Greek restaurant. This had an enduring effect on his use of the language, for while the man was fluent in eight major European languages, and was fluent reading scholarly English, he had never learned to speak it until he arrived at Ellis Island. There he was confronted in Customs by an Irishman from south Boston who was barely literate, and it was only through the good offices a Pakistani standing behind him in line and acting as translator that Levnikov was able to get into the country at all.

Applying at several local universities Levnikov found New York too well supplied with doctorates from prestigious European schools, and took the first job he could get, driving a hack. At first he communicated with his passengers using written notes, but after the first couple of weeks working on his spoken fluency hanging out in the company garage at odd hours, he was able to make himself understood. The result of attending this particular language school was not only a very literate English spoken with a deep Bronx accent overlaid with strains of Scots brogue, but also a fluency in three languages of the gutter patios of New York. Now when Zakhar Levnikov hit the roof, one got one's ass thoroughly and eruditely chewed, with no dangling participles.

The morning after the Pulitzer binge Zakhar was standing by the water cooler talking with someone else when Quinn walked by seeing nothing and no one outside his immediate line of vision. He obviously felt as rough as he looked and Levnikov shook his head sadly. "Hey, Quinn!" said the man standing beside Zakhar. He was young and had not been with the paper long. "I hear you won a Pulitzer!"

"Yeah," mumbled Quinn, taking an aspirin box out of his pocket and lurching toward the water cooler. "Big fucking deal."

The young man was shocked. He looked at Quinn like he man had just shat in the holy Grail. "Big fucking deal? Christ, man, what do you want? You should be happy. They don't hand out Pulitzers every day."

"Oh joy, oh rapture," growled Quinn tossing down four aspirin. He nodded to Zakhar. "Morning, Zak."

Despite Levnikov's warning look, the youngster plunged ahead. "What's with you, man? I don't get it. This is an honor."

"Right," said Quinn, looking at the young man through eyes so bloodshot they appeared a mass of red. His skin color was pale, sickly green, and the pupils of his eyes were the size of dots made with a pencil. While he was freshly bathed and shaved, he still carried the faint smell of stale beer and too many cigarettes. "It's a big fucking honor and they give you a impressive fucking certificate. With that certificate and a dime you can go anywhere in the United States and buy a cup of coffee. Except New York. Coffee costs fifty cents there. So what?"

"So what? So every reporter I know would give his eye teeth to be in your shoes right now." The young man was angry now. "Doesn't that mean anything?"

"Yeah," answered Quinn, "you're right, it does. It means there are a lot of fucking stupid people around."

Outraged, the young writer stalked off in a huff and Zakhar chuckled. "Just what you needed for breakfast, Martin," he said. "Fresh raw meat." The way he said Quinn's first name, dragging out the first syllable, sounded like it had a double vowel. "We need to talk, I think."

"Oh, shit," said Quinn. "What did I screw up now?"

"No, no," said Levnikov, reaching in his office and taking down a jacket people around the office swore must have been a gift Zakhar's grandmother gave her husband when they were first married. "You screwed up nothing. At least, no more than usual. No, I think I need to buy you breakfast. Then we talk about this big fucking deal you just won that pisses you off so much."

"Oh, God," murmured Quinn clutching his stomach. The thought of food turned him a shade greener.

"I think we start with a bite of the hare that dogged you," Zakhar said, pulling Quinn into his office and shutting the door. Taking a nearly full bottle of clear liquid and a shot glass from a drawer of his desk, he filled the glass half full and offered it to Quinn. "Drink," he said.

Quinn shook his head. "I've had too much..." he started to protest.

"Drink!" Zakhar commanded, not raising his voice but leaving Quinn no option.

Quinn took the glass with a shaking hand, tossed it down in one gulp. "Jesus!" he gasped, dropping into a chair beside Zakhar's desk and laboring for breath. After a few moments color began coming back into his face. "What was that?" he asked when he could get his voice again.

"It's called Everclear," smiled Levnikov, putting the bottle and shot glass away. "The closest things Americans make to good vodka. One hundred and ninety proof." He laughed. "I use it mostly for paper cuts these days."

"I can see why," Quinn said. "That must be like drinking Sterno."

"Sterno has more taste," Zakhar assured him, taking Quinn by the arm and leading him from the office. "We're taking the rest of the day off," he told his secretary on their way out the door.

"The publisher wants to see Mr. Quinn," the young lady sitting at the desk answered. She was new, too. "And you have an editorial meeting in a half hour."

"We have a case of the twelve hour flu," Levnikov answered. "Tell them that. Mr. Quinn already has it and I'm coming down with it." The secretary started to argue with him but he cut her off with a wave of his hand. "They don't like it, they can fire us both. *Verstehen Sie, liebschen?*" She nodded dumbly. "*Gehen vir!*" he commanded Quinn who popped his heels and snapped a Nazi salute, wincing as the sound of his heels coming together assaulted his ears.

"You're playing fast and loose with my job," Quinn observed as they climbed into Zakhar's battered car. He regretted not being in shape to drive. Riding with Zakhar Levnikov was a sobering, if not terrifying, experience on the best of days. Hung over it was beyond imagination. The man had never driven until his first day as a taxi hack, a fact which lost him his job four months and twelve multiply crinkled fenders later when the owner of the taxi company found out. Nor did Zak consider dented fenders or the age of his vehicle esthetically displeasing.

"They get you more room on the street," he once told Quinn, chuckling. "Those barstards in their fancy cars don't get so pushy when they see my heap." Now he looked at Quinn gravely. "I'm playing fast and loose with your job?" he asked. "Jesus, Mary, and Joseph, Martin. What in the hell do you think you're doing?"

They drove in silence to the restaurant, and in silence they ate their meal. Despite his earlier queasiness, Quinn found himself almost ravenous, demolishing two scrambled eggs, a short stack of pancakes and an order of sausage almost as soon as they were set on the table. For a chaser he downed a large glass of orange juice and sat sipping his coffee and smoking a cigarette. He was beginning to look human again.

"Seems you were hungry," Levnikov observed dryly, barely a third done with his meal. "When did you eat last?"

"I don't know," Quinn admitted. "I can't remember much about the last few days."

"Why am I not surprised?" the older man said.

"Look, Zak," Quinn said, almost pleading. "You're a good friend and I appreciate your helping me sober up, but no lectures, OK?"

"Certainly," Levnikov answered at once. "My experience is that lectures don't work." Quinn nodded and relaxed and the other smiled. "With me, at least, they never did. When I'd paid a high enough price, or, when I'd had enough pain, I did something about it. Until then all the lectures in the world did was to make it harder for me to quit."

"Thanks for understanding," Quinn said.

Zakhar nodded. "You're welcome, although I can't claim much virtue there. I only understand because I did a number of the things I see you doing. I'm really not a very sympathetic soul, Martin."

"You couldn't prove it by me," Quinn said, beginning to get bored with the whole conversation. "Looks like Lombardi is off to another winning season," he added, changing the subject.

"He is, indeed," Levnikov answered. He looked at Quinn gravely. "I'll talk football with you all day if you want, Martin, but I wouldn't be very much of a friend if I saw you stepping off a cliff and didn't at least try to say something."

"I probably can guess what you're going to tell me," Quinn answered.

"You might be surprised," Levnikov replied, taking a deep sip of coffee. He looked at Quinn, waiting.

"So tell me and get it over with," the other almost snapped. He was instantly contrite. "Sorry, Zak. You don't deserve that."

To his surprise the other man chuckled. "I can't ever remember letting that stop me." He shook his head. "No, what I was thinking was something else. I was thinking that winning your Pulitzer may be one of the worst things that could happen to you right now." He nodded, seeing Quinn's look of astonishment. That's right, although I don't know anyone more deserving of winning. As a matter of fact I was the one who submitted your work."

"I guess it would be ungracious of me to point out you did it without letting me at least know, much less get my consent, "Quinn grinned.

"Minor details," Zak shrugged it off. "You can always turn it down."

"No dice," Quinn laughed. "I want to see our illustrious publisher's face when he has to give me a raise. Not that I need the money. The books have done well and my needs are very simple."

Levnikov nodded and continued to eat slowly, savoring every taste as if it might be his last. It was a carryover from the war. Quinn sat thinking. After a while he asked, "Why do you say that?"

"Sorry," Zak admitted. "I was distracted by the honey they serve here. It must be from vetch. Very light taste." He looked up at Quinn as if surprised to see him there. "I seem to have lost the thread. What were we talking about?"

"About the Pulitzer being one of the worst things which could happen to me."

"Ah," Levnikov nodded. "Yes, just this. When I was doing what I see you doing now I was living in hell. Even though I was very successful, none of my success did me much good. It only made things worse when I finally crashed." Quinn was surprised by the look of compassion in Levnikov's eyes. The man held up a thumb and forefinger about an inch apart. "You know, you came this close to getting fired."

"Fired!" Quinn was as indignant as he was flabbergasted. "I'm the best you got."

The other nodded. "You are without question the best writer we have, and the best reporter, too. Despite those facts, our management made a decision last week not to renew your contract when it comes up next month." He looked at Quinn levelly. "I have to say it is a decision with which I agreed."

"You agreed!" Quinn's face flushed. "I thought you were my friend."

"I am your friend, Martin," Levnikov asserted. "Whether you know it or not. Despite my personal feelings for you," he smiled, "or maybe because of them, I hold you in too high regard to do you the disservice of protecting you from the consequences of your personal choices. So after a great deal of soul searching, I concurred with their decision." He gave a hollow laugh. "Now you've won the Pulitzer, it's a whole new ball game. I bet the meeting I'm missing with our illustrious publisher is about reversing that decision, and I have no doubt mine would be the only dissenting vote at the editor's meeting. Not that it would do you any good to fire you now. You would have six better offers by five o'clock."

"What did I do to piss you off?" Quinn wanted to know.

"This isn't about being pissed off, Martin," Levnikov answered. "It's about loving you enough to allow you to stub your toe so you can learn something you need to know. Now, when you hit crash and burn, it's going to be even worse."

"If I crash and burn," Quinn argued. "You're assuming it's a done deal."

Zakhar nodded sadly. "It is, my friend. As sure as the night follows the day. The only question is when and how it will happen. Believe me, I am delighted for you that you won the Pulitzer. It's a grand feeling I remember well. Yet while it's grand for your ego, I think you may find it hell for your soul. It was for mine. I did not possess the humility to truly receive the honor."

"Hell for my soul?" Martin laughed. "When were you ordained?"

"Just before the War," Levnikov replied. "Although that fact is not well known and I don't publish it. I was an Orthodox postulant before I was conscripted Stalin's army and sent to the front. For some reason they ordained me priest just before I was sent." He laughed a grim laugh. "Perhaps they thought I could save a couple of agnostic Russian souls before I was blown to pieces myself."

"You never followed it up after the War?" Quinn wondered.

"No, there was too much blood on my hands to celebrate the Mysteries. Far too many women in my bed, too, or so I thought at the time. I've had second thoughts of late, disturbing second thoughts of doing something totally whimsical." Levnikov laughed. "You are good, very good. That's the sign of a damned good reporter, to get me talking about myself and going after my story."

Quinn shrugged. "You taught me well, Zak. So you're an ex-priest, too?"

"No," Zakhar Levnikov said sadly. "There is no such thing as a former priest, Martin, no matter what the Church may say. Once a priest, always a priest. Something mysterious happens and it is forever." The older man got a far away look in his eye and murmured something softly to himself. "Disturbing second thoughts," he said. "I found myself on the Bishop's steps one day this last week, wondering how many years of penitence he would give me coming back."

He sighed and looked at Quinn sadly. "You're very good, Martin, the very best talent I've known. I hate to see you sacrifice greatness for being the very best."

"I wasn't aware I was doing that." Quinn's attention was no longer wandering.

"I know, my friend," Levnikov murmured, shaking his head sadly. "I know."

"So what do I have to do to be great?" Quinn asked.

"You must first discover the truth, my friend," Levnikov said softly. "You must first find the absolute truth about yourself. I assure you that will be painful. It was for me and it seems to be for everyone. Yet I assure you if you do this, it will set you free. It will set you free to love yourself, and in doing that, to love others without condition and become all you were put into this world to be." The look in the older man's eyes left no doubt in Martin' mind the man believed everything he'd said. "I cannot tell you what that may be," Zakhar continued, pointing his finger like a pistol at Quinn's breast. "Yet I can tell you it will be a marvelous surprise to all concerned, most of all to you." He gave Quinn an enigmatic smile and took another sip of coffee.

Quinn shook his head. "I don't know how I seem to do it," he said, "but I do."

"How you do what, Martin?" Zakhar asked gently.

"How I connect with people like you." Quinn laughed a dry laugh "You know, you're not the only former priest I've come across. My closest friend in New Mexico was a former Jesuit. He sounds a lot like you."

"Then perhaps you should listen," Levnikov laughed back. "Why do you think you're the one making the connection? That's pure arrogance."

"What do you mean?" Quinn demanded.

"Well, there are at least two possibilities I can think of at the moment," Levnikov said, "and I am sure there are more. Neither of the one which come to mind you will like. One is that there is an international conspiracy to connect one Martin Quinn, AKA the famous author, up with former priests. While that is a rather paranoid notion, it may be the more comfortable of the two possibilities. Or the least frightening."

"Oh?" Quinn replied, knowing Levnikov was waiting for him to ask the other. "I think you're right. That is paranoid." He paused, but could not out wait the older man. "So tell me, what's the second?"

"The second is that there is Someone abroad, a spiritual power, who is stalking you like the Hound of Heaven and putting into your life the very people you need to meet to become whomever you really are." Levnikov nodded. "When I first confronted this possibility in my own life, that was when I found things really terrifying."

Quinn thought a moment. "You don't seem very terrified right now."

Levnikov laughed aloud. "I'm not. These days I'm convinced my Pursuer is an unrequited lover who will stop short of almost nothing to have me. Yet it took me a long time to get to this place. When I came to understand what sins I had committed as a priest of the Church, I was terrified." He looked at Quinn intensely. "While I did not believe much of what they taught me about heaven, hell was all around me and I knew it well. It is a common saying among the Orthodox that there are more priests in hell than bankers or lawyers."

"I'll drink to that," Quinn laughed, lifting his coffee cup.

"Indeed," Levnikov answered, saluting him back with his own cup. "I did just that, for many, many years." The look he gave the younger man was strange, haunting.

"What?" asked Martin Quinn.

Zakhar Levnikov shook his head. "No," he said. "It's only a thought, a passing fancy of an old man's imagination."

"Then what harm can it do to tell me?" Quinn wanted to know.

"It could terrify you," came the swift answer. "It's probably nothing but my fertile imagination. I must be getting senile, losing the thread of conversations, having wild flights of pure fancy." He tried to shrug it off. "The gears must be getting rusty in the belfry," he said, pointing to his head.

"Your mind's about as rusty as a well oiled bear trap," Quinn said. "What is it?"

Levnikov raised his hands in supplication to the heavens. Then, seeming to get no answer, he looked at Quinn so directly the younger man felt as if Zakhar were assaying the contents of his soul. "My thought was simply this," he said, as if assured by what he saw there. "It was that quite often it takes one to know one. I always thought you would win a

Pulitzer, and you did." He shrugged. "Now you know."

"What's so terrifying about...." Martin began and stopped in mid sentence as the full implications of what Zakhar had said settled in his mind. "Oh, Jesus!" he exclaimed. "No. You're dead wrong. Not me."

"So you have thought about it," Levnikov nodded. "You find it as terrifying as it was to me."

Quinn didn't answer. He seemed to be having trouble breathing. A waiter, seeing his distress, rushed to the table quickly. "Is he choking?" he demanded of Levnikov, not waiting for an answer before starting to position Quinn for a Heimlich squeeze. As the waiter moved him, Quinn caught his breath, taking in deep gulps of air, as if he'd been underwater for several minutes.

"No, he's not choking," Zakhar assured the waiter, patting him on the arm. "He's just had something of a shock, I'm afraid. I believe the Hound of Heaven just nipped him on the butt." The waiter looked around, confused. There was no dog in sight. Levnikov smiled and shook his head. "Forgive me. An old man's hyperbole. Why don't you bring us the desert menu?"

Reassured by having something familiar to do, the waiter scuttled away toward the kitchen, giving them an odd look as he went. "Woof! Woof!" grunted Quinn, and the man almost broke into a run. Levnikov cackled.

An hour later they were seated in the park watching nurses and young matrons pushing prams, catching the unseasonable warmth of the sunshine. "So I wasn't the first to suggest it," Levnikov asked.

"No, Zak," Quinn admitted. "I remember one conversation with Ramos but I told him he was as full of shit as a Christmas turkey. He never brought it up again."

"I can imagine," Zakhar chuckled. "I haven't heard that expression in years." He thought for a minute or two, then looked at Quinn. "I'm going to take a chance," he said. "There are some people I want you to meet."

"Who?" asked Quinn. "Some monks?"

Levnikov laughed. "No, quite the contrary. They're drunks, not monks."

"Drunks?" Quinn was doubtful. "Geez, Zak, I just came off a royal bender. Give me a little time to recuperate."

"Well, not really drunks, either," Zakhar told him. "Alcoholics."

"What's the difference?"

Levnikov chuckled. "Well, as one of my alcoholic buddies put it, drunks don't have to go to all those friggin' meetings."

"Meetings? Oh, you mean AA?" Quinn was offended. The other nodded and Quinn continued. "Come on, Zak, the last thing I need now is a lecture on the demon rum. You know me better than that."

"You have a dollar on you?" Zahkar asked. Quinn nodded and when the other held out his hand, took out his billfold and handed him one. Zakhar laid it carefully on the bench between them. Taking out his own wallet, he laid a hundred dollar bill beside it. "You're a betting man," he said, not in question, but as a statement of fact. Quinn nodded and Zakhar continued. "I'm giving you an assignment and I'm making you a bet. The odds I'm giving are a hundred to one. You hold the money."

"All right," said Quinn, picking up the money and glancing around uneasily. This part of the city wasn't bad but one could get one's throat cut just about anywhere flashing that much money. "At a hundred to one I'll bet on almost anything. What's the bet?"

"This is your assignment, and it's a tough one because you're going to have to do it at the same time you're doing other assignments. I want an in-depth piece on AA here in the city and I want it done from an investigative approach."

"Come on, Zak, that's a kid's assignment." Quinn was indignant. "That's been done eighty-seven times already."

"You think so?" said Levnikov, taking another hundred dollar bill and laying on the bench. "Let's make another bet. If you can still honestly say that after doing the full assignment, that's yours, too. Same odds." Quinn could see the man was not kidding.

"All right," he growled, "but I won't pull any punches. Any sacred cows are fair game," he demanded.

"Done!" said Zakhar. "But you've got to do the assignment the way I outline it."

"Now wait a minute, Zak..." Quinn tried to protest, but Zakhar cut him off.

"Martin, do you really think I'd do anything to hurt you?" he asked, sadly. The other shook his head. "Good," Levnikov said. "I would never endanger our friendship doing something like that. The reason I insist on outlining the approach is strictly slant. I want you to look at AA as someone coming in for the first time. Have you ever been to an AA meeting?"

"No," said Quinn. He grinned sheepishly. "It's been suggested more than once, but I've never been."

"Good!" said Zakhar. "This needs to be approached with no preconceptions. What I want you to do for the next three months is to evaluate the program. I want you to go to at least five meetings a week and to make a total of ninety meetings during that first three-month period. AA calls it doing the ninety and ninety and I want you to go at it whole hog. Sometimes the meetings are a pain in the butt but I want you to hang in there. Most of all, I want you to connect with newcomers and to follow up with them. The question is what makes the program work for those who succeed and why it doesn't work for those who don't. I want you to follow the program as they suggest you follow it, regardless of your personal feelings."

"You mean you want me to stop drinking for the next three months?" Quinn was suspicious. " Zak, is this an attempt to get me off the sauce?"

"No, you don't have to stop drinking," Levnikov answered, his gaze level. "Unless you want to do so to further the assignment. I don't know if that would matter or not. I suspect not." He shook his head. "I also suspect you may see something you've never seen, but I don't want to compromise your objectivity. When you're done we'll talk about it and compare notes. I want an objective outsider's view."

"Why haven't you done the story before? Why not do it yourself?" Quinn was truly puzzled. Haven't you gone to meetings and met some of the people?"

"Yes, I have, but I'm not objective," said Zakhar. Reaching in his pocket he pulled out a small brass medallion, about the size of a Kennedy half-dollar, and handed it to the younger man, giving him a strange smile.

Quinn looked at the medallion. It was marked with a raised equilateral triangle inside a circle formed by the whole disk. Between the triangle and the edge of the medal was the legend, "To thine own self be true." Along each side of the triangle appeared a single word. One was "unity". Another was "service" and the third was "recovery". In each corner of the triangle there was a single letter, spelling "HOW" and on a raised circle within the triangle was a single Roman numeral, "X". Quinn turned the medallion over and on the back was a simple prayer that began, "God grant me the serenity to accept..." In the center of the back was a circle with the legend "HOW" stamped again.

"What's this?" Quinn asked.

"People in the fellowship call it a chip." Zakhar explained. "The 'X' is for ten years of continuous sobriety."

Quinn looked at Levnikov, astonished at what he'd heard. "I had no idea, Zak. I know you had a drinking problem when we first met, but it seemed to resolve itself."

"About ten years ago, but you're wrong. It was resolved, at least for today, but not by me." The older man smiled as Quinn started to pursue his inquiry but held up a hand. "I don't want to be your first source on the story, Martin," he said gently. "I think it would be better, more objective, if you dug it out on your own. However, I'll promise you this. I will tell you what I have to say after you write the story. And if I tell you anything you haven't heard, I'll give you plenty of time to rewrite."

"Plenty of time?" Quinn asked dryly. "What's plenty of time, Zak."

"For you, a couple of hours," laughed Levnikov. "Three at most. More than that and you'll overdo it, but I don't think you'll have to rewrite. Or even want to. What you'll have will be your story, not mine."

"Care to place another bet at the same odds?" Quinn asked casually.

"Sorry," said Zakhar, laughing. "I'm fresh out of hundreds."

"Good," Quinn answered, laughing as he showed the other his empty wallet. "I don't think I could cover it, anyway."

"You're holding two hundred of mine," Zakhar pointed out.

Quinn looked at the older man as if Zak had just peed in the pool. "Zach, that's different," he said. "That's bet money I'm holding! That's sacred."

8. A Gathering Of Men

Messiah - *from the Hebrew* mashaia *and the Aramaic* meshiha, *the terms means "anointed". One of the earliest usages was applied to Cyrus of Persia who was seen by the author of Isaiah as the one YHWH had chosen to deliver the children of Israel from bondage. Note that anointing was done frequently in the Old Testament whenever a king was crowned, beginning with Saul, who was anointed by Samuel.*

The term is applied to the person of King David, and after the Exile, the Jewish messiah was considered to be another David sent to restore Israel to its God-ordained primacy among all the nations. By the time of Jesus of Nazareth, whom disciples claim is the Messiah, popular belief was looking for the Palestinian equivalent to the modern day Che Gueverra, a revolutionary hero who would cast off the bonds of Roman rule. According to Christian belief, Jesus of Nazareth came with the message that the true messiah was to be something much different. "He who would be greatest in the Kingdom of Heaven must be the slave of all," he taught his disciples, turning the normal order of things upside down and insisting the real power behind the universe is the power of love, not fear. I have to admit, the man practiced exactly what he preached. Yet, as so many messengers to those who do not wish to hear, he was killed for his kindness.

Was Jesus the Messiah? I wish I knew. I wish I could believe he was. We so desperately need someone who can set things straight among us. Yet I cannot make the leap of faith seemingly required of believers, even seeing the effect such faith has in the lives others. I find myself in the position of Hillel, the liberal rabbi of the time. I wait and see. Yet it does appear true that after the time of John the Baptist and the crucifixion of Jesus, no real prophet has appeared to Israel. (from Martin Quinn's writing notes)

October 1982. Their first acquaintance was awkward, the way it often is when strangers are thrown together. It was the tall black man who detached himself from the crowd talking around the base of the large oak and made his way across the clearing to where Martin Quinn was standing by the central fire. Pouring himself a cup full from the coffee pot simmering there in the coals, he nodded to Quinn. "Nice drum," he said, his eyes falling to the primitive instrument standing by Martin' feet.

"Thank you," Martin replied, smiling. For some reason he felt shy, almost self conscious. "It turned out pretty well, didn't it?" he added lamely. The drum by his feet was about fifteen inches tall, perhaps an two or three inches less across the head, and was made of heavy rawhide stretched across a redwood frame. The sides of the barrel were mitered, between two and three inches wide and fit tightly together, with two strips of turquoise leather covering the bindings which held them together top and bottom. The outer surface was finished to a soft, satin sheen, and what looked like an oak peg stuck out at right angles from the bottom of each side slat to secure the head. The rawhide head was pulled tightly across the top of the wooden frame, being stretched there while still wet and was held in place by a narrow strip of raw hide making zigzags up and down between the head and the oaken pegs holding it in place.

The result was a primitive drum of great beauty, as much a work of art as a musical instrument. When it was played, the voice of the drum was deep and mellow with a surprising resonance, almost like that of a large brass bell which continues to ring long after it is struck. Yet it was the bold designs painted on barrel and on the head of the drum which captured attention. For painted in black and outlined in gold, the huge track of a raven spread itself across half the width of the head, and around the outer circumference a line of canine tracks circled the raven's print. These, too, were in black, except that every fourth track, outlined in gold, was of a different color, alternating among white and yellow and red and a deep charcoal grey which was almost indistinguishable from the black prints.

"Did you make it yourself?" the tall black man asked.

Martin was pleased by the other man's admiration. "Yes, I did," he said. "The flyer for this thing said we were supposed to bring a percussion instrument, so I made one." He shrugged. "It never occurred to me it could be something as simple as a couple of sticks."

The other man laughed and nodded. "I know what you mean. I'm one of those who seems to make things more complicated than they need to be. Where did you come up with the design? I haven't seen one made like that before. Most of the frame drums I've seen run the other way." He made a large circle with his coffee cup.

Martin shrugged and smiled. "I kind of made it up as I went along," he answered. "I got the basic idea from pueblo drums and a redwood planter I saw in a garden shop. That was the only thing I could find strong enough to hold the hide when I stretched it, and I didn't want to go to the trouble of trying to find a cottonwood to hollow out. The biggest problem I had was finding a planter with straight sides. When I did, I took it apart and glued the sides together so they're a solid unit. I think that's what makes it sound the way it does." He picked up the drum and stroked the head lightly.

The black man nodded. "You must have put a lot of yourself into it, too. What's the significance of the design on the head?"

"It's a personal totem," Martin told him. For some reason, he felt a bit reluctant to talk about it. "I've had it a long time. I used twelve sides to represent the months and the different colored tracks represent the seasons and the colors of the medicine wheel." He pointed to the design painted on the barrel. Running around the barrel was a series of green triangles tipped in white with two dark blue triangles pointing down from the base of each green one. "That's decorative, mostly. It was a design I saw at San Juan and I think the green is for the sacred mountains and the blue, for the Rio Grande."

The other nodded thoughtfully, looking at the design on the head. "I thought so. So you're wolf and crow. That's powerful medicine taking each separately, but together it's really something."

"Wolf and raven," Martin corrected automatically. "The wolf is the black wolf." He smiled, thinking to himself, humping wolf, but said nothing more to Dill.

The tall man whistled softly. "Wolf and raven, too. That's potent stuff you've been given. I take it you're aware of the significance?"

Martin nodded, almost embarrassed. "I know what I've been told, and at different times in my life one or the other has appeared, totally unexpected. Once it was both." At the other's look of surprise, something shifted within him and Martin felt his reserve melting quickly. The man was a good listener and Martin found himself telling the story of the raven and the wolf, and of the old man singing with the flute by the grave.

When he was done he felt a bit self conscious, but the other's response put Martin at ease. "So you've been there," he said, nodding. "A full tribal initiation. Those are nice to have, but they are better to have behind you." He nodded at the question in Quinn's eyes. "That's how I came by that shield and spear over by the tree." He grinned. "My totem is the lion, the red lion. I'm eternally thankful I only had to meet that sucker once. I'm up to tell the story tonight at the fire and I think you'll see the parallels."

Quinn looked at the man, impressed. "I'm familiar with that tradition," he replied. "I take it you got it in Africa?"

"The hard way," the other laughed. "The ancient way. It scared me so bad I shit my pants. Or, rather, my loincloth. Nobody wears pants there. But nobody thought less of me for it. I got brother lion before he got me and that's what counts. That's his blood on the shield and I wear his mane when I dance." He shook his head. "I've been in a lot of tight spots, but that was the scariest."

"A hundred and eighty or ninety pound man against an eight hundred pound lion?" Quinn said. "I can see how it might be. Sounds like we both came pretty close to dying."

"Yeah," the other nodded. "But here we are, Raven Wolf and old Shit-In-His-Pants-But-Got-His-Lion. That's what the name they gave me means and I'm proud of it. By the way, my common name's Dill," the man told him, extending a hand. "Willie Dill."

"Quinn," Martin responded, taking the offered hand. "Martin Quinn. I don't think I've ever met anyone named Dill before. I know of the poet, of course, W.J. Dylle. I don't suppose you're any kin to him, are you?"

Dill nodded. "Guilty as charged," he laughed, showing a wide expanse of large white teeth. "I spell it differently, but that's me."

"No kidding? You write good stuff," Martin told him. "I have two books of your poems, and a book of your essays."

"Music to a writer's ears," Dill replied. "People who buy his books. You're not so bad yourself," he added. "I believe you're a writer, too, if I'm not mistaken. A Pulitzer prize and two major novels?"

"I am a writer," Martin told him. "I was a journalist, but most of the time I'm a novelist now. I've been lucky. My books have done pretty well and I don't have to do much else these days."

"The way you write is not a matter of luck," Dill observed. Yet at that moment the ringing of a large steel triangle interrupted whatever else he may have added. "Damn, that thing's loud," he complained.

Quinn nodded. "Charley really gets into his work," he agreed. "I guess it must be time for lunch."

Dill nodded. "I'm glad he's as enthusiastic about his cooking. If you like biscuits, you've come to Mecca."

During their meal Quinn and Dill continued to visit, discovering in the process a surprising number of common friends. "Yeah," Dill said. "I know Clarence Powers. I grew up in the Midwest, but we went to the same college and hung around together quite a bit. I was in psychology and he majored in sociology, but we took a lot of the same classes and used to study together. I guess it's been fifteen or twenty years now since I've seen him. How is he?"

Quinn told Dill about his stay with the Powers family in the South and of his coming across the sculpture of Aunt Ruth Matthews, of how it moved him with it's simple grace and how he and his photographer blackballed their boss into letting them cover it. "I remember the article," Dill told him. "You did a good job and the photographs were superb."

"Rosalind is very good," Quinn acknowledged. "She has a feel for her subjects and she and Aunt Ruth really connected. By that time we'd worked together for almost five years and she knew what worked well with my style of writing."

"Was?" Dill asked. "Is she dead?"

"No," Quinn laughed. "She married our boss, Othello McLeod, after his divorce. It really pissed me off, too," he added, laughing. "I must have asked her to marry me a dozen times and she always turned me down."

"McLeod?" Dill asked. "What is he, a Scotsman?"

"He's darker than you are, Willie," Quinn replied, "and better looking than Harry Belafonte. But he can't sing worth a damn."

Dill frowned. "Interracial marriages are tough," he said. "My own is no exception. Your friend chose a tough row to hoe."

"No," Quinn told him, "other than putting up with Othello, but she has that down pat. Rosalind is black, too."

"Ah," said Dill. "So she chose not to marry a white men."

"I've often wondered how much that had to do with it," Quinn replied, nodding. "However, I was drinking pretty heavily and doing some pretty self destructive things at the time. I honestly believe that's what happened and I can't say I blame her. I drank myself out of a lot of things those days."

"You in recovery now?" Dill asked.

Quinn nodded, reaching in his pocket and pulling out a brass token about the size of a half dollar and showing it to Dill. It was almost exactly like the one Zakhar showed him almost four years before. On one side there was a triangle stamped in relief and enclosed by a circle made by the outer rim of the medallion. Just inside the rim was the quotation from the Bard, "To Thine Own Self Be True," and long each leg of the triangle the words "Unity," "Recovery," and "Service" appeared. The only difference, other than wear, was the Roman numeral encircled in the very center.

"I have nearly three years' sobriety now," Quinn said, "by the grace of God and with a little bit of help from a lot of good friends in the Fellowship."

Dill nodded. "You'll find a lot of good men in recovery here this weekend," he said. "As a matter of fact, one of my closest friends is in AA, too." Then he changed the subject and Quinn was left wondering who this friend was. His news instincts told him Dill was keeping something back. *On the other hand*, he thought, maybe *Dill is just respecting his friend's anonymity.*

"Tell me about Clarence," Dill was asking. "We were close but we took different paths and lost touch. How are things with him now?"

"I haven't seen him in years, although we talk on the phone from time to time," Quinn said. "He's still a pastor, but I from what he says, I get the idea he may be burning out or looking for something else. You did know about that, didn't you, his being a preacher?"

"Yeah," Dill chuckled. "There's some irony there. He became a pastor and I became a soldier, and we both ended up warriors, spiritual warriors. So as it turns out, our different roads have lead us into the same realm and onto the same field of battle."

"All roads lead home," Martin misquoted. "I never thought about preaching that way, as being on a field of battle, but it fits." He laughed. I asked Clarence once how things were going and he told me he was doing battle with the Christians. I've heard a lot of other preachers talk about doing battle with the Devil, but most of those seem to be zealots with more mouth than brains, and I've thought what they were doing was intended more to entertain than inspire." He shrugged. "That may sound cynical, but that's how it came across to me."

Dill laughed and nodded. "That sounds like Clarence. He told me once he was a lion God threw to the Christians. I think what you've said about some of the others is on target. A lot of the preachers I've known want to be activists at heart, but most of them seem more willing to talk than do something. There are some exceptions, but that's how it seems. Good brother Clarence is cut from different cloth."

Quinn nodded. "Yeah, he is. From what I've seen, most preachers seem to think they need to be Mr. Nice and make everyone feel good, and they seem to have about as much backbone as a wet noodle. Not Clarence, but most of them. Clarence puts it on the line all the time and sometimes I wonder how he gets away with it. So far he has, but it wouldn't surprise me to hear he'd been shot, either."

"I know," Dill answered. "Me, either. But going back to what you were saying about pastors, from what I've seen, very few soldiers are true warriors, either. They train us to be pretty efficient killing machines, and a lot of men never get beyond that. They either avoid what they've been trained to do by going into supply or staff work, or they succumb to it and become ruthless destroyers. Very few become true warriors."

"So what's a true warrior?" Quinn asked. "For you?"

Dill laughed. "You're good, Martin. That's what this weekend's about, finding the warrior within ourselves. But I think you'll find what we do is raise more questions than give answers. At least, that's how it's supposed to be."

"I know that's the drill," Quinn replied. "But you have your own answer and I'd like to know what it is." He shrugged. "Off the record. Strictly for my information."

Again Dill laughed. "You can put it in the record, if you want. I don't think many people would understand." He thought a moment. "There is a short answer and a long answer to your question. The short answer is this: a true warrior is a man or woman who has come to understand that the only real adversary worthy of one's attention is oneself, and that the fight to come to terms with oneself takes place in the realm of the human heart and the human spirit. To put it in a nutshell, it's the struggle between love and fear."

"That's interesting," Quinn replied. "That's what they teach us in the Program. Most people I know would say it was between love and hatred."

"Hatred is not the opposite of love," Dill said softly, as if reminding himself yet again of something he wanted never to forget. "The real opposite of love is fear, but that's hard to understand."

"It sure is," Quinn replied. "It was for me. The old man who's my spiritual father told me that exact thing many years ago but I've only recently come to understand even a little of what he was telling me."

"Ain't that the truth!" Dill declared. "It was my dad who first taught me that, but like any young stud, I was way too full of piss and vinegar to listen to an old fart like him."

At that point their conversation was interrupted by someone arriving at their table who needed to talk to Dill about the coming weekend. "I'll catch you later," Quinn said as he cleared away their dishes. "I want to wander around a little while I have the chance." Dill nodded and turned his attention to the newcomer, and Martin went to his tent. There he retrieved his flute before wandering into the woods to find a quiet place to play.

Walking away from the camp, Martin noticed a barely visible deer trail leading off from the path he was following. Following it he found it turned uphill for a short way before it turned again between two large trees and was lost to view of the main trail. Going on, Martin found the trail led further and farther from camp and deep into the depths of a dense thicket of scrub pine and brush, and within only a few minutes it felt as if he were walking where no one else had gone before.

After traveling what seemed like a long distance winding through the thicket, but which was probably a half to three quarters of a mile, the trail came out at a clearing about thirty yards across at its widest, and almost too perfectly groomed to be natural. Looking across the clearing, he saw the trail end beside a stone face from which a stream of clear water fell a dozen feet into a crystal pool. From the lower end of the pool he could see another trail leading away from the clearing and into an even deeper thicket down stream. After a few yards the stream turned and the trail following it vanished.

Martin seated himself on one of several rocks which seemed to be placed there for a purpose and took out his wooden flute. After a moment of silence he began to play. The early afternoon sun was warm on his face and chest, and as he played, Martin tried to follow the song of the stream, playing in counterpart to its melody.

At first, his fingers seemed clumsy and Martin had trouble anticipating the changes in the water's song. Then, shutting out all conscious thought, he began to let the flute call his fingers to their dance over the pipe, drifting with the mood of the stream in the bright afternoon. After a while the connection took place. He found the groove and the sound of his flute intertwined with that of the stream, becoming one voice.

Later, Martin would have no idea how long he played this way. It may have been a few minutes or it might have been an hour, but at some point he heard the sound of the stream become like that of another flute playing in counterpart to his lead. Surprised and delighted, he let his mind touch the memory of the Canyon, of the night he first called the black wolf. His soul responded, claiming back his fingers and he found himself playing the song of the old man singing by the grave.

Suddenly he realized there was another voice, another flute singing with him and the falling water and the old man. Without stopping he opened his eyes, saw Willie Dill seated on another rock nearby, his eyes closed and playing flute much like his. Smiling, Martin shut his eyes again, continued to play as the song led them into flight with the condor, with the eagle, with the raven flying into the Great Unknown which lies at the center of all things and from which all things come, until a long while later, their song finally ended and they sat in silence.

"I hope you didn't mind," Dill said quietly at last. "I was headed here to play myself when I heard your song. I started to leave but it was just too beautiful, so I sat down to listen." He shook his head in wonder, looking down at his own instrument. "I don't even remember starting to play."

Martin smiled. "You know, I don't, right now, either. I'm glad you stayed. That was incredible." He nodded, looking around the clearing. "This whole place is an incredible...." Then he stopped, shocked into silence as his eyes widened in surprise, staring at the far end of the clearing.

Seeing his look, Dill turned his head slowly to follow Martin' gaze, his own eyes widening as he saw what Martin was staring at. "Be very still," he whispered to Quinn with quiet urgency and without moving his head. "Don't move or smile or grin. I think he's just curious."

I hope so, Martin thought, hoping the huge beast at the other end of the clearing could not read his thoughts or smell his fear. Then he stared at the other man in disbelief as Dill raised his flute slowly and began to play quietly for the huge cat which sat watching them from the edge of the woods.

Am I going crazy? Quinn wondered as he sat looking at the puma. *Am I really seeing this?* Yet, real or imagined, he knew for certain if he tried to run or leave the clearing the mountain lion would be after him in a flash. Then, not knowing exactly why, he raised his own flute and began to play with Dill.

Suddenly the puma yawned, showing a vast expanse of deadly white teeth, and stretched. A hoarse croak from above drew their eyes to the sky, where a large bird circled the clearing, its black feathers bright, almost iridescent in the sun. Looking down, Quinn saw the puma was gone, and looking up again, he discovered the raven had disappeared, too. The only other creature in the clearing was his companion, sitting open mouthed and staring in surprise. "Jesus!" Quinn whispered reverently.

"Mary and Joseph, too," Dill whispered back. "Did you see what I just saw? Or were we hallucinating?"

"Hallucinations don't do that," Quinn observed, pointing at a splattered bird dropping on one of the other rocks.

Touching the splatter Dill found it smeared. "It's still fresh," he said, washing his hand in the pool. "Was it there when we came?"

"I don't think so," Quinn responded. "But I can't be for sure. I looked at the rocks before I sat down and I think I would have seen it." Shaking his head, he got up and walked to where the puma had sat at the other side of the clearing. The grass is mashed down," he said, "but I can't see any tracks."

A deep chuckle rose from the throat of the other man, growing into a belly laugh. Someone seems to be up to his usual tricks," he said. "And full of ambiguity. Now you see it, now you don't."

"What are you telling me, Willie?" Martin asked, curious, but irked at the other man's calm humor. His own heart was still pounding.

Dill nodded and chose his words carefully. "Oh, every once in a while the Universe seems to give us a glimpse of a whole different reality," he said. "When it happens it's more real than anything we've ever experienced, but then it's gone almost as soon as it comes, and we're left wondering what we saw and if it was real. You know, the little man who really wasn't there."

"You said someone was tricking us," Quinn persisted, shaking his head. "What did you mean by that?"

Dill nodded. "I was talking to myself, but that's how I choose to think about it," he said. "Call it the Prime Mover or the Universe, or call it God or Yahweh or Allah or anything else. It really doesn't matter except maybe to us because what we're talking about is something none of us can comprehend very well at all. My experience is that this Something Out There is driven by a desire to create, and by a sense of humor that includes deep appreciation for the absurd." He looked at his companion. "I'm not trying to get you to go to my church, Martin, but when two flute players call up a panther and a raven, as one of them has done before, and when the animals called up just happen to be the medicine totems for each of the players, I don't think we can call it coincidence. So the question is why the gift was given and how we respond to the giver."

Quinn opened his mouth to answer, then stopped as he stared at the large black canine which stood watching them from the path he'd followed to the clearing. Seeing the beast, Dill laughed. "No, Martin, that ain't no black wolf. That's one of the rancher's dogs. Here boy!" he called and the dog trotted over to them. Sniffing Quinn cautiously as he passed, he jumped up and licked Dill's face. "He took to me right away," Dill told him. "That's strange because I usually don't much like dogs. Buddy's something else."

Reaching in his pocket Dill took something out and commanded the dog to sit, which it did immediately. When Dill tossed him what looked like a piece of bread. Buddy likes the biscuits," he said. "I think it's because cookie makes them with bacon drippings."

Taking his seat on the rock again, Dill continued to pet the dog. "Well, our weekend has started with a bang," he laughed. "Usually it takes a day or two for things to really start happening."

"With openers like this, I don't know if I can handle the game," Martin answered, resuming his seat on the other rock. Buddy, having gotten all the attention he could from Dill, came over and forced his nose under Quinn's hand, tossing his head so it moved down his neck. Martin obliged and began petting him. "Found another soft touch, didn't you, boy?" he said gently.

"Ever been on a men's retreat before?" Dill asked after a moment.

"Not this kind," Martin replied. "I've been on the usual camping trips with scouts and stuff like that, but nothing like this." He shrugged. "I came because my editor is interested in these gatherings of men. I think he wanted to come himself but he wasn't sure what a 'wildman weekend' was, so he sent me, instead." He grinned. "He'll never come if I tell him how mine began."

"You were curious enough to try it," Dill smiled. "Or maybe right now you may be thinking, 'dumb enough,' instead. I assure you, what we've just been through is wilder than most of them get. You feeling nervous?"

Quinn nodded. "Yeah, I was, but not now. Still, that's reassuring to hear." He thought. "I guess it was mostly because I didn't know anyone here yet. I tend to be a loner, anyway."

Dill nodded. "You were smart to come on out early, then. Working with the other guys helping set up does help. And there are no surprises, either. We tell you up front what we're going to do."

"No surprises, huh?" Martin quipped. "After what just happened I'd like to know what you might call a surprise."

"That's not what I meant," Dill laughed. "Surprises always happen on these things, but not because we planned it that way." He nodded. You could help us out a bit, too, Martin. Half the guys have never been to one of these things, either, and you could help showing them around and helping them feel welcome." He nodded at the clearing. "This is a very special place and we normally don't bring people down here right away. When we come here it's usually alone or in small groups. We call it the Quiet Place and it's reserved for meditation during the weekend."

"So I need to find another place to play?" Martin asked.

Dill nodded. "I'll show you a couple of places I found the time I was up here before. One of them is a little hard to get to, but it has a magnificent view. I'll take you up there during free time tomorrow." He was thoughtful for a moment, then looked at Martin and asked. "Were you going to write this up as a story?"

Martin nodded. "That was the plan. Does that create a problem?"

Dill shook his head. "No, as long as people understand that's what you are doing, and as long as you respect their privacy. I think we need to let them know you're here and what you're doing up front."

"Sure," said Quinn. "What's your concern."

"Many of the men who come here for the first time open up in ways they haven't ever done before," Dill answered. "We create a place where it is safe for them to do so, and when they do, they find it a very liberating thing."

Martin nodded. "Then it's not that different from AA. I tell you what. I won't quote anyone or publish their pictures without written consent. Why don't you tell them that when we start tonight?"

"How about if you tell them yourself?" Dill asked. "I think that would be much better."

Quinn nodded. "You're probably right." He glanced at his watch. "Do you have something you have to do, or can we talk for a while? I'd like to know more about you. Do you mind?"

Dill thought a long moment. "Martin," he said, finally, his features drawn with concern. "I need to tell you something about myself you need to forget immediately. All right?" Quinn nodded, and Dill went on. "I'm in sensitive work now," he said. "So I have to be very careful. As Willie Dill, I'm off limits. There can't be any photos." He grinned. "That's why I'm the only one who can take pictures, and only then at certain times."

"Are you in government work?" Quinn asked automatically.

Dill shook his head. "Martin, I can't even answer that," he told him. "I can tell you only what I've already said. Your not respecting it could get some good people killed, not least of whom is me."

"We're only as sick as our secrets, Willie," Martin answered.

Dill nodded. "Yes, but this is not just my secret, and it's not a personal secret. The anonymity is to protect others, including my family. Your ninth step covers what I'm talking about. Unless you agree, I'll have to leave."

"You're really serious about this, aren't you?" Quinn observed.

Dill nodded. "I have to be. Too many good people's lives are on the line if I don't." He thought a moment. "You can report anything I say here, Martin, but not my name or anything that can identify me, like race or what I do for a living. Fair enough?"

"Fair enough," Martin responded. "Since you know Clarence Powers I need to ask you something completely off the record."

"You're free to ask," Dill pointed out. "However, I may not be able to give you an answer. All right?"

Martin nodded agreement. "One of the stories we were digging into about six or eight years ago was domestic surveillance of leaders in the civil rights movement by the CIA. I was getting pretty close to a good story when Othello called us off. There were some loose ends I've always wondered about. Is there anything you can tell me about that? Not for publication but just for my own curiosity."

Dill shook his head. "I didn't have anything to do with that, Martin. I was busy in Southeast Asia at the time. Doing military service," he added. "You probably know more about it than I do, and personal curiosity outside of professional activity is not something my boss would encourage. At least, not in terms of discussing it with a journalist." He looked at Quinn. "I'm surprised no one ever approached you," he said. "A journalist is a natural for intelligence work. They're supposed to snoop around and ask questions."

"They didn't," Quinn told him. "At least, not that I was aware of it. I was pretty anti-establishment in those days and pretty vocal about it."

"All the better," Dill laughed. "Who would ever suspect a radical gadfly?"

Martin looked at Quinn thoughtfully. "Are you trying to recruit me, Willie?" he asked, his voice very quiet.

Dill chuckled. "No, but my boss might. He likes drunks, especially those in recovery." He paused. "Are you asking for an interview?"

"No, although I'd like to talk to him," Quinn laughed. "I'm sure he's got some stories I could tell."

"Well, don't be surprised then if someone comes to talk to you. Or if no one does. I'll let him know, but that will be the end of it for me." Dill's expression told Martin the subject was definitely closed.

"Your boss must be a recovered alcoholic himself," Quinn guessed. Dill said nothing, but a flitting look of surprise in his eyes gave Quinn his answer and he shrugged. "Who else would like drunks, Willie?" he asked. "Drunks are crazy, obnoxious people."

"When they're drunk, yes," Dill said. "Those in recovery are some of the sanest people I know."

The two men continued talking for a long while and gradually a picture of Willie Dill came together in Quinn's mind. A black orphan, he was raised by a white family in the Midwest and given the name William James to honor both his grandfathers. Only later did it occur to his parents they had given him a curious burden to carry through life with the name of an American philosopher, but by then it was too late. "Fortunately, most of my school mates had no idea who William James was," Dill told Martin. "Or I'd have had be faster with my hands than I was. Things were bad enough being the only black kid in an all white school, but that's the way the town was. There were no black families there, and I guess I must have been four or five before I saw my first black adult. It scared me," he admitted sheepishly.

"That's also how I got drafted," he said a few minutes later.

"You mean being black?" Quinn asked.

"To be honest, I'm really not sure," Dill answered. "I thought so for a long time, but now I think it was just envy." He sighed. "Being black only aggravated the situation. The bitch who was the clerk at my Draft Board hated my guts. I don't think she liked anybody much, but I had the gall to beat her son out as valedictorian and captain of our football team. I think if it had been just the football team she would have been all right, but it was both, and when my student deferment ran out, I got my notice."

"That's interesting," Martin told him. "Just watching you I would have pegged you for a lifer. You have a very military bearing."

Dill laughed. "You'd be right there, too. After I got over being pissed off I decided I liked the military. For one thing, back then it was the only really integrated institution in the country. I found I had an aptitude."

"Better an aptitude than an attitude," Martin observed.

Willie Dill laughed and nodded. "You took the words right out of my mouth."

"Actually, out of one of your essays, I think," Martin corrected him and the other nodded. "So you ended up a career soldier? An odd choice for a valedictorian."

"Not really," Dill told him. "At least, not for me. Like football, it was a socially sanctioned way to deal with the anger I felt and it worked, at least for a while. It was anger that helped me survive and to become the very best, so it worked for me and made me very successful."

"For a while," Quinn reminded him.

Dill nodded. "That's when I really started writing. Black rage, poured out on white paper." He shrugged. "At least it kept me from killing people I wasn't supposed to. Or didn't need to," he added, after a moment, his eyes bleak. "For a while I could have gone either way, I think, but something pulled me back from the brink."

"Something or someone?" Martin asked quietly.

"Man, you're good, baby," Dill told him. "You're sharp. It was both I guess, because it was my father's love that did it."

"You mean God?" Quinn asked.

"No, actually, I mean James Dill, the man who raised me," Willie told him. "We had our cross moments but there was never any doubt in my mind the man loved me, even when he was so pissed off he could have wrung my neck. That's what I'm talking about." Then he chuckled. "Of course, my father had his faults like all of us, but when it came to Sunday School, I had no problem believing in a loving Father-God. Maybe that was where he learned it. He was always a deeply devout man."

"Who passed it on to you," Quinn nodded sadly. "You don't know how lucky you were, Willie. I'd give everything I've ever accomplished just to have had a dad like that. Sorry," he said as tears came to his eyes.

"You never have to apologize for your tears, Martin," Dill said gently. "Not ever. They weren't something you gave yourself."

Despite his grief, Quinn laughed through his tears. "No, at least not at first, but later on I did a good job of that, too."

"We all do, man," Dill told him. "We all do."

Later Martin would look back on the time he spent with Willie Dill as the best he'd spent with another man since he'd left the Canyon. While nothing could replace the warm companionship of the old man, ever, between Dill and himself there was a bonding which sometimes happens when two strangers meet and connect as if they have been friends for years upon years. With Willie Dill Martin experienced an easy familiarity which not only accepted their differences, and their respective shortcomings but assumed them as honored gifts. "We must have known one another in another life," Martin remarked at one point in the weekend.

"Or been poured from the same mold of the soul," Dill answered. "I cannot ever remember being as quickly familiar with anyone, and I'm a suspicious soul." A couple of men were horsing around as he spoke and he looked at them and smiled.

"I know you must be," Quinn chuckled. "I certainly am. With the world we live in, that's a survival trait." He frowned. "The only trouble is, it is also a trait that can turn around and bite. I know I've put a lot of people off with my attitude."

Dill grinned and nodded. "Yeah, I know. Or I think I do. You mean 'fuckem and feedem fish guts', don't you?"

"Took the words right out of my book," Quinn laughed in return. "The old 'eff-cube-gee'. Or 'Semper Fi', as the boys in the Marine Harmonica Band say."

"I'm amazed you've never been in the service," Dill responded. "You seem to have that mental set."

"I've always respected soldiers," the other told him. "Especially since the Six Days' War. They put it on the line I sleep behind."

Dill nodded. "A lot of civilians don't realize that. They may know the concept, but they don't realize just how true it is." He looked at Quinn and asked, "How you coming with your article? Are the guys talking to you?"

Martin nodded. "The problem is I have too much material already. I'll have a hard time boiling it down when it comes to the end of the weekend. It may take me a few weeks to sort it out."

"Yeah, I know. Catching the spirit of the thing without talking it to death is what you and I are about." He paused. "Just for my own benefit, when it's over I'd like to know what you found most significant personally."

"I can tell you that already," Martin answered quickly. "When Fred was talking Thursday night and spoke about our absent fathers, that really touched me. The whole idea we're the only ones who can give ourselves what we never got from our parents as children blows my mind. I've got it written down, but I can't remember exactly what he called it. Something about nourishing ourselves as children."

"Nurturing the child within," Dill reminded him.

"That's it," Martin said. "Nurturing the child within. If I didn't know better, I'd think Fred was reading my mail. His dad and mine were peas in a pod. I've been thinking about it, and the only thing my dad gave me was an attitude. He would deny it, but that's how it was for me."

Dill nodded. "That touched a lot of men. Believe it or not, it did me, too. As good a man as James Dill was, there were some shortcomings with my raising, too." He frowned. "I want to say something, Martin. I may be crossing a line here and be out of bounds, but I need to say it. I know your dad was never there for you, but I would also have to point out you are far too good a man for him to have been a total asshole."

Martin agreed. "When I was really young, it was different, somehow. I really liked being with him, even though it was obvious he liked my brother more than me. It changed at some point and he became abusive."

"Some day you may want to find a good therapist and take a look at that," Dill suggested. At Martin' startled look he quickly added, "I'm not saying you need therapy. I'm just saying you might find it useful. It's hard work, but I think it's worth it."

"Why would I need a therapist?" Martin wanted to know.

"Why do you need someone else for a Fifth Step?" Dill asked.

"To keep me honest," Martin said. "I see what you mean."

"I'm not sure you do," Dill said. "Therapy carries a bad name, but I look at it like an athlete having a professional coach. There's only so far a person can go by themselves. With professional coaching, athletes can do things they never could before, and the same is true of us as human beings. A good mentor can do the same, and from what you've told us, the old man in the Canyon was a mentor to you."

"He is my spiritual father," Quinn said simply. "Not that he didn't screw up, but when he did, it wasn't often, and he always made amends to me right away."

"How long since you've seen him?"

"Too long. I write three or four times a year, but I move around a lot and it's been hard for him to write back. I guess it's been three or four years since I've had a letter." Martin looked sad. "I really miss him, Willie."

"There's a good cure for that," Dill smiled. Go down and see him. What keeps you from doing it?"

"Up to now I've been in denial, and he's always read me like a book. So part of it is not wanting to tell him the truth." Martin answered, and then changed his mind. "No. Let me put that another way. Most of it has been not wanting to look at the truth about myself. I don't want him to know the kind of man I've become."

Dill sighed. "One of these days you're going to have to give up your shitty view of yourself, Martin. I guess that's what being your own father is all about. Unconditional love of yourself, warts and all." He looked at his new friend. "I've pushed the boundary, so I'll push it a little farther. From all you've told us, your dad apparently convinced you that you were a piece of shit as far as he was concerned. Right?"

"Yeah," Martin said. "That pretty well sums it up." A well of grief opened up behind his eyes and tears began to form.

"Well, I'm here to tell you he was dead wrong," Dill said. "What he did to you doing that is one of the gravest sins a father can commit against a child."

"He was doing exactly what his father taught him to do," Martin said.

"Right. 'The father has eaten sour grapes and the child's teeth is set on edge,'" Dill said softly. "It gets passed right on down from generation to generation to generation."

"So there's no hope for us?" Martin asked.

"Horse shit!" Dill responded. "That's what this weekend is all about, learning new ways of being a truly good father, to ourselves as well as to our children. That's a big part of what the way of the warrior is about."

"All right," Martin told him. "But all I've got is a very destructive role model. So far, I know what not to do, but where is the positive side? Where is something that tells me what to do? How to be?"

Dill looked at him gravely. "Do you remember the rabbi's story of the waiting father, Martin?"

"No," Quinn said, interested. "I've never heard of that one. Where is it, in the haggadah?"

"No," Dill smiled. "It's actually in the Bible." He seemed almost apologetic.

"There's nothing wrong with that," Martin told him. "I'm not really much of a believer, but there's a lot of wisdom there."

"No," Dill smiled self consciously. "That's not what's going on. I just don't want you to think I'm setting you up. It's New Testament, in the book of Luke. It's also called the Parable of the Two Sons."

"The prodigal son?" Martin asked.

Dill nodded. "That's the one. Most people think it's about the sons, but if you look at the context, I think you'll see it's a teaching about how to be a good father."

"I don't have a Bible with me," Martin told him. "I'll look it up when I get home."

"Do so," Dill said. "When you do, look at what happens when the wayward son decides to come home, and read between the lines."

"What do you mean?" Martin asked.

"Read what's not said there, but what is implied," Dill answered him. "The parable talks about how the son realizes how good he had it and makes up this speech to give his dad when he gets home. He thinks maybe he can talk his way back in. Then when he gets home, what does the old man do? That's what I'm talking about. What does he do, and what does he not do? The real message of the parable is right there." He smiled and nodded and stopped speaking.

"Come on, Willie, you going to leave me hanging? What did the father not do?" Martin was hooked.

"It would be better if you thought that up for yourself," Dill told him, looking troubled. "My answer may not be yours. I think one of the guys has a Bible. I'll see if he'll let you use it."

"Why don't you just tell me, Willie?" Martin implored. "Then I'll look it up when I get home and see if I agree."

Dill thought a moment. "All right, so long as you understand this it is my personal interpretation. It's right for me, but there are lots of others."

Martin looked at him. "Which you consider full of shit, but are far too polite to say," he observed dryly.

Dill chuckled. "You got me pegged, Martin," he said. "Takes one to know one. All right. The point is the father does not ask the kid anything. He doesn't even make him come to him. When he sees his kid coming, the father runs to meet him. The kid tries to make his repentance speech and the father blows it off, doesn't even hear him. He starts getting ready to party. His son is home. That's all he cares about. His son was dead to him and now he's alive. Nothing else matters to him. He doesn't even ask the kid not to do it again. That's how happy he is to see his son, and that's the model I'm talking about. Right or wrong, this is my son, and that's the bottom line. Nothing else matters."

Tears appeared again in Martin' eyes. "God," he said. "It would be nice to have a father like that."

"You do," Dill said. "With the old man."

"Not with God?" Martin asked. "I thought that was the point of the whole parable, Willie."

"Oh, it is," Dill said softly. "But you know that already and I never was one who liked a pastor preaching to the choir. What I was trying to suggest was a model you could use for being a good father to yourself. It doesn't matter if you are a believer or not, it's a good model."

"I don't know. It seems almost permissive."

"Permissive?" Dill almost shouted. His intensity was almost frightening. "Jesus, Mary, and Joseph, Martin! Don't you understand that freedom was the way the universe was created?" He was instantly contrite. "I'm sorry, man. You touched a nerve."

Martin shrugged and laughed. "That's all right, Willie. You made amends before I had time to get pissed. You want to talk about it?"

Dill shook his head. "It's something I've been fighting all my life, and I see it just about everywhere I turn. It doesn't matter what brand of religion you look at, there seems to be this underlying assumption that human beings are shit. Nothing is farther from the truth of the universe as I've observed it. Even shit is a part of the process of life. Can't grow roses without it."

Martin suddenly chuckled. "I'm not making fun of you, Willie," he assured the other man. "I just had this flash that life is very much a rose garden, a wild one with just a few flowers among a lot of thorns."

"Not bad," Dill said. "You're a gardener. Do you know how roses are grown. Good ones?"

"No," Martin replied. "Most of my effort was directed toward things I could eat. The ornamentals I raised were all desert plants."

"Well, what you do is take this scraggly little looking root thing and plant it in a big hole with old manure mixed in with the dirt. Then you try to drown it or soak it to death. After a while the damned thing begins to grow new vines and you let it think it's going to get away with this for a while. Then you cut it back just before winter and try to freeze it out. When spring comes you dump more old shit on it and give it the water treatment again. Then you ignore it until the bugs hatch, when you dump poison on it. And despite all these efforts to kill it, the damn thing flowers! That's how you raise good roses!"

Martin was laughing by the time Dill was done, as were two other men who happened by and heard him talking. "You're right, Willie," one of them remarked. "There used to be an old rose bush in our yard that my mother wanted me to dig up. I mowed it off, instead, and forgot about it and it came back with the prettiest roses you ever saw. As a matter of fact, I did that every year."

"Makes for an ugly looking vine," Dill assured them, "but it sure as hell raises great roses." He grinned. "While some of us have no claims on great physical beauty, they sure bear fruit."

"A flail, a rose, and a walnut tree," the other man said, bending the platitude. "The more you beat them, the better they be."

"Something like that," Martin said, getting to his feet. "I think we're beating a dead metaphor, gentlemen, and I hear the dinner bell."

"Are you saying better read than dead?" one of the men asked.

"As in Society of Read Poets?" the third man added.

"Or to beat it than eat it," said the fourth, and while it wasn't really that funny, they all laughed as they gathered for supper.

9. Demon Of The Noonday Rum

*N*ew Year's Day, Year IV. Tonight I bring in the New Year walking *through the city. Every year I am told this is dangerous to do, yet here I am, walking now until dawn, sometimes approached but never accosted once in the three years, no four, I have been doing this. No one asks me any more why I do this, why I bring in the New Year walking the streets of this desolate place they call Denver. When they do my answer is always the same. I walk the streets looking for the Messiah. I always say this with a smile, challenging them to actually take me seriously. No one ever does, of course, and no one ever accepts my invitation to come with me.*

Tonight, as is my custom, I end my walk at the news room, looking over the fire and police reports. Some years are better than others, and some worse, and I end my vigil writing another page or two in my journal, first reading what I wrote the first year I did this. The questions I asked still haunt me, and the answers are even worse. The truth is, I am packed and could be on my way home in two minutes. I even keep the bag here in the office these days. Yet I never do it. And why? I am a coward. I am afraid.

It's a fine thing, isn't it, when a man is afraid to be free? Lord Byron was right, it is not iron bars which make a prison. Prisons lie in the human mind and in the human heart, and the bonds are nothing but fear. Or so it is for me. I left the Canyon because I felt stifled there. I thought there was more to life than growing a garden and being neighbors, so I set out to find something. I set out to see the world and to write about it and I did. When people liked what I wrote, I wrote more and more. Somewhere along the line the Big One, the great American novel I would write someday became more important than anything else. Somehow, while I was hoeing my carrots, the dream became more important than the land I loved, or the orchards I planted, or the people I loved and who loved me. It became my passion, my obsession, the one thing I could have being denied the woman I loved. So I pursued it. I pursued it with all my mind and all my strength and all my soul. I went after it the way I now believe I should have pursued the first love of my life, making her mine, stopping only short of murder, if then.

Now I understand I was afraid. I was afraid her love might consume me and leave nothing but a dried up shell. Or to put it another way, I was afraid of taking the risks of learning to truly love another. I was afraid of the challenge it offered, the challenge to love enough to trust in the goodness of life itself, the challenge to live life simply, one day at a time. So I took the tragic way out. I took one mistress, then another, and what passed for love of them consumed my longing for a while.

The first mistress I took was the land itself, a harsh mistress who I thought only needed love and attention to bring her to fruition. I poured myself into her, into the soil itself, nurturing, tilling, pruning, clearing away stones to plant orchards and gardens in her for children. I came to know her every way, through her moods and her seasons. I learned to speak the rich language of her humus, and with gentleness and time she responded to my care, bringing forth a richness of harvest not known in years, if ever.

Yet she was not enough to fill the longing of my soul. So tiring of her, I cast the land aside and pursued my craft. At first I wrote simply for the joy of creation, simply trying to produce something which could be published. I did so, but that was not enough, either. Having published I strove to do even more, and then to be the very best. No accomplishment seemed to satiate my craving always more, and to achieve my ends I pursued one thing after another as if the hounds of hell were hot on my trail. There was no place I would not go, no risk I would not run diving into the hell holes of the world, often under enemy fire, to get the story, to see history as it happened, to get the precious stuff of life those who write call material. I took risks which make me shudder now, took risks seeking those life experiences which would enable me to write the Big One. Wherever trouble brewed, there I was, drawn to it like a fly to a shit wagon.

Now the Big One is written, four times over just to assure myself I really could do it. I am told completing a major novel is much like having a baby, both in terms of time and emotional investment. Yet seeing my four Big Ones lined up on the shelf, side by side in the order of their birth, how I now wish they were children, flesh of my flesh and bone of my bone, children of my beloved fathered in love by me. Now I see the choices I made in the stark light of the city streets each New Year's morning and I am far from pleased. The fruit of my labor now seems empty and hollow, a sad reflection of my own vanity and willfulness. All my accomplishments make no sense in the light of the way I see things now. Yet they are mine.

Or, perhaps I should say, they were mine. Now it is an open question who is the possessor and whom is the possessed. For the choices themselves seem to hold me here now. They tell me there is no going back, no hope of recapturing what might have been in returning to the road not taken. They tell me that those who try are fools, fools lost to their own folly and pathetic in their ever more desperate striving. The Chinese say a man can never step in the same river twice, and I believe they are right. People either outgrow times and places, or they become shadows of what they were, clinging to a history that will never happen again.

So I sit here in the cold morning light of another New Years morning, alone with the ghosts of my choices. Within their company I realize I have been lying to myself all these years, telling myself I would go home again after I did what I set out to accomplish. The truth is that I left for fear of staying longer. I left fearing the devils within me would destroy all I held dear. So I banished myself to a wilderness of my own making, a vast wasteland of the human soul. I came to this wilderness we call the City of Denver and there did I battle the devils which plagued me. There I encountered the darkness which lies within myself, and doing battle with my devils, I wrote the Big One four times. Yet each time it was as ashes in my mouth, for each time the exorcism failed. The devils remain, beyond my power to overcome, and every New Years eve as I walk the streets they torment me with memory of the Canyon, of the people I knew, of the woman I love, and of the only place I ever called Home.... (Martin Quinn's journal)

The speaker's voice was low and husky, a whiskey voice tempered by thousands of hours researching smoky bars, consuming countless shots of rye whiskey and smoking an endless chain of cigarettes. Though the air of the room was free from smoke, the speaker paused from time to time, coughing and clearing her throat before resuming her reading. When she was done she looked up from the podium, took off her reading glasses, and cleared her throat once again. "My name is Tillie," she said. "I am an alcoholic."

"HI, TILLIE!" the other people in the room chanted in unison. The room held perhaps a hundred chairs fanned out in rows from the long wall behind the podium and there were only about a fifth of them not taken, mostly toward the back.

"By the grace of God," Tillie continued, "and with the help of many good people like yourselves, I have not found it necessary to drink today. One day at a time, it has been twelve years, seven months and twenty-two days now since I had my last drink. For that I am very grateful." Tears came to her eyes, as they always did when she said this, and there was no question Tillie meant exactly what she said.

Tillie wiped her eyes and looked around the room, grinning. "As some of you are aware, some of those days it's been one hour at a time. Alcoholic that I am, I could once tell you my sobriety in hours." An appreciative titter went around the room. "But by the grace of God I've been delivered from even that particular form of insanity, too!"

This time the chuckle was louder. Tillie looked around the room. "I see a lot of new faces here tonight. At least they're new to me. So if there are any visitors from out of town or other groups who would like to be recognized, please raise your hand and introduce yourselves."

Four people raised a hand and Tillie pointed to each, who gave their first names and told where they were from. Each was greeted by the others as Tillie had been greeted, and there was a loud "Yeehaw!" from the back when one of the visitors mentioned he was from Ft. Worth.

"All right," Tillie said when the visitors were done. "It's good to have you all here. You know, it's been so long since I've chaired a meeting I've forgotten exactly how it goes, so please cut me a little slack. I think at this point I'm supposed to welcome you all to the evening meeting of Clean Air Group North. I assure you it's good to see you all here tonight. This is a closed meeting, which means that anyone is welcome who has a desire to stop drinking."

Tillie grinned. "For newcomers I'd like to point out you don't have to stop drinking to come to AA. You only have to have the least little bitty desire to do so. But I will point out this. The Big Book is right when it says people rarely fail who follow our method. So just keep coming here and listening to what we have to say, and I think eventually you'll find what you're seeking. You may also discover you have no desire to drink any more. At least that's how it was for me."

Someone said something and Tillie exclaimed, "I'm coming to that, Jimmy. Cool your jets, man." Looking at the crowd she observed, "Drunks are a pushy bunch, aren't they?" There was laughter around the room, including Jimmy who merely shook his head.

"Anyway," Tillie said, holding up a bright silver medallion, "we have a desire chip for anyone who would like to try our way of life for twenty-four hours." She waited a couple of moments, but no one came forward to take the chip. "Well, it's not your last chance," Tillie said. "Jim will remind me to offer it again at the end of the meeting." She winked at Jim, who laughed with the others and nodded.

"There's one other announcement for those of you who missed the signs, or the significance of our group name. This is also a non-smoking meeting." There was laughter at this for on the wall directly above the speaker's podium, and about a foot above was a black sign with six inch lettering in bright orange proclaiming "*SE PROHIBE FUMAR*" with "NO SMOKING" in parentheses below it. A similar sign was posted on each of the four walls of the meeting room and above the door coming in.

"What can I say?" Tillie asked. "We're dealing with alcoholics here, folks. When I came in through these doors I'm not sure I'd have noticed the signs, either. It took me about four years of continuous sobriety before the fog really started lifting."

There was silence at this, and many appreciative nods. Tillie looked at something on the podium. "I see this is supposed to be an in-house speaker meeting tonight," she announced. "Does anyone know who the speaker is supposed to be?"

No one spoke up and several people looked at one another uneasily. "I know, I know," Tillie said. "Whoever chairs these meetings is supposed to line up a speaker, but Bob called me an hour ago and asked me to fill in for him. Being an alcoholic, of course, it didn't occur to him to tell me it was a speaker meeting or to mention the name of the speaker." She grinned at the group. "And being an alcoholic like many of you people, my first thought now is that Bob's speaker backed out at the last minute and that's why Bob couldn't make it." There was a ripple of laughter. "Because he's probably out hunting the turkey down!"

A roar of approval went up from the crowd "Of course," Tilled added with a smile, "that would be taking brother Bob's inventory and that's not what the program of AA is about. Not that it stops us from doing it, but the program teaches us to take care of our side of the street. So maybe I owe Bob amends for having such a suspicious mind."

She smiled again. "What I'm here to tell you, however, is that Bob did me a real favor asking me to chair the meeting tonight. I say that because I've learned there are three things I need to do to live a life that's sane. One is to seek God, or, as Dr. Bob put it, to trust God. The second is to clean house, to clean up my own act and not worry about yours.

And the third thing I need to do is serve others. Chairing a meeting is one of the most delightful ways I know to serve, and so I'm very grateful to be here tonight."

Tillie took a drink of coffee. "So, boys and girls, what's your pleasure? Our options are simple." As she spoke, Tillie counted on her fingers. "One, we can open this up and have a discussion meeting; two, we can have a speaker if someone here is willing to speak 'contempor-anx-iously', or," she laughed, "there's a third option. We can sit here together and have an hour of silence followed by the serenity prayer." There was uneasy laughter at this. While it was true Tillie was joking, the old tim-ers in the room knew she was perfectly capable of doing just that.

"Tell us your story, Tillie!" someone shouted from the back. "I've been here four years now and I've never heard it."

"Sure you have, Martin," Tillie insisted. "Although you may not know it was mine. My story is the same as yours, the same as many people in here. But of that's what you want...?"

She paused and there was a round of applause. "All right, then," she said. "I think you'll see the only difference is in the gory details, but someone once said God is in the details." She stopped, looked bewil-dered." Do you know, I still haven't figured out what that means? Men-tion details to me and the first thing my pickled mind thinks is shaken, not stirred." Some of the group laughed. "I'm here to tell you, God's name isn't Martini, at least, not the last time I checked." She paused. "Or James Bond, either. But it's been a while since I checked that one out."

"You bragging or complaining, Tillie?" someone hollered.

"Why, sweetheart! What a terrible thing to suggest. I'm complaining, of course." The group laughed and clapped and Tillie raised her hands in apology. "All right, folks, enough foolishness. Down to the business of staying sober. My story is very simple. I used to drink in order to deal with the stuff of life, but after a while that way of dealing with life backfired and my drinking became a serious problem, so serious it was destroying the lives of those I loved as well as my own. Then a miracle happened and I came into AA. Now, after a couple of slips, I hope I am here to stay, but now I know it is by the grace of God I am sober. It is through good people like yourselves I discovered a way to deal with life on life's terms without having to self-medicate with booze, drugs, food, sex, or cigarettes." She grinned. "Not necessarily in that order." There was an appreciative titter at this.

"So what happened? Well, I don't want to give you a full blown drunk-alogue. I don't like them, myself. After all, you can fill in the details from your own life and it won't be far off. What I want to emphasize is the miracle which took place and how it happened, because I suspect a lot of you newcomers feel as hopeless as I felt when I first came in here. If there is one thing that gets through the fog to you tonight, I hope it is that message. There is hope for you."

There were many nods around the room. "We talk about having to hit bottom around here, and people are always arguing about high bottoms as opposed to low bottoms for alcoholics. Supposedly people who have high bottoms are those who get in here without having lost everything, but I also hear a lot of pride taken by those who claim low bottoms." She looked around the room. "For me that whole argument misses the point by the whole width of heaven. When I reached my bottom, I'd learned to despise myself completely and I don't see how anything could be worse than that."

There was deep silence in the room and Tillie let it grow before going on. "I don't know of anyone who came in here really liking themselves, much less loving themselves. Yet that's what this fellowship has taught me to do, to learn to love myself by learning to love you, who are like me." She smiled, tears once again blurring her vision. "That, dear people, is the miracle I was talking about. Because if despising myself is the lowest I can get, and despising you, too, then learning to love is definitely something which came from a Power much greater than me."

Tillie had them now, and as she briefly related the details of her career as a drinker, she emphasized attitudes and feelings, and there were many nods around the room. One woman who came in obviously suffering a major hangover listened intently for a while before her own eyes began to run. When the people sitting on either side reached out and touched her, she began to beginning to sob in earnest and someone passed along one of several boxes of tissues sitting here and there.

Tillie looked around the room and smiled. "You know, this is the real miracle of this program. Here we are, a gathering of the most self centered people on earth, but there are few in this room who are not concerned for our sister here." One of the women in the room about the same age as the woman who was crying went to her, whispered something and took her into one of the empty adjacent rooms. "Thanks,

Rita," Tillie said. The other woman waved as she closed the door.

"There's a lot more I could say about my own experience in recovery," Tillie continued," but what you've just seen is what the program is about, one alcoholic helping another alcoholic in need. You have to understand that there is nothing altruistic about this program. Through reaching out to our sister Rita is being helped to sustain her own recovery. That's why we do what we do, and for us it's a life or death matter."

Tillie looked around the room. "I want to open the meeting up for discussion now. First, I'm going to call on people who are new to the program and have less than a year. Would someone with at least ninety days but less than a year like to speak?" Three hands went up. "I'm going to call on all three of you," Tillie said, "but I know Mike's name, so I'll call on him first."

Mike thanked Tillie and began to speak, sharing his own experience of how the program worked for him. When he was done the meeting moved on from one person to another. About half way through the discussion Rita came back in with the woman who had been crying and rejoined the group. At the very end of the meeting, when Tillie offered a "desire chip" to anyone who wanted to try the program for twenty-four hours, the woman held up her hand and came forward. There was applause as Tillie hugged her and asked her first name. "Let's welcome Joan," Tillie said and the group responded, "HELLO, JOAN!" After the meeting closed with an well known prayer, several people came forward to greet Joan.

"Good meeting, Tillie," said a middle aged man, giving her a hug. "I haven't seen you around in a while."

"Hello, Martin!" Tillie answered enthusiastically. "I've been in Florida over the winter with my sister. She was sick."

"I hope she's doing better. I know I am, seeing you."

Tillie beamed. "You charmer! But, yes, she's doing all right now. How's Adam? I haven't seen him around since I've been back." Adam was Martin' long time sponsor in the program.

A pained look came across Martin' face. "He died a couple of months ago, Tillie. The cancer finally got him, but he died sober." He smiled a sad smile. "You know Adam. He's so hardheaded when it comes to anything related to the program. I had to yell at him there at the end to get him to take the pain killer his doctor prescribed."

Tillie laughed. "That sounds like Adam. Hard core all the way." She looked at Martin gravely. "I bet you haven't found another sponsor yet, have you?" she asked, gently and Martin shook his head.

"No," he admitted. "There are people I talk to, but no, I haven't." He grinned at her. "Why? You want the job?"

"I don't know," she responded seriously. "Why don't you buy me supper and we'll talk about it?"

They went to a little Thai place she knew about not far away, a place which served vegetarian as well as the normal menu. Through supper they visited, caught up with the events of one another's lives until at coffee after, they came to a long silence. "So," Tillie said. "What's going on in your recovery, Martin?"

Martin reached in the backpack he carried in place of a briefcase and took out a thick spiral notebook. He flipped to the first entry, the one with which he'd begun this year's journal after his walk through the city. "What I keep coming back to is this," he said. "Not a day goes by but it comes to mind at least once, and sometimes it's on my mind all day long." He looked down. "That's the closest I come to drinking these days, Tillie, when I can't get it off my mind."

Tillie took out her reading glasses but paused before starting to read. "I have to suggest that may be because you're trying to do it yourself, dear. I think if it's that bad it has to be a God deal." He nodded and she began to read through the entry. "You have good, strong handwriting," she murmured. "Easy to read, too." Then she chuckled as she got into the body of the text. "A marvelous way with words, too, but you know that, of course."

When she was done Tillie sighed. "So you're still in love with her," she observed. Martin nodded and Tillie gave him a wry smile. "Martin, what makes you so sure it would have worked out with her? Even if you had gotten married and had children?"

He shook his head. "I don't know. That's what I've always thought. I've never loved anyone the way I did her and I think she loved me."

"So what happened? Why didn't you marry?"

He shook his head. "I was my stupidity. She was away at school and I ended up in bed one night with her cousin."

"That might have something to do with it," Tillie said dryly. "How did you end up in bed with her cousin?"

"It's a long story," Martin told her. He glanced around. "It looks like they want to close up here."

"Then why don't you come over to my place and tell me about it?" Tillie said gently. "You have any place you need to be?"

Martin shook his head, but looked doubtful. "I'm not inviting you into my bed, Martin," Tillie assured him. "Nor am I trying to seduce you. I am old enough almost to be your mother and, believe it or not, dear, I prefer men my own age."

"Sorry," Martin said. "I guess I was off base."

"Not at all, dear. You're a very attractive man and there was a time I might have gone after you. 'I slept with the author' sort of thing." She laughed at his surprise. "What the hell? I'm an alcoholic. So it's just as well we make it clear this isn't about thirteenth stepping. It's about sponsorship."

Something occurred to Martin but he shoved the thought aside almost as soon as it came to mind. Yet at least a fleeting shadow must have reached his face because Tillie laughed. "No, sweetpea, this is not about 'I sponsor the famous author,' either."

"I don't know what's the matter with me..." Martin began but Tillie cut him off smoothly.

"Come on, bubba!" Tillie scolded. "You're an alcoholic and you have every right to be suspicious of another alcoholic." Her face turned grave. "I am dead serious, friend. Have no illusions about me. That's the only way it will work with you and me. There was a time in my life I'd have screwed your brains out just for trophy value." She gave him a bawdy grin. "As I said, bubba, you're quite a hunk, but thank God I've been delivered from putting men in the place of a bottle." She shook her head, grimacing. "At least, for today. It was awful."

A half hour later they were seated comfortably in front of her bay window high above the city. Since it was night, the brownish yellow smog which hangs over the city by day was not visible, and only the absence of stars against the night sky hinted it was still there. The lights of the city were below them and lighted the sky with a faint reddish glow. "Nice view," Martin said, settling himself into one of the easy chairs.

"Yes, it is, isn't it?" Tillie answered. "It used to be much better before so many people moved here."

They fell silent, Martin lost in thought and Tillie waiting patiently for him to begin. After a few moments he took a sip of coffee and cleared his throat. "I don't know where to start," he told her.

"Why don't you start in the beginning. Tell me how you and she met. Not the cousin, but you and..." She paused, thinking. "Damn!" she said. "I seem to have lost too many brain cells. I can't remember her name."

"Her name is Stephanie," Martin said, grinning. "I think the reason you can't remember is that I didn't tell you."

Tillie chuckled. "That could have something to do with it," she said. "I never was much good at mind reading, although I'd never admit it, of course. So how did you and Stephanie meet?"

So Martin told her, beginning with the day of their meeting at Posadas and leaving nothing out. When he was done Tillie nodded. "You met your soul mate, I think, Martin," she said quietly. "That doesn't happen very often in this world, and I'm sorry for your sake it came to an end. Tell me how it happened."

Martin sighed, resting his forehead in his hand. "It was almost like an accident," he said. "If I had not been drinking, it would have never happened the way it did." He looked up at Tillie, tears in his eyes. "I guess that's what drunks say when they've killed someone in a wreck."

"Go ahead, Martin, tell me and get it out on the table. It's been eating you alive, dear." Tillie's voice was gentle but insistent.

Martin nodded. "The old man was sick," he said softly, remembering the day clearly as if it were happening before him. "It was the spring of '66, the year I left and went to Illinois. The old man was sick and Luiz brought Carmelita up to help take care of him. That's her name, Carmelita Maria Gallegos de Ramos. She'd just graduated from high school and didn't have much to do that summer. There aren't many jobs there and she was waiting to go to the University in the fall...."

The blast of Luiz's diesel horns brought Ramos and Martin around from the back of the house where they'd been repairing the fence around the old man's chicken yard. Or to be more accurate, they came from where Martin had been repairing the fence while Ramos supervised from a cane bottom straight chair leaned against the shed. As they came around the house, the old man was leaning heavily on Martin' arm.

"Hey, Tio!" Luiz shouted. "I brought you some help this time."

Carmelita got out of the car smiling shyly at Martin as she walked up to greet the old man. "How are you, uncle?" she asked, kissing him on the cheek and nodding to Martin. "Hi," she said, shyly.

"Oh, I am a thousand times better just at this moment," Ramos beamed gallantly. "All I needed was the kiss of a beautiful young girl."

"You still look like a frog to me," Martin said dryly, and Carmelita laughed. The old man gave him a wry look, but ignored the jibe. "Come on in, pretty one," he said. "We'll let smarty mouth help Luiz with the things."

They went into the house while Martin walked down to Luiz's old car. "Not much to help with," Luiz said, shaking his hands. "You can get Carmelita's bags if you want."

"Oh, is she staying a while?" Martin was surprised.

"Yes," Luiz answered, laughing. "That is, if Tio Emil will let her. Her mother is convinced he's dying up here alone without anyone to take care of him, so she sent Carmelita."

"I'm here," Martin replied, a bit indignant. "I can take care of him. As a matter of fact, I have been for the last three days."

"You don't count to Tia Estrella," Luiz told him. "After all, you're a man and she thinks you're probably starving up here, too." He laughed. "Hey, man, enjoy it while you can. Estrella is the best cook in town and I hear Carmelita is almost as good. I bet she'd even clean your house if you ask nice."

"I don't want my house cleaned," Martin growled. "I like things just the way they are." Then he smiled and shrugged. "On the other hand, I'll be able to do some things I've put off. I've had to stick pretty close to home with Emil sick."

"They ever figure out what was wrong with him?" Luiz asked.

"The doctor thought it might be a kidney infection," Martin answered. "He wanted to put the old man in the hospital, but Emil wouldn't have it. He said if he was going to die he'd rather die at home."

Luiz nodded. "I could have told you that, man. I think he's right."

"I guess that's the way I'd feel about it, too," Martin admitted. "But it scared me not being able to get him to the doctor sooner."

Luiz shrugged. "He's a pretty tough old *hombre*," he pointed out. "If it wasn't for you, he'd have had to wait for me."

"Well, let's see what he has to say about Carmelita," Martin grinned.

That night Martin ate one of the best meals he'd ever eaten. Though he was used to good fare at Ramos' table, and was no tyro himself when it came to cooking, even Caroline's *flautas* barely measured up to the meal Carmelita prepared them. Nor was the old man upset with her being there. Far from it, he seemed genuinely glad to see the young woman, and while he was still too sick to eat much, he came to the table and laughed at Martin as the young man gulped down his food. "You're lucky she doesn't come up here more often," the old man said. "You'd be as fat as Luiz."

Another time, when Carmelita was out of the room he said softly in English, "You're lucky Stephanie's already claimed you, youngster. This one's half in love with you and she'd make you the fattest man in the county."

"Come on," Martin protested. "She's just a child."

"She's the same age as Rosa when she married your father," Ramos told him. "I know. She told me."

Carmelita reappeared a few moments later with a dish of *flan* which she set in front of Martin. Martin looked at her carefully and realized the old man was quite right. Below the simple cotton dress was the body of a woman, young but ready to bear children. Carmelita caught his look and smiled self consciously. Lundberg cursed himself for a fool, but smiled back. "If I eat this I'll burst," he groaned. "If I don't I'll always wonder what I missed." Taking a teaspoon and taking a taste he groaned with pleasure. "Carmelita," he said. "Your husband is going to be the best fed man in the whole state."

Carmelita flushed with pleasure, ducking back into the kitchen and appearing with two more dishes of the dessert. "If Tio Emiliano doesn't want his you can have it tomorrow," she said lightly. "I think it's just as good a day old as it is fresh. Maybe better." Suddenly embarrassed by the length of her declaration, Carmelita looked down and devoted her attention to her own dish of *flan*. Yet like a cat ignoring a dog, Martin knew she was aware of his every move and found himself becoming aroused. *Shit!* he thought, berating himself for being so fickle. *That's all I need, to rob the cradle.*

As if reading his thoughts, Carmelita asked. "So what do you hear from Stephanie? She should be home from school soon."

"That's what I thought, too, but apparently not," Martin answered, thinking of the letter Luiz brought that afternoon. While it was filled with endearments the last paragraph disturbed Martin greatly.

I have decided to take the grant, sweetheart. I know this means my being gone for the next six months, but it's too good a career opportunity to pass up. I will be working with the world's very best authority on preliterate people, and I can use the research I do for my doctoral thesis. Who knows? Maybe if I impress the great man he will offer me something as an assistant. Either way, it can't help, and the government is footing the bill. I know this means setting our plans back, but we've waited this long. Surely a little longer will not matter in the long run....

"Oh?" asked the old man, nodding. All evening he'd been aware of something bothering his young friend, but thought it was the presence of his niece. Curious as he was, he didn't press.

"Oh, that's too bad," Carmelita said, responding to his disappointment. "What happened?"

Martin shrugged. "She got some kind of research grant that was too good to pass up," he said. "So she's not going to be back for six months."

"Six months isn't so long," said the old man. "I'll keep an eye on things whenever you want to go see her."

Martin shook his head. "No, it's too expensive. She'll be going to South Africa and won't be back until the project is done. As a matter of fact, she may be leaving school early to join the research team." He shrugged, looked down. "I'll have to be the one who travels if we're to see each other before she leaves. I'll have to go to Boston."

"When does she have to leave?" Ramos asked.

"Three weeks," Martin answered. "That doesn't give us much time."

"Then you better go," the old man said. "Carmelita and I will do fine."

Lundberg shook his head. "No, I don't think so. It's too complicated. Too expensive, too. I'd have to fly out and she'd be busy winding things up. We wouldn't have much time, anyway. I'll call her when I can."

Ramos started to say something but decided to remain quiet. Were they alone he would have pursued the subject, but his sense was Martin did not want to talk in front of Carmelita. She was looking at Martin curiously, as if she were about to ask something, so the old man asked her, "Carmelita, my angel, is there any more tea? I think that would do me well. Bring my pills, too, if you will."

"Of course, Tio," she answered, immediately concerned for the old man but efficiently clearing away the dessert dishes as she went. When she was out of the room Ramos raised a questioning eyebrow at Lundberg, but the younger man shook his head. When Carmelita brought the tea in he smiled and said something, drawing a titter from her. *Careful, my friend,* thought the old man. *You may think of her as a child, but she's as old as Eve when it comes to offering the man she chooses the apple.*

Martin Quinn fell silent and Tillie nodded. "So Stephanie took off for Africa and Carmelita closed in."

Quinn looked up, startled. He started to frame a sharp response, then laughed. "Something like that. I'd think it was funny if it wasn't so painful. Sounds like something out of a situation comedy, doesn't it?"

Tillie nodded. "Yes, it does. But most romances do. Let me ask you something, Martin," she said. "I want you to really think about it before you answer. Do you think Stephanie was really serious about marrying you?"

He nodded. "You know, I've wondered that a long time. I've always wondered whether she was telling me how she felt or what she thought I wanted to hear. I've been afraid of the answer. I know she was scared but I think she did want to marry, at least when she was with me. I think when she wasn't she must have had grave doubts. God knows I did, even though I was the one pushing to marry right away. Maybe I pushed too hard and scared her away, but, yes, I had my doubts. Yet, I've never loved anyone like I loved her, Tillie." He handed her a letter. From the condition of the envelope Tillie could see he must have carried it with him for years. "Maybe I should have gone to Boston. I don't know. I got this two weeks after Stephanie left."

Tillie read the letter through twice and nodded. "I hate to disagree, Martin," she answered. "But I think a more accurate statement might be you've never carried a torch for anyone the way you've carried a torch for Stephanie." She folded the letter and put it carefully back into its envelope. "Despite the fact she is rather clear in what she says. I think going to Boston would have only postponed the inevitable."

"Maybe so," Martin agreed. "But what's the difference?"

"What's the difference between loving someone and carrying a torch?" Tillie asked and Martin nodded. "Well, my experience is that truly loving one person prepares us to love others. It's a flesh and blood thing, real people loving real people. Carrying a torch is different. It doesn't seem to have much to do with flesh and blood people. It's romantic in the worst sort of way, like the love between Romeo and Juliet, untouchable and always beyond reach. It's tragic in a bittersweet way and compared to really loving someone, it's safe and pretty exclusive."

"I don't understand what you mean," Martin confessed, confused.

"I'm not sure I do, either," Tillie answered. "I'm trying to put feelings into words and it's hard. Something I know for a fact is you've been romantically involved with other people since. I seem to remember someone named Sandy not that long back. The two of you were a pretty hot item for a while as I recall." She smiled. "Of course, that may have been when you were still drinking."

"It was," Martin said. "But I didn't feel for Sandy anything like what I felt for Stephanie."

"You didn't?" Tillie asked. "You couldn't prove it by me, and I'd been sober a while then. You two seemed pretty tight. Pretty passionate, too, and very much in love." She looked at him gravely and asked, "So you're saying that the whole time you were with Sandy you were wishing it was Stephanie, instead of her?"

"No," Martin said. "Of course not. I'm not that cynical. Sandy is Sandy and that was very special in its own way, but it wasn't like the way I felt about Stephanie."

"You never carried a torch for Sandy? You never missed her?" Tillie looked skeptical.

"Of course I did, Tillie. I missed her so much I almost left town to keep from seeing her with other people. It still hurts when I do, but it's different from what I felt for Stephanie."

Tillie nodded. "I'm sure it was different." She thought a moment and then said, "Let me put it another way. From what I can see, Stephanie is the safest person in the world for you to carry a torch for. At first she was far away, physically far away and not on the scene. So you didn't have to deal with the flesh and blood person, not really. It's easy to present our best side when we don't have to sustain the act very long."

Tillie raised a hand to halt his immediate objection. "No, let me finish, Martin. You can be pissed when I'm done, but let me have my say." He shrugged and nodded, looking down. "I'm not saying she did this cynically, Martin. It's just the way things happen when people fall in love. They don't want their lover to see their dark side."

Martin nodded and looked up again, paying attention. "So, first she was far away and you didn't have to live with her imperfections. Now she's safely married to your cousin and best friend, and so you don't have to do anything about it. That's why I say she's a safe person for you to carry the torch. The acid test is this. Suppose something happened to your cousin, or that their marriage fell apart, for whatever reason. How fast would you get there? Or would you even try?"

"You've got a nasty mind," Martin snapped.

Tillie laughed. "Of course, I do. Almost as nasty as yours. We are alcoholics, dearest, nasty, suspicious misanthropes. We spot the defects very easily, but that doesn't answer my question. Would you do it? Would you go after Stephanie if nothing was in the way? Would you take 'no' for an answer?"

"I don't know," Martin said, more than a little surly. "Depends."

"There's your answer, Martin," Tillie said gently. "Your heart is divided and that's hard to admit. Stephanie's easy to pine for because you never really loved her as a human being. You never loved her for her faults as well as in spite of them. I know that's painful to face, but is it possible I am right?" Martin nodded. "Then tell me," Tillie continued in the same quiet voice, "wasn't there anyone else before Sandy? Wasn't there anyone who was really special?"

"Yes, there was," Martin answered and tears came to his eyes. "There was a woman I knew in Jerusalem. We were going to be married but she was killed by a car bomb in the Old City. Fucking Arab terrorists killed her!" As the tears poured down his face he told her about Tovah Sharon and about the child he lost with her when the car bomb exploded.

"Oh, Martin, I'm sorry," said Tillie when he was done. "I went too far. I am so sorry you lost her."

"No," he said, wiping away his tears. "This really helps put it all in perspective. I'm beginning to see what you mean. I think you may be right, too. I really loved Tovah in a way I never loved Stephanie. It's just a little unsettling to believe something such a long time and then to realize I had it all wrong."

"We do the best we can," Tillie answered softly. Suddenly she began a yawn, unable to contain it. "Oh, pardon me," she said. "It's been a long day for this old lady. You want some more coffee? It's decaf."

"No, I better get on home," Martin answered. "It's a long drive from here and it's pretty late." The clock on the wall read half past one.

"Would you do me a favor?" Tillie asked. "I worry about your driving this late. You must be beat, too. Would you take the guest bedroom tonight? It has its own bath and you can borrow some of Jerry's clothes tomorrow if you want fresh ones. Or we can put your things in to wash." Jerry was her youngest son, away at school.

It was an offer too good to pass up and Quinn agreed. Taking a quick shower, he dried himself with the rough towels laid out and fell into bed wondering if he would have a hard time drifting off as he often did sleeping in strange quarters. Within fifteen seconds of his head touching the pillow, however, and after uttering a brief prayer to Whomever gods might be for the soul of Tovah Sharon, he fell into a deep, dreamless sleep that carried him far into the morning.

When Martin finally awoke, it was the smell of fresh coffee that drew him from his bed. Taking a quick shower he picked out the oldest pair of jeans he could find and a tee shirt which had seen better days. There were small tears in the fabric of the shirt, as if it had been hanging out to dry when a shell exploded not far away, sending shrapnel through the fresh laundry. As a matter of fact, Martin had seen this very thing in Jerusalem.

He found Tillie sitting in the same place she sat the night before, with a cup of coffee and the morning paper. A low pressure cell must have passed through, bringing winds from the east, for most of the smog normally seen hanging over the city was gone and the view was magnificent. "Good morning, Martin," Tillie greeted him. "How did you sleep?"

"Like a log," he said, nodding toward a carafe on a nearby table. "Is that what I think it is?"

"Help yourself," Tillie answered. "I made it about thirty minutes ago." She smiled at his outfit. "I see you found some fresh clothes," she laughed. "You know, that's Jerry's favorite outfit."

"It is?" Martin asked, surprised. "I picked the oldest thing I could find. I didn't want to take his good stuff."

"Haven't you heard of grunge?" Tillie asked. "It took him months to get those looking that way."

"Maybe I better change, then," Martin said, carefully setting his coffee on the floor by his chair.

Tillie shrugged. "If you want to, go ahead. This time pick what you like best and I bet that will be his least favorite."

Martin changed quickly, picking out a much newer set of chinos and a dark green polo shirt. When he came back Tillie laughed. "Good thing you didn't take my bet," she said. "Jerry wouldn't be caught dead in those."

"These are nice clothes," Martin protested. "They're the best thing he had in his wardrobe. Except for the suit."

"My sentiments, exactly," Tillie agreed. "That's why I bought them for him one Christmas. Jerry was very polite and thanked me, but he hasn't worn them once in three years. Wear them home and keep them. I hate to see them go to waste."

"Thank you," said Martin, taking his seat. "They fit perfectly and I have some old stuff I can replace them with."

"Jerry will be your friend forever," Tillie laughed. "Do you want me to fix you some breakfast?"

Martin shook his head. "No, thanks. Just coffee."

"Me, too." Tillie looked him over with a critical eye. "You look like you're feeling better this morning," she observed. "I think there's something on your mind. Want to talk about it?"

"Not really," said Martin. "I woke up thinking about Carmelita."

"I'm not surprised," Tillie answered. "You may owe amends there but I hope you talk it over with me or someone else first." She smiled and added, "Someone in the program."

Martin nodded. "I will, for sure." He was thoughtful. "I wonder what has become of her. I've been out of touch so long she may have ten grand kids by now."

"Your cousin could probably tell you," she answered, "but maybe it would be better to ask someone else."

"It probably would," Martin agreed. "But Max would know," he said. "He'd tell me and he'd understand keeping quiet about my asking about her, too."

Tillie asked who Max might be, so Martin told her how they became friends at first and how Max was now living in his old place. "I probably need to deed him part interest by now," Martin added. "I set up an escrow for insurance and taxes before I left, but Max has put a lot of himself into the place if I know him."

"You're not exactly hurting for money, either," Tillie observed. "Or maybe you are, I don't know. Still, that's very generous."

"No, I doubt money will ever be a problem again," Martin said. "I pay my taxes on time and I bank most of what I've made."

"Goodness," Tillie teased. "Maybe I was a little hasty turning you away from my bed. You must be the most eligible bachelor in town."

"The least available, too," Martin laughed. "The whole singles scene around here is awful. I avoid it like the plague."

"Gives new meaning to the word 'carnivore,' doesn't it," Tillie nodded. These days the women are just as predatory as the men."

"And there's a plague on the horizon," she added. Martin nodded and they sat a long while in silent companionship, enjoying the sun and the view. Finally Tillie asked, "So what are you going to do?"

Martin was blank for a moment. Then he smiled. "You know, the old man used to do exactly the same thing to me all the. I was miles away, just drifting actually." He frowned. "I don't know. It might be best to just let things be. I've caused her enough heartache already."

"Horse hockey, kemo sabe," Tillie replied, laughing at Martin' start. "I wish I could take credit, but that's one of Jerry's."

"I want to meet him," Martin said. "He sounds like a pretty good source of material."

"Bring old clothes and you will," Tillie said. "But as a sponsor..." She stopped and looked at him seriously. "I am your sponsor, am I not?" Martin nodded and she went on. "As your sponsor, I need to hold your feet to the fire about this. You may not know it, but I cut my teeth in recovery with ten years on the other side of the hall." She winked at him. "So just remember you're talking to a black belt Alanon."

Martin laughed politely. "All right, but what are you saying?"

"We have our own slogans on the other side of the hall," Tillie said. "I happen to like the three 'Cs' best, Cause, Cure and Control."

"Sounds like a law firm," he quipped.

"It does, doesn't it? What the Three C's say is that when we're dealing with someone else's problem or someone else's pain we must remember we didn't Cause it, we can't Cure it, and we can't even Control it."

"But I did cause it," he argued.

Tillie sighed. "For such a smart man you can really be a dumb shit," she observed. Martin flushed and Tillie said, "Martin, you can get pissed off if you want, but I'm only reminding you of exactly what you've said yourself in meetings. Let me go to the bottom line. Are you Carmelita's Messiah?"

"Of course not," he snapped.

"Then stop nailing yourself to a cross over this," Tillie said. "Even if you were responsible for her pain, it wouldn't help." He looked unconvinced. "Let me put it another way, what good is it going to do Carmelita right this minute for you to flog yourself?"

Martin shrugged. "None," he said grudgingly.

"Even if she were here it wouldn't do her much good, would it?" Tillie bored in. "Even if it gave her momentary satisfaction, it would feed her own sickness the same way going after vengeance does alcoholics."

Martin thought about this, then nodded again. "So the question is what you can do that will help you as well as her, and that's what I'm asking. What can you do about Carmelita to make amends and lay this ghost to rest?"

"I guess the first step is to find out what I can from Max," he answered. "Then go from there."

"Then talking to me is the second step, and only then do *we* decide where you go from there," she corrected. "If I'm going to be your sponsor, dear, you need to use me, and I do mean often," she added. "None of this crap of checking in with me at the New Year and on the Fourth of July. Agreed?"

"Agreed, already!" Martin retorted. "Damn, Tillie, I thought Adam was hard-assed for a sponsor."

"A gentle touch won't work with you, and you know it, love." Tillie was grinning but Martin said nothing. "Don't you, damn it?" she said, almost laughing.

Martin laughed with her. "Oh, hell, yes. That's why it's been so hard to find a sponsor. Everyone is so nice."

"Nice makes for a good funeral," Tillie snorted. "I hate nice people. I never know where they're going to stick the shiv. My former associate is a case in point." Tillie never mentioned her former spouse by name or as her former husband, but only as her former associate. "Nicest guy in the world, so everyone said, and he took me for damned near everything I had. Not that I didn't help him," she added. "There are no victims here, just volunteers."

"Rigorous honesty hurts, doesn't it," Martin commiserated.

"Not as much as the lie," Tillie shot back. "I think lying is one of the most violent things people do to one another." She looked directly into his eyes. "I love you too much to lie to you, Martin. That's why I may sound like a bitch from time to time. I may be wrong about any given thing at any given time, but I'll tell you what I think is the truth as gently as I can. That's a promise, and this deal will work better if you will do the same with me."

Two weeks later they were seated in an all night diner on the outskirts of the city, a place with the original name of Joe's Eats. At first glance, the place looked old, vintage greasy spoon, an ambiance the owner had worked very hard to achieve when the cafe was built a year or two before. Yet on the other hand, the place wasn't quite right. It didn't really smell greasy spoon, for one thing, and the non-smoking signs on the door and at the cash register were out of place. A closer examination revealed the table tops had been a little too uniformly distressed, the alleged cigarette burns a touch too artfully done, and despite its grimy appearance, the paint still looked new. Even so, the place attracted the affluent grunge crowd, who couldn't tell the difference, and it looked like it was making a killing from the expensive cars massed in front, even at this early hour. Martin had once come in late quite by mistake, thinking the place was a truck stop and discovered there was standing room only.

"I've never been here," Tillie said. "I'll have to tell Jerry about it. He'll absolutely love it."

Martin laughed. "I thought he might. The reason I chose it was it's about half way for both of us."

"You must live a long way out," Tillie answered. "It took me forever to get here."

The waitress came just at that moment to take their order, and when they were done Martin reminded Tillie, "Remember, this is on me."

"Tonight it is," Tillie replied. "After this we'll take turns, no argument, either." She spread her napkin carefully in her lap and cut to the chase. "So what did you find out? I'm dying to know."

"Not a whole lot," he answered. "When Max wrote back he gave me a phone number and so I called. It surprised me he had a phone put in but I guess it's his place now. Anyway, the last Max heard Carmelita was living in Albuquerque finishing up her schooling. Apparently she dropped out during her second semester at the University and never finished. Then, about two years ago, she went back."

"Any idea why she dropped out?" Tillie asked.

"Max remembers hearing she dropped out to have a baby," Martin answered. Tillie raised an eyebrow but he shook his head. "I wondered the same thing but the timing isn't quite right."

"What about the time in between?" Tillie wanted to know.

"Apparently she took up with a real loser when she went to Albuquerque," Martin continued. "He apparently treated her pretty badly before getting himself killed robbing a liquor store." He frowned. "As near as I can tell, that was about five years later, but Max thought they had just the one child. Carmelita came back to town after the kid's father was killed and has lived there pretty much ever since. For a while she was cleaning houses and doing laundry. Then she got a job as a cook for one of the restaurants in town and did well enough to be able to go back to school now."

Tillie nodded. "Nothing dishonorable about any of that, Martin."

"No," he said, "but I hate to think of her being mistreated and having to do laundry to stay alive."

"I agree," Tillie said. "However, that was the consequence of some of her choices and she's probably a better person for it." She looked at him and asked. "So what else did Max tell you?"

"Not getting much by you, is there?" Martin said.

Tillie shook her head. "As your sponsor I wouldn't be doing my job letting things slide, which you understand quite well. So what is it you don't want to tell me."

"Max thinks the child is living with Luiz now," he added, a strange look on his face. "Luiz raised him." He paused to take a deep breath. "Max tells me Carmelita named him Martin."

"You're sure it's not yours?" Tillie asked.

"Almost positive," he replied. "Of course, only Carmelita knows for sure, if anyone does."

"That's what I was thinking," Tillie told him. "For your sake, and the sake of the child I think you need to know what she has to say."

"I was afraid you were going to say that," he said, nodding. "I think you're right. I need to know."

"Do you think she'll tell you the truth?"

"I don't know," he said. "I think so. I've heard there are some kind of genetic tests they've developed to make sure."

"I read the same article," Tillie said. "Those are still experimental, but all this is irrelevant. The question is, when are you going to do it?" There was no question Tillie was pinning him down and expecting specifics.

"I'm booked on the first flight out Tuesday morning," he answered, grinning. "Unless you think I ought to wait."

"You turkey!" Tillie declared in mock outrage. "You love doing that, don't you? Sandbagging people! But, yes, I think you need to go," she went on. How are you going to find her?"

"Come on, Tillie, I'm a reporter. I know where to dig." He handed her a slip of paper covered with his clear handwriting. Carmelita's name was as the top, followed by an address and telephone number. "She's gone back to her maiden name," he observed. "Or maybe the bastard never married her."

"I forget sometimes, Martin," she laughed. "You come across as such a sweet young man I do forget that behind the facade lurks the mind of an unabridged alcoholic."

"Hey, I like that," he said. "'Unabridged alcoholic.' May I use that in one of my things?"

"Be my guest," she laughed. "I just have one question for you."

"Shoot," he replied.

"Well, two actually. The first is how you're going to approach her. It might not be such a good idea to just drop back into her life after so many years. She may or may not appreciate it."

"I understand," he said. "I dropped her a letter simply saying I would like to get back in touch again if she were agreeable. I told her about my program and that I thought I had amends to make to her. I gave her my unlisted number to call if she doesn't want me to come."

Tillie nodded. "Fair enough, although it would have been better to have talked to me first. Let me see the letter." Martin showed her his copy and she nodded. "Very clean. Now, my second question. How do you feel about all this, Martin?"

"Scared, Tillie," he said gravely. "Scared spitless. To tell the truth, I'd rather be ducking a mortar attack in some rice patty."

"Good," she replied. "A little bit of the right kind of fear can be a good thing. Too much is what gets us in trouble. Trust your program, Martin," she said urgently. "It really works, so work it. Connect with someone down there for local support and call me every day."

"I will," he said. "I will. But you know what?" Tillie shook her head. "I'm also looking forward to seeing her again."

"I was thinking that," Tillie said. "So be careful, Martin, be very, very careful, not only for her sake, but for yours. You're very brittle right now and I would hate to see you change your sobriety date."

Eight days later Tillie came in late to find a message on her recorder. It was from Martin, giving a phone number where he could be reached. All the message said was, "I'll be here all night. Please call me as soon as you can. There is a problem."

Part III. Coming Home

A silent look
A moment passes
Which lasts forever
And something else, too
Passes from I to thou
And thou to me
Its passing changes
Us forever

Souls touch forever
Within the moment
Of our eyes

Angelica
Jubilate!

W.J. Dylle
The Early Years

1. Reunion

Albuquerque, New Mexico. There is great irony in the fact that 1984, the year that titles George Orwell's famous work, begins on Sunday, which Christians call the Day of the Lord, but also commences with the Feast of the Holy Name in the ancient Church Kalendar. I've wondered if Orwell intended that, which would certainly fit his fertile imagination. Or was his choice a form of gentle cosmic humor, as some of the faithful would assert? I don't know, and nothing I've come across has cleared up the mystery. Yet I know this: that many who read Orwell's work approached the coming of this year with something bordering on superstitious dread, and that many of us, myself included, will heave a slightly self conscious sigh of relief when it is over. After all, we're rational folk. We believe in an orderly Universe, and when something touches our deepest fears, as Orwell's Big Brother does mine, we find ourselves reaching for a rabbit's foot, or a Messiah, despite what our rational minds tell us. For so often irrational disorder seems to poke itself through the rational fabric of our universe. (Martin Quinn's journal)

The hotel restaurant was quiet at this hour, the lunch crowd gone and those who came in for mid afternoon coffee scattered around the large dining room, their voices quiet in the emptiness of the room. Quinn glanced at his watch. He was almost an hour early and he considered going back to his room for a while. Yet he wanted to be there first, so he took out a pen and pocket sized spiral notebook to make notes to pass the time.

This was a habit he used well in tense situations all over the world, a way of moving his mind away from worry and focusing on whatever story was going down. Yet today the habit failed him. After a few attempts to jot something, anything down, the effort stalled and he found himself doodling. Seeing what he was doing he smiled to himself and put the notebook away, closing his eyes and concentrating on his breathing. Nor was he surprised to find himself slip into the mantra he used so often these days, his own short from of the prayer for serenity. *O God, my friend.* His thought as he breathed in was a prayer. He held his breath and the thought just for a moment. *Help me now,* he went on, finishing the prayer as he exhaled. Folding his hands in his lap, he let his chin rest on his breast as he continued, drifting away with the calming surf of his mantra repeating itself endlessly as he sat. *O God, my friend... help me now... O God, my friend... help me now....* He felt the tension drain slowly from his body as his soul took flight and...

...he found himself flying high above the desert mountains, every detail of the stony ground etched clearly on the filament of his mind. Tall pines rose out of the coulees and were scattered along the ridges where a narrow stream wandered its way down the valley, fanning out into a broad pond formed by a slide damming its course. The light was dim, almost hazy, as if something were clouding his vision, but whatever it was did not impair the clarity with which he could see even the pine needles and the small birds flitting among the trees.

As he soared he became aware of wind moving through his finger tips, and looking to his right he discovered they were not fingers at all, but long straight feathers spread like fingers to grasp the fabric of the air. Looking to his left he saw his other hand spread out the same, his arm transformed into a long mighty wing easily holding him aloft without motion.

I am condor! he realized, excited with his discovery. *This is my domain.*

Suddenly it was as if he were not only looking through his own eyes at the desert below, but as if he could see himself through the eyes of another as a large black vested bird riding the convection currents of the desert air. A scream of primal joy rose within his throat...

A gasp brought Martin Quinn back to earth. Opening his eyes he found himself staring into those of a young woman in her late thirties and he was struck speechless. She was stunning. Her clear eyes were blue grey, the color of the sky at dawn, startling against the deep tan of her face. She wore only a hint of makeup, and though there were small lines beginning to form around her eyes, these only accentuated the flawless texture of her skin. Her features were strong and angular and her long dark hair, drawn back from her face into classic braids, was beginning to show faint hints of silver. Yet he could see clearly within her the girl of so many years ago, and he could not take his eyes from her face.

"Mr. Quinn?" she asked, apologetically, but all he could do was nod. Then she smiled, filling the room with a radiance he remembered well and sat down opposite. "I'm sorry," she rushed on. "I recognize you from your dust covers, but for a moment when I saw you sitting there, you reminded me of someone else. Someone I used to know a long time ago." Then she frowned. "It's a strange coincidence, but his name was Martin, too."

Quinn started to say something, strangled on his own words, a painful knot forming in his throat. He began to cough, so painfully he could not see and reaching for his water he knocked the glass over, spilling it her direction. As quick as a cat she ducked out of the booth, letting the water splash on the seat. Still choking, Quinn rose to his feet and grabbed a water glass from another table, taking a quick drink and outraging the matron sitting there. "I beg your pardon," he croaked, his eyes watering furiously. "I'm choking."

The matron got to her feet, glared at Quinn, and stalked from the room. Two waiters appeared, ushering Quinn and his companion into a clean booth and bringing them more water. Quinn drank half of his and held up a finger. "Give me a moment," he whispered and both the waiter and the lady nodded.

"Are you all right, Mr. Quinn?" the waiter asked anxiously. "Can I bring you something else? A brandy?"

Quinn shook his head and pointed toward the table just deserted by the matron. "Put her meal on my ticket," he whispered. "Be sure to add the usual fifteen per cent."

"Oh, thank you, sir," the waiter said, smiling. "The ... lady usually only tips five." He hurried away.

Quinn looked at his companion carefully. He could see she must be tall and slender now, with the lean beauty of a thoroughbred playing harmony with the angular planes of her face. Her features were too strong to be classic beauty, but there was a strength there few ever attained, a repose of face and body many might find disquieting. Her rich dark hair hung in braids, framed a silver and turquoise squash blossom necklace and drew the eye to the hint of deep full breasts covered by her simple chambray blouse. A denim vest matched her skirt, and on her feet were thick soled sandals.

As the lady sat quietly, studying him back as frankly as he was her, the deep grey eyes were troubled. "It's uncanny," she said. "You could be his brother, Mr. Quinn."

"I beg your pardon," Martin said, recovering his voice and a bit of his poise. "I owe you an apology. I really do."

"That's what your letter said," the young woman replied. "I am quite familiar with twelve-step programs and the need to make amends, but I'm not aware of any harm you've done me." She frowned. "Unless you are the guy who totaled out my car in the parking lot last fall."

"No, not that," Quinn said, shaking a hand and clearing his throat. In an almost normal voice he continued. "I haven't been here in at least a couple of years. It's my name. I write under the name of Martin Quinn and I've gotten in the habit of using it for everyday life, too. So I signed your letter that way without thinking."

"I don't understand," said the woman. There was concern bordering on fear in her eyes. He wondered what could elicit such fear in this beautiful, strong woman.

"Carmelita," he said in quietly Spanish. "*Yo soy Martin, Martin del canyon de Ramos.* Martin Lundberg." I am Martin, the Martin from Ramos' canyon. Martin Lundberg.

"No!" she cried, looking at him as if seeing a ghost. "You can't be. He's dead. He was killed in the war fifteen years ago. In Palestine."

"No, Carmelita, it's me" Martin replied gently. "It really is me. The Martin from the old Vasquez place. That news report was wrong." He could see she was having trouble accepting his being alive. "They made a mistake in identifying one of the civilians who was killed. I put my coat over the man because he was badly wounded and going into shock. Some of my papers were in the coat when they evacuated him. He's the one who died, not me. But they thought it was me." He stopped, feeling like a fool for rambling.

Carmelita sat, stunned, staring at him wide eyed, emotions running the spectrum across her face. Completely in a daze she opened her purse and took out a pack of cigarettes. Opening it she lit one, her hands shaking as she reached for the ash tray, her eyes fastened to his face. As she did her arm bumped a water glass, spilling it in Martin' lap and he jerked back, wiping the icy water from his lap and started to climb out of the booth. Yet, seeing her face he stopped, sat back down. It was drained of color, a sickly yellow olive below her tan. Reaching out Martin gently took her hand in his. He found it limp, unresponsive to his touch, as if she were under the effect of a powerful sedative. The cigarette burned unnoticed in her other hand and Carmelita's eyes retreated from his face, fixed in the middle distance.

"Mr. Quinn!" said the waiter rushing over. Then seeing Carmelita he stopped. "Is something wrong?"

"She's just had a great shock," Quinn replied, his eyes never leaving Carmelita's face. "I told her something I thought she knew."

"Do I need to call an ambulance, sir?" their waiter asked, worried. "She looks awful."

"I think she'll be all right," Quinn replied. "Let's give her a moment." Very gently he removed the cigarette from her limp fingers, laid it in the ash tray so it couldn't fall out. Then he took both her hands in his and simply waited quietly, watching intently.

After a long while Carmelita blinked and the color began coming back into her face. Pulling her hands from his she covered her face for a moment, then looked up. " God," she breathed. "It really is you."

"Yes," he answered softly. "It really is me. Martin Lundberg."

"I never recognized you from your pictures," she said. "I saw the resemblance right away, but of course, I thought you were dead."

"I should have realized," Martin responded. "That happened with a lot of people when I first came back. Not many people saw the correction they ran after the story of my death. But that was years ago. Almost sixteen years now and it simply didn't occur to me you wouldn't know." He shook his head again. "I should have known. Jack and Stephanie didn't know either when I saw them, but that's been years now. I'm surprised you didn't hear it from them."

"God," she said. "I'm feeling so strange. Like my mind has been disconnected from my body."

"Do you need to lie down?" he asked. "I'm staying here if you do."

She nodded dumbly and he took her arm gently and led her from the dining room. "Send a pot of coffee up to 407," he told the waiter. "I'll take care of all this later."

"Yes, sir!" said the waiter, waving for a bell hop, who helped them across the lobby and into the elevator. Without having to ask, he pushed the button for Quinn's floor and helped them into his suite.

"Stay with her while I change," Quinn told the bell hop, careful helping Carmelita into one of the overstuffed chairs in the siting room. "I'll just be a moment."

Quinn quickly stripped off his soaked pants and underwear, replacing them with a dry set of shorts and a set of soft blue jeans. Kicking off his new Oxfords, he slipped his feet into a pair of soft, worn moccasins and pulled a oversized colored tee shirt over his head. Stepping back into the siting room he tipped the bell hop generously and asked him to send a doctor around if the hotel had one on call.

Turning back to Carmelita he found her eyes focused again, this time fixed on him. "Now I recognize you," she smiled weakly. "In those clothes you look like the Martin I knew."

Martin pulled another chair closer, facing hers, and said," Don't talk if you don't feel like it. Can I send for something?"

Carmelita shook her head. "No, just let me sit for a while," she said. "This has been quite a surprise."

A few moments later a soft knock at the door announced the arrival of the jug of coffee. The waiter wheeled it in on a service cart. "I put together some sandwiches and a bowl of fruit, sir. Compliments of the staff." Quinn tipped him and he disappeared, shutting the door quietly behind him.

Martin poured a cup of coffee and offered it to Carmelita. She shook her head and he sat quietly. After a long silence Carmelita said, "They sure give you good service here." Her voice sounded as if she were speaking from a great distance away.

Martin nodded "I tip well and being well known occasionally has it's benefits." He looked at her with concern. "Could I get you a glass of water? I'm afraid I don't have anything stronger."

"No, thank you," she responded. "I don't drink."

"I don't either," Martin replied. "At least not any more."

"So it's really you. You're really Martin Quinn the author, too?" He nodded and she thought. "How long has it been?" she asked. There was a sudden wariness in her eyes he'd not seen before.

"It's been eighteen years, Carmelita," he said softly. "Eighteen years, almost to the day." He shook his head in wonder. "Yet seeing you now, it's almost like it happened yesterday."

"Yes," she answered. "Yes it is. But it's not yesterday and that's not what I meant. How long's it been since you quit drinking?"

"I passed eight years about a month ago," he answered. "I came into the program sooner but I had a couple of slips at first." He looked at her, saw her nod. "How about yourself?"

"I've been clean over fifteen years now," she said. "Alcohol was never a problem but I don't want to stretch my luck."

Martin nodded. "Yeah, addictive people seem to do it with anything, don't they? Even things like love and religion."

They fell silent. "I probably shouldn't be here," she said after a while. "It's a very nice room, but I think I better go."

"We can go somewhere else if you want," he answered. "Or if you don't want to talk right now, we can wait and talk later."

"What if I don't want to see you at all?" she asked. "Have you considered that?"

A look of deep sadness came over Martin' face as he nodded. "I know that's a possibility and I could understand that," he said. "I will respect it if that's really what you want. I'm here to make amends and if that means staying out of your life, I will certainly respect your wishes. There are some things I need to know, mostly to know if other amends are needed, but we could do that some other way."

"Amends," she said, an edge of bitter anger in her voice. "So you're here to say you're sorry and to ride off into the future."

"Not at all," Martin replied, not taking offence. "I'm here to make amends, not apologize. I will do whatever it takes to set things as right as I can, as soon as I can and within reason."

"Within reason?" she asked, skeptical. "What does that mean? If it isn't too much trouble?"

"It means I'm not going to shoot myself, Carmelita," he said. "Or to allow myself to be used as a door mat or a whipping boy. That won't do anyone any good. Aside from that, I will take whatever time and whatever other commitment it takes."

His manner of speaking left little doubt he meant what he said, but Carmelita was still doubtful. "As soon as you can. What does that mean and how can I be sure you'll carry through?" she asked. "I know lots of recovered alcoholics who don't."

"I can't speak for lots of alcoholics. All I can do is speak for me and all I can suggest is that you watch and see," he told her. "Don't listen to what I say. Listen to what I do."

Carmelita shook her head. "I wish it were that simple, Martin, but it's not. There are other people involved besides you and me."

"I know," he answered. "There's your son."

She looked at him, her eyes suddenly guarded. "How long have you know about him?" she asked.

"About three weeks," he answered. "I learned quite by accident. When I did, I called Max right away to find out more." He nodded to the phone on the lamp table. "Call him if you don't believe me. Please."

She looked at him critically. "All right," she said. "I'll take your word for that. What else do you know?"

"Everything I know is secondhand information," he answered. "That's why I came to you. I've heard you were involved with a man who mistreated you, and maybe your son, too. I heard he was killed robbing a liquor store and I heard that after that you moved back home. I've heard you've been through some really hard times and that now you're back in school trying to finish. I've heard Luiz has helped you raise your son."

"Yes," she said. "Although not all you've said is true. One of the things I did right was protect my son from that. I took him to Luiz after the first time Ronnie hit me. What else do you know?"

Martin looked at her levelly. "Well, I thought he was Ronnie's child from what Max said. Then Max told me what you named him."

"It's not a common name," she shrugged, looking down at her hands. "But I've always like the name and it is a saint's name, after all." She sounded more than a little defensive.

"It's also my name," Martin answered, reaching out and gently lifting her chin. Carmelita pulled back from his touch, but she held his gaze. "That is why I'm here. He is my son, isn't he?" he breathed.

Tears suddenly filled Carmelita's eyes and she wiped them away with a tissue held tightly in her hand. Not trusting her voice she nodded. Martin sighed. "I thought so," he said. "What does he know about me, Carmelita?"

"He believes you're dead. When he was six he asked me about his father and I told him everything I knew about you," Carmelita said. "Later on Luiz told him even more." She smiled for the first time in an hour. While it was weak, Martin felt as if the sun had suddenly found a hole in the clouds of a dark, rainy day and revealed itself briefly in a resplendent bow. "The story he likes best," she said, "is when Luiz tells him about *el lobo de navidad* and how his father chased the wicked witches out of his house. When he was troubled as a child, his favorite thing to do was go up to visit the house where you lived." Then she sobered. "Martin, he thinks you died in the war in Palestine just before he was born. I even told him the truth about your not knowing about him before you died."

"How did you explain that?"

Carmelita looked sad. "It's one of the few lies I told him," she said. "I would have never done it if I thought you were alive." Martin waited quietly for her to continue. "I told him I never told you."

"Well, that's the truth," Martin pointed out.

"I told him you had to go there to work and that I didn't want you to worry about me, about us. So I didn't tell you." She looked at him. "That's the lie I told him. Now I wish I didn't."

Martin shrugged. "It's close enough to the truth for now," he said. "So what's he like now? He must be what, seventeen? Tell me, what's he like?" There was no mistaking the eagerness in his voice.

"Almost eighteen," she answered, smiling again gently. "He's a very sweet young man who looks just like his papa. Luiz guessed right away, as did Tio Emil, although he never said much." She shrugged. "I suppose everyone did, everyone who really knew you. Luiz has been a good father to him, too, even though Martin wasn't his own son. He calls Luiz his dad." She looked at him pleading. "That's why I said it's more complicated than just you and me. Or even you and me and Martin. There's Luiz, too. He considers Martin his son."

"I was closer to Luiz than I was my own brother and I am glad you took our son to him," Martin nodded. "I know it's complicated, but I need to set things right with Luiz, as well as Martin. There's no reason he can't have two father's, is there? Luiz is his dad, and I wouldn't change that for all the world. He always wanted a son. But I am his papa."

Carmelita looked at him searchingly. "Why can't you just stay dead?" she asked. "At least to him."

"You know the answer to that," Martin answered gently. "It simply would never work. Sooner or later he's going to find out anyway, and think of how hurt he will be when he does if we don't tell him now."

"I know, Martin," she said. "But he's at such a critical time in his life right now. He's about to graduate from high school and his mother has left. He didn't say much and he even encouraged me to go ahead last year, but I know it bothered him. I'm afraid this will be too much."

"I don't think there will ever be a good time," he told her. "I also think you underestimate our son. Right now I just found out, and so did you, so there's nothing he has to forgive but some choices we made in ignorance a long time ago. I think our lying to him by our silence would be far more destructive than anything we could say now."

She nodded. "You may be right, but I need time to think. Please. It's all happened very fast."

"I understand that," Martin replied. "May I call you tomorrow?"

She thought for a moment, then nodded. Taking an index card out of her purse, she wrote her first name and a phone number with a cheap automatic pencil and handed it to him. The number was the same as the one he'd been given for her. "I'll be up early," she told him, "but you'd better not call until at least after noon. My room mate works until late at night and we turn the phone off in the morning." Carmelita rose and gathered her things, and Martin followed her, intending to open the door. However, she was too fast and was out of the door and half way to the elevators before he could reach it.

Yet, suddenly turning back, Carmelita walked up and stood close to him, so close he could smell her scent distinctly. "Martin," she said softly, looking deeply into his eyes. "I don't know how things will turn out. I'm afraid for us, for you and me and for our son. But I need to tell you something. I'm glad you're alive." Then she was into the elevator and gone before Martin could respond. Walking back into his room he picked up the phone and called Tillie.

The old restaurant was busy but quiet at this hour. Later, when the evening crowd arrived, the happy noise of people enjoying good food would grow, but it would never be loud in this place. For one thing, the rooms were of good size but the tables were never crowded together. For another, the thick adobe walls prevented much sound from travel-ing from one room to another, and were set in such a way that most of the noise was absorbed by plants in the atrium. As he sat waiting, Martin Quinn was impressed by the skill of the architect in giving the whole place the atmosphere of an open air garden somewhere along the Mediterranean.

Carmelita arrived not long after he was seated. She spoke to the hostess, and Quinn waved when she pointed in his direction. Carmelita waved back and followed their waiter to the table. She sat down when her chair was pulled back and rewarded the waiter with a smile. Turning to Martin, she reached out and patted his arm. "Good morning," she said. "Or good afternoon, I guess" she said, glancing at her watch.

Quinn was relieved to see she was in a good mood, and he was once more struck by her strong beauty. "Well, I'm sure it's still morning in San Francisco," he laughed. "Have you eaten?"

"No, I'm starved", she replied. "I was up late studying and almost missed the bus."

"The bus?" he asked, reaching for a menu. The waiter handed him one and asked what they would have to drink. Both ordered tea. "I thought you had a car.... Oh," he said, remembering and nodded.

"That's right," she reminded him. "Someone totaled it in the parking lot last fall. So I travel by bus mostly these days."

Martin nodded. "You never found out who did it, I gather." Carmelita shook her head and studied the menu for a moment before closing it. "It is my treat," Martin said. Carmelita started to argue but he insisted. "Please. I wanted to treat you to dinner last night but...." He shrugged.

Carmelita looked at him levelly. "All right, Martin, I will. I have to admit I am a struggling student these days and have to be careful."

The waiter returned and they ordered. Carmelita saw his surprise at her ordering a full dinner plate and laughed. "You let yourself in for it. I'm a starving student and I don't get offered a free lunch every day."

"I find that hard to believe," he countered.

"Why do you find that so hard to believe?" she asked, teasing.

"The first time I ever met you I thought you were one of the most beautiful people I had ever seen. I still do. It's hard to imagine you don't get offers for dinner all the time."

"Oh, there are plenty of offers," she replied. "There just aren't many I would consider taking." She shook her head, waving at her body with her hands. "Most men can't see beyond this."

"I think you're wrong," he argued. "I don't know how else to put it, but when you smile it's like you light up the whole room. I think that's what they see. They may be looking at your body, but I think what attracts them is the light inside."

Carmelita looked down. "Martin," she murmured, shaking her head. "Please don't."

"No," he said, "I'm not making a pass, Carmelita. Nor am I being gallant. I'm simply telling you the truth as I see it. You're a beautiful woman and you always will be because your beauty comes from the inside out."

"You're embarrassing me, silly," she said, flushing. "Please stop."

"Oh," he said, surprised. "Sure. Sorry."

"You don't have to be sorry," Carmelita told him. "Just don't be so... direct. I'm not used to it." She looked up at him. "How would you like for me to sit here and tell you what a handsome fellow you are? And how you must have to beat the women off with a stick?"

He laughed. "I should be so lucky. Go ahead. I promise to take it like a man."

"Which means your hat won't fit if I did," Carmelita laughed. "You're awful!"

They sat looking at one another for a while. The waiter brought their food and for a few minutes they ate in silence, regarding one another like two cats, trying to figure out their next move. Martin finished first, having only a salad plate for lunch, and sat back, lighting a cigarette. "Why don't you tell me how it's been with you while I finish eating?" Carmelita suggested and Martin nodded. After a moment he began talking, starting with leaving the canyon and taking a job with his first paper in down state Illinois. He told her about Othello McLeod, the first article which got him the interview with Flayed Newman, and how he ended up in Jerusalem at the beginning of the Six Days War.

As he talked, Martin kept mostly to his professional work, shying away from much of his personal history. Carmelita noticed he skipped over certain periods very lightly, and given his expression as he touched on these, she knew they were still very painful to him.

Yet when he came to the time he stopped drinking and the period which followed, Martin was far more open and personal, and his descriptions of some of his conversations with his sponsor, Adam, kept her laughing. Then he told her of his conversation with Tillie the morning after their marathon session, how Carmelita's name had come up and how it was he came to seek her out.

"It's probably just as well I misunderstood who you were," Carmelita told him. "I don't know if I would have agreed to see you." She was very thoughtful for a while. "So Tillie suggested I'm a ghost from your past that needs to be laid to rest," she said finally, more than a little bitter.

"No!" Martin said emphatically. "That's only her way of talking. The ghost she was talking about is not making amends. You're real people to me, Carmelita. You always have been and you always will be. Among many other things, you're the mother of my child."

"So we're back to the 'a' word," she said softly. "And you tell me you want to make amends, not offer apologies. Amends to me. What if I asked you to never see your son. Staying out of his life would be one way to make amends to us both."

Martin nodded. "I know you think that, but I need to set things right with him, too, Carmelita. I just don't know exactly how to go about it." He looked at her. "I don't want to do him any harm by showing up now, but I do have responsibilities toward him. For one thing, he must be about to graduate from high school and I can send him to any school in the world if he has the grades and wants to go."

"Oh, he has the grades," Carmelita answered. "He's close to the top of his class right now, and he even skipped a grade, too." She smiled, thinking of her son. "Next fall he starts his senior year and he's interested in music. So he wants to study sound physics at MIT."

"Then consider it done," Martin said. "I'll have a trust set up when I get back to Denver."

Carmelita looked troubled. "Martin, I'm serious about your not seeing him. If you do that he'll have to know about you," Carmelita argued. "He'll have to know you're alive."

"He's going to know that anyway," Martin said. Carmelita started to argue but he held up his hand. "Carmelita," he sighed. "I hate to have to put it this way but my amends to him is between me and him," he told her. "It's not about me and you. It's about my son and his father. He's been without his father far too long as it is. So he's going to know."

Carmelita glared at him stubbornly. "Because you want him to," she snapped. "It seems to me, Martin, that you're considering your wants and needs rather than his."

"I understand your saying that," Martin went on gently. "I also understand your concern for him. But listen to me, please. My father died two years ago, without my ever really knowing him as a man. I'm not about to put a burden like that on my son." He looked at her bleakly. "I don't want to lose your friendship, Carmelita. Yet I'm willing to put it on the line for this. I will respect your wishes in every way I can. What I'm asking of you is to work with me, not against me." He shrugged. "I really don't understand your reluctance. What do you have to lose? What does he?"

"What do I have to lose? My son," she told him flatly. "You took away my life, Martin, and now you're trying to take away my son. I won't let you do it. I won't."

"I would never even try to turn your son against you, Carmelita," he answered sadly, overlooking her accusation. "I wish you could believe me about that. For one thing, it simply wouldn't work. For better or worse, you will always be his mother, and for better or for worse, I am his father. I wish you could trust me."

"How can I?" she asked. "I don't know you, Martin. I came to your bed a foolish young girl who thought she was in love with you. I gave you myself. Then you went away and I never heard from you again. How can I trust you?"

"Hold it!" Martin asserted. "Hold it just one damned moment. I was not the one who left. When I went up to Ramos' the next morning to find you, Emil told me you'd already gone. When I went down to Luiz's that evening to find out where you lived, he told me you'd decided to take the bus to Albuquerque a day early. I wrote you several letters and none of them ever came back. Yet you never answered any of them."

Carmelita was crying. "You're right," she admitted. "I never opened them. Not until after I heard you died and then it was too late. I almost killed myself. If it hadn't been for the baby I probably would have."

"Why didn't you open them?" he asked. "Why did you run from me?"

"Well, we had just betrayed Stephania," Carmelita told him. "Me even more than you. She's my cousin and I tried to take away her finance." She shook her head. "I still feel bad about that."

Martin sighed. "There's something I want you to read," he said. "I think it may put your mind at rest. It came the same day you came up with Luiz to say goodbye to Emiliano." He handed her a blue envelope, its edges worn from years of being carried around, but the address and post mark were still quite clear. The stamp was foreign, cancelled in Johannesburg, South Africa a full two weeks before the day young Martin was conceived.

Carmelita looked at Martin. He nodded. "Please," he said. "Just read it. Then you'll understand."

Carmelita touched a brown stain along one edge of the envelope. It looked like thick brown ink. "What's this?" she asked.

"That's the blood of the man I covered with my jacket," he answered. "That was why they thought he was me. They found the letter."

"You've carried this with you all these years," she said, wonderingly. "Everywhere you've gone?" He nodded and looked down, a desolate cast etched across his face. Carmelita opened the envelope and took out a sheet of blue paper, stationery she recognized as belonging to Stephanie. She saw the longhand was hers, as well.

"*Dearest Martin,*" the letter began, "*This is the most difficult thing I have ever had to do. And maybe the most loving thing I can do for your sake, as well as mine.*"

Knowing what was coming, Carmelita read on, quickly coming to the heart of the matter. "*When I am with you, there is no other place on earth I want to be, nothing more I want to do than be your wife, the mother of your children and the maker of our home. Yet when I am here, doing the work I love so well, days can pass without my thinking of you and me together. I don't know why this is, but I know it tells me clearly I am not being fair to you. I have loved you as I have loved no other man, but for me, that is not enough. Perhaps some day it will be, but not now. Nor can I ask you to wait until it is, for I am not sure it will ever be.*"

Carmelita paused for a moment, overcome by her cousin's anguish and the pain it must have caused her lover. Then she continued to read. "*I am breaking our engagement, Martin. I hope you will find someone much more deserving of your love and goodness than me. I am sorry for the hurt I know this will bring you, but I believe it will be less hurtful to you than my living a lie. Goodbye, dear Martin. I do love you, believe me I do, and I always will, but love alone is not enough....*"

Carmelita carefully folded the worn paper and started to put it back into the envelope when something caught her eye. "What's this?" she asked taking out a white piece of folded paper almost exactly the same size as the envelope. She opened it and started. She recognized the writing immediately and was too stunned to cover her surprise.

"I don't know," he answered, puzzled at her response. "I always thought it was part of the envelope." Taking it from her he read it quickly. "Oh Martin," it said. "I am so sorry. Please forgive me. And please don't tell S. I don't want to ruin your happiness together." It was signed, "C."

"It's from you," Martin said. "It's the note I found on my dresser the day you left. I thought I had lost it. I looked for it for years." He fell silent, looking at her and remembering, knowing she was doing the same.

The silence hung heavy between them for a long moment. Then Carmelita spoke. "So as it turns out, I really didn't betray her," she said. "Neither did you." Martin nodded. "Although to be completely honest, I didn't know it at the time," Carmelita added. "So I really did betray her."

"A priest would point out you repented," Martin suggested gently. "I personally think you've done ample penance."

"There's something I want to know," Carmelita told him. "I thought of it on the way home last night. What do you think you have to make amends to me for? What did you do to me in your mind?"

"I got drunk and I used you without thinking," Martin replied quickly. "I didn't know about our son or I'd have done something long before now." He looked down. "That's what I came here thinking, anyway. Right now I wonder if I don't owe amends for not trying harder to see you."

"What would you have done if you had known about him?"

"I would have tried to get you to marry me. At the very least, I would have made sure you had everything you needed to raise him." Martin looked at her levelly. "I'd have tried to make sure you stayed in school, too, if you wanted to. I'm prepared to do that right now, if you will let me," he added. "I can't force it on you."

"I'd like to believe you, Martin," she replied. "I really would. At the moment you sound too good to be true. Or maybe I'm just scared. Maybe I want to believe you too much. Do you understand?"

Martin sighed. "I can't promise I won't screw up. I make mistakes like anyone else. I can promise to try to always admit it and make amends when I need to. So like I said, listen to my actions." He poured himself another glass of water from the pitcher on their table and took a bite out of one of the remaining chips in their basket. "The first thing I'd like to do is see our son. After that I'm going to set up separate trusts for you and for him."

Carmelita started to say something but he said, "I want to hear what you have to say, but let me just finish. Please?" She nodded. "I've thought about how to set it up so it never becomes a bone of contention. The money in the trust will be put there for you to use however you see fit. There will be enough you will never have to ask me for money, and if you don't use it, then it will go to Martin after your death, or to the University if both of you refuse."

"The money troubles me, Martin," she told him. "It feels like you're trying to buy our love. I know you don't mean it that way, but that's how it feels." She shrugged. "I don't know if I can use it."

Martin nodded. "I know. That's why I set it up the way I did. Either you use it or it will become the Emiliano Ramos fund for scholarships. The choice is yours, not mine, and I will never know if you choose not to tell me."

"Seems you've thought of everything," she said.

"There's one thing that really bothers me that I haven't been able to figure out yet," he told her. "I hate your having to ride the bus. Would you at least let me buy you a reliable set of wheels?"

Carmelita gave him a direct look. "You really know how to tempt a girl, don't you?" Martin started to protest and she laughed. "I'm teasing. I would be forever grateful, but..." she stopped. "I hate to say it."

"Then I will," he countered. "No strings attached. You have time to do it this afternoon?"

"Tomorrow afternoon would be better. I have a mid term exam in the morning." She shrugged.

"All right," he answered. "You can me what you like and I'll do some scouting around this afternoon. Give me something to do." He took another drink of water. "Now," he continued, wiping his mouth, "What do you think would be the best way of letting our son know I'm alive? We need to do it soon, so what I'd suggest is writing him a letter, and then giving him a call."

"No," she said. "You're his father. You write the letter and I will take it to him and answer his questions the next time I go home."

"I really want to see him," Martin countered. "Can you take a couple of days off to drive up so you and I can see him together?"

"I don't want to shock him the way you shocked me," she argued.

"Please, that was completely unintentional," Martin told her. "I really thought you knew who I was." He thought. "Why don't you call him and tell him you're bringing someone you want him to meet? Warn Luiz who it is so we don't shock him."

"I don't want him thinking you're a boyfriend," Carmelita declared. "If I tell him I'm bringing someone I want him to meet that's what he'll think."

"Ouch!" Martin complained. "I guess I let myself in for that. Tell him I'm not a boyfriend but someone you knew a long time ago who wants to meet him. That will work."

Carmelita sighed. "All right. I can go day after tomorrow. I just hope you're right about this."

"I do, too," Martin told her. "God, do I ever."

Carmelita nodded and picked up her purse. "It's been quite a day," she said, getting to her feet, "but I need to go and I've got to catch the bus."

"Let me send you home in a cab," Martin offered. "That way we could maybe grab a bite of supper later."

"Thanks," Carmelita responded. "I'm afraid my stomach's still a little too full to eat much more today." She smiled. "Besides, I have a date."

"Oh," he said, crestfallen. "Well, at least let me get you a cab."

"Actually, it's a date with a book. I have a history exam tomorrow and that's why I can't go with you until Thursday." She took a heavy text out of her large purse. "I was planning on reviewing it on the bus."

"History?" he asked, suddenly enthusiastic. "That was my field and I graduated with honors. Need a tutor?"

"Martin," Carmelita said, "please slow down. I like you but I need some time to sort all this out in my mind."

"Carmelita," he answered. "When I said tutor, I meant tutor. We have a son in common and we need to get to know one another better.

I really am not pressing at you. Let's find a quiet restaurant where I can review you while we eat. When we're done I'll put you in a cab home and I'll come back here. My treat for a starving student."

"Well," she said solemnly. "All right, but you'll have to promise me one thing." He nodded. "You have to promise on your word of honor not to embarrass me by knocking over water glasses." Then she flashed him a quick smile, filling the room with radiance and reminding him of the day he first saw her in the town square. "Let me use the phone and I'll save you cab fare. It's too late to go there and back and I need to call my room mate. We were supposed to study together this evening. We're taking the same class."

"Tell her to join us," Martin suggested. "I'll treat us all."

"Him," Carmelita corrected. "No, it's not like that, silly," she said laughing at his expression. "He's my cousin. Besides that, he's gay." She looked at him questioningly. "Do you have a problem with that?"

"No," he told her. "Just so long as he understands I'm not."

The morning was bright and beautiful. The night before a torrential rain stormed through with a front, washing the air of dust and leaving it clean and clear. As Martin and Carmelita drove north toward Berna-dillo, the rolling plain to their left was bright with hints of new green, while the Sandia peaks high to their left brooded in a deep study of blues and purples. The air was chill, as well as clear, this early in the morning, though it was late spring, and they drove with their windows rolled up.

"So," said Martin to Carmelita, who was driving. "How does it feel?"

"Oh, I like it," she answered. "It's really responsive and I like the way I can scoot around in traffic." She smiled at him. "I think you were right about the bigger engine, but I don't understand why you bought it new when there was a perfectly good used one on the same lot. You would have saved a thousand dollars." They were talking about the brand new Tercel station wagon they picked out the afternoon before. It was white, although Martin encouraged Carmelita to get the red one she really liked better. "No," she'd replied. "I really like the white one, too. White is a much safer color on gray rainy days."

Martin nodded and smiled to himself. *There aren't too many of those kind of days around here*, he thought but kept it to himself. After all she was right, and every morning and evening presented low light situations.

Nor was he about to argue against safety. Carmelita had really wanted a little yellow Volkswagen bug, and he had talked her out of that citing the crash fatality figures.

Martin nodded. "I used to feel that way, too. But I don't spend my money on much these days, and when I do I always go for quality first." He shook his head. "It took me a long time to understand that I didn't have to worry about money any more. I'm not extravagant and it seems to pile up faster than I can use it. I give a lot of it away."

"What does that have to do with this?" she asked.

"My own comfort. I'd rather pay the extra thousand and have the peace of mind knowing you were just that less likely to break down somewhere. That's why I also had a CB radio put in. You may never, ever need it, but it's there if you do." He shrugged. "I appreciate your humoring me."

"Oh, I like it," Carmelita laughed. "What do you think my CB 'handle' should be? How about Red Hot Momma?"

"That would get you a lot of attention," he agreed. "Whether it's the kind you want or not is the question."

"Well, what would you suggest?" she challenged.

"How about Sister Carmen?" he laughed.

"Then they'll think I'm a nun," Carmelita protested indignant.

"Not if you tell them you're a psychic and Tarot reader," he laughed, referring to a sign they'd passed. It advertised a psychic reader.

Yes!" Carmelita laughed again. "I can tell them I can read palms over the air waves. All they have to do is lay their hand on the radio."

"And if you get it wrong, you can accuse someone else listening in of confusing the reading by laying their hand on the radio, too!"

Their laughter tapered off and they fell silent as they drove, passing the turnoff to Santa Fe and continuing on toward Las Vegas. Carmelita drove confidently and well, and Martin was pleased to learn she was no stranger to the mysteries of the manual shift. Passing the turnoff to Glorieta he turned to her and asked, "How are you feeling?"

"Scared," she admitted, briefly glancing his way and quickly back to the road. "I want this to work, Martin. There are so many things that can go wrong."

He nodded. "Same here. I'm glad it's out of our hands now. They know we're coming and there's not much we can do except tell the truth and be as loving as we can."

"Yes," Carmelita said. "But Stephanie was right. Sometimes love is not enough. Trying to love harder doesn't work very well, either."

"No," he agreed, "it really doesn't, does it? What I'm saying, though, is that the outcome is not up to us. It's a higher power thing."

"I'm afraid I'm not much of a believer these days, Martin," Carmelita said. "God seemed to be conspicuously absent when I needed him most, and who came to my help were some good people, not God."

Martin nodded. "I can't answer that for you, Carmelita," he responded. "My own experience is that God works mostly through other people in my life, people like Adam and Tillie. I wouldn't be here this minute if it weren't for Tillie, and I don't see it as a coincidence we both were at that particular meeting and that we connected."

"So you see it all as a grand plan God has?" Carmelita wanted to know.

"Not a rigid plan," he answered. "No, it's more like God lets us choose and act, then works it out to the best for all."

"Tell that to a starving child in Albuquerque!" Carmelita snapped.

Martin sighed. "Carmelita, I have seen settlement camps with tens of thousands of children starving to death. Not because there wasn't food but because men with fucking guns kept them from getting it! And only because other governments did not want to get involved. I've seen children used as carriers of bombs set off by remote control to kill enemy soldiers, children sent to die that way. There's not much human nastiness I haven't seen, and yet in the middle of the nastiest symphony of human evil, there are grace notes written all over the score. What I came to understand very clearly is that I don't know jack shit when it comes to how the universe works."

Carmelita was quiet. After a while Martin sighed deeply. "I beg your pardon, Carmelita. End of sermon." Carmelita glanced at him again, was surprised to see tears in his eyes, pain cut deep into the lines of his face. He smiled and nodded. "That's why I used to tell myself I drank. To avoid the pain I saw. The only problem was, in avoiding the pain, I shut out joy, too."

Carmelita reached over, took his hand, squeezed it gently. "I know, Martin," she murmured. "I really do understand. I didn't know how well you did. My higher power is simply the goodness of the human spirit."

He nodded and they drove on again in silence, passing Serafina and then Romeroville on their right. "I'll certainly drive if you're getting tired," he told her.

Carmelita grinned. "Are you kidding? You don't know what it's like being without wheels at my age, kemo sabe."

Martin laughed. "Carmelita, I've thought about timing and there's one thing I don't understand," he said. "Martin must have been born in February, wasn't he."

"Yes," she smiled. "February fourteenth. He was a love child and I almost gave him Valentine for a middle name."

"I wish you had," Martin said. "What did you give him instead?"

"Stephen." Martin started and she nodded. "Yes, I named him for her, too. She brought us together and I thought it might make up for my betrayal. I know now that was foolish thinking but I was young and confused."

"Does she know?" Martin asked.

Stephanie shook her head. "No, or if she does, she hasn't said anything about it."

Martin looked at her. "I'd be willing to bet that even if she knew about us she wouldn't think you betrayed her. In her mind, he'd already broken it off with me."

Stephanie shrugged. "What did you want to ask me?" she interjected, changing the subject.

"Well, Martin was born in February," he answered. "And I didn't 'die' in Palestine until June. Why didn't you get in touch with me before I went overseas? You had about three months."

"I was very hurt and very scared and very guilty," she answered. "So I thought it was God's punishment for my betrayal, having to raise a child all by myself. Then when you died, I was sure of it."

"Jesus," he breathed. "No wonder you have a hard time with the God thing now. I was raised the same way, but that's not at all like the God of my understanding now." He shook his head. "I'm sorry you had to go through all that alone."

She sighed and shrugged. "They say it takes what it takes. So for better or for worse, as a friend of mine says," she teased, looking at him out of the corner of her eye, "it's made me who I am now."

Martin looked at her and smiled. "I take it we are friends now?" She nodded. "Do you... have any interest in... seeing if there's more there?" he asked, choosing his words carefully.

Pulling the car off the road she stopped it and set the brake, then she looked at him gravely. "I don't want to push things, Martin. Let's be friends one day at a time and see where that leads. The night we made love was one of the most beautiful experiences of my life, and the birth of our son was the only thing greater. I don't want to risk that memory trying to recapture it." She opened the door and climbed out. "I need to find a bush. Why don't you drive when I get back."

When Martin started the car and resumed their trip Carmelita looked at him and smiled. "Does that answer your question?" He nodded. "Just to be very clear," she said, "what I am saying is a highly qualified 'yes.' I'd like to be able to slay 'YES!' but I can't right now. Maybe later."

Martin nodded. "Thank you," he said. "It helps to be clear." Then he continued. "So, how are we going to handle this when we get there?"

"I've been giving that some thought," she replied. "Here's the way I'd like to handle it." Briefly she outlined her plan. "Is that agreeable with you?" she asked him.

Martin nodded. "That would do very well. There's only one other thing I think we need to do. After we do all that, I need some time alone with just him and me."

"Marvelous," Carmelita said. "I was going to suggest it if you didn't."

"There's not getting much by you, is there?" he teased.

"Just remember that and we'll do famously," she retorted. "Actually it's very simple. Just do what I want and we'll do fine."

"That's funny," he answered, laughing. "You took the words right out of my mouth."

2. Patri Et Filie

So it was that the adam, the red earth creature created in the likeness of Him who makes all, and in His image, beheld what the Earth Maker had created from his rib. And the adam shouted, "At last! This is bone of my bone and flesh of my flesh!" Which is why a man leaves his father and a woman leaves her mother and the two become one flesh.

Book of Beginnings 2:23-24

Northern New Mexico 1984. The town square hadn't changed much in the last eighteen years. Martin Quinn saw a gap like a missing tooth, now used for a parking lot. There a wooden frame building housing a hardware store stood for fifty years before burning to the ground one night eight years before. Quinn was sad to see it gone, for every time he came to town he once spent hours probing the secrets of its musty, dimly lit racks and shelves. On two occasions, having become friends over the years with the owner of the store, he was admitted to the holy of holies, the vast, cluttered store room at the rear. Both times the owner almost had to drag him out so the man could close the store for the evening.

Though he missed the hardware store, Martin could see the rest of the buildings on the square were still standing. Some of them housed different businesses now, and one or two were vacant, but their stone or adobe walls kept them safe when the paint department of the hardware store exploded into flames. Anchoring the eastern side of the plaza was the adobe Roman church complex, whose thick adobe walls would stand for a thousand years as a home to the faithful and as a beacon of hope to those whose faith would remain known to God alone.

Whether one attended services or not, the mass of the building there, and perhaps the massive number of Masses celebrated for the masses, lent a comfortable sense of the presence of the unchanging in a world of shifting sands. Businesses came and went on the square, people were born and died, but within the adobe walls the *ecclesia christi* was still in business after two thousand years. Though its form and rituals did change from time to time over the centuries, its presence and proclamation were the same: *hoc est corpus meus*, which infidels transliterated into hocus pocus, but which lost none of its power to their efforts. "This is My Body," it said. "You are My people."

Martin stopped the car and moved his gaze on around the square. The bank still stood next to the church, facing it at right angles, and further down the row was Mama Lupe's, still in place almost fifty years after opening its doors, and one of the finest New Mexican food restaurants in the state. Not long ago it had unfortunately been discovered by the food editor from the Albuquerque newspaper. While this had not changed the quality of food, local folk often found it hard to get a table on weekends and during vacation season. So Lupe had taken the obvious step and reserved her best, largest room for local trade. While this it might have been violation of the law, prices were much lower in the local room. Nor was this altruistic. Lupe knew it was local business which built Mama Lupe's over the years. The locals would remain loyal long after the *tourista chingadas* were gone.

Martin drove the Tercel around the square slowly, smiling and pointing as he did. Turning down the street between the bank and the church, he was surprised to see how many cars now lined streets once mostly vacant. Nor were they junkers and it seemed to him the town must have a higher number of expensive German luxury cars per capita than Dallas. He said as much to Carmelita who nodded and pointed to a spot where someone was pulling out from the curb. "Why don't you take that one," she said.

Martin waited for the other car to move. "We're still two blocks from Luiz's," he pointed out.

"I know," she answered, "but we may not find anything closer. Tina opened a bakery across the street and sometimes it's impossible to find a place to park at Luiz's."

Martin nodded, although it took him a moment to remember Tina was Luiz's older sister. "Is she living with them?" Martin asked.

"Yes," said Carmelita, giving him a strange look. "I forget you've been out of touch. Tina moved in not long after Luiz's wife left him about six years ago. Martin and I were living there, too and it got a little crowded, so she and I shared a room." She smiled. "We're very close, but she wasn't too sad to see me go back to school."

Martin laughed. "I remember her now. Hasn't Luiz remarried?"

"No," Carmelita replied. "He's a good Catholic and it would hurt his business in town." She shrugged. "Of course, it she dies...."

"She'll probably outlive us all," Martin said, distracted by something and not wanting to believe his eyes. "When did they put in parking meters?" he asked, indignant.

Carmelita gave him a wry grin. Most local people shared his feelings but were aware that tourists bore most of the brunt, and the income was welcome in city coffers. "Several years now. Ever since Dickman and his crowd took over the Chamber of Commerce and tourists started pouring into town."

"Why do they come here?" Martin wanted to know. "One of the reasons I came here in the first place was I didn't see much here to attract most tourists."

"That seems to be the 'in' thing these days," Carmelita answered, locking the car. "That's another thing I've had trouble getting used to," she added, holding up her keys. "Having to lock everything up all the time. Doing that in the city makes sense, but here?"

Martin appreciated the delicacy with which Carmelita put all this, most of all about his being out of touch. He nodded his appreciation for what she was not saying, and they stood there a moment, neither moving. They looked at one another, each knowing their moment of truth had arrived but both very reluctant to take the irrevocable first step. "Are you ready for this?" she asked quietly.

"No," he answered honestly. "I was champing at the bit this morning, but now we're here, not at all." He looked at her. "How about you?"

"I could very easily be talked into backing out of this," she told him. "But I don't believe we should."

Martin reached out a hand and took hers. "You're a good woman, Carmelita," he said simply. "I'm glad I know you."

Carmelita did not withdraw her hand. "You don't really know me," she said. "Nor do I know you. Yet I think you're a good man."

"Sometimes a person has to trust their feelings," he replied. "I find it much easier to say than to do, but when I do, I'm almost always right." He touched her lightly on the sternum just below her neck. While it surprised her, still she didn't pull away. "What I see in here, where it counts, is an incredibly beautiful soul, and I trust that sense of you."

Carmelita was struggling, he could see. It was obvious to him that while she wanted to believe what she was hearing, there was a frightened part of herself it would take years of trust to reach, if ever it could. As much as he wanted to see his son, ached to see him for the first time, he did not want to lose this woman. "Carmelita, this may not be the day to do this," he suggested. "Why don't we just walk abound a while and let our feelings settle."

Carmelita smiled and squeezed his hand. "To be perfectly honest," she said, "I'm afraid my feelings would settle on terror. We better do it if we're going to. I'm afraid I'll chicken out later."

"All right, then, let's go see our son," he said. "Ladies first?"

Again she smiled. "You know the way as well as I do," she told him. "Down here it's customary for the man to go first to protect the women and children."

"Is that what it is?" he asked, offering her his arm. "I thought it was just basic chauvinism."

"Chauvin was a Frenchman, not a Spaniard," she replied, mocking. "I know because we just studied that in history." She took his arm and they started off in the direction of Luiz's house.

"That's right," he remembered. "You did. You seemed to like history. Or was it the tutor? Most people tell me they find it boring."

"Not me," she answered. "I love history. You don't find it boring, do you?"

"Only when I make the same mistake more than three times," he laughed. "Disraeli was right, you know. Those who forget history seem to end up repeating it."

"That's a sobering thought," Carmelita said. Then she started to say something else but stopped.

"Are we repeating it, you think?" Martin asked lightly.

Carmelita glanced at him sharply. "That's uncanny," she told him. "It makes twice now you've done that."

"Done what?" he asked, not sure what she was talking about.

"Spoken the exact thought I was having," Carmelita responded. "It's three times, actually. I thought the first two were coincidence."

Martin stopped, turned her toward him. "Carmelita," he said soft-ly. "Whatever we may think about what happened with us back then, something very special happened between us. I didn't realize that until I talked to Tillie before coming down here. I don't know what it is, or was, but I do know it wasn't something passing. Somehow our souls touched and I think maybe neither of us has been the same since."

"Martin," she said, looking down. "Please, don't. It's too soon."

He nodded, gently raising her chin so her eyes met his. "I know," he said. "I think it may be a good while before we talk about it, and I'm not pushing. I'm just letting you know. You are important to me, and not just as the mother of my child. That's what I'm saying." He lifted her hand gently to his lips and kissed it.

Carmelita suddenly hugged him quickly, then took his hand and pulled him in the direction of Luiz's. They were only a half block away and Luiz must have been watching for them. As Martin started to knock, Luiz opened the door, leaving him standing there with his fist raised foolishly.

"Martin!" Luiz shouted, grabbing him in a bear hug. "*Mi paisano*! Man, it's good to see you! We all thought you were dead."

"Man, it's good to see you, too, *cunado*," Martin replied, returning the *abrazo*. "All of you," he laughed, looking his friend up and down. "There's more of you now." Luiz laughed and hugged Carmelita. "I'm surprised Jack or Steph didn't say something," Martin added. "I ran into them in Denver four or five years ago."

Any answer Luiz might have given was interrupted by a young man coming into the room. He was of medium build, taller than Martin, with the same dark features. Carmelita smiled and crossed to him. Hug-ging him she said, "Paco," causing Martin to start by using a pet name Rosa once used for her son, "Here's the old friend I told you I want you to meet."

"I know," said the young man. "He's my father everyone thought was dead. Dad told me."

Luiz nodded. "Yes, I thought it best not to surprise him." Carmelita was clearly not pleased but shrugged. Men!

Martin was thunderstruck. Looking at his son he felt a strange sense of deja vu, or as if he were standing in front of a magic mirror which peeled the years away. Taking a black and white photo from his jacket pocket he showed it to Carmelita, whose eyes widened. The picture was one of a young man in football uniform standing looking at the camera with a gaze of cool detachment, his helmet held casually under his arm. The bright white number 18 showed clearly against the dark jersey and anyone seeing the picture for the first time would swear it was of Paco. Only the date written on the back indicated it was not.

"Goodness," Carmelita said, showing it to Luiz, who looked at it and laughed, handing it on to Paco. "*El lobo de navidad,*" he agreed.

Paco took the photo Luiz handed him and looked at it. He blinked, but other than that showed nothing. Tough guy, Martin thought. Just like his old man. Studying it carefully he nodded and grinned. "Well," he said, "it can't be me. I never wore a flat top." Then looking at Martin curiously, he asked with the easy candor of youth, "How come everyone thought you were dead?"

"It was a dumb mistake that never got corrected," Martin said. "Why don't we sit down and I'll tell you how it happened."

"Good idea," Luiz said. "I just made more coffee and Tina sent over some fresh sweetbreads from the bakery."

"No wonder there's so much more of you now," Martin quipped. "You have your own in-house bakery."

An hour later they were gathered around the large kitchen table. A demolished plate of sweet breads lay in the middle of the table with nothing left but crumbs, and somewhere in the middle Martin had scrambled eggs to go with them. "Man, you sure haven't forgotten how to cook," Luiz told him. "I remember how you used to feed us out of your garden."

Martin nodded. "It always tastes better with fresh ingredients." He looked at Paco. "I need to stretch my legs. Want to come with?" Paco nodded and they left the house, aimlessly walking the dusty streets until they came to the city park down by the river. Martin seated himself at a table under a huge cottonwood and Paco followed suit. "This part of town hasn't changed much," Martin observed, nodding across the creek to a herd of goats in a large pen. I see Musquiz still has dairy goats."

"That's his son," Paco answered. "His dad died a couple of years ago."

Martin was surprised. "I'm sorry to hear that. He was a good man. I think the son must be the fourth generation on that land."

Paco nodded and said nothing, studying the grass. "So what do you want to know?" his dad asked.

"How do you know I want to ask anything?" Paco challenged.

Martin suppressed a grin. "I have strange occult powers," he replied solemnly. "Ever since the aliens kidnapped me and worked me over in their space ship." For a moment it hung in balance. Then Paco snorted and rolled his eyes. "Hey, you do that good," his dad told him. "I bet it drives your mother batty."

Paco simply looked at him. "All right," Martin said. "I'll cut the crap. I don't know that you want to ask me anything. Yet you are a very intelligent fellow, so I'm told. I am, too, and in your place I'd have dozens of questions."

"Maybe I do," Paco replied. "Maybe it's not time to ask now."

"Fair enough," Martin said. "You like cars?"

"How could anybody be raised by Luiz and not like cars?"

"I don't know," Martin told him. "Maybe it didn't take." He looked at Paco directly. "Look, Paco. I know this is all a big surprise. I was blown away when I found out and I still am. I've only known for three weeks. We don't have to talk if you don't want to right now. Or ever, if that's your choice. I'm going to be around a long while, so there's no rush."

Paco said nothing. Martin nodded and got to his feet. "All right, Paco. I'm going back to the house. Let me know."

Paco remained seated, but looked up. Martin was about to leave when his son said, "Yeah, I like cars. I've got my own I'm building up. Luiz taught me how. A 'Fifty-seven Chevy."

"Good choice," Martin said, nodding and taking a seat again. "It's a classic. Would you care to show me?"

Paco looked at him and grinned for the first time. "I thought you'd never ask."

As they walked to the garage where Paco was restoring the old car, it was if a plug had been pulled from a water spout. Paco described in exacting detail exactly what he had done, and appreciated the questions Martin asked. When his son opened the garage door, Martin was impressed by what he saw there. "Goodness," he said, running an appreciative hand over the surface of a fender. "You've done a super job."

Nor was he being kind. The gleaming white and chrome machine was trimmed with turquoise along the high fins and through the new windshield he could see fresh new upholstery. It looked like leather. Brand new whitewall tires and plain chrome moon hubcaps shod the beast and the wide chrome "V" front and back proclaimed it had the power to really move. "Looks finished to me," Martin told Paco. "What else do you have to do?"

Paco shrugged and looked embarrassed. "The engine," he said. "I did it last and I found the block was cracked. I'm waiting until I have the money to get a new one."

Martin was thoughtful. "Most people would have done that first," he observed. "There's enough money in that upholstery to do a new motor. Why did you wait?"

"I wanted it to be perfect before I drove it," Paco said. "I don't want to drive around in a primered heap like some guys do."

"All or nothing," Martin said, nodding. "I'm the same way. We have more in common than you may realize."

"Dad never understood why I waited," Paco said. "He would have been driving it a year now." He looked at Martin. "So what do I call you?" he asked. "Father? Mr. Quinn?"

"Good question," Martin said. "Luiz is your dad and I'm honored to have you call him that. Father is way too formal." He shrugged. "How do you feel about using my first name, calling me Martin?"

"Mama would probably chew me out if I did that," Paco laughed.

"I'll fade the heat there," Martin responded. "But use the Spanish pronunciation. I like it better."

"Martin," Paco said, listening to how it sounded as he pronounced it. "I've never known anyone else with our name."

"I'm relieved," Martin said. For a moment Paco stared at him not comprehending. Then Martin added, "Two of us is plenty, don't you think?" and he laughed.

"I don't know," said Paco. "I always wanted a brother or a sister my own age. Dad's kids are all older except for Josephina and she's a pain."

"Sorry I didn't think of that," Martin answered, and they both laughed. "Not to get heavy," he told Paco, handing him one of his business cards. "If you do want to know something, you don't have to wait until you see me. I have an answering service who always knows where I am and can track me down. All you have to do is tell them you're my son. That's the first number. The one I've written in is the unlisted one at my apartment. You can call any time day or night."

Paco nodded and put the card in his wallet. Martin continued. "You'll be graduating soon and I'd like to give you a present. Would you let me give you an engine for this rig?"

Paco was thoughtful. "Thanks," he said. "I'd like that, but I'd like the money put in my college fund better. He nodded toward the car. "I can always finish this later after I get done."

Martin nodded. "Your college is already paid for," he told his son. "My parents paid for mine and I'm paying for yours, if you will let me. All you have to do is carry a full load and keep your grades up, same as with any other scholarship. My attorney is putting together the trust right now."

"What about Mama," Paco asked. "Could you help her, too?"

"I will, if she'll allow it," Martin replied, shaking his head doubtfully. "I don't know, she may not. She can be pretty hard headed sometimes."

"Tell me about it!" Paco laughed. Then he grew serious. "Are you all...?" He paused, not knowing how to ask.

"We're not lovers now," his father told him. "We weren't even lovers back then, not really."

"I don't understand," Paco responded. "I thought you were."

So Martin told him how he'd been conceived, holding nothing back. When he was done Paco nodded and asked, "So why didn't you try to find her? Weren't you in love with Mama, then?"

"I was too messed up to be in love with anyone," Martin said. "When Stephanie broke off our engagement...."

"Stephanie?" Paco asked, shocked. "Alicia's mother?"

"I don't know," Martin shook his head. "The lady I'm talking about lives up the canyon and is married to a man called Jack Bear."

"That's Alicia's dad," Paco assured him. "Wow."

"Sounds like a soap opera, doesn't it?" his father agreed. "The point is, your mother was very much in love with me. Or she thought she was. I was very lonely and very confused. I wish I could tell you it was different, but I can't. I like her very much and I always have, but I wasn't in love with her the way she was with me."

"So she lied to me," Paco replied, looking angry.

"Not really," Martin told him. "Look at it from her point of view. She may have stretched things a little to spare your feelings, but she basically told you the truth."

"A lie's a lie!" Paco insisted.

"No," Martin contradicted him. "I've told you the truth as I know it, but she understood things differently."

"She told me you were lovers."

"From her perspective we were. Remember she was very young and couldn't understand why I didn't feel the same." He looked at his son with concern. "Paco, the last thing I want to do is to come between you and your mother. Please believe me. Your mother may not have had her facts straight, but she told you the truth as she knew it."

For the moment things hung in balance. Then Paco nodded. "I know," he said. "I don't know why I said that."

"Hey, cut yourself some slack," his father replied. "A whole lot's been thrown at you today." He thought. "To answer your question, your mother and I are working at establishing a relationship right now. I don't know what it will be and neither does she, so we're going very slowly. I know this. I care for her a great deal. I hope it develops into something more."

Paco nodded, was thoughtful. "Well," he said, "I think I'd like to have the engine. That way I can take this to college." He looked at Martin. "Can you help me put it in?"

Martin laughed. "You don't know what you're asking, Paco, so I won't hold you to it. I can change a flat and basic stuff like that, but that's about all I am confident doing. You and your dad are the members of the family with mechanical skill. Tell you what, let me be your swamper."

"What's a swamper?" Paco wanted to know and their talk returned to working on cars and other manly addictions.

The auto parts store was open on the square and they stopped by on the way home to order an engine. Paco started to order a short block, but Martin persuaded him to go ahead and order the fully rebuilt engine. "A short block is a false economy, Paco," he said. "A full engine will save time. There's is no way we can rebuild the upper end as well as a machine shop." His son still looked doubtful and he added, "Did you do the upholstery yourself?"

"No way!" Paco answered. "I wanted it done right."

"The same principle applies here. Yes, we could do it, but a factory engine will go twice as far before needing another overhaul, and the motor is the heart of the car. I think you'd be better off spending your time somewhere else." He shrugged. "Whatever. It's your choice."

Paco nodded and grinned, then ordered the full engine a new battery, and a full set of tires. He watched impassively as Martin paid the bill with a credit card. "How about one of those, too?" he asked.

"Those you have to do for yourself, my friend," his father laughed. "One step at a time, all right?"

Paco nodded and grinned back. "It didn't hurt to try, did it?"

Carmelita looked up anxiously when the two Martin' returned to the house, was relieved to hear them laughing with one another as they came in. "Hey, Mama," Paco told her. "Martin is going to help me with the car." Seeing her face he quickly added. "He told me to call him that." His father nodded agreement.

"Well I don't like it," she stated in no uncertain terms. "Why don't you call him papa?"

Martin intervened. "Carmelita, papa is something children use. We're a little beyond that, I think." Over Carmelita's shoulder he could see his son begin to smile. "We're getting to know each other as grown men and Quinn is what most of my contemporaries call me. I guess he could use that but it sounds too distant." He raised an eyebrow in question and Paco nodded.

"So call him *el patron*," Luiz contributed, walking into just in time to catch the tall end of the conversation.

"Sounds too much like *el cabrón*," Martin objected. The three men laughed and Carmelita rolled her eyes and threw up her hands. "What did I do to deserve this?" she asked the Anyone beyond. Yet she was not really displeased. "You need the money for college," she reminded Paco.

"I thought you understood I was taking care of that," Martin told her. "My lawyer will have trust papers drawn up for me to sign when we get back to Albuquerque and I took out a short term policy to protect you both until he does." Martin fished in his coat and came up with a flat folder he handed her. "You'll never have to worry about money again unless you want to."

She opened the folder, looked at the papers. "We're not for sale, Martin," she said, handing the folder back.

Martin took it and handed it to Luiz who took it as if he were being offered a live snake. "I know you're not, and I'm not trying to buy you," he answered. "I'd just hate the state and feds to get it all and for you to get nothing. The holographic will is legal and there's an original on file with a lawyer in Albuquerque. I know him from when I was here before." He looked at her directly. "It's one way I can make amends," he told her. "Not only to you, but to Luiz, as well. You three and my mother are the only people I have, so I'm naming you. Whether you take it or not is your choice." Out of the corner of his eye he saw Paco's smile begin to broaden into a grin. Not many could get away with speaking so directly to his mother. *Damn*, Martin thought. *I need to be careful. I don't want to undercut Carmelita.*

Carmelita, however, had seen the grin, too, and her jaw began to set. "I mean it, Martin," she responded.

"I mean it, too," he answered. "I am not trying to be unpleasant, but I intend my for son to enjoy the fruits of my labor if I'm not around to share them with him."

"He's still a child," Carmelita said, trying to get the argument back to safe ground. Paco frowned hearing this and shook his head, but said nothing. "And I'm his mother," Carmelita continued. Until he's grown I'll decide what is good for him."

"My son is a man grown," Martin told her, pointing. "He is as tall as I am and I don't think we should talk in front of him like he's a little child." He turned to Paco. "You'll be eighteen in not many months and legally on your own. You need to respect your mother in every way but you need to make your own decisions. What I'm telling you is that you don't have to worry about school, or professional school, either." He smiled. "So long as you keep your grades up. My lawyer in Albuquerque will be your banker until you're twenty-five if I'm not around and after that you're on your own. Fair enough?" Paco nodded solemnly while Carmelita frowned.

"So if I bump you off that means I'm rich?" Luiz laughed, trying to defuse the conflict.

"I think the law might frown on that, Luiz," Martin laughed. He looked at Luiz seriously. "You may not know it, my friend, but you are already one of the richest men I know. I don't know anyone who has more friends. Compared to you I'm a pauper."

Luiz didn't know quite how to respond. Carmelita came to his rescue. "That's right, Martin," she said taking Luiz's arm. "When it comes to friends, I don't know anyone who has more than our Luiz."

"And all of them want to borrow money!" Luiz complained. Grinning, he pointed to the papers. "We better keep this quiet, Martin. You know how people can get about money. I'll never have any peace if word gets out."

Martin smiled and spoke to Carmelita. "Could you and I have a word in private?" She looked at him a moment, then nodded and led him out through the kitchen into a small walled courtyard behind the house. Without having to ask Martin knew this was a special place to her, a place of refuge which bore the small marks of her touch, her own self. Taking a seat beside a wrought iron picnic table she sat, looking at her hands as she waited for him to speak. "Carmelita," he said softly. "Please believe me. I'm really not trying to get in the way between you and our son."

To his surprise she nodded. "I know, Martin. I really do. I know you *are* right about his being a man. He is already, even though he's not yet eighteen." She looked up at him, eyes wide and countenance clear. "That's the reason I went to school this last year rather than waiting. I know he doesn't need me any more and that hurts."

"Oh, no, Carmelita, you're wrong," Martin assured her. "He needs you and he always will. I still need my mother after all these years, but it's not in the same way as it was when I was a child."

She nodded. "I really do know, Martin. He really doesn't need me the same way but it's hard to get used to the change. I know I need to let him go and be on his own, but it's hard to do that, too." She looked at him directly, then reached out and touched his arm. "For so long he was all I had. I don't want him to be hurt. Or spoiled."

"I can't promise I'll never hurt him," he responded. "Because I'm sure I will. Not intentionally, but I will. I have bad days, too." He looked at her, his eyes reaching out, caressing hers. "One thing I can promise. I will never abandon him the way my father did me." He smiled gently. "I'll never abandon you again, either. That's why I've set things up the way I have, so you'll never have to feel you're coming to me begging. That's very important to me. I've been on the other end."

"It must be," Carmelita answered, giving him an odd look. "What if I take it and run? What would you do then?"

"Once I became convinced you didn't want me in your life, I would butt out completely," he answered, smiling. "I hope you don't do that because I like you. I like being around you." He shrugged. "I guess that's the risk I have to take, but it's only money."

"You like me," she said. It was a flat statement, spoken as if she were looking at it closely but reserving judgment. "You don't know me very well, but you like me."

"Yes, I do, Carmelita," he answered, sighing. "I know you better than you think." She glanced up sharply, but he waved her concern away. "No, I haven't had anyone snooping around. I know how to read people and I can see your integrity written all over our son. I respect what you've done raising him and I really like you as a person. I like being with you...."

Martin stopped, the thought left unfinished. After a moment Carmelita asked, "But what?"

Martin looked at her levelly. "Not a but, at least not about you. I was going to say I like you in a way I think could grow into love, but I'm not sure I know what love is. Or that I'm capable of loving the way you deserve."

"Well," she answered, smiling shyly. "I'm not so sure I do, either. So I guess we'll just have to wait and see."

"Do you mind if I court you?" he asked, his tone intent but casual.

"Isn't that what you've been doing?" she laughed. Then she reached out to touch his arm again. "I'm sorry. I have a wicked sense of humor. The answer is yes, I'd like that very much. Just please, be patient with me. Don't push me too fast."

"Good," he said, taking her hand and kissing it gently. "I won't. We'll take it a day at a time and take it easy. I don't want to scare you away again."

Carmelita got to her feet, came close to him when he arose. "You may be the one who gets scared," she said, coming into his arms and giving him a kiss which left him gasping. "That's just to seal the bargain," she whispered, gently pulling back. "I've wanted to do that for two days."

"You don't have to stop," he answered, finding his voice.

"Oh, yes I do," Carmelita laughed, squeezing his hand. "I don't want to shock our son. We'd better go back in."

Martin nodded. "He'll be wondering what we're talking about" he said, raising her hand to his lips and kissing it. "Speaking of which, I'd like to take him up to the place to see it. Would you like to come along?"

"No," Carmelita answered. "I want to visit with Luiz and Tina, and I think you two need some more time by yourselves. Men stuff."

"Male bonding," he agreed, nodding. "Scratch ourselves, spit on the ground, make primal noises. Argh, gronk, patooie! Me Urzuk!"

"You do that well, Mr. Quinn," she laughed, leading the way back into the house. "Maybe you could give your son lessons."

"It's genetic," he assured her. "Just like..." he stopped abruptly, biting off his words and almost choking on them.

"Making thunder," she laughed, walking ahead of him into the kitchen. "It's good to know you can be embarrassed."

Three-quarters of an hour later Martin and Paco were carefully picking their way up the road to the canyon. The road had not improved with age. If anything, the surface seemed rougher than before, and in some spots it was obvious it had been months, if not even years, since the blade of a grader had given it the grace of its attention. Nor did the fact Paco was driving do much to smooth their ride in Martin' opinion, though he said nothing. To be fair, his son seemed to be trying hard, perhaps too hard, to be gingerly with his mother's new car. "Damn!" Paco said, as a rock ricocheted off the fender well with a loud clank. "We should have brought Luiz's truck. Mama will kill me if I scratch this baby."

"You're doing fine," Martin lied, drawing a look of gratitude from his son. "I think we should have rented a tank." The road couldn't be too much worse and still be passable. "Don't they ever grade out here any more?"

"Not since *El Zapo* got elected county commissioner," Paco told him. "Dad says he doesn't do anything up here."

"*El Zapo*?" Martin asked. The name was oddly familiar although he couldn't remember exactly who it was they used to call The Toad.

"A *gringo* named Dickman," Paco told him, swearing under his breath as he turned the wheel hard to avoid a deep pot hole. Then, realizing what he had said, he looked at Martin as if expecting disapproval.

"That's a good way of describing the *chingada*," his father laughed. "Sometimes you have to call things by their Christian names."

"Mama doesn't like it when I swear," Paco told him. "She says it's a lack of intelligence."

Martin nodded. "It can be," he said. "Some people don't seem to know how to say anything else or express things any other way. It can be a real art, too, however." He broke into a fluent burst of harsh utterance.

"That sounds nasty," Paco said, impressed. "What did you say?"

"It's an old Turkish insult going all the way back to the Mongols," his father informed him. You've got to be a real horseman to appreciate it, I suppose. What it says is, 'Wipe the shit off your saddle, you incompetent farters! You stink so bad even your own goats won't copulate with you!' It loses something in translation."

Paco laughed. "How did you say it?" he asked, and Martin spent the next five minutes teaching him the slur phrase by phrase. Like himself, Paco had a gift for tongues, and soon they were moving around the globe with his father teaching him bits and phrases he'd picked up in his travels. Then the road suddenly became smooth and Martin remarked on it. "Alicia's dad keeps it fixed from here on up," Paco told him, pointing to a homestead not far distant. "You want to stop by?"

While it was apparent to Martin it was Alicia, not her parents, Paco wanted to see, he shook his head. "Maybe on the way down," he said, evading an issue which troubled him. Seeing Jack Bear and Stephanie was more than he wanted to take on for the day. There would be time for that later. "I want to get on up to the place," he said.

"You going to see Tio Max?" Paco asked.

"On the way down, yes," Martin answered. "Right now I'm anxious to see the old man. It's been way too long since I've seen him." He looked at his son. "Has he told you much about himself?"

"Tio Emil?" Paco asked. Martin nodded and he smiled. "Yes, but I don't know what to believe. What he says is pretty far out."

Martin laughed. "I thought that, too, when I first met him. What I think you'll discover is he has only told you what he thinks you might believe. When I had time I checked him out, and, if anything, what he told me was far too modest." He laughed. "I even talked to the rector of the seminary he attended in Spain. Come to find out they started the same time and shared a cell together."

"A cell?" Paco was surprised. "Like in prison?"

"No, but now I think about it, they are probably not all that different." He thought a moment. "The original meaning of the word probably meant a small room, but in a monastery that's what they call the monk's rooms. They were free to leave, and that was the difference."

Paco nodded. They were passing the old Vasques place and Martin saw someone working in the garden and waved. The gardener looked up as he did and waved back. There's Max," Martin said. "We'll stop and see him if he doesn't come on up." He rolled down the window and stuck his arm out to point toward to the Ramos place. The gardener held up a thumb and nodded before going back to his work.

Paco looked uncomfortable. "That's not Max," he said. "That's Carlos, Max's... room mate." He glanced at his father, then concentrated a bit too much on his driving.

Martin turned and looked at his son directly. "You mean his lover?" Paco nodded guiltily. "Does that bother you, Paco?"

Paco shrugged. "Well, I know what they say. And I know what the Church teaches. But when I see them together they're very kind and gentle to each other. Almost like...." He stopped, searching for words.

"Almost like a married couple who really love each other?" Martin said gently. Paco shrugged and nodded. "I don't know how you feel about it," his father told him, "but Max is one of the most beautiful souls I know. I think we have to recognize the gift of love no matter what form it may take." He looked at Paco directly. "Stop the car for a moment, son."

Paco looked at his father sharply, but did as he asked. Halting the car, he turned and held Martin' gaze. "I an sorry, Paco. I didn't mean to sound patronizing." He smiled. "Literally. The only time you will ever hear me call you son is when I really want you to hear what I have to say, and I promise never to use it as a term of disrespect. If I do I want you to call me on it, all right?" Paco nodded and relaxed.

"The kind of relationship you've just described is what I would like to develop with your mother," Martin said. "I believe we are moving in that direction, but it may take some time."

"What's the big deal?" Paco asked, puzzled. "Why don't you just do it? I mean, you've already...." Suddenly he realized how his words could be taken, and embarrassed, he broke off. "I'm sorry. I didn't mean..."

His father smiled gently. "You didn't mean any disrespect, I know. We already have been physically intimate, yes," Martin nodded. You are living proof of that and we are both glad you're around. However, one thing that's been true for me is that physical intimacy is much easier to do than emotional and spiritual intimacy. Not to be crude, but getting it on as a man and woman is much easier than really loving someone, particularly someone of the opposite sex. We're easing our way along there."

Paco nodded and they sat for a moment. Then, glancing at Martin, he said, "I hope it works out." Then he started the engine and drove on to Emil Ramos' drive.

The old man was sitting on his porch as they drove up, much the way he had so many years before when Martin first came to the canyon. As he rose from his chair, however, Martin could tell time had taken its due, for the old man seemed stiff and he braced himself with a cane. Nor did Ramos at first recognize him. "Good afternoon, sir," he called out in classic Spanish. "Are you lost?"

"I don't think so," Martin shouted back. "Although I might be a strain even on God's grace. Most people ask if I have been saved."

Apparently the old man's hearing had faded with the years, as had his eyesight. Looking puzzled he responded, "I certainly hope you have. What service can I do for you, sir?"

"I'm looking for an old brujo named Emiliano Ramos!" Martin said. "This young man told me I might find him here."

The old man frowned and squinted at Paco. "Hey, you're Carmelita's boy, Paco, aren't you?" he asked. The young man laughed and waved. "Who is this rude *pendejo*?" he asked Paco, who laughed all the harder.

"I don't know," Paco answered, shrugging. "I picked him up on the road. He claims he knows you."

Martin suddenly realized he was being had. He covered his face with a hand. "I see you're still up to your old tricks," he said, bounding up the steps and giving the old man a bear hug. "Corrupting the young."

"Most of them don't need corrupting," Ramos answered, hugging him back with surprising strength. "Especially those from Minnesota. *Hijo*, it's good to see you! How is our dear Rosa?"

What struck Martin later about their conversation that afternoon was that it seemed as if he had been only gone a matter of days, not years. Only the old man's physical stiffness seemed different, and Martin remembered times before when the old man suffered the same affliction when the weather changed. Yet there was no question he was older. His salt and pepper hair was now snowy white and the lines in his face were much deeper. Yet his eyes were clear, as was his mind, and there was no mistaking his delight.

At first Paco followed their conversation intently, but after a while Martin noticed his attention was wandering and caught him glancing back down the canyon. Laughing he said to Ramos, "Paco is very polite, but I think there is another house up here he'd rather be visiting." Paco nodded and grinned shyly and Martin told him, "Go ahead on down and see if Alicia is home. I'll walk down later or get Max to drive me down."

"Thanks, Martin," Paco said, loping down the walk and climbing into the car before his father could change his mind. "I'll check back later on. Do you mind if I take Alicia for a ride?" Martin' face must have reflected his concern, for Paco added, "I'll stay on the smooth part of the road."

"Sure," Martin replied. "Just remember it's your mother's car, not mine and you'll have to answer to her if you scratch it up."

"Carmelita is doing very well to have such a nice car," Ramos noted as they watched the new Tercel carefully make its way down the drive.

Martin shrugged. "It makes life easier for her and I can easily afford it," he answered. "I don't spend half of what I make these days."

The old man nodded. "So Paco knows who his real father is now?" he asked. The other nodded and the old man continued, "I wondered when she named him after you, but I wasn't sure. That *ladrone* she was with looks a little like you, too, and I thought Paco might be his. So I said nothing." He smiled. "Seeing the two of you together now, there is absolutely no doubt in my mind. He looks very much like you did the first time I ever saw you."

"I wish I'd known," Martin said. "I could have helped out a bit."

"I started to write you more than once," the old man told him. "Yet I was not sure, either, or I would have. How did you ever get in touch?"

Martin told him of his conversation with Tillie, and how he came to look Carmelita up. "I can't get over it," he said when he was done. "She really thought I was dead all these years. I would think someone would have said something to someone else, but somehow it never happened."

"Perhaps it only happened when it was time for it to happen," Ramos suggested. "Perhaps it would not have worked well earlier."

"There's a time both of us remember that I would have argued with you," Martin responded. "These days I try not to second guess the HP."

"HP?" Ramos asked, confused. "Highway Patrol? Or did I not hear you right?"

"Higher Power," Martin laughed. "I've been in recovery for several years now, Emil. That's what a lot of my friends call God."

"Ah," the old man nodded. "I knew you turned a corner there from your letters. Not so much from what you said, but how you said it. I can see it quite clearly comparing one of your recent letters to one of the early ones."

"You saved them?" Martin asked.

"Of course," Ramos laughed. "All the journal entries you sent as you wrote them, too. Or had you forgotten?"

"I guess I did. Could I see them? Not now, but sometime?"

"Of course, you can," Ramos nodded. "Although since you've become famous I may have to charge you."

"I guess they're worth something," Martin laughed.

"I was saving them for Paco mainly," Ramos told him. "He has always been interested in *el lobo de navidad*."

"I suppose I'll never outlive that," Martin said, not altogether happy about it. "At least, not around here."

"Why would you want to?" Ramos inquired. "It is very much who you are, my friend. So is the writer, but the Raven Wolf is more ancient, I think."

"Raven Wolf," Martin murmured. "You know, it's funny, but that's been on my mind a lot lately."

"I'm not surprised," Ramos answered. "Especially if you have spent much time with Carmelita."

"I don't follow," Martin confessed.

The old man sighed. "I don't want to offend you, my friend, but so little of what human beings sometimes do is conscious."

"I can't promise not to get pissed," Martin said. "But I can promise to forgive you if I do. Is that good enough?"

"You've always been very good about that with me," Ramos said. "I think at times you were more patient than I deserved."

"I probably was, but it worked both ways," his friend replied. So what it is about Carmelita that has me thinking of the Raven Wolf?"

"Well, remember the day you followed him?" Martin nodded. "It was the night after you called him to your fire. We had a lot of fun with it when you told me about it, but do you remember what he was doing when you finally caught up with him?"

"How could I forget?" Martin laughed. "But what does that....?" He broke off suddenly. "Oh, shit!"

"Precisely," the old man said. "Raven means black. And who was there when you earned the name?"

"You were," Martin told him. "At least, you came out with Luiz later on when Ignacio called you."

"You're forgetting, my friend. It was not Ignacio who called and asked Luiz to bring me." Ramos looked at him intently.

Martin shook his head as if dazed. "No, it wasn't, was it? It was...." He stopped as the realization hit him. "It was Carmelita."

"She was there the whole time," the other pointed out dryly.

"That's right!" Martin said. "She was. She wanted to come see the pottery Ignacio's aunt made, so I invited her to ride with me. Then, when I was ill, she nursed me."

"I think pottery was a lesser attraction," the old man observed dryly. "Later on she chose the black wolf, the raven wolf, for her mate."

"Jesus!" Martin breathed, reverently.

"Or maybe his Mother," Ramos said, smiling. "I think you're thinking about the Raven Wolf for a reason. A call of the wild, so to speak."

"Carmelita may not agree," Martin pointed out.

"Oh, I think she will," the old man told him. She's loved you from the moment she first laid eyes on you in the square." He nodded. "I think it goes the other way, too."

"It does," Martin confessed. "But we're both very afraid."

"The hound of heaven will take care of that," Ramos assured him. He yawned. "I'm thirsty. Why don't you fix us some tea?"

"I bet everything is still in exactly the same place," Martin teased.

"Of course," the old man laughed with him. "How else would I ever remember where it was?"

3. Point Of Departure

New Year's Day, 1992. Again, tonight, I bring in the New Year as I have for many years now, walking though the city streets. Those I know and love no longer tell me this is a dangerous thing to do, although our city grows more violent and bloody with each passing year. Or does it? I am told our perceptions do not match the hard figures the police derive from their arrest reports. Yet who can say? Perhaps the lower crime figure only shows we are getting used to it and no longer report what once we might have considered outrage but now shrug off as the stuff of life. I do know that in all the years I have walked these streets, I have never been accosted or mugged or threatened, not even by the half wild dogs and cats which come out to scavenge the alleys.

Tonight, as remains my annual custom, I end my vigil at the news room, reading over the fire and police reports. While some years are better or worse than others taken as a whole, what I have noticed, which is even more significant to me, is that in some years the spread between the good news and the bad news is greater. In those years in which disasters seem to abound, so does something I have learned to call grace, and the outcomes of these disasters is often far different from what one might expect. What I have witnessed is that where disaster brings human loss and anguish and grief, more often than not it also brings about profound change not only in those who suffer, but also in others whose lives they touch, making them different, and subtly better, human beings.

There are many who would argue this with me, but this is my personal witness and testament, and one which continues to surprise me. As a news reporter it was easy to be cynical given the nature of what we see and report each and every day of the year, and cynicism became a habit of soul which almost destroyed me. Then something happened in my life, the miracle I call sobriety. With it came new vision. For what I was hearing day after day as I sat listening of the stories of those who sat there with me was witness to miracles which were as commonplace as the disasters which haunted me.

I first saw this in the lives of these others who helped give me a new way of looking at the world, a 'new pair of glasses' which saw more clearly, more charitably. I began to see what happened as they looked at the world with eyes of love and compassion rather than with fear. Then I began to notice this in my own life as I came to realize I was not a victim of circumstance in a hostile world. More than a victim, I was a player in a process of bringing an imperfect world which is still being created into the fullness of all it could be, to its perfection in a universe shot through with grace. Not least in the process was seeing the fear which had driven me change to concern and even liking of those I once despised. God help me, I found myself even feeling charitable toward Arabs, who had murdered my wife and child.

With this realization, the news I covered took on a different cast, for I began to look for the miracles behind all the seeming disasters I was sent to cover. Looking for these, I found them in numbers which were bewildering, and I wondered how I could have ever been so blind as not see them before. They were there for the eyes of those who could see them, and seeing the small day to day miracles of healing and reconciliation, I began to see the larger miracles of love which lay behind them.

This last year is a case in point. The year began with Desert Shield, which turned into Desert Storm. A hundred hours after it began, the war had destroyed the fourth largest army in the world with thousands upon thousands of dead and the world facing ecological disaster from the fumes of hundreds of oil well fires set by the retreating army. Cholera broke out in Peru, claiming the lives of hundreds, and a week later four white LA police officers were videotaped viciously beating a black motorist they stopped, revealing the institutionalized racism in one of the largest cities in America. Six weeks later a huge cyclone stuck Bangledesh, claiming the lives of an estimated 120,000 people and leaving millions more without shelter. Late in May the premier of India was assassinated, Mount Pinatubo erupted in the Philippines in June, compounding the threat of the Kuwaiti fires, and August brought race riots between blacks and Hasidic Jews in Brooklyn. This was less than a week after neo-Nazi skinheads marched in the streets of Bayreuth to mark the fourth anniversary of the death of Hitler's deputy, Rudolph Hess. The same week, hardliners in the Soviet Union attempted an unsuccessful coup to oust Gorbachev a week before Soviet deputies voted to dissolve the world's second largest nation.

Miles Davis died in late September and earlier that month it was re-

vealed that the government of France had been carrying out industrial es-
pionage against major American corporations in France. A black judge of
dubious competence was confirmed to the Supreme Court in October after
a scandal which many felt would have disqualified a white candidate, and
we witnessed the public trashing of a whistle blower by the powers that be.
A civil war which broke out in Yugoslavia earlier became more intense, and
Serbs shelled the historic city of Dubrovnik, threatening the destruction of
'the pearl of the Adriatic'. There was good news in November when the last
of the Kuwaiti oil well fires was extinguished, but this was overshadowed
two days later by the news that Magic Johnson had tested positive for AIDS.
Then Pan Am's last flight landed in Miami on December 4 and on Christmas Day Mikhail Gorbachev resigned, bringing to an end what Ronald
Rayguns called 'the evil empire'. Looking to the arts, the mood of the year
seemed to be summed up in the title of the latest Arnold Schwartzeneger
movie, Terminator 2: The Final Judgment.

Quite a crop for a single year, and on a personal level, 1991 was one of
the most difficult I have ever had to live through. With the passing of the
old year came the death of Emil Ramos, who died on his birthday, January
6, at age 80. I was surprised when I learned he was born in 1911, for I
had thought him much older than that, and his death was devastating. For
months I wandered around from one thing to the next, hardly able to finish
a project or begin anything new, and I know I was not there much of the
time for Carmelita, my wife of five years now, and Paco, my son. Only our
three year-old daughter, Rosita, seemed to be able to pull me out of my gloom
and the three of us spent much of the first half of the year walking the beach
and collecting shells.

The death of the man I consider my spiritual father was bad enough, but
in March we learned my mother had cancer. The surgery was successful and
she responded well to chemotherapy, but there remains a large question mark
over her future, even though the physicians tell us it was caught early and
they believe they got it all. Then came August, when one of my best friends,
Othello McLeod, was killed in a plane crash, leaving his widow, Rosalind
with three children to raise. Without Carmelita I don't know how I would
have gotten through it, and Rosalind seemed particularly grateful for her
calm presence. Yet when I try to express my gratitude, Carmelita tells me
payback time is coming and I owe her, big.

So where is the grace in all of this? Oddly enough, it is in the very act
of grieving, for standing in my sense of loss, beautiful memories have come

flooding back, the gift of times and places and events I never thought of that way when they were happening. Oddly enough, after a while the pain goes away, but the joy in those memories remains. So when the blues come in the early hours of the human spirit, I read over the many notebooks I have filled with these memories, and always the grace of newer memories and their joy comes. No, I am not denying my loss. I am standing in grief even as I write these words, the tears of loss making it hard to see what I have written, yet I know the tears will pass and I will find joy this morning. For in this last year I have experienced the healing of my deepest wound and a grief I thought I would carry to the grave. With this healing, I have been given a gift of joy beyond anything I could imagine.

That is the grace upon grace I have seen this year in my own life. I remain convinced if you take the very worst of the news stories of this last year and were able to see with God's eyes into the lives of all those who suffered and survived, you would see grace upon grace taking place in their daily lives. Nor would many of them be aware of exactly what is unfolding before them or what it means. (Martin Quinn's journal)

November 1991. The late afternoon sun was warm in the Canyon, even now, the Friday before Thanksgiving. Martin stood on the porch of the old Ramos place, which now belonged to him, watching his wife and his daughter play their simple games in the yard. Hearing something on the road up from the Vasques place where Max still lived, he looked up to see a car approaching. Nor was it one he knew. "Someone's coming," he said to Carmelita, squinting in the bright light for a better look. "It's not Luiz and I don't recognize the car. Do you suppose it's Paco?"

Carmelita picked up Rosita and looked down the road. "Not unless he's gotten a new one. He told us he won't be here until next week. Tuesday at the earliest."

"I know," Martin replied. "I wonder who it is?" He stood a moment longer, then turned into the house. "I better put water on for tea just in case."

The preparations took longer than Martin thought, and he heard a car door slam just as he was putting water on the hot spot of the cast iron stove. As he moved through the house toward the front porch he heard Carmelita's voice calling him, "Martin, there's someone here to see you." There was a strange tone in her voice and, worried, he hurried out onto the porch.

There was a young woman standing in the yard talking to Carmelita and Rosita, her back to the door. She was of medium height with long dark hair hanging almost to her waist and wearing jeans that fit very well. Oddly enough, there was something very familiar to him in the way she stood.

Hearing the door, she turned and looked at him over her shoulder in a way that sent a shock wave through his mind, and seeing her face, the blood drained from his. "Tovah?" he called out, reaching toward her. Then he pitched forward onto the porch in a dead faint.

When he came to, Martin found himself lying on his back and look-ing at the ceiling of his front porch. Carmelita was looking down at him, a wash cloth in her hand and a look of concern on her face as she bathed his brow with the cloth. "What happened?" he asked, trying to sit up, but Carmelita restrained him. Then he remembered. "I thought I saw Tovah," he said, looking from side to side, but no one was there.

Carmelita smiled gently. "I know," she told him. "What happened to you is what happened to me when we met again in Albuquerque. When I thought you were dead."

"Tovah's alive?" he asked, incredulous. "She's here?"

"No," Carmelita told him. "You didn't see Tovah, Martin. You made a mistake. You saw her daughter."

"Her daughter?" he asked, confused. "She didn't have a daughter. Our child was her first born."

"This is your daughter, too," Carmelita told him, watching him closely, waving for someone to join her. The door of the house opened and the young woman he'd seen stepped out.

"I look like my mother," the young woman said, reaching in her pocket and taking out a photograph. She handed it to Martin.

"I remember when this was taken," he responded. "That's the house where she lived in the background and my mother snapped the picture for me. I had a copy made and sent it to her." He showed the photo-graph to Carmelita who looked at it with an odd look on her face.

"She looks just like her mother," Carmelita smiled. "She looks like you, too, Martin."

Quinn sat up, despite the protests of the two women and sat in the rocking chair on the porch. Little Rosita, feeling herself shut out and wanting some attention, came to her father and climbed into his lap.

Carmelita started to take the child but Martin shook his head. "This is your little sister, Rosita," he told his daughter. Then he frowned. "I'm sorry, I don't know your name." He was clearly embarrassed.

"I'm Rose, Rose Sharon," the young woman told her sister. "You have almost the same name I do."

Rosita giggled and Martin exchanged an odd look with Carmelita, who shrugged and looked down. He couldn't tell what she was feeling, yet she did not seem displeased so much as surprised. "I'm having a little trouble with this," he said to Rose. "This has been very sudden."

She nodded. "Would you like me to leave and come back later? I will if you want me to." The expression on her face told them clearly this was not what she really wanted, but that she would if they wished.

"Of course not," Carmelita said, reaching out and taking her hand. "I am just as surprised as Martin is, although maybe I shouldn't be by now. He did the same thing to me and Paco, your brother. We all thought you were killed when your mother died."

Rose nodded. "I know. I got mixed up with another baby. Mother wasn't killed by the bomb right away. She went into labor and delivered me right there on the street. A medic picked me up and cleaned me and handed me to a woman whose child had been killed in the blast. She was in pretty bad shape too, and it was several days later, after she died, they discovered their mistake. Her child was a little boy." She shrugged. "Since mother wasn't married I was given to some of her *kibutzim* to raise."

"Why didn't they try to get in touch with me?" Martin asked. "I would have come for you."

"I asked my mom, the woman who raised me, that," Rose told him. "She knew mother wanted me raised as a sabra and they were afraid if they told you that you'd bring me to the United States. So they raised me as one of their own children. I didn't know I was adopted until I went to school and even then I didn't hear the whole story." She frowned. "I only found out about it a year ago, when I was being checked for a security clearance, and then I had to drag it out of mom. She is afraid I'll leave and never come back, but I wouldn't do that."

"No," Martin murmured. "Of course not. Not if you're your mother's daughter. She could be pretty stubborn at times."

Carmelita laughed. "Look who's talking!" she told Rose. "You must have gotten it from your mother because he still has all his."

"Why's your name Rose?" Rosita asked her.

Martin laughed. "What else could it be?" Turning to his daughter, he asked. "Do you know where you got the name?"

"No, I don't," she told him. "My mom told me it was a name mother picked for me before I was born, but she didn't know why. She always said it was because I was mother's Rose of Sharon."

"You were named for my mother, Rosa," Martin told her. "Just like little Rosita here."

"Oh. Is my grandmother...dead?" Rose asked, tentatively.

"Oh no," Martin replied. "She's been sick and we're worried about her, but she's still very much alive. I want you to meet her just as soon as you can. She'll be here for Thanksgiving."

"We'll need to break the news to her ahead of time so it's not such a shock," Carmelita reminded his. "Can you stay?" she asked Rose.

"Oh, yes," Rose whispered softly. There were tears in her eyes. "I want that, too." She hesitated, then said, "Daddy? May I call you that?"

"Sure," Martin responded, opening his arms. Rose came into them and hugged him, trapping little Rosita, who giggled and hugged them both back.

Carmelita hesitated just a moment and then sighed happily and joined the hug, putting her arms around them all. "Welcome home, Rose," she said softly, repeating herself in Spanish. "*Bienvenidos a tu casa y a tu familia.*"

"*Gracias,*" Rose replied. "*Me gusta mucho conocerle.*" Thank you. I am very glad to meet you.

"*Yo tambien,*" Rosita cried out in a muffled voice. Me, too!

Letting go of her father, Rose picked up her little sister. "This is going to get confusing!" she told the toddler, continuing in fluent Spanish. There are three Roses in this family. There's little Rosita," she said, tickling the child, "Grandma Rosa, and me, Rose. What are we going to do?"

"Granny's name is Granny," Rosita objected, speaking English. "I'm Rosita, and you're Rosysharn."

"Where did you learn to speak Spanish?" Martin asked. "You're very fluent, almost like a native."

"Berlitz," Rose laughed. "I have an aptitude for languages and the government sent me to school in New York. "I work as a translator for our delegation to the United Nations," she explained. "It didn't pay as much as I'd like but they sent me to school and I get to travel." She laughed. "I even have a diplomatic passport."

"Why don't we go into the house?" Carmelita said. "Martin put water on for tea and we have some fresh sweet breads. I'll show you your room."

"Oh," said Rose. "I don't want to impose."

"You're not imposing, dear," Carmelita assured her. "You're family and we want you to stay. There's plenty of room."

The following morning Martin and Rose went for a long walk, just the two of them, although Rosita begged to come along and wasn't satisfied until Rose promised to play with her after lunch. Walking down to what he still called the old Vasques place, although Max had lived there now for more than twenty years, Martin showed her the goat trail up the face and pointed out where he once had fallen into the stream below going home one night. He told her what he knew of the history of the place, of how it had been when he first came there and all the work which went into restoring it.

"It's so beautiful here," Rose said as they approached the drive to the house old house. "So peaceful and quiet. I see why you settled here but I don't understand why you ever left."

Martin chuckled. "There's a short answer and a long answer to that," he said. "I have to warn you the long answer is a journal I've kept for the whole time. It's about thirty notebooks worth now. The short answer is I didn't find what I was looking for here and my life has been the search. It was here, but I didn't know how to find it here." He touched his breast. "As a wandering rabbi once said, the Kingdom is within us. I could have stayed if I'd known that, and been very happy, but I didn't know."

Rose nodded. "I'd like to read it sometime, if you don't mind. Who lives up here now?" she asked.

Martin told her about Max and his long time partner, Carlos. "He's one of the most beautiful people I know," he added as they approached the gate. "Remind me to tell you about calling the wolf." He opened the gate and an old dog lying by the door sleeping in the sun lifted its head and gave a half-hearted wheeze, which was the best it could do for a bark these days.

"Hello, Oscar," Martin called and, hearing his voice, the dog's tail went up and down twice, thumping the earth although he didn't get up. "Oscar is almost fifteen," Martin told her. "Like a lot of men his age, he spends most of the day dozing between meals." Oscar heaved a deep, contented sigh, and resumed his nap.

A handsome young man stuck his head out the door and smiled when he saw Martin. "Hey, Max," he called into the house. "It's Martin and he's got a pretty girl with him." Coming out of the house he gave Martin a big hug and smiled at Rose. "Welcome to our house. I'm Carlos. Max will be out in a minute." Not pausing for a response or even a breath he prattled on. "We wondered who came up in the little blue car last night and never went back. Are you family? You look just like Martin. Are you staying over for Thanksgiving?"

"Goodness, Carlos," said another man, coming out of the house. Give the lady a chance to speak. I'm Max, dear," he said.

"Hi, I'm Rose," she answered, offering her hand.

Max kissed her hand and then opened his arms. "The custom here is hugging more than hand shakes, dear," he told her, "especially among the family." Smiling, she hugged him gently, then Carlos. "Carlos doesn't get to see people often enough, I'm afraid." Max explained, like an indulgent mother. "He gets very lonely here with just me for company."

"Now, Max, that's not true," Carlos laughed. "You know perfectly well if it weren't for me you'd never go anywhere." He turned to Rose, as if to a lifelong ally, and waved Max off with a careless hand. "What would these old men do without us, dear? If we weren't around to get them going they would lie around all day like that old dog."

Martin laughed, hugging Max. "I'm afraid it's true for me these days, Carlos. I don't seem to have the drive I used to have." Walking arm in arm with Max he followed Carlos and Rose into the house.

"I bet you're here for the Cook's Tour," Carlos said to Rose, and began to show her around the house while Max and Martin took seats at the kitchen table. Max watched his partner with an amused look and offered tea, which Martin accepted.

"Who is that?" Max asked him. "She looks just like you."

"Remember me telling you about Tovah?" Martin asked. Max nodded. "That's the child I thought was killed with her in the bombing."

"That must have been quite a shock," Max observed, and listened very closely as Martin told him her story. "Goodness," he said when Martin was done. "That's twice now, isn't it?"

"Makes me wonder," Martin replied. Then he realized what he'd said. "No," he told his old friend, shaking his head. "I didn't mean how many other children I have I don't know about. I mean, the way this has all happened. I know there's no answer, but it makes me wonder why."

Max nodded soberly. "No shit," he whispered. Then he laughed as Rose and Carlos passed out the back door on their way to the gardens. "He really does need to see more people," he murmured. "I'd hate to lose him but he needs to get out more."

"He's not going to leave you, Max," Martin reassured him. "He's doing exactly what he wants to do right now. He loves you. Where else would he go? You're here and that's why he's here."

Max sighed and shook his head. "I'm feeling our age, Martin."

"We're not so old," Martin argued. "I'm only fifty-four, and you're a lot younger than me."

Max nodded. "I'll turn fifty next month, but you don't understand, my friend. You've lost a lot of people your age, but most of them are still alive. For me it's different. So many of my friends my age are dead now, it's like I'm thirty years older. Most of my friends my age are gone." He sighed and added. "Most of those were lost to AIDS."

"I'm still around," Martin told him. "So is Jack."

"You don't understand," Max said. "I'm getting old. Carlos is my last chance for a partner. If he leaves, who would want an aging queen?"

"Horse shit!" Martin snapped, startling Max. "You're just scared and I'll make you a bet. We'll go to Santa Fe, just you and me, and hang out a few day around the square. We'll just see how long it takes for someone to give you the eye."

"I'm not talking about cruising, Martin," Max answered. "Anybody can cruise and get laid. I'm talking about a committed relationship."

"Why do you think Carlos has stayed?" Martin asked him. "That's what he's about, too. He loves you, Max, and he's committed. To you." He looked at his long time friend. "What set this off? Did something happen?"

Max nodded. "I got a letter from a friend of mine in San Francisco."

He got up and went into another room, bringing back an envelope. You can read it if you want to. He's an artist and is quite successful. Lots of money. His lover of ten years cleaned out the bank account and left him high and dry."

Martin looked at his friend and smiled. "You know, you're not exactly loaded, Max," he replied gently. "I doubt he's after your money."

Max nodded and sighed. "You're right, Martin. Thanks. I guess I've been brewing a tempest in my teapot."

"Yes," Martin nodded, "but I wouldn't be one to know anything about doing that, now would I?"

Max laughed. "You always tell the truth, even when you're lying. Maybe it's me who needs to get out and see more people." He smiled at his friend. "I'm glad you came by this morning. Will you stay for lunch?"

Martin shook his head. "No, I packed us something. We need to talk and I thought I'd take Rose up to the thinking place. Why don't you all come for supper? Carmelita's expecting you." He frowned. "I'm not sure what I need to tell her, Max. I mean about me and Carmelita and Paco. I'm not sure what she can handle."

"Everything," Max told him. "Tell her only the truth and then tell her only as much as she wants to know. From what you've told me, you're the only source of information she has about her mother as a married woman. She will want to know it all, just as Paco did."

"That's what I'm afraid of," Martin responded. "Some of what I had to tell him bothered him for a long time."

"Yet he got over it," Max replied. "Which he couldn't have done if you had not told him. Believe me, it would have been worse if you'd held out."

Martin sighed. "Thank you, reverend father," he whispered. "Pray for us sinners now and in the hour of our trial."

"Always," Max smiled, making the sign of the cross as if blessing his friend. "*Pax vobiscum.*"

"The church lost a great priest in you," Martin replied, smiling.

"Ah, but I gained my soul," Max whispered back. "As did you." He shrugged and smiled. "We do all right, Martin. The apostolic hands may not have been laid upon our heads, my friend, but we do well as brothers of the wolf."

"*Si, pero somos los lobo de navidad passeo,*" Martin said softly. Yes, but we are the wolves of Christmas past.

"*No, mi hermano, el lobo viva aqui,*" Max corrected him, reaching out and touching Martin' breast. No, my brother, the wolf lives here.

When they reached the sitting place, Martin built a small fire and took out his flute while Rose caught her breath. "I don't know what's the matter with me," she said, concerned. "I'm having trouble breathing."

Martin smiled. "It's the altitude. Where we're sitting is just over seven thousand feet. The same thing happened to me when I first came up here."

Rose thought a moment. "Over two thousand meters. No wonder. I had no idea it was so elevated. Is that why the air is so clear?"

Martin nodded. "That and the lack of cars and people. It's also very dry up here, more than you might think."

"I know my skin has felt dry," Rose said. "New York is so humid."

Martin began to play his flute quietly. Without giving it much thought he drifted into the song of the wolf and raven, and, although he'd not played it in years, his fingers found their way surely over the wooden pipe. When he was done, they sat in silence for a long while.

"That was incredible," Rose whispered. Martin nodded and pointed with his chin toward a pinion on the rise above them. There she could see the form of a large dark bird sitting quietly. Yet even as she looked, the bird gave a harsh croak and flew off. "What was it?" Rose asked. "A crow?"

"A raven," Martin smiled. "One usually shows up when I play that tune. Either that or a wolf."

Rose looked at him as if she wanted to believe him and he laughed and told her of the night in this very same place when the *penitentes* were scared away by Max and the black wolf. "You can ask Max," he said. "He saw the tracks, and he certainly saw the men."

"It's all so..." Rose began, but stopped, her eyes wide. Looking in the direction she was staring, Martin saw a large male coyote sitting at the edge of the clearing, watching them gravely. Gently picking up his flute, Martin began to play, and as he did, the coyote began to howl. Not loudly, but with a soft keening moan. Then, looking at them as if smiling, the huge beast left as quietly as he had come and disappeared down the trail.

Rose blinked. "Am I going crazy?" she asked.

"No," Martin said. "But there may be some things about yourself you don't know. That's the first time I've seen the raven and the coyote together. The last time it was a mountain lion."

"If I hadn't seen what I just saw, I'd think you were lying," Rose said with a sense of wonder. "There is something very strange going on here."

Martin could tell she was a little alarmed. "Nothing to be afraid of," he told her. "I'm sure there's a very natural explanation, but I'm not sure what it is. Have you ever seen a coyote before?"

"Is that what it was?" she asked. "It's beautiful." She looked troubled, but Martin did not push. "It's strange, but there is a creature like that in many of my dreams. I thought it was a wild dog."

"That's what they are," Martin told her. "They can be domesticated and they're very smart. The Indians call them the Trickster." He looked at her unsure how much he should say. "I have a book at the house that will tell you about Coyote. I think you will find it interesting."

"Do they come up to you like that?" she asked.

"This is the first time, ever," he replied, smiling. "I don't think he was coming to see me." Rose gave him another strange look but said nothing, so he moved the conversation to safer ground. "Rose, I'm sure you have a thousand questions," he said. "Where do you want me to start?"

She smiled back, almost in relief. "Why don't you start by telling me how you met mother. Why were you in Israel?"

"My boss needed someone to cover the Israeli-Syrian talks in January of 1967 and I was the only one available to go. That one trip made me an 'expert' on the Middle East and when Israel shot down Syrian jets in April I happened to be in Greece and was sent back to cover that. Things were tense and they wanted me to stay, so I was there when the first mobilization began."

As Martin spoke, the memories began to flow and he told Rose of being wounded and of the first moment he saw Tovah. "I think I fell in love at that moment," he said, "Later Tovah told me it was the same for her." He went on to relate being called back to Chicago and not being able to see Tovah for six months, and then, when he found she was pregnant, of his mother's trip to Jerusalem. "We were to be married in June," he said, "and I was studying with Rabbi Cohen. I planed to immigrate to Israel and convert to Judaism."

The happiness which marked his features when he spoke of this turned to sadness as he told Rose of having to leave and never seeing his lover again. Then he told her of the empty years, the years he tried to destroy himself with work and drink, and of how he had finally been almost dragged into recovery by Zakhar Levnikov, his editor. "I told Zak one time that, while people in the Program may not be saints, he, himself, was an angel of mercy," Martin laughed. "You should have seen his face. I thought he was going to choke on his coffee."

Then he told her of his growth in recovery and how making amends to all he had harmed led to his renewed relationship with Carmelita and the discovery of the son he never knew he had. Nor did he hold back telling about the difficulties they experienced building a relationship as a family.

"Paco and I hit it off right away," he told Rose, "but with Carmelita it took a long while. It was almost six months before we became lovers again, and it took me another six months to win her hand."

He looked at his daughter and smiled. "Believe me, I had to win it. When Rosita came, everything seemed to come together for a while."

"Now I'm upsetting the balance," Rose said, suddenly unsure of herself. "Maybe it was a mistake to come here."

"Absolutely not!" Martin declared. "Sorry," he added in a calmer tone. "I didn't mean to yell. I'm delighted you're here and so is Carmelita. She told me that last night, and she wasn't just being polite. Your grandmother is going to love you. She was just as devastated as I was when Tovah was killed."

Rose thought a moment, then nodded, accepting what he said. "So how did you and Carmelita meet?" she asked.

"You're really rattling the family skeletons," Martin laughed. "At the time I was engaged to her cousin Stephanie." He stopped, considered for a moment himself, then went on. "The Program teaches us we're only as sick as our secrets. I don't know how Carmelita would feel about my telling you all this, but I will, anyway. Just respect her feelings, all right?"

Rose held up her hands. "Maybe you better not tell me. I don't want to cause problems."

Martin shook his head. "I think you need to know. After all, you're as much family as Paco, and he knows." Then he told her the story of how he first came to the Canyon and of the Posadas when he met Stephanie. When he was done he looked at Rose gravely. "One thing I want you to understand very clearly is that I acknowledged you from the beginning as my child. In my eyes you are the daughter of my first marriage."

Rose nodded. "With the wars and all, we look at that a little differently in Israel," she said. "I know I'm your daughter and I feel it, too. I guess right now I'm a little overwhelmed by how it took place. I'm lucky to be here."

"Oh, yes," he said. "It was a miracle Tovah delivered you."

"No, that's not what I mean. I mean, if you'd known about Paco I'd have never been conceived. It's strange how it worked out."

Martin nodded. "Some people would say that was God's plan from the beginning, but I don't think so. I think life is as much a mystery to God as it is to us, at least in terms of the outcomes. God or Adonai or El-Shaddai or whatever you want to call Him or Her seems to play the course the way we leave it lie. The thing you and Paco share is that you are beautiful gifts born into the world as a result of other people's choices. I think you're God's way of redeeming those choices."

"How do you mean?"

"Well, our choices and our pigheadedness, mine and Carmelita's, made for a lot of pain for ourselves and for others. I can only speak from my own side of the street, but Tovah was God's redemption of my choice to leave the Canyon rather than wait for Stephanie or to try to change her mind. I don't know what I was redeeming for her. What I do know is that we are God's gift to one another and to ourselves, and your coming here is a special gift of grace to Carmelita and me and Rosa."

Martin grinned. "Probably Paco, too. He gets a little full of himself and needs a sharp sister to keep him in line." He looked at her and smiled gently. "I suspect in time you will discover how we all are gifts to you."

Rose looked at him seriously. "I wish I had your faith," she said. "I try, but I don't." She shivered and pulled her jacket tighter about her. The sun was beginning to set and the fire was almost gone, with darkness chilling the mountain air quickly.

Martin stood and opened his arms, hugging his daughter gently.

Then taking her by the hand he led her on up the mountain to another special place, one from which the sunset could be seen clearly. This evening it was more breathtaking than usual, and they watched until it was gone.

Then Martin turned to her and said, "You will, Rose. You will. Keep seeking it and the gift of faith will be given. How the gift is given may come as a surprise. It did for me. Some people find it in the forms of the Church but I first found it out here in the sacred mountains. Then I discovered what I was seeing outside was only a reflection of what was within my heart all the while. Keep seeking. Keep looking within."

Rose looked at him silently for a long while. Then tears came to her eyes and she nodded. "Let's go home, daddy," she said, shivering as she took his arm and held it tight. "Let's go home."

A Canticle For Lazarus

So it is I have come to the end of one journey and the beginning of another. I often remember my words to my daughter, Rose, with wonder and a deep sense of awe. For in speaking to her, I was speaking to myself, *ex cathedra*, knowing I was proclaiming the utter truth even as I spoke. I remember these words in the dark times of the soul, and they give light to walk farther along the way. Keep the faith. Keep seeking. An answer will always be given in the fullness of time.

Now it is time to bring this chronicle to an end. I think this new part of my journey deserves a journal of its own, and there remain only two things left to be said here before moving on to that. One is that not much has changed in the world except my awareness of how the fabric of human life is inextricably interwoven into patterns and purposes within a universe we can only dimly begin to perceive. The bottom line, as bean counters are fond of saying, is that we don't know jack shit, and that our belief that we do know, or even can, is pure vanity and a "striving after wind." We can speculate and we can form opinions, yet we must always keep in mind these may or may not have much to do with the true nature of things. We simply don't know much and to pretend otherwise is spiritually risky, at least in the sense that it can lead us to "have wandered long in a land that is barren and waste," just like the 'apiru, the poor trash who followed Moses.

Yet as I write I am reminded that any journey of the spirit is always a journey of risk, for once begun, nothing will ever be the same. Our discontent may drive us out of the comfortable fleshpots of Egypt, but to reach our Promised Land, we must experience the astringent grace of the desert. There seems to be no other way.

The other thing I need to note, is that while many companions have walked with me along the way, drifting in and out of my life as unsuspecting messengers of the divine, there is only one who has been constantly with me at every turning, although often I have not known this companion was there. This is the desert runner of my recurrent dreams, the master of Black Wolf and Raven, who brings me again and again through the desolate Valley of the Weeper to the oasis by the Emerald Pool. The irony is that this was the one whom I sought these many years I have walked in the New Year, looking into each passing human being for the face of one "whom...mine eyes shall behold, and not as a stranger." This is who was with me all the while.

So while I still walk the streets of Denver each New Year's eve, I no longer look for the messiah. I no longer look now because I know I am never alone, and never have been. The messiah is with me every step of the way, and whenever I need to recognize I am in the presence things celestial, for whatever purpose, I know the messiah will be revealed in a way I cannot possibly mistake, as he was the day I talked to Rose. I find freedom in this, and incredible liberty. For since I have no doubt in my mind, I am now free to simply walk and behold this world, and to look at it through eyes of love and grace. And in looking for grace, I find it.

So how do I know this? How do I know what I see is the benevolence of a guiding Intelligence? How can I be certain I am not simply fooling myself or indulging in wishful thinking? I don't and I can't, and at this point it doesn't matter to me. There is no proof we can offer of the existence of the divine except the difference such things make in our lives. There is always a measure of doubt. What I do know is that something else happened this last year that touched me in a way that flung me off the high perch where I clung to the safety rail of caution, and cast me into the depths of Joy. Some call this making a leap of faith. I don't see I had much choice. For me it was a leap of utter desperation I am not sure I could have made if my Companion had not snuck up like the Indian he is and startled me out of my wits.

The way it happened is funny, truly absurd. I was trying hard to work the Eleventh Step, to improve my conscious contact with God through prayer and meditation. I was trying to pray only for knowledge of God's will for me and the power to carry that out after a week straight from the depths of Hell. All the promises I'd made came due in one way or another that week and I was stressed to the max running from pillar to post and on to the next.

To put it another way, it was a week I spent so much time giving to others that I had no time to be still and quiet and refill my own spiritual tanks. I was literally given out, too hungry, too tired, too lonely and too angry, and I knew I was off the beam and needed to reconnect. So I got up early that morning and went to a little chapel they open early on Saturday at one of the churches downtown. I go there often when I am empty, and never have I come away unrefreshed.

One of the odd things about that little chapel is that there is a pay phone there. When I'm downtown I go there sometimes to use the phone, for it's quiet there and out of the weather. And while I've always wondered why the phone is there, I've never asked. I like to think it's for souls on the brink of despair to call for help, but I don't know that for sure. I do know other people use the phone from time to time, but in all the times I have been to the chapel, I have heard the phone ring only three times. All three were on that Saturday morning I was in such urgent need.

Sometimes there are other people in the chapel when I go there. This morning there was no one, and I was deeply grateful for the solitude. Taking out the prayerbook Tio Emil gave me so many years ago, I began to read from the Psalter. The psalm I chose was appropriate to my mood and one I often use when I take Creation to task for the way things are. It began, "Out of the deep have I called unto thee, O Lord; Lord hear my voice and let thine ears consider well the voice of my complaint." After giving out all week, I thought that was the very least my Higher Power owed me.

Reading the psalms calmed me, as it does, and I was deep into the mystery of silence when the phone rang. At first I thought it was something else, but it rang again and again and again. It rang fifteen times before it stopped, and with each jangle both my resentment and my determination not to answer grew. This was my time and, by damn, I was going to have it. Then the ringing stopped and I relaxed and began to make amends to the Power greater than myself. Surely I had strayed off the beam in taking such poor care of myself that the simple ringing of a phone could stir up such a fiery storm of resentment.

Then the phone rang again. This time it would not stop, and after the twentieth ring I jumped up in a rage and stalked to the back of the chapel. Just as I was violently snatching the receiver off the hook, ready to fire a blast of invective, it stopped ringing and I was left listening to a dial tone.

I stood there, thinking for a moment and calming down. Then it occurred to me that perhaps someone was calling in desperate straits, and I waited for a long while alone there in silence, resolved to answer calmly when whoever it was called again. Nothing happened for fifteen minutes, and sighing in relief, I made my way back to the seat and picked up my prayerbook. I turned to the prayer attributed to St. Francis, and I began to read, praying for someone to respond to the soul I was now sure was in need. Now I wonder how I could have been so blind to my own hypocrisy.

> Lord, make me an instrument of your peace:
> where there is hatred, let me sow love;
> where there is injury, let me give pardon;
> where there is discord, let me bring union;
> where there is doubt, let me lend faith;
> where there is despair, let me give hope;
> where there is darkness, let me shed light,
> and where there is sadness, let me bring joy.
> O Master, grant that I may never seek
> so much to be consoled as to console,
> to be understood as to understand,
> or to be loved as to love.
> For it is in giving that we receive,
> it is in forgiving that we are forgiven,
> and in dying that we are born to eternal life.

As I read, I was not aware of the personal irony in those magnificent words. So Someone decided to rub my nose in it. I had barely finished reading this prayer when the phone rang once more.

This time I answered on the third ring. The caller was in the city jail and really needed help, he said. When I asked what he was in for he told me he'd gotten drunk the night before and torn up the house of a friend where he was staying. He was passed out when she got home and woke up in a cell. He guessed she had called the police. I told him that was highly probable and I could understand why. So could he, he told me.

"All right," answered. "What do you need? Bail?"

"No," he said. "My brother is on the way down here with bail but he won't be here until late this afternoon. I'm out of cigarettes."

He was out of cigarettes? Can you imagine how pissed I was when I heard this? Here I was trying to refuel my own spiritual tanks and some frigging drunk calls me from jail to bring him a pack of cigarettes? Yet I was once a smoker and knew exactly what the man was suffering. As bad as the feelings which go with hangover may be, or the remorse for what one has done, the withdrawal pains from addiction to nicotine are worse. That was what got to me, for even now, seven years after I quit, the craving for a smoke still strikes me at times, as strong as ever.

"All right," I said, somehow managing a tone which was almost civil, and asked the man's name, which he told me. Then, growling and grumbling, I left the chapel, bought his frigging cigarettes at a newsstand, and took off for the city jail.

The jailer on duty that morning made a mistake. When I told him a guy had called me at the chapel at St. Mary's, he thought I was a parish priest. Being a good catholic himself, he let me in. "I wish you guys would wear your collars these days," he grumbled, leading me back into the cell block. I was surprised but I followed. My intent was to drop off the cigarettes and get back to the chapel, having fulfilled my duty, but after a cursory examination of the packets, the jailer handed them back and led me upstairs. For some reason I followed him.

I do not know if you have ever been to the city jail. If you have you know it is a very basic cage made of concrete and heavy steel bars on the top as well as the sides. The bars are painted, quite often in that pale green used during the 'Fifties to cover institutional walls. When I was in school it was called mint green, and compared to shit brown, it might seem beautiful. Our name for it growing up was puke green. I have no idea why it was so popular, except that it invariably communicates the idea one is in a public building and therefore is under the authority and control of the guardians thereof. Or maybe, knowing how unpleasant school is for many, it was simply used to make jails as unpleasant as possible for inmates in the system. The last is an explanation most alcoholics can relate to, in or out of recovery.

The man was in a green cage with two other prisoners, both much younger than he was. When the jailer called his name he came over and I told him who I was and handed him the cigarettes. The others came over and asked me if I had any more, and I told Steve, the man who called me, to give them one of the three packs I'd brought. "You can call me if you run out," I told him, wondering why I was saying that.

"So tell me about it," I added, not knowing why.

The jailer showed me the bell to ring when I was done and left me in the hallway. Steve began to talk and the other prisoners became bored and returned to their bunks on the other side of the cage, which was fairly big. I have thought many times about what he said, and the questions I asked as we stood there. Yet, I cannot remember any of this.

What I do remember is his eyes, a deep, almost startling blue grey and very clear for his having been drunk the night before. It was the eyes that spoke to me, looking out between the massive green bars of his cage. And as I stood there listening something strange began to happen. Another face began to take form behind Steve's and I found myself looking into eyes as dark and piercing as those of the raven.

I blinked, surprised. Such flashes have happened to me before but have always been fleeting, disappearing quickly. This time was different. With my blink the features snapped into sharp focus and I was looking at a dark Semitic face with a rich black beard. Yet it was the eyes that touched the very depths of my soul, examining everything there with a compassion that brought tears to my eyes. And while I had never seen this face before, it was one I knew well, and not as a stranger. Nor was there any doubt in my mind whose face I was seeing.

A friend of mine, a psychologist I was consulting then, claims I was seeing the younger face of Ramos, my spiritual mentor. When I told him I had never seen a picture of Emiliano Ramos at a young age, he spoke at length of age reversal with photographs. This uses sophisticated computer software to produce an accurate younger image from a photo taken at a much older age. What my friend suggested is that my mind had done much the same.

I thanked my friend for his concern and turned the conversation to other things. Yet when Carmelita asked me about it later, having heard the whole conversation, I told her the man was wrong. For I knew the young Emil Ramos, having seen him many times in the laughter and joy of the old man during the years we shared in the Canyon. I knew him well and he was not the one whom I had seen staring out at me through the pale green bars of City Jail. For even as I stood there, so close I could reach out and touch him, I knew beyond a doubt that I was looking into the eyes of the Messiah, the Master of Wolf and Raven.

About the Author

Joel Reed has been many things in life—a parish priest, a farmer, a building contractor, a university professor, a photographer—so, it isn't surprising that his publishing house, White Turtle Books, is delivering such original material. This jack of many trades has actually written eleven novels, and one of his latest works, *Murder in the Choir,* received a Finalist Award in 2005 from USABookNews.

An avid photographer, Reed spends his leisure chasing light in South Dakota and southwestern Minnesota. He makes his home with his family in their tree house overlooking the Minnesota River.

Acknowledgements

U nless otherwise noted, all material quoted in this work is taken from sources in the Common Domain or from the author's own writings. While most of the specific usages are noted below, brief references and quotations are not.

p. 3 *Psalms of David* based on *The Book Of Common Prayer, 1979*

p. 91 *Psalms of David* based on *The Book Of Common Prayer*

p. 91 ff *Las Posadas* – traditional Central American lyrics

p. 136 "whither thou goest" selection taken from the Book of Ruth, *Holy Bible,* Authorized Version (1611)

p. 245 Song of Songs – transliterated from *Holy Bible*, Authorized Version (1611)

p. 246 *Ascent of Mt. Carmel* – St. John of the Cross (1542-1591) (see www.ccel.org)

p. 251 *Softly and Tenderly* – lyrics by Will L. Thompson (1880)

p. 251 *Psalms of David* quoted and transliterated from *The Book Of Common Prayer, 1979*

p. 257 *Psalms of David* quoted and transliterated from T*he Book Of Common Prayer, 1979*

p. 312 *Psalms of David* quoted and transliterated from *The Book Of Common Prayer, 1979*

p. 556 Prayer of St. Francis – from the *Book of Common Prayer, 1979*